THE DREAD

"Ready?"

Donelan nodded once more.

Felix began to pour the blood in a thin stream onto the cloth doll. At the same time, Donelan's ghost became less solid, like fog dissipating on the wind. Tendrils of white fog unwound from the figure of the dead king and twined around the blood, disappearing into the *nenkah*. When the chalice was empty, Donelan's ghost was almost translucent, and the *nenkah* was soaked in crimson. Felix put his hand over the *nenkah*, and Donelan placed a spectral hand atop his. Felix murmured one last incantation, and the gems he wore flared with sudden light, blindingly bright in the gloom of the crypt. A spark of blue-white fire leaped from Felix's palm into the *nenkah*, which jolted and shuddered.

Cam realized he was holding his breath.

Beside him, Rhistiart fainted.

The *nenkah* was breathing.

BY GAIL Z. MARTIN

The Chronicles of the Necromancer
The Summoner
The Blood King
Dark Haven
Dark Lady's Chosen

The Fallen Kings Cycle
The Sworn
The Dread

GAIL Z. MARTIN
THE
DREAD

THE FALLEN KINGS CYCLE: BOOK TWO

www.orbitbooks.net

ORBIT

First published in Great Britain in 2012 by Orbit

Copyright © 2012 by Gail Z. Martin

Excerpt from *The Heir of Night* by Helen Lowe
Copyright © 2010 by Helen Lowe

The moral right of the author has been asserted.

*All characters and events in this publication, other than
those clearly in the public domain, are fictitious
and any resemblance to real persons,
living or dead, is purely coincidental.*

All rights reserved.
No part of this publication may be reproduced,
stored in a retrieval system, or transmitted, in any
form or by any means, without the prior
permission in writing of the publisher, nor be
otherwise circulated in any form of binding or
cover other than that in which it is published and
without a similar condition including this
condition being imposed on the subsequent purchaser.

A CIP catalogue record for this book
is available from the British Library.

ISBN 978-1-84149-914-7

Typeset in Times by Palimpsest Book Production Limited,
Falkirk, Stirlingshire
Printed and bound by CPI Group (UK) Ltd, Croydon, CR0 4YY

Papers used by Orbit are from well-managed forests
and other responsible sources.

MIX
Paper from
responsible sources
FSC® C104740

Orbit
An imprint of
Little, Brown Book Group
100 Victoria Embankment
London EC4Y 0DY

An Hachette UK Company
www.hachette.co.uk

www.orbitbooks.net

For Larry, Kyrie, Chandler, and Cody, who have to live with a writer and who make the best of it.

1

"I had hoped that Isencroft wouldn't see war again in my life-time." King Donelan of Isencroft took a deep breath and swirled the brandy in his goblet. "I had my fill of it in my younger days. It was a bad bargain then, and it hasn't gotten any better."

"It's not by your choosing, m'lord." Wilym, the head of the elite Veigonn warriors and a close personal friend of the king's, set aside his drink. "Temnotta's made the first move."

Donelan sighed. "Spare me any words about a 'good war.' There is no 'good' war. The only thing worse than war is slavery. I know we have no choice, dammit. I know Temnotta cast the die. But it's a funny thing about war. Even when you win, you lose. There are several thousand men having a good night's sleep tonight who won't be breathing by war's end. There are villages that won't exist when the fighting's through. I never thought a king's reputation was earned on the battlefield. I always thought it was earned by making sure fields never saw battle. War is easy. But keeping peace for any length of time—well, that's the tricky part."

Donelan downed the last of his brandy in one gulp, and for a moment, Cam thought the king might pour himself another draught. Instead, Donelan let his head rest against the chair and closed his eyes. And although Cam had been the King's

1

Champion for years, never had he thought Donelan looked so worn and tired. "There are no thoughts in my head fit to fall asleep with," Donelan said, his voice gravelly with fatigue. "Tell me just one good thing before I turn in for the night. I'd rather not dream of war."

Cam exchanged worried glances with Wilym. "Think on the packet you received this morning from Kiara," Wilym said. "You told me her letter says that she and Cwynn are doing well, and that the baby has a fine appetite. The portrait she sent showed a healthy, strong boy. And they're safe from this madness, far away in Margolan." He chuckled. "I've heard it said that no one except Martris Drayke himself ever breached the walls of the palace Shekerishet. Count that as your good thing to sleep on, Your Majesty. Kiara and Cwynn are safe."

Donelan seemed to relax. The king was known both for his appetite for strong drink and for his ability to seem utterly untouched by it. Cam wished that tonight the brandy might overcome the king's tolerance and give Donelan a few candle-marks of untroubled sleep.

"Aye, that's a fine thing," Donelan agreed, his voice a deep rumble. "A fine thing to sleep on. Thank you."

"The firesetter's been to your room a candlemark ago," Wilym replied. "The chill will be off and the fire should be banked for the night. We have a few more days before the army heads for the coast. Perhaps you should enjoy a bed while you have the chance." He chuckled. "Even the finest cot gives a poor night's rest once we're in the field."

Donelan stretched and twisted in his chair, as if to loosen his shoulders. "I think I will," he said, and he smiled, but Cam saw that it didn't reach his eyes. "Thanks to you both for sitting with me a while. I'd best let you get some rest as well." Donelan stood and walked across the sitting room to where a guard stood by the door to his bedchamber. He glanced over his shoulder. "Mind that you're careful going about your business. I'll need both of you beside me when we ride for the coast."

The door closed behind Donelan, and the guard resumed his place. "I'm worried about him," Cam remarked quietly.

Wilym was silent for a moment. "Donelan drew his first blood on the battlefield when we were still sucking on our mothers' teats. Does it surprise you that it gets tiresome after twenty-some years? By the Whore! I'm wholly sick of every campaign by the end of the first battle, and I haven't seen as much of it as he has."

Cam nodded. "I've never met a sane man yet who enjoys battle, even if they love soldiering. I'm just not used to seeing Donelan look so haggard. Now it seems his dreams are dark. Makes me worried—"

A man's scream cut off the rest of Cam's words. Cam and Wilym jumped to their feet as the guard threw open the door to Donelan's chamber.

"Sweet Chenne," the guard whispered, blanching. Cam and Wilym shouldered past him at a dead run and stopped at the foot of the king's bed.

Six stout pikes thrust up through the bed, spanning from one side to the other. Donelan lay impaled, with one of the spikes protruding from his chest. Blood spread down the king's nightshirt, soaking the bedding, enough blood that Cam was sure the spike had taken Donelan through the heart.

"Get Trygve!" Wilym shouted. He grabbed the guard by the shoulders and spun him around, shoving him out the door. "Run, dammit!" He turned back to the king. "Hang on, Donelan. Trygve will be here in a moment."

Donelan's whole frame shook. His hands opened and closed convulsively, grasping at the covers. The king's eyes were wide with pain and shock, and his mouth opened and closed, gasping for breath. Wilym took the king's hand. "Hold on, please. Just hold on."

Cam drew his sword and made a thorough inspection of the room. The king's private quarters were large, but by design, they offered no easy hiding place. Cam flung open the wardrobe doors but found nothing except dress robes. The garderobe alcove was empty, with an opening too small for even a slender boy to navigate. Then he looked at the high four-poster bed. The frame was at least two feet off the floor, tall enough that two steps were required for Donelan to climb onto the mattress, and it was skirted with heavy tapestry material. When Cam knelt to look under the bed, he caught his breath.

"By the Crone!"

"What?"

Cam climbed to his feet. "Someone's rigged a bow contraption beneath the bed. Must have gone off once there was weight on it."

Trygve barreled through the doorway, followed by the guard, who seemed close to panic.

"Mother and Childe!" Trygve swore under his breath, never breaking stride until he reached Donelan's side. Cam and Wilym melted back along the wall, giving the healer room to work. Trygve was one of the finest battle healers in all of Isencroft, but by the set of his mouth, Cam could tell that Trygve was worried.

"We've got to remove the stake, and the moment we do, he'll start bleeding harder." Trygve's voice was clipped.

"Tell us what to do," Wilym said, as he and Cam stepped forward.

"Can you retract the weapon from below? I'd rather not try to lift him."

Cam dropped to his knees. "I think so. It's been bound to the frame with rope."

4

"Then on my mark, with one of you on each side, slice the ropes while I try to staunch the bleeding." Trygve climbed up on the bed and straddled the king's body so that his hands were best positioned above the wound. "On three: one . . . two . . . *three*."

The two swords swished through the air simultaneously, slicing through the ropes and hitting the bed frame with a thunk. The stakes dropped, but did not completely retract.

Trygve cursed. "Get on your knees. On my mark again, grab each side of that cursed thing and pull straight down."

This time, the apparatus gave way. Cam and Wilym climbed back to their feet. Donelan gave a sharp cry, and Trygve murmured healing incantations while his hands cupped over the hole in Donelan's chest. Blue healing light glowed beneath Trygve's hands. But from where Cam stood, Donelan's skin looked ashen, and his body had gone still. Trygve's tension gave Cam no reassurance.

Blood spattered Trygve's healer's uniform and his hands were slick. Donelan's breathing was slow and labored. Trygve leaned closer, and the blue light flared. Donelan murmured something Cam could not hear, and then, with one heavy breath, the king lay still.

"Donelan!" Cam said, starting forward.

"No!" Wilym cried.

Trygve bowed his head and his shoulders sagged. "I'm sorry. It was too much damage. Perhaps if we'd had a summoner to bind his soul, we might have bought more time for healing. The stake . . . it tore through his heart . . ." His voice faded. Slowly, he climbed down from the bed and drew up a sheet to cover Donelan's body.

Cam turned to the guard at the door. The young man stared wide-eyed at the king's body. "Who beside the firesetter entered the king's rooms tonight?"

It took two tries for the guard to find his voice. "No one, m'lord. There's been a guard at the door to the king's bedchamber all day. The chambermaids set out his night clothes, but they come on the watch before mine, just before supper."

"We'll find the firesetter and the maids and the previous guard." Wilym's voice was tight and emotionless, and only his eyes revealed his sorrow. "I handpicked the king's guards myself, and I'd swear to their loyalty on my own life. As for the servants, we'll get to the bottom of it."

Cam looked at Wilym and Trygve. "The army's about to head to war, and the king's dead."

Wilym took a deep breath. "How fast can a *vayash moru* travel from here to Shekerishet?"

Cam met his gaze. "A few days." He paused. "You're not proposing—"

"Yes, I am." Wilym's expression was resolute. "Kiara may be Queen of Margolan, but she is also the rightful heir to the Isencroft throne. We have no choice except to call her home to lead her people. Alvior's behind this. He'll count on chaos slowing our response. Maybe he's betting that without Donelan we'll fall into a full civil war and he can sweep up the pieces. The army can move without the king. But the people need someone who can rally them, someone to remind them why they fight."

Footsteps in the doorway made them turn. Both Cam and Wilym drew their swords. Kellen stepped into the room, followed by Tice and Allestyr. "By the Whore!" Kellen swore softly. Tice froze, a look of shock on his face. Allestyr swallowed back a sob.

"It's true, then." Allestyr was the first to speak. Tears ran down his cheeks. "The servants found us when the guard came for Trygve. Is he—"

Wilym nodded. "Donelan is dead. And if Isencroft is to survive, the six of us must make it happen."

*   *   *

The Dread

The next candlemarks passed in a blur for Cam as Donelan's closest advisers prepared for the burial of the king. Allestyr sent messengers to the Council of Nobles, while Tice recruited Cam's squire, Rhistiart, for help with the formal funeral arrangements that protocol demanded. Wilym went to break the news to the Veigonn in person and dispatched messengers to the generals who had already taken troops afield. Cam kept vigil beside Donelan's body, waiting for the king's last official visitor.

The door opened. Cam stood, knowing that the guard had orders to admit only one person. A white-cloaked figure entered, and Cam recognized the newcomer as an Acolyte to the Oracle of the goddess Chenne. He made an awkward bow. "Your Grace," he stammered, unsure of the proper acknowledgment.

The Acolyte nodded in response, but said nothing. Cam watched her in silence. The hood hid the Oracle's face in shadow, and her long sleeves covered her hands. Cam wondered if it was his imagination that she glided rather than walked, or whether the Acolyte's communion with the goddess had altered her enough to make her no longer of this world.

Cam stepped back as the Acolyte approached the bed. She moved in silence; not even footsteps broke the pall. The Acolyte bent over the king's still form as if listening for breath.

"He's well and truly dead, if that's what you're checking," Cam mumbled, as grief gave way to irritation.

"Magic did this." The Acolyte's voice was a murmur, barely above a whisper.

"Beggin' Your Grace's pardon, but there's a row of stakes beneath the bed and each one longer than my forearm. Must've run on some kind of spring," Cam argued.

The hooded head turned toward him, and he fell silent. In the shadow of the cloak, Cam could not make out any features, or any glimpse of a face at all. She considered him without speaking, and that moment of silence felt like it lasted forever.

"Magic, not mechanics, sprang the trap. The man you arrested, the firesetter, was bewitched. He was not the only one." She held out a hand above the king's corpse, as if sensing something in the air. "Two others have handled the weapon. One merely carried it, perhaps unknowingly. The other stinks of blood magic."

"We've got a pretender to the throne headed this way with dark mages and a navy. There's rioting in the streets, and now the king's dead. If your Mistress or the Lady Chenne has any suggestions on what to do about it, I'm sure we'd all like to hear it right about now." *Keep it up, and she'll probably turn you into a frog.* It took an effort for Cam to bottle his anger and grief and swallow the rest of his comments unspoken.

Once again, the Acolyte turned toward him, and Cam felt as if she were taking his measure. "You loved him."

Cam swallowed hard. "More like a father to me than my own father he was, that's for damn sure. I'd have died to save him." Cam fell on his knees in front of the Acolyte. "Can the Oracle— or the Goddess—bring him back? Take my life instead. Please, m'lady, I beg of you." Cam smeared away his tears with the back of his sleeve.

The Acolyte inclined her head. "It isn't given to my Mistress to bring back the dead, and Our Lady Chenne keeps her own counsel. While your grief is sincere, and your offer heartfelt, I can't give you what you seek."

Before Cam could answer, the Acolyte swept from the room. Then, with a silent bow toward Donelan's body, Cam blew out the candle in the lantern and left the bedchamber.

Just a few candlemarks before dawn, a solemn group assembled in the seneschal's chambers. Tice, the king's closest adviser; Allestyr, Donelan's seneschal; Kellen; Trygve; Wilym; Darry, the armsmaster; and Rhistiart were seated around a table. With them was Brother Felix, the king's favored scholar and an Acolyte of the Oracle. Cam joined them and accepted the warm mug of wassail Wilym pressed into his hand with a nod of thanks. No one spoke until Allestyr cleared his throat.

"I know we all have duties that demand our attention, as well as our own grief. But I thought it was important to gather this group before things get any more complicated." Allestyr's voice was tight and his eyes were red. In all the years Cam had known the seneschal, he had never seen Allestyr look as worn and sad.

"You're here because your loyalty is certain," Allestyr continued, his voice growing firmer. "By dawn, Count Renate should arrive at the palace. As the most senior member of the Council of Nobles, he is empowered, under Isencroft's Covenant of the Lords, to step in as Regent for up to ninety days until an Heir of the Blood is crowned."

He paused. "Renate is an honorable man, and his loyalty to the crown has never been doubted. He even volunteered to raise a private army and hunt down the Divisionists himself, but Donelan persuaded him that it was a matter best left to the king's troops."

Tice nodded. "He's a bold man, and good in a fight. We could do worse for a Regent, that's for sure."

"Since we learned of the king's death, we've allowed no one to leave the palace. We wanted to keep the news from spreading until Renate could be installed as Regent and until Wilym had a chance to speak with the generals," Allestyr continued. He shook his head. "I don't know what will happen when word reaches the streets. I fear the worst. We have to crown a new monarch before Alvior lands his armies on Isencroft soil, or he will claim a right by blood to the throne, and I don't know how many might throw their allegiance to him out of sheer panic."

Cam leaned forward. "Kiara is in Margolan. By fast horse, it's a two-week ride. She's recently given birth, and it was hard on her. We may well be at war before she can reach Isencroft."

Allestyr nodded. "There's no helping that. And although Kiara is an excellent warrior, she can't be expected to fight so soon after the birth, nor would we put her in that kind of danger."

"Wilym asked me to contact my friends among the *vayash moru*. They can travel more quickly than mortals. Antoin will take the news to Kiara in Margolan. He'll leave tonight. It should take him only a few days." Everyone turned toward Brother Felix. "Antoin's loyalty is beyond doubt. He can be trusted to carry word to the princess."

Allestyr and Tice exchanged glances. "Thank you," Allestyr said. "In the meantime, we had something a bit more arcane in mind."

Wilym raised an eyebrow. "Oh?"

"There is a way to crown a new king—or queen—in absentia," Allestyr replied. "It hasn't been done in several hundred years. We need a mage, preferably one of the Oracle's Acolytes. It also requires eight witnesses, one for each of the Faces of the Lady. There's a very particular way to carry out the ceremony. For one thing, it has to be done in the necropolis."

"Why in the tombs, for the Lady's sake?" Rhistiart clapped a hand to his mouth as he realized his outburst.

Allestyr gave a wan smile. "It has to be done in the necropolis because that's where the dead monarchs of Isencroft are buried. The only way to crown someone in absentia is with the agreement of the ghosts of the fallen kings."

"There is precedent." Once again, Brother Felix drew their attention, although his voice was scarcely above a whisper. "Aldo the Wise was crowned in such a manner, over two hundred years ago. He was on a visit to Dhasson when King Zoccoros the Third choked on a piece of venison at dinner and died. A group of loyalists and an Acolyte petitioned the dead kings and consecrated the crown. Something about the ritual activates the regent magic that's carried in the royal blood. Once done, it can't be undone by writ."

"So once the crown is consecrated for Kiara, the regent magic can't be conferred on anyone else, even if Alvior found some traitor lords to crown him?" Wilym leaned forward earnestly.

Brother Felix nodded. "If the ceremony is done right, then the crown can't be claimed by another—unless Kiara dies."

Wilym crossed his arms over his chest. "Just what does this 'consecration' ceremony involve?"

Allestyr looked to Brother Felix. The scholar took a deep breath. "It's very old magic, and somewhat controversial. There are reasons why it fell out of favor in recent generations. For one thing, the spirits of the dead kings can be temperamental. They don't like to be disturbed. There are legends—"

"Save the ghost stories for another time, Felix," Allestyr prompted gently.

"Right. Well, assuming you don't bring the wrath of the dead kings down on you—which we shouldn't, I hope—then, a small figure is created using items that were used frequently by the heir, either things she wore or things she valued highly, and dirt from the burial place of the kings. The items are placed inside a piece of cloth cut and sewn to be the shape of a person, like a child's doll without the stuffing. The Acolyte petitions the dead to come. It's up to them whether they do, unless the Acolyte happens to be a summoner, which none of the current ones are."

"Skip the details, Felix, please, or we'll be here all night," Tice muttered, but there was affection in his voice.

"Sorry. Sorry." Felix rubbed his bald head. He was obviously warming to his tale. "The warding and ceremony are not unlike a ritual wedding—each of the eight witnesses must contribute a few drops of blood into a chalice, which is mixed with wine and sacred herbs. Then we each lay hands on the effigy and drink from the chalice and the Acolyte says the words of power. The dead kings lend their magic, and the doll becomes a *nenkah*. Magically, it 'becomes' Kiara until she arrives to take its place."

"You want us to do blood magic?" Trygve's voice was a warning growl.

Felix sighed. "I told you it was controversial. That's one reason why it went out of fashion. But anyone who makes a ritual wedding uses a form of blood magic when they cut their palms and mix the blood with wine. It's not like there's a human sacrifice."

Tice cleared his throat. "I took the liberty of reading over Brother Felix's shoulder when he retrieved the old scrolls. There are a few potential complications."

"Complications?" Cam asked warily.

Tice nodded. "Because the items that are used to make the *nenkah* are very personal to the heir, they have a strong physical and emotional tie. When that link is activated by magic, the *nenkah* shares that magic with the person who owned the items. In exchange, the heir shares a glimmer of life force with the *nenkah*."

"This thing is alive?" Cam's voice reflected his horror.

Tice sighed. "In a manner of speaking, yes. That's how it can be crowned in the princess's absence with the force of law. It creates a way for Kiara to be in Margolan and here at the same time. But if the *nenkah* were to be captured, or destroyed . . . well, the records aren't entirely clear. It's possible that whoever controls the *nenkah* may control the princess so long as the *nenkah* exists. And there's at least a suggestion in the records that destroying the *nenkah* might be able to wound Kiara through it—maybe kill her."

"I don't like this." Wilym sat back in his chair, arms crossed and face set. "What happens after Kiara arrives? How do you get rid of the damned doll?"

Brother Felix shrugged. "According to the scrolls, once Kiara is crowned and the regent magic is activated, the *nenkah* becomes nothing more than a rag doll filled with an odd collection of items."

Kellen leaned forward. "While I have to say that I share Wilym's concerns, what choice do we have? Without the *nenkah*, Alvior might be able to have himself crowned and invoke the blood magic before Kiara could take the throne. I agree there are risks. I don't like magic. But even with the *vayash moru*'s help, it will take weeks for Kiara to reach Isencroft. We can't leave the succession open."

"What of the Regent?" Trygve shifted in his seat.

Allestyr shrugged. "The *nenkah* must remain our secret. We'll need Renate as our public face. As far as everyone at court knows, there's only Renate. But the crown is both legal and magical. Renate covers us as far as the legal matters go. But for the magical, we need the *nenkah*."

"Does Antoin have everything he needs to leave for Margolan?" Cam asked, turning to Brother Felix.

"All he needs is a letter—I was assuming Allestyr would want to write the message."

Allestyr nodded. "Very well. I'll do it immediately. While I'm busy with that, I'll need your help to make ready for our little ceremony." Cam could hear a touch of distaste in the seneschal's voice and he guessed that Allestyr was as uncomfortable about the ritual as the rest. "Trygve, I'm hoping nothing goes wrong, but I'd like you to have your healer's kit with you, just in case. Cam and Tice, I need you to go to Kiara's rooms and find some things that belonged to her that we can use for the *nenkah*. Kellen, I'll need you to prepare the ritual chamber. We haven't used it since Kiara left for Margolan."

"What about me?" Rhistiart had been nearly silent, but now he sat forward. "I want to help."

Brother Felix regarded him for a moment. "There have to be eight witnesses. You'll be the eighth man." He stood. "Gentlemen, this kind of magic is best done at dusk or dawn. We'll meet in the crypt chamber at fifth bells. And may the Goddess look kindly on our souls."

When the group assembled in the necropolis beneath Aberponte, Cam could not recall seeing them ever look so ill at ease. His own stomach was tight as if anticipating a battle, and he caught himself pulling nervously at the collar of his uniform. Rhistiart was pale, and although the crypt chamber was cool, a light sheen of sweat showed on his forehead. None of the others looked any less nervous.

The necropolis was ancient, older than the Isencroft monarchy, going back at least to the time when warlords ruled the clans that would someday unite to become a kingdom. The newer sections of the necropolis, still centuries old, were tunnels of stone with barrel ceilings and bricked floors. Crypt rooms opened off the walkway, and many corridors branched off into darkness. The walkway led into several large rooms ringed with ornately carved catafalques, monuments to Isencroft's dead kings and queens. Cam swallowed hard as he filed past the tomb of Queen Viata, Kiara's mother, and noted the as yet incompletely carved catafalque next to it that would hold Donelan's remains.

As they descended, the cut stone and bricked corridors gradually became tunnels in the rock, and many of the openings appeared to be natural cave rooms enlarged and embellished over the centuries. Bones were stacked in alcoves cut into the walls, neatly piled with the skulls facing out so that, in places, the walls on either side of the corridors appeared to be made from yellowed, grinning skulls. The deeper they went into the necropolis, the more ornate the ossuary became. Cam shuddered at the macabre decorations left behind by long-forgotten priests. Bones were set into the walls in complex designs to make crests and murals, while in other places whole skeletons posed in a lifelike tableau were cemented in place.

Hundreds of tunnels formed an ancient labyrinth beneath the Aberponte palace, filled with tens of thousands of shrouded corpses or yellowing bones. Finally, Brother Felix stopped at a locked room with a thick, oaken door bound with iron and drew a key from a ring on his belt. They waited outside as Felix entered and lit the torches that hung in sconces around the room, and Cam noticed that Felix chanted as he moved.

Cam looked around when Felix bade them enter. Felix locked the door and then raised a circle of warding behind them. The torches were only partially successful at driving back the shadows, and Cam realized the room was larger than he had first thought. He could not tell whether this room was part of the natural caves or man-made, but it looked as if it had been in use for centuries. The floor was worn smooth at the doorway, and the walls around the sconces were blackened with soot. Around the walls were a series of intricate mosaic crests, and Cam realized that they were the heraldic emblems not of the Isencroft kings but of the eight ancient clan lords. Where the walls met the ceiling, runes were carved into the smooth stone, and a row of ancient skulls were set beneath the runes, angled so that they appeared to be watching what transpired below. The runes shifted as Cam stared at them, and he wondered if it were merely a trick of the flickering light.

In the center of the room was a large, raised oblong altar. Its base was worked with symbols, and its surface was worn smooth with use. The stone had dark stains whose origins Cam did not care to ponder.

Brother Felix seemed to be most at ease with the night's work. He wore his formal white robes. Silver embroidery edged the cuffs and hem, more symbols that Cam did not recognize. Over his robe, Felix wore a large gold pendant set with five of the gems sacred to the Goddess and her eight Aspects: ruby for fire, sacred to Chenne the Warrior; sapphire, blue as the skies, for the Childe; diamond, clear as air itself, for the Formless One; sea-green emerald, for the Mother; amber, the color of the Goddess's eyes, for Istra, the Dark Lady. A wide gold cuff ringed Felix's right wrist with the last three gems: onyx for Sinha, the Crone; red garnet for the Lover; and bloodstone for Athira, the Whore. Felix carried a large silver chalice that was set with the same stones. On his left hand, he wore a silver ring set with a large ruby. At his belt was a silver dagger with a jeweled hilt.

Felix motioned for the men to take their places in a circle around the altar stone. Before joining them, he warded the doorway so they would not be interrupted. Cam glanced around the room. Every man except Brother Felix wore a sword, even Tice and Allestyr, who usually did not go about the palace visibly armed. Cam wondered if, despite Felix's wardings, each of them was unnerved enough by the necropolis to feel the need for protection.

When they took their places around the altar, Felix closed his eyes and lifted the chalice toward the ceiling. "Powers that be, hear me! Goddess of Light, attend! We call to the fallen kings of Isencroft and to the Lady in all Her sacred Faces for both witness and power. Hail to the eight clan lords, who raised a kingdom from anarchy. We invoke your presence as we consecrate Kiara Sharsequin, only born of King Donelan and Queen Viata, as the Chosen of Isencroft, daughter of royal blood and descendant of the clan lords of old."

The temperature of the crypt, already cool, grew colder until

Cam could see his breath. The hair on the back of his neck stood up. Beside him, Rhistiart gave a muffled squeak and his eyes grew round. Along the northern wall of the chamber, mist began to solidify into the forms of men and women, until a solemn row of figures stood in silent witness.

Cam looked down the line of ghostly newcomers and was startled to recognize some of the faces from paintings and tapestries in the castle. A tall, gaunt man with short-cropped hair and a neatly trimmed beard was the ghost of King Rowan, dead for more than two hundred years. The next figure was equally familiar from the portrait over one of the sitting room mantels: Queen Tanisia, a wise and steady ruler, who had lived and died a hundred years ago. The spirits of eight monarchs stood silently, but Cam did not recognize the others. The ghosts represented only a few of the monarchs who had ruled in Isencroft's history. Some of the spirits wore garments of a style that suggested they had ruled so long ago that likenesses of them had not survived the ravages of time, and Cam wondered if they numbered among the original clan lords. Cam was disappointed not to see Donelan among the spectral monarchs.

"We gather to invoke the ancient powers," Felix continued, and as he spoke, he lifted the chalice in turn to the four corners, and then to the cross-quarters. "We claim the powers to name a new successor to the throne, and to animate this proxy until Kiara Sharsequin can take this power for her own. Let it be so."

A cold wind moved through the sealed chamber, gusting hard enough to make the torches flicker. *Well, someone's heard us, that's for sure*, Cam thought nervously.

Rhistiart elbowed Cam and held out an inlaid box. Cam, as King's Champion, bore the duty to take the next step in the ritual. Cam squared his shoulders and approached the altar, holding out the box to Felix.

Felix laid aside the chalice to receive the inlaid box. From within his white robes, Felix withdrew a piece of muslin sewn in the rough shape of a person, with the stitching open on one side. The figure had no features and no markings. Felix murmured under his breath as he opened the box and withdrew a piece of silk that Cam had cut from the seam of one of Kiara's gowns. Felix lifted the bit of silk to the four corners and slid it into the cloth doll shape.

Next, Felix took out a silver disk from one of Kiara's childhood necklaces and then a small dirk, well worn from Kiara's lessons in the salle with Darry. These he lifted to the cross-quarters and then placed them in the doll with the other items. Finally, Felix removed several strands of Kiara's hair and a piece of paper Cam knew to be one of Kiara's most recent letters to her father, covered in her neat, small script. Felix offered these to the four corners and then put them into the doll form. Then with a murmured incantation, he touched the rough edge of the open seam and it knitted together under his hand.

The *nenkah* lay lifeless but complete, a rough, featureless doll. Felix looked around the group and met each man's eyes in turn. He took up the chalice and raised it over his head in salutation.

"By the power of creation and chaos, of light and darkness, I call on the magic of blood and bloodline to anoint this proxy until our new queen can be crowned." Felix lowered the chalice and stood before Tice. Tice held out his left hand, and Felix withdrew the jewel-handled dagger. With one swift movement, Felix drew the blade down Tice's palm, raising a thin stream of blood that flowed into the chalice. Cam could hear Felix chanting in a low voice, but even when it was his turn and Felix stood in front of him, Cam could not make out the words.

More ghosts joined them as Felix made slow progress around

the circle. As Felix drew the blood of the last participant, Cam gasped. Next to the stone altar stood a new ghost, who appeared nearly solid enough to touch. Cam heard the sharp intake of breath as the others recognized King Donelan's shade.

Felix appeared to be the least shaken of the group, and Cam wondered if he had expected Donelan's participation. When Felix had stirred the last of the blood into the chalice, he stepped closer to the altar, standing directly across from Donelan's ghost. Cam studied the late king's face. Donelan looked neither surprised nor upset by the ritual, giving Cam to wonder again if Felix had anticipated the king's presence. The expression on Donelan's face was as worried and weary as it had been lately in life.

Felix looked to Donelan's ghost. "You understand our purpose?"

Donelan nodded.

"Are you familiar with the ritual?"

Again, the ghost nodded.

Felix drew a deep breath, and for the first time, Cam noticed that the Acolyte's hand was shaking. Felix's voice began a somber chant. He dipped the blade of the dagger into the mingled blood and withdrew it, making an eight-point circle around the *nenkah*. Then he looked up to meet Donelan's eyes.

"Ready?"

Donelan nodded once more.

Felix began to pour the blood in a thin stream onto the cloth doll. At the same time, Donelan's ghost became less solid, like fog dissipating on the wind. Tendrils of white fog unwound from the figure of the dead king and twined around the blood, disappearing into the *nenkah*. When the chalice was empty, Donelan's ghost was almost translucent and the *nenkah* was soaked in crimson. Felix put his hand over the *nenkah*, and Donelan placed a spectral hand atop his. Felix murmured one

Gail Z. Martin

last incantation, and the gems he wore flared with sudden light, blindingly bright in the gloom of the crypt. A spark of blue-white fire leaped from Felix's palm into the _nenkah_, which jolted and shuddered.

Cam realized he was holding his breath.

Beside him, Rhistiart fainted.

The _nenkah_ was breathing.

2

"What news do the spirit guides bring?"

Jair Rothlandorn, heir to the throne of Dhasson and Rider with the Sworn, leaned forward so as not to miss a word. Talwyn, just returned from walking the spirit paths, took a deep breath and accepted a cup of *vass*. She took it down in one gulp, as if its strong flavor and potent kick would fortify her, grounding her once more in the realm of the living.

"They believe we have three dawns before the war begins." Talwyn was the shaman of her people and next in line to become their chief. Her role required her to communicate with the spirits of the Ancient Ones, the gods worshipped in the Winter Kingdoms long before the cult of the Sacred Lady came to these lands, the gods who became the Consorts of the Goddess.

"That's something." Pevre, Talwyn's father and chief of the Sworn, sat back, watching Talwyn with a worried gaze.

"They weren't reassuring." Talwyn looked grim. "The spirit guides had little to add to what our own rune scrying has told us. Dark magic. Much bloodshed. Invasion by the living and destruction from the risen dead. If you were hoping for a cheery prediction, I'm afraid you're out of luck."

"We appear to be out of luck everywhere we turn." Jair reached out to touch Talwyn's shoulder, and she clasped his hand. The intricate tattoo that wound around each of their wrists marked them as married by the custom of the Sworn, although the royal court of Dhasson would never accept their union, nor their son, Kenver, as a legitimate heir to the throne.

Pevre tossed a handful of ground anise into the fire for protection, and its fragrant smoke rose into the night air. In the distance, Jair heard a single horn blast one sharp note: the report of the night guards marking both the hour of the night and an uneventful watch. "What of the Dread and the Nachele? Did the Spirit Guides bring word from the barrows?" Pevre asked.

Jair stole a glance at the three large, grass-covered mounds behind them. The ancient burial sites stretched from the coast of the Northern Sea in Margolan south through Dhasson to the Nargi border, and at one time, legend held that the barrows continued through Nargi into the steppes of the Southland tribes. One look at the dark hair and golden skin of the Sworn, and it was impossible not to guess that their bloodlines harkened to those same Southland tribes and to the people of the long-destroyed Southern Empire.

Imprisoned in the mounds for more than a thousand years were the Nachele, dark beings entombed to stop them from preying on the living. Their guardians, the Dread, were as fearsome as the things they guarded. Both were known only through tales passed from generation to generation, since neither had walked among mankind for ten centuries. The shamans of the Sworn were the only living people with whom the Dread communicated, and then only on the paths of spirit and by the Dread's rare invitation. Talwyn and her father, both shamans of the Sworn, had seen the Dread, heard their long-dead voices. Jair suppressed a shiver, glad he shared none of his wife's magic.

"The Dread are . . . agitated." Talwyn chose her words carefully, and Jair wondered whether the spirits that dwelled in the large mounds bothered to listen to the living. "The magic is wrong. It was harder than it should have been to raise the Spirit Gods, difficult to walk the paths, more tiring than usual. It's like there is a strange hum in the background that shouldn't be there."

"A *hum*?" Jair shook his head. "I don't understand."

Talwyn sighed and leaned against him. Jair realized that it was for support as much as it was a gesture of endearment. "I don't understand it either. It's hard to find a word for it. Hum is the closest I can get. Like there are voices talking in the distance. Only it's not voices. It's in the magic itself, and I think it's coming from the invaders."

Jair looked north, beyond the barrows, toward the shore of the Northern Sea. They were well behind the lines of battle, positioned by agreement with King Martris Drayke of Margolan, Jair's cousin. In the cold light of the moon, the shadows seemed sharper-edged, and Jair was glad for the reassuring warmth of the fire in the early-autumn chill.

Talwyn closed her eyes. "The war may not have started yet, but somewhere, there's been blood spilled. The Nachele are stirring in the barrows, and for the first time since I've been a shaman, I sense that the Dread are uneasy."

Jair frowned and looked from Talwyn to Pevre. "If no one's dying yet in battle, then where is the blood coming from?"

Talwyn shrugged. "I guess it's up to us to figure that out— more of that bad luck you mentioned."

They looked up as footsteps came closer, and Jair's hand automatically fell to the *stelian* sword at his belt, the weapon he carried as one of the Sworn's elite *trinnen* warriors. Mihei, one of Jair's fellow *trinnen*, was approaching with an unfamiliar guest. Mihei reached the edge of the firelight and stopped, bowing to Talwyn and her father.

"My apologies for the interruption, Cheira Talwyn, Chief Pevre."

Pevre shook his head. "We've finished the working. Who's this with you, and how did we come to have a visitor on the eve of battle?"

The newcomer stepped into the firelight, and Jair raised an eyebrow, recognizing the cut of the man's jacket to be Dhasson military issue, although it was stripped of its insignia. "Honored Chief and Cheira," the man said, making a deep bow. "My name is Captain Davin, and I've come with a message for Prince Jair, from King Harrol."

Jair motioned for Davin to join them and be seated. Mihei returned to his post. "These are dangerous times for a ride through Margolan," Jair said cautiously, trying to read Davin's face and posture. "Is Father well?"

Davin made the sign of the Lady in warding and then cast a glance toward Talwyn and her father, as if he feared they might take offense at the gesture. "The king's well, thank the Lady. But I'm afraid these are dangerous times in Dhasson as well. Plague has spread from the Margolan border, and it's reached the outskirts of Valiquet. So many farmers have died or fled from the plague that food is becoming scarce in the cities. The king sent soldiers out to recover what he could of the harvest, since much of it was left to rot in the fields and on the trees. I'm afraid we'll eat through the winter stockpile long before spring."

"And hunger means unrest," Jair murmured. Davin nodded. "What else can you tell me, Captain?"

"Your father's called up all the regiments on high alert. Dhasson doesn't have coastline on the Northern Sea, but there's plenty of shoreline along the Nu River, and the chroniclers warned the king that the last time invaders came from the north, their raiders went as far south as Trevath before they were beaten back."

"So Father's going to make sure they don't get past Dhasson this time?"

"Yes, my prince." He shook his head. "Granted I've been on the road for several weeks, but when I left, the army had its hands full keeping the peace. Frightened people drink more, and pick more fights. It's as if there's been a month of full moons, what with people losing their senses. The wretches at the madhouse went on a rampage and broke down the gates. No one knows why, or where they've gone. Even the Sisterhood is having a grim time of it. Word has it that some of their mages have been frightened out of their wits by something only they can see." He shivered. "We're past the Feast of the Departed, but there are ghosts walking in every crossroads and burying ground. They won't lie still, and even the hedge witches can't make them rest quietly. These are bad days, m'lord. Never seen the like of them."

Davin reached into his jacket and withdrew a folded parchment. It bore the royal seal pressed into scarlet wax. From the way the seal made a dim glow as Jair broke it, he guessed that it had been spelled to open only for him.

"Problems?" Talwyn asked, turning to watch as Jair read down through the bold, sweeping pen strokes.

Jair's mouth formed a hard line as he scanned the letter. "They've had more problems with the Black Robes," he said dryly. "Damn Shanthadurists. He put an armed guard around the barrows while the Sworn is on the northern leg of the Ride, but there've been grave robbings and goat killings at cairns and crypts all around the kingdom. Amulet sellers are making piles of gold off people's fears, and the farmers won't put their flocks out to the autumn pastures because they're afraid of what might happen to the animals and the shepherds."

"No wonder the Dread are restless," Talwyn murmured. Davin paled.

"He's sent three regiments to patrol the Nu River in case the Temnottans try to move inland. He also sent a division to watch the Nargi border. Seems some of the nobility think the Crone Priests might be behind all the grave robbing, and while Father says he doubts that, he wouldn't put it past Nargi to make a move while everyone's busy fending off invaders from the north."

"Anything else?"

Jair managed a wry half smile. "Father sends his regards to Pevre, and his love to Talwyn and Kenver. He says he'd far rather be on the Ride with us than where he is." He frowned. "He's asked you to pray to the Spirit Gods to bless Dhasson. He says he's asked the same of the Lady's seers." He glanced up to meet Talwyn's eyes. "He must really be worried. Father's not exactly observant when it comes to religion. I've never seen him pray except in public on feast days, and then the seneschal has to write out the words on a paper Father keeps in his sleeve." Jair carefully folded the letter and slipped it into a pouch at his belt.

"I'm sorry to bear worrisome news, m'lord."

Jair shrugged. "It's not as if you were the cause of it. What instructions did Father give you once the message was delivered?"

"I'm to return with your reply, if it's possible to do so with war in the offing. If I can't return, then I'm to offer my services to you or to King Martris."

"And your assessment of the road between here and Dhasson?"

Davin was silent for a moment, as if something he had seen warred with his bearing as a soldier. "Speak your mind, Captain," Jair encouraged.

"Twice on the road, I was set upon by *ashtenerath*," Davin said in a quiet voice. "Fortunately, only one or two at a time, and they smell so bad I had warning of their coming. I saw ghosts aplenty and even though I know how to set stones for a night warding, many a night I couldn't sleep because there were *things* out there, just beyond the wardings, wanting my blood.

I came upon the body of a peddler near a crossroads, and the man and his horse looked as if they'd been torn apart by something, but it wasn't any animal I could name. The bite and claw marks were wrong. Magicked beast or *dimonn*, I didn't stick around to find out. I passed villages without a living soul in them from the plague, and at night, I could hear their wights calling me to join them." He shivered. "I'd prefer to face a whole army in battle, Your Highness, than take that road again. But I'll do as you command."

"Perhaps one of the *vayash moru* could be persuaded to carry your reply to your father," Pevre suggested.

Jair nodded. "I was thinking the same thing. Right now, there's nothing urgent I have to tell Father that won't wait." He looked at Davin, and the soldier averted his eyes, as if ashamed to admit his fear of a return journey. "You're a brave man, Davin, and a clever one to make that trip in one piece. I'd like you to carry a message for me to the Margolan battlefront, to King Drayke. You need to tell the king what you've told me."

Davin drew a deep breath, pride in his eyes at the unexpected praise. "I would be honored to do so, my prince."

"Good, then it's settled." Jair gestured to Mihei, who had waited just beyond earshot. "Davin's going to need provisions and a place to stay the night."

Mihei inclined his head in assent. "Done." He looked to Davin. "Please follow me."

Jair watched Davin and Mihei leave the edge of the firelight. Talwyn laid a hand on his arm. "What are you really thinking?"

Jair sighed and stared into the fire as if a sign from the spirits might appear. "I'm worried, about Father and about Dhasson. I'm too far away to do anything, and besides, we've got more than our share of problems here. Between his report of strange goings-on in Dhasson and Davin's stories of what he saw on the road, I have to think that it's more than just the Shanthadura

Black Robes trying to revive the worship of a long-forgotten goddess. It's too close to what you heard from the Spirit Guides, about something disturbing enough to upset even the Dread and the Nachele. I don't look forward to going up against a power that has the Dread worried."

Pevre nodded. "I was thinking the same thing. I've spent my life riding these barrows, and more than once, I wondered whether the whole thing was just a myth. After all, the Dread haven't stirred in a thousand years, and generations of Sworn have ridden from one end of the barrows to the other time after time without anything noteworthy ever happening. But now . . ." His voice drifted off and he looked up at the star-lit sky. "Now, I'm afraid I have the answer I was looking for, and it's one I'd have rather done without." He looked from Jair to Talwyn. "It's late, and there's no telling what morning will bring. Best you get some sleep while you can, before Kenver wakes you up at dawn."

When Jair and Talwyn reached their tent, the fire inside was banked and the embers cast a dim light around the interior of their *gar*, the portable circular dwelling that the Sworn called home. Jair could just make out Kenver's sleeping form underneath the woven blankets. The tent smelled of incense, and Jair guessed that Talwyn had scattered some herbs and scented wood in the fire before they left.

As if seeing them for the first time, Jair took stock of the painted images and symbols drawn on the interior of the dwelling's cloth walls, and of the crystals and talismans that hung from the support poles. Despite Talwyn's position as cheira and chief's daughter, their home was nearly identical to those of the rest of the Sworn. For all the years Jair had ridden with the Sworn, he had never fully thought about the paintings and talismans beyond their value in teaching the nomadic people's history to the children of the tribe. Now, after hearing Davin's story and reading Harrol's letter, Jair wondered about the protective nature of the decorations, and whether the markings, passed down from parent to child across generations, harkened back to more dangerous times.

Kenver did not stir as Jair and Talwyn settled into their bed. Jair closed his eyes, enjoying the night sounds outside the *gar*. The sounds mingled with the scent of burning embers and incense, and Jair sank into the comfort of the sensations, wishing once again that he could remain on the Ride forever. None of the comforts of Dhasson's palace ever made him feel as much at home as he did on the Ride, and each year, the months slipped by too quickly, until it was time for his return to the palace city. *The war might be more adventure than you bargained for*, he reminded himself silently, and he inched closer to Talwyn, who was already asleep. Tired as he was, worries about the war would have to wait, and Jair drifted off to sleep.

He awoke with a start, unsure of what had awakened him. By habit, his hand fell to the pommel of his *stelian* in the scabbard that lay next to the bed. Nothing stirred in the darkness of the tent, and the glow from the banked embers was nearly gone. Across the way, Jair could make out Kenver's form, assuring him that Kenver was still where he had been candlemarks before. Jair reached out to rouse Talwyn, but he withdrew his hand with a gasp.

Talwyn's body was cool. Jair shook her, swallowing back rising fear, but Talwyn did not rouse. She grimaced in pain, as if about to scream, but no sound came from her, even as Jair shook harder. Talwyn's hands were fisted, and her body was rigid. Fresh gashes, like claw marks, raked her arm and cheek, though no paw prints of an attacking animal led away from where she lay.

"Daddy, what's wrong?"

Jair felt Kenver behind him, and only then became aware that he had been calling Talwyn's name loudly. "Mommy's sick. Go get Grandpa. Run!"

Jair drew a deep breath, forcing himself to think instead of feel. Talwyn's skin was unusually cool, but not devoid of warmth like a corpse. Her muscles were clenched tight, though not with the rigor of death. To his relief, he found both breath and pulse, although Talwyn did not rouse, even when he splashed her face with water.

Pevre and Kenver were beside him in minutes. "What happened?" Pevre asked, taking in Talwyn's condition with detachment.

Jair moved back to permit Pevre to examine Talwyn. "I don't know. Something woke me. There was nothing unusual in the tent, no strange noises outside. I reached over to Talwyn and found her like this."

Pevre frowned in concentration, and he extended one hand, palm down, over Talwyn's face. Slowly, he moved his hand down the center of her body, just above her skin. He closed his eyes as he moved his hand and began to chant under his breath in a low voice. Finally, he opened his eyes and looked at Jair.

"Someone . . . or something . . . has sent dream magic against her. She's rigid because she's fighting for her life in the dream realm against something we can't see or hear but that is very real to her. Her body is cool because whatever it is drains her life force, the same way a *vayash moru* drains blood."

"Fighting for her life," Jair repeated quietly, and instinctively he put a protective arm around Kenver, drawing the small boy close. "So it's real to her, even in the dream realm?"

Pevre nodded. "Very real. This kind of magic is old. It takes power to wield it, and skill. It's considered gray magic at best because the potential to misuse it is so strong. You can imagine what such a thing could do to a political rival, or a spurned lover, for example."

"How do we break it?"

Pevre rocked back on his heels, thinking. "I need my ritual bag from my tent," he said with a glance to Kenver, who ran to fetch it. While they waited for Kenver to return, Pevre motioned for Jair to help him move Talwyn closer to the fire. Lifting her by shoulders and ankles, they carried her near the fire pit and laid her on a mat. Pevre added wood to the fire and lit the lanterns. Kenver returned with the ritual bag, and Pevre set it down near Talwyn. He made a gesture of warding over the bag and opened it reverently, and then he walked a larger circle of warding around Talwyn, carefully keeping Jair within the circle and motioning for Kenver to step back so that he would be outside the warded space.

"I don't know who sent this, or how strong their magic is. I'll need your help to fight it," he said with a nod toward Jair. "But I'd just as soon Kenver stay outside the warding. My magic should be strong enough to keep it contained."

Pevre withdrew a shaman's mantle from the ritual bag and carefully laid it around his shoulders. Then he took four carved images from the bag, one for each of the Spirit Gods the Sworn honored—the Bear, the Eagle, the Wolf, and the catlike Stawar. These he placed in a ring around the fire. As he placed the images, he bowed to each one.

"Guardian spirits, we honor you," Pevre said in a low rumble. "Walk with me on the dream paths, and give me your strength to overcome the attacker."

The fire glowed more brightly, and Jair thought he glimpsed movement in the shadows of the four images, and he wondered if it were a trick of the light. Pevre removed several polished disks of amber and agate from his bag and placed them at Talwyn's head, feet, shoulders, and hips. He took a smooth piece of onyx and pried open Talwyn's fist, closing her fingers around the disk. Then he motioned for Jair to kneel beside Talwyn.

"Hold her hand in your left hand, and your *stelian* in your right. Concentrate on the onyx she's holding. I'll open up the dream realm for you. A shadow of your weapon should follow you into her dream. Use the onyx to bring both of you back to the waking world."

Jair nodded and began to breathe deeply as Pevre began to chant. Inhaling the smoke and incense, Jair closed his eyes and let himself enter a trance, keeping his mind focused on the onyx disk in Talwyn's fist. At first, Pevre's voice was loud, sounding just behind him. Over the span of several breaths, the voice grew more distant, until it was so faint Jair could no longer hear it.

Talwyn's scream and the growl of a wild beast jolted Jair into action. Warrior training overcame instinct, and he rose with his *stelian* ready for battle. They stood on a stark plain that was devoid of color. Few trees or plants rose from the barren ground that stretched to the horizon, broken only by one or two rocky outcroppings. In the gray of twilight, it was difficult to make out the shape of the enemy, and then Jair spotted them and caught his breath. Shadows, not predators, were encroaching on Talwyn, who barely kept them at bay with a hand raised in warding and a gnarled broken branch wielded like a weapon. She looked exhausted, and the gashes Jair had seen on her sleeping form were fresh and seeping.

A ring of shadow forms circled Talwyn. At first, the shadows lay flat against the ground, and then one of the shadows rose out of the dark ring, amorphous at first, until it solidified into the shape of a man. It reached toward Talwyn with taloned hands, slashing at her and nearly getting inside her guard.

Jair hurled a rock at the shadow. "Leave her alone!" The rock sailed right through the figure. There was a guttural sound like many deep voices conferring in the distance, and the shadow ring began to move swiftly toward Jair across the dirt.

"Don't let them touch you!" Talwyn's voice was sharp with warning, but Jair could hear the pain and weariness that tinged it. She looked haggard and drained, with an unnatural pallor. He ran toward her, taking a zigzag path and doubling back on himself, eluding the shadow forms until he stood between them and Talwyn.

The guttural sound grew louder, and the shadows seemed to boil, as if his action displeased them.

"Where's the onyx?" Jair shouted to Talwyn without taking his eyes off the roiling shadow that had doubled its size, coming toward them like a wave on dry land.

"I don't have it!" Talwyn replied, dropping to her knees to scrabble in the dust searching for the stone. "Where was it on the other side?"

"Pevre put it in your hand," Jair replied, bracing himself for the onslaught.

Behind him, Talwyn searched for the stone as the shadows drew nearer. Jair wielded his *stelian* as he would have in the waking world, unsure of its worth against their enemy. "What are these things?" Jair called to her.

"*Esiteran*. Life-drinkers. They drain energy instead of blood."

"Will my *stelian* hold them off?"

"For a while. Sooner or later, they get inside your guard, as you can see."

The shadows surged forward, and Jair struck at them with his *stelian*. The sword felt as solid and deadly in his hands here in the dream realm as it did in the waking world, although how it had moved across the gap between realms with him, he did not know. The *stelian* met the darkness, slicing through it like light. The shadows shrieked and drew back, only to rush at him from another angle, forcing him to pivot sharply to meet their advance with another blow of the *stelian*. A tendril of darkness snapped out and cut through the cloth of his pants, tearing into his leg. Jair gritted his teeth against the pain and slashed at the shadow, forcing it back.

The shadows were massing. Jair wondered if they had been merely toying with Talwyn, and whether his arrival had pushed them to action. He struck again at the shadows and a whip-thin edge of the darkness sliced down, lashing him across his shoulder and chest. He cried out at the pain and swung his *stelian* until the shadows drew back again.

"I've got it!" Talwyn found the onyx disk and clasped it between her two hands. "Lay a hand on my shoulder, and don't let go," she said to Jair. He complied, keeping his *stelian* ready in his right hand. Talwyn raised her hands overhead and murmured words of power, and she then held up the onyx between thumb and forefinger.

A brilliant flare of light streamed from the polished stone. The shadows hissed and receded, like a dark tide. The light traveled down Talwyn's upraised arms, until Jair and Talwyn were encircled in a pillar of light.

With a sudden shift, Jair found himself back in the tent, kneeling next to Talwyn, his *stelian* gripped in his hand. He glanced down at his ruined shirt and the vicious slash that had laid open both cloth and skin. Jair shifted, painfully aware of the gash on his leg that had begun to throb. Talwyn's eyes snapped open. Color had come back to her skin, and her whole form relaxed. Beside them, Pevre stopped chanting and drew a deep breath. He let his head hang for a moment, as though the effort had exhausted him, and then looked from Talwyn to Jair.

"You're back," he said, a note of tired pride in his voice.

Talwyn reached out to touch Pevre's sleeve. "Thank you."

Pevre shrugged. "The question is, how did you become trapped in the dream realm?"

Talwyn struggled to sit, and Jair helped her rise. "I'm not sure. I keep wardings set around the tent to avoid problems just like that. When we came back last night, the wardings were in place. Either something broke the wardings or someone is doing powerful blood magic nearby, strong enough that it penetrated my wardings."

"Wouldn't you know if someone tried to break the wardings outright?" Jair asked. Pevre was busy making a paste from liquids and herbs in his bag to clean their wounds. Jair winced when Pevre applied the thick salve.

"The sting of it can't be helped," Pevre grumbled. "The wounds are most likely poisoned."

"Yes, under most circumstances," Talwyn said, answering Jair's question. "It should have awakened me if anyone tinkered with the wardings at all, long before they were broken. So either something was able to get past the protections without actually breaking them or we're up against a mage who's good enough to be sly with his power."

"Will you be all right?" Kenver's voice was thin and reedy, and Jair could hear the boy trying to hide the way his voice trembled. Pevre dismissed his own warding with a gesture, and Kenver ran to Jair and Talwyn, throwing his arms around them.

Talwyn tousled the boy's hair, and Jair drew him close. "We'll be fine as soon as your grandfather's poultices do their work," Talwyn said, though Jair could hear the exhaustion in her voice.

Pevre took a seat against one of the support poles of the tent. "It's still the middle of the night. I suggest you three get some sleep. I'll stand guard. I doubt anything will try again tonight to harm you, but if it does, I'll be ready."

Kenver would not return to his own bed, insisting to be between his mother and father. For once, Jair didn't feel like arguing. Despite Pevre's medicine, his wounds still throbbed, and he wondered if he could possibly sleep. But sleep found him, and this time, he did not dream at all.

*　　*　　*

Light was already streaming through the smoke hole in the roof of the *gar* when Jair awoke. Kenver was sleeping soundly beside him, but Talwyn had rolled onto her side, awake, absently stroking Kenver's dark hair. In the light, the slashes on her cheek looked even worse than Jair remembered from the night before. Carefully, they extricated themselves from Kenver's wide-flung arms and moved quietly outside the tent, where Pevre joined them.

"It's going to take a few days for those wounds to heal," Pevre said, taking in their still-tender injuries with an appraising eye. "Nature of the beast that got you. Could have been worse. At least it wasn't teeth."

"I didn't know shadows had teeth," Jair muttered.

"Those weren't exactly regular shadows," Pevre replied, his voice rough from lack of sleep. "If you hadn't figured that out already. The line between waking and sleeping is just like twilight or daybreak, or the solstices. It's a place where the threshold between our world and other realms is thinner, easier to cross. Sometimes we cross over; sometimes something else does. Just like a summoner's magic can cross between the realms of the dead and the living, other magics can invade thoughts or dreams, even memories. We're lucky such magics are rare. They can be a terrible weapon."

"Chief Pevre! Cheira Talwyn!" One of the *trinnen* warriors came running up to them. He stopped and made a quick bow. "Two elders from one of the nearby villages approached our night guard. They said they have no one else to turn to, and they need our help."

Jair and Talwyn exchanged glances. "I thought the villagers along this route pretty much ignored or avoided the Sworn?" Jair murmured.

"They do," Talwyn replied. "They keep to themselves, and so do we." She looked to the guard. "Why did they come to us? Why not go to the king's patrols?"

The taller of the two warriors nodded. "I asked the same thing. With the preparations for war, it appears that patrols in the area are almost nonexistent. I think they were desperate. We've heard a little of their story, but I think you should be there for the rest. Their problem may have more to do with us than they know."

Talwyn, Jair, and Pevre followed the taller guard, while the shorter man stayed behind on Talwyn's orders to guard Kenver while the boy slept. The guard led the way to the large common lodge. The Sworn's *gar* were large circular structures held up by an easily collapsible frame of light but sturdy wood. The heavy cloth of the *gar* and the fanlike ceilings could be insulated for warmth in the winter with a layer of cloth batting or sheepskin, or left to be a single layer of cloth in warmer seasons. The lodge was the largest of the moveable structures, and the entire tribe of guardian warriors could fit inside for important rituals when the need arose. Now, the large *gar* held only three guards, a half-grown boy, and a ragged man.

"What has brought you to our camp?" Talwyn stepped forward. Despite her injuries, she was fully in command as the Sworn's shaman. She spoke Common instead of the Sworn's consonant-heavy language, but the ancient language of the nomadic guardians accented her words.

Both the man and the boy made awkward bows. "Forgive us for disturbing you," the man said, "but we had nowhere else to go. The king's soldiers are gone to the war, and there's no other justice within several days' ride. Please, m'lady, we need the help of a mage. My village won't last another night."

Jair could see from Talwyn's expression that she was both intrigued and moved by the man's entreaty. Talwyn gestured for them to sit, and everyone but the three Sworn guards did so. By unspoken agreement, the guards remained standing, just a few steps behind their unexpected visitors.

"Tell me why your village needs a mage," Talwyn said.

"It started when someone began stealing the bodies of our dead," the man replied. Jair watched closely as the man spoke. At first glance, he'd taken the stranger for being in his middle years, but as Jair looked more carefully, he saw that hard work and deprivation had etched the man's face more than time, and he revised his estimate of the visitor's age downward by twenty seasons. The boy, whom Jair guessed to be twelve or thirteen summers old, seemed to shrink into himself as if wishing to disappear, or to be completely overlooked. *Something's scared both of them badly*, Jair thought. *That's the only thing that would bring them here.*

"A week ago, someone or something tore up our burying ground. They dug up the bodies and dragged them off."

"Was there anything left behind, like sacrificed animals or rune markings?" Talwyn asked, leaning forward with interest.

The man looked surprised. "No, m'lady. Nothing at all, not even tracks. We thought it might be looters, but what little was buried with the bodies was left in the graves. Our village is too poor to bury anything of value with the dead, when the living make do with little."

Talwyn nodded, and her smile gave the man courage to continue. "A few nights after that, two of the shepherds came screaming back to town in the middle of the night. They'd been out in the fields since before the grave robbings, and no one had been out to tell them about it. Swore they'd seen dead folks walking out along the ridge, and named them, all the ones taken from the burying ground. Scared nearly out of their minds they were, and these aren't children. These are young men who have fought off wolves and robbers."

"The dead were walking? Where were they going?" Jair watched the men as they spoke, but nothing in their manner seemed false. Like Talwyn, he was riveted by their story.

The man gave a bitter chuckle. "The shepherds didn't stick around, or follow. They lit out of there as soon as they realized what they'd seen. Said the dead were headed north, and that they moved sluggishly, as if pulled along by strings instead of free to move on their own."

"Is that why you came here? To ask for help in binding your dead to their cairns?" Talwyn asked gently.

Their visitor shook his head. "No, m'lady. While I would not like to see them disturbed, the dead are dead. I wouldn't risk the living to bring them back, if they've taken to wandering, so long as they leave us in peace." His voice caught. "But that's not the worst of it. Last night, it was like madness struck our little village. M'lady, you'll think we're awful people, but we're just a small village of herders and farmers, scraping out a living and trying to pay our taxes. Even when Jared the Usurper—Crone take his soul," the man said, spitting to the side to ward off evil, "took the throne, we didn't run away, the way so many did. We hunkered down and let the worst of it pass us by. But we're paying for it now, m'lady, because something's found us. Something evil."

"You said that madness struck. What do you mean?" Talwyn's voice was soothing, and Jair knew that its calming effect was enhanced by her shaman's magic.

The man shifted uncomfortably. He refused to meet her eyes. "Last night, ten people in our village were murdered. M'lady, there are only forty of us, just a few families. There warn't no reason for it. Can't blame strong drink, because the ones who have too much to drink on a regular basis slept through it all." He shook his head, and dared to look up. His eyes were red-rimmed, as if he had been among the grieving.

"In the space of two candlemarks, it was like a shadow fell over the village. Husbands and wives who had never quarreled took a hammer or a hatchet to each other. Parents who loved their children with all their breath wiped out their whole families. Brothers set on each other or on their parents. There's no one untouched, no one who didn't lose someone. And we can't even bury the dead, for fear that they'll be stolen away."

At the word "shadow," Jair and Talwyn exchanged a hurried glance. "Did anything unusual happen just before the murders?" Jair asked gently. "Anyone new visit the village or pass by? Any strange symbols or markings on the trees or rocks?"

The ragged man shook his head again. "No one's been by our village in weeks. What with the talk of war, the traders don't travel our way. It's several days' ride into the nearest real town of any size. We don't have enough coin for the peddlers to make an effort to come to us, and there's no inn or tavern nearby." He thought for a moment.

"But there was one thing. A few days before the murders, the hedge witch in our village went raving mad. She'd been complaining of headaches that even her potions couldn't set right, but no one else had them. When we found her, she had gouged out her eyes and was slamming her head against a rock until she was bloody. She'd been clawing at her ears until they were practically torn from her head, and her nails were stripped down to the quick. All she'd say was that something wouldn't stop calling her, wouldn't stop humming in her head."

"And where is she now?" Talwyn asked.

The man took a long breath. "Last night she got away from the ones who were watching over her. She ran into the fire and danced while she burned, and she used her magic to keep anyone from saving her. She didn't want to be rescued. The last thing she said before she died was, 'It stopped. I can't hear them anymore.'"

Talwyn and Pevre stepped away to confer in low voices. Jair sat silently beside the man, completely at a loss for words. The boy clung to his father, hiding behind a mop of unruly dark hair that covered his face. His posture and actions made Jair think of a much younger child, one just Kenver's age. *He's seen horrors that would drive grown men out of their wits*, Jair thought. *Let him take his comfort where he can.*

After a few moments, Talwyn and Pevre returned. "I'll visit your village and see if there's anything I can do to help, although I have to warn you, I'm not sure I can set things right," Talwyn said. She held up a hand to stave off the man's protestations of gratitude.

"We'll go tomorrow. I'm too spent to work the kind of magic such a visit requires. You and the boy may stay the night in our camp. You'll be safe here."

It was apparent to Jair that the man chafed at the delay, even as he realized the necessity. The stranger nodded in acquiescence. "As you wish, m'lady. We're in your debt."

Talwyn spoke to the guards in the language of the Sworn, instructing them to make the strangers comfortable but to keep them under guard without implying that the visitors were prisoners. When the guards had shown the man and the boy out, Talwyn looked to Pevre and Jair.

"Once again, I have the feeling that our enemy across the sea isn't waiting to bring the war to us," Talwyn said. Jair could hear the fatigue in her voice, and he saw the tiredness that lined her face. "Even worse, they . . . or it . . . has the power to cause damage far behind the battlefields. And with all that power, whoever or whatever is behind this wants to free the Nachele to make it even worse."

3

Martris Drayke, the Summoner-King of Margolan, watched over the seer's shoulder, giving rapt attention to the scene that was unfolding in a basin of still water. Beyral, one of the king's rune scryers and far-seers, held her hands on either side of the basin, near but not touching the bowl. On the still surface of the water was an image of a battle being fought miles away, out on the Northern Sea. The fighting was beyond the acute eyesight of the most eagle-eyed scout, even armed with a small telescope. And so the king and two of his generals watched anxiously, breathing shallowly so as not to ripple the water with their breath.

"Fishermen can't hold off an invading fleet for long," General Senne murmured.

"Pashka and his people may be fishermen, but they know those waters like the inside of their own homes." Ban Soterius was both a general and one of the king's boyhood friends. He leaned in over the king's shoulder. "Can Beyral make the image any sharper, Tris? I can barely see."

Despite the gravity of the moment, the king hid a slight smile. Soterius was one of a handful of trusted friends who still called him by his nickname. It was a fleeting reminder of the time, just over two years before, when Tris had been just a privileged second son with no aspirations to the throne, before coup and betrayal and war changed his destiny and the history of Margolan. "We can try," Tris said, lending some of his own magic to amplify Beyral's far-seeing.

The image sharpened and grew slightly larger. "Look there," Senne said, reaching out to point and only barely stopping himself before he disturbed the water and might have lost the image. "Are those actually ships?"

Tris and Soterius bent to get a better look. "Some of them are," Soterius said slowly, squinting to see better.

"But look at those ships, the ones on the right," Tris said, feeling a chill go down his spine. "They look like hulks, as if someone hauled a wreck to the surface and made it float."

Soterius met Tris's eyes. "Could a summoner do that? I mean, you can call spirits back from the grave and make them solid. You have the power to raise the dead, even if Light mages don't do such things. Can you raise 'dead' things like a ship hulk?"

Tris bit his lip. "Technically, yes. The wood in the ships was living at one time, so once it's cut, even though it's 'dead,' there is a thread of connection. That's the tricky part with summoning. If you're sloppy about how you cast a spell, in theory, you could get not only the ghost you're trying to summon but all the dead animals, insects, and plants in the immediate area."

"Are you telling me that Pashka's men are fighting ghost ships?" Senne's voice told Tris that the general was struggling to make yet another leap of faith to believe his king. Tris knew that while Senne's loyalty was absolute, the general wrestled to understand his liege's magic.

"Afraid so." As they watched, larger ships, carricks and caravels, entered the scene in the scrying bowl.

"Tolya's privateers are sailing to the rescue," Soterius murmured. His tone told Tris that Soterius might have accepted the privateers' help, but he didn't fully trust their allegiance.

"Look there!" Senne cried out, belatedly tempering his voice when he realized he had just yelled in the king's ear. Tris and Soterius shifted their attention. "Those damn ghost ships are ramming the fishermen's boats!"

The image in the scrying bowl was smaller than Tris would have liked, though holding even that size of an image required a large expenditure of power. But even in miniature, Tris could see a flotilla of wrecks and hulks with broken masts and shattered sides moving with impossible speed. No wind propelled them, yet they were moving quickly, and the small boats of the fishermen scrambled nimbly to avoid being run down. The bow of one of the ghost ships plowed into a small skiff, breaking it in two. Tris could see the tiny images of men throwing themselves to the side to escape being crushed by the hulk.

"Not just ramming," Soterius said grimly. "Someone's firing on Tolya's and Pashka's men from the ghost boats." Just then, the image rippled again, as Tris concentrated his power to refocus the scrying on one of the ghost ships. He could hold that clarity for only a few seconds, but it was enough to show a skeletal crew aboard the boat sending very real arrows toward the fleet of defenders.

Tris had no idea what the fishermen and privateers made of the spectral invaders, but to their credit, both groups held their positions. As they watched, the privateers replaced regular arrows with flaming missiles, gambling that even the dead might flee from flames. The battle raged for the better part of a candlemark, with Tolya's fire missiles scuttling a dozen of the wrecks. Pashka's fishermen used the smaller size of their crafts to their advantage, attacking near the waterline with pikes and hooked blades fastened onto poles, sinking several more of the attackers' ships. Where the hulks exposed their crews near the waterline, Pashka and his fishermen used their hooks to yank the skeletons into the water and bash them with the pikes.

The ghost ships pulled back, but before Senne and Soterius could exclaim in triumph, Tris saw the cause for the retreat and felt his heart thud. In the space vacated by the ghost ships, a small waterspout was beginning to form.

"Here's hoping that our mages are paying attention," Tris muttered under his breath. Even as he spoke, he saw their own fleet of fishing boats and privateer vessels also pull back, and then he saw the reason why. A wild wind rose out of nowhere, whipping toward the waterspout and buffeting it until it dissipated. Margolan's motley fleet bobbed with the winds, but they did not flee.

"Are the attackers moving backward?" Soterius wondered aloud. They strained to see, but as they watched, the ghostly hulks began moving in reverse, slowly at first, and then faster and faster. Tris pointed to a disturbance in the surface of the ocean, a growing vortex that pulled the Temnottan hulks back to their grave beneath the sea.

"Their side raises a waterspout, and our side sinks a whirlpool," Senne said admiringly. The ghost ships' skeletal crews remained in their positions, either stripped of reason or no longer afraid of death. The whirlpool widened, drawing more and more of the hulks into its maw. Margolan's "navy" of fishermen and privateers reversed course sharply, maneuvering their own ships out of danger. Even at the distance of the scrying, they could see the crews dancing in celebration aboard their vessels as the last of the ghost ships sank into the whirlpool.

When it became clear that, for now, the battle was over, Beyral waved a hand above the image and the basin once again held only clear water. "Now by your leave, m'lord, I need to rest." Beyral's voice was scratchy and Tris could hear the exhaustion in her tone.

"Yes, of course. Thank you." Beyral left Tris's campaign tent. The three men were quiet for a moment. "If they could raise a waterspout, why didn't their mages do something about the whirlpool?" Senne mused.

"And for that matter, why send ghost ships when we know they've got a fleet hidden?" Soterius added.

Tris considered the images they had seen in the scrying bowl. "I think both were meant to test us," he said finally. "It wasn't the first real shot of the war; it was a fishing expedition. They wanted to see if they could intimidate the fishermen and privateers into turning tail and running away. Maybe they wanted to inspire terror in anyone watching on shore. Perhaps they were hoping to draw out our mages and get an idea of their power to use it against us later."

"Their power—or yours," Soterius said quietly. "I noticed that you didn't rush in to use magic, even though someone on their side obviously was using summoning tricks to raise those ghost ships."

Tris shrugged. "Not necessarily summoning. Animating something isn't the same thing as bringing it back to life. We saw the same kind of thing at Lochlanimar, when Curane's mages made our dead move like puppets. They weren't summoners. They hadn't brought the dead back to being able to move on their own; the mages had to use their power for every step."

"What about the skeleton archers?" Senne was frowning as if the sudden discourse on magical instead of military tactics was straining his patience.

"That's what Tris is saying—they could be 'puppets,' too, like the corpses at Lochlanimar. Any mage who could move something from a distance could do it, right?" Soterius looked to Tris for agreement, and Tris nodded.

"If you think about it, the archers weren't particularly accurate. Their advantage was surprise and sheer numbers, but they didn't seem to be doing anything to steer the boats, and when the whirlpool opened up, they didn't look like they made any attempt to get out of the way."

"That's true." Senne's lips pursed as he thought. "Do you think it was a trap—for Tris?" He leaned forward. "Maybe we were meant to think another summoner was behind it, but perhaps they hoped that the king would use his power, risk himself to counter their magic. For all we know, there could have been something magical waiting to counterstrike."

A grim smile played at the corners of Tris's mouth. *This* was the general that his father, King Bricen, had so valued for his cleverness in battle. Senne might not be as comfortable with magic as Soterius was, but the general knew the value of any military advantage, whether he understood how it worked or not. And right now, Tris knew that the wheels in Senne's head were turning quickly, looking for a strategic advantage.

"I didn't sense another summoner's power," Tris said slowly, thinking back to the scrying and trying to remember what his mage senses were telling him. "Then again, we're quite a distance from the action, but I think I'd be able to tell that kind of power signature." He shook his head. "No, I'm certain. A mage of power, to be sure. It was a good trick, very convincing. But not a summoner's power. I'd have felt it."

"Could you tell, was something waiting to pounce if you had tried to use your magic?"

Tris paused again, replaying the events in his mind. Finally, he shook his head again. "Not unless whoever did it was very, very good at masking his power. We know there's a dark summoner out there. But he didn't show his hand tonight, and our ships held their own, so it didn't seem necessary to risk more of our mages—or give away anything about my magic—if we didn't need to."

"Well played, m'lord," Senne said with a note of honest

appreciation that made Tris smile. Senne was not free with his compliments, nor was he in the habit of fawning praise.

Senne rose. "I'd best go back to the troops," he said. "Take them some good news and have them ready in case the next salvo comes by land."

Tris nodded. "Have Tolya and Pashka come to my tent when they return. I want to hear about the fight firsthand. Maybe something they saw will give us a better idea of what kinds of magic we're up against." He paused. "And let's make sure that they get a hero's welcome. They deserve it for standing their ground."

Senne inclined his head in acknowledgment. "As you wish, m'lord."

Tris waved Soterius to sit. "Stay for a moment."

"Now that you're done watching water boil, can I interest either of you in supper?" Coalan asked dryly from the tent doorway. Coalan was Soterius's nephew, chosen to be Tris's valet because of his unquestioned loyalty and longtime friendship.

Despite the tension, Tris fought a smile. "And may I assume that you've already sampled tonight's fare?"

Coalan grinned broadly. At sixteen summers old, he was only six years younger than the king. He'd shown his mettle the previous year, in the war against Curane the Traitor, by killing an assassin meant for the king. But he was equally famous for his seemingly never-ending interest in food. "Stew again, and the war hasn't actually started yet," he reported, with an exaggerated sigh. "On the other hand, cook's bread turned out to be softer than rocks, so it's a good day."

"Rocks or not, dinner would be welcome. Thank you."

Coalan gave an exaggerated bow. "Coming right up. And I'll make sure to include two glasses of brandy." Only a conspiracy between Tris and Soterius kept the young man from the front lines, but after Jared the Usurper's treachery had cost Coalan most of his family, Soterius had begged Tris to keep him as safe as possible. So while most of Coalan's time was spent as Tris's valet, the sword on the young man's belt was a reminder that if anyone were to get past the bodyguards who surrounded Tris and the tent, Coalan had proven his ability to defend the king.

When Coalan had gone, Soterius turned to Tris. "You look tired, and the real fighting hasn't started yet. I don't think these magic skirmishes are what's losing you sleep. So what's the real reason?"

"We're getting ready for war. I'm worried about having to leave Kiara and Cwynn behind. Do I need more reasons?"

Soterius gave him a potent stare. "I don't think that's all of it."

Tris sighed. "I haven't slept well the last few nights. Bad dreams. It's been different each night. I haven't been able to decide whether they're warnings or just my nerves getting to me."

"What did you dream?"

Tris shifted uncomfortably. "One night, I dreamed about Alyzza, dancing in her cell at Vistimar. Only this time, she wasn't mad, and she wasn't singing in riddles. She looked like she did when we met her in the caravan. She looked at me and said, 'Look to the pages, Tris. There are answers in the pages.'"

"Pages? Does she mean the histories Royster brought you from the Library at Westmarch?"

Tris shrugged. "I'm not sure." Darker possibilities had occurred to him, ones he would not speak aloud. "The thing is, I've read through everything countless times, and nothing jumped out at me as being significant. Maybe the circumstances just aren't right. Maybe the meaning will be clearer later."

"Or maybe you just had a bad dream."

Tris grimaced. "Yeah. Maybe that too."

"Was that the only dream? You seem a little too tired to have had just one bad night."

"There've been others. I dreamed about Cwynn. He was lying on a huge pile of bones, and a current of wild magic, like the Flow, opened the ground under the pile and roared up toward the sky. I thought it was going to burn him, but it swirled around him. It was as if he were part of the magic, calling the power."

"But you've examined Cwynn and had the Sisterhood and Cheira Talwyn look at him. You said that as far as anyone can tell, he doesn't have any magic at all."

"As far as anyone can tell," Tris repeated tiredly. "He's only a few months old. Most power doesn't manifest until puberty. Talwyn thought he had something. She said he 'glowed' to her mage sight. She said she thought whatever we're fighting might be after him." Tris ran a hand over his face. "He's my son. How can I protect him if I don't know as much about him as our enemy does?"

Coalan returned with their dinner, taking great care to lay out their bowls, bread, and drink carefully. Soterius hid a proud smile at the young man's proficiency. As promised, two generous glasses of brandy accompanied the meal. "Who knows what we'll have tomorrow, or whether we'll have time to eat," Coalan said as he finished setting out the food. "So eat hearty!"

With that, Coalan settled down in a corner of the tent with his own meal, which Tris could not help but notice included a double portion of bread and a tankard of ale. Coalan had charmed himself into the good graces of the cook, who made sure that the young man never went hungry.

"Anything else?" Soterius brought Tris's thoughts back to the present. "Any other dreams?"

Tris paused to take a few bites of food, followed by a sip of brandy. "It's just as I told Sister Fallon: I've had each of those dreams several times. But there was one more. I dreamed about a burying ground, an old place where someone had been laying their dead to rest for a long time. I felt power sweep through the cairns, calling to the dead. It gave the spirits no choice; it tore them from their resting places, forced them to the surface.

"But it wasn't calling them just to rise. It began drawing the souls that hadn't crossed over to the Lady into itself. I could hear them screaming, but in the dream, I was frozen. I tried to use my power to block the magic, and I couldn't do it. I felt like I was watching at a distance, through thick glass. It didn't just pull the spirits into itself; it shredded them, tore them to pieces. It didn't want the souls. It wanted the energy in the souls. It consumed them, destroyed them." This time, Tris took a longer drink from the brandy.

"Can such a thing be done?"

Tris drew a deep breath. "Yes. The Obsidian King had the power to do that. All the accounts I read suggested that he had to do it one spirit at a time. This power pulled at many spirits at once. It hollowed them and left them shattered."

He paused. "What's left after Hollowing isn't really a ghost— there isn't enough of the original soul left for that. All that remains are random flickers of energy, but the entity is usually hostile. After the Mage Wars, my grandmother spent months wandering the countryside, releasing the spirits that the Obsidian King had hollowed. She was the last summoner of real power in Margolan."

"Until you."

"Until me. And whoever it is that seems bent on invading Margolan."

A commotion outside stopped conversation. Shouts, curses, and the sound of a fight nearby brought both Tris and Soterius to their feet. The guards closed ranks outside, blocking the doorway and surrounding the tent. Soterius stepped in front of Tris, drawing his sword. Coalan rose from where he was sitting, sword in hand. Tris, too, had drawn his weapon, and he stretched out his mage sense. Magic was close at hand, dark magic. Just

51

as Tris readied a warding, he felt Sister Fallon's power raise a protective barrier. Tris shouldered past the guards, followed by Soterius. The guards fell in behind them as Tris edged closer to the conflict.

The golden glow of magical wardings created a dome that covered two dozen men locked in hand-to-hand combat. Three men lay dead on the ground, bleeding from grievous wounds. A crowd had formed, and several of the lieutenants were ordering the onlookers back to their tents. Sister Fallon hurried over.

"What's going on?" Tris did not take his eyes from the fight, which grew more deadly moment by moment. Two more men were on the ground, and their assailants kept hacking with their swords although the downed men cried out for mercy. Both Soterius and Senne shouted for the men to lay down their weapons and stop fighting, but nothing slowed the violence.

"They can't hear you," Fallon said to Soterius and Senne. "Or if they can, they don't have control over their actions."

"Are they bewitched?" Senne's face reflected his disgust at the carnage within the warded circle, as men Tris recognized as seasoned fighters cut down their comrades with a ruthlessness rarely seen in the midst of pitched battle. There appeared to be no sides to the conflict, no reason for the attack. Within minutes, only one man was standing, and he was badly bloodied, his belly slashed open and his hands pressed against his flesh to slow the bleeding and force his entrails back into his body. The dying man collapsed to his knees, and for an instant, a look of absolute bewilderment and horror crossed his face, as if in his final moments, awareness of what he had done finally broke through a toxic haze of blood rage.

"Bewitched isn't exactly the right word for it." Fallon's belated explanation filled the awful silence as the man stared, stunned, at the massacre. "Do you remember the fear spells that Curane's blood mages sent against us at Lochlanimar? The terrors

Curane's mages created were enough to send seasoned veterans screaming from imagined horrors."

"This feels different," Tris said slowly, as he extended his mage sense further. "Dark magic, perhaps even blood magic, but whoever cast this is more powerful than the mages Curane had."

Fallon nodded. "This was a sending, but of rage, not terror. These men were going about their assigned tasks when they suddenly drew their weapons on each other and set to. Fortunately, I happened to be close when the shouting started. I threw up a minor warding at first, just to protect the onlookers and keep anyone else from joining what I thought was a brawl. As soon as one of the onlookers told me that nothing had happened to spark a fight, I guessed what had happened and cast a stronger warding."

Soterius looked at her with horror. "What's to keep whoever sent this from turning us all on each other? Or from casting something like this randomly, to keep the camp in chaos? Sweet Chenne, do you know what it could mean if something like this happened in the middle of a battle?"

Fallon nodded soberly. "Yes. I can imagine, and it would be bad. That's why while I was here containing this outbreak, the rest of the mages went to strengthen the camp wardings against this particular type of attack."

"Will it hold?" Senne had joined them. Apparently, he had not gone far from the tent before the brawl.

Fallon paused. "I believe so."

"But you're not certain."

"Unfortunately, magic isn't always predictable," Tris said in a dry voice. "I think what Sister Fallon is saying is that to the extent we can anticipate what kind of magic caused this, she and the mages have taken precautions to keep it from happening again. Unfortunately, that doesn't mean that the sender couldn't come up with a variation of the spell and try again."

"Yes and no, m'lord," Fallon said. "Yes, it's possible for the sender to tweak the spell and try again, but now that we've included this in the larger camp warding, whoever did this would have to change the power signature to get another shot. We've made the wardings as broad as possible, trying to anticipate just this sort of thing." She grimaced. "Obviously our imagination wasn't as good as we thought it was."

"Does your magic tell you anything about who did this?" Soterius looked from Tris to Fallon.

"It took a powerful mage to cast a sending this far. And no, before you ask, I can't tell where the spell originated, but I think it was quite a distance away," Fallon said.

"Anything else?"

Tris paused, searching for words to convey what his magic told him. "Like the ghost ships that attacked the privateers and fishermen, I don't think this was meant as the opening salvo of the war. Whoever is out there means to test us. They're probing our defenses, and I'm betting they were pretty sure we could shut down something like this. The question would be: How long would it take us and how far would it spread before we could stop it?" He nodded toward Fallon. "Thanks to our mages, the damage was limited."

"Surely they know that Margolan has powerful mages, and a summoner for a king?" Senne's eyes were hard, and Tris knew that the general would not forgive those who had squandered the lives of his soldiers.

"Maybe not," Fallon replied. "Temnotta has been isolated, by its own choice, for a hundred years. In all that time, have we ever caught a Temnottan spy?"

Tris thought for a moment, and then shook his head. "Not that I've ever heard tell."

"If they've been so isolated that they haven't even sent spies, their knowledge of anything would be badly out of date. That could mean that their information is from long before the Mage War over a generation ago. If they haven't engaged any of the Winter Kingdoms in that time, perhaps they're assuming their own mages are invincible."

"That's a bold assumption," Soterius murmured.

Fallon shrugged. "Arrogance usually sows the seeds to its own fall."

Tris frowned. "That doesn't make sense. If they know so little about us, why are they attacking? How did they decide to launch a war if they haven't even been gathering intelligence?"

Soterius stood hands on hips, eyes surveying the still-warded scene of the fight. "Just because we never caught a spy doesn't mean spies weren't sent. And even if they didn't send spies for many years, they could have stepped up their intelligence recently. Until we received the warning from Donelan, we weren't watching for outside invaders. We had our hands full with Jared, and then Curane. I doubt Jared expended any resources worrying about invaders from across the sea. He was too busy slaughtering his own people and trying to kill Tris."

"Meaning that we have had some big holes in our attention for the last couple of years." Tris's voice was bitter.

"It's been a busy couple of years."

"All the information we've been able to gather about Temnotta since Donelan's warning suggests that their invasion is somehow connected to the problems in Isencroft. If that's true, Alvior of Brunnfen managed to get the attention of someone important in Temnotta, who probably saw an opportunity. My question is, are the Temnottans seeing the same opportunity as Alvior?" Soterius looked from Tris to Senne. They nodded, following his reasoning.

"Meaning that Alvior may think he's found a partner, while Temnotta may have their own plans for Isencroft—and everyone else."

"Alvior and Isencroft may end up in the belly of the stawar for all his cleverness." Senne's tone conveyed his anger. "If this were really an Isencroft issue, Temnotta would only be threatening Isencroft. But our information suggests that Temnotta plans to attack the whole coast: Isencroft, Margolan, Principality, and Eastmark. That tells me their ambitions go far beyond helping Alvior seize the throne."

Soterius glanced at Tris. "Either way, it's our problem, isn't it?"

Tris nodded. "No matter how anyone feels about it, the futures of Isencroft and Margolan are bound together for at least a generation now. We don't dare support Isencroft with troops that cross their border. The Crofters would think *we* were invading. But it's clear that we share a common enemy. Any way that we can weaken Temnotta protects our kingdom and Isencroft. We can no more afford to have Temnotta successfully invade Isencroft than we can to let them march onto our coast."

Tris returned to his tent, followed by Coalan and the *Telorhan*, elite bodyguards who followed him everywhere. When Tris and Coalan were safely inside, the *Telorhan* guards stepped back into place, blocking the tent's entrance. Coalan began moving the table, basin, and chairs that had been used in the scrying aside and readying the tent for night. Tris sank into a chair, deep in thought.

Kiara and Cwynn are leagues away. How can I protect them and fight a war? A series of "what ifs," each more awful than the one before, came unbidden to his mind, and he was only able to make a halfhearted attempt to push them from consciousness. *I never wanted to have to choose between duty to crown and responsibility for the people I love.*

Coalan rearranged the lightweight, sparse campaign furnishings to set out Tris's cot and his own bedroll, and Tris realized how tired he was. Still, worries hounded him. *What if things go wrong in Isencroft? Kiara will have to go home, pregnant or not. She has a duty to her people. There's no guarantee she'll be able to sit out this war safe inside Shekerishet.*

His dark musings were broken when Coalan pressed a brandy into his hand. "Thought it might help you sleep better," he said with a smile.

"Thank you." Tris lifted the glass to his lips and stopped, his attention on drawings scratched into the dirt of the tent floor. "Coalan, what are those?" he asked, pointing.

Coalan fidgeted. "It's no secret to me that you haven't been sleeping well, Tris. You can't keep that from someone who sleeps in the same tent. You thrash and toss, and some nights it's as if you're having a fight in your sleep. I've tried to figure out what you say when you cry out, but it's not in either Common or Margolense, at least nothing I've ever heard."

"Who taught you the runes of protection?"

This time, Coalan blushed scarlet. "Do you know Elya? She's one of the air mages, the pretty one with the red hair? I see her when I go up to get our meals sometimes and we talk." He looked flustered, and Tris guessed that infatuation had helped to drive Coalan's frequent visits to the mess area, as well as the young man's appetite. "Anyhow, she taught me some runes for peaceful sleep, and I thought it might help. Are you angry?"

Tris smiled. "No. That was kind of you. But you know that both Fallon and I have put our own wardings in place?"

Coalan looked embarrassed. "I know. And believe me, I know nothing I scratch in the dirt could compete with the kind of magic the two of you have. But sometimes, when you can do big things, little things get overlooked, you know? Like you can have a guard at the tent flap and still get mice under the sides? I'm just keeping out the mice, so to speak."

Coalan was one of the few people who remembered how life had been before the coup, who knew him as Tris instead of as king. He and Soterius and Coalan had gone on many a hunt with their late fathers, and they shared memories of a life now forever gone. Tris recognized the friendship behind Coalan's effort, and it was the only bright spot in an otherwise gloomy day.

"Thank you," Tris said. "If you can keep out those damned 'mice,' I'll be very grateful."

Coalan rallied, grinning widely. "I'll add 'royal mouse catcher' to my ever-expanding title."

By the time Tris finished his brandy and changed into his nightshirt, he was feeling very ready for sleep. So it was irritation, more than curiosity, that he felt when he heard voices at the tent flap as a would-be visitor met resistance from the king's guards. Coalan jumped up to see what visitor dared bother the king so late into the night and spoke briefly with the guards and the newcomer. He returned in a few moments, visibly concerned, with Sister Beyral behind him.

Beyral gave a nominal bow. "I wouldn't have come at this time if it weren't urgent, m'lord. But I've read both the runes and the portents and cast over and over. Always I receive the same reply. I didn't want to believe the bones, but then I looked up and saw a ring around the moon. Tonight, a king has died."

Tris caught his breath, and he motioned for Beyral to enter the tent and sit down. "Do you know which kingdom?"

"I saw the ring when the moon was in the northwest sky."

"Isencroft. Donelan. Sweet Mother and Childe," Tris murmured, sinking into his chair.

"I'm sorry, Tris," Beyral said quietly.

Tris looked up at her. "We have to be sure. Isencroft is too far away for me to call to Donelan's spirit. Can you scry for me?"

Beyral nodded and brought a wide-rimmed, shallow bowl out of the bag she carried. "I'll need to fill it with water," she said, and Coalan ran to fetch a bucket. Tris stood back as Beyral set the scrying bowl on the table and filled it. When the water in the bowl had stilled, Beyral gathered her magic and stretched her hands out above the water's surface, palms down and fingers spread. Beyral closed her eyes with concentration, and Tris stood, leaning closer to watch as mist began to swirl in the still water. An image formed in the mist.

Tris caught his breath as the image grew clearer. He saw Donelan lying in his bedchamber, covered in blood. His eyes were open and staring. The mist swirled, and the image faded.

Tris swallowed hard, grappling with the loss. "It's not just that I thought well of Donelan. He was a fine king. But with Donelan dead, the crown of Isencroft passes to Kiara." He met Beyral's eyes. "She'll have no choice but to return to Isencroft."

"That thought crossed my mind. I cast the runes a second time, holding Kiara's image in my mind. The runes seemed heavy in my hand, as if they did not want to speak. And when they did, their omen was dark. The runes spoke of chaos, and of war in the places of the dead. This war will influence succession. But there was something else, something strange. The rune for 'son' lay connected to the rune for 'darkness.' *Son of darkness*. It was clear that the runes went together, but I have no idea what they meant, but whatever it is, it influences the rune of fate. The fate of the war depends on the son of darkness."

4

Jonmarc Vahanian, Dark Haven's brigand lord, swung into a high Eastmark kick. His opponent blocked the kick, and then pivoted, lashing out with his other foot and nearly catching Jonmarc on the jaw. Jonmarc smiled. His next move was low, taking out his opponent at the ankles. Down but not out, his opponent bucked to his feet in one fluid movement, swinging hard with his sword.

Seconds before the sword struck flesh, Jonmarc parried, driving the other man back. Their swords gleamed in the light, as the daggers they held made silver slashes, looking for an opening. Jonmarc's opponent opened a gash on his forearm. Jonmarc's sword slashed into the other's shoulder. Jonmarc's mouth was set in a hard line, all traces of a smile gone. His opponent wore a look of grim concentration. Kick. Block. Jonmarc dove and rolled, nicking the other man on the back of the right leg, a flesh wound right over the hamstring. The other man let out a string of curses in Markian, whirling seconds too late to catch Jonmarc with his sword before the other was on his feet, mounting another press.

Summoning a burst of energy, Jonmarc drew on his year of training with a *vayash moru* weapons master. His reflexes and responses, already honed enough to make him a legendary swordsman, showed an expertise that enabled him to hold his own against the undead. His very human opponent took another gash, this one to the shoulder.

"I yield!"

Smiling again, Jonmarc lowered his sword once his opponent dropped the weapons he held. "Not bad. Not bad at all," he said, sheathing his weapons and walking forward to shake the other's hand.

Jonmarc's opponent was a young man of nineteen summers. Long black hair, shoulder length, was caught back in a mussed queue. A complex tattoo, even darker than his skin, curled down the left side of his face from his eye to his chin. Emotions played across his ebony features: pride, disappointment, vexation. He noticed that Jonmarc was looking at him, or more specifically, at his tattoo.

"Why are you staring?" Prince Gethin of Eastmark's voice was colored with a mixture of teenage angst and royal pique.

Jonmarc shrugged. "Because the last man I saw with that marking ordered my execution."

To Jonmarc's surprise, Gethin made a show of spitting to the side and grinding his spittle under his heel in a gesture of contempt, a gesture accompanied by a rather vile curse in Markian. Jonmarc's Markian was rusty, but he had to admit that he remembered the curses pretty well.

"*Uncle* Alcion was a traitor," Gethin said, contempt thick on the family relationship. "He wanted to supplant my grandfather, King Radomar. Your defiance stopped him. The mark means that I'm third in line to the throne, as it did for Alcion. It relates me to my father, not to that worthless traitor scum."

"I know. But . . . let's just say that Alcion made a lasting impression on me." Jonmarc's tone was wry, but as they stood in the salle at Lienholt Palace in Principality, the memories of that other time more than a decade before seemed very near.

Shirtless for their fight, Jonmarc knew that Gethin could see the array of scars that covered his chest and back. Most people noticed four: a long scar that ran from behind one ear down under his collar, the faint parallel scars left from a Nargi fight slave collar, the puckered skin of a bad burn across his back, and twin pink bite marks on his shoulder, from a renegade *vayash moru.*

But there were more, many more. Raised welts covered his back, a "souvenir" from a flogging in Nargi. A thin white scar on his abdomen where he had been run through with a sword, a wound that would have been fatal without the magic of both Carina and Tris Drayke. High on his chest a discolored line of skin was the reminder of an assassin's poisoned dagger. And just below that, the mark of the Sacred Lady was branded onto his skin, a reminder of a vow sworn to Istra, the Dark Lady. Dozens of other scars from fights too numerous to mention covered his arms, hands, chest, and back. With his shirt on, Jonmarc Vahanian was a handsome man with dark brown eyes, shoulder-length brown hair, and a wicked, lopsided grin. Shirtless, he knew that people saw only the scars.

"Some of those are because of Alcion, aren't they?" Gethin's voice was quiet, and in it, Jonmarc heard a mix of shame and fascination.

"Yeah. A lot of them, actually. Especially the burn on my shoulder. Too bad for Alcion, the barn he locked me in and set on fire didn't actually kill me." The screams of the other villagers who weren't so lucky still haunted his dreams.

"My father regards you as a great hero," Gethin said, and Jonmarc heard honest regard in the prince's voice. "He saw you fight a magicked monster at King Drayke's wedding. He told me that you fight in the Eastmark style as well as any of our best warriors. I didn't believe him." The young man had the grace to look rueful as he glanced down at the fresh sword cuts on his arm and chest. "I do now."

Jonmarc drew a cup of water from a bucket near the wall and handed it to Gethin. Then he dug two strips of cloth out of a box and began to bind up the prince's wounds. "You fight well," Jonmarc replied, choosing to ignore the compliments rather than search for words to acknowledge them. "You're salle trained, but you've seen some battle, haven't you?"

Gethin's chagrin at being bested wasn't easily mollified, but he nodded. "Some. I was sent to the army at fourteen, and went on my first campaign against raiders at sixteen. I've been out a few times since then. It's all the campaigning there's been—until now." He managed to brighten. "Although if I have to lose in the salle, it's no shame to lose to you, of all people." He sighed. "You could have hamstrung me with that move, couldn't you?"

Jonmarc chuckled. "It's a street move that I like to use on all the young princes I end up having to train right before we go into battle against overwhelmingly bad odds."

Gethin frowned. "You do a lot of this sort of thing?" His Markian accent made his words clipped and gave his vowels a strange turn. The accent stood out, even in Principality's polyglot mix of peoples.

"Actually, only once before. An old mercenary friend of mine helped three young noblemen escape with their lives from Jared the Usurper. One of them, a prince who was your age at the time, wasn't fortunate enough to have even your battle experience. I will say, he improved quite a bit by the time it counted."

Gethin gave him a dry smile. "Might that unlucky prince have been Martris Drayke?"

Jonmarc nodded. "Tris was as green as grass back then when it came to real fighting. Not his fault: Margolan hadn't been to war in a generation, and his salle training had been mostly for sparring, not for real battle. I'll tell you what I told them: My 'technique' was learned one street fight at a time, which is the only way I know how to teach anyone. Oh, and did I mention— there are no rules."

Gethin smiled widely. "We have a saying," he began, and then lapsed into Markian with a look that dared Jonmarc to translate.

"A scar at the hand of a master brings no shame," Jonmarc interpreted dryly. "I know I speak Markian with a Borderlands accent, but when I was your age, I was a Principality merc hired into the Eastmark army and well on my way to becoming a senior officer. Until the court martial."

Gethin shouldered gingerly into his shirt, and Jonmarc worried for a moment that he had scored more deeply than he intended. But the look on Gethin's face kept him from inquiring. He had no desire to batter the prince's pride any more than his loss in the salle had already done. Despite himself, Jonmarc found that he liked the young man.

He put on his shirt and turned, only to find Gethin looking at him as if debating whether or not to speak. Jonmarc raised an eyebrow, inviting comment.

"You've known Princess Berwyn for a while, haven't you?" Suddenly, Gethin sounded every bit as young as his years. Whatever assurance Gethin had in his sword skills and his royal lineage, he seemed flustered by his new role as a peace-offering groom for a politically arranged marriage. For Jonmarc in his position as Champion for the princess, that boded well.

"I met Berry when we'd all been captured by slavers who'd been sent by Jared to hunt down Tris Drayke," Jonmarc replied, dipping a cup of water for himself. He took a long drink. "They'd captured Berry when she had traveled into Margolan to visit family, but they didn't know they had nabbed a princess. They thought she might be noble, and that someone might pay a ransom." He chuckled. "They got more than they bargained for."

"She's a fighter?" Gethin's voice revealed skepticism.

"Not exactly, although Berry understood the 'no rules' part before I ever met her. She slipped me a blade, poisoned the slavers with bad mushrooms in their stew, scalded the leader with a pot of hot soup, and in a brawl to the death with slavers, vengeful ghosts, and more magic than I care to remember, she was hopping from ledge to ledge dropping boulders on their heads."

Gethin smiled, and Jonmarc guessed the other was forming a mental picture of the events. "Then I'll try not to make her angry," he said with a grin. Just as quickly, he grew serious.

"I must admit, my lessons were a bit thin on how to woo a headstrong bride for a marriage of necessity." Gethin looked decidedly uncomfortable. "But just in the short time I've been here, I can see that Princess Berwyn won't be forced into something she doesn't want."

"Look, Gethin, I'm really not the best person to ask for advice about women," Jonmarc said, setting his cup aside. "My way of winning over Carina involved nearly getting myself beaten to death by a Nargi commander who was overdue for revenge."

"Truly?"

Jonmarc grimaced. "Yeah. Truly. So as I said, I'm maybe not the best person to consult."

"I have no one else." Jonmarc met his eyes and saw Gethin the young man, and not the self-assured Eastmark prince.

"All right," Jonmarc said and sighed. "Ask. But it doesn't mean I know any answers."

Gethin hesitated, and Jonmarc had a flash of insight. Gethin had been presented as a trophy groom to seal an alliance, accompanied by priests, ambassadors, and staff. None of his companions would be suitable for personal questions. "Am I correct in guessing that Princess Berwyn didn't know about the pact our fathers made—at least, not about me?"

"She knew they were working on an alliance. She didn't know it involved marriage."

Gethin sighed. "Is there a rival? Is her heart already taken?"

"Not to my knowledge."

At that, Gethin relaxed, just a bit. "That's for the best. I left no one behind, either. Perhaps that, at least, is in our favor." He dared to meet Jonmarc's eyes. "I've seen quite a few arranged marriages at court. At best, the couple grows fond of each other. Most merely tolerate a charade where each goes separate ways. At worst, they spend the rest of their lives ripping each other to shreds." He looked away. "I'm the extra heir. That meant chances were high that I would be sent somewhere for a political marriage. I've always hoped to manage the best of the three options, if love isn't one of the choices."

"Marrying for love almost started two wars in recent memory," Jonmarc noted. "From what I've heard, your grandfather didn't take kindly to your aunt eloping with Donelan."

Gethin grimaced. "No, he didn't. And the rules that forbade the royal family to marry outsiders were struck down by my father, as soon as he took the throne, in Aunt Viata's memory."

"But because your grandfather was spoiling for war, Tris's father agreed to an arranged marriage between his heir and the heir to Isencroft's throne, just to put Eastmark on notice. It managed to stop that war, but it created a real mess when Kiara ended up betrothed to Jared the Usurper and then sided with Tris."

"And if our intelligence is correct, Isencroft is on the brink of civil war over having a shared throne and a mixed-blood heir." Gethin closed his eyes and shook his head. "And people actually believe that the royal family can do as they please."

"What do you think I can tell you?"

"I believe that Berwyn and I will do our duty to our kingdoms, although she'll make me prove myself to her, as is her right," Gethin said, beginning to pace. "But can I win her heart?"

Jonmarc chuckled. "Berry was quite the matchmaker, trying to pair up Tris and Kiara as well as Carina and me. So I suspect she harbors some hope of an agreeable match. I'm not the best person to ask about winning hearts, but it's a good start to win her respect. She can't stand pretense or arrogance. She can forgive mistakes but not lies. And she has a wicked sense of humor."

"I'm relieved to find that she's not one of those fragile noble girls," Gethin confessed. "You know something of Eastmark. We train our princesses just as hard as our princes in the sword."

"I found that out from a turn or two in the salle with Kiara," Jonmarc said with a chuckle. "She held her own with me, and she said it was her mother's training."

Gethin looked down. "I know Viata only from my father's stories of her. He was much younger, and he mourned when Grandfather banished her. When Father took the throne, he found a court artist who remembered Viata and commissioned portraits of her. So in a way, she returned to the palace, at least in memory. I grew up hearing his stories about her and thinking how strong and brave she must have been to defy Grandfather. When I was a child, I was silly enough to hope that I would find a beautiful, headstrong princess like Viata."

"Then you've come to the right place." Jonmarc watched Gethin, surprised that the prince would be so open. That honesty, along with Gethin's sword skills, raised Jonmarc's opinion of the young man and made him somewhat more comfortable with the shaky alliance. "Berry's got a lot of fire, and she has a good head on her shoulders. She needs someone who'll admire that and support her, instead of trying to get the upper hand."

"I've thought a lot about Aunt Viata lately, because what happened back then is a great deal of the reason that I'm here, now." Gethin walked to the salle window and looked out toward the eastern horizon. "Eastmark has never willingly given one of its royal family for an alliance. Father's taken a risk with this. There are some among the nobles who still agree with Grandfather's ways. They don't want to see our blood 'polluted' by outsiders," he said scornfully.

"*Sathirinim*," Jonmarc murmured. The term meant "corpse flesh," and it was the view of many of Eastmark's older leaders that the pallor of outsiders' skin was evidence of deeper inferiority.

Gethin's head snapped up. "Don't use that word! Father made it a crime to say it, and he's done his best to root it out wherever he could from law and custom. Nothing enrages him more, not even blasphemy."

"But old ways die hard," Jonmarc replied, understanding Gethin's meaning. "Kalcen's gone out on a limb sending you here. It's the final defiance against what King Radomar did to his sister, isn't it? And not everybody likes it."

Gethin sighed. "No, they don't. If it doesn't go well, if the offering were to be refused . . ."

Kalcen would lose face among his nobles, and that can be fatal, Jonmarc said to himself, mentally finishing the sentence that Gethin left unsaid. "I think I understand. Principality is used to a mix of people. Hell, I met mercs from places beyond the Winter Kingdoms. As I recall, there were more than a few Eastmark soldiers who found their way across the border and settled down with Principality women, no matter what the old king thought. On the other hand, some of the mercs noticed that their 'bad blood' was good enough to spill on Eastmark battle-fields, but not good enough to win them an Eastmark woman. They'll be scratching their heads over why you're here, that's for sure."

"I need to make sure the alliance goes smoothly." Gethin's eyes looked older than his years. "These are dangerous times. Eastmark and Principality need each other." He paused. "For myself, I'd like it to be more than just an arrangement." He smiled sadly. "I'd prefer to win Berwyn's affection and not just her tolerance."

"Play your cards as straight with her as you have with me, and I think you've got a chance," Jonmarc said. "Now if you'll excuse me, I've got a war to plan."

A candlemark later, Jonmarc was seated at a large council table. As Queen's Champion, he sat at Berry's right hand. Berry had dressed for the occasion, attending the council in full formal regalia, to reinforce the authority of the crown.

At Berry's left was Jencin, the seneschal. Around the table, Jonmarc saw several familiar faces. General Valjan, the former leader of the War Dogs mercenaries, Jonmarc knew and trusted. Laisren and Serg, the emissaries of the *vayash moru* and *vyrkin*, had fought alongside Jonmarc. Hant, the palace spymaster, had thrown his considerable abilities toward helping Tris Drayke take back the throne of Margolan. Exeter, the head of the Mercenary Guild, was an unknown, as was Lord Alarek, the representative from the Council of Nobles.

"We've sent advance troops to the coast, and what ships could be mustered are in place," Valjan reported. "Thanks to the mercenaries," he added with a nod toward Exeter. "The Principality troops are split three ways: Most went to the coast with the mercs. Some will patrol the river to make sure none of the enemy ships slip inland. The rest will guard the palace."

"What of the mercs?" Berry asked. "How many troops can we count on?"

Jonmarc looked to Exeter. For other kingdoms, mercenaries were usually just extra hired muscle. But Principality had a long, complex relationship with the multitude of merc groups that called the small kingdom home. A few hundred years ago, Principality had been created by the surrounding powers as a way to keep the peace over its wealth of gem mines, mines that had been a near constant source of war as the neighboring kingdoms fought for control. Battered by fruitless and expensive fighting, the other kingdoms had created Principality as its own sovereign state, but it was too small to marshal a full army from its population.

The first king of Principality, in a stroke of genius, had made it known that all mercenary groups were welcome to winter within the kingdom's borders, provided that those merc companies swore that they would never sell their swords against Principality. Over the years, the best and most fearsome merc companies in the Winter Kingdoms found their way to Principality, as did the fastest privateers and some fleets that were probably more pirate than privateer. The kings of Principality had welcomed them all, along with their oath of fealty. As a result, Principality was heavily protected from within and rested in the assurance that no legitimate mercenary group would agree to attack them. Now, Jonmarc hoped that the age-old agreement would be enough.

"We've rallied the merc troops," Exeter reported. "Those that were traveling have been recalled, except for the ones that had already been recruited to serve the other kingdoms against the Northern threat. As for ships, we're still counting as they come in." Exeter grinned, showing a row of mottled teeth and a wolfish grin. "It's been a long time since there's been a war like this is shaping up to be. Any fighter worth his price is itching for a piece of it. And of course," he added with a calculating look toward Berry, "for a piece of the spoils."

"You'll receive your customary percentage, and a bonus if my commanders say it's been earned," Berry replied.

"Thank you, m'lady."

Berry looked to Laisren and Serg. "Were you able to recruit from among the *vayash moru* and *vyrkin*?"

Laisren was Dark Haven's weapons master, and Jonmarc knew exactly how dangerous Laisren could be on the battlefield. Although he was several hundred years old, he looked to be in his early thirties, with an angular face and dark blond hair that fell loose to his shoulders. The charcoal jacket that he wore made his pallor the more visible.

"Our numbers are fewer than they were at the beginning of the year due to the war with the rogues of our kind," Laisren said. "And we are always fewer in numbers than mortals believe. Some remain in Dark Haven to protect the manor. But four of the Blood Council broods have pledged themselves to support you, m'lady. They're still arriving, but we should have several dozen, at the least."

Berry frowned. "And the fifth Blood Council brood?"

Laisren exchanged a glance with Jonmarc. "Astasia and her people have gone missing. We believe she's thrown her support to the other side. The other houses are bloodsworn against her. We'll handle that matter ourselves, if it arises." Jonmarc could see the tips of Laisren's elongated eye teeth in the other's cold smile.

Berry looked to Serg. "And the *vyrkin*?"

Serg was a stocky man of medium build with brown hair and a close trimmed beard. His violet eyes were the mark of the shapeshifting *vyrkin*. "As with the *vayash moru*, the uprising in Dark Haven cost us many lives. But the plague brought many more *vyrkin* for sanctuary in Dark Haven, and these new wolf brothers and sisters are ready to fight in your service. There are fifty of us, and we expect more to come."

Berry nodded. "Very good."

"Your Majesty." Hant's quiet voice made the room fall silent. The late King Staden had once introduced Hant to Jonmarc as his "best rat-catcher." Hant was a small man with dark eyes that did not miss any motion. He said little, but knew everything that went on anywhere in Principality. Hant might not be a warrior like most of the others at the table, but Jonmarc knew the spymaster was equally dangerous in his own way.

"You have news, Hant?"

"Not as good as what the others have reported, but important nonetheless." Hant looked at the group seated around the table. "My sources in the city have continued to investigate the attack at the Feast of the Departed. The *serroquette*'s information was correct. More than a few of the Durim were active before and after the attack."

"Were?" Jonmarc met Hant's eyes, and the spymaster gave a cold smile.

"Were. My associates are very effective in rooting out vermin."

Jonmarc's smile mirrored the chill in Hant's expression. He'd gone up against the Durim himself, in that battle and before, in Dark Haven. The Durim were the fanatical devotees of a long-renounced goddess, Shanthadura, the Destroyer. Long ago, Shanthadura had demanded blood offerings and human sacrifice. Peyhta, the Soul Eater; Konost, the Guide of Dead Souls; and Shanthadura, the Destroyer had been worshiped as the Shrouded Ones, and their reign of bloody devotion had held sway in the Winter Kingdoms for centuries. Four hundred years ago King Hadenrul had displaced the worship of the Shrouded Ones with devotion to the Eight Aspects of the Sacred Lady, exiling or destroying those who would not abandon their murderous rites.

"I'd like to tell you that the problem is solved, but unfortunately, although we've captured quite a few of the Durim, someone or something is still causing problems. Buka, for one."

"Is Buka one of the Durim?" Berry leaned forward. "He seems to share their love of cutting up victims and leaving a bloodbath behind."

Hant frowned. "I don't think so. The Durim we interrogated seemed to be truly ignorant of his crimes." He shook his head.

"Unfortunately, I think we have a separate problem with Buka. And it's getting worse."

Jonmarc moved to see Hant better. "How many people can one man kill?"

Hant grimaced. "Apparently, this one has a talent for killing, and for not getting caught. That's bad enough. But there've been reports of other problems near the sites of the killings."

"What kind of problems?"

"Ghost attacks." Hant met Jonmarc's eyes. "You traveled with Martris Drayke. I believe you and the queen both saw, firsthand, just how dangerous angered ghosts can be."

Despite herself, Berry shivered at the memory. To escape the slavers that had imprisoned them two years ago, Tris Drayke had used his power, then mostly wild, raw, and uncontrolled magic, to set the wronged ghosts of a haunted forest on their captors. It had been more terrifying than any battlefield horror Jonmarc had ever experienced. The ghosts had been merciless taking long-overdue vengeance, so much so that only bloody bits of the slavers remained after the fighting was over.

"I remember," Berry murmured.

"Now imagine ghosts like that in a tightly packed city, bound to the place where the body was found. We've tried all the normal ways to set spirits to rest, even called on the mages we could find, but nothing's worked yet." He sighed. "Unfortunately, we're short on summoners, and Tris Drayke has his own problems in Margolan." He met Jonmarc's eyes. "Do you think that the *serroquette* you brought with you could help? What was her name?"

"Aidane," Jonmarc replied. "As I understand it, Aidane's gift lies more in being possessed by spirits than in dispelling them. If this Buka favors young women victims, then we could end up with a bigger problem if the ghosts were to take her over."

Hant nodded. "I thought of that. And I agree, it's too risky to take her near the places that are being haunted. But perhaps, with her skills, she's heard something from the spirits? I don't pretend to know how these things work, but I'd like to talk with her."

"Agreed." Berry gave her consent, but with a glance to Jonmarc that made him sure Berry would expect him to be present to watch out for Aidane's safety.

"I'm placing General Valjan and General Gregor in charge of establishing a line of defense along the coast," Berry said. "They'll be leaving with their troops within a few days. As Queen's Champion, Jonmarc will serve as my proxy. He and Prince Gethin will lead another division north as soon as we're sure that the situation in the city can spare them."

Jencin frowned. "Prince Gethin is a guest, m'lady. Is it wise . . . ?"

"Gethin petitioned the crown in person, accompanied by his ambassador, asking for the privilege of representing Principality in the conflict," Berry replied shortly. "I understand the sensitive nature of his position, which is why I've assigned him to Jonmarc."

Jonmarc kept his face neutral, even as his fingers began to drum against his chair under the table. *First I've heard of this. Gethin had to know when we were in the salle, and he didn't tell me. He'd better expect a good pounding the next round I go with him.*

Berry gave him a slight, knowing smile. "Your presence is required at dinner tonight. Our guests will be the prince and his ambassadors."

Jonmarc gave her a look that he knew she would read correctly. "I'll be looking forward to it."

Berry regained her solemn expression and returned her attention to the seated group. "Gentlemen, you know what we're facing. The Winter Kingdoms hasn't seen an invader from beyond the Northern Sea in generations. You and your forces are the only thing standing between Principality and invasion. I pray to the Lady for your success." With that, Berry rose and swept out of the room, followed closely by Jencin and surrounded by the palace guards. The rest filed from their places without conversation and scattered in different directions as they left the war room.

Jonmarc headed down the corridor toward the stairs that would take him to Aidane's rooms. After the briefing, he'd come up with quite a few questions for the *serroquette*.

"Vahanian! I'd like a word with you."

Jonmarc's hand was on the pommel of his sword as he turned. He recognized the voice even before the figure of a man strode into the torch light. Gregor.

"You went over my head to Valjan and Hant. Why?" Gregor was a dark-haired man with intelligent brown eyes and a hard line to his mouth. Years ago, Carina had been unable to save Gregor's brother. Gregor had never forgiven that, and the few times he and Jonmarc had crossed paths had not been pleasant.

Jonmarc stood his ground, hand firmly on his sword. "Because I knew they'd listen. And you wouldn't."

"You brought that damned ghost whore into the palace."

Jonmarc clenched his jaw. "Aidane carried essential intelligence information to the queen at great personal risk, and she put herself further at risk to identify the traitors at the coronation. She saved the queen's life."

Gregor's lip twisted. "You'd know all about whores and that ilk. You shame the queen with your presence and with the vermin you bring with you."

A killing glint came into Jonmarc's eyes. "And what 'vermin' would that be?"

Gregor spat to one side. "Whores. Biters. Shifters. You probably had something to do with the fact that we're coddling that Eastmark prince, didn't you?"

"Gethin is here at the invitation of King Staden. I had nothing to do with it." Jonmarc paused. "And he hardly needs coddling. He's much better in a fight than you are."

Gregor reddened, and Jonmarc thought the general might swing at him. Veins stood out on Gregor's neck, and Jonmarc guessed that it was taking a great effort for Gregor to control himself. "I've heard the stories about you. My brother and I were mercs, too. We fought for those bloody Eastmark bastards who thought they were too good for us, for *sathirinim*. You should know that. They betrayed you worse than anyone."

Jonmarc was losing his fight to keep his temper. "So one minute I'm vermin, and the next I'm a martyr?"

"You leave a trail of dead men in your wake, Vahanian. I don't trust you, your biter friends, or the Eastmark bastards. They threw our mercs into the front lines first, to draw fire before they risked their own precious skins. And now they send one of theirs to marry the queen, and you, of all people, you're going to stand for it?"

Jonmarc saw the glint of Gregor's drawn blade and parried fast and hard. Practice against *vayash moru* opponents gave him an edge in strength and speed. He sent Gregor's sword scuttling down the corridor, and he body-slammed the general against the corridor wall.

"Take your opinions about Eastmark and shove them up your ass." Jonmarc's voice was a hiss, close to Gregor's ear. Gregor struggled, but Jonmarc kept him pinned with a blade at the general's throat. "I've been betrayed by too many people to blame it on anything more than old-fashioned greed."

He twitched the blade slightly under Gregor's chin, raising a thin line of blood. "This is the second time I've let you off without breaking some bones or running you through. So you say one more word to anyone about 'vermin' and I'll cut out that tongue of yours and pin it to the wall for a trophy. I'm expecting you to do your duty and keep your opinions to yourself." He poked the tip of his blade into the soft skin beneath Gregor's chin. "Do you understand?"

"Yes."

Jonmarc pushed away hard from Gregor, giving himself space and slamming his opponent into the wall again for good measure. He kept his sword in hand as Gregor straightened his uniform and recovered his sword.

"Is it your doing that my men and I are in the first wave while the Queen's Champion takes his time to reach the battlefield?"

"Thank the queen for that decision, not me. Perhaps you didn't notice that, so far, there've been more casualties here in Principality City than on the coast?" Jonmarc sheathed his weapon in disgust. "I don't have time for this. Now get out of my way or, by the Dark Lady, I'll cut a door right through your hide."

"I'm leaving." Gregor turned and strode away. Jonmarc did not relax from a ready stance until he was certain that Gregor was truly gone.

5

"Drink this." Kolin pushed a cup of *kerif* into Aidane's hands. Aidane accepted the strong, bitter drink gratefully and sipped at it as she sat beside the fireplace in her room. "Why didn't you tell me you were having nightmares?"

Aidane shrugged and looked up at Kolin where he stood beside the fireplace. The glow of the fire made his *vayash moru*–pale skin less pallid. His dark blond hair framed a sharp-featured face that was distinguished if not quite handsome. By comparison, Aidane had the coal-black hair and dusky skin of a Nargi native. Dark eyed and with high cheekbones, she had heard more than one courtier describe her as "exotic." She had yet to decide whether or not that description was meant as a compliment.

"I'm a *serroquette*. I should be used to dreams—my own, and others." She sipped the hot tea and repressed a shiver.

"Are the dreams always like these?" Kolin looked at her with a mixture of horror and sympathy. "You woke screaming and fighting for your life. If I'd been mortal, I'm not sure I could have contained you."

Aidane sighed and looked away. "I allow ghosts to possess me to make peace with their lovers. My sanity depends on being able to keep most ghosts at bay and allow only certain ghosts to possess me. But something's going wrong."

78

Kolin frowned. "So are you dreaming, or being possessed?"

Aidane sipped her tea again as she thought. "I think it's something in between. Not a full possession; I can tell that my own spirit is still in control. But more than a dream. And they're not just any ghosts. They're young women, and they've been murdered."

"By whom?"

Aidane met his eyes. "Buka."

Kolin's eyes widened. "The killer in the city?"

Aidane nodded. "He's not *vayash moru*, if that's what you're worried about. I've seen the ghosts' deaths . . . felt them. It's a knife, not teeth, that does the killing. But the funny thing is, I don't think he's Durim, either."

"Why?"

"Through the ghosts, I've gotten glimpses of what he does in the moments around the deaths. He . . . carves up the bodies," Aidane said, swallowing hard. "He takes pieces of them. But it doesn't feel like what we found on the road, when we came upon where the Durim had fouled the barrow. And yet . . ."

"What?"

"I think that Buka does make some kind of offering. He mutters to himself as he does the cutting. Sometimes, I can hear him. He says things like 'honor the master' and 'make the master welcome.' The Durim worship Shanthadura, a goddess. Whomever Buka is trying to please is a man." Aidane finished her drink and set the empty cup aside. She stared into the fireplace, trying to dispel the awful visions from her memory.

Kolin sat down across from her and gently took her hands in his. "Dying once was bad enough. I can't imagine what you've been though, reliving all those deaths." He paused. "What can I do to protect you? Are there charms, talismans that would keep out the ghosts? Can a mage help ward your chamber? Tell me, and I'll make it so."

Aidane squeezed his hands in appreciation before moving away to wrap her arms around herself. Although the fire was warm and the autumn night was not yet wintry, she felt a chill that had nothing to do with the weather. "Yes, I'd like to be free of the dreams. Of course. But . . . I think there's a reason the ghosts are trying to contact me. I don't know what it is yet, but I'm afraid that if they can't reach me, something worse will happen. They're angry. So angry."

"So you'll let them consume you instead?" Aidane heard anger in Kolin's voice, and his eyes blazed. "Maybe they're jealous that you're alive and they aren't. Maybe they intend to take you with them."

The thought had occurred to Aidane. "I think that if they meant to kill me, they'd have done it already. Maybe they just want me to carry a message."

"Do you get a choice?" he asked, and his eyes met hers with a gaze that was difficult to elude.

A sad smile crossed Aidane's face. "I'm just a ghost whore, Kolin. No one worries much about my choices."

Kolin's eyes darkened. "Even as a *vayash moru*, we choose how and where to slake our thirst."

Aidane turned away. "You wouldn't understand," she said quietly.

"No? What part of not having a choice do you think is beyond my experience?" There was an edge in Kolin's voice Aidane had not heard before. "It was not my choice to be brought across. When I was new in the Dark Gift, the hunger that drove me to kill like a wild thing didn't obey my choices until many years later. It was not my choice to submit to the will of my maker for a hundred years until Lady Riqua purchased my freedom. It certainly wasn't my choice to lose Elsbet to her father's rage." He struggled to temper the anger in his tone. "And it is not my choice to be denied the chance to ever walk in the sunlight again."

"I'm sorry. I didn't know."

Kolin looked at her as if he were debating with himself. "You have a dark gift of your own, I think. Why are you ashamed of it?"

Aidane looked up defiantly. "Who said I was?"

"If you really believe that with your gift you are 'just a whore' in Principality of all places, where they worship Athira the Whore and even the temple oracles join their bodies with the supplicants, then yes, I think you're ashamed. And I wonder, why?"

Aidane's heart was pounding. No one had ever questioned why she felt shame. Everyone, from her parents to the Crone priests to the other whores, all made it clear to her that being a *serroquette* was even worse than the common strumpets who sold their bodies but did not permit their entire being to be possessed for coin. "You, of anyone here, know what I am."

"You'd be hard-pressed to find a virgin in Principality, with the exception perhaps of our queen," Kolin replied. "They worship the Lover and the Whore, and the kingdom is full of mercs. 'Experience' isn't shameful here, Aidane. You're not in Nargi anymore."

Aidane wanted to flee the room. This was not a conversation she had ever imagined having with anyone, certainly not Kolin. And although she had told him that she retained no memory of the reunion between Kolin and the spirit of his dead lover whom she had channeled, she had remembered almost everything. It had been easy, over the years, to block out the awful experiences, the beatings, the enraged clients, the betrayed lovers bent on revenge. Those she could honestly say blurred into a jumble.

But Kolin's reunion with Elsbet had been so tender and his love for the ghost so sure that the memory burned brightly. *None of those feelings were actually for me*, she reminded herself sternly. *And the kindness now is just gratitude; it's because of the memory of Elsbet, not really for Aidane.*

"Did you know that a *vayash moru* takes more than blood with a bite?" Kolin's question pulled Aidane from her discomfort. He did not wait for her to answer. "We taste the life that's in the blood. With animals, there's a sense of its fears and abilities. A deer tastes of the forest, of flight from hunters. But with humans, it's much more."

Kolin usually kept his eye teeth hidden, but now she could see them plainly. "We can't subsist completely on animal blood. Sometimes, we'll feed lightly from a drunk or a willing donor. Through the ages, villages have tied their criminals outside the gates as an offering to us and to the wolves. There and in battle, over centuries, I've drained the life from hundreds of people. And in the draining, there is a . . . joining . . . of sorts. Not bodies but memories, consciousness, thoughts. You eat a piece of deer meat and need not really think of the deer. But with the blood, I drain life and self. It's a far more intimate twining than bodies can ever make." An edge of bitterness tinged his voice. "So who is the whore?"

Aidane looked up at him slowly, surprised and confused by his confession. "Why tell me this?"

Kolin's smile was self-deprecating. "I wanted you to know that we have more in common than you thought. I'm willing to bet that, through Elsbet, you saw me as Kolin and not as a *vayash moru*. I'm impressed by the *serroquette*, but I'm more impressed by Aidane."

"I don't understand."

This time, Kolin's smile held more warmth. "You stayed alive in Nargi, when it's not a healthy place for our kinds. When the Durim took you, you fought them. When my team rescued you, you took a huge chance to get us out of that ambush. You were willing to carry Thaine's ghost to warn Vahanian and the queen when holding her inside was difficult, maybe painful for you. And I'm betting that you lied about not remembering the night you brought Elsbet to me, for my sake."

Aidane blushed and looked away. "Clients prefer to think that," she mumbled.

"You have the heart of a warrior. You don't back down. And even though you're mortal, you risk that precious life—and that *is* a choice." He shrugged. "I'm impressed."

To Aidane's overwhelming relief, a knock at the door saved her from having to respond. Jonmarc Vahanian stood in the hallway.

"Sorry to trouble you, but may I come in?"

Aidane stepped back to permit him entrance. Jonmarc and Kolin acknowledged each other with a nod. "If it's about Thaine, she's really gone," Aidane said.

"I'm not here about Thaine," Jonmarc said. He glanced up as Kolin moved to slip out the door. "Please, stay. I don't want anyone running back to Carina with tales of me alone with a *serroquette*."

Kolin raised an eyebrow and suppressed a smile. "So I'm to be a chaperone?"

Jonmarc shrugged. "Call it what you want. Actually, I'd value your opinion on this, too. Berry asked me to find out if Aidane knows anything about the Buka killings."

Aidane and Kolin exchanged glances. With a sigh, Aidane motioned Jonmarc to a seat and gave a shorter version of the story she had shared with Kolin. She was pleased that this time, she betrayed little emotion, and she hoped that she shared the information dispassionately. Kolin said nothing, and she felt a flash of gratitude that he did not bring up just how much the dreams had bothered her. When she was finished, Jonmarc sat back and pursed his lips, thinking.

"So you've heard from the ghosts without ever leaving the palace. Am I right that taking you to the places the murders occurred wouldn't be a good idea?"

"I can't guarantee what would happen," Aidane said, trying to keep her voice steady, although her heart pounded at the thought.

"I think it would be a very bad idea." They both looked at Kolin. "When we were on the road to Dark Haven, Jolie and I both saw Aidane be attacked by spirits that wanted to possess her by force. We were able to stop that, but it was too close for my comfort. If the Buka victims are angry enough to distress her here in the palace, there's no telling what would happen if you took her to where the ghosts are actually stronger."

"When I traveled with Tris Drayke two years ago, the ghost of a murdered woman tried to possess Carina and steal her body," Jonmarc said quietly. "It took a summoner to cast the spirit away. I wouldn't put you in that kind of danger. But I had to ask."

Aidane nodded. "I understand. I've thought that the ghosts have some reason for seeking me out, because so far they haven't tried to force themselves onto me. That's why I told Kolin I don't want to banish them, not yet. Maybe they're trying to talk to me because they think I'll listen."

Jonmarc nodded. "Hant told me that he's doing all he can to find the killer, but I'm afraid his men aren't taking it quite as seriously as we'd like—"

"Because the victims are mostly whores," Aidane finished matter-of-factly. "It was the same in Nargi. Our lives had less value to some than the sewer rats."

"Hant doesn't see it like that, and neither do I. But with the war starting, the soldiers' attention is elsewhere. Although I'm quite sure that if it were nobles turning up dead, they'd find it easier to remember," Jonmarc added acidly. "I'll tell the queen what you've said, about not thinking Buka is with the Durim. Damndest thing is, if he's not with them, then we've got some other crazy person who's after blood that this Buka thinks is his 'master.'"

"Like a dark summoner?"

Jonmarc looked at Kolin. "Yeah. And that would be really, really bad. Foor Arontala wasn't a summoner, just a powerful blood mage, and he almost brought down two kingdoms. I've seen a real summoner in action, and I hope I never have to go up against that kind of power on a battlefield. Dark Lady help us."

Aidane shifted uncomfortably in her seat. "There is one other thing," she said, and both Jonmarc and Kolin turned to look at her. "Whoever or whatever this Buka is, even the ghosts are afraid. They think he can still hurt them, even after death. They kept repeating a word . . . 'hollowed.' That's what they're afraid of," she said, looking up to meet their eyes. "Being hollowed."

Jonmarc frowned. "What does that mean?"

Kolin pursed his lips as he thought. "I think I may know. My kind often takes shelter in crypts and burying places among the dead. Often, the grounds are haunted, but ghosts rarely bother us, and we do nothing to violate their resting places. A few times, over the centuries, I've encountered something much more malevolent. They were filled with rage, violent, mindless, and yet, there was also pain, as if something had ripped the ghosts apart and left an angry shadow."

"Hollowed?" Jonmarc questioned.

Kolin nodded. "That's what I was told when I asked about them. Even as a *vayash moru*, I feared them. I wouldn't have wanted to take my chances against them."

"What kind of power does it take to do something like that?"

Kolin shook his head. "Lady Riqua told me that a blood mage could do it. It requires more ruthlessness than power, or so I was given to understand."

"Great. So now we not only have a murderer running around and ghosts haunting Aidane, but we could also have *killer* ghosts?"

"Apparently so."

"If this Buka has actually hollowed anyone, those ghosts haven't come calling yet," Aidane said with a shiver.

"Could they?" Jonmarc asked the question, but both he and Kolin turned to look at Aidane.

"Maybe," she admitted. "If they're ghosts, then it's a possibility."

"So we've got yet another thing to worry about," Jonmarc murmured. He looked to Kolin. "Have you heard from any of the *vayash moru* outside the palace?"

Kolin was silent for a moment, as if trying to decide what to say. "Yes. There have been . . . problems."

Jonmarc nodded. "That's what Hant told me. Between the plague, the war, and Buka, people are jittery, looking for someone to blame. Whores are turning up dead, with crude notes left scratched next to them that say 'for Buka.' In the last few days, there've been two *vayash moru* burnings and several residences torched whose owners were probably undead." He sighed. "Valjan and Exeter said that some of the merc troops will accept *vayash moru* if they want to fight. By the Dark Lady, we could use them!"

"I have contacts in the city. I'll see what can be done. It serves no purpose to leave my people at the mercy of the mobs."

"I'll talk to Berry about it tomorrow," Jonmarc said. He paused. "Oh, and before I forget. Berry asked me to make sure the two of you are at dinner tonight. We're dining with Prince Gethin and his entourage."

6

No one told me there would be *Hojun* priests at dinner."
Aidane's voice would have been too quiet for mortal ears, but
as she made her way toward the dining room with Kolin, she
knew his *vayash moru* hearing was quite capable of picking
up her whisper.

"This isn't Nargi."

"They're priests. I wouldn't have worn this if I'd known there
would be priests." Aidane indicated her gown of blood-red silk.
She was dressed in the fashion of her profession as *serroquette*,
with a low-cut silk bodice, flowing slit sleeves, and billowing
silk pants with a skirt like slit panel in the front and back. Gold
adorned her neck, wrists, and ankles, and the small jewels in
her earrings glimmered in the candlelight.

"You're a *serroquette*. What were you planning to wear? A
cloak, fastened neck to knees?" Kolin chuckled.

Aidane struggled with very real fear. Her last encounters with
both Nargi priests and the Black Robe disciples of Shanthadura
had very nearly been fatal. "I shouldn't come. This is going to
cause a scene."

Kolin stopped and took Aidane by the shoulders. "Have you
ever been to Eastmark?"

"No."

"For one thing, Eastmark reveres the Lover Aspect of the Sacred Lady, which is just the mirror image of the Whore Aspect that Principality worships. They believe that the Lady speaks through the senses—*all* the senses—and that sensuality is the touch of the goddess. The *Hojun* priests speak for their Aspect of the Lady and her Consort, the Stawar God. I've seen the murals on the walls of some of Eastmark's temples, and I assure you, the Lady and her Consort seem to enjoy sex as much or more than anyone else." He chuckled.

"I thought it was only the Principality temple priestesses who . . . indulged . . . like that."

"They might be a little more straightforward about it, but since the Eastmark faithful have the example of their sacred couple, the *Hojun* priests not only carry messages from beyond, but they help the faithful achieve bliss and transcendence through . . . union."

Aidane gasped. "You're serious? Then why are they here with Gethin—oh," she said, and felt a rare flush creep into her cheeks. "Here all the time I figured they came along to make sure the prince and princess kept their distance until the marriage. You mean, they're not only here to make his sacrifices to the gods, but to . . . coach . . . him on achieving that bliss?" Despite the seriousness of the situation, Aidane could not fully stifle her giggles. "Does Berry know?"

Kolin smiled. "I have no idea. I truly can't see Jonmarc being the one to break it to her. That doesn't matter. The point is, you can stop being afraid that the *Hojun* priests will insist on using you to light the after-dinner bonfire."

Aidane let out a long breath. "All right. So all I have to worry about is paying attention to ghosts tonight, assuming there are any, and let you or Jonmarc know if any of them seem intent on getting a message through?"

Kolin gave her a reassuring nod. "That's it. Not too bad of an assignment, as spying goes."

"I thought spies were supposed to be invisible, not attract notice." Aidane gestured to her brightly colored and gold-glittering outfit. "I just failed that test."

Kolin took her arm. "You're just hiding in plain sight. That works even better."

The formal dining room at Lienholt Palace glittered with reflected light. A massive candelabra, filled with hundreds of glowing candles, hung suspended above the intricately carved and inlaid table. Queen Berwyn sat at the head of the table, with Jonmarc Vahanian, as the Queen's Champion, at her right hand. To her left sat Prince Gethin. Aidane took a few moments to observe the prince. He was dressed in the Eastmark fashion, with flowing robes in ochre and orange that set off his ebony skin. Long black hair framed his face. The ritual tattoos that marked the left side of his face from cheekbone to jaw seemed like elaborate shadows, and Aidane might have thought them a trick of the light if she had not seen the prince in daylight.

Next to the prince sat Avencen, an older man with close-cut, white hair. He was dressed in a similar manner as Gethin and wore a broad necklace of artfully wrought gold. Beside Avencen sat the two *Hojun* priests. The priests wore loose robes with elaborate embroidery, and small disks of copper dangled from the hems of their clothing, making a soft bell-like sound as they moved. Unlike Gethin or Avencen, the *Hojun* were shaved bald, and a complex web of runes had been cut into the skin of their scalps to remain as permanent, raised scars. Equally complicated tattoos circled their upper and lower arms, spiraling down to their wrists.

Kolin and Aidane were seated to the right of Jonmarc, with Aidane in between the two men. It was an arrangement that put Aidane directly across from Avencen, facing both of the *Hojun*. By the same token, Aidane was seated between the only two men in the room to wear their swords, other than the guards at the doorway.

When the formal greetings and introductions were finished, the talk turned to weather and war, and Aidane focused her listening skills for the whisper of ghosts. Throughout her brief stay in the palace, she had sensed the distant presence of spirits, although none of them attempted to contact her, and she had not gone looking for them.

Oddly enough, Aidane thought, spirits clustered around the *Hojun* priests, who appeared to be unaware of their invisible companions. Aidane smiled as if captivated by the conversation, and she poured her concentration into sensing the ghosts that accompanied the priests. Gradually, the images became more clear. A wizened old man who wore similar priestly robes. A magnificent stawar, dark furred, catlike, sinewy, and powerful. A wolf—no, she corrected, glimpsing the violet eyes—a *vyrkin*. The image shimmered to reveal a dark-haired, sullen-eyed young man. A young girl, perhaps only a few years older than the queen, dressed in lemon-colored robes. There were a few more spirits, and Aidane was so intent on getting a good look that the voice inside her mind made her jump in surprise.

Why are you staring at us?

The yellow-clad girl was looking at Aidane as if to take her measure. Aidane was vaguely aware of Kolin giving her a sideways glance, perhaps wondering why she startled.

You can see me, but you're not Hojun, and you're not a summoner, the girl's ghost continued.

I'm a serroquette, a ghost whore.

If the admission shocked the saffron-robed ghost, the girl did not show it. *Are you an oracle? An acolyte?*

No. Just a ghost whore. I help dead lovers reunite.

The girl considered that for a moment. *That is a holy calling, and a rare talent. You would be welcome in Eastmark. We would revere such a gift.*

Aidane felt herself relax, just a bit. She had been sure, up until now, that Kolin had been stretching the truth about Eastmark's beliefs. *I'll keep that in mind. I'm Aidane.*

The ghost nodded. *I'm Daciana. Are you here to be part of the wedding ceremony?*

Aidane's eyes widened. *Goodness, no! I mean, no, I'm not really here for the wedding ceremony at all. I had an important message to carry from a ghost for the queen, and now, with war coming, it looks like I'm a guest for a while.*

As Aidane talked with the ghost, her gaze wandered over the intricate bracelets and amulets worn by the *Hojun*. *I bet some of those contain the ashes of the ghosts*, Aidane thought. *That's how they're able to carry the ghosts with them.*

You're correct. Daciana's voice cut through Aidane's musings, but the ghost did not seem concerned over Aidane's curiosity. *We are advisers, seers, and protectors. We travel with the Hojun to help them access the Lady and her Consort.*

Do you possess the Hojun?

This time, it was the ghost's turn to seem surprised. *We advise. We do not enter their bodies, if that is what you mean.*

The group had been eating while Aidane was conversing with Daciana's ghost, and Aidane realized that the group was beginning to rise from their chairs on Berry's signal, to move into the parlor for further discussion. Kolin gave Aidane an inquiring glance, as if he guessed she was attuned to something he could not hear, and she managed a reassuring smile. But as they crossed the threshold into the sitting room, Aidane stopped in her tracks.

"What is it?" Kolin asked in a whisper only she could hear.

"There's something evil, something in here," Aidane said aloud, and both Jonmarc and Berry turned toward her as the

Hojun hung back, surrounded by their own frantically conferring spirit advisers.

A rush of cold air swept into the room from an open window at the side of the parlor. It struck Aidane hard enough to make her stumble backward as a hollowed spirit descended on her with the fury of a madman. Aidane's body went rigid with the effort to repel the invader, but the spirit shrieked in rage, forcing itself past her defenses. Jonmarc moved toward Berry, and the *Hojun* with their spirit advisers circled around Gethin. Kolin advanced slowly toward Aidane, watching her movements carefully.

Never before had Aidane felt a spirit in such torment. The hollowed soul screamed in agony, lashing through Aidane's body and violently pushing aside her own spirit. The possession was brutal, as if she were being pulled apart from the inside, and while Aidane fought her attacker, she knew she could not hold out for long. The two armed guardsmen had their swords drawn, but they looked around as if unsure what to do.

"Put down the knife, Aidane." It was Kolin's voice, and to Aidane's complete shock, she realized she was holding one of the knives from the sideboard that was set with an after-dinner repast of cheeses, fruit, and wine.

Aidane's entire body swayed with the effort to contain the hollowed spirit as Aidane fought for control. She called out to the palace ghosts to help her, but the other spirits fled from the dark power of the ghost that struggled to possess her. The dark spirit had no goal other than vengeance and a hunger to shed blood. Against her will, the revenant propelled her toward the others, although everything in her screamed for her body to obey her command.

I won't let it use me to do this. The ghost was wild, uncontrolled, and Aidane's movements were not coordinated. She knew at any second that Kolin would rush her, and she feared that she might plunge the knife into his heart, driven by the vengeful spirit that possessed her. Its howls of agony were making it difficult for her to think, drowning out her concentration in its consuming pain. Nothing would satisfy this tortured spirit except blood, and Aidane guessed that if she tried to cast the knife away, the spirit might find a new body to inhabit, one less able to fight it. If it possessed Jonmarc . . . Kolin . . . the guards . . . the result would be a bloodbath.

She was still halfway across the room from the others, who had pressed against the wall. The hollowed ghost was shrieking for her to run, and her body was beginning to carry itself faster and faster in lurching, unsure steps. Aidane glanced up and met Berry's eyes for a second, and then managed the only resistance open to her. As the ghost's attention focused on its would-be victims, Aidane turned the knife in her hand and let the momentum of her off-balance attack take her to the ground.

The knife plunged into her stomach, and the searing pain Aidane felt was her own, coupled with the screams of the hollowed spirit as it realized that this was all the death it would cause. As she fell, Kolin threw himself over her as one of the guard's swords sang through the air. Berry's cry of "Halt!" came an instant too late, and Aidane heard the sickening sound of the sword blade connecting with Kolin's flesh.

It hurt to breathe, and her hands were covered with her own blood. Then it felt as if something hit her hard, and Aidane realized that Daciana's spirit was forcing its way inside her dying body. Aidane was too spent to protest, but to her amazement, Daciana's spirit crashed against the tormented spirit of the hollowed ghost. Aidane thought the attacker would be thrown free, but Daciana's spirit glowed brighter as it fought the angry ghost, wresting it away from Aidane and binding it in strands of light.

I will fight for you. It was Daciana's voice, whispered from within Aidane's mind. The spirit adviser's voice was calm, but everywhere around them, voices raised in alarm.

Someone rolled Kolin from where he lay atop her, and Aidane could hear Jonmarc cursing under his breath. "Get a healer before we lose both of them!" Jonmarc shouted, and Aidane heard the distant pounding of footsteps as a guard ran to do his bidding.

"Mine looks worse than it is," Kolin said, his voice taut with pain. "I'll heal."

"Your back is laid open to the ribs."

"I'll heal. Take care of Aidane."

To Aidane's surprise, the queen knelt beside Jonmarc, heedless of the growing pool of Aidane's blood and Kolin's ichor that spread across the floor. "She did this to protect us, Jonmarc. I saw it in her eyes before she fell."

"I know." Jonmarc looked from Berry to the guards near the door. "Where is the healer?" His voice was angry, and his body spoke of frustrated motion, but in his eyes, Aidane read fear, and she knew just how well-founded that fear was.

Aidane felt a growing coldness. She had stopped trying to staunch the flow of blood, and although Jonmarc pressed a cloth against the wound, blood was slowly coloring the cloth a bright red. Kolin's cool hand gripped her own blood-soaked fingers.

"Help's coming, Aidane," Kolin whispered. She couldn't see the damage the guard's sword had done to Kolin's back, but she knew it must be substantial to cause the tightening she heard in his voice. He might have survived a strike that would have killed a mortal, but he was obviously in a great deal of pain because of it.

"Get over here now!" Jonmarc barked as a green-robed figure swept into the room. The healer knelt next to her, and Aidane could see a worried expression on the face of the older man as he let his hand hover over her, using his healing magic to read her condition.

"She's losing blood fast," he murmured. "I'll need help—"

"With the queen's permission, we offer our services." The voice was deep and rich, heavily accented in the consonant-heavy overtones of the Markian language. The hem of an ochre robe swirled into Aidane's line of sight.

"Please, do whatever you can," Berry replied, and for once, Aidane thought that the queen sounded like the young girl that she was.

A new face filled Aidane's view, although the images were beginning to blur and Aidane felt as if she were spinning. The ebony-skinned man met Aidane's eyes and fixed her with his gaze. He began to chant in a language she did not understand, but she caught one word: *Daciana*.

Inside her own head, the yellow-robed ghost girl responded with a singsong chant. Aidane felt Daciana's spirit fill her with warmth. Other ghosts were crowding close, drawn to the nearness of death, anxious to possess Aidane in her dying moments to own a living body once more, even if only for a few seconds. Aidane knew she was too weak to fight them off. *Don't let them take me*, she murmured in her mind.

I can't hold them all off and hold onto you, Daciana's spirit replied, *but my companions can. Will you open yourself to us?*

Too weak to reply, Aidane dropped the last battered vestiges of her mental shielding, trusting Daciana's companion spirits to reach her before the hungry interlopers.

Aidane's whole body bucked and began to shake as the spirits she had seen clustered around the *Hojun* priests slipped into her, filling her, leaving no space for the marauders who snarled and snapped in frustration.

"You're losing her!" Dimly, Aidane heard Kolin's angry voice.

Both of the *Hojun* priests were chanting now, and Aidane

could hear the healer's murmured words interspersed amid the chanting. She felt as if she were floating, and the shearing pain had dulled to an almost-bearable agony, though it felt distant, not really her own. The room around her was crowded, but inside her mind was crowded, too, and Aidane longed for the sweet peace of darkness that would make all the myriad voices be silent.

She is not Eastmark-born.

She is one of us in her gift. Can you not sense that?

Her ways are strange to us.

She reunites dead lovers, and you join body and flesh of supplicant and goddess. There's nothing strange about it. Aidane recognized the heated voice as Daciana's, and she was fairly sure that the other voice was of the old man's spirit that she had glimpsed in the company of the *Hojun*.

Not all blood likeness shows on the outside, old man. Look at me and my wolf. The sullen dark-haired spirit shifted into the image of a large, dark wolf. *She is more like us than not.*

The rhythm of the *Hojun* chant changed, and it caught the attention of the wolf-spirit. Whatever the priests were saying also brought the stawar spirit to attention. It was a massive cat, lithe and heavily muscled, the ultimate predator. Aidane saw both the wolf and the stawar freeze as if hearing something she did not, and their spirit forms tensed as if their prey was in sight. The *Hojun* priests uttered one guttural word in unison, and both of the spirit animals sprang forward.

At that same instant, Daciana released the shadowed remnant of the hollowed spirit that she had bound. The stawar and the wolf spirits sprang on it and Aidane felt the rush of their power surge through her, convulsing her body. Distantly, she heard a woman scream.

The stawar and the wolf seized their prey, using their powerful claws and teeth to shred through the shrieking revenant. Its screams filled Aidane's mind and issued from her mouth. Stawar and wolf were consuming the darkness, slashing it into dark ribbons and gulping it down, and Aidane felt the darkness tear loose, feeling as if fire flowed through her veins. Powerful hands gripped her shoulders as her body arched and writhed. Far away, she could hear arguing voices and the hum of a low chant.

Suddenly, she was free. Her body collapsed, utterly spent. Darkness of another kind, sweet unconsciousness, rushed up to salve her wounds.

You're safe now. It was Daciana's voice, and while the voice seemed close enough to have been whispered in her ear, Aidane knew that the spirit spoke within her mind. *I promise you, we will leave you more gently than we entered, when we are sure that no more harm will come to you.*

Aidane awoke in a bed. She lay on her back with fresh, clean linens beneath her and covering her, and the sleeve she glimpsed was of a nightgown she did not own. *I'm dead and they've prepared me for burial.*

The thought crossed her mind for a brief and frightening instant, and then Aidane realized that the fear caused her heart to pound in response. Not quite dead then ...

"You're safe." Kolin's voice sounded nearby. Aidane opened her eyes gingerly, afraid that light would hurt. She found Kolin sitting on a chair that had been pulled near the bed, and she realized she was in her room. He gave a tired smile, but Aidane saw concern in his eyes. "That was close."

Aidane listened in her mind for the voices of Daciana and her companion spirits, but all was quiet. "They're gone."

Kolin indicated the room around them. "Just barely. Those two *Hojun* priests insisted on following us when we carried you up here. Vittor, the healer, stayed with you for several candlemarks.

What's more is that the queen refused to leave your room until Vittor assured her that you would live."

"Does she know?" Her own voice sounded scratchy and faint. Kolin held a glass of water and gently helped her sit to take a sip.

"Know what?"

"That I meant her no harm. It was the spirit, the hollowed one . . ."

Kolin nodded. "The *Hojun* priests confirmed that there was an evil spirit, and they said their spirit envoys had destroyed it. The queen knew that you turned the knife on yourself to save her." There was a note of anger to his voice. "Dammit, Aidane! Why didn't you signal me? I could have held you back without nearly killing you."

"I was afraid . . . that it might try to possess you . . . or Jonmarc, or the guards. I wanted to destroy it."

"By destroying yourself?"

"If necessary."

Whatever reply Kolin intended to make was cut off when the door opened. Jonmarc entered, followed by Prince Gethin. Kolin's eyes widened for an instant, and he drew back. "She's only just awakened," Kolin said with an edge of reproof.

"Gethin insisted on coming, and neither of us wanted any sword-happy guards near Aidane, so here I am," Jonmarc replied with a shrug.

Gethin took a few steps to stand beside Aidane's bed. For a moment, he regarded her without speaking, and she could read nothing in his black eyes. "I came to thank you for your bravery," Gethin said in accented Common. "You stopped an attack that was clearly meant for Berwyn or for me. Either way, I am in your debt."

"The *Hojun* . . ." Aidane began, but her voice trailed off, and she found that just breathing required an enormous amount of energy.

"Along with the queen's gifted healer, the *Hojun* and their spirits cast out the attacker and helped you heal."

"One of them . . . wasn't sure about it. I'm glad he . . . changed his mind."

Gethin drew a breath before speaking, and a look of chagrin crossed his face. "For many years, my people kept many things to themselves, refusing to share them with the other kingdoms. We did not marry outside our own people, and we did not share our other . . . gifts. It led to great sorrows. My father decreed that all that should change. I'm here as part of that change. The *Hojun* shared with you something that has never been given to someone who was not of our blood." The last four words were edged with such a thick distaste that Gethin seemed to spit them.

"Thank you."

Gethin exchanged a glance with Kolin and Jonmarc. "I'm told that there are others like you, who share your talent, and that in Nargi, such a gift earns a death sentence. Jonmarc and Kolin told me that they're part of a smuggling concern to bring valuable people out of Nargi into Dark Haven. I've committed ten thousand gold *veneraj* from my personal account to fund their efforts, provided that they also bring out any true *serroquettes* that they might find. I can guarantee safe passage and sanctuary in Eastmark for you, m'lady, should you choose to come, and to others of your gift."

"Thank you," Aidane repeated, her voice a whisper.

"She needs to rest." Kolin's voice was firm. He walked the two men to the door, and there was a hum of muted conversation before the door clicked shut and Kolin returned. "Seems you're not only famous, but the queen considers you a national treasure. There are half a dozen guards outside your room, and Jonmarc's asked me to stay on as your bodyguard, even though I didn't do a very good job of it." He looked down, and Aidane caught the bitterness in his voice.

She managed to raise a hand to touch the place where his waistcoat and shirt were sliced open. The brocade and silk were dark with ichor. "Your side," she whispered.

"It's healed."

"Show me."

Kolin hesitated, and then pulled away the remnants of his shirt. A pale line ran from his spine diagonally to his waist. "By tomorrow, it will be gone." He managed a self-deprecating smile. "We heal quickly. It's one of the few benefits of being dead." He paused. "And I'll spare you the effort of looking for your own scars. The healer and the *Hojuns* fixed you up just fine. Not a mark on you."

"I heard Jonmarc say . . . you were cut to the bone."

Kolin looked away. "That idiot guard came after you like he meant to cut you in two. I just got in his way, that's all."

"He could have had your head."

Kolin met her eyes. "Better mine than yours." Kolin leaned forward and kissed her on the lips, a lingering, gentle kiss. Aidane found herself returning the kiss willingly. Kolin let his fingertips stroke her cheek and gave a sad half smile at the unspoken questions in her eyes. "When you fell on that knife and I saw the blood, I thought I'd lost you. And I realized that I care about you . . . more than just as your bodyguard."

Aidane realized that Kolin actually seemed ill at ease. "I've existed long enough to learn that important things shouldn't go unsaid," he said quietly.

Aidane paused, unsure of his meaning, and Kolin chuckled. "I don't want you to be Elsbet. I don't want you to be anyone but yourself. And I'm not looking for the services of a *serroquette*. I would like to be your suitor, if you'll have me."

She reached out to take his hand. "I'd like that."

Kolin's eyes registered a mixture of surprise and wonder. He touched the back of her hand to his lips. "I'm honored, m'lady," he said, and Aidane realized that he used the term without a hint of irony.

"It'll be dawn soon, and since the parlor off this room has no windows, I'll take my rest there," Kolin said, falling back into his role as bodyguard. He gestured toward the far wall, and for the first time, Aidane realized that heavy tapestries covered the window in her room. "Just in case, we had the window covered. I don't usually stir during the daytime, but I can if I need to, in an emergency, so long as there's no sunlight. The guards will be outside the door day and night, and I'll be close enough to hear if you need me, even when I'm resting." He saw her move to speak, and he laid a finger across her lips.

"Now, get some sleep." His voice was light, but his fingers gently brushed the hair back from her forehead. For an instant, he looked at her and something flickered in his eyes, and then he was gone so quickly Aidane did not see him leave. Too tired to think further about anything, Aidane closed her eyes and found sleep waiting.

7

The Goat and Ram tavern was the kind of place anyone who wished for a long life was well-advised to avoid. Jonmarc pulled the collar of his great cloak up to shield his face and entered, standing for an instant in the doorway to take stock of the room with his hand near the pommel of his sword.

The air smelled of ale and roasted goat. The tavern was about half full, with patrons playing cards or talking in hushed tones at the well-worn tables. Two hard-used trollops lounged at the bar in gowns that were several years out of fashion. Another strumpet sat near one of the men at the betting table. Conversation hushed for a moment as the patrons sized up the newcomer at the door.

Jonmarc chose a table where he could sit with his back to the wall. A chair and a stool sat next to the table, and Jonmarc hooked the rungs of the stool with his boot, drawing it into position against the wall. Unlike the chair, the stool permitted him a clear reach for his sword.

The innkeeper was a thin man with a face scarred by pox and fights. His angular nose had been broken and badly reset, and there was a notch out of one ear. As the man set a tankard of ale down, Jonmarc could see more scars on the man's hands.

"I'd advise you to drink your ale and be on your way." The

innkeeper's voice was rough, suggesting that he was fond of tobacco and fonder of whiskey.

"I've got business here," Jonmarc replied.

"Oh?"

"I'm here to see Scian." Jonmarc watched the innkeeper's face for a reaction but saw no flicker of emotion.

"That so? And why should Scian see you?"

"Because an old War Dog sent me." Although Jonmarc's voice was low, he knew that, despite their effort to appear otherwise, the conversation was being appraised by the other denizens of the tavern, one of whom was likely to be Scian.

"I'll handle this one, Ved." A figure emerged from the shadows of the kitchen passage. Jonmarc saw the silhouette first. High boots, slim-cut trousers, with a serious sword in a fighter's scabbard that slung low across the waist. Broadcloth shirt, narrow shoulders, and sleeves wide enough for Jonmarc to be certain they hid a variety of knives.

Obediently, Ved left the ale and returned to the bar. A rough voice just above a whisper spoke from the shadows. "Well, well. The new queen doesn't waste time. I thought she might send a messenger, but what should I make of this?"

"Scian?"

"Among other names." The shadowed figure shifted, revealing a lean woman with chiseled features that spoke of mixed blood. Margolan and Trevath, Jonmarc guessed. She leaned against the wall alongside Jonmarc, poised to see anyone who rose from their seats or entered from either the outside or the kitchen. "You don't seem surprised."

Jonmarc shrugged. "By the fact that the head of the Assassin's Guild is a woman? I'll be the first to acknowledge that women are more dangerous than men. I don't doubt you're good at your job, or I wouldn't have come."

"How do you know Valjan?"

"We were War Dogs together, long ago. He was my commander."

"Before you were betrayed and left for dead. I know who you are, Jonmarc Vahanian."

"So do we talk business, or do I drink my ale and go home?"

Scian's thin lips quirked upward into something that was almost a smile. "Follow me."

Scian led him into a private room and closed the door. She motioned for him to take a seat at a table near the fire. The room had just four tables, enough chairs for each table, and its own fireplace, which held a freshly fed fire. Jonmarc found a chair with a good view of the door, careful to make sure he had easy access to his sword.

"So what is the Queen's Champion doing on this side of town?"

"Business."

Scian raised an eyebrow. "And that business would be?"

"I want to know how your ghost blades are faring these days."

All amusement disappeared from Scian's face and her lips pressed tightly together. "And just how are you so well informed?"

"Because I've got as many friends in low places as you do." Jonmarc did not bother to hide his annoyance. "Stop playing games. I came with a warning."

"And that would be?"

"That whoever this Buka is, he—or she—has the nasty trick of hollowing the spirits of the victims. I think someone is using those hollowed spirits to attack anyone who can channel ghosts, like a *serroquette*—and a ghost blade."

Scian nodded solemnly. "Unfortunately, your warning comes too late. Within the last few days, two of our ghost blades killed themselves. It wasn't in their nature to do something like that, so we suspected dark magic, but couldn't prove it. Then one of our blades went mad and attacked several of his comrades. Two were killed. The others had no choice except to defend themselves, and the ghost blade was killed."

Scian leaned forward. "The men who were there said that as the ghost blade lay dying, his whole body began to shake and they saw a shadow leave him. The room grew cold and their breath misted. Once the shadow passed, the ghost blade was back in his right mind, but before they could call a healer, he died."

"What of your other ghost blades?"

Scian barked a harsh laugh. "You presume that we have an unlimited number of such rare weapons."

"I'm given to understand you employ about a dozen."

A hard glint came to Scian's eyes, and Jonmarc took it to mean his information had been more correct than the assassin preferred. "We've taken steps to protect them," Scian said. "Amulets, talismans, protective spells. But it's difficult to keep out just one type of spirit when a ghost blade's effectiveness relies on being able to channel the ghosts of our dead fighters."

"Then the job I bring you may be to your liking."

Scian regarded Jonmarc with suspicion. "You bring a job to us? From the queen?"

Jonmarc nodded. "Kill Buka."

Scian sat back in her chair and crossed her arms. "What do we care about a killer of whores?"

"Buka is more than a madman. He's not just a killer; he's using blood magic to hollow the souls of his victims. The revenants he leaves behind are like ghostly *ashtenerath*, mad with pain and blind with rage."

"You know this how?"

It was Jonmarc's turn to sit back with a cold smile. "That's restricted information."

Scian scowled, and for a moment she was silent, drumming her fingers against her arm as she thought. "If you know of the threat to the ghost blades, then you also know about the attacks in the city. We thought perhaps *dimonns* were behind them, but our mages proved us wrong."

Jonmarc nodded. "It's the hollowed spirits of Buka's victims. When they stay near where they died, they attack anyone unlucky enough to be in their way. When they find someone who can channel spirits, they possess the channeller and use the body as a weapon."

Scian drew a deep breath. "We've heard that the seers in the poorest neighborhoods have also been attacked, and the attacks sound like what happened to our ghost blades. It does seem to support what you say."

"What of the warrens beneath the city?"

"The mines that built Principality's wealth also run beneath the city. There's an anthill of tunnels and passageways underneath every part," Scian said. "It's the last refuge of people with nowhere left to go. Of late, we hear that whole sections of the warren have been taken over by people dying of plague. It's gotten so bad that, in some parts, the tunnels are clogged completely with bodies, and the smell even reaches the surface."

"Could Buka be hiding in the warrens?"

Scian shrugged. "He may hide there, but from what we've heard, he doesn't kill there. None of our sources from the warrens have talked of killings down there like the ones Buka's been blamed for above ground." She paused. "And yet . . . I think something about the warrens fascinates him. Of late, the murders have been close to entrances to the warrens, with the bodies placed near the openings to the underground, or hung in doorways."

Jonmarc felt a chill go down his back. "Hung in doorways?" he repeated sharply.

Scian nodded. "Does it matter?"

Jonmarc leaned forward intently. "Back in Dark Haven, we fought several battles against the Durim."

Scian nodded again. "So we've heard."

"I was part of those raids. The Durim seemed to prefer slaughtering goats—or *vyrkin*—while Buka apparently likes his victims to be human. But they made their sacrifices near the entrances to burial mounds, barrows, and cairns. We've caught them digging into the mounds, but we don't know whether they're trying to get in or let something buried get out."

"I've heard tell that mounds near the city have also been disturbed. What does that have to do with Buka?"

"Maybe nothing," Jonmarc admitted. "On the other hand, you might look at the warren as its own kind of barrow, where the desperate go to die. Buka's drawn to death—that much is certain. And the way he's killing his victims is binding their spirits here and driving them mad. The palace spymaster didn't think Buka was in league with the Durim. But what if . . ."

"What?"

Jonmarc shook his head. "I'm the last person to be speculating about magic, since I haven't a bit of it. But what if something is calling to both the Durim and to Buka, drawing them toward it, encouraging them to kill? Some kind of magic . . . something that they can feel and we can't?"

"Something like a dark summoner?"

Jonmarc grimaced. "Yes. Something with power like that, calling to them."

"Strong enough to raise the dead?"

Jonmarc felt the hair on the back of his neck rise. "What do you mean?" He could see that Scian was debating with herself on how much to tell him, and perhaps on whether he might think her mad for whatever she was about to say.

"We've seen some of the Durim's handiwork in the burying grounds out from the city, that's true," Scian said, and licked her lips nervously. "Your spymaster hired us to hunt down the Durim responsible, and we did. But there were other places throughout the countryside where the dead just . . . walked away. Not *asht-enerath*, because no one reported attacks. Not *dimonns*. Just bodies that walked out of their crypts into the night and vanished."

"Like puppets on strings," Jonmarc murmured.

Scian's head snapped up. "You've seen this?"

Jonmarc shook his head. "Not here in Principality City. But back in Dark Haven such things occurred. We didn't find the bodies."

"We haven't, either."

Jonmarc tapped the toe of his boot as he thought. "I have it on good authority that during the war in Margolan last year, the traitor lord's blood mages raised the bodies of the dead to terrify the Margolan troops and draw their fire away from the real enemy."

Scian's eyes narrowed. "Your 'good authority' about such things might be quite good indeed."

"Count on it."

"I thought only a summoner could raise the dead."

Jonmarc spread his hands. "That's where the magic gets technical, so I'm told. Apparently, it takes a summoner to return a soul to a body, actually bring someone back to life. I've had some experience being on the receiving end of that kind of magic. It works."

Scian raised an eyebrow. "Indeed."

"On the other hand, any mage who can move objects with magic can make a corpse walk. It takes blood magic to raise *ashtenerath*, but it's hard work. Making the dead walk is more like puppetry, so I'm told."

Scian considered his words in silence for a moment. "Do you think they're related: the Durim, Buka, the body snatchers?"

Jonmarc frowned. "Related, yes. Working together, no."

"Explain."

Jonmarc leaned forward, resting his elbows on the table. "I think there's someone out there, maybe that dark summoner you mentioned, who's the real threat. Whoever is doing this is powerful, very powerful. Maybe powerful enough that people attuned to that kind of magic can sense something, feel it calling even if they don't know what it is. The Durim call it Shanthadura. Who knows what Buka or the body snatchers make of it. But I'm sure of one thing: What the three groups are doing, whether they know it or not, feeds the power of the real threat. Blood magic, dark magic, dark summoner—I don't know what to call it, but I think the murders and the barrow desecrations and the body thefts are all part of someone's plan."

"So the war has actually begun."

"Absolutely. And right now, before the armies even attack, this is the front line. Kill Buka, find the missing bodies, and we might just win this particular battle."

Scian gave a scratchy laugh. "And is our young queen ready to dirty her hands with the likes of me and my assassins as allies?"

"If she wasn't, I wouldn't be here."

Scian gave him a hard look. "What's in it for us?"

Jonmarc leaned back and smiled. "Gold. Oh, you'll have the queen's gratitude, at least privately, but I figured you'd prefer a reward you can spend."

"Gold works. How much?"

"For Buka, ten thousand gold pieces." He gave a cold smile. "That should be enough to stir even your *vayash moru* assassins into action." The rewards were lavish, higher even than the bounties Jonmarc had on his own head in the not-too-distant past. High enough to put the Assassin's Guild in competition with every other bounty hunter in Principality.

Scian seemed to guess his thoughts. "Have the bounties posted yet?"

"I'm doing you a professional courtesy by telling you first."

For the first time that evening, Scian's smile seemed genuine. "You've just hired yourself some assassins, Lord Vahanian."

8

"Bad dreams again?" Cerise set a cup of tea in front of Kiara and gave her an appraising look. Kiara knew better than to evade the healer's scrutiny.

"It's the same dream, over and over. I haven't been able to sleep for the last two weeks, since I saw a ring around the moon. That's a bad omen, Cerise. It means the death of a king. I see a man stabbed through the heart, but I can't tell who the man is." She paused. "I see a rag doll in a box surrounded by bones. The doll has no features, no face, but somehow, I know that doll is . . . me."

She let out a long breath. "In the dreams, I see Mother, weeping. Since the dreams began, I've felt her presence more closely than usual." Her hand went to an amulet that hung from a gold chain at her throat. Inside the golden locket were a few of her mother's ashes, enough to allow the spirit to cross the distance that separated Kiara from Viata's crypt. "I feel it in my bones, Cerise, Father's dead."

Jae, Kiara's battle gyregon, lifted its head from where he lay on the hearth as if he knew she was distraught. Heedless of the two large wolfhounds that sprawled near Kiara's chair, Jae waddled over, his compact, reptilian body easily navigating between the dogs. The same attunement to her mood that made

Jae an excellent battle companion also drew him to her grief. Absently, Kiara stroked his smooth, greenish-brown scales and Jae settled into her lap.

"Is it just the dreams? Like scrying, dreams can show what might be instead of what is." Cerise cocked her head as if she knew Kiara was holding back information, and Kiara paused, then shook her head.

"My regent magic is different." Kiara knew Cerise could hear the fear in her voice. "Until now, it's never been very strong. A little scrying—imprecise at best—a bit of truth-sensing, that's all I could ever do, even when Father was sick and I was ruling in his stead."

"Perhaps it's because you couldn't rule openly. It's not as if you were crowned."

"Maybe. I wondered if the coronation ceremony here in Margolan would strengthen the regent magic. After all, it's supposed to provide a nonmage with special abilities that are useful to a ruler."

"And did the Margolan coronation change anything?"

Kiara shrugged. "I felt the regent magic stir when I was crowned queen, but nothing else happened. My magic has never compared to what a true mage like Tris can do, or even been as strong as Father's regent magic. I thought perhaps that it was because I'm the consort rather than the reigning monarch here in Margolan. I wondered if something different would happen when it came time to take the throne in Isencroft. But now, something feels different. If it's changed, I'm afraid to find out why."

Just then, there was a knock at the parlor doors, and one of the guards outside leaned into the room. "My apologies, Your Majesty, but there are guests to see you." The guard drew back, and Mikhail, Shekerishet's *vayash moru* seneschal, moved into view. Mikhail was accompanied by another man;

by the look of him, Kiara guessed he was *vayash moru* as well.

"My apologies for interrupting, but I'm afraid this can't wait," Mikhail said. He took a leather pouch from the courier and handed it to Kiara.

"This can't be good news." Kiara looked to the leather pouch in her hand and then back to the man who had brought it. She exchanged a worried glance with Cerise. That the courier was *vayash moru* signified a message too urgent to entrust its delivery to even the fastest mortal messenger. This particular *vayash moru* looked haggard, as if he had pushed even his abilities to their limit.

"This is Antoin," Mikhail said. "He carries with him verified papers from *vayash moru* in Isencroft who are known to me, and more important, whom I trust."

Kiara settled into a chair near the fire, staring at the wax seal with the mark of the king of Isencroft that secured the bundle. Kiara waved Cerise to sit beside her, fighting off a leaden feeling of impending ill news. She hoped no one noticed that her hand was shaking as she broke the seal and carefully unbound the message inside.

It's in Allestyr's handwriting, not Father's, Kiara noted, catching her breath. She drew herself up to sit straight and began to read the letter to herself.

Your Majesty, and my dearest Kiara, the letter began. *I dread being the one to bear this news. I can only hope that our long and fond acquaintance will help to soften the blow. Your father was murdered in his bedchamber by a conspiracy among servants with Divisionist sympathies.*

Kiara caught her breath so sharply that Mikhail and Cerise both moved toward her. Cerise placed a steadying hand on Kiara's shoulder, and Mikhail stood behind her protectively.

We have buried him with the full honor he so richly deserved.

The Dread

Despite the unrest that has troubled Isencroft, throngs of loyalists followed the procession in mourning. Unfortunately, even with the visible presence of both the army and the Veigonn, several violent incidents marred the ceremony, a tragic commentary on the difficult times in which we live.

In your absence, Count Renate has been named Regent, but this is, I caution you, a very temporary measure. Renate is a man of unquestioned loyalty, but he is not the leader our divided kingdom requires to navigate both unrest within and attack from outside. We have no choice except to beg you to return to Isencroft as quickly as you can. I know, my dear Kiara, that you have only recently given birth, and were our situation not desperate, I would not ask such a sacrifice from you. I know, as do the others who stand in the breach for Isencroft—Cam, Tice, Brother Felix, Kellen, Wilym, and Trygve—that it is dangerous for you to travel, and even more dangerous for you to return to Isencroft, with the ships of war on the horizon. But there is no other course if we are to preserve Isencroft. Without a monarch of the blood, I fear we will tear ourselves apart before any foreign enemy could lay waste to our shores.

The situation is dire. Alvior of Brunnfen has betrayed his vows to your father and returns with the invaders to seize the crown. His claim of consanguinity is stronger than Renate's position as regent. Only a more direct blood heir to both the crown and the regent magic of the fallen kings can hope to rise as both symbol and monarch and save our kingdom.

My dear Kiara, my heart breaks for you. I know it cannot be easy to weigh your duty to your child and to your husband, and the burdens of your responsibilities in Margolan, against the claims of the crown, and yet, I beg of you, please find a way to return to Isencroft as quickly as you can. Long ago, on the battlefield, you saw a vision of the Sacred Lady, of Chenne the Warrior, and your conviction rallied the troops to victory.

You are both heir and symbol, and it is that symbol of Isencroft around which our riven kingdom must rally.

Your father made his journey to the Lady on the tenth day of the month, just after the eleventh candlemark in the evening. Before fifth bells the next morning, ere the sun could rise on a leaderless kingdom, our small cabal of loyalists worked a magic that must remain unnamed to make you queen in fact as well as in theory. You may already feel stirrings of the regent magic; such is your birthright in ways I do not pretend to understand.

I ask an impossible choice of you, my dear Kiara, to leave behind your son and return to save your homeland, when war imperils both kingdoms. Yet I beg of you not to bring the baby with you as he would present too ready a target for those who would destroy the monarchy. I can only ask that you heed my pleas and return swiftly.

Trust Antoin. His loyalty is unquestioned. Ride with whatever guard you deem appropriate to the Isencroft border at Beirmoth. There, you will find a handpicked garrison of Isencroft soldiers awaiting you. I mean to cast no aspersions upon your new home, or upon the intentions of King Martris, but given the difficult history of our two kingdoms, it would be best that Margolan soldiers not cross into Isencroft. The soldiers who await you are sworn to bring you to the palace at any cost. Take every precaution. Arm yourself as if for battle and wear a cuirass beneath your cloak. These are dangerous times.

I wish your homecoming could be under better circumstances. You are not alone in grieving the loss of the king, although I know it is a double blow to lose both king and father. There is much more to tell you that I dare not trust to a letter. Come home as quickly as you are able, Kiara. Isencroft hangs in the balance. Your faithful servant, Allestyr.

Kiara slumped forward and leaned against Cerise's shoulder.

For a few moments, the room was silent except for the sound of her sobs. Kiara took a deep breath, shook herself, and then wiped her eyes with the back of her hand and lifted her head. "Father is dead. Murdered. Isencroft is in the middle of civil war, with a pretender to the throne among the invaders whose fleet is already off our shores." Her voice nearly broke, but she willed steel into her tone. "I have no choice. I must go home."

Cerise took Kiara's hand in hers. "What of Cwynn?"

Kiara knew that her grief and turmoil were clear in her expression as she turned to Cerise and glanced upward at Mikhail. "I don't dare take him with me. Yet I don't know how I can leave him. It's not quite three months since he was born. What if Talwyn was right? What if Cwynn is at the heart of this war? How can I leave him? How can I leave Margolan, when Tris has already gone to war?"

Cerise's grip tightened on Kiara's fingers. "You aren't the first mother who had to leave a small child. Think of the women who die in childbirth, and their babies survive. We'll find a wet nurse for him, someone the mages can certify is completely trustworthy. He'll need guardians, people you trust implicitly."

"Alle and Lady Eadoin," Kiara responded. "There's no one else I'd trust with Cwynn except Mikhail, and he'll have his hands full minding the castle."

"I appreciate your trust, m'lady, but I fear I have very little experience with babies," Mikhail said gently. "I will do everything in my power to keep Shekerishet safe and running smoothly until you—and Tris—return."

"I'll send for Alle and Eadoin tonight," Cerise said, "within the candlemark. We'll also have to speak with the mages the king left behind to watch over Cwynn. They need to know that the danger from Isencroft has risen to a new level."

Retreating into the distance of strategy and logistics made it possible for Kiara not to break down. There would be time for grief later and for the rest of her life. Now, the future of two kingdoms was on the line. Never before had Kiara felt more powerless.

"There's something else you must factor into your plans, Kiara," Cerise said, fixing Kiara with her gaze. "While you can leave Cwynn in Margolan, there's no helping the fact that the other heir goes where you go." She glanced pointedly at Kiara's belly, where the new pregnancy, just a few weeks along, had not yet begun to show.

"Allestyr doesn't know," Kiara murmured. "I didn't want to worry Father, so Tris and I agreed that I would wait a few months before I told him. There hasn't even been time for a regular courier to carry the news, if I had intended to announce it."

Cerise nodded. "For the best, perhaps. You're already a valuable target. There are some, in both kingdoms, who would prefer there to be no new heir."

Kiara shivered. She knew too well how right Cerise was. Earlier that year, a well-placed traitor within Shekerishet had very nearly managed to assassinate both Kiara and the unborn child, Cwynn, which she carried. While the attack had been foiled through the heroic action of Master Bard Carroway and Macaria, the poisoned blade had still managed to sicken Kiara dangerously during the last months of her pregnancy, and the effect of the wormroot poison on Cwynn was yet to be known. "I take one child with me, I leave one behind, but none of us is safe," Kiara said in a hushed voice. She rallied, willing herself to square her shoulders.

"There's no other choice. Cwynn must stay here, and I must go to Isencroft."

"Cerise, I know little of childbirth, as I've just admitted," Mikhail said. "But should Kiara ride, given the circumstances? Antoin made the journey in a few days because he's *vayash*

116

moru, but at a swift pace, two weeks is the fastest Kiara can hope to reach Aberponte and a carriage would take even longer."

I risk the kingdom if I move in greatest safety, and the baby if I move with speed, Kiara thought miserably.

Cerise looked thoughtful for a moment. "Granted, Kiara had a difficult time of it with Cwynn. But that may have been because Cwynn was special from the start." She met Kiara's eyes. "You and everyone else have been blaming the wormroot on that damned knife for Cwynn's 'differences,' and that may have a grain of truth to it. But this pregnancy is already going more smoothly than it did the last time. Perhaps Cwynn's 'differences' also made your pregnancy so difficult, and the fact that you've had an easier start to it this time bodes well for what you now find yourself called to do."

"So what you're saying—"

"What I'm saying is that I believe you can ride swiftly, with precautions. And of course, I plan to ride with you." Cerise crossed her arms and set her jaw. Kiara knew from a lifetime of experience that Cerise's decision in the matter was not open to debate, or to the fiat of a queen.

"I'll choose from among the *Telorhan* guards myself," Mikhail said. "And I'll add a few of the *vayash moru*—those I can vouch for personally—to your guard." He smiled, making his eye teeth plain. "You may not be able to take guardsmen with you into Isencroft, but *vayash moru* and *vyrkin* wear no uniform. I'll rest better knowing that you're guarded by some of our own, going into such a dangerous situation."

"Thank you," Kiara murmured. "It's just so much to take in, all at once."

"Antoin and I have preparations to make before dawn," Mikhail said, with a glance toward their visitor. "I'll bring you a report at nightfall. How soon do you plan to leave for Isencroft?"

Kiara caught her breath. What had been unthinkable a few candlemarks ago was now a foregone conclusion, and an urgent one at that. "It depends on how quickly we can make arrangements for Cwynn, and how soon I can be packed." She shook her head. "Packing shouldn't take long, not with the circumstances. I'll need a plain tunic and trews to blend in on the road, and provisions. Almost everything else Cam and Allestyr will have for me in Isencroft." She paused. "Mikhail, can you please send a messenger right away to Alle and Eadoin at Brightmoor?"

"As you wish, m'lady."

Cerise gave a comforting smile. "I'll come to help you pack necessities. It might be best to leave after dark tomorrow, to reduce suspicions. We should have everything arranged by then."

"We haven't even talked about how to handle this with the Margolan court," Kiara said, feeling breathless. "This isn't going to go over well, I'm afraid. I suspect Margolan's nobles assumed that when I married Tris, I left Isencroft behind for good, despite all the talk about a 'dual throne' and a 'joint heir.' It's entirely one thing to bandy such terms about; it's another to see your queen ride off for another kingdom when the king's gone to war."

Mikhail grimaced. "The timing is bad; no doubt about it. On the other hand, if we weren't at the brink of war, the situation wouldn't have arisen at all."

"We have no idea how long I'll be gone, or when Tris will return. And no matter how we explain it, there will be some gossips who will say that I've abandoned my husband, my child, and my vows to Margolan and run for home."

Cerise sighed. "I'm afraid you're right, and what's more, I don't know that there's anything we can do to keep that from happening. You're likely to be gone months, not days. We can say that you've taken to your bed with the pregnancy. After the last time, it will be what people expect. That might buy us some time."

Mikhail nodded. "The fewer people who know the truth the better, at least for a while. I have a few ideas, but I need until tomorrow to pull what I need together." He glanced at Antoin. "Come with me. We have a lot to do."

For a few moments after Mikhail and Antoin left, it was quiet. Kiara stared down at the parchment in her hands. *One letter changes everything. And how will I tell Tris?*

Cerise patted Kiara's hand. Kiara turned to see a sad smile on the healer's face. "*Skrivven* for your thoughts."

Kiara shook her head. "I'm afraid there are too many thoughts for just one *skrivven*," she said quietly.

"If it's any consolation, your mother faced these kinds of decisions many times."

Kiara gave a harsh chuckle. "I doubt she faced quite this same set of choices."

Cerise's gaze seemed far away. "Perhaps not. Then again, when she was pregnant with you, her father, King Radomar, demanded that she return to Eastmark and raise you there."

"Radomar can't have expected her to obey."

"Kings become quite used to expecting every order to be followed. He not only demanded that Viata return to Eastmark; he sent agents to take her by force."

"He had to realize that kidnapping the queen of Isencroft—and the heir—would start a war. He could have sent the entire Winter Kingdoms into war!"

Cerise shrugged. "From your grandfather's perspective, it was Donclan who had done the kidnapping, and since Radomar never recognized the wedding as legitimate, he considered her pregnancy to be tantamount to rape."

Kiara gasped. "What happened?"

"As you can imagine, Donelan and Viata had no intention of

doing what Radomar demanded. King Bricen in Margolan had done all he could with the betrothal contract to avert one war. So Donelan had no one to turn to among the kings for help. But your father was a clever man," Cerise said. "He declared that the remaining months in your mother's pregnancy should be considered a festival in her honor, and he spent a fortune in gold to bring minstrels and merchants with Eastmark goods to Isencroft. It became fashionable for Isencroft women to wear the silk clothing your mother preferred, and to copy her style of jewelry. Not only that, but the good women of Isencroft actually began to tint their fair skin with teas and berry juice to make them nearly the same ebony color as Viata!"

Kiara chuckled, glancing down at her hands. Her own skin was much lighter than her mother's pure Eastmark coloring, more the shade of *kerif* with cream. "But how did that help? The Eastmark agents had only to look in the palace to find Mother."

"That's where I'm certain you're truly Viata's daughter, in nerve as well as fact. Donelan hid Viata with a troupe of traveling Eastmark performers who were wintering in the countryside. One of the lesser nobles was glad to play a part in the ruse and opened his manor to the troupe for the winter. Radomar's agents were searching a city full of Viata look-alikes, while your mother was leagues away, sheltered in an unremarkable country home passing herself off as a disgraced actress."

Kiara managed to smile at the audacity of the ploy, but the smile soon faded. "I can't bear to think about leaving Cwynn," she said quietly. "I have a duty as queen and heir, but my heart tells me I have a duty as a mother, too. He's so small, so vulnerable, and there are so many dangerous things afoot right now. How can I leave him, maybe for months, when we still don't know for certain what troubles his sleep or why he might be important to the war?"

Cerise refilled Kiara's cup and held the steaming tea out to her. "Cwynn would be a pawn in the war no matter what because he's the heir. It complicates matters for both you and Tris to be far away, but again, you're not the first royal parents to make difficult decisions for the sake of your kingdoms."

"I know. And I'll do what I must. But I don't have to like it," Kiara said softly. Jae stirred in her lap and Kiara scratched the gyregon lightly under its throat. With a trill, Jae settled himself and went back to sleep.

Cerise shook her head. "No, my dear. You don't have to like it."

Lady Eadoin and Alle arrived by noon the next day. Alle, Lady Eadoin's niece and the recent bride of General Ban Soterius, was quick to greet Kiara with the exuberance of an old friend. Jae, Kiara's gyregon, stirred from his customary spot near the hearth to greet the visitors and presented himself for attention, preening as Alle bent down to stroke his scaly neck.

"Your Majesty," Alle said solemnly with a mischievous glint in her eye as she curtsied low. She bounded up and clasped Kiara in a tight hug that was returned with equal vigor. "It's so good to see you, Kiara! We came as quickly as we could when Mikhail's messenger told us what was going on."

Alle's blonde hair was pinned up after the fashion popular among noble ladies, as befitting the wife of a general who was also one of the king's best friends. But Kiara knew that Alle much preferred to have her wild curls down, and that any appearance of sedate acceptability was merely a performance for onlookers. During the war to take back the throne from Jared the Usurper, Alle had left the comfort and relative safety of

Eadoin's estate to join the Resistance, passing herself off successfully as a barmaid to spy against Jared's soldiers.

"It's wonderful to see both of you. I can't believe how much I've missed you." For the first time in many weeks, Kiara felt a genuine rush of pleasure.

Lady Eadoin chuckled quietly. She walked with a cane, moving slowly across the room. In her day, Eadoin had been one of the most sought-after beauties at the Margolan court, and even now remained a staunch patron of music and art. Both Eadoin and Alle had been among Kiara's loyal protectors amid the court intrigue when Tris besieged Lochlanimar, and they had become the queen's closest friends.

"Good to see you as well, my dear. Came as soon as we could. My people at Brightmoor will send the rest of our things along." Eadoin's voice, though reedy, was full of dry humor. "I'm a bit old for saving the kingdom, but I'll do my best."

Eadoin made as deep a curtsey as age allowed, and Kiara lifted her with a gentle grip on both hands to stand before warmly embracing the dowager. "I'm so glad you've come," Kiara murmured.

Eadoin regarded Kiara with a knowing look. "As one grows older, the opportunities for clandestine adventure become few and far between. One must never pass up such rarities when they occur."

Kiara patted Jae's head and the gyregon lumbered over to rub against Alle's ankles, catlike. Jae's mouth opened in contentment, baring his sharp teeth. Around the palace, Jae might pass for a pampered pet, but Kiara had seen the gyregon in his true role as a hunting and battle companion and knew that a well-trained gyregon put even the best falcons to shame.

Cerise joined them after half a candlemark. She brought Cwynn with her and handed the already fussing baby to Kiara.

"Meet Cwynn," Kiara said in a voice that mingled both pride and exasperation. "And yes, he's always like this."

Alle and Eadoin murmured the expected pleasantries, as Cerise helped Kiara loosen the bodice of her gown so that Cwynn could nurse.

"He looks quite healthy, with good lungs," Alle observed as Cwynn finally quieted down to eat. "So the wormroot had no effect?"

Kiara sighed. "We're still not sure. There are so many things that have been unusual, not the least the way he seems to be affected by magic in ways that even Tris doesn't understand. As far as we know, Cwynn has no magic of his own. I wouldn't expect him to; he's far too young.

"He stymies every attempt Tris has made to read his life force, yet Cheira Talwyn of the Sworn believes that Cwynn has great power. She thinks at least some of this fussing is because he hears something in the magic, something the rest of us don't. Something that might even be related to the invaders from the north." Kiara began to gently stroke Cwynn's downy hair. "He's already seen far too much excitement for just a babe, and I'm afraid it's only the beginning."

"We gathered from Mikhail's note that your rather sudden journey would require some special help with the baby," Eadoin said, clearing her throat. "I've taken the liberty of bringing with us one of my ladies' maids, a lovely young girl by the name of Verley, who is a new mother herself. She's brought her own baby with her as she's nursing, you see. Verley's mother and grandmother have been part of my household for their entire lives, and I trust them implicitly. Souls of discretion. So if part of your concern comes from worrying that the child will go hungry, Verley is amply prepared to meet his needs along with her own child's."

Kiara felt a wave of gratitude and relief, followed by a cold pang of jealousy at the thought of sharing so intimate a moment as nursing with a total stranger. *You don't have the luxury to begrudge this*, she chided herself. *It's the price of the crown.*

"Part of me wishes I dared send him away to Brightmoor, safely out of the palace," Kiara murmured.

Alle and Eadoin exchanged glances. "I remember what happened when we tried to move you someplace we thought would be safer," Alle said. "That didn't work out well. The assassin still found us. Let's stay here at Shekerishet this time."

Kiara shivered. "I agree."

Kiara felt something rustle against her skirts and looked down to see Tris's two favorite wolfhounds stirring. The dogs paused for a friendly sniff at the nursing baby, and then greeted Alle and Eadoin as old friends, with their long tails wagging. Kiara knew that wherever the two wolfhounds went, so went the ghost of a mastiff, the third of their "pack," unseen by everyone but Tris.

Cwynn ate with gusto, and Kiara cradled him against herself fiercely. Alle and Eadoin talked merrily about the recent harvest and the news from Brightmoor, Eadoin's estate. But while Kiara smiled and nodded, it was a struggle to swallow back her tears.

I don't want to leave Cwynn, kingdoms be damned! Look how small he is, she thought as one of Cwynn's tiny hands curled around her finger. She closed her eyes, reveling in the warmth of Cwynn's small body against her flesh, trying to permanently sear the feeling of his eager suckling into her memory. *Who will watch over him, if neither Tris nor I return from war?* Kiara felt a stab of pain at the thought. She stroked Cwynn's back gently, letting her fingers memorize the feel of his smooth skin and his downy hair.

Finally, Cwynn ended his meal with a contented sigh and nestled against Kiara, eyes fluttering closed in sleep. Kiara watched the even rise and fall of Cwynn's chest, and when the nurse came to take him from her, Kiara shook her head.

"You'll have months to hold him when I'm gone," she whispered. "I only have tonight."

Alle brought a shawl to cover Kiara's shoulders and Kiara shifted enough to permit the return of her bodice to a more modest position. In her arms, Cwynn mewled softly and then settled into slumber. For a few moments, no one spoke, and all eyes were on the sleeping prince.

"The thought of riding into battle doesn't terrify me," Kiara said quietly, eyes still fixed on Cwynn. "No more than it should for any rational being. I've seen battle before, and I've been trained for it since I could hold a sword."

She shook her head. "Leaving Isencroft, seeing Tris ride off for war—each time I thought my heart would break." Tears welled up and she struggled for composure. "Father's death would be enough of a blow. Taking the crown in the middle of an invasion and a civil war troubles me, but it's a military exercise. It can be done. But leaving Cwynn," she said, and her voice caught. "I feel as if leaving Cwynn behind will stop my blood and take my breath." She looked up at Alle and Eadoin. "There's no other course, Goddess help me. But right now, I don't know how to survive it all."

Alle and Eadoin rallied around her, encircling Kiara with their arms so gently that Cwynn did not stir. "You'll survive because you're strong," Eadoin said, meeting Kiara's eyes. "And so is Cwynn. Neither of you will be alone. And I have no doubt that you—and Tris—will be home again to see this little one grow up." She smiled. "Now, my dear, it's time to let Cwynn sleep. You have things to prepare, and you'll need your rest."

Reluctantly, Kiara let the nursemaid take Cwynn. The baby stretched and turned, and a scowl darkened his face for a few seconds until he settled in the nurse's arms. Kiara permitted herself a deep sigh, and then she straightened her shoulders and fastened the rest of her bodice. "Thank you. I'm sorry to be so overcome. It's just—"

"It's never easy to leave the ones we love, even when we have no choice," Eadoin reassured her. "I've found that business is the best cure for heartache. Let's get you ready to go."

9

"The problem is, Your Majesty, it's damned near impossible to hold the whole coastline secure indefinitely." Tolya, captain of the ship *Istra's Vengeance* and leader of the Northern Fleet, leaned forward. He had come straight from his ship, and tonight, he wore none of his looted finery.

Instead, Tolya wore a loose tunic shirt smudged with soot and darkened in places with blood. His breeches were similarly marred, and his high boots were scuffed. The gold rings and gemstones he had worn on his first meeting with the king were absent, the better for him to grasp his cutlass. His black hair was plaited into a thick braid, and dark eyes glinted beneath heavy brows.

"Do you think their purpose is to break our line or to wear us down?" Tris looked from Tolya to Sister Fallon, one of his most gifted mages, who sat to Tolya's right. "When our mages aren't conjuring up storms and rough seas to trouble the invaders, they're fighting back against the Temnottans' magic to raise havoc here."

"The last two weeks have felt like a test of strength," Fallon replied. "We know from the spies and from the reports out of Isencroft that the brunt of the attack has been aimed at breaking through on the Isencroft coast. Whoever is behind this attack may be trying to keep us busy so that we don't send our resources to Isencroft's aid."

"I wonder if wearing us down isn't closer to the truth." They turned to look at Pashka, the chief of the fishermen whose flotilla of small boats augmented the privateer vessels Tolya and his captains lent to the war effort.

Tris grimaced. "An expensive gamble, if that's all there is to it."

"Each salvo grows fiercer, as if the invaders originally thought to land their ships without challenge. I know little of battle magic, having experience only with the fishwives and hedge witches of our villages, but even they hesitate to use a greater magic when lesser power would suffice," Pashka said. He was a man in his middle years, gray templed, with hands broadened and callused by hard work. "I wonder if, now that we've frustrated their intent to make an easy landing, it's taken them some testing to determine what might be required to break our line."

"The invaders can't sit in the harbor forever," Tris mused. "For one thing, it's a tremendous drain on their mages to animate the dead. I suspect there are more soldiers in those boats, soldiers who are very much alive. Our troops and ships are on home territory. We can resupply easily. They're limited to the food and water they brought with them, unless they can land and replenish."

"And, undoubtedly, that's what they mean to do," Fallon said. "But have you noticed: The magic so far has been minor workings, nothing on par with what we might expect from the 'dark summoner' King Donelan warned about. Most of the attacks so far have been physical."

"There are several ways to read that," Tris thought aloud. "The Temnottans could be keeping us pinned here as a diversion. We don't know how good their spies are, and they've been isolated from the rest of the Winter Kingdoms for over a hundred years. Perhaps they don't realize the politics that keeps Margolan from marching its army to the defense of Isencroft."

"That's one possibility." Fallon crossed her arms and leaned back in her chair, staring at her empty cup of tea in thought. "Their dark summoner might not be as powerful as Donelan feared, or perhaps he's doing his best to draw us out, to gauge how well we might withstand his attack."

"Which is exactly why I've avoided interceding in the magical attacks so far," Tris finished for her. "But the men are growing restless. We can't stay in the field forever. An army this size consumes a huge amount of provisions, and we have little enough to spare."

"What do you feel in your magic, Tris?" Fallon asked.

Tris drew a deep breath. "I feel a storm coming. There's power out there, holding back. I think they've been looking for a weak spot, and there's no telling whether they think they've found one."

"What about us? Have we found a weak spot?" It was Pashka who spoke, and Tris knew that the fishermen and his flotilla captains had spent the last two weeks harrying the invading fleet, easy targets for arrows and hot-oil grenades.

Tris met Fallon's eyes and nodded. "I believe so. I think that the Temnottans never expected to find an army in the field waiting for them. So our first strike was preemptive. They've hung back, having already revealed their intention to make war, but finding it harder to attack than they expected. It's time for the next strike on our part."

Tris looked from Pashka to Tolya. "Tonight, our weather mages will bring in a heavy fog to give your ships cover to withdraw. Pull back to safe harbors and wait. Once you're clear, the water mages will cause a sea surge, driving the Temnottans in toward shore. At the same time, the land mages will shift and raise the sand bars. We plan to drive the ships into range of our catapults and trebuchets, or run them aground on the sandbars."

"And once they're wrecked or aground, my ships can help you make short work of them," Tolya said with a wolfish smile. "That's the best news I've heard all week, Your Majesty. We're ready to fight."

"Get word back to your ships right away," Tris cautioned. "We move in five candlemarks."

"I hate being this far behind the lines," Tris grumbled to Fallon. They stood atop a wooden platform well behind the front lines. It was high enough to afford a view of the harbor but not so tall as to become a target. Tris tapped his telescope against his leg nervously. The spyglass might help with detail, but the tower afforded an adequate view without help of lenses.

"You're the king, not a foot soldier," Fallon chided. "And I don't believe for a moment that you'll weather the entire war without having a hand in the action. Right now, we can manage without your sword or magic. Be grateful. It won't last."

"I know. It's just that—"

Fallon looked at him appraisingly. "Another premonition?"

Tris nodded. "I have a very strong feeling that we'll break the stalemate today. I wish I knew how or when. But I don't. Magic can be damnably unclear."

Fallon glanced at the swords that he carried. "You're carrying Nexus. That alone tells me you're expecting whatever happens today to be as much about magic as it is about fighting."

In the scabbard at Tris's belt hung the finely forged sword he preferred for combat. But in a back scabbard waited another sword, Nexus, the sword that had once belonged to the legendary summoner Bava K'aa, Tris's grandmother. Nexus had a sentience and power of its own, and while Tris had not yet fully learned the extent of the sword's capability, he knew its value in arcane battle firsthand. Even the warning that Nexus required a breath of the user's soul in payment for its protection did not deter Tris from carrying the sword this night.

As planned, a heavy fog shrouded the bay. Below in the camp, Tris heard the bells strike nine times.

"Now." Fallon's voice was quiet, full of anticipation. And although Tris did not contribute any of his magic to this attack, he could feel the power weaving warp and weft around him, wrenching violently against the tide.

In the distance, Tris heard the heavy thud of the catapults and the whoosh of the trebuchets as the bombardment began. From their post, they saw only shadows sailing into the fog from the heavy armaments that ringed the high ground. "There's no way to see if we're actually hitting anything," Tris muttered.

Suddenly, the night grew bright as day as light and flames flared from the direction of the waterline. A wall of flames replaced the dark line of the shore, and Tris could hear the screams and cries of soldiers scrambling to get out of its way.

A curtain of seawater rose to douse the flames, but instead of extinguishing the fire, the water scattered the flames, which burned even hotter than before. Another wave of fire streaked through the night sky, landing even farther inland. Tris felt the buffeting of sudden winds, no doubt the response of the air mages to the assault, but like the water, wind only fed the flames.

"Whatever they're using isn't magic," Fallon said as she strained to see. "It's alchemy, and I wish our man Wivvers had invented it first!"

Behind them in the camp that stretched as far as the eye could see, something caught Tris's attention. He stared into the night, unsure of what had alerted his mage sense to trouble. He caught a glimpse of shadow, followed by a man's hoarse scream. "Come on," Tris said, already starting down the ladder to the ground. "We've got trouble."

The night was cold enough for Tris to see his breath, and a haze of campfire hung over the camp. The scream had roused the camp, and all the soldiers who had not been called for positions near the shoreline stirred from their fires and tents to see what was going on.

More shadows caught Tris's attention. Moving fast, they swept in from the edges of the camp, shrieking as they came. The shadows shifted form as they moved, becoming the silhouettes of nightmarish beasts, with sharp fangs and long, pointed claws. The shadows swept across—through—two soldiers, and the men cried out in agony and then fell to the ground.

"*Dimonns*," Tris breathed, readying his magic. He reached for Nexus, and as he drew the sword, runes along its blade burst into fire and the blade itself glowed.

Fallon leveled a barrage of blue-white mage lightning toward a swath of darkness that was heading toward them. Tris gathered his magic and stretched out his left hand, willing power out into the night. A glowing, translucent warding snapped into place, covering Fallon and himself. In the distance, Tris heard shouting and saw flashes of mage lightning, assuring him that more of the battle mages recognized this threat from the rear.

The shadows poured over their warding like black oil, shrieking and battering against the energy. Beyond the warding, Tris could hear the shouts of soldiers, and he saw torches blaze as the fighters realized that they confronted a supernatural enemy. In the distance, along the far edge of the camp, Tris heard more commotion and the sound of running footsteps.

"Something else is coming in from the eastern edge of camp,"

Tris said, leveling another blast of mage lightning at the shadows that swarmed over their warding, blasting them clear.

"Somehow, the wardings around the camp have been breached," Fallon replied, using her magic to blast at the shadows that were flying low and swiftly across the camp. "The *dimonns* shouldn't have been able to penetrate."

"We can't keep picking them off one by one. There are too many. But I have an idea. On the count of three, we drop the shielding, and instead of blasting the *dimonns* individually, we send out a sheet of lightning across the camp, over the heads of the men."

"If that doesn't work, we'll be too drained to be much good for a while."

"We can't maintain the power to keep up the wardings and send lightning surges all night," Tris countered. "And the men out there don't have any wardings at all. I'm counting on the other mages to join their power when they see what's happening."

"Start counting."

On the third count, Tris let the wardings fall and concentrated his magic along Nexus's blade. The sword glowed white with power, its fiery runes blindingly bright. Tris held the sword over his head as the power thrummed through him, his own magic and Fallon's combined, finding focus in Nexus's blade and release in the lightning that exploded from the sword's point.

Instead of streaking across the night, the lightning formed a blue-white canopy, crackling with power just over the heads of the soldiers. The observation tower Tris and Fallon had just deserted burst into flame. *Dimonns* shrieked and winked out of existence as the canopy lanced through them. Other *dimonns*, caught below the canopy, became easy targets for the battle mages who did not send their fire aloft. The night smelled of sulfur and of burning flesh. In the distance, Tris could hear the sound of fighting. The air around them was charged so thoroughly with the lightning's energy that Tris felt his hair rise. Within minutes, the last of the *dimonn* attackers fled or vanished. Tris and Fallon warily dropped their defenses.

"Head for the rear. Whatever's over there wasn't affected like the *dimonns*."

Tris lowered Nexus but did not sheath it. The sword no longer glowed, and its runes were the same dull gray as the rest of the blade, but Tris could sense the sword's power awaiting his command.

By now, the battle at the shoreline bathed the night in flame. "Sweet Chenne," Tris murmured as he and Fallon neared the action. The smell of rotting flesh and decay hung heavy in the night air. All along the eastern border of the camp, soldiers battled a gray line of attackers streaming from the nearby underbrush. Ragged figures shambled toward the soldiers, showing no fear of the swords and battle axes, or of the scythes and pikes. Even the glow of the firelight could not warm the pallor of the attackers' faces as they surged forward. Swords swung through the air, severing limbs, but the attackers continued their silent press, undaunted. Only fire caused them to change their course, when a soldier thrust a burning torch close enough to illuminate the rotting features of the invaders.

"*Ashtenerath?*" Fallon murmured.

Tris shook his head. "Too emotionless. *Ashtenerath* are driven wild by pain and fear. They're alive, at least when they attack, although the magic that drives them kills them soon enough. No," he said. "These are corpses. Stolen bodies."

"The work of a summoner?"

"More like a puppeteer. They aren't even armed." Tris's features darkened in anger. "They were called from their graves to be a distraction, not a real threat. The souls are elsewhere. This desecration must end."

Tris spoke a word of power and brought his hands together at chest height and then swept them to the sides, palms down. Like marionettes with severed strings, the corpses halted and then fell to the ground, still.

A cheer went up from the soldiers as they realized that their enemy was defeated. Tris dropped to one knee next to the nearest corpse and let his open palm hover over its decaying rib cage. "Just a shell," he murmured to Fallon, who remained standing, alert for danger. "The soul is long gone." He stood and looked over the corner of the camp where the fight had been. Hundreds of corpses littered the ground, felled in midstride.

"Someone's been planning this," Tris said, his voice tight with anger. "These aren't soldiers. It's not like at Lochlanimar, when Curane's mages animated our war dead against us. Someone's been raiding tombs, civilian graves, and gathering them for a strike like this."

"Could there be more?"

Tris shrugged. He looked into the distance, into the scrubby vegetation and thin trees that stretched behind the camp to the horizon. He could sense no glimmer of magic, no indication that more animated corpses waited, hidden, for another strike. "It's possible. Even though it doesn't take the same kind of power to animate corpses as it does to actually force a soul back into a dead body, it still required a substantial amount of power to move that many bodies at once."

Fallon nodded and began to wander toward the edge of the camp. "Look here." She pointed at the ground and used her magic to allow the spelled boundary of the camp to glow dimly. "I'm guessing that while our attention was on the attack from the harbor, whoever controlled the corpses attacked the wardings. That's what allowed both the corpses and the *dimonns* into the camp."

Just then, a young man in a lieutenant's uniform walked up

and saluted Tris, snapping to attention. "Your Majesty, sir. What would you have us do with the bodies of the . . . things . . . that attacked us?"

Tris looked out over the ruin the attack had made of the southern corner of the camp. "Once it's daylight, shovel them beyond the edge of camp and burn the bodies, so they can't be disturbed again. That should be enough to keep disease down."

"Yes, sir."

Tris walked a few steps to where a soldier lay dead on the ground. This was a fresh kill, not one of the long-dead. The man lay in a pool of blood where the claws of a *dimonn* had torn his chest open. Again, Tris knelt and let his hand hover over the corpse. When he stood, he said nothing.

"You look troubled," Fallon observed.

Tris took a deep breath. "It's not the usual *dimonn* kill. I want to check the others, see if it's the same for them. Usually, *dimonns* are content with blood. After a *dimonn* attack, the souls are freed at death to take their rest in the Lady or remain near the place of death."

"And tonight?"

Tris turned and met Fallon's gaze. "The souls are missing."

The northern horizon was lit with an unnatural glow, as if the bay itself were on fire. The sounds of bombardment had ended, and Tris could see the outlines of the massive catapults and trebuchets standing idle. Cautiously, he and Fallon worked their way forward, until they could see that the flames still burning were from ships in the harbor stranded on sandbars. Sandbars that had not existed just a few candlemarks before, raised by the Margolan mages.

Tris spotted Soterius at the center of a knot of soldiers, giving orders and dispatching the men in every direction. Fallon headed in another direction to seek out the mages most involved with the waterfront battle. Soterius looked up as Tris walked closer.

"Thank the Goddess you're here; it makes the reporting easier."

"What happened?"

Soterius's face was soot-streaked, and his uniform was stained with dirt and blood. "We had a good plan, driving the ships in where we could hit them with the catapults and stranding them on the sandbars. Unfortunately, they had a good plan, too."

"Which was?"

"Fire. I'm sure they would have used it sooner or later without our attack, but it was obviously something they'd been saving for the right moment. We didn't trap all of their ships, so Goddess help us if the rest of them have the same capability. As soon as they were close enough for our missiles to hit them, they retaliated with fire."

"From what Fallon and I could see, it didn't act like regular fire, but it wasn't magic, either."

Soterius shook his head and gestured with a sickened expression down the blackened beach. Charred bodies littered the ground, and the dirt was scorched from the waterline halfway back to the camp. "The mages might say it wasn't magic, but it wasn't normal fire; you're right. Senne says he's heard legends of such a thing, from the traders who venture into the far west, to the Harran Sea and beyond."

He ran a hand through his hair. "We've already got Wivvers trying to figure it out. It burned on the surface of the ocean, and dousing it with water only spread it farther. Wind scattered it but didn't put it out. The only way to stop the damned fire was with dirt, and so the land mages brought a rain of dirt down on us and that worked."

"They set their own ships on fire?"

"No. That was our doing. Between the mages and the catapult

crews, we were able to give them a taste of their own poison. The good news is that the new sandbars and the wrecks should make it that much harder for them to invade, at least here. The bad news is that quite a few of their ships weren't touched, either by the catapults or the sandbars. The Sentinels tell us that there are fewer ships at the mouth of the bay than there were this morning. We don't think they've gone home," he said, meeting Tris's gaze. "We think they're moving down the coast, to make another strike, maybe a landing."

Soterius paused for a moment, taking in Tris's appearance. "You don't look like you've been watching from a safe vantage point. What did I miss?"

Tris exhaled tiredly. "*Dimonns*. Soul thieves. Animated corpses. I don't know whether the mages on the ships were coordinating with collaborators on the ground behind us, or whether it was just a coincidence. Maybe they meant to strike from the rear, and it just happened that our attack made it a two-front battle."

"Soul thieves?"

Soterius listened with a grim expression as Tris explained. "Is this the same as your hollowed ghosts?"

"Similar, but not quite the same. Hollowing a ghost leaves consciousness behind. The spirit goes mad with the pain of having its soul wrenched away, making it violent, like *ashten-erath*. There was no consciousness left behind with these dead. The soul is gone."

"Were all the battle dead soul-stolen?"

Tris shook his head. "No. We had only a couple of dozen casualties—it could have been far worse. Of that, just a handful were soul-stolen. But it's troubling, on several accounts. First, if the souls have been . . . kidnapped, for lack of a better word, then the dead aren't free to pass over to the Lady. They're imprisoned, against their will. It reminds me too much of the kind of blood magic that the Obsidian King used. I don't like the possibilities this raises. It takes a summoner to wrest a soul loose and imprison it. We haven't seen the 'dark summoner' Cam warned us about, but I'd say this proves there's merit to the rumor. The question is: What does he want with the souls?" He managed a bitter smile. "I don't think I'll like the answer."

10

"Hold the line!" Cam's voice was a hoarse roar. The foot soldiers set their pikes and held their swords at the ready, while behind them, heavily armored cavalry awaited the order to strike.

Dozens of warships that had hovered for days near the horizon now sailed for the bay. It was, Cam had to admit, a perfect place to attempt a landing. The land around the bay was relatively low, giving no advantage for the Isencroft army's catapults and trebuchets, which would have benefitted from positions on higher ground.

Between the troops on the beach and the incoming ships, the Isencroft navy sailed out to meet the enemy. From Cam's vantage point, the ships appeared to be well-matched, both in size and in number. He fought down a tightness in the pit of his stomach. Isencroft's strength lay in its army, not its navy, which had always lagged in both number of recruits and in the quantity of ships. Threats from neighboring kingdoms had kept the focus of Isencroft's kings on their land forces, while no threat had arisen from across the sea in over one hundred years.

The ships appeared to steer straight for their opponents, meaning to ram or grapple. Iron-clad bows on the ships fitted with ramming pikes dared the captains of opposing vessels to shift course or face the consequences. The ships were fast, and their high aft and forecastles were designed to deter boarding and afford archers and mages the best shot at their opponents with maximum coverage.

A runner stopped just a few paces from Cam's horse. "The beach is secured, sir. As you ordered."

Cam nodded. "Well done, lieutenant. Have your men take their places." He looked across the beach toward the water. Anticipating an attempted landing, Cam and Wilym had ordered their men to make the beach impassable. Crude fences made of logs scarred the beach, a way to slow down troops that waded ashore. Traps—magical and otherwise—pockmarked the shoreline. The land forces were ready.

"Why aren't their ships moving?" Cam fretted under his breath. A cold feeling of dread sank into his gut. His soldiers had laid traps on land, but a nagging premonition warned him that Alvior's navy may have done the same on the sea.

A flash of light as bright as the sun flared from the Temnottan ships on the horizon. A solid horizontal layer of flame blasted from the Temnottan line, overtaking the Isencroft ships before they had time to change their course. The flames enveloped the ships, setting masts and rigging on fire. Cam could see men jumping off the burning decks into the water, only to hear their screams as the surface of the water itself became an inferno. As fire reached the pitch and resin stored below decks for use in flaming arrows and catapulted missiles, one after another, the Isencroft ships exploded, sending men, timber, and rigging into the air in a bloody, flaming hail.

Catapults began lobbing iron balls at the invading ships that neared their range, but even at a distance, Cam could see that many of their shots missed the targets. Suddenly, the sea swelled and a burning tide rose between the invading ships and the beach, a wall of what should have been water but was now fluid flame.

"Fall back!" Cam shouted as he realized the danger. "Fall back, now!"

Men and horses scrambled to outrun the flaming wave, deadly both from the fire and from the crushing weight of the water. The wave rose high into the sky, momentarily obscuring the enemy ships behind it, and then raced toward the beach, crashing down onto the shore with its full weight.

What defenses weren't crushed by the huge wave's power burned as the water spread the flames. Within minutes, the fences were gone and the beach was wiped clean of the pits and traps so carefully laid to snare the enemy.

A heavy blanket of smoke covered the shoreline. In the distance, Cam could hear the regular thudding of the catapults and trebuchets. Another wall of flame erupted from the invading ships, and the tall frames of the catapults became fiery towers. Across the water, Cam could hear the screams as the artillerymen burned with their machines, unable to outrace the flames.

The wall of water had washed the flames onto the beach, lighting afire the debris from the ruined ships. But the huge wave had cleared the fire from the surface of the water, and the masts of the invading ships loomed nearer through the choking haze of smoke. The air was thick with the smell of burning wood, vegetation, and flesh.

"You've seen the worst they have to offer. Hold fast!" Cam shouted. Down the line, he heard Wilym second the call.

Nothing in Cam's worst nightmares had prepared him for this day. The shallows of Fainrun Harbor were red with blood, strewn with the wreckage of ships and bits of human flesh. The invading fleet sailed into the harbor, their tall masts rising above the smoke, sails billowed by a wind that was more the creation of mages than of nature.

The Temnottan ships dropped anchor, and smaller ships began

to fall from their sides, filled with soldiers. Cam saw the battle mages move forward, preparing their own attack.

As the invaders drew near to the shoreline, many of the soldiers leaped overboard to drag the boats ashore. Suddenly, the shallow water around them that had so recently been aflame now began to boil. The invading soldiers screamed, trying to leap back into their flat-bottomed boats or run for the shore. In the panic, several of the small boats capsized, sending their occupants into the boiling sea. The harbor wind stank with the smell of cooked fish and roasting meat.

A sudden wind blasted toward shore, cold as the dead of winter. Water that a moment before had been boiling now calmed, and then began, in the shallowest parts, to form a thin skin of ice. The wind howled across the ruined coastline, extinguishing the last of the flames, strong enough to make the men in the front row of foot soldiers fall back a pace to brace themselves.

Propelled by the sudden gust, more landing boats filled the harbor, bristling with men and weapons. The small boats crunched through the ice, beaching quickly and unloading their deadly cargo. Heavily armed soldiers formed ranks and marched up the beach, trampling the charred remains of men and ruined ships.

"Get the mages behind!" Cam shouted, raising his sword. "Charge!"

Footsteps thundered as thousands of men moved as one, followed by the clatter of hoofbeats. The chill wind fell quiet as the shouts of soldiers filled the air. To Cam's eye, the Isencroft troops had the advantage of mounted soldiers and more men. Yet the invaders moved forward undaunted, against superior numbers.

Something's not right, Cam thought as he swung his sword. An attacker on his right fell to the ground, cleaved from shoulder through the rib cage. The invaders swarmed toward the defending troops, heedless for their own safety, like men possessed.

Cam nearly lost his saddle as one of the Temnottans launched himself into the air brandishing his sword. Cam's horse reared just in time, giving Cam the leverage to deflect the attack with a kick of his boot and a thrust of his sword. For an instant, the attacker hung in midair, impaled on Cam's blade, and Cam saw ferocity past the point of reason in the man's eyes. It chilled him to the bone. The attacker fell to the ground and then struggled to his knees, apparently heedless of the gut wound that would quickly prove mortal. Blood poured from the man's abdomen as entrails began to slip from the gash, yet the fighter came at Cam again, swinging his sword like a wild man.

"They're bewitched!" Cam shouted. "Watch yourselves!"

A bolt of mage lightning struck down Cam's would-be attacker, and Cam looked up to see one of the battle mages. Before he could nod his thanks, the mage had turned to loose another blast against two more soldiers who were headed straight at them. Across the battlefield, Cam could see flashes of mage lightning crackle through the press of battle, reflected in the haze of smoke that still hung over the battleground.

What the Temnottans lacked in number they made up for in frenzy. Yet these were not *ashtenerath*, Cam realized. These men had none of the dead-eyed look of the drugged and magicked *ashtenerath*, men so broken by torture and potions that they resembled wild beasts. The Temnottan attackers moved with the skill and strategy of soldiers, yet to a man, they seemed to lack any desire for self-preservation.

Are our enemies so enamored of their king to swear themselves to mass suicide? Cam wondered as he fought. Despite the day's chill, sweat ran down his forehead and back, soaking through his shirt. His warhorse reared again, kicking with its deadly hooves, smashing in the heads of two advancing Temnottan soldiers.

All around Cam, the battle raged. The Temnottans, showing absolutely no fear, took on the Isencroft troops relentlessly. One Temnottan, fighting in a fury of motion, could hold his own against two or three Isencroft soldiers, at least for a while. *What is possible when men care nothing for their own lives?* Cam wondered, simultaneously amazed and horrified.

The smoke was clearing, and as he spared a gaze for the horizon, Cam spotted the flags that had risen on the masts of the invaders' ships. Unfurled on the cold wind, Cam could see the bold colors of the Temnotta flag, and large in its corner, the crest of Brunnfen.

Alvior! May the Crone take his soul, and may I be the one to send him to the Abyss! Cam cursed his brother under his breath, finding new energy in the anger to take on another crazed attacker. The Temnottan's uniform was ragged, burned, and bloodied, and his left arm was a bleeding stump, hastily tied off with rags. Anger burned in the man's eyes, not unreasoning rage but intelligent fury heedless of cost.

Cam blocked the man's lunge. He was carried back a half step, although he outweighed the Temnottan, yet the man ran for him at full speed, sword swinging. The force of the man's swings reverberated the length of Cam's sword, making his forearm shudder. Although he deflected the worst of the blow, the point of the man's sword cut into his shoulder. The fresh blood raised a shout of triumph from the attacker, who doubled the speed of his press. This time, the man's speed amplified Cam's swing, which severed the soldier's head from his shoulders, carrying the headless body forward two or three steps before it fell.

Cam stepped back, sword raised, ready for another attack. Two Temnottans rushed at him, swords at the ready. Just as suddenly, they stopped, a look of bewilderment on their faces. Cam and a nearby soldier seized the advantage, running at them with a battle cry. To Cam's astonishment, the Temnottans fell to their knees and raised their hands in surrender.

All around the battlefield, Cam saw the scene repeated, as

soldiers that had, moments before, charged into unwinnable odds heedless of survival stopped dead in their tracks and dropped their weapons. While their numbers were far reduced from the original invasion force, Cam had expected them to fight to the last man. Their sudden shift left him baffled and suspicious.

"Tie them up and take them for questioning," Cam shouted. "Don't turn your back until they're secured." He watched as his soldiers moved to comply, braced for treachery. Then he spotted the battle mages, arms outstretched, faces rigid with concentration, as the last of the attackers laid down their swords. After a moment, the nearest mage turned with a weary, bleak smile.

"The fight's gone out of them," the haggard mage said, tiredness clear in his voice. He was a young man, not much older than Cam, with a thin face and dark, intelligent eyes. Blood stained his torn robes, and in many places, there were burn holes from flaming debris.

"What drove them? They looked too . . . sane . . . to be *ashtenerath*."

The mage nodded. "They weren't. But they were bewitched. Your shout helped me realize that. Their master didn't break their will, as *ashtenerath* are broken. He just removed all fear, including the fear of death." His eyes hardened. "It's an abomination to do that to men, to rob them of their will to survive. No Light mage would do such a thing."

"Obviously, our enemy doesn't worry about niceties."

The mage grimaced. "Once we realized what was going on, we were able to use our magic to break the spell. When they saw how outnumbered they were, the men came to their senses and surrendered." He looked out across the carnage and shook his head. "Men should not be driven like pigs to slaughter, even in war."

Cam sighed, too tired to argue the realities of war. "What about the fire? Was that magic?"

The mage wiped a grimy hand across his forehead, trading a streak of soot for the sweat that ran down his temples. "No. It wasn't. I've never seen anything like that, though I've heard rumors that such things exist, far beyond the borders of the Winter Kingdoms, past the western horizon."

"What, then? Do you have any idea?"

The mage shrugged. "A mixture from the alchemists, no doubt. Something that won't mix with water, or be quenched by it. I assure you, when this day is over, we mages will be digging through our texts for anything we can find to avoid a repeat of today."

Cam's attention strayed to the harbor. The Temnottan ships, disgorged of their human cargo, had withdrawn to the mouth of the bay. In their wake they left the burned hulks and wreckage of the Isencroft warships that had, just a few candle-marks earlier, proudly defended their shore.

"Cam!" The shout brought Cam's attention back to the battlefield, where Wilym was striding toward him. The head of the Veigonn looked as worn as Cam felt, with his uniform sliced and torn and one sleeve caked with blood.

"You're hurt," Cam said, with a sharp glance toward Wilym's left arm and its bloodied sleeve.

"It's not bad, considering." Wilym glanced at the mage. "I assume you've just heard what's been behind all this?"

"Just now."

Wilym nodded. "I was briefed by one of the other mages. Damn Alvior!"

Cam turned to look down the shoreline toward the eastern horizon. "Do you think they've struck all the way down the coast?"

Wilym grimaced. "I've sent men on horseback to find out, but we won't know until tomorrow. If you're wondering about Renn—"

"Of course I am." Renn, Cam's younger brother, had vowed

to hold the family manor, Brunnfen, against Alvior's return. "Did you see the flags?"

"Yes. I guess Alvior isn't making any secret of his allegiance." Wilym swore, and spat as if to ward off evil. "I'd love the chance to send him to the Formless One myself, if you hadn't already claimed the honor."

"I was ready to kill him just from what he did to Renn," Cam replied, his expression hardening as his hand gripped the pommel of his sword. "After today, I'll feel no regrets at all, blood ties be damned."

"Once we mop up out here, I'm calling the commanders to my tent to regroup," Wilym said. "Mages, too," he added with a nod to their companion, who acknowledged with a half bow and then moved away into the crowd. "I want to know what our options are when Alvior and his ships return, and how to avoid this kind of . . . carnage."

"Don't you think this is just what Alvior wanted? To return not just with force but with terror?"

Wilym nodded. "Oh, I believe all of this was a very carefully arranged first strike. What we don't know is how much these theatrics cost Alvior and whether the Temnottan command is willing to sacrifice their troops so blithely on every engagement."

"Meaning?"

Wilym shrugged. "I'm hoping that Alvior staged this to make his point, but that his next move will be more conventional. This was an extravagant move, difficult to sustain. So the question is . . . does Temnotta have the resources to squander, or is Alvior betting that a good entrance will do his fighting for him by putting fear into the hearts of our soldiers?"

"For all our sakes, I hope he's more bluster than substance."

"So do I."

* * *

After ninth bells, a sober group gathered in Wilym's campaign tent. The three generals assigned to the defense of Fainrun Harbor filed in, followed by their commanders. Benhem, the senior battle mage, followed, looking haggard.

Wilym motioned toward a decanter of brandy on the table in the center of the tent. One by one, all but the mage filled their cups before they sat down. Cam was already on his second brandy, able to attest that not even the strong liquor could wash away the bitterness of the day's fight.

It felt more than odd to sit at Wilym's right hand, in the place Donelan should have filled. As King's Champion, that was Cam's right and duty when the king was unable to preside. Even when Kiara returned to Isencroft, Cam would still take Donelan's place at the forefront of the battle, since Kiara could not be risked. He did not relish convincing Kiara that she should stay behind the lines, and he only hoped that tales of this day would help to make the point that discretion was prudent.

"For the record," Cam said, clearing his throat. "I think we can call today a victory for our side, given the bravery with which our soldiers met such a terrible enemy."

The generals nodded, but the weariness in their eyes gave Cam to understand that they knew just how high a price such victory commanded. "If Alvior makes us fear his next move, then the victory is his." Cam met their eyes defiantly. "We can't let that happen. So I ask you, what can we pluck from today to give us an advantage when he returns, as he surely will, and soon."

Benhem, the mage, spoke first. "We learned that their Destroying Fire is not magical. I have a theory, should we have the unfortunate chance to face such an assault again. We fought back with water and wind, which were no match for this unnatural weapon. But dirt can smother a fire, and we didn't try that tactic since we had no land mages among us. We've put out a call for more land mages, and we'll make sure that they're spread among the regiments."

Wilym nodded his approval. "What of the fury of the attackers? Can we expect more of that?"

Benhem frowned. "Such magic can't be sustained for long. It comes at a great price, draining the mage who casts it. Its power also seemed to wane with distance, since the Temnottan mages remained on their ships in the harbor. We did counter it successfully, and if we face it again, we'll be able to move more quickly. Spells of confusion, panic, and feeblemindedness are relatively easy to cast."

"Take care that you hit your target with your magic, and not our own troops," Wilym objected.

Benhem gave a wan smile. "That part is easier than you may think. We cast our spells to follow the trail of the other mages' magic, striking only those who were under its pall. Our fighters felt nothing, while theirs were freed of their delusions."

"Well done," Wilym said, inclining his head in acknowledgment. He turned to look at the generals. "What of the navy?"

Edgeton, an older man with graying hair and a scar that ran across his left cheek from ear to chin, shook his head sadly. "No survivors. Neither ships nor men."

"Do we know how badly today went for our troops?"

Edgeton nodded. "Our headcount is down by five hundred men, not counting the sailors lost with the ships. Given the assault, it could have been worse."

"Agreed," Wilym said, nodding.

"I believe that Alvior meant to make a statement today more than he expected to be able to land his troops unopposed," Cam said. "He wanted us to know that he's backed by powerful allies, not mere Divisionists. Message delivered. Next time, I think we'll find out just what true force Temnotta means to bring against us. They can't stay anchored in the harbor forever. They'll be anxious to get their troops on the ground where they can forage for their own food and water. We'll need to be ready."

"We've got men mining the harbor with the wreckage," Edgeton said. "And others are replacing the obstacles on the beach, this time, with stone and trenches that won't burn. We won't stop them, but we can make the going slow for them. We're also replacing the artillery with new catapults and trebuchets, moving them into more protected locations with an eye toward hammering the beach and the invasion force rather than the ships."

"What of the mages?" Wilym asked, turning back to Benhem.

"We can't stop an invasion force," the mage replied, "but we can make it costly. I have my mages working with Edgeton's men, adding some nasty surprises to their traps. Now that we have a sense for the Temnottans' magic, we'll be working on counter spells and defenses." He sighed. "Unfortunately, we don't have the sheer numbers to do something sweeping and dramatic, as I'm sure you'd prefer. So we can't take the offensive directly, although we can make targeted strikes. We'll be ready."

When the group filed from the tent a candlemark later, Cam lagged behind. Wilym clapped him on the shoulder. "Your men held their positions today. They fought well. You should be proud."

Cam nodded wearily. "Proud—and tired. I want nothing so much as my bedroll and a good night's sleep."

Wilym gave a wan smile. "I feel the same way. We both know how rare an uninterrupted night is once the battle is underway."

Just as Cam turned to leave, Rhistiart, Cam's valet and squire, stopped at the tent doorway. "A messenger's just arrived from the palace with orders to speak to no one but the two of you."

Rhistiart stepped aside to reveal Kellen. Kellen's cloak was covered with dust and mud from the road, and he looked weary from the ride. Wilym waved him in, and Cam also stepped back inside, motioning for Kellen to sit. Wilym went to pour Kellen a brandy.

"What brings you out to the front? Aren't you supposed to be guarding the Regent?"

Kellen nodded wearily and accepted the brandy, closing his eyes as he sipped. "It was Renate who sent me," he said, his voice hoarse as the brandy burned down his throat. "Had a few things he thought you should know about that he didn't want to trust to paper. And since I was headed this way, I took the liberty of bringing this along for Cam." He reached beneath his great cloak and withdrew a sealed parchment letter, which he handed to Cam.

Cam looked down at the seal. "It's from Renn."

"First, let's hear what Kellen rode all the way here to tell us," Wilym said, leaning back in his chair.

Kellen nodded. "It's been tense in the city since the troops left. Seems like every day there's something—a riot in one of the city quarters, a block of buildings catches on fire, or the guards around the palace are attacked by some fool with more anger than brains. It's been like that for two weeks now."

"How's Renate dealing with life as Regent?" Cam asked.

Kellen grimaced. "He's managing. He's not a military man, and not inclined to fancy himself as such, thank the Goddess, so at least he isn't trying to interfere with what the soldiers are doing to keep peace in the city when things get out of hand. Most of the time, he signs the paperwork that Allestyr puts in front of him and looks out from his window over the city toward whatever's burning at the moment."

"That bad?" Wilym leaned forward. "Divisionists again?"

"Hard to tell. People are afraid and angry. Our spies tell us that there's been talk in some of the taverns that Alvior is a legitimate heir, come to take what's rightfully his. Hard to squelch that kind of thing once it starts to make the rounds. It would help a lot if the princess were here."

Wilym nodded. "No word then from Antoin? There's been

more than enough time for him to reach Margolan. Dare we assume that, without news to the contrary, he reached Kiara with the message and she's on her way to Isencroft?"

"By the Crone, I hope you're right," Kellen replied. "The whole city's a tinderbox full of rumors and lies. Even the countryside isn't safe from the madness. Three of the magistrates from villages a day's ride outside the city gates came to the palace to complain that someone is desecrating their burying grounds."

Cam frowned. "What do you mean?"

"Gruesome stuff, to hear them tell. Bodies dug up and taken away. Runes marked on the entranceways to crypts. Cairns and barrows vandalized. Animal sacrifices, too, if you can believe it." Kellen shook his head. "Just what we need, blood magic on top of everything else."

"No idea who's behind it?" Wilym tented his fingers as he spoke, deep in thought.

Kellen shrugged. "People report seeing men in black robes, but nothing more specific than that. So far, we haven't been able to catch them at it, so we don't know whether they're with the Divisionists, aiding the Temnottans, or creating a whole new threat." He leaned forward. "But Brother Felix thinks that the desecrations just might be related to something that happened a few nights ago, at the palace."

Kellen paused, declining an offer by Wilym to refill his brandy. "You remember the . . . ceremony . . . we held to protect the crown until Kiara can return?"

Cam and Wilym exchanged glances. The creation of the *nenkah* wasn't something easily forgotten. "Of course," Cam said.

"Two nights before I left, a night terror came upon Count Renate. I have no better description. He went to bed tired but in good spirits, and roused much of the household with his screams in the middle of the night. Neither the healer, Davon, nor Brother Felix could rouse him at first. It was as if Renate was a prisoner within his own nightmare."

"How did you free him?" Wilym's whole attention was fixed on Kellen.

"It took both Davon and Felix to do it, a mix of magic and medicine. Davon sedated him with a mixture of powders and wine. When Renate was still, Felix was able to decipher the magic against him and break the spell."

Cam looked up, alarmed. "How was hostile magic able to affect Renate? I thought Brother Felix warded the palace."

Kellen sighed. "Aberponte is a very large place. And apparently, wardings must be rather specific to be effective. But Felix doesn't believe it was actually a spell that affected Renate. He thinks magic worked elsewhere followed connections of our own making, with the unfortunate effect of troubling the Regent's sleep."

"Say on," Wilym urged, his face intent.

"The next morning, the guards found a dead goat at the entrance to the necropolis beneath the city. The beast had obviously been sacrificed, because it hung by its back hooves, gutted and headless, with its blood used to mark runes on the stones all around the outer doors and its entrails left in carefully arranged heaps that Felix said were old magic, very dark."

"Did they enter the necropolis?" Cam asked.

Kellen shook his head. "No. The outer doors carry very strong magic to protect against assault and invaders. But Felix thinks that whatever magic was done there at the gates—and similar magicks that appear to have been done in the countryside at the same time—were powerful enough to cast a shadow over the magic that binds Renate and Kiara to the crown—and to the *nenkah*."

"Is the *nenkah* safe?" Wilym's voice dropped low on the strange word, as if to say it aloud invited trouble.

"Yes. Felix went to make certain after we were able to rouse Renate."

"What of Renate's nightmares?" Cam asked, drumming his fingers on his thigh, impatient that there was no immediate action to take in order to avenge the attack.

"They were, indeed, troubling, although they offered little useful information," Kellen said. "When the sleeping potion Brother Felix gave Renate wore off, he was only able to recall a few images. He saw a large shadow—a woman's shadow, he said—rising from the dead places, burying grounds, and cairns, marshes, and sickly swamps. The shadow made the ground shake and brought with it fire and flood. Everything was swept away before it, and the wretches who survived fell down on their knees and worshipped it."

Cam looked grim. "What else?"

"He saw the shadow fall on Aberponte, and it made the foundations of the castle shake. He saw the sun turn from its normal course to rise in the north, and he saw a strange flag fly above the palace. He says there were other images, terrible sights, but he doesn't remember them, or can't put words to them." Kellen looked from Cam to Wilym. "What do you make of it?"

"Unfortunately, some of it sounds familiar." Cam's voice was tight. "When I left Dark Haven several months ago, Jonmarc Vahanian was having problems with the Durim, black-robed fanatics who wanted to revive the worship of a long-banished goddess, Shanthadura, the face of Chaos. The sacrifices you mention, and the desecration of tombs, sound like what Jonmarc encountered. The Durim work blood magic, and they especially like to use the blood of the *vyrkin* and *vayash moru* to invoke their power."

Kellen shuddered. "I don't know what chills me more, that these things are happening elsewhere, or that the Black Robes would desire such an end for all of us."

"The other images appear all too easily read," Wilym added. "The sun rising in the north would appear to mean a new day, one ruled by power from the north, which would seem to describe Temnotta. And an unfamiliar flag is clear enough. Whoever worked this magic would see a change of kings for Isencroft."

Cam shook his head to clear the headache that was beginning behind his temples. "What worries me is the way the vision melds the two: Divisionist and Durim. In Dark Haven, the Durim—the Black Robes—appeared to care nothing for mortal kings. Their fight was with the Sacred Lady, to replace her worship with that of Shanthadura. Yet Renate's vision seems to suggest that there is a connection between the Durim and the Temnottan invasion, which is the doing of Alvior and his Divisionists." He met Kellen's eyes. "I would like to be wrong about that, but I don't see how else to read the omens."

"While I'm glad for the warning, I'm also just as happy to leave reading omens to Brother Felix," Wilym said, stretching. "I'm a military man, and I prefer to spend my time fighting enemies that I can see."

Cam looked back at Kellen. "You never said—did the *nenkah* appear to be affected by Renate's nightmare?"

Kellen met his eyes. "Our ceremony gave the *nenkah* breath, as the proxy of the new queen, but not movement. When Brother Felix felt it was safe to go into the necropolis and check, he found the wardings strong and undisturbed. And yet, the *nenkah* lay curled up on itself like a frightened child, a rag arm covering its face. No one had moved it, and yet, it had moved."

Wilym let out a long breath. "I don't know whether to wish that Kiara arrives soon, to end the regency and the issue with the *nenkah*, or to hope that she stays far away from Isencroft until this cursed business is finished."

"Before I forget, let me see what the news is from Brunnfen," Cam said, breaking the seal on the parchment. "It's from Renn, all right," Cam confirmed. "His writing is so small and cramped it strains my eyes."

The Dread

Dear Cam,

I hope this letter reaches you quickly, and finds you as safe as current circumstances permit. Captain Lange from the garrison has been true to his word, keeping troops here on watch in case Alvior tries to come back.

Ships appeared two weeks ago at the mouth of the bay, but the snags you and Lange laid for them seemed to foil their plans. Two of the ships sailed right into the snags and ripped out their hulls. Lange's archers made quick work of the crews when they tried to flee the ships. The other ships didn't try to enter, and after a day or two, they sailed away. Lange torched the wrecks, as a message.

I'm not convinced it's the last we'll see of Alvior's bunch, since he seemed intent on setting up a headquarters in Brunnfen. We've sent patrols up and down the coast, but it's long been a favorite for pirates for all the little inlets, and I have no doubt Alvior could use it to his advantage, if he wanted to. And while we were able to keep the large ships out of the harbor, we might not fare as well if they return with small boats. I can only hope that the enemy doesn't share my imagination!

Give my best to Rhosyn, when you see her next. I've had the chance to do some more work toward creating an alehouse and distillery in town, and I think you'll be pleased. If we all survive this war, I've got just the location for a brewery and tavern that might put coin in our pockets once more. I pray to the Lady that this madness ends soon and we can focus on more pleasant prospects, such as ale. I fully expect you to keep your promise and return safely from your duties. Until then, rest assured that Brunnfen is in good hands.

Your brother,
Renn

Cam gave Wilym and Kellen a shortened version of the letter as he folded it and slipped it beneath his tunic. "By rights, I should be at Brunnfen with Renn and Captain Lange. He's hardly more than twenty summers old, and he's already managed to outfox Alvior twice—once as his prisoner, and now foiling his return." Cam shook his head. "I feel wrong to claim the title of Lord of Brunnfen and let my little brother protect the manor."

Wilym clapped Cam on the shoulder. "It's no shame to leave your manor in the care of another to serve your king, and by the Lady, Isencroft needs you here with the army."

Cam sighed. "I know I had no other choice, but it doesn't mean my conscience rests any easier. Renn's smart and tough, and Captain Lange has the experience Renn lacks. I don't doubt that Alvior will make more attempts to return there. We found a secret room he'd outfitted for a mage, and by the look of it, a dark summoner. Renn and I destroyed all of the equipment that we dared and managed to get one of the Sisterhood mages to cart off the rest of the magical items. But I regret leaving Renn to defend it on his own."

Wilym chuckled. "I happen to know Vyn Lange. His garrison has a reputation for doing the impossible against the odds—as I'm betting you well know. You've hardly left your brother to handle the threat alone, backed up by several hundred of the toughest soldiers in Isencroft. So let your conscience rest and keep your mind on our problems here."

"We have enough to keep us busy, don't we?"

Wilym's smile faded as he sobered. "That's the Goddess's own truth. As soon as Alvior and the Temnottans regroup, I think we'll have our hands full."

11

Kiara Sharsequin Drayke, Queen of Margolan and Isencroft, shivered in the cold autumn rain. It was past the midnight bells, and she was sore from riding. Her traveling cloak was long ago soaked through by the wet fog, and though she wore a woolen tunic and trews beneath her cloak, she was chilled to the bone. Cerise looked equally miserable, huddled in her sodden cloak. Jae rode behind Kiara, perched on the packs behind her saddle, and the gyregon scolded the weather with hisses. Royster seemed unfazed by the rain, and he hummed a ditty under his breath. Of all of them, Royster seemed happiest about their journey; he had jumped at the chance to extend his sabbatical by accompanying Kiara to Isencroft, eager to witness the war for his chronicles.

"Not too much farther. Look, from this hill, you can see the palace city, maybe the lights of Aberponte itself." Balaren, one of Kiara's new companions, urged her to nudge her weary horse up to the summit. Kiara sidled her horse up beside Balaren for a clear view. She gasped.

"Something's very wrong," Kiara said, looking out over the expanse. "Look there! Part of the city is on fire!"

The rest of her traveling companions clustered closer to see. Dense smoke poured from the northernmost corner of the old walled city. Across the valley, the muffled sounds of shouting carried on the night air.

Balaren turned back to Kiara with a worried expression. "Under normal circumstances, I would suggest spending the night at an inn and making the rest of the journey by daylight, but we're too close to the palace for you to risk being recognized." He paused. "I'd thought about suggesting that one of us," he said, indicating the other *vayash moru*, "fly you past the city and palace walls and get you safely into Aberponte through a balcony, but since we've had the warning from Lord Vahanian that some of the *vayash moru* have joined the enemy, the palace defenses will be set against us 'dropping in.'"

Kiara saw a mix of concern and determination in the faces of the other riders. She had left Shekerishet accompanied by seven mortal soldiers, three *vayash moru* bodyguards, and three *vyrkin*. The Margolan men-at-arms had delivered her to a small group of Isencroft soldiers who had awaited her covert crossing at the border. While Kiara did not know the Isencroft soldiers personally, Balaren, one of the *vayash moru*, could vouch for them. Kiara shivered beneath her cloak. She was grateful that Balaren and the other *vayash moru* and *vyrkin* would remain with her at Aberponte for as long as she stayed in Isencroft. Her hand dropped to her belly as she added a fervent prayer to the goddess that her stay in her homeland would end before it was time to deliver this new heir.

"You're right," Kiara conceded. "We don't dare stop so close to the city. If that's the case, then let's ride, as I'd like to be out of the weather as soon as possible."

They headed for the city riding three abreast, with Kiara safely on the inside. The road was rutted from heavy travel and recent rains, splashing mud onto their cloaks with every step of their horses. *You've gotten spoiled*, Kiara chided herself as her teeth chattered. *Remember what it was like when you rode with*

Tris to take back the throne? There were cold and wet enough times then, going without meals and hunted by Jared's soldiers. You've survived worse.

It took another candlemark's ride before they reached the outskirts of the newer section of town, the buildings that had sprung up over the past hundred years outside the ancient city walls. The light from the windows of the buildings that hunched along the sides of the street could not compensate for the heavy fog and the lack of moonlight, and the shadows seemed ominously dark. But the feeling of dread, of anticipation of a coming storm, had little to do with the rain, Kiara thought. The whole city seemed to be holding its breath, waiting for something to happen. And Kiara felt it in her gut that whatever was in the offing wasn't going to be good.

"Can't imagine how anything manages to burn in this weather," Balaren murmured. The streets were nearly empty, but it felt to Kiara as if eyes watched them from every window that they passed.

"Ho, there. State your business." Two guardsmen stepped from the shadows, blocking their way.

Kiara fidgeted as Captain Remir, one of the Isencroft body-guards, edged his horse slightly in front of the group. "We have urgent business at the palace. We travel at the summons of the Regent."

"You're out past curfew," the guardsman barked. "Do you have papers to show for yourselves?"

Remir dismounted and dug into his pouch for the letters of passage Count Renate had sent for them. Kiara kept her head down. *Things must be even worse than Father told me, if the palace city is under curfew and papers are required to travel. It's as if the city itself is under siege.*

The guardsman studied the papers so long that Kiara wondered if the man could read. Finally, he returned the documents to

Remir and waved them through. "Stay on the main road if you know what's good for you. There's been trouble in the north ward tonight. The sooner you're inside the walls, the better." He stepped aside for them to pass, but Kiara felt the guardsman's gaze on them as they filed past.

Kiara looked around as they passed through the outer city's narrow streets. It looked as if a war had recently been fought in its alleys and ginnels. Some blocks of buildings were untouched, while others bore the obvious scars of recent fires. More than once, she spotted crude slogans scratched onto the brick with charcoal or cut into the wood with knives. Misspelled and profane, they called for a "free" kingdom and the end of a "traitor" king. She shivered again, though not from the cold.

Isencroft was hungry from bad harvests, but we hadn't come apart at the seams when I left. Has so much had time to go wrong just since Father's death?

Twice more they encountered guards who demanded their papers as they wound their way uphill toward Aberponte. At the gates to the walled city, the guardsman returned the papers to Remir and still refused to let them pass.

"Let me see your faces. Papers can be forged." The guard took down a lantern from under the overhang of the guardhouse roof. He moved in turn from one of Kiara's companions to the next, but only when he neared her did she guess his true purpose. *He's a mage*, she thought. *He's doing his best to truth-sense, or at least check for glamours. Sweet Chenne! It must be dire for things to have come to this.*

Kiara kept her head down until the man reached her, hoping that a quick glimpse would suffice. The guard thrust his lantern close to her, forcing her to jerk back or be burned. His eyes widened as he saw her features, and she feared that he would cry out.

"Please, say nothing," she hissed.

Whether he recognized her or whether his power recognized the signature of her regent magic, Kiara did not know. To his credit, the man said nothing and kept up the ruse of examining the remaining members of her group before declaring them fit to pass through the gates. On the other side, Kiara heaved a sigh of relief.

"He recognized you." Balaren's voice was quiet.

"Apparently."

"Let's hope that he's on our side."

Aberponte Palace lay at the end of the cobblestone roadway, set on the crest of a hill. Growing up, Kiara had always loved the sight of the palace at nighttime, sitting like a jewel among the stars inside its own set of walls and gardens. Now, although the lights at the windows burned as brightly as ever, Kiara imagined that Aberponte looked worn and beleaguered, as if it hunkered down against not only the weather but the vast darkness of the night itself.

To Kiara's relief, they passed no more checkpoints until they reached the outer wall of the palace. Once more, Remir showed their papers, but this time, he lowered his cloak, expecting to be recognized. After a terse exchange with the gate guards, Remir swung back up to his mount and motioned them forward. Still in their formation from the road, they approached the palace from the rear, using the servants' entrance instead of the sweeping front steps and massive entry doors of the palace. *This used to be home*, Kiara thought. *Now, it looks like a fortress fit for a siege.*

"Come in, come in!"

Kiara recognized the voice at once, and despite everything, a smile touched her lips as she turned to see Allestyr standing on the steps, barely shielded by the cloak he held over his head. "Your runner arrived a candlemark ago. We've been anxious to see that you made it here safely. Now hurry up, before you catch your deaths from the cold."

Servants rushed to take their horses. Kiara swung down from the saddle, glad that the need for concealment had allowed her the function and relative comfort of traveling in a tunic and trews. *Thank the Lady I don't have to navigate in yards of sodden silk!*

Kiara opened the flap on a large saddlebag, and Jae climbed out, hissing his dislike for his hiding place. "Sorry, but we had to hide you." Kiara chuckled. "You're the only gyregon in Isencroft."

Yet even here, on the steps to the palace, Kiara sensed that Allestyr was holding back, and it made a growing knot in her stomach clench even tighter. *What's gone so wrong that Allestyr fears to speak to me in front of the palace staff?*

Inside, Tice met them and servants came to take their wet cloaks. "Allestyr, what—" Kiara began, but Allestyr gave her a warning shake of the head.

"Let's give you a chance to get out of your traveling clothes and into something dry," Allestyr said. "I'll have some refreshments brought to your father's sitting room. You can join us there after you've refreshed and changed."

Kiara looked to Balaren and the rest of the *vyrkin* and *vayash moru* who had accompanied her. "These men came with me from Margolan as bodyguards. They're *vayash moru* and *vyrkin*, sworn to protect me. Since Margolan dared send no soldiers across the border, this was the compromise."

"I'll have the servants see to their accommodations," Allestyr said. "We have rooms in the cellars that should suit for the *vayash moru*. I'll have the cook draw blood from the herd animals and prepare some raw meat for our *vyrkin* guests." He gave a small bow. "We appreciate your efforts to bring our queen home safely."

Balaren smiled, making his eye teeth plain. "We're honored to serve."

Captain Remir looked to Allestyr. "My men will remain on

guard. We'll take shifts to clean up and eat, so that the queen is never without protection."

Allestyr nodded. "Thank you." He met Kiara's gaze. "After what happened to your father, we've had mages sweep your room for any type of traps, magical or otherwise. I've taken the precaution to limit the servants who access your room to half a dozen, those who have been in our employ the longest and whom the mages have assured me are loyal. They've been given charms against magic, to prevent anyone from bewitching them. To be cautious in the extreme, I'd like to limit your personal assistants to just Cerise and Tarra, my niece."

"Thank you," Kiara replied tiredly. "That will be fine."

Kiara had the odd feeling of being a guest in her own home as she followed a servant upstairs. Captain Remir and his guards followed at a respectful distance. As the servant showed them to their rooms, Kiara realized that the only retainers she had seen were people who had been in the service of her father for decades. *Allestyr's not taking any chances with the loyalties of newcomers*, Kiara thought. She sighed. Having to watch over her shoulder for threats within the palace as well as on the battlefield was a reality of war, but it stripped the last remnants of happiness out of her homecoming.

Too large to perch for long on Kiara's shoulder and too constrained by the stairway's walls to fly, Jae scurried up the steps behind them, his claws scratching on the stone steps as his compact, reptilian body undulated with the movement. The group fell silent as they were shown to their rooms.

Kiara closed the door as Cerise and Jae hurried inside. Servants had already placed their travel bags on the floor near the fireplace. A young woman with long, curly red hair was laying out a tray of cheese, hard sausage, bread, and warmed wine. There was even a small bowl of raw meat for Jae. She smiled as they entered, and made a low curtsey.

"Your Majesty. I'm Tarra. Uncle Allestyr asked me to attend you."

Despite how tired she was from the ride, Kiara managed a smile. Tarra was noble-born, as was Allestyr, and she had been around the palace for as long as Kiara could remember. "Thank you, Tarra. It's good to see you again."

"I'm pleased that Your Majesty remembers me," Tarra replied with a grin. "Now I'd best leave you to your food and a hot bath, but I'll be back in a candlemark to check on you, and Father's put Cerise and me in rooms on either side of yours, so you can call for us if you need to." Tarra slipped out of the room, and Kiara threw herself down into a chair near the fire. Jae curled up on the hearth next to her feet.

"Can you believe it, Cerise? Riots and fire in the palace city. Father's barely been gone for a full month, and everything is coming undone."

Cerise moved to stand behind Kiara, placing a comforting hand on her shoulder. "I think it's more correct to assume that everything had started to come undone before your father's death. Knowing the king, I suspect that he kept the worst from you, hoping that it would end before you had reason to return to Isencroft."

Kiara stared into the dancing flames of the fireplace. The exhaustion of the hurried trip and the realization of just how desperate the situation in Isencroft had become all crashed down on her at once. "But we're in the thick of it now, aren't we?" she murmured quietly.

She turned in her seat to look up at Cerise. "Father had been king for decades. He stared down King Radomar's threat of war with Eastmark. He fought raiders on the western border. How can I hope to rule Isencroft as well as he did, with war and revolution on our doorstep?"

Cerise came around to kneel next to Kiara's chair and she

took Kiara's hands in hers. "I'm sure Tris felt much the same way when he accepted the crown of Margolan. After all, his father, Bricen, was legendary, even before his death."

Kiara nodded. "Even with all of Tris's magic, he couldn't imagine ever being as good a king as his father was." She swallowed hard. "And yet, he's found his way, hasn't he?"

"Tris is a fine king," Cerise consoled. "He's wise and just, and he cares about what's best for his people. He may not approach problems exactly as Bricen did, but he has gifts Bricen did not. It's not about stepping into your father's shoes, Kiara. It's about finding your own path to rule with the gifts you've been given."

"It's just so . . . overwhelming. Father might have easily lived another twenty years. I had hoped—"

"That twenty years from now you'd know just what to do?" Cerise chuckled. "Fate doesn't allow for our choosing, Kiara. And truth be told, we're never ready for some responsibilities. We just have to do the best we can when they fall to us."

Kiara squeezed Cerise's hands. "Thank you for coming back with me. I know the ride was hard on you."

Cerise stood slowly, leaning on the arm of Kiara's chair for support. "My old bones don't take the cold as well as they used to, nor the saddle. But after a hot bath, I warrant that I'll feel fit again." She eyed Kiara. "Speaking of which . . . I hear the chambermaid drawing a bath for you. Go take it. You'll feel better, and you wouldn't want to be crowned queen covered with mud from the road!"

Kiara rose and glanced around the room. In many ways, the room appeared unchanged from when she had lived at the palace. The personal items she left behind remained in their usual places. And yet, Kiara felt as if the room had become unfamiliar, although she could not put the feeling into words. Home, she realized, had become Shekerishet, with Tris and Cwynn.

Kiara permitted Cerise to hurry her toward the tub in the adjacent chamber, but although she tried to let the steaming water and fragrant bath salts clear her mind, she found that she was as troubled afterwards as before.

A candlemark later the group reconvened behind locked and guarded doors in the king's private sitting room. Allestyr turned to Kiara with a welcoming smile.

"How I wish I were seeing you under better circumstances, my dear!" Allestyr and Tice both gave a token bow and then embraced her as old friends as Remir and the others stood back. Kiara introduced Royster, who barely contained his excitement despite the long journey. Antoin and the *vayash moru* and *vyrkin* guards patrolled the corridor outside the room, giving Captain Remir's men a much-needed opportunity to eat and rest. For the first time in several days, Kiara struggled to choke back tears, trying hard not to think about all that had changed since she had last been inside the palace walls.

"What's going on? We saw part of the outer city in flames, and we were stopped time and again by guards who reminded us of the curfew and demanded our papers. There's a mage at the palace gate—"

"I know, Your Highness. Or should I say, Your Majesty," Tice replied with a sigh, seeming not to notice when Kiara winced at the title. "I'm afraid that the letters you've received in the last months from your father, and even the most recent letter from Allestyr, dared not convey just how dire things have become."

"The outer city looks as if a war has been fought there."

Tice moved toward the fireplace, beckoning for them to take their seats. A table filled with breads, honey cakes, and dried fruit waited there, along with a decanter of brandy and a pitcher of warmed wine. "I'm afraid that 'war' is an apt description.

Despite the valiant efforts that Cam and the Veigonn, along with the army, have made against the Divisionists, Isencroft is only a breath away from civil war." Tice looked more tired and much older than Kiara remembered, and his shoulders slumped as he shared the news.

"In the weeks since your father's death, there have been riots. With most of the army in the field to meet the enemy from the north, we had no choice but to enforce a curfew and restrict movement throughout the city." He shrugged. "You can see from the fires in the north ward how well that's working."

"What purpose does burning down the city serve?" Kiara demanded as Balaren forced a hot cup of tea and a wedge of cheese into her hands.

"None at all, save as a message that frightened, angry people feel that events have gotten out of hand," Allestyr replied. "This year's harvest wasn't enough to make up for the past several bad years. In fact, by normal standards, this was a poor harvest. That it looked good by comparison only tells you how bad it's been lately."

He sighed. "Few people are starving, but there's little to go around in some parts of the kingdom, and not enough surplus elsewhere to make up for it. Margolan and the other kingdoms had poor enough harvests that there's no relief to come from importing grain. People look to the king to make it right, but there's little the crown can do. We've already stopped patrolling the kings' forests, leaving them open for poachers who need to feed their families. By the end of the winter, I won't be surprised if much of the kingdom is getting by on potatoes and rabbits."

"And the war?"

Allestyr gave a bitter smile. "Which one? Even the Veigonn couldn't keep peace in the city. The army scattered the Divisionists, but I don't think they're really gone. There've been fires throughout the city for weeks now, ever since the bulk of the army left for the war front. The guards say that there have been murders, down in the ginnels, in the worst sections of the city. Butchering is more like it. Not even the burial mounds are safe. Why someone would want to dig up the dead is beyond me, but then again, people snap when the fear and the anger get too bad."

Kiara sipped the tea, welcoming its warmth and hoping that it would steady her as the weight of Allestyr's revelations sank in. "How was the news received when Father died?" she asked quietly.

Allestyr looked pained. "We waited to announce the death until Count Renate was sworn in and other . . . precautions . . . were taken. Most of the city reacted with mourning. In some quarters, however, the mood was more . . . triumphant."

Kiara winced. "I'm assuming no public ceremony was held?"

Tice shook his head, taking a few steps closer. "We didn't think a large gathering was prudent, given the circumstances. Bells were rung to call the city to mourning, but the body was burned on a pyre in the inner courtyard, with only the Council of Nobles and the palace staff as witnesses. Even then—" He hesitated, and Allestyr gave him a sharp warning glance.

"If I'm to be the queen in fact as well as name, you can't hide unpleasant truths," Kiara said evenly. "I'm not a child."

Tice look a deep breath. "Apologies, Your Majesty. Those who care about you want only to protect you. But you're right. You must know. Even with so small a crowd, one man came at Wilym with a butcher knife. The man was the father of the servant who set the mechanism in place that killed your father, the servant who was hanged for the murder of the king. The father was screaming about his child being bewitched, about avenging the family's honor."

Kiara looked at him, appalled. "What happened?"

Tice grimaced. "The man was struck down by one of the

170

guard's arrows. Count Renate came to no harm. The pity is, I wouldn't doubt that the man's story was true. It's possible that the servant was bewitched, or at least didn't fully understand the seriousness of what was being done."

"How is Count Renate adapting to his regency?"

Allestyr chuckled. "Well enough. But he has asked every day if we'd heard when you were due to arrive. He'd like nothing better, I wager, than to quit the city with its fires and riots and leave for his country home."

"And yet, with war coming, even that's not assured to be a haven, is it?" Kiara mused, watching the tea leaves swirl in the bottom of her cup.

"No, m'lady. I'm afraid not."

They were silent for a moment. Kiara finally set aside her cup. "Well, I'm here. What must be done?"

Ticc and Allestyr exchanged glances. "We've crowned you by proxy, but now that you're here, it's best to waste no time to make everything completely official. Tonight, we'll convey the crown. By law, you must make a public appearance as the new queen a day after accepting the crown to show that power has transferred from the regent to you as the rightful ruler. You can make your appearance from a palace balcony, far away from the crowd."

Kiara shuddered. "Tris was nearly killed by an archer in the palace crowd."

Tice nodded. "Brother Felix will construct a warding between you and the public. That lesson was not lost on us."

Kiara frowned, going over Tice's words in her mind. "You said I had been crowned 'by proxy.' What exactly did you mean? I've felt the regent magic stir for several weeks now, as if it's grown more powerful. Would naming Renate as regent cause that?"

"I'm afraid it's a bit more complicated than that." Allestyr began to pace. "I'd prefer to have Brother Felix explain it. He should be joining us soon. Since we weren't sure exactly when you would arrive, there are some final preparations to be made." He paused. "We'll need to explain the ritual and coach you on your part. While Brother Felix attends to the magic elements down in the necropolis, Tice and I can help you prepare." Allestyr glanced over to Royster, who was doing his best not to look like he was eavesdropping.

"As the Head Keeper at the Library of Westmarch, Royster's spent his life studying and archiving scrolls and other magical items," Kiara said. "Perhaps he can be with us while I prepare. He might have some insights into how the regent magic is tied into all of this." At her words, Royster beamed and practically danced over to join them.

"As you wish," Allestyr replied. "It will take about a candle-mark to have the ceremony ready. In the meantime, rest and eat, and then we'll begin your preparations."

There was a knock, and one of the guards opened the door for Count Renate to enter. "Your Majesty!" Renate hurried over. He was in his middle years, with dark hair touched by gray at the crown and temples. The man made a low bow and knelt to kiss Kiara's hand. "Welcome home, Kiara."

"Count Renate," Kiara murmured, motioning for the man to rise. Renate had been one of her father's favorites among the nobility. He was plain-spoken and without the affectation of some of the lords. Renate was an intelligent man with a quick wit, deep loyalty, and, to Donelan's great admiration, a sixth sense about where to find deer in the forest. Now, as Kiara met Renate's gaze, the man looked much older and more worn than she remembered.

"Thank you for all that you've done for Isencroft, safeguarding the crown in my absence."

Renate made a dismissive gesture. "I appreciate your thanks, m'lady, but it was the least I could do for such a friend as your father has been to me over the years."

"You don't look well," Allestyr said with concern.

"Just a poor night's sleep," Renate replied. "Dark dreams. They look ridiculous by day, but in the middle of the night, such visions are troubling."

Kiara met his eyes. "Please tell me, what were your dreams?"

"Nothing to trouble you about, my dear. Just an old man's indigestion."

Kiara took his hand. "My husband is a powerful mage. I've learned that things like dreams are not to be dismissed lightly."

Renate sighed. "Very well. I dreamed that there was a dark, swift river running under the palace. I saw a bridge, swept away on a flood swell and carried along the river's course. Beside the river, where the bridge had been moored, I found a small rag doll, a poppet like children play with. That's the strangest thing. It was warm in my hand, and I swear that I saw it breathe." He gave a sheepish grin. "Then I awoke. As I told you, m'lady, I'm sure it was no more than the legacy of last night's dinner, returned to haunt me."

Kiara saw Tice and Allestyr glance sharply at each other, though they said nothing. "I'm sorry that your sleep was troubled," Kiara replied. "I hope that your rest tonight will be unbroken."

"And yours as well, m'lady. Although I wish it were under happier circumstances, welcome home." Renate bowed and took his leave.

Tice looked to Kiara. "There's much to be done. Let's go to the library so that you can prepare for tonight's ritual without being disturbed. There's a litany you'll need to learn, and we'll talk you through what you'll need to know when you go before the Oracle—and the spirits of your Ancestors." He glanced around. "You left Jae in your room?"

Kiara nodded. "He was happy by the fire."

"Very well then. If you'll follow me, Your Majesty." Tice motioned for Kiara, Cerise, and Royster to follow him up the stairs. Balaren and Antoin fell into step behind them. Patov, one of the *vayash moru* guards from Margolan, and Jorven, a *vyrkin*, walked a few paces behind.

Within a candlemark they had completed their preparations. Tice led them from the library into the necropolis. Kiara repressed a shiver. The necropolis seemed different than the last time she had visited these dark passageways, more than two years before. Now, Kiara was aware of the presence of silent figures in the shadows, as if the ghosts whose bones rested in neat piles along the corridors gathered along the walkways, watching. The air seemed heavy with power, making it difficult to breathe. Magic, old and powerful, clung to the passageways. It reached out to her, as if it were looking for a sign, a confirmation.

Brother Felix awaited them in the room where the ritual would be performed. Antoin and Captain Remir stood guard next to the doorway. Tice, Allestyr, Kiara, Cerise, Balaren, Royster, and the *vyrkin*, Jorven, filed into the room, and Antoin pulled the heavy, iron-bound oak door shut behind them, locking it. Torches flared in sconces around the walls, casting the room in a play of light and shadows. Kiara glanced toward the ceiling. The line of runes marked at the top of the walls were shifting and growing brighter and darker; it was no trick of the light or her imagination. Beneath the runes, a row of skulls stared down into the room, and Kiara could hear whispers, as if the spirits of the skulls awaited the night's working. Around the walls were intricate mosaics in the heraldic patterns of the eight clan lords, the warlords who had forged a kingdom out of warring tribes centuries ago.

Brother Felix bade them take their places in a circle around the room. He moved behind them, chanting a warding. Kiara could hear only snatches of his words, but she knew that he invoked the spirits of the fallen kings of old and asked for the protection of the ancient clan lords on the night's working. She looked at the faces of those who had accompanied her, both witnesses and guardians. In every face, she saw a flicker of apprehension that mirrored her own.

A stone pedestal stood in the center of the chamber. On it was an ornate silver chalice and a wooden box. The box was covered with Noorish inlay, and the complex parquetry formed an intricate design. Next to the chalice lay a golden crown set with jewels.

"Welcome, Your Majesty." Brother Felix knelt in front of Kiara and kissed her signet ring. "I'm sorry that Cam and the others can't join us for this ceremony," he said. "They were present for the working that crowned you by proxy, but they've gone to the battlefront."

"Let's get started," Kiara said, hoping she did not sound as nervous as she felt.

Brother Felix motioned toward the items on the pedestal. "Tonight, we activate your full regent magic and convey the crown in both power and law. The public coronation ceremonies are for show; they carry on the tradition in front of the people, but the real conveyance takes place here, as it always has."

He picked up the goblet, which was filled with red wine. "In many ways, the ceremony is similar to a ritual wedding. Your blood and the blood of witnesses are mingled in the wine, which you drink. Some of the wine will be sprinkled on the crown, sharing your life force with it, as it were. We hold the ceremony here in the necropolis so that the transfer of power from one generation to the next is witnessed by both the living and the dead.

"As we've discussed, after the ceremony, you will spend the

night in the mausoleum room, where the kings of Isencroft and their most trusted seers have been laid to rest for hundreds of years. It's then that the regent magic is activated, and you stand among the bones and ashes of your forefathers, who give you counsel."

Kiara nodded. "And the box?"

"A magical item was used as a proxy for you, so that we could assure that nothing could challenge your claim to the throne. When the full regent magic activates, the power will pass from the proxy to you."

Kiara took a deep breath. "All right then. I'm ready."

12

Brother Felix removed a coil from his belt. What Kiara had at first glance taken to be rope, she now recognized as a sorcerer's cord, used to create a second circle of warding. Tice, Allestyr, Kiara, Cerise, Balaren, Royster, and Jorven stood in a circle, close enough to touch each other, with the pedestal in the center. Antoin and Captain Remir remained outside, on guard. Felix chanted in a low voice as he moved slowly around the small group, letting the coil slip to the ground to form a circle as he walked. Kiara felt the tingle of strong magic and thought she glimpsed a faint iridescence in the air when Felix had closed the circle.

Next, Brother Felix withdrew a jeweled ceremonial dagger from his belt. It glinted in the torchlight. A large ruby, a gem sacred to the Aspect Chenne, gleamed in the handle. Taking the chalice in one hand and holding the dagger in the other, he moved to Tice first. Tice held out his right hand, palm up. Felix made a cut on Tice's palm deep enough to coat the edge of the blade in blood and then let the blood drip from the blade into the chalice so that it mingled with the wine. Slowly, Tice moved from person to person repeating the ritual, until he stood before Kiara.

Tice took Kiara's hand. She steeled herself as the blade bit into her palm, cutting a thin line from the base of her longest finger to the heel of her hand. Blood welled up from the cut, and Brother Felix used the gleaming blade to flick drops of it into the goblet of wine.

"In the name of the kings and queens who came before," he intoned, "we recognize Kiara Sharsequin as the true Queen of Isencroft." More drops slipped down the blade into the wine. "The blood of her forefathers and foremothers runs through her veins, tying what is to what went before. Spirits of the fallen kings, hear me! Open your daughter to the magic that is hers by birthright. Let power flow through her like her sacred blood. Anoint her with the regent magic, and let what once was proxy now be fact."

Felix passed the goblet to Kiara, who began to drink. Power crackled in the dusty air of the crypt. The wardings flared golden, plainly visible. Though the chalice was cool against her skin, the wine burned as it flowed down her throat, taking her breath like the strongest whiskey, sending a tingling sensation from her scalp to her feet that had nothing to do with alcohol. She tilted the goblet back and let the last drop of wine drip from its rim.

The box on the pedestal began to rock back and forth wildly.

Everyone startled and stared at the inlaid box, which continued to tremble. "What in the name of the Sacred Lady was that?" Kiara asked, her voice rough with the strong elixir.

"Don't break the circle!" Felix warned. "We must complete the ceremony and then deal with the box." The others stayed where they were, though they continued to stare at the trembling box.

Felix took the golden crown from the pedestal and nodded for Kiara to kneel. She bowed her head to receive the crown. "In the names of your forefathers and foremothers, in honor of the blood of kings and queens that flows through your veins, and by the power of Chenne, our Warrior and Protector, I crown you Queen of Isencroft."

Felix ran his finger across the inside of the chalice. It emerged red with wine and blood. Reverently, Felix touched his bloody finger to the crown of Kiara's head, and then to her forehead, throat, and breastbone. He wiped more bloody wine from the chalice and touched four gems on the crown, in front and back and on each side. He began to chant, swaying from side to side, as he lifted the crown into the air above Kiara's head. The words were unfamiliar, but Kiara thought she recognized the language as the ancient form of Croft, used on rare ritual occasions.

Felix lowered the crown to hover just above Kiara's head and made a pronouncement in the ancient language. "With this circlet, the power of the throne and the regent magic of your blood become yours, Kiara Sharsequin, Queen of Isencroft."

Felix set the crown lightly on Kiara's head. Although Kiara could not see the crown, she did see a cloud of golden light that enveloped her from the top of her head to the soles of her feet. The light extended a slender glowing cord toward the inlaid box on the pedestal, enveloping it in the same nimbus. Once more, the box began to tremble, and the golden glow began to swirl, shifting from golden into a light blue.

Before Kiara could react, an image forced itself into her consciousness, of Cwynn, alone in the darkness. At the same time, she felt a jolt of power travel down the length of her body, coming to rest in her abdomen, which clenched lightly and then released. The image remained vivid in her mind, as did the unshakable feeling that somehow, Cwynn was present.

"The crown conveys the full regent magic." Brother Felix's voice seemed to come from a great distance away. "Use it!"

Compared to Tris's power as a summoner, Kiara had come to believe that her own magical abilities were lesser gifts, despite Cerise's vague predictions that the regent magic would someday fully open for her. Now, Kiara drew on the fragile threads of power within herself, surprised to find that they glowed with a new vividness, golden and strong. Where the regent magic had been random and chaotic as it emerged since her father's death, now the power felt coherent and whole. In her mind's eye, Kiara saw the threads weave together, over and under, melding together into a warm, golden glow that filled her and surrounded her. Kiara willed the glow back along the blue thread to the inlaid box on the pedestal. She caught her breath. The sense of Cwynn's presence was so strong, so tangible, that a sob tore from her throat.

Whatever was in the inlaid box reacted to her touch, and across the nether, she felt the presence lurch toward her, clinging to the golden glow as if to life itself. Kiara felt her abdomen tighten again, as if in recognition, and she felt a pulse of magic that began in the center of her body, flowing from her womb, up through her chest, and then out to envelop the inlaid box that ceased its trembling and now lay quiet. The image of Cwynn in her mind, still vivid enough to touch, relaxed, bathed in a golden glow.

As suddenly as it came, the glow dissipated, and Kiara fell forward onto her hands and knees, spent. Dimly, she heard Brother Felix murmur the words to break the warding, and Cerise rushed to kneel beside her.

"What did you do to her?" Cerise's voice was tinged with anger and fear. Kiara tried to catch her breath. She could feel Cerise's healing magic flowing over her, a warm, comforting blanket of power.

"I've studied the conveyance ritual thoroughly, and I've never read of anything like this before."

"What is in that damn box?" It was Balaren who spoke. He took a step toward the pedestal, but Allestyr blocked his way.

Cerise helped Kiara to her feet. Kiara wondered if she looked as pale as she felt, and from the expressions on the others' faces, she guessed that she did. She met Allestyr's gaze. "You said that you took 'precautions' to assure my throne. What have you done?"

Brother Felix sighed and moved to the inlaid box that now lay quietly on the pedestal. He murmured a few words of power over it before lifting it gently in his hands. "We were afraid that if Alvior landed troops on Isencroft soil before you were crowned in the full ceremony, he could claim blood title to the throne. There is an ancient working to crown you by proxy, creating a 'you' to be here in Isencroft until you actually arrived in person." Felix opened the lid of the inlaid box.

Inside lay the *nenkah*, a crude rag doll. Felix caught his breath. The *nenkah* lay curled into a fetal position, and its linen chest rose and fell with slow, steady breath. Cautiously, Kiara stepped forward to touch it with a finger. The linen was warm.

Balaren looked at the box with a mix of curiosity and horror. "What breathes in that box is not fully alive, but not dead or undead. Even to my senses, it has the feel of gray magic."

"A rag doll on the banks of a river, warm like life," she murmured, remembering Renate's nightmare. Once again, the touch brought a vivid picture of Cwynn to mind, and an overwhelming feeling of fear, of being hunted, of escape that it almost tore a sob from her throat.

"We borrowed from your life force when we made the *nenkah* out of personal items," Felix explained, shaking his head as if at a loss. "The ancient texts said that the life force would return to you when the ceremony was completed, and the *nenkah* would become just a bit of rags once more. I have no explanation."

"It never occurred to you that you might be drawing on two life forces, did it?" Cerise's voice was sharp.

Brother Felix looked at Cerise blankly, stunned. "Two?"

"Kiara is pregnant."

181

Allestyr paled. "We didn't know. We had no idea," he said, eyes growing wide at the implications.

"When the magic came on me, it touched the child inside of me," Kiara said quietly. "But I also saw an image of Cwynn, felt his presence. When I touched the *nenkah*, it happened again, as if his presence is bound here somehow." She looked up at Felix and Allestyr sharply. "We don't dare withdraw the power from the *nenkah*, not until we know what it means for my children."

Brother Felix let his hand hover above the *nenkah*. The figure did not stir, like a sleeping child curled into a ball. After a moment he withdrew his hand and turned to them. "A whisper of your life force remains within the *nenkah*, but there is another force as well. Something is different about the second life force. Like yours, it's incomplete, divided. I can't explain it. Whatever it is, it's powerful even though it's not whole. If it's your son's energy, then he is likely to be an even greater mage than his father."

Kiara shook her head slowly. "But none of the mages—not even Tris—has been able to read Cwynn's magic. Cheira Talwyn of the Sworn believes Cwynn is very powerful, but there's something very different about whatever power he has. She was afraid that it was different enough that Cwynn might be the real prize behind this war."

"You have many questions," Allestyr said, stepping up to stand beside Kiara. "You'll spend tonight in the company of your ancestors' spirits, and tomorrow, tradition demands that you make a pilgrimage to the Oracle of Chenne. Together, they may be able to explain what has happened, since we cannot."

Kiara nodded, but her gaze traveled back to the curled shape of the *nenkah*. Brother Felix closed the inlaid box gently and gave her a sad smile. "The *nenkah* will be safe here. The magic of the box and the power of the wardings help to sustain it.

We'll take good care until we know how to free your energy—and Cwynn's."

Kiara and the others waited in silence as Brother Felix dismissed the wardings around the circle. Once they made their way to the door, Felix laid down the cord around the pedestal that held the *nenkah*'s box, chanting under his breath as he raised new wardings of protection. He knocked at the door to signal Antoin and Captain Remir, and Kiara could hear the heavy key scrape in the iron lock. The door swung open and a cold blast of air filled the room as they stepped into the necropolis corridor.

To Kiara's heightened vision, the darkened passageways and crypt rooms teemed with ghosts. They did not speak, nor did they try to touch her, yet Kiara felt as if she were being scrutinized closely. The group waited for a few minutes while Brother Felix locked the door to the chamber and replaced the wardings at the entrance. When he was finished, Kiara turned to him.

"How is it that suddenly, I can sense spirits all around us here? Is the regent magic a kind of summoning?"

Brother Felix considered her question in silence for a moment. "There's been no record that activating the regent magic ever created a summoner in a king or queen who did not already have that talent. Certainly not someone with the range and depth of the talents that Martris Drayke has, or his grandmother, Bava K'aa.

"At the same time, part of the full regent magic involves being able to take the counsel of your ancestors. Your father was never truly comfortable with that part of the magic, and it may not have manifested as strongly in him as it does in you. After all," he said with a faint smile, "you also bring the blood of the Eastmark royalty into the equation. We have no idea how their magic works."

"So I can see these ancestors and speak with them? Just tonight? Just on Haunts? Or at other times?"

"We really don't know. Nothing has been recorded. You can ask the spirits, but they may not be able to answer you, either. Every monarch is different. For example, your father's magic manifested in superb battle instincts. He had an uncanny way of knowing where the enemy was hidden, of anticipating their strikes. It was too accurate to be luck, too consistent. He swore he didn't know how he did it, but he didn't complain when it helped with the hunt as well!"

Kiara managed to smile, remembering how fond Donelan was of hunting stag.

"Unless I can use that kind of magic from afar, that won't do us much good this time. I can't risk the baby by taking my chances on the front lines."

Cerise nodded thoughtfully. "Your mother had scrying magic. Sometimes she helped your father prepare for battle by using her talent behind the lines and feeding him the information via messenger. Your own abilities in that area are probably the legacy of her gift."

Brother Felix led the group deeper into the necropolis. Antoin walked at the front with Brother Felix, while Captain Remir followed them, and Kiara noted that even here, the two men had unsheathed their swords, ready for danger.

They stopped when they reached a large mausoleum room where the bones or ashes of the monarchs of Isencroft rested, the place where Kiara was to spend the night. The door to the room was ornately carved mahogany, and the stone door frame and lintel were embellished with a complex pattern of knots and woven strands. Brother Felix held up a hand to keep her from reaching for the door.

"There are a few details to attend to before you enter," Brother Felix said with a reassuring half smile. "While you are in the crypt, the rest of us will hold vigil in this side room," he added, pointing to a dark opening across from the mausoleum room that Kiara had not noticed. They waited in the corridor as Felix lit the torches in the smaller room. The light revealed a room with several empty raised pedestals for the vigil keepers to rest, as well as a low wooden table and two wooden benches. On the table, someone had already set out a large basket and a smaller basket, several wineskins, and a flagon of what appeared to be blood. A folded blanket lay on each of the raised pedestals, as well as on the benches, a nod to the comfort of the vigil keepers. The side room itself was notable for its complete lack of ornamentation. Brother Felix gestured for them to enter, and he bade everyone sit.

"While the mausoleum will be warded for your protection, at least one of us as well as one of the *vayash moru* will be awake and on guard all night long," Felix said. "We'll know if something unexpected happens, and if the spirits will permit us to enter, we'll be there to help."

"If the spirits will permit you to enter?"

Felix shrugged. "This part of the conveyance ceremony is not in my hands." Felix paused and met Kiara's eyes. "Tonight will be a long night, and you'll be among spirits. Before you enter the mausoleum, you must ground yourself for the magic by eating and drinking."

Although a knot in the pit of her stomach cancelled out hunger, Kiara forced herself to eat from the breads, meats, and cheeses that were set out for her, and to sip from the watered wine Felix offered.

Kiara turned to Felix. "If the spirits of the crypt can't tell me how the magic of the *nenkah* affects Cwynn and the babe that I carry, might the Oracle know?"

Brother Felix looked thoughtful. "You'll have the chance to ask. A visit to her grotto is required after your journey into the mausoleum is complete. Your question might be best suited for her wisdom."

"I can't say that I'm comfortable with either the mausoleum or the Oracle," Kiara said quietly. "I'm not sure I'm wise enough to ask the right questions, and Father always said the Oracle was damnable about playing hide-and-seek with the truth if the question wasn't phrased just right."

Brother Felix chuckled. "Your father did not seek the Oracle out often, but even he acknowledged her wisdom when the situation warranted it. She came to him with a prophecy not long before his death, with words that unfortunately seem much clearer in hindsight. Perhaps she will speak more plainly to you."

Kiara finished the food and wine, although she was so preoccupied with her thoughts that she tasted nothing. When she was finished, Brother Felix met her gaze.

"It's time." He helped Kiara to her feet, and then reached for the small basket on the table and handed it to her. "Everything you need for the ritual is in the basket. You know what you need to do to make it through the working. We'll be here, keeping the vigil, and we'll see you in the morning."

Brother Felix and Antoin accompanied Kiara from the vigil room, and the others murmured their blessings and charms for protection as she left. At the entrance to the mausoleum, Antoin stood to the side, on guard. Felix took the iron ring from his belt and found a heavy iron key. The door's lock was as ornamental as its carvings, forged of black iron covered with the raised images of complicated knots. The key turned in the lock, making a soft thud as the mechanism opened. It took an effort for Felix to open the heavy door. Brother Felix did not enter the mausoleum; instead, he used magic to light the torches around the perimeter of a large circular room.

He turned to Kiara. "I can go no farther. The spirits are ready for you; I can feel it in the magic. Walk carefully, Kiara, and may the Goddess go with you."

The Dread

Brother Felix stepped back, allowing Kiara to approach the entrance. She took a deep breath, reaching out to the nascent regent magic, and entered the room. As she passed by the carved door frame, she noticed the four-headed dragon seal of the Isencroft royal family, as well as the heraldic icons of the eight clan lords. Kiara shivered as she crossed the threshold, feeling as if she had walked through a curtain of power.

The room was more ornate than many of the other crypts, and the walls and entrance were covered with carved runes and elaborate mosaics of glass, colored stone, and precious gems. Kiara realized that the images in the mosaics echoed the carvings in the doorposts. One panel was a huge depiction of the four-headed royal dragon. The mosaic glittered as the light caught the red gems and crimson glass, held together with gold.

Eight other panels covered all but one portion of the walls, one panel for each of the clan lords' patron images. One mosaic showed a huge bear standing on its hind feet, paws raised to attack, the symbol of Clan Kirylu. In the next panel, a large silver wolf with violet eyes stood beneath a full moon, patron of Clan Dunlurghan. Clan Finlios's patron was a huge eagle, depicted with its wings spread wide. A stawar with luminous citrine eyes represented Clan Skaecogy. Clan Dromlea's icon was the gyregon, shown plunging as if into battle, its talons bared. For Clan Tratearmon, a stag with huge antlers. The patron of Clan Veaslieve, a massive black warhorse, looked down from the wall with ruby eyes. Clan Rathtuaim, the last of the old clans, was represented with a huge falcon, its beak open in a war cry. Kiara recognized each of the patron images from the stories she and every Isencroft native had heard from birth. Though the clan lords were long dead, every Crofter claimed to be a descendant from at least one of the clans, and Kiara knew that all of the lords were reputed to be ancestors of the royal line.

The only part of the circular wall not covered with mosaic panels held row upon row of sealed square openings, recesses that held the bones of the dead kings and queens of Isencroft. On the floor at the base of the mosaics, at least a dozen large marble biers ringed the mausoleum room. Atop each bier was the elaborately carved form of the monarch whose death the bier memorialized, and carved into the marble on all four sides of the pedestal were runes and sigils.

The floor of the mausoleum was as ornate as its walls. Colored tiles traced a large circular labyrinth that took most of the floor. A ring of white candles burned all around the edge of the labyrinth circle, lit by Felix's magic. The twisting tile pathway led to four colored candles, and Kiara knew that as she walked the labyrinth, she would come face to face with her spirit guides.

Kiara drew a deep breath as the door closed behind her. Her preparations had been hurried, but complete. She paused, mentally reviewing what she must do. The shadows seemed to move slowly out of the way of the light, as if they did not want to withdraw. In her left hand she carried the basket with the ritual elements. She knelt in the circle of light cast by the torch and opened the basket.

As she worked to prepare the offering, Kiara felt as if she was being watched from the shadows. She had felt the nearness of spirits in the necropolis corridors; now, the revenants crowded in on her. As she set out the elements of the offering, the room grew colder, so that her breath misted.

Kiara made her way carefully through the narrow opening in the candles that traced the outer edge of the labyrinth floor tiles. The path had a single entrance and exit. Followed correctly, the path she took would take her through the intricate, circular twists and turns of the labyrinth and bring her back to the beginning. Kiara took a deep breath and closed her eyes, focusing her energy and struggling to calm her thoughts. Clearing her mind, she began to follow the tiled path, toward the first candle.

After a few moments, Kiara stood before the candle. It was red, for Chenne, the Warrior Goddess, patron of Isencroft. She looked around the labyrinth at the other candles. White for the Mother and Childe. Pink for the Lover and Whore faces of the Goddess. Black for protection and the favor of Istra, the Dark Lady. Only the two darkest faces, Sinha the Crone and the Formless One, were not invoked.

Turning her attention back to the red candle, Kiara took the piece of charcoal Felix had placed inside the basket and marked a rune. *Katen*, the rune of succession, lay between the white and red candles. She made her way slowly to the white candle, where she marked another rune.

Telhon, the rune of family, lay between the white and pink candles. At the pink candle, she marked *Eshan*, the rune of power, between the pink and black candles. Finally, Kiara reached the black candle and marked *Rahn*, the rune of fate, between the black and red candles. Kiara made the sign of the Lady over the candles and then made her way to the center of the labyrinth. She removed a scroll from the basket with the words of the ritual. As with all of the monarchs before her, the ritual had been altered subtly for her and the circumstances under which she found herself coming to the throne. Kiara took a deep breath and began.

"Honored fathers. Esteemed mothers. I come before you to claim my birthright, the throne of Isencroft. I am Kiara Sharsequin, daughter of Donclan and Viata, heir to the crown. Honor me with your presence, grandfathers and grandmothers. I ask you to share your wisdom."

A breeze fluttered through the windowless chamber. It buffeted the candle flames but did not extinguish them. The torch flames swayed from the moving air, sending shadows dancing across the floor. Yet within the darker shadows near the opposite wall, Kiara sensed the presence of movement.

Slowly, four shadows separated themselves from the darkness. The first to step into the light was a gaunt man, dressed in the manner of the Isencroft kings several centuries before Kiara's birth. He had sharp features and hollow cheeks, with deep-set eyes that looked at Kiara as if he would see her soul. He took his place between the black and red candles. Next to emerge from the shadows was a tall woman, strongly built, with the stance and manner of a warrior. She wore the ghostly image of ancient armor, and her hair was caught back in a battle queue. This ghost stopped between the pink and black candles, above the rune of power.

The third spirit was a portly man who looked to be in his middle years. Broad shouldered with a large belly and a full beard, the man had a pleasant look about him as he came to stand between the white and pink candles, next to the rune of family. Finally, the ghost of a thin woman in a long cloak emerged from the darkness. Her pale face was surprisingly young, appearing no more than thirty summers old, but the gown she wore was at least several generations out of fashion. This final spirit glided to a stop just beyond the rune of fate. Kiara swallowed hard, forcing back a wave of disappointment that Donelan's spirit was not among her spirit counselors.

Kiara gave a low bow. "Honored ancestors. Thank you for heeding my call. I have received the crown according to the ritual, and now I come to seek your wisdom."

"We cannot speak of the future, only of the past," said the tall, gaunt-faced spirit. "It's not given to us to know what will be. But the four of us have been called by the runes and ritual, because something we know may be of value to you. Ask your questions, Kiara Sharsequin, daughter of Donelan. We will answer as best we can. It will be for you to interpret how our stories may yet affect the days to come."

"How is it that my father is not among you?"

The heavy-set ghost gave Kiara a sad smile. "Donelan's spirit was not drawn to the runes because he struggled with the same questions that you do, and he had not yet discovered answers. In time, he will be able to come to you for comfort, as does the spirit of your mother. This is not a time for consolation, Kiara. We are a war council, gathered for you by magic and the will of the Lady. Make good use of what we have to offer you."

Kiara nodded in acknowledgment. "Share with me your wisdom, and help me save our kingdom." She realized she was clutching the scroll in her hand hard enough to crumple the parchment. Now that she faced the ghosts, she hoped that the questions she had chosen would make the most of the opportunity to seek guidance.

She turned first to the gaunt, hollow-eyed man who stood near the rune of succession. "Tell me, honored Father, how can I protect the crown from the invaders and help the people of Isencroft accept my sons as the rightful heirs to the throne?"

The thin ghost regarded Kiara with a sharp, unforgiving gaze. "You have returned to your homeland and accepted the crown. Complete the ritual, and the full power of the crown cannot be taken from you by force. The regent magic will elude usurpers, weakening their rule until descendents of the true regent line return to take back what is theirs."

"And my sons?"

"You are not the first to wed an outlander. Your father's marriage scandalized the Winter Kingdoms. At the time, many swore they would never accept the child of that marriage as the true ruler of Isencroft. Yet time passed, and now it is not you but your sons to an outlander king whose legitimacy to rule is questioned. So it was in my day, when I married a daughter of the Western Raiders to bring peace to our borders. There was great outcry that our son would grow up and deliver our kingdom into the hand of our enemies. He did not. Rule wisely and with strength, Kiara, and make sure that your sons are seen in Isencroft and know our ways. Such tempests are quickly forgotten once there is peace and bread enough for all."

"Thank you, wise Father," Kiara said with a bow. The gaunt spirit stepped back, his image becoming less solid, though he stayed near the circle of the labyrinth. Next, Kiara turned toward the warrior queen. The queen wore leather armor emblazoned with the image of a wolf, the symbol of Clan Dunlurghan.

"Honored Mother. How can I lead my armies to victory when I dare not risk the child I carry in the heat of the fight?"

The ghost of the tall, warrior queen regarded Kiara silently, as if she were taking Kiara's measure. "You have trained for battle, and you have drawn blood in battle," the ghost said, watching Kiara closely.

"Yes, honored Mother. I take no joy in either, but I have done what I had to do when the times demanded it."

The warrior queen nodded. "Exactly so. Then this time, also, you must do what must be done as the times demand it. Tell me: If the babe you carry were already born, would you count it shame to hide him out of reach of the enemy?"

"Of course not."

Once again, the ghost queen nodded. "Then why do you count it shameful to hide him before his birth, when both you and he would be a tempting spoil of war? There are many ways to fight an enemy. Swords are often the least effective, though we turn to them first more often than not." The hint of a smile softened her features. "Generals and heroes can lead an army to victory, but none can be a rallying point like the one who wears the crown. Now, more than ever, you *are* Isencroft embodied. You are Donelan's daughter, the crowned monarch. And you carry within your body the next heir to that throne. You are the nexus of past, present, and future, and that is a powerful focus for your magic."

"But I'm not even sure what my regent magic is!" Kiara's voice carried a hint of desperation. "We don't have time for me to find out by trial and error. There's an invading fleet ready to attack."

The ghostly queen's face hardened. "Battle proves the warrior, as fire tempers steel. I was the daughter of Leksandr, lord of Clan Dunlurghan, wife to Lord Gavrill of Clan Finlios. I saw many battles and fought alongside my husband. No soldier knows with certainty what sets him apart as a fighter until the battle. Is it his reach? Stealth? Speed and sure-footedness? Cleverness and guile? Brute strength? These are proven in the heat of battle. Since it is not for you to cross swords in this war, then you must use the gifts you have to change the tide."

Kiara bit back her frustration and bowed her head in deference. "Thank you, honored Mother." Again, the ghost took a step back and faded to a dim outline.

Kiara turned next to the spirit of the burly, bearded king. While the other three ghosts looked forbidding, this wraith had a hint of mirth to him that set her somewhat at ease. "Honored Father, I fear for the lives of both my sons, and for my husband. My oldest child, Cwynn, may not be suited to rule, due to a difficult birth. The child I carry would claim both thrones, since it isn't advisable for me to have a third. Yet the prospect of a joint throne has brought Isencroft to civil war. What wisdom do you have for me?"

Although the bearded king's expression was thoughtful, his eyes were kind. "Well-fed subjects rarely revolt. Find relief for their hunger, and you will undermine the traitors' greatest advantage, because they claim to offer what the king could not provide. This war will force your enemies to reveal themselves, as it will show the true colors of the monarchy. Let your people see the real horror against which the army stands to protect them, and they will rally to your cause."

"Thank you, honored Father," Kiara said quietly as the ghost retreated to the shadows.

Hesitantly, she turned to the last of the ghostly counselors. The thin woman wore an ornate dress with intricate beading that was a work of art even though its style had long passed from fashion. Kiara could see sorrow in the ghost's pale features.

"Speak, honored Mother. You were drawn to the rune of fate. I fear to ask, and yet I must. If your gift is not to speak of the future, then what can you tell me of my fate, and that of my kingdom and kin?"

"I came to the throne quite young, without the benefit of advisers among the nobles or the castle staff whom I could trust," the ghost replied. "Doubting myself, I put my faith in seers and rune scryers, and in the words of the Oracle. I took their prophecies and omens at face value, without testing them for deeper meanings. Without intending to do so, I abdicated the throne by ceding my decisions and choices to what I believed was fated for me.

"By acting on what *might* be as if it were what *would* be, I narrowed the options open to me and brought about the future I most feared. Omens and prophecies are meant to alert you to what is possible, but do not believe that what is foretold is certain. The victory comes most often to those who deny their fate and forge their own paths. Do not make my mistake."

"Thank you, honored Mother," Kiara murmured.

"You have chosen your questions well." It was the first ghost, the gaunt old king, who spoke. "We leave four gifts for you. Use them wisely. Remember that the blood that flows through your veins gives you not only the magic but the wisdom of all those who came before you, if you will but open yourself to the power."

The Dread

The gaunt king raised his hand in blessing, and the other ghosts did likewise, making the sign of the Lady. One by one, their shadowed forms blurred and then disappeared, leaving Kiara alone with the circle of candles. Where each ghost had stood, an item lay on the floor next to the runes and candle. Kiara saw that the path out of the labyrinth would bring her close enough to each of the candles to retrieve the gifts. She made her way carefully through the labyrinth, stopping at each of the colored candles to whisper thanks to the spirit who had appeared before gathering the gift. At each candle she smudged the rune before extinguishing the flame.

In the place where the gaunt king had stood lay an intricate necklace made from silver and glass beads in a fashion Kiara did not recognize. It looked very old and was of fine enough craftsmanship to be worthy of royalty. Near where the portly king's spirit had been lay a weighty piece of glass. At first, Kiara thought it to be a scrying ball until she lifted it in her hands and found it to be flatter than a sphere, yet convex on either side.

By the spot where the young, thin queen had been lay a handful of rune dice, rectangular polished pieces of bone inscribed with runic symbols. The calligraphy on the rune dice was magnificent, and in the dim light of the crypt, Kiara thought she saw the intricate symbols glow with an inner fire.

The final gift was from the warrior queen's ghost. It was a finely forged sword, and as Kiara hesitantly lifted the weapon, she realized that it was very old. The crest of the crown of Isencroft was worked into the guard and four gems were set into the end of the pommel in the shape of a cloverleaf: sapphire, onyx, emerald, and ruby. Kiara frowned, trying to match the gems to the faces of the lady, and then she noticed writing etched into the blade. She moved closer to the torch to see better.

Inscribed along the blade were the eight names of the ancient clans of Isencroft. Once the followers and families of long-ago warlords, the clans still retained a powerful hold on the imagination of Crofters, and even those who had lived for generations mingled in Isencroft's cities could proudly trace lineage back to one of the eight old clans.

Eight for the clans that became a kingdom, the first lords of Isencroft, who chose among themselves for its king. Raise this sword, Goddess Blessed, and remind your people who they are. It was the voice of the warrior queen that sounded softly in Kiara's ear, close enough to be whispering over Kiara's shoulder. When she stepped across the opening to the labyrinth, air and magic stirred through the room, extinguishing the ring of candles around the labyrinth's edge.

She placed the gifts in her basket, then turned and made a deep bow.

"I am grateful, honored spirits. Thank you for your wisdom."

To Kiara's surprise, the heavy door unlocked of its own accord. Kiara pushed the door open, feeling the magic of the threshold tingle as she stepped back into the corridor. Jorven and Balaren were waiting for her. Relief and exhaustion flooded over Kiara as they walked her back to the vigil room. Kiara's companions crowded around her, and Cerise helped her sit next to the low wooden table. Kiara realized that she had no idea how much time had passed. Cerise shooed the others away until she could verify to her satisfaction that Kiara was well. Only then did the healer permit the rest of the group to ply Kiara with their questions.

"Can you tell us what you saw?"

"Did the kings appear to you?"

"What did they tell you?"

"Did they leave anything for you?"

Cerise brought Kiara a chalice of watered wine and a hunk of bread with honey, nudging her to eat before launching into long explanations. Gratefully, Kiara finished the food. The others waited, trying to mask their impatience to hear her story.

When Kiara finished recounting the counsel of the spirits, Allestyr looked thoughtful. "The advice appears sound to me. A bit vague, but that's to be expected." He managed a tired smile. "You weren't really expecting an otherworldly checklist, were you?"

Tice chuckled. "I'm intrigued by the first ghost's comments. Which of the gifts did you think might have been his?"

Kiara laid out the ghosts' gifts on table, placing the sword next to the smaller items. Tice hunkered down next to the items and raised an eyebrow. "Now, that's interesting."

"What is?"

Tice gestured toward the beaded necklace, although he was careful not to touch it. "It's been my privilege to be the archivist to the crown for some time now. I catalog the gifts and important purchases. This necklace is similar to another in the 'crown jewels' collection. Or perhaps it's the same piece, 'spirited' from there to here by our friendly king." He looked up at Kiara.

"It's every bit as old as the first king's spirit claimed to be, and I'm betting it was King Vestven who was among your advisers. He was the monarch who created the longest-standing truce with the Western Raiders, and his reign enjoyed great prosperity. Vestven did indeed marry a chieftain's daughter, which raised a fuss here in Isencroft but brought him high esteem among the Raiders."

Tice smiled. "A bit of trivia. Did you know what the Western Raiders call themselves?" When Kiara shook her head no, Tice grinned. "The Adares of the West. 'Raider' is a mispronunciation of their language into Croft. They're actually a very sophisticated society with thriving commerce. We forget that their scholars, seers, and mathematicians have contributed a great deal over the centuries to knowledge in the Winter Kingdoms."

"Then why did they make war on Isencroft?" Kiara asked, sitting back and sipping at the watered wine. "Father had to fight them several times. Once, I went with him."

Tice nodded. "Every kingdom or people have the misfortune to have a bad leader once in a while. The Adares had father and son rulers who fancied themselves the eighth kingdom in the Winter Kingdoms and wanted to do their share of pushing and shoving to get respect." He shrugged. "That was nearly a decade ago, and I understand from our spies that when the son's rule was cut short by an untimely and mysterious death, the new ruler led the Adares back to a more traditional outlook."

He drew a deep breath, thinking. "About eight years ago, an envoy came to the palace from the Adares with a peace offering. Donelan was skeptical, but in the time since then, while the border lords are constantly whipping the villagers up in fear of the Raiders, there's been no organized action beyond some minor bandits. I believe the Adares were sincere."

Kiara frowned. "What does it mean for us now? Why would the ghost bring that up? There has to be a connection."

Tice and Allestyr exchanged glances. "The most obvious connection would be grain," Allestyr said. "The ghost mentioned that 'well-fed subjects rarely revolt.' While the Winter Kingdoms, and especially Isencroft, haven't had good harvests recently, the western plains have. Your father was too proud to approach the Adares to see about purchasing wheat and barley. But if I'm correct, Vestven is advising you to use this necklace and remind the Adares that you share a royal bloodline with them. They're a culture that takes blood ties very seriously. For example, it's considered a fault of the highest order not to share your food with blood kin who are hungry."

Kiara smiled slowly. "What are we waiting for? How quickly can we send an envoy to the Adares?" She chuckled. "Let's keep it quiet though. The Divisionists are angry enough about my ties to Margolan. They'll be livid if they hear that we're trading with the Western Raiders!"

Allestyr gave a slight bow. "A wise decision. I'll see to it tomorrow, or rather, later today," he said, stifling a yawn.

Kiara turned to Brother Felix. "What do you make of the glass and the runes? At first, I thought it was a scrying ball," she said, indicating the oddly shaped glass, "but it's the wrong shape."

Felix picked up the weighty glass and turned it in his hands. "I haven't seen many of these," he said with a touch of awe in his voice. "There aren't many mages who can use one." He looked up at Kiara. "It's a mage lens, a mage's burning glass."

"Burning glass?"

Felix nodded. "Anyone without a hint of magic can take a piece of glass shaped like this and hold it in the sun to start a fire. But a *mage's* burning glass is different. There's a very secret, ancient process to make the glass. Something about the glass in a *mage's* burning glass focuses magic, not light. It's a tricky thing to do, and it's easy to singe your hair if you get it wrong."

"Kiara's had some experience with exploding scrying balls," Cerise noted dryly.

Felix raised an eyebrow, and Kiara felt compelled to explain. "On the journey to help Tris take back his crown, we had a couple of bad experiences with scrying balls when too much power was concentrated through them. We were all picking glass shards out of sensitive places for a long time," she added ruefully.

"Well, then," Felix said with a chuckle, "you'll appreciate the genius of the burning glass. It's designed to contain and amplify that power, rather than let the power blow it apart. Most mages don't have the gift for it. They can barely harness their own power, let alone focus the power of several mages—"

"Wait. This glass lets a mage focus more than his own power?" Kiara asked with sudden interest.

Felix nodded again. "Not just mages' power, but the power of magical objects as well."

Kiara frowned thoughtfully. "Magical objects . . . what about magical places?"

Felix shrugged. "I'm not sure. Not much has been written about the burning glasses because they're too rare. Perhaps the Oracle, or the Sisterhood, would know."

"I'm glad Royster is here," Kiara said with a sigh. She glanced at Tice. "I want you to give him access to all of the palace archives. He's spent a lifetime studying magical lore. Let's see what he can find out for us about all of the gifts."

Kiara was thoughtful for a moment. "And in the meantime, can you please start thinking of the magical items it might be handy to focus with the glass? It might also not hurt to start thinking about the local places of power: temples, shrines, sacred mounds, haunted caves, that sort of thing. Plot them on a map. Maybe we'll come up with something. There has to be a reason the ghost thought it was important for me to have this."

"As you wish," Felix said. A glint in his eyes told Kiara that the quest intrigued him, and that his mind was already churning with possibilities.

Kiara picked up the polished bone runes and was about to let them spill through her fingers when Brother Felix caught her hand before the first rune could fall. "Please don't do that, Your Majesty," he said breathlessly.

"Why not?"

Felix helped Kiara return the runes to the velvet cloth. "Rune magic is a delicate thing," he said. "Many seers believe that to spill the runes is to invite fate. One does not do so lightly."

"I understand." Kiara's finger stroked the smooth bone surface of a rune. "I think these are the gift of the queen who believed too much in fortune-tellers. An odd gift, don't you think?"

"She was called by the rune for fate?" Felix asked.

Kiara nodded. "She said that believing in predictions brought them about, and that she should have forged her own path rather than trying to find or evade what others said was fated for her."

"Then you have a lot in common with her." Cerise's observation startled everyone. "After all, the Divisionists think you're a traitor. The Durim aren't likely to believe you're really 'goddess blessed' if they don't recognize our particular goddess. Alvior and his foreign navy think you're either not going to return to Isencroft or are too weak to hold the throne. It's up to you to follow your own path and prove them wrong . . . and prove us right," she added with a smile.

"I think I'll take these to the Oracle and see what she makes of them," Kiara said, wishing that she had a hot cup of *kerif* instead of the watered wine that threatened to make her sleepy.

Balaren knelt beside the sword, studying it carefully without touching it. "I'm old enough to remember the eight clans," he said ruefully. "Funny thing about immortality. If you exist long enough, useless information may one day become valuable."

"What do you recall?" Kiara asked, leaning forward and hoping that shifting her position would help to keep her awake.

"Lord Gabriel and I are from the same times," Balaren said quietly. "We remember when the Winter Kingdoms were wild lands ruled by warlords. Even among men who respected no law but their own, the eight clans of Isencroft were feared and given their due." He paused, looking into the distance as he remembered a time long past.

"When I was mortal, I was a soldier in the army of Warlord Ifran in Margolan. Ifran's lands were on the border of what are now Margolan and Isencroft. War was nearly constant in those days, as the great lords fought for territory, trade routes, even women. The Margolan warlords were brutal and ruthless. Yet

I'd have gone up against them any day rather than face the armies of the eight clan lords of Isencroft."

"Why?"

"Legend said that the eight clan lords were descended from the direct offspring of the old gods. Back in those days, before the time of the Sacred Lady, most people worshipped their family spirits or the spirits of the rocks and trees and rivers where they made their livelihood. But many people worshipped the Shrouded Ones: Peyhta, Konost, and Shanthadura. Legend has it that the Wolf God came disguised as a man to each of the Shrouded Ones and seduced them. When they realized he had tricked them, it was too late. They were already pregnant with his seed.

"The Shrouded Ones hated the Wolf God for his trickery, all the more so when they realized that each bore more than one babe. Each of them gave birth to triplets, and when the babes were born, the Shrouded Ones decided to destroy the Wolf God's sons. Peyhta threw her three sons into a deep cave. Konost cast hers into the ocean. Shanthadura set her sons on the top of a mountain and called down fire and lightning. Yet the babes did not die."

"What happened?" Kellen asked, with an attentiveness that made Balaren smile.

"Konost's sons were found by fishermen and raised near the coast, where they became rich traders. Shanthadura's sons were found by goat shepherds, who took them in and taught them how to become prosperous farmers and herders. Two of Peyhta's sons were found by miners, where they learned to find precious stones underground. The third of Peyhta's sons is said to have crawled away and gotten lost, finding his way to the surface far away from his brothers, among a nomadic people who were excellent horsemen. That son, by the way," Balaren said with a glance toward Kiara, "is credited with becoming the founder of the line of Adares kings."

"If the eight warlords are the children of the Shrouded Ones, won't that sword play right into the Durim's quest to bring back Shanthadura's worship?" Cerise asked, aghast.

Balaren chuckled. "Who do you think banished her worship in Isencroft in the first place? When the sons of the Shrouded Ones were grown and learned how their mothers had tried to kill them, they swore vengeance and forbade the worship of the three goddesses. They were rather ruthless about enforcing the ban, slaughtering the priests and priestesses, destroying the shrines, murdering the faithful, and seizing any valuable temple goods. Within a few years, the old ways were gone, except among those in the most remote areas and a few who kept the rituals in secret."

Kiara grimaced. "Which explains where the Durim came from."

"I'm afraid so."

Kiara gently lifted the sword and turned it in her hands. It warmed to her touch immediately, though the grip was obviously made for a man. She turned to Balaren. "So if the legends are right, the eight clans were the mortal enemies of Shanthadura and the Durim?"

"That's correct."

She smiled. "Then this might be just the sword for the war we face, don't you think?" With a groan, she rose and stretched. "If it's not already dawn, it must be close to it. I'd best ride for the temple to see the Oracle before I fall asleep."

Balaren gave a deep bow. "Patov and I must remain here in the crypts until nightfall, but Jorven can accompany you," he said with a glance toward the *vyrkin*, who nodded.

"Captain Remir and four of the guards will ride with you," Allestyr added. He held up a hand to forestall Kiara's objection. "Until you see the Oracle and make a public appearance, you haven't quite completed the requirements to convey the throne.

We need to take every precaution to keep you—and the baby—safe."

Reluctantly, Kiara nodded. "Let's go then. I suspect it would make a poor impression for me to fall asleep during the Oracle's prophecy." She gathered up the items in the velvet cloth and carefully lifted the sword, lost in thought as they wound their way out of the necropolis and back to the corridors of Aberponte.

All too soon, Kiara and her protectors were on their way to the temple of the Aspect Chenne, where the Oracle resided. "You've been to the temple before, haven't you, m'lady?" Remir asked, riding beside Kiara.

"A little over two years ago, before I went on my Journey. It was the Oracle who sent me to Westmarch, and because of that, I met Tris and, well, everything changed."

Remir raised an eyebrow. "Including the history of the Winter Kingdoms."

Kiara looked away uncomfortably. "I guess so."

"Aside from the fact that you've been up all night, you don't seem very excited."

Kiara sighed. "I agree with Father. I prefer advice that isn't wrapped in riddles. And after the ghost's warning about predictions, well, it didn't make me feel any better about this whole thing."

Remir chuckled. "Then you'll be following both the spirit of your father and the advice of the ghost queen if you're skeptical. That's not a bad thing. Queens shouldn't believe everything they hear."

The forest seemed unnaturally silent when they hitched their horses to trees just outside the edge of the temple grounds. The Oracle's temple was in a large clearing. The last time Kiara had visited was by moonlight, and she had been awed by how the white marble glistened even at night. In daylight, the temple shone and a reflecting pool sparkled in the sun. Beyond the pool, altar fires burned. The clearing was ringed by a ravine-shrine on three sides. In the glade, Kiara could see the statues of Isencroft's military heroes, favored by the warrior-Aspect Chenne.

Falcons shrieked and fluttered as Kiara and the others passed the mews. Kiara breathed a sigh of thanks that she had left Jae at home. She stopped, and then motioned the others to follow her as she left the path, heading toward a large monument.

"Looks like Balaren knows his legends," Kiara murmured. The marble carving showed eight men crouched or standing with swords upraised over the prone form of a shrouded woman. She touched the pommel of the sword the ghost had given her and felt a faint hum of energy in response.

"It's probably not a good thing to keep the Oracle waiting," Remir prompted.

With a glance over her shoulder at the monument of the eight clan warlords, Kiara turned back to the path. Ahead of her was a raised marble platform with eight broad steps, surrounded by eight gleaming marble pillars. Standing in the center of the platform was a white-robed woman. Kiara approached slowly and knelt, bowing her head. From her basket, she withdrew a gift of honey cakes and ale, the traditional offering to the Sacred Lady.

"Your offering has been accepted, Kiara Sharsequin, daughter of Donelan, Queen of Isencroft. Rise, and ask your questions. If it is given to me to answer, I will do so."

Next, Kiara took out the items the spirit counselors had given to her and laid them at the feet of the Oracle. She drew a deep breath and squared her shoulders, hoping the Oracle could not see how nervous she was. "My Lady," she began, relieved her voice was steady, "I would hear your wisdom on the gifts of my spirit counselors, but more than that, I seek to understand what magic ties the *nenkah* to the child I carry within me, and the babe I left in Margolan."

The Oracle's cowl obscured her face, and the long sleeves of her robe covered her hands, making Kiara wonder if any physical being was beneath the robes. Yet she knew from her last encounter that the Oracle was actually not one woman, but many, and that the priestesses of Chenne would be called by the spirit of the goddess to prophesy in her name.

"Wise questions for a new queen." The Oracle inclined her cowled head to survey the items laid at her feet.

"Consanguinity. Focus. Fate and charisma. Powerful tokens. Magic, all of them."

"All?" Kiara asked, giving a questioning look at the beaded necklace.

"Blood conveys magic, as blood draws magic. Only fools shed blood to work magic. The most powerful magic courses with the blood through living veins. Blood ties are among the strongest magic."

The Oracle moved her arm to point to the sword. "The ability to rally men to fight against great odds is also powerful magic. Blood alone does not guarantee it, nor does a crown. Yet for those who possess it and would use it wisely, it can turn the tide of fate."

Next, the Oracle pointed to the burning glass. "Pick up the glass."

Kiara complied, holding it with both hands along its narrow edge.

"Hold it above the runes and draw on not just your own magic, but the magic around you, from this place, and from me."

Kiara shut her eyes and held the burning glass over the bone runes. She called to the place in herself where she had always found the faint magic to do scryings, and to her surprise, power leaped to answer her call. Kiara visualized that power flowing through her chest and into her arms, her hands, and, finally, the lens of the burning glass. Tentatively, she stretched out her senses to the grotto around her, aware for the first time that magic clung to every statue and tree, to the fountains and the still waters of the reflecting pool. Gradually, she felt the warm rush of magic answer her call, felt what her mind pictured as a gossamer sheath of golden light flow toward her from everything in the glade, and felt that power glide down her arms, through her hands, into the lens and channeled the magic to the runes.

"Open your eyes, Kiara. Behold."

Kiara opened her eyes and saw that the burning glass in her hands glowed with golden light. Diffuse at the edges, too bright to stare at in the center, the light streamed down through the curved base of the lens and bathed the runes in its glow. As Kiara watched, the runes began to tumble of their own accord until they lay still in a new configuration.

Unbidden, the golden light began to withdraw, washing back like a receding tide, and Kiara felt her own magic subside. The glow faded and disappeared, and Kiara lowered the burning glass.

"Look to the runes, Kiara of Isencroft. *Est*, the rune of darkness, lies at cross-quarters to *Telhon*, family. *Telhon* in this position is masculine, and means father or son. The tip is pointed downward. Son. Son of Darkness. *Sai*, the death rune, faces *Aneh*, the rune of Chaos. Beside them is *Vasht*, the rune of burial. Most unusual. These three runes lie akimbo, signifying war. War among the dead, in the places of the dead. Whether Chaos is the outcome or originator, I cannot tell. But *Katen*, the rune of succession, depends upon the outcome of that war." The Oracle paused. The next bone rune lay blank side up. "Most unusual. This rune follows *Katen*. It should speak to succession, yet it refuses to speak."

"When my son Cwynn was born, every rune lay blank side up. The runes refused to speak," Kiara said quietly.

"There is one more rune. *Tivah*, the rune for the Flow of magic. *Tivah* fell out of order. It should be between *Katen* and the rune that is blank, and yet it chose to fall last. It is a portent that the Flow plays an important part in what is to come." The Oracle's hand dropped to her side. "That is all the runes say to me."

"Thank you, m'lady," Kiara said, making the sign of the Lady. "But what of my sons? Why do I sense Cwynn's presence near the *nenkah*? How is it that the *nenkah* breathes and is warm to my touch when the coronation should have transferred its power back to me? How did it reach out to the child I carry?"

The Oracle inclined her head as if listening to a voice only she could hear. She did not speak, and Kiara feared her questions would go unanswered. Finally, the Oracle returned her attention to Kiara.

"Your son, Cwynn. I see a knife, poison."

"Yes, m'lady. An assassin stabbed me with a knife tainted with wormroot when I carried Cwynn. I almost lost him. He seems healthy, but he's not . . . right. Tris can sense no power in him, but Cheira Talwyn believes he is stronger than we know. I fear he may not be able to take the throne."

"Wormroot blocks a mage's power, but so much, so early, has opened Cwynn to the power of the Flow long before he can control that power. He is lost in it, adrift, too young to know it from himself."

"And the *nenkah*?"

The Oracle was silent for a moment. "Someone hunts your child. They seek to use his power. After you left him, he fled the darkness. A child follows its mother. Some part of his consciousness found your magic in the Flow and followed you here, where he found your spirit in the *nenkah* and took refuge. Your magic was imprinted on the *nenkah* and part of your spirit, and so he took refuge there."

"Can he be made whole?" Another terrifying possibility occurred to Kiara. "Does he live?"

"He lives. But he is not whole. Dispel the darkness, and he can be led back to himself and the last of your spirit will return."

"How can he live if his consciousness is here, in the *nenkah*?"

"Consciousness I sense, but not a soul. His essence has been split."

"Did the . . . darkness do that? Cwynn's too young to know—"

"Fish emerge from their eggs and swim. Hatchlings fly. Turtles walk as soon as they leave the egg. Abilities do not have to be understood to be done." She paused. "Cwynn's consciousness searched for you and recognized you, and the energy of the babe you carry. Guard the *nenkah* as you would your son."

"And the child I carry?"

"The future is uncertain. A War of Unmaking is upon us. If you survive the battle, the son you will bear will be a great leader, but not a mage. Whether he is a king or a renegade depends upon the outcome of the war. He will rise up against his enemies and challenge the Abyss itself." The Oracle grew quiet. "Leave me now. I have told you all I see. The blessing of Chenne be upon you."

13

Tris Drayke fled for his life. Darkness itself pursued him, neither living nor dead nor undead. Ancient and evil. Powerful. The darkness lapped at his heels like water. It snapped at his legs and slipped like a snare around his feet. To fall into the darkness was to perish. He could feel the darkness pull at him. It hungered for the light of his life thread. It thirsted for his magic, his power. It wanted his soul.

Tris ran for the clear, pale moonlight, but as he neared it, the darkness threatened to overtake him. He scrambled up a tumble of boulders to reach high ground lit by moonlight.

"*Lethyrashem!*"

The banishment spell pushed back the darkness, but Tris could feel the strength of the darkness warring with his own. He cast out his power, drawing on the Flow beneath him and on the spirits of the dead buried deep within this land that had once been a killing ground. He pulled that power into himself, mingling it with his life force, and cast it forward, toward the darkness, with a word of power.

"*Lethyrashem!*"

This time, the darkness scattered, receding like the undertow of the ocean. Tris felt it pull back, beyond the tree line, beyond the forest, back and back until he knew it was gone. He collapsed to his knees, utterly spent, as a blinding headache pounded.

"Tris? Tris, wake up. Come on, Tris, you're scaring me. Wake up now!"

The voice was barely audible, coming from a great distance, and the pounding in his head made Tris wonder if he was imagining it.

"Come on, Tris. Wake up now!" The voice was closer, more insistent, and there was a sharp crack of pain that blurred his vision. Another snap of pain dissolved the forest and the moonlit night. Tris woke on his cot in his own campaign tent, with a blinding reaction headache, his face feeling as if it were on fire. His vision became clearer, and he saw Coalan, his valet, standing over him, one hand raised as if to slap an errant child. When Coalan saw Tris's eyes open, the young man gave a weary smile and relaxed, dropping his hand.

"Beggin' your pardon, Tris. I know it's probably a hanging offense or worse to strike the king, but I'd already tried putting cold water on your face and nothing roused you." Coalan looked shaken, and Tris managed a reassuring smile.

"I imagine that slapping the king in the middle of a rescue is permitted under dire circumstances," Tris murmured.

Coalan hurried to pour a brandy for him and steadied him as Tris sat up. With practiced ease, Coalan withdrew a pinch of herbs from a pouch in the bag at the head of Tris's cot and mixed the herbs with a small amount of wine. "Drink this first. You sound like you've got one of your magic headaches."

Tris complied, grimacing. Just moving his jaw to swallow hurt. "The headache isn't magic. It's caused by magic."

"You get them often enough to make me quite glad I'm plain old Coalan, and not a mage."

Coalan had shown enough pluck and valor that Tris hardly thought of him as "plain," but his head hurt too much to argue.

"That wasn't just a bad dream." Coalan gave him an appraising look. Tris grimaced, realizing how often this sort of thing must happen for Coalan to recognize something few people other than mages ever experienced.

Tris set aside the wineglass and sipped the brandy. "No. It wasn't a bad dream. There was power. Not a vision. Something was after me. It didn't want my life or my magic. It wanted my soul."

"Soul thief. Can someone hollow the living?"

Tris managed a wry half smile. "You really are listening when you're sitting in the back of the tent, aren't you?"

Coalan gave a broad smile. "My father always told me foolishness pours out of an open mouth, but wisdom sneaks in through the ears." Despite the seriousness of impending war and soul-thieving darkness, it was clear that Coalan still regarded his service to Tris as the greatest adventure of his life.

"I've never heard of such a thing as hollowing the living, but then again," Tris said, groaning as he shifted position and his head pounded, "I'd only heard rumors of soul harvests and hollowing before this war."

"Uncle Ban thinks Temnotta has a dark summoner," Coalan said, all mirth gone from his voice. Tris looked up at Coalan and saw a resolve that told him Coalan probably had a better understanding of the war at hand than many of the ranking officers.

"I think that's not just likely; it's certain. I can sense power just beyond where I can reach it. It feels dark, and strong."

"You've fought dark mages before, and won. And you destroyed the spirit of the Obsidian King. If you could do all that, then can't you beat this one, too?"

Tris closed his eyes, letting the potion work its healing, warming the chill deep inside that had nothing to do with the autumn night. "Jonmarc Vahanian is the best warrior in a generation, but I've seen him nearly die, twice. Once from being run through by a sword, and once from an assassin's knife. You can be the best and strongest, but it only takes one mistake."

"Uncle Ban said to tell you that he's sent reinforcements and scouts down the coast to the east. He said he thinks it's likely the invaders will look for a less defended harbor to land and flank us. They should be in place by morning."

Tris finished the last of his brandy and let it burn down his throat. "Good. Because I don't think the fleet is just going to go home."

Voices outside his tent flap drew both men's attention as a newcomer argued with the guards. "I have an important message for the king."

Tris and Coalan exchanged glances, recognizing a familiar voice that was out of place on the battlefield.

"It's the middle of the night," one of the guards challenged.

"I'm quite well aware of that," replied the newcomer.

"What's Mikhail doing here?" Tris asked, as Coalan rushed to the door of the tent just as a guard stuck his head inside.

"Begging your pardon, Your Majesty, but Mikhail is here to see you."

"Send him in."

Mikhail stepped through the tent flap as the guard returned to duty. He looked from Coalan to Tris and frowned. "Other than it being the middle of the night, did I come at a bad time? I get the feeling you weren't sleeping."

"It's a long story," Tris said, motioning for Mikhail to have a seat. "Is Kiara well? And Cwynn? What could possibly bring you out to the front lines of a war to carry a message?"

Mikhail met Tris's gaze. "It's not the kind of message I'd care to entrust to paper—or to a messenger. The first news is, King Donelan is dead."

"Mother and Childe," Tris murmured. "Beyral's omens predicted it, but we had no way to verify. How did he die?"

"Murdered. Someone bewitched one of the servants."

Tris felt grief well up in his chest. He had admired Donelan, and from their brief meeting at the royal wedding, Tris had looked forward to getting to know Kiara's father. "I'm so sorry. How is Kiara taking it?"

Mikhail's gaze was direct. "The letter that bore the news asked her to return to Isencroft. She rode for Isencroft weeks ago, with a handpicked guard, as well as Cerise and Royster. An Isencroft guard waited for her at the border. The Margolan soldiers reported transferring her safely to the Isencroft guards. Patov, Jorven, Antoin, and the other *vyrkin* and *vayash moru* who accompanied her as . . . civilians . . . will remain with her as protectors."

"What about Cwynn?"

Mikhail nodded. "Kiara was especially concerned about leaving Cwynn behind. She called for Alle and Lady Eadoin to care for him, along with Sister Essel and Sister Nardore. We tripled the guards on the palace to keep him safe from intruders."

Tris drew a long breath and let it out slowly. "It's too early to have heard anything back from Kiara. We'd talked about what might happen if the war went badly for Donelan, but truly, I never expected it to cost him his life." The herbed wine and the brandy were beginning to take the edge off of his headache, but he could feel new tension building in his neck and shoulders at Mikhail's news.

"How is Cwynn?" Tris paused and ran a hand across his eyes, rubbing his forehead. "I have to admit, she made a wise choice in calling Alle and Eadoin to the palace. There's no one I'd trust more to care for him."

Mikhail's pale features looked like they had been chiseled from stone, and his eyes did not reveal any emotion.

Tris felt his heart sink. "Something's gone wrong," he said quietly.

"I'm afraid so. Three nights after Kiara left Shekerishet, after the mages reinforced the wardings, something struck at Cwynn in his sleep. He began screaming and crying, and nothing would console him. The healers couldn't find anything amiss. Eadoin thought he acted terrified of something.

"Cwynn went limp. He breathes, he'll suckle, and his body functions as it should, but he hasn't awakened since then. He responds to no one, not to voices or chimes or even loud noises." A sad smile touched Mikhail's face. "Even your dogs can't rouse him. Cwynn usually laughed when they visited him. He loved it when they licked him and his happiness was very . . . loud. He was also fond of the ghost dog, your mastiff. It often sleeps next to Cwynn's crib." Mikhail frowned. "It was very odd . . . Right before Cwynn began screaming and crying, we all swore we heard a dog barking angrily, as if it was trying to frighten away an attacker or warn its owner. But your wolfhounds weren't in the room at the time."

"What do the mages say?" Tris swallowed hard to keep his voice even. He tried to breathe deeply, stemming the rise of panic he felt. *What use is it to be a king, and a mage, if I can't protect the ones I love?*

"Sister Essel and Sister Nardore used all the magical resources they had available to investigate," Mikhail replied.

"Did they find anything?"

"Nardore detected a . . . residue . . . of power that breached the wardings. She believes that whatever attacked Cwynn was looking for him in particular. No one else was troubled, not even by bad dreams," Mikhail added.

"And Essel?"

Mikhail met Tris's gaze. "Essel's magic focuses on energy.

She believes a part of Cwynn's soul was taken from him. All that remains is an empty shell."

Tris and Coalan exchanged an alarmed glance. "Soul harvest," Tris murmured.

"Hollowing," Coalan whispered.

Mikhail looked from one to the other and sat in silence as Tris described the attack he had just withstood. As Tris spoke, Mikhail's expression grew more somber. "What could the attacker hope to gain? Cwynn's just an infant."

Tris shrugged. "It could be a challenge to me, a way to call me out to fight someone who's certain that I'll defend Cwynn."

"So they took his spirit as a hostage," Mikhail replied.

Again, Tris gave a nod. "The second possibility worries me more. Cheira Talwyn believes that Cwynn has great power. She said he was a 'bridge.' Alyzza, the old sorceress at the Vistimar madhouse, warned me to 'protect the bridge.'"

He looked from Mikhail to Coalan. "Talwyn was right. Cwynn's been part of this, somehow, from the beginning. Whoever it is out there," he said, gesturing toward the coastline, "has more of an inkling about Cwynn's true power than we do."

"What are you going to do?" Mikhail's voice was level.

"One way or another, I'm going to get my son back."

Outside the tent, Tris and the others heard raised voices as the guards challenged another visitor. "You can't go in there."

"It appears your king is not asleep." The voice was unknown to Tris, who listened more closely.

"He's in a meeting. You can't just barge in—" the guard argued.

"My matter is pressing. I bring news from the Sworn. The information can't wait."

Tris nodded to Coalan, who stepped to the tent flap. "It's all right. We weren't getting any sleep anyhow," Coalan said, with a nod of thanks to the guard.

The Dread

Their visitor wore the rough-woven clothing of the Sworn. His black hair was woven into small braids with intricate silver talismans. The man's dark eyes were bright and alert, and he glanced around the small group assembled in the tent until his gaze lingered on Tris.

"Your Majesty. I bear an urgent message from Cheira Talwyn." He made a perfunctory bow and handed Tris a folded piece of parchment. Tris frowned, recognizing the handwriting as that of his cousin, Jair Rothlandorn.

"I wonder what made Jair send a rider in the middle of the night," Tris said, carefully breaking the seal.

Tris—I'm writing this on behalf of Talwyn, who said to tell you that her written Common is as imperfect as her spoken Common, and that both carry a heavy accent. Talwyn was preparing for the feast of Sohan, when, to her surprise, the Dread did not wait for her to come to them. They sought her out in dreams with a warning. The warning was for you.

She dreamed of a broken lock and a missing key, of a sailor adrift on the currents of a swift river, and of two soldiers battling atop a bridge. Then she said it was as if a fog lifted, and she felt the presence of the Dread. "We would speak with the Summoner-King," the Dread told her. The dream ended.

Neither Talwyn nor I know what to make of this, Tris. I can't advise you on whether or not to accept the Dread's invitation. Such requests are not made lightly. At the same time, we don't know whose "side" the Dread are on or whether or not they intend to take sides. Please, Tris, use caution.

If you come, Emil will guide you to our camp. Talwyn and I trust him with our lives. Talwyn also begs you to accept the amulet Emil has for you. Talwyn crafted it herself, and her magic is strong. She said that it will protect you on your journey through dark places.

I know that a king cannot lightly leave his troops at such a time, but Talwyn believes it is critical for you to make the journey. You know you are welcome and safe among the Sworn. May the Lady cover you with her protection. Even in such dire times, it is always good to see you, Tris. Ride carefully. Jair

Tris read the letter aloud to the others and drew a deep breath. "I'm open to your thoughts about this," he said, looking to Mikhail.

"In light of what has happened at Shekerishet," Mikhail said, "I don't see how you have a choice. You have to go."

Tris nodded. "That's what I make of it, too." He looked to Coalan. The young man had put a fresh pot of water on the brazier and busied himself setting out a repast of hard rolls and sausage, though dawn—and breakfast—was still candlemarks away.

Coalan looked sheepish as he realized Tris was watching him. "Sorry. I just figured that with all the company, you'd want some food and some hot tea." He glanced at Mikhail. "I'll get fresh blood from the butcher."

"Go find Soterius. Senne, too. Might as well wake up Fallon and Beyral. Tell them we've got a 'situation' to discuss and it won't wait." He paused, then sighed. "And after that, tell the stable master to have my horse ready. I'll need you to pack a bag for me." He frowned, thinking. "Set out both swords."

"Both?"

Tris nodded. He understood why Coalan hesitated. Tris rarely carried Nexus, leery of its not-yet-fully understood power, and the warning that its use stole a breath of the user's soul. Still, if he was going to seek out the Dread in the places of the dead, he doubted that his regular sword would be of much use.

"Cheira Talwyn bade me give this to you," Emil said. He held out a small pouch. It was made of cloth painted with runes and markings Tris did not recognize, but as soon as he took the small package, he could feel the signature of her magic.

An amulet on a leather cord spilled into his palm. A round slice of agate was bound with hair, rough twine, and a thin copper wire to a piece of hematite. Tris recognized all of the stones as charms for warding and protection, amplified by the hair, hemp, and copper. Tris bowed his head and permitted Emil to fasten the amulet around his throat.

"You do us a great honor to wear Cheira Talwyn's gift," Emil said.

Coalan set the tray of rolls and meat out for them as Tris motioned for Emil to sit. Then Coalan disappeared from the tent with a hurried aside to the puzzled guards. Tris and the others sat in silence, making only a halfhearted attempt to eat. Before long, Soterius ducked past the guards and into the tent. He gave a startled glance toward Mikhail and Emil.

"I was wondering what made you call for a war council in the middle of the night," he said, taking a seat next to Tris on the floor of the tent. "Bad news from home?" he said with a look toward Mikhail.

"From home . . . and the Sworn," Tris replied.

Gradually, the others filed in and sat on the crowded floor of the tent. Tris gave a brief recap of the news Mikhail brought from Shekerishet, followed by Jair's letter.

"You're going to go, aren't you." It was more statement than question, and Tris knew from the tone just what Soterius thought of the idea.

"I'm inclined to," Tris admitted. "That's why I called the group together. We've already had one attack from the invaders.

So far, I've tried to use a minimum of my magic, to not show our hand too early in case the invaders are trying to size us up. But the next attack might be in earnest, and my magic might be needed here to turn the tide."

Senne frowned. "How far away is the Sworn's camp?"

"A half-day's ride behind the lines and to the east," Emil replied. "But soon our Ride will bring us within a few candlemarks of the battle lines."

"It's not the journey that worries me," Sister Fallon said. "We don't know what kind of magic will be involved once Tris arrives at the camp. It might be a candlemark—or days—before he can return."

"Can we trust the Dread?" Senne's raspy voice broke in. "How do we know they're not in league with the invaders, trying to lure Tris into some kind of trap? For all we know, they had something to do with what happened to Cwynn."

"Possible," Fallon admitted, "but I don't think it's likely. The Dread have avoided getting involved with mortal conflicts for over a thousand years. From what Tris and Cheira Talwyn have said, the Dread are stirring now because someone—or something—is threatening to raise the Nachele, the dark spirits the Dread guard. I don't think the Dread have called for Tris to help us with our problems. I suspect their interest is more self-centered. We may have a common enemy."

"And in war, the enemy of my enemy is my friend," Soterius finished for her.

"Exactly."

Tris looked at Soterius and Senne. "What are the scouts reporting? Have you heard anything from the Sentinels or the fleets? How likely is an attack over the next few days?"

Senne shrugged. "Good commanders don't give away their moves in advance. I don't think they're going to give up and go home."

Soterius leaned forward. "When the Temnottan ships pulled back from the harbor after the first engagement, they moved out of range of the Sentinels. Nisim and I think they've dispatched ships to the east, where the coast makes an easier landing spot. They'll try to flank us."

"You've sent troops?"

Soterius nodded. "All we could spare. I bet a division on it."

"It's a gamble, no matter how you play it," Senne grumbled. "Your father was a man who believed in intuition. Whether you call it regent magic or damn fine luck, his guesses worked out far more often than they didn't. So how about it, Your Majesty? What is your gut telling you?"

Tris took a deep breath. "I think Soterius is right, the Temnottans are going to make a move very soon. That makes this especially difficult. Someone went to a great deal of trouble to attack Cwynn. He's my son. I would have to go because of that. But I believe that he is a key to this war. And I intend to bring him back."

"I'd recommend you ride in disguise," Soterius said. "Not that I doubt your fighting skill," he said with a glance from Emil to Tris, "but I'll feel better sending half a dozen of the *Telorhan* with you—just in case." He held up a hand to forestall Tris's protest. "Once you reach the Sworn camp, I know you'll be safe. But there are still Durim out there as well as whatever it was that tried to attack you tonight, and we don't need an opportunist getting off a lucky shot."

Reluctantly, Tris nodded. "Anything else?"

Soterius gave him a grim, lopsided grin. "Yeah. Just remember what Jonmarc used to say. 'If you get your royal ass fried, the rest of us hang.' It's still true, so be careful."

14

Just moments after Tris and Emil and the five *Telorhan* guards reached the outskirts of the Sworn camp, Tris spotted a tall man running toward them. Jair Rothlandorn was dressed like the rest of the Sworn warriors and armed with a broad, deadly *stelian* sword. "Ho there! Are you come to keep the feast with us!"

Despite the circumstances, Tris could not keep from smiling. Jair answered Tris's smile with a grin of his own, welcoming Tris with a slap on the back and an embrace when Tris swung down from his horse.

"We came as quickly as we could," Tris said as he walked with Jair farther into the camp. Emil and the guards fell behind them, allowing a respectful distance and the semblance of privacy for their conversation.

"I know this is a bad time for you," Jair began.

Tris waved off his apology. "More than you think." Briefly, he explained the attack on Cwynn and the unsuccessful attack he had fended off himself.

"You think that the two attacks are related to Talwyn's vision—and the Dread's request?"

Tris shrugged. "These days everything seems to be related." He met Jair's gaze. "If there's a chance that the Dread might know how I can rescue Cwynn, well, I can't pass that up."

Jair's gaze wandered to where a small, curly-haired young boy practiced in the center of the camp with his bolas. "If it were Kenver, I'd feel the same way." He paused. "Come on. Talwyn's waiting for you."

Tris looked around him as they walked through the camp. Despite the obvious war-readiness of all of the young men and women of fighting age, there was an unexpected air of celebration to the camp. In the center of the temporary village created by the Sworn's *gars* was the beginning of a bonfire. Boys and girls too young to fight carried wood to the fire pit. Large wooden bowls filled with apples, pinecones, and acorns were gathered to one side of the camp's center.

As Tris watched, several of the old women came to the camp center with their aprons bulging. The young girls ran up with empty bowls and unloaded the delivery of eggs, seeds, and more nuts. Near where the fire would be, Tris saw a strange, bean-shaped pod made of cloth and twine hanging from a post. He also noted that he and his guards were not the only strangers among the Sworn.

"Is all this for the harvest feast?"

Jair nodded. "War or no war, the Sworn take Sohan very seriously. It's the last of the autumn festivals, after the Moon Feast and Haunts, but even though it's after the equinox, it's special to the Sworn. It's the Feast of Changes."

Tris looked again at the offerings in the bowls. "Eggs become chickens," he said quietly. "Nuts become trees. Seeds grow into plants." He looked at Jair questioningly. "But what about all the outsiders?"

Jair chuckled. "Shapeshifters, all of them. Some *vyrkin*, but also some who can shift into the other forms of the Lady's Consorts: the stawar, the bear, and the eagle. We'll have a few *vayash moru* as well, who understand transformation between the living and the dead."

223

"And that thing hanging from the post?" Tris asked, jerking his head toward the odd-shaped object.

"An effigy of a caterpillar's cocoon. At the festival, it's Talwyn's honor and duty to bless the offerings. Then she uses her magic to let a small bevy of birds loose from the cocoon." He shrugged. "The Sworn live with the land even more closely than farmers do. Sohan honors the death of autumn and the coming of winter before the year is reborn in the spring. I hope you'll have the chance to pass the feast with us."

Tris sighed. "That depends on the Dread."

When he entered the *gar* Jair shared with his family, Talwyn jumped to her feet and greeted him with a smile of welcome and an embrace. "I'm so glad my message reached you. I didn't sleep well last night, fearing that Emil might not be able to find you." Although Talwyn spoke Common with the heavy accent of the language of the Sworn, her voice was lilting and musical, and not for the first time, Tris saw what tempted Jair away from the throne of Dhasson.

"Last night brought many messages," Tris said.

"Oh?" Jair asked. Talwyn grimaced at him.

"Despite war and festivals and even the Dread, we need to make your cousin welcome," Talwyn said, beckoning for Tris to sit near her on one of many large cushions on the floor. "Please don't think me frivolous. There is power in ritual, even something as simple as welcoming a guest correctly. That's why we keep the feast days, even when it is not convenient. Hearth magic is strong protection, and we bypass it at our peril."

Talwyn went to an ornate metal pot that sat over its own small fire. From it, she poured the thick, dark tea the Sworn preferred, its nutty flavor softened with syrup made from sweet grass. She brought him the tea in a copper cup that matched the pot's intricate decoration, and Tris recognized sigils of warding and protection worked into the beautiful scrollwork. Talwyn brought him a plate of goat cheese with honey and pieces of thin, hard bread. Tris accepted the food gratefully, hungry after the ride. Afterward, she brought out a carafe of *vass* and poured a small amount for each of them. Then Talwyn settled back onto her cushion with her legs crossed.

"Tell me of your other messages, Tris. Please, hold nothing back."

Tris did as Talwyn requested, and both Jair and Talwyn listened in silence as he recounted his vision and the attack on Cwynn.

"You were right about Cwynn being a pawn in all of this," Tris concluded.

Talwyn frowned and shook her head. "Important, yes. But not a pawn. Such power, even at a young age, takes its own course."

"It had crossed my mind, before Emil arrived, to ask your guidance and perhaps even seek counsel from the Dread. That they've asked for me now—"

Talwyn nodded. "It cannot be a coincidence. But be wary. My dreams have been dark. The Nachele no longer sleep. Never before have I felt concern from the Dread. They are not exactly fearful, but they are not pleased. Any help they give to you is likely to come at a price."

"My child's life and my kingdom are on the line," Tris said. "It's already a high-stakes wager."

By sundown, the festival in the center of the camp was well underway. Talwyn had completed her duties as shaman and as the daughter of the chief, leaving Pevre to oversee the festivities and watch over Kenver.

Talwyn, Tris, and Jair stood in the center of a warded workspace Talwyn had created next to the nearest barrow. The *Telorhan* stood a short distance away, on guard to make sure they were not disturbed. Talwyn had marked a circle of runes and sigils. She was dressed in her shaman's robes, and the embroidery along the hem seemed to move and pulse.

Tris carried Nexus in a scabbard at his hip. His regular sword was easily drawn from a back scabbard, but he doubted it would do him much good. Around his neck, he wore the amulet Talwyn had made for him, and Marlan the Gold's talisman. At Talwyn's nod that all was ready, Tris closed his eyes and centered his magic.

"The Dread have asked to meet with you on the Plains of Spirit. That rules out using the smokewalkers and the Spirit Guides," Talwyn said. "It's as close to face to face as you can get without entering the barrows, and it's only possible because you're a summoner."

"You don't like it."

Talwyn shook her head. "It makes you more vulnerable than if we walked the smoke. More of your life energy will be between realms. But the Dread are the ones dictating the terms."

The autumn air was cold, misting his breath. Tris let his magic flow down through his body, through the soles of his feet, down into the cool ground. He opened his mage senses, aware of the hum of magic that surrounded both the living and the dead. His summoner's magic sensed the powerful life forces of the Sworn and the shapeshifters, and the different energy of the *vayash moru*.

Stretching out his senses, Tris heard the rustle of dry bones and ragged shrouds, and the whispers of the dead reached him. He did not turn his full attention to them, and they did not cry out to him.

Tris listened for the voice of the Dread. He stretched out his magic toward the ancient mound and listened. He could feel the layers of strong power that interlaced over and through the burial mound, magic placed long ago and reinforced age after age, both from outside and from within. The magic carried the signatures of many wielders, too many to count. He felt the magic of the Sworn, and other, less benign powers.

You heeded our call. The voice sounded in Tris's mind, seeming to come from everywhere at once and nowhere at all. It was a low rumble, and Tris felt it as much as heard it.

I came.

Walk with us on the Plains of Spirit.

Tris let his magic shift inside of him, allowing his consciousness to separate from his physical form, moving into the Nether realm between life and death, the Plains of Spirit.

Tris was glad for Talwyn's protections, both the wardings that she set and her constant chant. The Nether was a dangerous realm. More than once, he had encountered *dimonns* in this realm. Whatever power had attempted to hollow him might also find the Nether to its liking.

They cannot harm you. The low voice seemed closer now. *Those things that you fear, fear us more. They will not trouble us while we meet.*

Tris forced down his apprehension and focused on Cwynn. There was a ripple in the Nether, and Tris saw a dark shadow roll across the burial mound. He could sense the personality, and the great age, of the shadow.

Why have you called me from battle?

We have merely called you from one battle to another, Summoner-King. The war to which we call you is one your army cannot fight.

Why should I fight a second battle? Name the enemy and his prize.

Tris could hear the distant rumble of voices, as if the Dread held a muted conversation among themselves.

A dark summoner has risen in the East. He is called Scaith. He would raise the Nachele to do his bidding, and for the first time in a thousand years, the Nachele have roused from their slumber. Many have tried to do this; none have succeeded until now.

The Nachele are yours to guard. Can Scaith take them from you?

Tris heard the weariness of ages in the deep rumble of the Dread's voice. *It required a War of Unmaking to seal the Nachele within the barrows. We hoped never to see such destruction again, nor to be the cause of it. Even now, we hope that such a catastrophe can be averted. We are a match for the power of the Nachele, but Scaith has worked powerful blood magic to strengthen himself. Those you call the Durim, the Black Robes, have called on the power of the Shrouded Ones, strengthening Scaith with their sacrifices. The Durim are not alone. Scaith feeds his power with bloodshed and with the stolen souls and hollowed spirits of the dead. If you wish to prevail against Scaith, you must strengthen yourself.*

How?

You are the mage-heir of Bava K'aa, and of Lemuel, who became the Obsidian King. You wear the talisman of Marlan the Gold, who was your forebear.

Bava K'aa and Lemuel were my grandparents. Marlan was my ancestor. Their magic and their blood flow through me.

The Obsidian King was nearly as powerful as Scaith. He was called by many names: Darkness, Blood-Sower, Slaughterer. He gained through blood sacrifice a very rare magic: the ability to meld his magic with the Flow so completely that they became nearly indistinguishable. Scaith does not possess this magic. You must gain it, if you hope to fight him. Even then, it does not guarantee your success, only a fighting chance.

Tris felt his temper rise. *You want me to practice blood magic? You ask me to turn against everything I've learned, everything I am?*

More than one road leads to a destination. The Obsidian

King gained that power through blood magic. But there is one who possesses that power by accident of birth. Your son, Lemuel's great-grandson, the one you call Cwynn.

Tris caught his breath in surprise. *Cwynn's only an infant.*

The poison that endangered his birth opened him to great power. Even now, Scaith seeks him. And infant though he is, his will to survive has enabled him to hold off Scaith—at least for now.

Hold him off? How?

Scaith moved in the Nether to hollow your son's soul and take Cwynn's power for his own. Cwynn's instincts served him well. Like a rabbit knows how to flee a predator almost from its birth, Cwynn instinctively sent a part of his life force into hiding. His consciousness followed the child's mother to a relic far away from the threat. His vitality, that which breathes and makes the heart beat, remained in the body his consciousness left behind. Scaith could not hollow an incomplete soul. Your mage's wardings were sufficient to rush Scaith, who stole what was easiest. He stole the child's essence, his eternal being. You must regain what was stolen. You will need it as an ally in the war that is to come.

Tris struggled to understand. Part of Cwynn had followed Kiara—or her regent magic—to refuge in Isencroft. A remnant of his soul remained to keep his physical body alive—for now. But his essence, his eternal self, the portion that would, at his death, cross the Gray Sea to rest in the Lady, was Scaith's prize of war. Tris felt rage at the violation, and he used that rage to fuel determination.

Tell me what I have to do to bring him home.

Again, the Dread conferred among themselves. *What are you willing to pay, Summoner-King, for your child?*

Tris raised his head to glare defiantly at the shadow. *Everything I have.*

Your life, certainly. Your kingdom?

There is no choice. If I allow Scaith to keep Cwynn's essence, he may be too powerful to destroy. Either way, my kingdom is forfeit.

Your soul?

If that is the only way, yes.

Well spoken, Summoner-King. We have watched you from afar. You have shown great courage. To save your son, you must enter the Abyss. Scaith has struck a deal with Konost, the Guide of Souls. Cwynn is a prisoner in her realm. You must bring him back.

Konost—one of the Shrouded Ones?

The shadow shifted in a way that Tris took as an indication of assent.

Scaith has made a blood pact with the Shrouded Ones to restore their worship in exchange for the Winter Kingdoms. Peyhta, the Soul Eater, hollows the souls and shares the feast with Scaith. Shanthadura bathes in the blood of sacrifices, sparing a few drops for her chosen champion. Konost has been promised a feast of death on the battlefield, with legions of new souls to torment.

You would have me fight a goddess? I'm most certainly not a god.

In the distance, Tris sensed what sounded like the rumble of grim laughter. *It's well that you are clear on that point, Summoner-King. You are indeed not a god. Nor do you need to be in order to prevail.*

Stop talking in riddles. Tell me what I have to do to save Cwynn. I have a war to fight.

For a moment, the shadow was silent, and Tris cursed his impatience.

Return here tomorrow night at dusk, on Sohan. Before the bells of midnight, light magic will be favored over dark. Bring

*with you Marlan's talisman, your spirit sword, and the amulet
you wear. They will serve you well. Take these with you also.*

The shadow stretched toward him, an opaque fluid movement,
and Tris fought a primal urge to flee. The tide of darkness
receded, leaving a small pile of objects at his feet.

*Our "gifts" exist in both the Nether and the mortal world.
When you return to us, we will open the barrow to you. You
must pass through eight gates in the Underrealm to reach the
Abyss. At each gate, a guard will ask for your passage token.
Give the gifts in the order in which they lie at your feet. You
will be able to pass through the gates. Take nothing, and do not
eat or drink anything, or you cannot return.*

*Once you pass the eighth gate, do not call to your son. Next,
you must face Konost. She will demand your soul as the price for
Cwynn's return. If you can win against her, you can retrieve
Cwynn's essence.*

And if not?

You will join him.

Tris looked at the items that lay at his feet. First was a wide
vambrace of polished silver. He placed it on his left forearm.
Next to the vambrace was a neck plate the size of his palm,
made of hammered gold. He clasped it around his throat. Beside
that was a thin circlet of bronze. The fourth item was a string
of grave beads. Fifth was a ring set with a beveled gem of onyx.
The sixth gift was a dagger chiseled from polished obsidian.
He gathered the items and placed the ring on his left hand and
the circlet on his head, and he slipped the other gifts into a
pouch at his belt. Tris took a second look at the seventh gift. It
was a human heart.

*Go back to the realm of the living. Keep the feast. The Cheira
is correct. There is great power in such things. Prepare yourself
for the battle. We will meet you at dusk.*

The shadow withdrew as quickly as it came, and it seemed

to Tris as if magic itself went with it for a moment. Had he been outside the Nether, he would have thought that the air had suddenly gone out of the space, leaving his chest heavy and burning. Grimly determined, Tris bent to retrieve the heart and then focused his magic on finding his way back to his body through the Plains of Spirit.

He returned to himself abruptly, with a thudding reaction headache from the strong magic. His knees buckled and he slumped to the ground. He could hear voices shouting around him, but they seemed distant and muted.

"Tris! Tris, come back to us. Come all the way back. All the way."

It was Jair's voice, and Tris heard an edge of fear in his cousin's tone. With effort, he released the last of his magic and shuddered. Strong hands grasped him by the shoulders and rolled him face up on the dry, brown grass. In the background, Tris could hear Talwyn chanting, dispelling the wardings.

"He's back." Jair turned to call over his shoulder, and Talwyn made a bow of thanks to the spirits before she rose and joined Jair at Tris's side.

"You were successful?"

Tris swallowed hard, blinking against the headache that pounded in his temple. "In reaching the Dread, yes. And I know what happened to Cwynn." Tris looked down at his right hand, where the heart had been clasped in his grip. His hand was empty.

Jair helped him sit with his back against a tree, while Talwyn brought him a cup of *vass* and a chunk of bread. "Eat. Remind your body that you are among the living," she urged.

They waited until Tris had taken a few sips of the strong drink and managed several bites of the bread. "I have a name now for the Temnottan summoner. Scaith," he told them. Jair and Talwyn listened in silence as Tris recounted his exchange with the Dread.

"If you're looking for the passage tokens, they're set out just as you described, in a line near where Talwyn was keeping vigil," Jair said with distaste in his voice as his gaze lingered on the gray heart that lay on the ground.

"You can't really mean to enter the Abyss," Talwyn challenged.

Tris drew a deep breath. "Is there a choice? Not only is Cwynn my son, but his fate seems to be tied up with this whole war, as you said. If Cwynn is a conduit to the Flow, then we don't dare allow Scaith to access that kind of power."

"The Dread said that it wasn't a guarantee of victory." Jair's voice reflected his concern.

"They said it wouldn't guarantee victory for *me*," Tris replied. "They never really said whether it would be enough for Scaith.

"I had the distinct feeling that my grandfather's power is involved in this somehow," Tris added. "When I get back to camp, I think I need to spend some time with that third diary of his. He tried to possess the same kind of ability to channel the Flow that Cwynn was born with. Maybe there's something in what he wrote that can help us . . . assuming I survive the journey into the Abyss," Tris added grimly.

Talwyn made a sign of warding against evil. "I believe it works in your favor that this battle occurs on Sohan night," she said quietly. "It's the third of the harvest feasts. First, the Moon Festival, to welcome the long nights and the autumn moon. Then, Haunts—the Feast of the Departed, on the equinox, to honor the dead and speak with their spirits.

"But Sohan is a darker festival," she mused aloud. "It's the feast day when the Sworn renew their vow to guard the Dread. It's also a requiem for the death of summer. In legend, the Summer King is killed by his brother, the Winter Prince, who rules from the Underrealm until the spring equinox, when the Summer King returns and slays his brother to take back the throne. In the legend, the battle begins at dusk and rages until midnight."

"When the Summer King dies."

Talwyn grimaced. "Well, yes. But it isn't permanent. The Summer King isn't destroyed. And no one said you had to relive the legend."

"Let's hope not."

"Uncle Tris! Wake up, you're missing the festival." A young boy's voice shrilled from the doorway of the tent. "Mother said you have to get up. Come on!"

With a groan, Tris rolled over, and then, blinking, sat up. Kenver stood in the doorway, silhouetted against the bright daylight.

"I'm coming. Give me a moment."

The headache of the evening before was gone, but a leaden feeling of anticipation for the night to come had replaced it. Tris dressed hurriedly, deep in thought. Even so, Kenver's unabashed enthusiasm managed to rouse a weak smile as his nephew grabbed him by the hand and dragged him out into the daylight.

A small fire burned in the center of the camp where a bonfire had raged the previous night. Already, the air smelled of roasting meat and baked goods. Musicians played an upbeat tune near the fire, and throughout the camp, Tris heard the shouts of children. Tris's guards followed him at a discreet distance.

"They're racing the horses, Uncle Tris. Come on!" Kenver tugged harder at Tris's hand, and Tris let himself be pulled toward the edge of camp. The Sworn were well known for their horsemanship and the fine plains horses that they rode. Tris had heard Jair's proud comments that as young as Kenver was, he showed every promise of following in his tribe's abilities. Kenver pointed excitedly as the older boys and girls, most of them younger than fifteen summers old, put their horses through exacting turns and leaps.

"If I live to be a hundred, I don't think I could ever learn to ride as well as Sworn children do by their tenth birthday," Jair observed from behind them. Kenver grabbed his father's hand, letting go of Tris.

"I suspect Kenver will be out there long before he's ten," Tris replied. Some of the riders showed horsemanship skills as good as any cavalry soldiers, and Tris did not doubt that the Sworn's renown as warriors was due in no small part to their skill astride a horse.

"Just so long as he doesn't expect me to keep up with him!"

Although the coming confrontation was never far from Tris's mind, he allowed Kenver and Jair to escort him through the camp. While he found his mind wandering back to the conversation with the Dread, Tris did his best to accept the hospitality of his hosts.

No matter where they wandered, Tris found himself offered food. He started to decline, only to have Jair say something in the consonant-heavy language of the Sworn to the woman who offered Tris a trencher of meat. Jair took the meat and handed it to Tris.

"Talwyn was very specific. She said I'm to make sure you eat and drink today so that you're grounded in this world before your journey tonight."

They found a place to sit in the shade of a large tree. The leaves had turned to brilliant shades of red, and a light breeze rippled through them, dappling the ground with sunlight. For a moment, the smells, sounds, tastes, and sights of the camp seemed more intense than ever, reminding Tris of what he would be leaving behind when he entered the Underrealm.

"There's a little matter I need to discuss with you," Jair said as Tris finished his food. "About adoption."

"What?"

Jair chuckled. "Blame Talwyn. She had the idea. Do you

remember her mentioning that Sohan is when the Sworn reaffirm their vow to the Dread?"

"Yes."

"Well, it's also when the Dread renew their promise to defend the living against the Nachele. Most years, it feels like a formality. This year it's more of a pressing issue."

"What's this got to do with adoption?"

"Talwyn and Pevre decided that it might not hurt to have you acknowledged as one of our blood, a member of the Sworn. It's not something that's done very often. In fact, it's been long enough since the last time that Pevre had to consult the old writings to remember how the ceremony goes. You should be honored."

"I am. But didn't they adopt you?"

Jair shrugged. "My case is a little different. There's a perpetual bond between the Sworn and the heirs to the throne of Dhasson. I was born into it." He paused. "Anyhow, Talwyn thought that having you made one of us would mean that the reciprocal vow with the Dread applied to you as well."

"You mean, it would include me in their protection?"

"That's what Talwyn and Pevre believe."

Tris mulled over Jair's words for a few moments. "Half of the Sworn's Ride runs through Margolan, so it makes sense. Is there a reason they haven't made a pact with the Margolan kings like the one they have with Dhasson?"

Jair shrugged. "I don't know. The pact with Dhasson is very, very old."

"Would it mean my sons would be committed to the Ride?"

"I would guess so. The challenge there is persuading them to come back home to take the crown." Jair's voice was joking, but Tris could see in his cousin's eyes the tension between his commitment to the Sworn and his duties as heir to the throne.

"If my magic is likely to be passed down through the line of Margolan kings, such an agreement would make sense."

Jair smiled. "Good. I'll tell Pevre. There is some preparation to be done. He'll make certain we can complete it before dusk."

Just then, Tris's attention was caught by the strains of a familiar song. It took him a moment to recognize the tune.

"Please tell me that's not the song I think it is."

Jair grinned widely. "Ah, but it is. I believe it's called 'The Forest Is Dark No More.'"

Tris groaned. The song was one of bard Carroway's most popular, celebrating and romanticizing Tris's quest to win back the throne from Jared the Usurper, and his cleansing of the haunted Ruune Videya forest. As Tris recalled, the ballad had an interminable number of verses and a tune that was difficult to forget. It was also, to Tris's way of thinking, an overwrought and embarrassing ditty that would not die. The only person Tris knew who hated the song more than he did was Jonmarc Vahanian, who figured prominently in the ballad's heroic story.

"Just wanted to give you a taste of home. It's very popular in the Dhasson court. If you ever came to visit, you'd probably be serenaded wherever you went."

"I heard Jonmarc banned it from being played in Dark Haven."

Jair chuckled again. "I couldn't resist. And I must say, the musicians here in camp have really enjoyed the new material."

Tris rolled his eyes. "When all this is over, and Carroway is back at Shekerishet, I'll set him to immortalizing you, and we'll see how you like it."

When they walked back to the fire circle, Tris was greeted with clapping and cheers. He gave a good-natured bow in acknowledgment and shot a glare in Jair's direction when no one else was looking. The rest of the afternoon passed with a lighthearted holiday spirit that managed to draw Tris out of brooding over the evening's work to come.

* * *

Late in the afternoon, Pevre and Talwyn came to the fire circle and held up their hands for the attention of the group. Voices hushed, and others who had been busy with preparations drifted closer.

"Amid the celebrations of the feast day, we have our solemn duty to renew our vow as the guardians of the Dread," Pevre said. "For the last thousand years, the Sworn have guarded the barrows of the Dread, as the Dread guard the living from the Nachele. Each year, the vows are renewed, reforging the bond between the Sworn and the Dread. That bond is more important now than ever before.

"Today, we are honored to have yet another duty, a joyous and rare event. Today, we gain a brother among the Sworn." He held out his hand to Tris, who stepped forward. Tris took Pevre's hand and made a low bow.

"Martris Drayke, king of Margolan, summoner, and blood kin to my son-by-marriage, the Sworn claims you as one born among its number, blood of blood, breath of breath. You will be numbered among us, and you will share in our duty to stand watch over the spirits of the Dread."

Talwyn removed a thick pillar candle from the sleeve of her shaman's robe. The candle was yellow like beeswax, with streaks and swirls of a much darker, reddish-brown color throughout. The candle sat in a stone bowl engraved with runes. She held the candle between Pevre and Tris.

"Mingled with the wax of this candle is a drop of blood from every member of the Sworn. This is the Vow Candle, which will be used to affirm our oath to the Dread. Will you add your blood to ours and become one of us?"

Tris drew a deep breath. "I will."

Pevre withdrew a silver knife from his belt, and he took Tris's left hand. Holding Tris's hand high enough for all to see, Pevre made a swift cut in the center of Tris's palm and held his hand above the unlit candle until four drops of blood fell into a depression in the top of the broad candle. With a murmured word and a flicker of Pevre's magic, the cut healed as if it had never been.

Another whispered word called the wick into flame. Pevre took the candle from Talwyn and held it up. "As the flame melts the wax, the blood of our new brother mingles with our own. We will reshape the wax, to make it anew as we make our vow to the Dread anew. Celebrate the birth of your new brother within the family of the Sworn."

Next, Pevre motioned for Tris to extend his right arm. "Gather your sleeve to the shoulder," he commanded. Tris did as Pevre ordered.

"A child marked as one among the Sworn is forever one of our people. What is done cannot be undone." Pevre touched Tris on the upper arm, just below his shoulder. His touch burned, radiating around Tris's arm, and with the burn came a tracery of shadow as the tattoo that marked each of the Sworn with their family and clan wound its way across Tris's skin. It took only a moment, and when the burning sensation was gone, Tris saw a complex marking that matched the pattern on Pevre's arm and on Talwyn's.

"This is my son, from this day forward. Rejoice that new life has joined us."

At that cue, the musicians struck up a joyous tune, and the onlookers crowded around Tris to embrace him. When he had greeted all of those gathered around the fire, Talwyn motioned for them to sit, and gestured for Tris to sit next to her.

"When a child is born among our people, we share *vass* and bread and *tepik* together," she said. Tris glanced toward the loaf of hard bread and flagon of *vass* set next to a wide bowl of *tepik*, a heavily seasoned vegetable mash. "By joining in our birth feast, you become one of the sons and daughters of the Sworn." Talwyn lifted the hard loaf of bread, broke off a piece of it, and then handed it to Tris who did the same. Next, she dipped the bread into the *tepik* and ate her portion, passing the bowl to Tris to follow her example. She took a drink from the flagon of *vass*, and as Tris gave the bowl and bread to Jair, he took the flagon and steeled himself for a mouthful of the strong liquor. Slowly, bread, bowl, and flagon moved around the circle, until all had partaken.

Pevre was the last to eat and drink, consuming the last piece of bread and bit of *tepik* and then emptying the flagon. He held the empty vessels aloft. "Rejoice. Our numbers are increased. Together, we renew our bond to each other, to the Spirit Guides, and to the Sacred Lady as keepers of the Dread."

Once again, joyous songs rose from the musicians, and everyone in the camp began to dance, drawing Tris in among them. Amid the celebration, Tris saw Pevre take the candle that had spread into a puddle of warm wax in its stone holder and reshape the soft wax into a new candle. Still singing and dancing, the group followed Pevre down the path to the barrow.

The sun was quite low in the sky, just a candlemark before sundown. At the barrows, Pevre and Talwyn stepped forward. Pevre lit the candle and held it aloft.

"Ancient Dread, keepers of the barrows and what lies within, accept the renewal of our vow to defend your sacred places from all who would desecrate them." Pevre repeated the oath in the consonant-heavy language of the Sworn, a language that sounded to Tris like the murmur of the wind. To Tris's amazement, the language now needed no interpretation, and he realized he understood every word.

"Yes, it's an effect of the ritual," Jair murmured to him. "Be glad. I had to learn it the hard way."

Talwyn moved to stand beside Pevre, and Tris saw that she carried a tray with an offering of bread, *tepik*, and *vass*. "Honored Ones, keep the feast with us. Accept our gifts and accept our oath. As in the past, so tomorrow, and for all days." She set the offering next to the burning candle.

The song of the crowd became a chant. Tris could feel old magic rising around them. The magic rose from the ground and every living thing around them, and was answered by a wave of magic from the barrows.

The air around the candle and food offering began to shimmer, like the ripple of heat in the air on the hottest of days. The air itself bent and shimmered, and when it cleared, the offering was gone. Where the offering had been, the ground was scorched bare. Talwyn raised her hands and turned to the cheering crowd. Slowly, the group made its way back to camp.

Tris remained behind, along with Jair, Pevre, and Talwyn. Tris felt his stomach tighten, knowing that the time had come for him to enter the barrows. He thought again about Scaith's attack on Cwynn, and fierce anger dispelled his fear.

"I'm ready," he said, meeting Pevre's gaze.

Pevre held out a leather bag to Tris. Inside were the passage tokens the Dread had given him. He put on the items that could be worn and left the other gifts in the bag. Nexus hung in his scabbard, and his steel sword was a reassuring weight in the scabbard on his back.

Talwyn motioned for Tris to lie down. He stretched out on the ground near the barrow, while Talwyn and Pevre set eight candles in an outline around his form. Jair stood back and was soon joined by Emil, both of them heavily armed with daggers and their *stelians*. Tris knew that their task was to keep Talwyn and Pevre from being disturbed during the working.

"Can you work the keeping spell?" Tris hoped his voice did not belie his nervousness.

Talwyn nodded. "It's as you said: Breath and the beating of the heart are like bellows and pump. I will keep them going while you enter the Underrealm."

"If I don't return—"

"We will wait for you for as long as your journey takes," Pevre said. "We will break our vigil only upon your return, or upon the report of the Dread that you are lost to Konost." He met Tris's gaze. "I believe you will return to us. Know that it is not just Talwyn and I keeping vigil. The whole camp keeps vigil with you. Such a thing has its own magic." Pevre paused. "Remember that you'll have to pass a series of gates. Each gatekeeper will demand a gift. Make your offerings, and you should be able to pass." Pevre raised a hand in blessing. "It's time for your journey. May the Spirit Guides and the Sacred Lady walk with you."

Tris closed his eyes and centered his magic. He could feel Talwyn's magic close to him, reassuring and strong. With a thought, he loosed the bonds that connected his soul to his body. He felt his body still for a moment, and then a rush of Talwyn's magic began the rhythm of breath and heartbeat as he moved away from the pale, prone form on the ground.

Already, he could feel the power of the Dread. He took another step toward the barrow, and where its surface had been unbroken only moments before, now Tris saw a dark gash in the mound. Cold, ancient power radiated from the barrow, unlike any magic he had encountered in the mortal world. He moved into the Plains of Spirit and entered the barrow.

Welcome, Summoner-King. The voice that greeted him was the same as the one he had encountered before, and as Tris neared the opening in the mound, he saw the shadows shift and move. He kept a firm grip on Nexus's pommel as he stepped into the shadows.

What are you? Tris sensed the presence of the Dread guide with his magic, able with his mage senses to separate the animate shadow from the darkness around them.

Millennia ago, we were much like your people. Magic was

more common among us, and it bred true so that as the years went by, nearly all of our people harbored some power. Ours was not the elemental magic your people possess, the magic of air, land, water, and fire. Nor was it exactly like your summoning magic. Our gift was thought magic, and we had the power to read, shape, and alter the thoughts of outsiders and even of supernatural beings. The stronger among us could also manipulate those who were younger or weaker. Magic of any kind invites corruption, as you have learned yourself.

How did you come to be the guardians of the Nachele?

We grew bored with the conquest of other mortals, and we grew arrogant in our power. We turned our attention to the beings of the Nether, and of other realms best left untouched. We awakened beings that were beyond our power to control, and because of our magic, gave them a new and dangerous sentience. We loosed a bloodbath upon our time that nearly wiped out all living beings from the lands you know as the Winter Kingdoms—and beyond their borders.

A War of Unmaking.

If so, then the gods had no part in bringing cataclysm down upon us. We did that to ourselves.

The Nachele were the beings that you set loose?

Our discovery, and our burden. In our desperation, when only a few of the most powerful among us were left, we found a way to bind what we had loosed—but at a terrible price. So long as any of our kind remained among the living, the Nachele would also roam the world. To bind them, we would have to become their jailers, for eternity. So you see, Summoner-King, why we cannot allow the Nachele to be awakened once more.

I see. Must I pass among the Nachele to find Konost?

No. We bound the Nachele in a place between realms that is not of the living, but also not of the Underrealm. Even with our power, we were not gods. Yet the opening to the Underrealm

lies near here. I can take you to the first gate, but no farther.
When—and if—you return, I will guide you back to your body.

Tris followed the voice through the long descent into the gray
half light of the Underrealm. It was silent, without the distant
sound of insects or animals, or even of wind through dry
branches. There was no scent from the moist ground, the vegetation, or the wind, just the distant smell of the grave.

Tris looked down at himself. He wore the spirit-remnants of
his clothing, as well as the passage tokens the Dread had given
to him. He drew Nexus and as it cleared the scabbard, its runes
flared and rearranged themselves. *Light sustains*, read the
inscription. It was the same message that the sword had given
him on the occasion of Cwynn's birth, and he hoped it was a
good omen.

Ahead of him stood a large stone wall. It seemed to go on
forever in either direction. The stone was weathered, ancient,
and thick. In the center of the wall was an arched opening with
an iron gate and a large lock molded into the shape of a serpent.
Tris fingered the silver vambrace on his left arm, and squared
his shoulders. He strode up to the gate.

"Gatekeeper! A word with you."

The lock came apart, reshaping itself into the form of a large
gray metallic serpent. The serpent languorously twined itself
over and through the wrought-iron bars. The snake stopped and
raised its head to look at Tris. Tris saw that the serpent was as
thick as his upper arm, and its coiled body looked powerful.
Black, depthless eyes fixed on his.

"I bring a gift to pass this gate. Allow me to enter and return
and the gift is yours."

The serpent stretched forward, its long fangs plainly visible.
Just as Tris thought that the snake meant to strike him, it stopped,
head raised, as if waiting. Tris removed the silver vambrace
from his arm and slipped it over the snake's head.

As soon as the snake's body passed through the silver vambrace, its skin lost its metallic luster, and as Tris watched, the snake took on the supple, scaled appearance of a normal serpent. The vambrace fell to the ground, and the serpent uncoiled itself from around the gate, letting the doors swing apart to admit Tris.

Wary that he had passed the first gate only to enter a more dangerous place, Tris nodded his thanks to the serpent and followed an overgrown and long-disused path that stretched from the stone wall down a long, rocky hill. Tris could hear no rustle of his passage on the path, no footsteps in the dead grass, no whisper of his breath.

He continued down the path until he reached the edge of a large forest. Like the stone wall, the forest stretched to the horizon on either side. Where the path entered the tree line, there stood a gate with two intricately carved posts and an equally ornate lintel. It appeared possible to go around the posts and lintel, but an indentation in the ground showed that the pathway led through the wooden gate.

Tris stopped just short of the gate. When he grew closer to the posts, he could see that the carvings were of totemic animals, each atop the other, and that carved into the lintel was the wide wingspan of an eagle. At the foot of the right post was a large blank space, as if the carved animal figure had been removed.

A movement at the edge of Tris's peripheral vision made him turn sharply, Nexus drawn. A figure was emerging from the forest with the low, menacing growl of a large watchdog. As the figure moved into the dim light, Tris saw that it was the skeletal remains of a dog nearly as big as his own mastiff.

"Allow me to pass and return, and my gift is yours."

The skeletal dog lowered its head threateningly, but Tris did not move. It circled him, and its bones made a cold, rattling noise. Tris loosened the neck plate and held it out toward the bone dog without moving closer. The dog sat down next to the blank space on the right post of the gateway and lowered its head as if awaiting the neck plate. Tris bent down and fastened the neck plate around the dog's throat like a collar, and then stood back.

As he watched, flesh formed over the bones and the skeleton became a living dog. Then the dog leaned back against the post and the wood expanded, forming a sheath over the dog until, at last, the dog appeared as a perfect carving, completing the post. Around the throat of the carved dog was the neck plate.

Tris opened the wooden gate and walked cautiously into the forest. He summoned a ball of blue hand fire to light his way. The sky was a uniform gray that gave no indication of the movement of sun or moon. Time meant nothing here.

The canopy of the forest closed over Tris's head. A trail wound through the forest and stopped at the edge of a rocky cliff. A large canyon split the forest floor. It was too steep to climb down and cross on foot, and much too far to leap across.

Tris stood at the edge of the cliff and looked over the divide. He saw no gateway, and the path ended abruptly in the shattered rock at the lip of the gorge. Yet when he turned back to the forest, he could see the path clearly. There had been no branching paths. Unsure of what to do, Tris looked out over the cliff.

"Gatekeeper, I have a gift for you. Show yourself. Permit me to pass and return and the gift is yours."

From behind him in the darkness of the forest came a loud scuffing sound and the snort of a wild animal. Tris turned, Nexus in hand, to see a large black boar charging at him. With the cliff at his back, Tris had nowhere to go. The canyon floor was far below the edge, and Tris was sure that a fall here in the Underrealm would be just as lethal as in the mortal world.

The boar continued its headlong charge, heedless of the path ending in thin air.

"Gatekeeper! Show yourself!" Tris took a wide stance, digging in his heels as best he could, and he readied his sword like a pike, certain that the boar meant to drive him over the edge.

Just before the boar would have spitted itself on Tris's sword, the large animal came to an abrupt stop. It stood staring at Tris, its small, close-set eyes watching his every move.

"Are you the Gatekeeper?"

The boar made no movement, and Tris removed the third gift, the circlet.

"I bring a gift to pass this gate. Allow me to enter and return and the gift is yours."

He held out the circlet in his left hand, carefully approaching the large animal. When it made no move to gore him with its tusks, Tris set the circlet on its head.

The outline of the boar shimmered and rippled like sunlight on water. As Tris watched, the shoulders broadened and the thick body elongated, its pelvis flattening. The skull grew rounder and the features shifted until a naked man stood before him. The man gestured for Tris to follow him.

The gatekeeper walked to the edge of the cliff and stepped off. He disappeared from view, but Tris heard no scream, nor did he hear the thud of a body rolling its way down the steep, rocky incline. He walked to the place where the gatekeeper had disappeared and looked down. The man stood below him, balanced on a path so narrow that, without a guide, Tris knew he never would have found it.

At the bottom of the chasm, the guide stopped, motioning to where the path continued across the flat ground.

Tris turned to the man. "Thank you," he said. The man looked at him in silence. "Will you return to the shape of a boar, or stay a man?"

"I will stay a man." The guide's voice was rough, and the words came out slowly, as if he had not spoken in a long time.

"If you return this way, the path will show itself to you." With that, he bounded up the narrow trail, leaving Tris alone in the floor of the chasm.

Tris walked on, following the remnant of a trail that wound across the rocky ground. The trail led out into hilly ground that became a grassy plain. Across the plain, Tris could see a white marble building with steps leading up to it. The path led in that direction.

As he grew closer, Tris realized that the building looked like a crypt. Broad steps led up to a large, circular landing made of gleaming white stone. Tris followed the path up the steps, but as he was about to cross the landing, he heard a sharp noise overhead and felt a rush of air. A huge, scaled bird landed in front of him and gave a sharp cry. The bird had a wingspan easily twice Tris's height, and a sharp, dangerous beak. Instead of feathers, the bird was covered with small reflective scales. It had long talons at the end of its powerful feet and a whiplike tail.

"I seek the gatekeeper. Is that you?" Tris asked the huge bird. "Allow me to pass and return and the gift is yours."

Tris had no desire to get within the reach of either the bird's beak or its talons. Reaching into his pouch, he withdrew the string of grave beads and tossed it toward the huge bird. With a raptor's cry of victory, the bird grabbed the string of beads, tossed it into the air, and swallowed it down.

As Tris watched, the bird spread its wings, reaching from edge to edge of the landing. The bird's form became thinner, until it slipped onto the landing like a picture painted onto parchment and became part of the elaborate mosaic tile of the landing. The way was clear for Tris to enter the crypt.

Inside the crypt, a set of stone steps led downward. Halfway down, the gloom became impenetrable, and Tris called hand fire to light his way. Only three passage tokens remained in his bag.

He was relieved not to have needed to fight the gatekeepers, preferring to reserve his strength for the confrontation with Konost.

The bottom of the stairs opened into a torch-lit cavern. The path ended abruptly at the edge of a large, still pool. Far across the water, Tris could see where the path picked up again and headed deeper into the cave. There was no telling how deep the water ran, nor what lay beneath its placid surface. Tris watched the water and saw a ripple. In the torch light, shadows glided beneath the water.

"Gatekeeper, I have a gift for you. Allow me to pass and return and the gift is yours."

Tris walked toward the water's edge. His boot steps sounded deafening in the unnatural stillness. As he neared the path's end, a dark shape exploded from the water, thrusting its large, powerful reptilian head toward him. Huge jaws, easily the length of a man's arm, snapped inches from where Tris stood. The creature's mouth was filled with jagged, gleaming black teeth.

It reared back and thrust forward again, opening its maw wide. Two large, sharp fangs protruded from the left side of its mouth, but on the right, only one bottom fang jutted up. Tris stepped back and dug into the pouch. He withdrew the obsidian dagger and held it up. He had no idea whether or not the beast could see the dagger or make out what it was, but Tris gave an underhand toss and the beast caught it in its mouth.

The large beast rose out of the water, revealing four thick, muscular legs and a long, serpentine torso. It opened its maw to bellow, and Tris saw that the dagger had replaced its missing fang. Tentatively, hand on sword, he stepped forward to the edge of the water.

The reptile regarded him with cold, dead eyes, and then it began to sink low into the water. It stretched out both head and tail, leaving just enough of its body above the water to form a walkway across the pool. With a prayer for luck, Tris took the first step onto the reptile's head, expecting the beast to swing around and attempt to snap at him with its fangs. To his relief, the creature remained still, allowing him to cross.

When he stepped onto the path on the far side of the water, the reptile gatekeeper sank silently beneath the surface.

Tris looked longingly at the clear water of the pool. The path had been long and arduous. He was as tired and sore as if he had made the trek in his mortal body, and now, staring at the water, he felt parched. With effort, he reminded himself of the warning to take no food or drink, and he forced himself to walk farther along the path.

The cave narrowed to a tunnel barely wide enough for Tris to walk through without turning sideways. More than once, he knocked his forehead against low rock outcroppings, and blood began to mingle with his sweat, trickling down his forehead into his eyes. When the tunnel finally widened, Tris found himself in a room with three openings. In the center of the room stood an old woman. Torches in sconces set the room in shifting light and shadow. The old woman raised her head, revealing a sightless eye and an empty socket.

"Who is it? Who's there?"

"A traveler," Tris replied cautiously.

"Living, dead, or undead?"

"Not quite any of the three."

"Paths go to different ends, depending on which you be."

"I have a passage token, a gift for the gatekeeper. Are you the gatekeeper?"

The old hag gave a mirthless laugh. "Oh, I'm the gatekeeper, all right. But I have no need of gifts. I go nowhere, eat nothing, and see no one."

Tris dug the next-to-last token from his bag. Aside from the heart, all that was left was the onyx ring.

"Allow me to pass and return and the gift is yours." Tris approached the hag carefully, with his right hand settled on the grip of his sword and the ring held in his outstretched left hand. He moved close enough to place the ring in her gnarled hand.

The hag took the ring and stroked it with her fingers. She grinned broadly, revealing a row of broken, mottled teeth. "A good gift you've brought me, a very good gift." With that, the hag gave the onyx stone a sharp twist, freeing it from its mounting, and slapped the stone against the empty eye socket. When she withdrew her hand, a black eye filled the socket. She regarded Tris carefully.

"Living, dead, or undead?" she asked again.

"All, and none. I seek Konost. Permit me to pass and return."

The hag gave him a long look once again and then stepped aside, pointing to the middle tunnel. "I hope you have one more gift in that bag. There's another gatekeeper—one who isn't as pretty as I am," she said with a harsh laugh. "Then again, after you've been down here a while, you won't be pretty, either." She gave a mocking laugh. "Go."

The middle path descended steeply, growing colder with every step. Tris could sense the spirits of the dead nearby; their conversations formed a whispered hum just out of earshot. The path was narrow, requiring him to move sideways at some places, and the sharp rocks jabbed into his skin. Even though he was in spirit form, pain was real.

Gradually, the pathway widened. Tris entered a large cavernous chamber. Bones and skulls were stacked along the walls and embedded into the ceiling of the cave. Some of the bones were arranged in tableaus, with lines of dancing skeletons holding hands as if at a spring dance, or fixed in depictions of everyday life: sitting around a table, reclining on a picnic, or playing sports. In other places, the bones formed abstract patterns, runes, or a repeating motif of the three-bone symbol of the Shrouded

251

Ones. Along the back wall of the cave was an elaborate mural made from bones. Three figures—Peyhta, Konost, and Shanthadura—were carved into the rock, the only figures in the entire cavern not sculpted from bone. These three cowled figures accepted tribute from a long line of skeletal supplicants who came on foot, crawling on hands and knees, carried in the arms of others, or riding on bony horses and mules.

At the base of the mural was a large white building, also constructed from bone. Tens of thousands of human bones built its pillars and lintels, while its roof was tiled with flat shoulder bones. Skulls and pelvis bones adorned the walls in ghastly combinations, while smaller finger and toe bones edged the top of the wall-like ribbon. Between where Tris stood and the bone-covered temple was a wide river with only one bridge. Like the temple, the bridge was built of the bones of countless men, women, and children. It arched across the dark river supported by a latticework of long bones, suspended with the graceful curving strands of hundreds of human spines.

As Tris walked closer to the bridge, the smell of decay became stronger. A shambling figure with putrefying flesh peeling from its rotting frame blocked the bridge's entrance. Tris approached cautiously. Though the figure walked unsteadily while patrolling its post, Tris had no desire to find out just how quickly it could move if it detected prey.

Tris stretched out his magic. While the corpse of the gate-keeper was very old, strong magic kept it from disintegrating into dust. Tris's anger flared. Trapped within the eternally rotting flesh of the stinking corpse was a sentient spirit. To reanimate the dead by forcing an unwilling soul back into a rotting body was forbidden to any Light mage. Konost obviously played by her own rules.

Carefully, Tris reached into the bag for the last passage token: the human heart. It, too, was halted in a state of waxy partial decomposition. Tris could feel the vile magic that preserved it. Holding the heart in his hand, he approached the bridge.

"Gatekeeper! I have a gift for you. Allow me to pass and return and the gift is yours."

The shambling corpse stopped and turned toward the sound of Tris's voice. Its yellow, gelatinous eyes fixed him in their gaze. "Not unless you can destroy me."

"I have no cause to fight you," Tris replied, keeping his hand on Nexus's grip, ready to draw. "Take the heart and stand aside."

The gatekeeper moved forward warily, snatching the heart from Tris's hand. The gatekeeper pulled aside the filthy remnants of his shirt to reveal decayed flesh that barely covered the bare bones of his ribs. He pushed one hand through the rotting sinew to place the heart where it belonged inside his chest. As Tris watched, the putrefying flesh lost its green-and-black hue as it knit together. Oozing pustules of festering rot closed to become purple-and-brown lesions and then faded to the sickly gray of a fresh corpse.

The gatekeeper drew its sword from the ragged remains of an ancient leather scabbard. He began to advance, and where Tris had glimpsed sentience before, he now saw craft and intelligence. The gatekeeper swung his ancient sword, and Tris met the bone-jarring swing with Nexus. Nexus's blade flared with the contact, warming in Tris's hand as the gatekeeper swung again with lethal force. Here, on the Plains of Spirit, it was easy to let himself merge with the magic of the sword. He remembered his grandmother's warning: *The sword draws a breath from your soul.*

The gatekeeper showed no sign of tiring, and Tris wondered what magic imbued the corpse with its power. Tris knew he could not sustain pitched battle forever. His foot slipped, and the gatekeeper scored a deep gash to Tris's shoulder. The sight of blood oozing from the wound made Tris wonder if the damage sustained here in the Nether marked the body he had left behind.

The triumph of inflicting a serious wound distracted the gatekeeper. It was only for a second, but it was the opening Tris had been waiting for, and he lunged, driving Nexus between the corpse's ribs, into the newly returned heart. Nexus's blade flared once more, bright as the sun, and Tris felt the blade pull a surge of his magic down its steely length, even as the grip grew dangerously hot in Tris's hand. The corpse guard screamed as magic fused with Nexus's fiery glow, and Tris realized what the sword meant to do a second after it had begun to force life energy down the honed edge of the blade. His magic burst into the gray, dead heart, and then sent tendrils of white-hot power through every nerve and vein.

Spitted on the point of Tris's sword, the gatekeeper began to tremble, screaming, as the power surged through his body. As the return of its heart had forced back the putrefying flesh, now the blast of Tris's summoner magic drove out the deathly pallor of the corpse flesh, and in its wake, left living tissue.

The transformation took only seconds. Tris watched in horror as Nexus drew upon his power, until the body from which the blade protruded was that of a living, bleeding man.

The gatekeeper dropped his sword and sank to his knees, watching red blood flow from the chest wound in astonishment. He drew a shuddering breath, and he raised his head to meet Tris's gaze.

"You have passed the challenge and given me my freedom. Go—and if you can best the goddess, return in peace."

The gatekeeper slumped forward, dead, and Tris pulled the blade free. He half expected to see the form crumble into dust or reanimate, but the dead man's body remained crumpled where it fell. Tris wiped Nexus's blade clean on the hem of his tunic. He stretched out his magic, intending to offer to help the gate-keeper's soul to cross over, but the soul had vanished. Sword in hand, Tris walked across the bone bridge.

The weight of dead souls pressed around him. These souls had been stolen, hollowed, from deathbeds and battlefields throughout the course of centuries. Tris wondered if the gate-keeper's soul was among them. Konost's role, Tris realized, was more accurately "poacher" than "guide."

Souls crowded him, desperate for the touch of his magic. They wailed and screamed, cursed and begged. He knew that to yield to their pleas would be to allow them to drain him dry of magic, stranding him among them, but their cries tore at his conscience. He listened for just one soul, Cwynn's essence, but heeded the Dread's warning not to call to his son until he had first defeated Konost. As he approached the temple of bones, Tris let his power search out the shadows for the life force he recognized as his son. Just as he neared the bottom step to the temple, he felt a quiver of recognition. The essence that trembled in response to his magic was young, and for the first time, Tris could sense nascent power.

Stay hidden until I call for you. Tris wasn't sure whether Cwynn's soul could understand his warning. Whether it knew his meaning or gathered a warning from his tone, the essence did not come closer, although Tris marked its location in his mind.

Sword at the ready, Tris squared his shoulders and began to climb the temple steps. Where others might see only long-dead bones, Tris's magic resonated with the screams of the captured souls still bound to the bones that made up the grisly ossuary. They begged and pleaded for the release he had granted to the gatekeeper, and it took all of Tris's shielding to block them out so that he could focus on the task before him.

Inside the temple, walls of stacked bones were decorated with elaborate crests formed from even more skulls, ribs, teeth, and tibias. Swags made from hundreds of forearms and shin bones crisscrossed the open room as if awaiting a party. A huge chan-delier hung suspended from the ceiling, formed from every type of bone, with decorative pendants fashioned from the smallest finger joints. At intervals around the walls other complete skeletons had been positioned like skeletal guards, swords clasped in bony hands, forever at attention, awaiting the call of their mistress.

To Tris's mage sense, the temple stank of blood magic and death. Enshrined on a throne of skulls in the middle of the temple was a gray-shrouded form. The being stood, and Tris saw that it was a woman, so emaciated that every bone showed through her tissue-thin, gray skin. Lusterless dark hair fell lank to her shoulders. Her eyes were solid black. Ancient power radiated from the figure, and Tris knew he had reached his goal. This was Konost, and he fought a wave of mortal fear.

"Give me back my son, Cwynn, and I'll leave in peace," Tris said, although Nexus remained unsheathed and ready in his hand. It glowed, as if it alone possessed life in the realm of the dead.

"How dare you enter my lands to steal away my servants! I give you nothing." Konost's black eyes stared at him, unblinking. Her thin lips drew back from mottled teeth that protruded from gray, receded gums.

"Then I will take Cwynn from you, as I took your gatekeeper. You have no power over his soul. You cannot keep a soul that is not whole."

Konost's bony features twisted in anger. "I rule in this realm. Win the boy's soul from me if you can, summoner, but be prepared to forfeit your own."

Konost lashed out with magic. Tris felt the goddess's power wash over him like a tide pulling him beneath the heavy waves of the sea. He felt Konost's power robbing his body of its breath, draining the blue-white glow of his life force. Tris saw the skin on his hands grow shriveled and wrinkled like an old man, and he felt his body weaken. Konost, guide of dead souls, was calling his life and essence to her.

The sheer power of the attack forced Tris to stagger. Nexus flashed in his hand, its runes burning with the fire of the magic that forged it. For an instant, the sword's power halted the drain of Konost's magic. Tris knew his remaining life force could not sustain the power he would need to defeat Konost, and he reached deeper with his magic, drawing on the currents of the Flow. Tris forced his summoner's magic into this spirit form, warring cell by cell against Konost's deadly power, winning back breath and blood and sinew.

Konost gave a shrill cry of anger. She clapped her hands together, and the bones of the skeletal warriors that ringed the inner temple began to tremble. The warriors advanced on Tris, and Konost stepped back, laughing.

"Prove your power in battle, Summoner-King. If you want your son, fight for him."

Twelve skeletal warriors advanced, swords raised, forming a circle around Tris. He raised Nexus. Tris felt the magic of the old blade thrum through its grip, and as the warriors attacked, Tris drew on the magic of the Flow.

Nexus became a flaming athame, as light and magic flowed from the blade's tip like fire. The blaze forced the skeletons to fall back, but Tris knew he could not channel this much power forever. He focused his power on the dark magic that animated the dead bones. He sent his summoning magic along the channels of power, calling to whatever remained of the spirits and hollowed souls of the reanimated skeletons. Tris drew in as much of the Flow's power as he dared and wrested the dead soldiers free from Konost's grip. Konost's skeletal guards collapsed into a heap of bones.

"What right have you to invade my realm? Who do you think you are?" Konost shrilled. "I am the Guide of Dead Souls."

"And I am the Lord of the Dead." Tris met her eyes defiantly. Despite his victory, his life thread was growing dangerously dim, and he knew he could not remain separated from his body for much longer without risking his ability to leave the Underrealm. Weakened by hunger, thirst, and fatigue, he did not know how many more of Konost's onslaughts he could withstand. "Give me my son."

"I do not do the bidding of mortals!" Konost's black eyes glinted with rage, and Tris felt her power growing like a storm cloud. He rallied his own magic for one last defense.

"I call to your soul, summoner. And I will take what is mine!"

It felt as if a cold, dead hand reached inside his chest, compressing both heart and breath. Tris fell to his knees. Konost seemed able to pull the marrow from his bones. This was the goddess's true power, to call souls. Tris felt his soul, a glowing shadow of himself, straining against its mooring in the nerves and sinews of his body as Konost tried to wrest it from him.

Nexus burst into an arc of blue-white flame that seemed to drive the air from the chamber. In the flame, Tris saw a shimmering form, a ghostly image of his grandmother, the summoner Bava K'aa, the sorceress who forged Nexus. He saw his own image as well and recognized the stolen whispers of his soul. *Konost has no power over partial souls.*

Nexus engulfed him in a blinding ball of fire and Tris screamed. Konost's grip weakened, and then suddenly, his soul was free of her grasp. Every inch of his body throbbed, as if he had been skinned alive and then the flayed hide roughly reattached. Life returned as the fragile soul thread began to glow once more. And in that moment, another presence streamed through the conduit of Nexus's blinding light. At first, Tris thought it was Talwyn's magic he felt flowing through Nexus, but the tide of power was too strong. It refreshed his weary form, gave him strength to climb to his feet, rushing through his body in a cold, bracing wave. Tris remembered that Pevre had told him that the whole Sworn village would keep vigil. And then Tris knew: Talwyn was channeling not just her own life energy, but sustaining him with the life force drawn from the entire Tribe.

"You may be the guide of souls, but you have no power over life," Tris said.

Konost screamed, throwing herself toward him, bony hands and blackened nails outstretched. She touched the white-hot arc of light and recoiled, shrieking as if burned.

Tris flung out his magic to Cwynn, pulling his son's shattered soul to him and sheltering it within his own form. Cwynn's familiar life force huddled within him, and Tris felt it reach out reflexively to the Flow. The connection only lasted for an instant, but its power was blinding. For that moment, Tris felt the full power of the Flow channeled through him. Once before, when he and Carina had healed the shattered Flow beneath Margolan and Dark Haven, Tris had felt that magic run through him at its full strength, threatening to incinerate him with its power. Channeled through Cwynn, the Flow was no less fearsome, but it felt contained, as if it were taking its natural course.

A blast of power illuminated Konost's chamber, power that radiated from Nexus, the connection to the Sworn, and from Cwynn channeling the Flow. Brilliant light dispelled the shadows and a swell of power rose around Tris, making the ground shake hard enough that he nearly lost his footing. Lightning arced from Nexus's tip, striking the temple walls. The bone-inlaid crests fell, shattering on the stone floor. Overhead, the swags of smaller bones tore loose from their moorings, pelting him as they fell and raining down like hail. The massive chandelier swayed dangerously, and then its cord gave way, sending it to the floor with a crash. With a final salvo in Konost's direction to deter her from following him, Tris ran for the bone bridge and used his summoning magic to withdraw the trapped souls that held it together, letting it collapse behind him into the swift currents of the black river.

Konost was shrieking curses at him as he ran, carefully choosing his path over the treacherous footing. He refused to look back. Tris stumbled as Cwynn's attachment to the Flow winked out, and he knew that Talwyn was limited in how long she could draw on the life force of the Sworn. *Hurry, Tris*, he could hear Talwyn urge across the bond. *Attackers come. I can't channel the power to you if we're under siege.*

Nexus dimmed, still giving light enough to show their way back through the gateways and to dispel the menacing shadows that dwelled in the dark places of the Underrealm. He met no resistance from the gatekeepers, but he also knew that if his power failed him before he reached the world of the living, or if his mortal body died before he could take it back, he and Cwynn would never leave Konost's realm.

Tris felt himself weakening. The blue-white glow of his life thread was growing dimmer, and he knew he did not have the power left to draw on the Flow again without being lost beneath its roiling power. Moving on sheer willpower, Tris burst through the last of the gates, stumbling and falling, to make his way back to where the Dread waited.

Nexus's glow winked out and its fiery runes went dark as Tris fell to his knees at the threshold to the Dread's abode. *Well done, Lord of the Dead.*

Cold, ancient power flowed over him. Where Nexus had been fire and the Flow had been water, the magic of the Dread was unlike anything Tris had ever felt. The magic seemed to soak through his flesh into his bones, healing the injuries he had sustained in the Underrealm, restoring his life thread and soothing the places that still were raw where his soul had been battered.

A gift, for a worthy warrior. We honor our pact with your people. Release your son's soul. We will see to his safe return.

Reluctantly, Tris loosed his hold on Cwynn's essence, knowing that he did not have the power to accompany his son back to Shekerishet. Dangerous beings dwelled in the Nether, but Tris doubted that anything would be foolish enough to attempt an attack on the Dread.

"Thank you," Tris said, his voice thick with fatigue. "Now please, can you show me how to get out?"

The cold night air had never seemed so sweet. Even on the Plains of Spirit, as Tris emerged from the barrow of the Dread, the sounds and smells of the living world burst upon his senses, a stark contrast to the lightless realms below. His spirit rejoined his body with a violent spasm, and his mortal body felt heavy as he shifted from pure spirit to flesh and bone. A tremor shuddered through him, and strong hands held him by the shoulders.

"You're safe now, Tris. You're back." It was Talwyn's voice, but Tris could hear an edge that told him all was not well.

"You said . . . attack." Tris's voice was scratchy and dry, forcing breath into words.

"Durim," she said, helping Tris to his feet. "Can you stand?"

"Give me a moment, and I can fight," Tris said, grateful that the Dread had healed his wounds and replenished his magic.

"I fear we don't have that long," Talwyn said. She stepped away from him and drew her *stelian* from its sheath. In the moonlight, Tris saw a wave of black-robed fighters swarming across the plain and over the barrow as the *Telorhan* guards rose to block their path.

Willing himself to move, Tris sheathed Nexus and drew his battle sword. He heard the cries of Sworn warriors rise to shout down the chants of the Black Robes. Magic crackled in the air as the Sworn answered the assault of the Durim.

The Durim outnumbered the Sworn warriors and the *Telorhan* at the barrow. Tris hoped reinforcements from the camp were on their way. The Durim's swords could not hold against the large, flat *stelians* of the Sworn, but what the Durim lacked in weapons, they made up for in sheer fury, and Tris wondered as he countered the assault whether Konost had sent the attackers out of vengeance.

Dozens of the Black Robes ran from the shadows. Some emerged swinging their swords in a mad frenzy, while others sent bolts of red fire streaming toward the Sworn fighters. Tris reached for his magic and winced. The channels of power felt raw from his battle in the Underrealm, despite the Dread's healing. Tris reached beyond his own magic, not to the Flow, but to the old dead who lay buried in the ground around the barrow.

These were the bones of the Sworn, and of other ancient fighters interred in the shadow of the great cairns. Tris called on their spirits, and they yielded to him willingly, opening the flicker of their remaining energy to let him draw on them, fortifying him. Behind him, Tris could hear Talwyn chanting her spells, and mist rose from the cold autumn night, shaping itself into the form of the Spirit Guides.

One of the Durim sent a blast of red fire toward Tris, and he held out his palm, throwing up a shield of blue-white light, absorbing the blast. Seizing the moment as the attacking Durim regrouped for another attack, the misty figure of a huge wolf leaped for the Durim's throat. The sound of snapping teeth and the death scream of the Durim told Tris that the magic of the Spirit Guides was real, though the form of the wolf dissipated on the wind.

Tris heard Talwyn cry out. He turned to see the silver blade of a knife protruding from Talwyn's right shoulder. Her sword arm fell, numbed by the blow, and the Durim closed on her.

Rage fueled Tris as he wheeled to attack Konost's servants. He brought his sword down on the Durim nearest to Talwyn with enough force to cleave the man from shoulder to hip. He heard a battle cry from the left, and at the edge of his vision he saw that Jair had joined him. Fighting back to back with Talwyn protected between them, Tris and Jair swung their heavy swords with deadly accuracy. Across the field leading to the barrow, Tris saw Sworn warriors striking down the Durim, until the ground was littered with severed limbs and bloody black-robed bodies.

The battle was over even before reinforcements from the camp reached them. The last of the Durim fell to Jair's blade, and there was fury in Jair's face as he shoved his blade nearly hilt deep into the Black Robe's chest. Jair snarled a curse as he shook the Durim's body free of his *stelian*, and his blade whistled in the night air, neatly removing the head from the crumpled form.

For a moment, the battlefield was still, its silence deafening after the frenzy of battle. Warily, Tris and Jair surveyed the horizon, alert for a new attack. When no new foes appeared, Tris and Jair lowered their swords, and Jair knelt next to Talwyn. Emil and the other Sworn warriors along with the *Telorhan* guards formed a protective circle around them.

"We'll get you back to camp. Pevre can heal you."

"Not so bad," Talwyn murmured. Tris could see the pain in her face, but his magic told him she was in no real danger from her wound. "Pull out the knife. I can heal it."

Jair hesitated, and Tris met his gaze. "It's all right. I can help." Tris laid a hand on Talwyn's shoulder and used his magic to lend her power as she turned her own energy inward for healing.

263

Talwyn opened her eyes and looked up at Tris with a smile. "Thank you." Her smile faded. "Your journey—was it successful?"

Despite the healing the Dread had provided, Tris could feel exhaustion wash over him. A dull reaction headache throbbed in the back of his head, and he ached from the exertion of battle. "I made it out alive, and I retrieved Cwynn's soul. The Dread promised to see Cwynn's essence back safely across the Nether. As for the rest of what I saw . . . it makes an amazing story, but I don't think anyone will believe me." He paused. "I felt the power you sent to me—yours and the Sworn. Thank you. I couldn't have done it without your help." He drew a deep breath.

"You were right about the Dread. It mattered to them that I counted as one of the Sworn. When they healed me, they told me they would honor their vow to 'my' people."

Talwyn looked thoughtful. "That could certainly mean the Sworn, but it was Marlan the Gold who saw the Dread go into the barrows, wasn't it? If so, the Dread may also mean that whatever vow they made to Marlan, they recognize you as his legitimate heir and see the vow as still binding."

"Either way, I hope this means they're now on our side."

Talwyn hugged him and gave him a warm smile. He stood and then helped her to her feet. "It's too late for you to ride back to your army tonight. We'll clean up here and go back to our camp. There will be plenty of food from the Sohan feast, and I, for one, am starving!"

Tris and Jair watched as Talwyn moved away from them among the Sworn warriors and began directing them to secure the battlefield.

"Do you think it's a coincidence that we were attacked when you were in the Underrealm?" Jair asked.

Tris grimaced. "It's awfully convenient. I really hate to think of the alternative: that someone, somewhere is watching us closely enough to know our every move."

"I don't like it either," Jair said with a sigh. "But I'm beginning to think it's likely—and if it's true, it's going to make the battle even harder to win."

15

"Amazing how still it can be just before the battle starts."

Jonmarc glanced at Gethin. They stood near the Principality coast, looking out over a wide bay. Across the bay, a fleet of ships flying the Temnottan flag waited just out of reach of the catapults and trebuchets that defended the coastline.

"I hate waiting," Jonmarc muttered. "Let's get started and be done with it." He gave a nod toward the *Hojun* priest on the other side of the prince.

"It's time your priest buddy took you back to camp. I want you out of the line of fire when this blows open."

Gethin met his gaze levelly. "We've been through this already. I'm staying—and I'm fighting."

"No, you're not. I don't have time to watch over your royal ass."

"You've seen me fight. This isn't the first time I've been to battle."

Jonmarc took a deep breath and tried for patience. "I've seen you in the salle. That's not the same as on a battlefield. I have only your word that you've ever been in actual combat."

Gethin's lip quirked with annoyance. "In Eastmark, the word of a prince carries some weight."

"Then go back to Eastmark and see if your word carries

weight with your daddy. This is Principality, and I don't much care to have visiting nobles on the battlefield."

"I'm staying right here. What would it say about Eastmark's intent to ally with Principality if I were to turn tail and run at a time when every soldier is needed to protect the kingdom?"

Jonmarc glowered at him. His real focus was on the coastline. Though the ships were far out in the bay, every fiber in his body warned him on sheer gut instinct that the strike would come at any moment.

"They would say that you were smart enough to do what you're told and stay safe."

"Your princess might prefer that I die honorably in battle. It would solve one problem."

Jonmarc did steal a look back at Gethin at that, and saw a weary half smile on the prince's face. "Not really," Jonmarc replied. "I only just got your father to repeal the royal death warrant your grandfather placed on my head. I have no desire to have another one proclaimed because you got your fool self killed. Sending Eastmark's royal assassins against the Champion of the Queen of Principality just might qualify as a 'diplomatic incident.'"

To his surprise, Gethin chuckled and made a side comment to the *Hojun* priest nearest him. The priest, whom Jonmarc had not seen show any expression other than somber reflection, actually cracked a smile. "I understand what the queen sees in you—and why my father warned me that I might have more trouble winning your trust than that of the queen."

"Don't bet on that," Jonmarc replied, returning his attention to the coastline. "Berry's tough to impress."

To Jonmarc's left, the third of Principality's army headed by General Gregor stretched along the wide flat shoreline nearly to the horizon. To his right, General Valjan, newly called back to duty from his brief retirement, headed up a second third of the army.

267

"Do you think those things will really work?" Gethin nodded toward the array of nasty-looking contraptions Valjan called his "pride and joy." Valjan's "pride" was a small fleet of carriages with lethal modifications. Drawn behind armored horses, the low-slung war vehicles brandished wickedly long scythe blades that whirled and sliced through the air around them with every turn of the wagons' wheels.

"I think they're as likely to chop up our men as the enemy, but Valjan's thrilled with his 'killing machines.' I plan to stay the hell out of their way."

Behind Jonmarc was the final third of Principality's fighting forces. Exeter, the head of the Mercenary Guild, had agreed with Valjan to place his forces under joint command with Jonmarc. The *vayash moru* also fell under Jonmarc's command, along with the mages, to his consternation. Gethin and the *Hojun* priests insisted on being part of his unit as well.

"So the question is—can our merc navy do some damage before Temnotta has a chance to land troops?" Jonmarc didn't expect an answer. That question had been debated long into the night among the generals, to no satisfactory conclusion. Now, as they waited for someone to make the first move, the chill Jonmarc felt was not a product of the crisp autumn air.

"What about the *vayash moru*? Aren't you the Lord of Dark Haven?"

Jonmarc gave a tight chuckle. "Yes, I'm the Lord of Dark Haven, but that doesn't mean I hold any power over the *vayash moru*. Of the Blood Council, four members are on our side. The other, Astasia, has disappeared along with her brood. She might have gone elsewhere to sit out the war, or she may have made a deal with Temnotta. We won't know which choice they've made unless her brood attacks."

"Can the rest of the Blood Council send more *vayash moru*?" Jonmarc shrugged. "Gabriel and Riqua have their broods defending Dark Haven and hunting the Durim. Most of the *vayash moru* we have with us are from Rafe's brood, along with Laisren, who came with me. Uri is supposed to be on our side, but we might be best served if his brood just stays away."

"There! It's started!" Gethin pointed to the horizon, where Jonmarc had already seen a flash of fire that could not be mistaken for sunset.

"Let's hope our captains have a few tricks up their sleeves," Jonmarc muttered.

From beyond the bay, a new line of ships, Principality's merc navy, seemed to appear out of nowhere. Jonmarc smiled. If the Temnottans had expected to bottle up the kingdom's navy in the bay, they were sadly mistaken. The merc captains had already taken their considerable fleet out to sea several days before. A complicated communication relay between the mercenaries' fleet mages and Hant's spies and watchers let the captains know when to return.

The calm waters of the bay began to buck and heave. Huge waves tossed large ships up and down, and in the light breeze, it was magic, not wind, that would make navigation possible. As quickly as one wave would swell, the sea would suddenly quiet, testimony to a battle of magical power for control.

Lights flared against the sky as the merc ships traded magical volleys with the Temnottan navy. Flames streaked from the merc ships toward the sails of the invaders as the fire mages added their power to the fray. In answer, sudden explosions rocked half a dozen of the merc ships as the fire mages of the Temnottans returned the volley.

For a candlemark, the ships pounded each other. As the setting sun gave way to night, only the moonlight and the occasional flare of flames gave a hint to what was happening beyond the shoreline.

"There go the *vayash moru*," Jonmarc said as dark shapes

raced through the night sky toward the invaders' ships. "Let's hope the Temnottans aren't looking up."

"Let's also hope their fire mages are the first to die, or your men could have problems," Gethin commented.

Vayash moru attackers dropped onto the decks of the Temnottan ships, while others slipped silently across the water to levitate up along the sides. Even at a distance, Jonmarc could hear screams as the *vayash moru* fighters began their slaughter.

"What are they doing?" Gethin pointed toward the ships, where dark shapes flitted among the rigging and the sails, only to drop large objects back to the deck.

"Laisren was willing to gamble that the Temnotta mages wouldn't be quick to light their own sails on fire, so he gave orders for the *vayash moru* to haul their kills aloft."

"Ready your mages—there's something in the water!" Laisren seemed to appear out of nowhere at Jonmarc's side.

"What's out there?"

"Several large forms, moving fast."

Jonmarc lifted a burning brand, the signal to mages along the coastline to stand ready. He could see ominous ripples heading toward shore while the fight between the Temnottan ships and the merc navy raged on the water.

"Sweet Chenne, what are those?" But even as he spoke, he knew. Huge, sodden hulks rose from the bay in the shallow water, followed by smaller shapes. Reptilian heads sat atop powerfully built sea-slick bodies with muscular legs and clawed feet. *Magicked beasts*, he thought, as his blood ran cold.

Already, the mages and troops were responding. Jonmarc heard the cries of commanders rallying their men to battle stations and heard the crackle of lightning as mages sent volley after volley of red and blue magic fire against the lumbering beasts.

Smaller, quicker beasts ran from the water. They were black,

270

thin, and fast, with long, taloned hands and wide, toothy maws. The small beasts set on the nearest ranks of soldiers with a shrill, unnatural cry.

"Torches, we need torches," Jonmarc shouted, sending the aides scurrying to comply. He swung around to grab a runner who was awaiting instructions. "Fire's the only thing that stops those beasts. I want a torch in every soldier's hands, and I don't care if you have to burn down the camp to do it."

The runner took off to spread the word, shouting to other messengers to join him. Jonmarc turned back to Laisren.

"Call off your men. There's nothing you can do with so much fire, and you're as likely to burn as the beasts."

Even as he spoke, a wall of flame rose from the deck of one of the Temnottan ships. It caught on the dry rigging and sailcloth and sent the masts ablaze. Fire rose from another and then another of the Temnottan ships. The Temnottans were dropping skiffs from the inland sides of their ships, leaving the burning hulks to keep the merc navy from intervening.

With a stricken expression, Laisren took flight to gather what remained of his *vayash moru* fighters.

The horrors that first waded from the ocean ignored the skiffs behind them. Now, Jonmarc saw why. What had looked to be men aboard the small landing craft blurred in the moonlight, dropping to all fours as they shifted into wolves and huge bears. Heedless of the clang of swords and the smoke that rose as brand after brand flared into flame, the enemy shifters launched themselves into the fray, scrambling around the larger magicked beasts.

"We've got big problems." It was Scrg, one of the *vyrkin* leaders. That he was still in uniform told Jonmarc the other had not yet shifted to fight.

"Really? You just noticed?"

"Sorry. I forget that you can't feel magic as we do. Those

aren't normal shifters. They've been . . . compelled . . . to shift. Driven like rats at the edge of a forest fire. They're more afraid of what's behind them than what's in front of them, and with those damn monsters out there, that's saying a lot."

"How many?"

"More than we have. If I had to bet, I'd say they've had mages playing at cursing normal men into animal form. Nasty stuff."

"Make sure your people know that they're a valuable asset. I don't want them wasting their lives. We're not going to win this hand-to-hand."

"Done."

The slope down to the beach was ablaze with torches and burning brands. Jonmarc drew his sword and looked at Gethin. The young man's jaw was set with a grim expression.

"Any tricks your *Hojuns* have would be appreciated right about now. I've fought these things before, and they don't go down easily."

Gethin's gaze flickered to the long scar that wound from Jonmarc's ear down beneath his collar. "Then let's get started."

Jonmarc swung up onto his battle steed and gave a cry to start the charge. Gethin and the *Hojun* priests were in their saddles and ready to go. Hoofbeats pounded in the night air, thunder to the lightning of the burning brands and the blazing ships. The air stank of smoke and blood. Jonmarc let battle coldness take him, let it drive out fear until nothing existed except the quarry in front of him. His horse charged forward, and Jonmarc rode for the smaller beasts. They were faster than the great lumbering monsters, and he hoped that meant easier to kill.

Not far to his right, one of the large beasts swung its great, clawed arm and swept three soldiers off their feet. A cluster of fighters rushed forward, torches thrust ahead of them, forcing the monster back. Jonmarc heard a throaty growl and turned just as a huge wolf sprang at him. He swung his sword, catching the large wolf through the ribs, letting its forward motion drive the blade deeper. The wolf snarled and swiped its wide, powerful paws at him, forcing him to duck to avoid the sharp claws. Just for a moment, Jonmarc met the wolf's eyes. These eyes were the shape and color of a man's eyes, wild with rage and pain. The light in the wolf's eyes dimmed, and it went limp, sliding dead from his blade.

To his left, Gethin dug his heels into the ribs of his battle stallion. It reared up to send the iron-shod hooves kicking into the swarm of small beasts that swarmed around him. Jonmarc reached the fray a moment later, slashing with all his might to cut through the magicked beasts' tough, scaly skin.

The small beasts fell, but in their wake came a dozen wolves. They were larger than normal wolves, and Jonmarc wondered if the mage that forced them into their animal shapes had tinkered with their bodies, making them into weapons of war. Behind the wolves, Jonmarc saw a new wave of the deadly small beasts. All around them, the Principality soldiers fought in desperate bands of two and three, overwhelmed by the enemy advance. Neither the magicked beasts nor the Temnottan shifters seemed deterred by the threat of death, and so they pressed forward heedless as their fellows fell to the blades of the soldiers and the arrows of sharpshooters. Somewhere in the fray, Serg and the other *vyrkin* battled the alien shifters. The battleground was littered with bodies of men and *vyrkin* and horses, and the layer of smoke that hung over the land glowed red as blood by torchlight. *We could die here tonight*, Jonmarc thought grimly.

Just as the Temnottan wolves poised to spring, a wall of what appeared to be smoke rose from the ground between the wolves and where Jonmarc and Gethin readied for the onslaught. Unlike the torch smoke, the heavy mist did not waft with the wind. As Jonmarc watched, this new smoke swirled and began to take shape, forming into a ghostly line of powerful stawars. The smoke-stawars drew back on their powerful haunches and then launched themselves at the wolves with an otherworldly shriek.

The wolves ran, but not fast enough. Ghostly stawars pursued the fleeing wolves, and all-too-solid claws ripped through the wolves' skin. Jonmarc and Gethin swept behind the stawar-spirits, delivering killing blows to the maimed and dying wolves in their wake. The *Hojun* priests stayed where they were, hands raised and faces set in concentration. Jonmarc wondered just how many of the ghost cats the *Hojun* could call, and how far their creations could range afield.

More of the gray-skinned monsters rose from the sea to take the place of those the soldiers slaughtered. The howling of wolves and the fearsome snarls of bears vied with the shrieks of dying horses and the cries of men.

Six of the small beasts surged after Gethin. The beasts had grown bolder, and smarter, and they eluded the prince's deadly blades. Instead, they struck for the horse's underbelly and left deep gashes in his mount's hindquarters. Gethin leaped free of the saddle as the horse crumpled from its injuries, and with a curse, Jonmarc drove his stallion straight into the midst of the fray, sword swinging.

Around them, arrows and quarrels rained down from archers on higher ground, barely missing the soldiers as they struck the beasts and bears. Flaming arrows soared through the night sky like falling stars. Jonmarc sincerely hoped someone had warned the archers that a number of the wolves were *vyrkin*.

Jonmarc jumped from his wounded horse, surrendering it as a diversion to draw off the beasts. He came after Gethin's attackers swinging his sword in one hand and a burning torch in the other. One of the beasts turned and came after him, and Jonmarc wheeled into a high Eastmark kick, catching the beast in the ribs and sending it backward with enough force to take two more of its companions off their feet.

Jonmarc heard a cry from one of the *Hojun* priests. His Markian was rusty but good enough to catch the meaning of a hurried warning. A ring of flames shot up from the ground, circling Jonmarc and Gethin. The beasts shrieked in fury but withdrew a pace or two from the flames. As they drew back, a second outer ring rose out of nowhere, trapping the beasts between sheets of fire.

The flames were close enough that Jonmarc felt the heat ripple against his skin. Though the night was cool, within the protective circle it was as hot as a blacksmith's forge.

"Wonderful. We've got the choice of being eaten or being roasted."

Gethin was cursing under his breath in Markian. "I hadn't really planned on either."

As Jonmarc watched, the inner and outer rings of flame began to move toward each other, sandwiching the screaming beasts between them. Within a few heartbeats, the fire engulfed the beasts, sending noxious dark smoke into the air. When the beasts were dead, the flames vanished.

"My lord, are you hurt?" Tevin the fire mage emerged from the smoke. His face was smudged with soot and his mage robes were stained with blood.

"We'll live," Jonmarc replied. "Thank you." He looked out over the battlefield. A glance told him that the night was going badly for the Principality forces. Valjan's trebuchets and catapults were lobbing large flaming projectiles where the beasts were massed, but it was an imprecise attack at best, likely to kill as many soldiers as it saved.

"Can you rally the mages? Do what you just did but on a much bigger scale?"

Tevin nodded. "Aye. What timing did you have in mind?"

"When we begin the retreat, lay down a line of fire to cover our backs and then set another at the edge of the beach. Maybe we can trap the majority of those damned beasts so they can't follow us."

Tevin nodded grimly. "What of the injured men in the strike zone? And the dead? You won't be able to save the wounded or bring back bodies."

Jonmarc looked down over the scarred slope at the battle that raged amid the blood-red smoke. "They're beyond help. I want to save enough of the army to fight another day."

How Tevin planned to communicate with the other mages Jonmarc did not know. He only hoped that the fire mage could rally his companions fast enough to avert a total rout. Fighting back to back, Jonmarc and Gethin managed to hold off another wave of beasts, and all around them, the *Hojuns'* smoke-stawars snapped and clawed at the wolves and bears that slunk around the edges of the fight.

When Jonmarc was fairly sure Tevin had had the time he needed to get into position, he dropped the still-burning torch to the ground and reached for a horn that hung at his belt. With a deep breath, he blew the four-note clarion that signaled retreat.

For a moment, he feared that the call could not be heard over the din of battle. Then down the line, he heard Valjan answer, and after a long pause, Gregor as well.

Retreat was as bitter as it was necessary. Jonmarc and Gethin stumbled over the fallen dead. Behind them, they heard the first curtain of fire roar into life. It sounded like a huge tide rushing in from sea, or the blast of a storm wind. A wall of fire rose high into the night, blocking their view of the burning hulks in the bay. Around them, men ran for safety. It was easy to spot the less-seasoned soldiers, who scrambled for their lives, compared to the experienced soldiers, who stayed in something resembling formation.

At first, beasts and shifters pursued the fleeing soldiers, taking a heavy toll on the rearmost line. Tevin's second wall of flame flared from nowhere. Screams rose on the night air from the men and beasts caught in the conflagration. Jonmarc spotted three of Valjan's killing machines aflame amid a mass of dead enemy bodies. The machines, Jonmarc thought grimly, had served their purpose.

The night air stank of roasting flesh, and Jonmarc's stomach clenched as old memories threatened to resurface. He resolutely forced down any reaction except the cold logic needed to survive the retreat, and he bent to retrieve a torch that lay guttering on the ground. Seizing one of the abandoned horses, Jonmarc swung up in the saddle, the better to see his troops and be seen by them. He stopped on the slope midway between the battlefield and the camp, shouting at the soldiers to hurry, hoping that his visibility as a commanding officer might help the panicked fighters remember their training and rise above their terror.

Smoke made visibility difficult, but as Jonmarc squinted to see, he was sure that Tevin and the mages had begun to move the concentric walls of flame toward each other. The death cries of men, shifters, maimed horses, and magicked beasts raised a nightmarish keen in the darkness. Above the howls of the dying, Jonmarc heard the sound of battle close at hand, and he rode toward it. The slope was bathed in firelight, hot as a midsummer noon. Set in the shifting red light and dancing shadows was a small group of soldiers battling about a dozen of the small magicked beasts that had slipped beyond the ring of flames.

Gethin was among them, fighting on foot. Jonmarc did not see either of the *Hojun* priests, but in the heavy smoke, it was difficult to see more than a few feet. More of Valjan's killing machines smoldered just this side of the flames, but the horses that drew them were gone. With a loud cry, Jonmarc rose in his stirrups and charged at the knot of beasts from its flank.

One of the beasts launched itself toward Jonmarc with an incoherent, guttural howl. The beast was solid black like a moving shadow, with long, thin arms and wicked claws. Its claws slashed at the flank of Jonmarc's horse and caught Jonmarc on the thigh, opening a wound that poured blood down his leg. Jonmarc's horse, terrified by the attack, reared. Jonmarc let himself fall back in the saddle, close enough to thrust his torch down the maw of the beast as it leaped up at him. He barely got his hand out of the way as the wicked teeth snapped, but the torch snapped off, leaving its burning end in the monster's mouth. It fell away, shrieking, as the flames engulfed it.

Drawn by the downed beast and the smell of blood, the knot of beasts shifted their attention from the soldiers to Jonmarc. His wounded horse could never outrun them; Jonmarc had seen just how fast the small magicked beasts could move. Out of the corner of his eye, he could see that Gethin and the other soldiers had fallen back a pace or two, regrouping for another attack. He was close enough to the flame wall that Jonmarc felt its heat like a furnace, and he saw the beasts scrabbling to put more distance between themselves and the fire even as they kept their prey in sight.

"Gredic vo!"

A man's voice roared above the din, and Jonmarc translated the Markian call before he had the chance to realize how out of place it was. A hunting call, a shout to let the others in the hunting party know that the hunt had begun in earnest, a sound completely out of context on a Principality battlefield. Motion caught Jonmarc's eye, and he managed to wheel his horse barely in time to avoid both the attack of the small beasts and the swift movement of a flaming wagon bristling with scythes and blades.

Amid the smoke, Jonmarc caught sight of one of the *Hojuns* with his hand outstretched, even as the second of the killing machines rumbled down the slope, narrowly avoiding Gethin and the soldiers, headed straight toward the black-scaled monsters. Jonmarc dug his heels into his horse, wrestling the panicked beast into position where he could close off one route of escape even as Gethin and the soldiers sealed the other flank. Caught between swords and torches and the careening war wagons, the monsters were pushed back into the wall of flame. Their magicked forms caught fire with a hiss and they wailed like the damned, twisting and shriveling in the inferno. In a moment, they were gone, and with them the war wagons that had rolled on into the curtain of fire.

The slope had grown quiet except for the sound of the flames. From what Jonmarc could make out through the dense clouds of smoke, most of the others had made it up the embankment and were out of sight, probably most of the way back to camp. The two *Hojun* priests rode toward him out of the haze, one from each side. Gethin and the handful of soldiers stayed where they were, swords and torches in hand, watching the flames as if they expected new horrors to burst forth at any second.

"Thank you," Jonmarc said in Markian to the *Hojuns*, who nodded.

"What did you think you were doing?" Jonmarc said, turning toward Gethin as the prince left the other soldiers and strode up to him. Gethin's dark skin was covered with ash, making it plain where sweat streaked down his temples. His arms were marked with gashes and burns, as were Jonmarc's.

"Fighting a war, as I was trained to do," Gethin replied in Markian, and Jonmarc guessed that in the heat of battle, the prince did not even realize that he had abandoned Common for his native language.

"Your wound needs tending." One of the *Hojun* had drawn up alongside Jonmarc even as the adrenaline of the battle began to fade and Jonmarc became aware of the pain in his thigh and a light-headedness that had nothing to do with the smoke.

"Damned beasts have rot on their claws," Jonmarc replied.

He gripped the pommel of his saddle as a wave of vertigo washed over him. "Can you keep it from festering?"

The *Hojun* priests exchanged glances, and the second priest rode up next to the first. They began to chant in the harsh, guttural tones of their language, but although Jonmarc spoke Markian well, he could not follow what they said. An orange glow moved from the downturned palm of the *Hojun* to Jonmarc's injured leg. His leg tingled from hip to ankle, the familiar residue of strong healing magic, and as the *Hojun* continued to chant, Jonmarc felt the vertigo recede as the flesh around the gash knit into wholeness. The *Hojun* moved his hand to do the same for the horse's injured flank.

The barest of smiles touched the *Hojun*'s face. "Your leg should be fine now," he said in heavily accented Common.

"Thank you," Jonmarc replied. Weariness had replaced the heat of battle, and he knew, with a glance toward the camp, that his night was far from over.

16

Gethin trudged alongside Jonmarc as they made their way back to camp.

"Why don't you have one of the healers tend you?" Jonmarc asked. A quick appraisal of Gethin's injuries gave Jonmarc the impression that the collection of burns and gashes were painful but probably not life threatening. Mostly, he hoped to deflect the prince before heading into a debriefing with the other generals.

Gethin gave him a withering glare. "The *Hojun* knew that without their help, you might have lost the leg. If they weren't worried about me, you shouldn't be. There are men with much more serious wounds who need their help."

Jonmarc's expression did not change, but his estimation of the Eastmark prince rose. "Do your *Hojun* allow you river rum . . . for the pain?"

A tired grin spread across Gethin's face. "Eastmark is hardly Nargi. I'd welcome some rum if you have it."

Jonmarc took a flask from his belt and handed it to Gethin. Despite the prince's protestations that his wounds were minor, the way he knocked back a generous swig of the potent rum let Jonmarc know the truth. "You don't have to come with me to the meeting, you know. You've made your point."

"Which would be?"

Jonmarc sighed and rolled his eyes. "This obviously wasn't your first real fight. I get that. For what it's worth, it took Tris Drayke quite a while to get sword skills like yours. I'm . . . satisfied."

Gethin chuckled and gave Jonmarc a sidelong glance. "Just . . . satisfied. Certainly not . . . impressed."

Jonmarc's eyebrows rose. "Dispel a forest full of murderous ghosts single-handedly, and I'll be impressed. Until then, you'll have to settle for what you get."

Gethin fell into step beside him despite Jonmarc's offer to let the prince leave. Jonmarc was bone weary, both parched and hungry, and he knew Gethin had to be equally uncomfortable. To Gethin's credit, the prince made no complaint.

Jonmarc headed across the camp toward Valjan's tent, guessing where the generals would congregate.

"Jonmarc! Thank the Whore you made it back!" Valjan came striding out of the haze of smoke that hung over the camp. Soot-streaked, his armor cut and bloodied, Valjan looked like he, too, had been in the thick of the battle.

"I was just heading to your tent. Figured Exeter and Gregor would do the same. We need to regroup—assuming we have the men."

Valjan's expression was sober. "Aye, we have the men. It was bad, but not that bad, thank the Lady. I had my valet run to bring brandy and whatever food is at hand. I dare say we're all barely standing at this point, and I, for one, would like a drink."

"How bad?"

Valjan let out a deep breath and looked out over the camp. "Don't know yet. I've sent for a count, but that will take some time. My guess . . . we lost at least two or three thousand men, out of the ten thousand we deployed."

"What about the merc ships? After the Temnottans sent their ships afire, we couldn't see what became of ours."

Valjan's jaw tightened. "Nothing, yet. I asked Laisren to scout it out, and to let us know the casualties among the *vayash moru* and *vyrkin* as well." He gave a brisk nod toward his tent. "Go in and make yourselves at home. I need to find Exeter . . . and Gregor."

"That will be a treat," Jonmarc muttered.

Jonmarc and Gethin had just gotten themselves settled in Valjan's tent when others began to join them. First Exeter, who looked as war-weary as Jonmarc felt, and then Valjan, followed by Gregor. Of the four commanders, Gregor looked as if he had taken the worst of it. One eye was purple, nearly swollen shut. His left shoulder was bound in rags, evidence of a recent healing. Something about the tightness of Gregor's mouth and the way he held himself as if in pain convinced Jonmarc that, perhaps, Gregor had earned his healing.

Behind Gregor came Valjan's squire, who was doing his best to juggle food and a bottle of brandy. "Begging your pardon, but it was the best I could find on short notice," the young man said as he set the bundle down in the center of the tent among the men and handed the bottle to Valjan.

For a few moments, the group made a meal on the hard bread, dry cheese, and sausage. When they had finished, and the bottle of brandy had been passed round, Jonmarc sat forward.

"How bad was it?" Jonmarc looked from face to face.

"Still counting the dead, but I'd say my command is down one-third, not counting the wounded that can be patched well enough to fight again soon," Exeter grumbled.

"We've lost several hundred men as well," Gregor added, but the venom in his voice did not seem to be directed at Jonmarc; instead, the Temnottans appeared to be the intended recipients. "Crone take their souls! What whore-spawned commander hides behind beasts and shifters to do his blood work for him?"

"His name is Imri." The voice came from the entrance to

Valjan's tent. A slim *vayash moru* in a dark purple robe stood in the doorway. One look at his eyes gave Jonmarc to know that this newcomer was among the eldest of the Old Ones.

"This is Ansu," Valjan said, as the man entered the tent. "He arrived just before the battle."

To Jonmarc's surprise, Ansu stopped in front of him and inclined his head in greeting. "Hail, Lord of Dark Haven. Lord Gabriel found me and asked for my help in this matter. He also sent this for you." Ansu reached inside his robe to withdraw a folded parchment. At a glance, Jonmarc recognized Gabriel's precise handwriting and the wax seal with his crest.

The others watched in silence as Ansu took a seat on the other side of Gethin. "What do you know of the Temnotta commander—and how do you know it?" Jonmarc asked. He fingered the parchment, debating whether or not to open it, and then slipped it into the pouch on his belt to read later.

Ansu gave a cold smile that bared his eye teeth. "Four hundred years ago, I fought the Temnottans, as did Gabriel. I'm an air mage, not quite the gift with spirits as a full summoner, but possessed of magic that is tolerably close in some respects. In that war long ago, the Temnottan mages, the Volshe, were a formidable foe. It appears that, despite the passage of time, some things do not change."

"How do you know the name of their commander?" It was Gregor who asked, his expression skeptical to the point of hostility.

"In the last few months, two *vayash moru* mages from Temnotta have sought sanctuary in my lands, far to the north, on the border with Eastmark. It was . . . unusual . . . for it to happen once, let alone twice, considering that after the war, Temnotta did not consider me to be . . . welcoming."

"Maybe they were spies, or sent to spread false information," Gregor grumbled.

If Ansu noted Gregor's insolence, he did not show it. "I doubt it. Both men expected me to kill them, and they preferred death by my hand than being part of the Volshe's schemes in Temnotta."

"Which were?" Exeter's voice was a growl.

"The Volshe have returned to the ways that were forbidden after the Long War four centuries ago. Then, as now, they conspired to use their magic to tamper with shifters to create a perfect living killing machine." Ansu's eyes glinted, a hint to just how strongly he felt about the subject. "That was after they tried—and failed—to magically alter *vayash moru* toward the same ends."

"And this Imri? Where does he come in?" Valjan pressed.

"Imri is a powerful shifter, but more than that, he's also a mage. And his specialty is bending other shifters to his will," Ansu said. "Imri's 'gift' won him the jealousy of the Volshe and the attention of the Temnotta king, especially after the king began to harbor expansionary plans."

"If you knew Temnotta was up to something, why didn't you say something before now?" Jonmarc's temper was clear in his tone.

"The mages didn't know what the king was planning, only that he suddenly took an unusual interest in magic, and in a type of magic better suited to offense than defense," Ansu replied. "Neither of the two were senior enough among the Volshe to be privy to strategy meetings. There was nothing to do but watch and listen."

"What does this get us that we didn't have before?" Exeter's mood sounded every bit as dark as Jonmarc's.

"An opportunity," Ansu said, with a hint of a cold smile. "Temnotta's choice to invade the Winter Kingdoms brings their magic into our territory. Imri didn't bother looking into how the last such invasion fared. The magic of the Sacred Lady works differently than the magic of the Volshe. Tomorrow is Sohan. The Temnottans do not celebrate it, and so they overlook it at their peril. It's a festival of change, the change from autumn into winter." Ansu's smile broadened into a predatory grimace. "And on Sohan, souls compelled into a form against their will may be set free."

Valjan straightened. "I don't know much about magic, but are you saying that if we engage Imri's forces tomorrow night, on Sohan, you and the mages can break his hold over the shifters he commands?"

Ansu's eyes glittered with a cold light. "I believe so. The magicked beasts are also unnatural creatures, held together by the will and power of their creator. We may well be able to break Imri's power over his beasts. Once broken, such power is almost impossible to reestablish. Imri may find that his beasts are as ready to turn on him as on us."

Gregor leaned back and crossed his arms, skepticism clear in his face. "Is Imri a fool? If he's vulnerable, why would he choose now to attack?"

Ansu shrugged. "As I said, the Temnottans don't celebrate Sohan, so the date would be of no consequence to them. Imri might not have had a choice in the date. We know now that Temnotta's attack ranges from Isencroft to Eastmark. It's likely that Imri is only a general under orders." He paused. "Then, as now, Temnotta's arrogance may be its undoing. In its isolation, Temnotta has bothered to learn little about the lands around it. Always, the Volshe assume that their ways are best. It may never have occurred to them to explore the customs and magic of our people because the Volshe would have assumed them to be mere superstition, nothing of substance." The cold smile returned. "We will prove them wrong."

After another candlemark of strategizing, the weary generals finally took their leave of Valjan. Jonmarc was the last to leave. Gethin stepped ahead of him out of the tent and into the night air, and Valjan laid a hand on Jonmarc's arm. "Even considering the circumstances, you looked a bit preoccupied in there. Anything I can help with?"

Jonmarc sighed and shook his head. "Afraid not. I'm just worried about Carina. It's only another week until she's due to have the twins, and it's pretty certain I won't make it home in time."

Valjan nodded. "I was on campaign when both of my sons were born. I understand." He glanced down at the scar from the ritual wedding that marked Jonmarc's palm and back up to meet his gaze. "If she's fiery enough to win that kind of commitment from you, I dare say she'll be able to manage. Women do, you know. We men are much more essential at the beginning of a pregnancy than at the end."

Jonmarc chuckled, but the laughter did not reach his eyes. "True enough, I suppose. Still, I'd rather be there, even if there's little I can do."

Valjan clapped him on the shoulder. "You left her with Lord Gabriel? Then she's in good hands. Save your worries for the battlefield, my friend. The rest will take care of itself."

When Jonmarc finally reached the privacy of his own tent, he pulled off his boots and sat on the edge of his cot, lighting a candle from the embers in the brazier. He withdrew the parchment from inside his pouch and broke the embossed wax seal. Inside, he found two letters, one inside the other. The outer letter was clearly from Gabriel; the inner one in Carina's neat script.

He forced himself to read Gabriel's short update first.

Jonmarc—I hope this letter finds you as well as can be expected. I have located someone I believe will be an asset to you in the war, a very old vayash moru *named Ansu. It was difficult to find him, and even more of a challenge to give him a reason to involve himself, but in the end, his need for vengeance against the Temnottans won out. He's a dangerous man.*

Vygulf is headed your way with a dozen more vyrkin. Word spread among the refugees, and the newest among them insisted on joining the fight once they were well enough to do so. Take care, Jonmarc. The magic of Sohan night is powerful, and it weighs especially heavy on those of us for whom change is our essence. Look to Ansu and Vygulf to guide you. I know that you understand how greatly magic can affect war. I fear it will be even more so in the battles to come.

The manor and the holdings are secured. After we discovered and destroyed a small scouting party that had been dispatched by the Temnottans up the Nu River, we snagged the river near Dark Haven to prevent further incursions. When war is past, we can make the river navigable again, but for now, perhaps, you can sleep better at least on that accord.

Carina is in good hands, with Lisette and Sister Glenice looking after her. I fear that you will not be free of the war in time for the birth. If that is the case, know that I am pledged to the safety of Carina and your daughters. I pray to Istra that these times will quickly be behind us. Gabriel

Jonmarc rubbed his palm across his eyes. Outside, a gong sounded second bells. Jonmarc unfolded the letter from Carina carefully.

My dearest Jonmarc. I could not pass up the chance to send my note to you along with Gabriel's more urgent letter. Things are going as well as can be expected, and both Lisette and Sister Glenice are watching over me closely enough to drive a person to distraction. I'm very ready for the girls to be born, and have already set the servants to loosening every knot in the manor to speed

*the birth. Carroway and Macaria have pitched in to help
with the refugees, doing even more than they did before,
and Macaria has promised to play for me when my
time comes, to ease the pain. It seems a minor triumph in
the face of all that is going on, but Carroway's hand is
nearly as good as new, though it may always pain him in
the cold. We may be under siege, but we have the best
music in the Winter Kingdoms!*

*I miss you terribly, and mind Berry's absence as well,
though I know you both have duties you can't avoid. Think
of me, but don't worry overmuch. I'll be waiting when you
come home, with our daughters.*

With all my love, Carina

Jonmarc blew out the candle and stretched out on his cot.
Weary as he was, sleep proved elusive.

Despite the rout of the night before, the Principality army and its
mercs rallied quickly. Jonmarc stood outside his tent, nursing a
cup of black *kerif* and hoping the strong drink would make up
for a night that had afforded little sleep. He watched the preparations for the counterstrike and wondered exactly what—or who—
would meet them on the battlefield. He looked out across the
camp and spotted Exeter striding across camp, heading his way.

"I figured you'd be up early."

Jonmarc shrugged and took another large gulp of the bitter
kerif. "Sleep is for the dead." He paused. "Any word on how
our ships fared?"

Exeter scowled and let loose with a few choice curses that
were creatively obscene, even for a mercenary. "Not well. Some
of the *vayash moru* scouts came back last night, and we've
gotten a few mortal runners in early this morning. Temnottan

ships showed up from farther out at sea than we expected. Our ships were caught between the burning hulls in the bay and the attack. They fought their way out of the trap, but many of the ships were seriously damaged. We hope to have the seaworthy ships ready for the attack tonight, but I don't like the idea of even more Temnottan ships out there."

"And I'm betting these will have a mix of men and shifters," Jonmarc replied. He drained the last of his *kerif*, grimacing at the dregs. "The beasts are too unstable—probably took a lot of magic just to keep them from tearing the ships apart."

"Unless their mages can just make the beasts go to sleep until they're needed."

Jonmarc scowled at him. "Aren't you just full of cheery ideas."

Exeter shrugged. "Foreseeing bad outcomes is my job." He stood in silence, watching the camp for a moment before he spoke again. "Do you think the mages can do it? Break Imri's spell on his shifters?"

"Don't know. If they can't, we're going to be in for a bad time of it." Jonmarc shook his head. "Tevin and the other mages were going to huddle with the *Hojuns* and figure something out. Ansu said he'd join them at sundown, but by then, we'd damn well better have a battle plan."

Exeter's eyes were unreadable. "For all our sakes, I hope they know what they're doing."

The troops rallied in the late morning, summoned by the call of a horn. Jonmarc caught a glimpse of Gregor at a distance. Gregor wore a uniform coat, but from the way he sat his horse, Jonmarc wondered just how badly Gregor had been wounded the night before.

Gethin was waiting with the rest of Jonmarc's division when Jonmarc and Exeter were ready to head out.

"I was hoping, now that you've made your point, that you'd head back to the palace," Jonmarc said.

Gethin grinned. "Sorry to disappoint you, but I'm here for the duration. And so are the *Hojun*. They're already in position, with the rest of the mages."

Valjan's soldiers were the first to march out, followed by Jonmarc's division and then Gregor's troops. As they retraced their path from the night before, the toll of the battle was clear. Bodies, human and otherwise, littered the slope, lying where they fell in the tall grass. Farther toward the coast, a wide stretch of land was burned bare, scorched and blackened. The smell of death hung over the battlefield.

"Where's Gregor going?" Gethin scanned the ranks of marching soldiers.

"East of here, farther down the coast. The *vayash moru* scouts and the mages confirmed there were ships headed in that direction." The weather had turned colder and wet, roughening Jonmarc's voice. "Damn Principality coastline—plenty of inlets and places for ships to hide. We don't have enough scouts—or *vayash moru*—to search them all."

Gethin watched him closely. "You think it's a trap?"

Jonmarc shrugged ill-humoredly. "Could be. Gregor knows that. We can't afford to have Temnotta land ships in those inlets and flank us."

Gethin considered the possibility in silence for a moment. "What if the ships were just to draw us off, make us spread the resources too thin?"

Jonmarc acknowledged him with a grunt. "That's the problem with battles. You only have one shot to get it right. Trust me, we argued half the morning. In the end, the evidence seemed strong that the Temnottans could be planning to land down the coast. It was as much of a risk to leave ourselves open to a flanking attack as it was to divert the resources." He shrugged again. "We'll know which was right when we win—or die."

Throughout the night, the privateer vessels of the Principality merc navy had regrouped enough to harry the Temnottan ships, keeping them too occupied to land troops until the army could get into position. Jonmarc looked out over the beach and out to sea. The sunken hulls of the ships set afire the night before had burned down to the waterline. A fleet of Temnottan ships held the mouth of the bay, but the small, quick mercenary vessels used the morning fog to strike and retreat before the larger, slower-maneuvering ships could respond. The pirate ships had done their job keeping the Temnottan fleet busy.

"What makes you think they'll attack again so quickly?" Gethin's attention was on the battle that raged at the mouth of the bay.

"The longer they stay on those ships, the harder it's going to be for Imri to control and feed his 'creatures,'" Jonmarc replied. "They can't sail farther west and land easily; the coastline's too rocky and there are too many cliffs. Go too far east, and they've got to march for days before they reach any kind of real target, like Principality City. They'd be vulnerable." He shook his head. "No, they've got good reasons for wanting to land here—and we've got the same reasons for waiting them out."

Once again, they were waiting for the battle to start. War, Jonmarc had long ago discovered, was mostly boredom broken up by short bursts of mortal terror. Given the choice, he decided, he'd rather face the terror.

When the fog lifted, the Temnottan ships hoisted their sails and broke the line of their blockade to go after the privateer vessels. Soon, only the masts were in sight from the shore, but by the look of it, the Temnottan commander had decided to put an end to the merc ships' harassment. The soldiers watched grimly as the Temnottan warships hunted their prey, attacking the privateering ships with fire arrows, heavy iron balls hurled from small, on-deck catapults, and blasts of mage fire. Within two candlemarks, the privateering ships had scattered, and the

Temnottan fleet sailed back to the bay, entering as far as they dared without snagging their hulls on the burned remnants of the sunken ships.

"I don't like this," Jonmarc muttered. "They can't believe that we'll just let them offload men and monsters without picking them off in the landing craft. Something isn't adding up."

Suddenly, shouting at the rear of the formation broke the quiet. Jonmarc dug his heels into his horse's sides and rode back to see what the commotion was about, with Gethin right behind him.

A ragged line of soldiers straggled across the fields toward them. Their uniforms torn and streaked with blood and dirt, men limped and staggered until they reached the waiting army.

"They're coming," the first soldier to reach them panted, eyes wide with fear. "We tried but we couldn't hold them. Dark Lady take my soul! They're coming."

Jonmarc felt a hard knot form in the pit of his stomach. "Where's the rest of your division?"

"Dead. Burned. Eaten. Gone, all of them—"

"Soldier, report!" Jonmarc snapped. "I need to know what happened."

"It was bad, sir." The voice came from another soldier, a man who looked to be about Jonmarc's age and had the manner of a professional fighter. "They were waiting for us. Must have given the sentry ships the slip or blinded them with magic. Somehow, they got around us and landed up the coast in the inlets. There were thousands of them, and they're headed this way."

Jonmarc lifted his face to the wind, looking out over the slopes of tall, waving grass in the direction the soldiers had come from. "How long?"

"Maybe a candlemark. Not much more than that."

"General Gregor?"

"Dead, sir. Fought like the Crone's own, to the end. I saw him go down myself."

Jonmarc swore. Much as he disliked Gregor, this was the wrong way to be rid of him. "All right," Jonmarc said. "We'll be ready when they get here. Valjan's going to have to handle whatever happens in the bay." With that, he rode down the line, shouting orders to his captains to get their men positioned to defend against an attack from the flank. Runners scrambled to take news of the new attack to Valjan and Exeter.

The sun slipped past its height before the distant sound of footsteps reached them.

"Here they come!" The cry started with a scout and echoed down the line as soldiers readied for the onslaught.

Animals, not men, led the advance. Wolves and bears covered ground with long, loping steps in a line of attack that Jonmarc guessed to be several hundred long. Row upon row followed them before the columns of regular soldiers appeared.

"Hold your positions!" Jonmarc shouted. Pikemen set their long, stout pikes into the ground at an angle readied for the attack. Behind them, archers lifted their bows. Neither the pikes nor the archers were likely to stop the attack, but they could make the enemy's advance costly and decrease the numbers that made it through to battle the foot soldiers.

The cold fall air rang with the snarls of wolves and the roar of bears. Imri's compelled shifters had a wild, mad look about them, not driven past the point of sanity like *ashtenerath*, but far beyond the point of caring for their own safety. The beasts launched themselves at the pikes, heedless of how many of their number fell to the ground impaled on the sharp tips. A hail of arrows rained down on the attackers, but the shifters never broke stride as their fellows dropped with arrows prickling from their bodies.

The line held for only moments before the shifters crashed

through. Once the pikes were gone, the archers could not hold off the press themselves.

Foot soldiers waded to the fore, assisted by mounted men at arms, while the surviving archers fled to find new, more protected vantage points. In the fray, Jonmarc lost sight of Gethin, but the onslaught left no time to worry about anything except holding off wave after wave of the desperate shifters.

It was obvious that the Temnottan soldiers were content to let the shifters bear the brunt of the battle. Jonmarc did not doubt that the soldiers would sweep in to take care of any Principality fighters left standing when the shifters were through. The shifters fought with an unnatural fury, and if the men inside the beasts' forms knew that the Temnottans considered them expendable, it did not blunt the ferocity of their attack.

Packs of wolves in groups of threes and fours attacked soldiers, while the huge bears took on up to six men at a time. These shifters seemed driven to fight, no matter how uneven the odds against them. The unsettling rage in their eyes made Jonmarc wonder how much of the relentless attack was the effect of Imri's curse, and how much was mass suicide by men pushed past reasoning.

Whether fear or anger drove the attack, the results were devastating. Jonmarc had personally killed a score of wolves, but he was tiring, and he knew his men could not hold out forever. The Temnottans held back, as if they were afraid of their own shifters, and perhaps, Jonmarc thought, they had reason. Whatever pain and compulsion drove the shifters to attack might wish to turn itself on their captors, though Jonmarc doubted Imri's compulsion permitted it. The field was littered with more dead shifters than Principality soldiers, but exhausted by the fight, Jonmarc knew the numbers would change as soon as the Temnottans made their attack.

The sun was low in the sky, and the moon was large just

above the horizon. *Ansu said that the curse could be lifted on Sohan night. He'd better mean early evening, because there won't be enough of us alive by midnight for it to matter by then.*

The light was fading as a fog rose from the ground. It was too sudden to be natural, and while the fog did not deter the shifters, Jonmarc saw consternation among the waiting Temnottans. Without warning, dozens of wolves appeared over the crest of the ridge behind Jonmarc's troops, and Jonmarc fought a wave of despair at the thought of a renewed attack.

But these wolves did not head for Jonmarc's weary soldiers. They ran at the Temnottans, teeth bared, snarling and snapping. Jonmarc saw the Temnottans scrambling to defend themselves, and the Volshe that controlled the shifters shouted spells in vain at the new wolves.

One of the Volshe collapsed under the weight of a huge, gray wolf, still shouting counter spells until the wolf snapped its powerful jaws on his neck, silencing him. The other Volshe screamed and ran, making it only a few steps until two more of the attacking wolves leaped together to bring him down.

When the Volshe fell, the Temnottan shifters seemed momentarily dazed, as if they had been driven on by a maddening drumbeat that suddenly stopped. Before the Temnottans could rally for an attack, Jonmarc's soldiers seized the advantage, setting on the shifters before they could regain their wits.

The fog was swirling around the remaining shifters and the now-rattled Temnottan soldiers. The air had grown markedly colder, although the sun had not yet completely set. The fog took on the shape of wolves, and as the mist-wolves grew more solid, they joined the attack against Imri's shifters and the Temnottan soldiers.

The Temnottans held their ground until the first of the attacking mist-wolves leaped at—and through—their line, emerging with a freshly torn heart in its massive jaws as the soldier fell dead behind it.

By now, the moon had risen, large and yellow. A sudden cold wind blew across a stand of trees, carrying a blizzard of golden leaves across the battlefield and stirring the tall grass. The wind's intensity grew, and Jonmarc felt the hairs on the back of his neck rise, not from cold but from the insistent prickle he knew was magic.

A dull orange glow settled with the falling leaves, bathing the battlefield in an unnatural luminescence. The mist-wolves seemed unaffected, as did the wolves that had joined on the Principality side of the battle, wolves whose violet eyes marked them as *vyrkin*. The glow surrounded the Temnottan shifters like a nimbus, and the attacking bears and wolves stopped in their tracks. The wolves began to howl, and the bears roared, but as the nimbus grew brighter, their cries became high-pitched, and they fell to the ground writhing.

Jonmarc kept an eye on the Temnottan line of soldiers, but they held their ground, staring at the downed and glowing shifters. The shifters' shapes began to blur, and a dull ripping sound echoed across the battlefield, as if someone tore a knife down through tanned hides. The shifters' cries had become shrieks of pain and fear, as the wolf and bear bodies tore themselves apart in the orange glow, leaving in their place bloody, naked men.

Cries of fear rose from the Temnottans, who without their Volshe could not counter this sudden turnabout. As Jonmarc and his soldiers rounded up what remained of the compelled shifters with weary remorselessness, the *vyrkin* and mist-wolves ran the Temnottans to ground. No matter where the panicked Temnottans fled, the fog rose to meet them, until the twilight was filled with the howls of wolves and the snap of teeth. The *vyrkin* continued to harry the Temnottans, running them to ground or herding them back toward where the mist-wolves could finish them off.

Jonmarc chanced a look toward the ridge behind them. Vygulf stood in the moonlight, arms outstretched, face set with concentration. Farther down the ridge, Jonmarc could see Ansu, hands raised in a gesture of warding. Jonmarc turned back to the battlefield and was relieved to see Gethin making his way toward him. The Eastmark prince's cuirass bore deep gouges, and his tunic and pants were spattered with blood. One arm bore a nasty gash. Only after he had noted Gethin's injuries did Jonmarc stop to realize how many bruises and slashes of his own he had taken in the fight.

"What do you want us to do with the lot of them?" One of Jonmarc's captains stood beside the shivering form of a Temnottan shifter. The man lay facedown, with his hands clasped behind his head.

Jonmarc looked up toward where Vygulf stood on the ridge. The *vyrkin* shaman slowly lowered his arms, lips still moving in a warding, and then walked down to where Jonmarc stood. Ansu joined them a moment later.

"Will they shift back if we leave them alive?" Jonmarc asked Vygulf with a jerk of his head toward the downed shifter. "The fight's gone out of them."

Vygulf looked across the field. Dozens of the shifters lay unmoving, distinguished from the corpses by the Principality soldiers standing over them, swords ready. "The Sohan night magic has stripped the compulsion from them. So long as they don't rejoin the mage who cast the curse, they should remain human." He shrugged. "Cage them if you like. If they shift, your archers can take care of them, but I don't think you'll have a problem."

Jonmarc let out a silent sigh of relief. Killing in battle was something he had learned to live with long ago, but he had no desire to skewer surrendering troops. He turned back toward the soldiers who were awaiting orders. "Tie them up, cover them up, and march them back to the holding area," he shouted.

He met Vygulf's gaze. "Thank you. Between your magic and whatever the mages did for Sohan, it saved our hides." He glanced to Ansu. "I really don't want to think about how this would have gone without you."

Ansu nodded. "I'm pleased to have arrived in time."

Vygulf looked out over the fields in the direction the Temnottans had retreated. "My wolves will harry them back to their camp and report their location and numbers. Come morning, you can do as you please with the survivors."

"Pleased to see you and your men on your feet." The newcomer's voice startled Jonmarc, who turned to see Laisren striding out of the shadows.

"How did Valjan fare?"

Laisren shrugged. "The Temnottans landed a force of men and shifters, but the mages worked their Sohan magic on them." He gave a grim smile. "Fortunately, such magic does not affect those of us for whom change is voluntary. We were able to help with the attack, much as the *vyrkin* aided you." He licked his lips. "It was an expensive evening for Temnotta."

Behind Jonmarc, captains called their troops to order and men gathered the wounded and the prisoners. In daylight, they would return to make a pyre of the dead. Jonmarc gazed over the fields toward where the Temnottans had fled.

Jonmarc looked from Laisren to Ansu. "If Valjan can spare the *vayash moru*, I want you to find General Gregor's division. We received warning from men who said they were the only survivors, that Gregor and the rest had been killed." He met Laisren's gaze. "We need to know if that's the truth, and if there are survivors, we'll need them back at camp. It's too dark for me to set out now with a search party, but I don't like the idea of wounded men lying untended all night."

Laisren nodded. "Let me rally the other *vayash moru*, and we'll report what we find." He looked out over the darkened battlefield. "As expensive as we made it for the Temnottans, I dare say we've paid a high price ourselves."

"The question is—how many more do they have to send against us?" Jonmarc paused as a thought struck him, and he turned to Ansu and Vygulf. "If this Imri and his Volshe could compel their own soldiers into wolves and bears, can he turn something like that against our men?"

Vygulf thought for a moment, and then shook his head. "Doubtful. That kind of magic takes a great deal of energy. I don't think their mages created such a large number of shifters quickly. They've been preparing for this invasion for quite some time, I'd say. Our mages have placed wardings around the camps; I dare say after this, they'll do some more powerful workings. I think you're safe from seeing your men turned into wolves."

"As Laisren said, the nature—and magic—of *vayash moru* are different. We are immune to this type of magic," Ansu replied. He met Jonmarc's gaze. "I have some thoughts about how to assure that our prisoners will not fall victim to the same magic again. I'll test my theory, and let the other mages know what I find." With that, he strode off in the direction the captives had been taken.

Jonmarc's attention returned to Gethin. The Eastmark prince had stood silently throughout the whole exchange. "Had enough excitement for one day?" Jonmarc asked, taking in Gethin's appearance.

A bitter half smile touched Gethin's lips. "You'll have to let the queen know that despite the odds, I survived to be a problem for another day."

"Nice to know you can hold your own, even when your *Hojuns* are elsewhere."

"I was thinking the same thing myself." Gethin grabbed at the reins of a stray horse and swung up into the saddle. He looked out over the still bodies that lay sprawled on the battlefield. "What happens next?"

Jonmarc drew a deep breath. "I don't know, Gethin. That's what worries me."

17

I *know you can hear me.* The spirit's voice was insistent.

Aidane closed her eyes in concentration. *I don't want to hear you. Go away.*

My wife is dying. She has the plague. Please, carry my message to her. Let her know I await her by the Gray Sea.

Go away!

"M'lady? Did you say something?" A servant bringing hot tea and biscuits glanced up from her work to where Aidane sat near the fireplace in her room at Lienholt Palace.

"No, sorry. Just thinking out loud," Aidane murmured, embarrassed.

"Will Lord Kolin be joining you?"

"He should be here any minute."

"Very well, m'lady. I'll have a flagon of goat's blood sent up right away. Just ring if you need something," she added, and slipped out of the room.

Aidane poured herself a cup of tea and smiled to herself. Love was a luxury few whores ever had the chance to experience, and Aidane had been certain she would be no different. But these last several weeks with Kolin had made her begin to hope, and he proved himself to her by his constancy. More to her surprise, despite the fact that she could tell that Kolin was attracted to her, he had not tried to take her to his bed. Instead, Kolin pursued her with a charming courtliness, as if she were actually a lady. And as the days wore on, Aidane finally admitted to herself that Kolin's gentle pursuit had won her love.

The door on the other side of the parlor opened, and Kolin entered. It was early evening, not long after sunset, and he had left immediately upon rising to feed. Aidane rose and met him at the door, and he took her into his arms and kissed her. His lips were warm. Aidane let herself lean into the kiss.

"Do we really have to go to the banquet tonight? I'd rather stay in and talk." They spent most nights by the fireplace, curled up together, sharing stories. She was fascinated by Kolin's tales of all that he had seen over the last two centuries, and to her surprise, he seemed genuinely interested in learning more about her past.

Kolin grinned. "Berry's counting on us. She says we're the only hope she has of not being trapped in boring court talk."

Aidane sighed and slipped out of his arms. "Are you sure it's wise for us to go as a couple? There's bound to be gossip."

Kolin took her hand and turned her to face him. "Then it's about time they talk. I care about you, and I have no intention of hiding the fact that we're together." He paused. "Unless you're embarrassed to be escorted by a *vayash moru*."

"I don't give a damn about that. You know it. But to the court, I'm just a fancy whore."

"You're a guest of the queen's. A hero. You have more right to sit at the queen's table than most of the nobles. And there's no one else I'd rather have accompany me." He drew her close to him again, holding her against his chest. "Let them talk. We have nothing to be ashamed of."

After a moment, he drew back from her. "I have something for you," Kolin said with a hint of a smile. He led her to a chair near the fire. From the pocket of his waistcoat, he withdrew two small silk-wrapped packages.

"Here. Open these. They're Sohan night gifts."

Aidane laid the packages on her lap and carefully unwrapped them. The larger held a beautiful garnet necklace. It was far more expensive than anything even the wealthiest of Aidane's clients had ever given her, and it had obviously been made by a master craftsman. "I can't—"

"It's from the queen," Kolin said in tone to settle her objections. "A token of her gratitude, and, truth be told, it's also because she likes you."

"It's beautiful."

"Go ahead, open the other one."

It took her a moment to untie the smaller package. When the silk wrapping fell away, inside was a finely wrought bracelet of silver and onyx. Aidane gasped. It was every bit as beautiful as the necklace.

"You like it?"

"It's lovely. Just beautiful."

Kolin's smile widened. "Good. That one's from me."

Aidane looked up, questioning, and Kolin looked away, a blush creeping into his cheeks. "In my day, Sohan night was a time for a young man to give a gift to the lady who caught his fancy. It's true that after two hundred years, I'm no longer exactly 'young'—"

"And I'm not really a lady," Aidane said quietly.

Kolin knelt in front of her. "We've been through that. I don't care about the past. But I do care about you, Aidane."

Aidane felt her throat tighten. Her hand closed around the bracelet and she met Kolin's eyes. "I'm not Elsbet."

He gave a sad smile. "I know. Elsbet is well and truly gone to her rest. Don't you think two hundred years is long enough to grieve? I don't want you to be Elsbet. I like Aidane just fine."

Kolin leaned forward and kissed her gently. She moved closer and returned the kiss. He drew back and cupped her cheek gently with his hand. "I want to make sure you understand my gift. I'm not trying to bed you, Aidane. I want more than that. I love you."

Aidane blinked back tears at this unexpected and over-whelming admission. "I love you too," she murmured. She glanced up. "But I didn't know the custom. Nargi doesn't keep Sohan. I don't have a gift for you."

Kolin's blue eyes were bright. "I hadn't dared hope that you felt the same for me. If you truly do, that's gift enough," he said, as he drew her to him to kiss her again.

When they drew apart, Aidane looked up at him. "Can you stay until it's time to get ready for the feast?"

Kolin shook his head. "Afraid not. The queen asked me to take care of a few things for her before the formalities. I'll be back in time to escort you down to the great room." He smiled. "I can't wait to see you in the gown Berry sent for you."

"You know about that?"

His smile widened. "I helped her choose it." With that, Kolin excused himself and left to take care of the queen's business, leaving Aidane alone with her tea. But to her chagrin, as soon as he left, the voices of the ghosts crowded around her.

The onslaught of spirits had begun days ago, during the preparations for Sohan. As the Festival of Changes grew closer, the voices had grown more numerous and more insistent. Others might focus on the seasonal shift from fall to winter, or from autumn-planted seeds to the expected spring crops, but for Aidane, the change most apparent at this time was the ever-present cycle of life and death. She wondered if seers, mediums, hedge witches, and summoners also felt the restless dead most strongly on such feast nights, and how they managed to keep the dead at bay.

Her own protective measures were not sufficient. She had tried warding with salt, and it had done well enough to keep the spirits from taking form in her room, but their voices called to her across the threshold, begging for help.

I'm not really the right person, Aidane thought tiredly. Spirits did not sleep, and lately, neither had Aidane, unable to shut out the ghostly voices that called to her. *I'm a ghost whore, and if their loved ones are dying, it's definitely the wrong time to arrange a tryst.*

It's a message we seek, not trysting. The voice came from the sad-eyed ghost of a young woman whom Aidane guessed to be in her late twenties, just a few years older than Aidane herself. The young woman's face was already careworn, her eyes tired, and Aidane wondered how many children the ghostly woman had birthed before death found her.

The plague tore us from our families, from the people we love, the woman's ghost continued. She did not beg for Aidane's favor, as so many of the other ghosts had done, harrying Aidane's sleep. Nor did she rail or threaten.

Is that why you linger?

I stayed to watch over my family, and one by one, the plague took them. The last of my children died just two nights ago. I saw them all to their rest in the arms of the Lady.

Yet you stay behind. Why?

My husband is the only one left alive. He grieves for us, and he doesn't know that I watch him from afar. It's not for a . . . joining . . . that I want your help. Just to go to him, to tell him that the children rest with the Lady, and that I'll wait for him until his time comes.

Aidane shook her head, and then feigned a cough, fearing the maid would think her mad for conversing with "empty" air. *There are too many of you. I can't—*

Please, m'lady. My husband is a groomsman in the stable, here at the palace. T'will take but a few moments of your time. Please, m'lady, I beg of you—

Aidane sighed. The spirit had no true idea of how much it cost her to permit possession, even for something like conversation. But there was something about the ghostly woman that overcame Aidane's resistance, even though she feared it would just make the other ghosts harder to decline. *All right*, she conceded. *But just a word with him. Nothing more.*

Aidane finished her tea and set it down, resigned to go through with her promise. The maid had already left the room, and Aidane lingered a few minutes more to let the servant get ahead of her on the steps before she let herself out of the door. She made her way to the servants' stairs, rather than the main stairway, all the better to avoid prying eyes. When festivals or official events did not require her to dress the part of a *serroquette*, Aidane had taken to wearing plain dresses that did not call attention to her or her talent. Queen Berwyn's welcome had been sincere, and it was the queen who insisted Aidane stay on at the palace, but Aidane was well aware of the whispers and dark glances she received from many at court and tried to remain unnoticed as much as possible.

As Aidane headed for the stables, the ghost remained with her, unseen by others but quite audible to Aidane. The servants' stairs felt more comfortable to Aidane than the gilt-railed sweeping central staircase. *After all, what's a whore but a different kind of servant, one at the bottom of the pecking order?* she thought as she made her way down the steps and across the courtyard to the stables. When she reached the stables, she hesitated. Dozens of men bustled about the large building, tending to the horses, mucking out the stalls, and grooming their precious charges.

There. That's Jodd.

Aidane followed the ghost's urging and saw a haggard-looking man who appeared to be a few years older than the ghost. He swept the stable with his eyes downcast and mumbled a terse reply the few times he was spoken to. Aidane waited until he left the busy main area of the stable and followed him around to the back of the building. At first, she feared he had gone outside to relieve himself, but then she saw that he moved a ways down the wall, away from the stable bustle, and took a pipe from his pocket. Stuffing a bit of pipe weed into its bowl, Jodd lit the pipe with a spark and leaned against the wall as if he would have liked to collapse.

Speak to him. Let me in.

Aidane braced herself for the possession and let the ghost fill her. This time, she did not withdraw into her hiding place, since she had no intention of allowing the ghost to go further than a conversation. The ghost's memories washed over her. The woman's name had been Detri, and she had four children, all young. Grief, loss, and yearning washed over Aidane like a tide. *Let's get this over with*, Aidane said.

"Jodd." The voice was her own but not hers, and as the man looked up, his eyes widened. He made a sign of warding and looked as if he might bolt or faint.

"Please, don't go. It's me, Detri. My . . . friend . . . allowed me to use her to speak to you."

Jodd's face went pale. "It sounds like Detri, but it can't be. Detri's dead."

The dead woman's mannerisms came naturally to Aidane, who found herself approaching Jodd with a striding step, the movement of a working woman, not the mincing step of a well-born lady with voluminous skirts and impractical shoes. "I'm dead, that's true. But I miss you. I helped the children cross the Gray Sea. They're safe now, in the Lady's arms. I'll wait for you."

The pipe slipped from the man's fingers. "Will I die, too? Is that what you mean?" His voice rose into a panicked squeak.

"No, Jodd. No."

"Then what do you mean? An accident? How will I die?"

Aidane could feel the sorrow that filled the ghost and Detri's frustration at Jodd's misunderstanding. "May you live a hundred years, my love. I only meant that I'll wait for you, on the shore of the Gray Sea, until your time comes so we may cross together."

Jodd considered Detri's words, and he relaxed a little, losing his panicked expression. "How did you . . ." His words trailed off, but his meaning was clear as he tried to reconcile Aidane's appearance with the obvious presence of his dead wife.

"She is a—" Detri started to say "ghost whore" but Aidane drowned her out with a purposeful cough. "She has a talent with spirits," Detri said after a stern mental rebuke from Aidane. "Remember me and the children, Jodd. I can't come to you again, but I'll watch over you and wait."

Her message delivered, Detri's spirit slipped away from Aidane, leaving Aidane momentarily light-headed. Jodd grabbed Aidane's arm as she turned away.

"Was that some kind of trick?"

Still feeling the effects of the possession, Aidane pulled her arm free, trying not to move too quickly for fear she might faint. "No trick. I have a . . . way . . . with spirits."

Jodd's eyes narrowed. "Is it true? That Detri will never leave me?"

Aidane saw a trapped look in the man's eyes that made her heart sink. "That's what she said."

Jodd swore. "By the Lady! I'm twenty and nine years old. Am I never to take another wife? Oh, Detri was all right, but we were young and my parents arranged it. I'd have stayed with her, for the children, if things had worked out differently, but now—"

Aidane felt her temper flare. "Now that she and your children are barely cold in their graves, you've already given thought to her replacement, is that it?" Aidane had always found that the moments just after a possession faded were difficult emotionally. A side effect of relinquishing control was sharper-than-usual feelings: joy, sorrow, fear. Now, the gap between Detri's sorrowful faithfulness and Jodd's desire to remedy his widower status sent a surge of anger through Aidane.

"I'm still alive, aren't I? I didn't mean I'd take a wife right away," he said, taking a step back as he saw the anger in Aidane's face. "Maybe not till the springtime—"

Aidane spat on the hard-packed dirt. "You don't deserve Detri. It would serve you right if she crossed the sea without you. Pox take you." At that, Aidane turned on her heel and left, paying no heed to the sputtering man behind her.

She was so worked up about Jodd's faithlessness that she did not hear the footsteps behind her until the newcomer was close enough to lay a hand on her shoulder.

"Well, who do we have here?"

It took Aidane a moment to place the man who stood with a firm grip on her shoulder. She had seen him a few times at court and knew him to be the son of one of the lords. After another few seconds, she remembered which lord and felt uneasiness turn to fear. The man had the dark looks of his father, Lord Norden, a man whose coloring spoke of Trevath blood. She had seen Lord Norden make all of the appropriate gestures of support to the queen, yet the few times she had happened by when Norden was talking with his friends, the lord had been a sharp critic of the new queen and her unorthodox champion. From what she had seen of Norden's son, Antony, he was as critical and cynical as his father.

Aidane tried to shrug out of Antony's grip, but the young man grabbed her by the arm and yanked her into an alcove where the tack was stored. "Let me go. I have business at the palace."

"Whore's business, is it? Friendly with the stable hands, too?" Antony pushed Aidane up against the rough wall of the tack room and let his fingers stroke her cheek. "You're a pretty little trollop. I bet you're a feisty wench between the covers."

"Let me go!" Aidane gave a sharp kick against Antony's shin, hoping he would drop his hold. He howled in pain but gripped her arm tightly enough to bruise and he slammed her back against the wall.

"You don't have a choice." His voice had lost its mock seduction. It had become as hard and cold as Antony's eyes. "I'm a lord's son, and you're just a fancy whore. Now give me some of what you do for your clients, and if I'm satisfied, there might be a gold piece in it for you."

Antony's hand fell to her bosom, and Aidane took a sharp breath. The rage she had felt for the faithless Jodd swelled again, and with it, her power surged, drawing all of the woeful spirits to her she heard clamoring outside the city wall. She twisted away from Antony, but he brought his right hand down with a sharp crack across her cheek.

"Just for that, I won't be gentle, and there'll be no gold," he hissed. "Hold still, or I'll see you thrown out of the palace into the gutter where you belong. You're an embarrassment to the court. My father can make it expensive for the queen to keep you. Do you really think she'd favor you if the price was her reputation?"

There was no one around to help her; even if someone had come upon them, Aidane doubted any of the servants would raise a hand to stop a lord's son from having his way with a whore. Desperate, she opened herself to the press of spirits, letting them fill her. Their emotions swept over her, giving her the burst of strength she needed to break free of Antony's grip. He lunged after her, and she grabbed the first thing that came to hand: a bit and bridle. She swung it hard, catching him across the temple and opening a gash on his forehead. He tore it from her hands and threw it across the room.

Antony cursed and lunged after her, catching her by the ankle. "When I'm done with you, whore, even Buka wouldn't have enough pieces left to play with."

The pounding of Aidane's heart fed the swell of the spirits' emotions. More spirits crowded to her, thrumming with borrowed energy. Aidane kicked at Antony and landed a heel on his shoulder. He grabbed at her free foot with his other hand, and the pressure was nearly enough to break bone. Aidane felt around desperately for something, anything to fend off her attacker. Her hand fell on one of the metal combs the groomsmen used to curry the horses. With a cry, Aidane used the spirits' energy to heave Antony away from her, bringing the horse comb down hard on his hand when he reached for her. The sharp tines of the comb sank into his hand, starting a stream of blood.

She scrambled to her feet and ran for the door, yanking it open just barely ahead of Antony.

"I'll fix you for this," Antony shouted behind her. "Just wait. I'll fix you."

Aidane ran back across the servants' courtyard and up the back steps. By the time she reached her room, her arm had begun to ache and her eye was starting to swell shut. She closed the door behind her and collapsed against it, sobbing for breath.

I should have known it would come to this. I'm a whore. I don't belong in a palace. I've done everything I can to help the queen; now I'm just a burden, and an embarrassment. The queen's so young; she doesn't need trouble from the likes of Lord Norden on top of the war and the Durim.

Aidane took several deep breaths, steadying herself. She looked around the room. A maid had already laid out a dress for her to wear to the Sohan festival this evening. She felt a twinge of regret. The palace celebrations would be filled with magicians and conjurers doing sleight-of-hand tricks and real magic in celebration of the Feast of Changes. Men and women would exchange outfits and go about "changed," parodying each other. Food, wine, and ale would be plentiful, and musicians would play for their costumed audience until the dawn.

I need to leave. The truth was as clear as it was painful. Lord Norden's son would not forget that she had bested him. He and his father were well positioned to make trouble at court for Berry. And though Berry had welcomed Kolin, Aidane knew that the welcome for *vayash moru* was always fragile at best. It wouldn't take much for the court gossip to turn on Kolin, isolating the queen further. *Staying in the palace puts Kolin and the queen at risk. I can't take the chance that harm will come to them because of me.*

Aidane sat down at the writing desk that stood beside the darkened window. Night had fallen, and already, beyond the window, Aidane could see the flickering of newly lit bonfires in the courtyard. Everyone would be busy with the festival. They wouldn't notice that she was gone until she was far away.

A knock at the door startled her. She ignored it, but the visitor knocked again. "Aidane? It's Kolin. Let me in."

Aidane gasped and looked down at her dress. It was dirty and torn from the scuffle in the stable, and she was almost certain her cheek had begun to purple. "I'm not ready," Aidane called.

"Aidane?"

Aidane moved away from the writing table and turned her back to the door. "Come in."

She did not turn to look as Kolin entered the room. Other than the click of the latch, he moved soundlessly, though how he managed to keep his boots from betraying his footsteps, she did not know. She smelled warm apple cakes and heard Kolin set something on the table by the fireplace.

"I happened to intercept the servant on her way up with some cakes for the feast night," Kolin said. "I figured I'd bring them myself, since I was already on the way."

"Thank you," Aidane said, still refusing to turn.

Kolin chuckled. "Why so shy all of a sudden?"

"I . . . don't feel well. I'm sorry. I'm really not fit for company."

Kolin was beside her before she ever heard the rush of air that was the only warning of his movement. "What happened, Aidane? Something's wrong."

Aidane bit her lip, forcing back tears. "Nothing. Just . . . feast night jitters. Please, I'll be all right—"

Kolin touched her shoulder and she winced, the memory of Antony's grip too fresh in her mind. She let him turn her to face him, saw his expression move from shock to rage, and felt the same lethal coldness that she had glimpsed when she had seen him fight the Durim.

"Who did this?"

"Please, don't. It's not important."

Kolin's voice was icy. "You are a personal guest of the queen, under her protection. Whoever did this didn't just injure you; he struck a blow at the queen herself." But in Kolin's eyes, Aidane saw something she had never seen before, protectiveness.

Aidane felt the weight of the last few candlemarks come crashing down, overwhelming her reserve. She sank to her knees, holding Kolin's hand. "Please don't make a fuss. It's not so bad. I don't want to embarrass the queen. Please don't—"

Gently, Kolin raised her up and met her gaze. He was angry enough to kill, of that, she was certain. "Tell me what happened."

If he kills Lord Norden's son, there'll be the Crone to pay. Kolin will be sent away—or worse—just when the queen needs his protection most. She'll be discredited, and Norden will make it all the harder for her to rule. I'm not that important.

Aidane looked down, sniffing back the last of the tears. "I

went down to the courtyard because a ghost called to me. Someone . . . jumped me . . . between the buildings. I got away from him." She swallowed hard, embarrassed. "It's over."

Kolin stood so still that she might have thought him carved from stone. She knew he did not need to breathe, but now, he did not blink, or move at all. "Jumped you," he repeated in a cold voice that told her he had filled in the details she omitted. "On the palace grounds, someone tried to force you—"

"I'm just a whore, Kolin. It's not like my virtue was at stake."

"Sweet Istra, Mother of Shadows," he murmured.

Against her will, the tears began to flow, and Kolin took a step closer, folding her into his arms and letting her cry against him. He was warm; she guessed that he had fed recently. "Have you seen a healer?"

"I don't want there to be talk."

Kolin steered her to a chair near the fire. He took a wash rag from the basin on the stand near the bed and wrung it out, and then he opened a window and held the wet rag in the cold night air for a few minutes. He walked back and knelt in front of her, gently holding the cold compress to the bruise on her cheek.

"Thank you," she murmured.

"It will take some of the sting out, at least. I'll get the servants to bring up some herbs. I think I still recall how my mother made a poultice for my brother and me. We were always banging ourselves up," he said, and went to the door, where he conferred in low tones with a passing servant. In a moment, he returned, and Aidane could tell from the look in his eyes that he had not abandoned the idea of retribution.

He said nothing until the servant brought him what he had requested. Kolin mixed a paste of herbs and gently spread the mixture with his fingertips on the worst of Aidane's bruises and cuts. His touch was so gentle that Aidane struggled not to cry at the unaccustomed show of tenderness. When he was finished, Kolin sat back and met her gaze.

"Who did this?" he asked quietly.

Aidane looked down. "He threatened to create problems for the queen. He could make it difficult for you, too. Please, you can't do anything."

Kolin's blue eyes had a haunted look. "I knew Elsbet's father could be violent, but I didn't think he'd really hurt her. I didn't act quickly enough, and he killed her. I made that mistake once. I won't make it a second time." Kolin folded Aidane's hand between both of his. "I promise you I won't do anything before the festival tonight. But afterward, I need you to tell me the truth. I need to protect you and the queen."

"Who will believe a whore's word? If I were a noblewoman, someone might care about a threat to my virtue. But I'm not noble, or virtuous. I've heard the talk when people thought I wasn't around. There's no shortage of courtiers who would be glad to see me gone. You can't risk the queen's credibility. I'm not worth it."

Aidane saw a stubborn glint in Kolin's blue eyes. "Let me be the judge of that." His expression softened, and he kissed her gently on the top of her head. "It's time for you to get ready for the banquet."

Aidane reached up to touch her bruised cheek. "I can't go out like this. People really will talk. I'm so sorry. I was looking forward to going with you. Please, make my excuses to the queen. Tell her I'm not feeling well." The latter was true, both from the bruises all over her body that were beginning to throb and from the ache in her heart at Kolin's devotion and the knowledge that it didn't change her need to leave.

Kolin hesitated, and then nodded. "All right. But I'll hold you to your promise of a dance at the very next opportunity."

Aidane felt tears well in her eyes, and she hoped Kolin misread the reason as disappointment over missing the festivities. *I don't dare stay, even for Kolin. He can't protect me without damaging the queen. For both their sakes, I have to go. When I finally find what I've always wanted, I can't keep it.* "That would be wonderful," she said, her throat closing on her words.

"I'll be up to see you after the festival is over. You should be safe here in your room." He gave her a kiss on the forehead at the door. Aidane closed it behind him and covered her face with her hands.

She had been correct in her guess that no one would notice one more hooded traveler amid the feast night revelry, Aidane thought bitterly. She carried only the small sack with the clothing she had brought with her, leaving behind the gowns the queen had given to her lest anyone accuse her of theft. On the writing desk, she left a note for the queen, thanking her for her kindness and explaining that she did not wish to be an embarrassment and so must leave. Wrapped in the note was the garnet necklace. The letter to Kolin had taken longer to write. No matter how many times she worked through the wording in her mind, it never came out quite right. In the end, the best she could do was to tell him that, while she loved him, he deserved much better, someone less shopworn. She left the onyx bracelet in the folds of the note, but not before she had tried it on again and held it to her heart.

Aidane slipped unnoticed from the city gate, leaving the revelry in the courtyard behind her, though the sound of the musicians' tunes and the voices of the revelers carried on the cold night air, echoing down the narrow, winding streets.

In the common grazing area at the edge of town, a different type of gathering marked the feast night. A burning length of rope was stretched between two iron posts. Next to each post were shocks of burning cornstalks. Aidane recognized it as the

317

Need-fire, a gathering more to do with the fear of plague and a crazy butcher loose in the streets than with any deity or festival. Villagers young and old lined up to pass through the fire, driving their frightened children, sheep, and cattle on before them. Passing through the flames was thought to drive out the ill humours of the plague, and it was said by some to protect against madness. Aidane shivered, giving the commons a wide pass. Deep inside, she doubted that either plague or madness was so easily held at bay.

She had left the palace in a rush, but now that she stood outside the wall in the cold night air, she faltered, unsure of where to go. Although Jolie had offered her a position, Jolie was in Dark Haven, and Aidane knew that leaving Principality City was not an option, with the army gone to war and invaders off the coast. *I'm certainly not going back to Nargi*, she thought wryly. The borders to Dhasson and Margolan were closed. Both kingdoms were even more ravaged by plague than Principality, and she was uncertain of the welcome someone with her gifts might receive.

No, Principality with its mercs and traders from across the Winter Kingdom was the most likely to enable her to disappear among its many colorful wanderers. It was also a kingdom that did not look too closely at one's papers or parentage, a place where the disgraced and those with nothing left to lose reinvented themselves as smugglers and mercenaries. Just right for a *serroquette* with powerful enemies.

After the bright flames of the Need-fire, the shadows in the twisting alleys seemed darker than ever. Aidane hugged her cloak closer, wary of every sound. She had a few coins from the journey to Principality, enough to pay for a cheap room and enough bread and cheese to last a few days. She dared not work as a *serroquette*; the gift was rare enough under any circumstances, but it was all too likely to give her away now that she needed to remain hidden. But there was always work for whores, especially in a place like Principality City where most people were just passing through.

This time, instead of burying my gold for an escape fund, I'll save it, maybe open a little shop, she mused. *I won't have my looks and figure forever. I wouldn't open a brothel. No. Perhaps I'll buy a spinning wheel and some dyes and spin wool to make warm shawls for the winter—*

A sudden noise in the shadows stirred Aidane from her thoughts. Too late, she realized that she hadn't been paying attention. Now that she concentrated, she could feel the pull of spirits calling to her. Some were the newly dead, taken by plague, who wanted her to carry messages to the living. Others recognized her gift and offered her gold to let them lie one more night with a lost beloved. Darker spirits hovered at the edge of her consciousness, eager to seize on any weakness for the chance to possess her and take her life for their own.

This part of the city was deserted, strange for a feast night when Aidane expected to see even the poorest abroad in the streets. The buildings were in disrepair, and their windows were dark. Aidane quickened her step. The air grew colder, proof not only of it being late autumn but also that spirits were near.

Her footsteps echoed on the cobblestones. The spirits crowded around her, begging, seducing, warning.

You're cold, let me fill you.

Take me to my lover, I beg of you.

Please, just one more night.

He's coming. Run!

The last voice was louder than the rest, and at its warning, Aidane felt a thrill of terror run through the other spirits that badgered her. *It's him! Get away! Run!*

Heeding the spirits, Aidane began running, though she had no idea of where she was going, or whether she would blunder

319

into whoever it was that the spirits found frightening. As quickly as they had come, the spirits fled, all except for the one who had warned her.

The ghost who stayed with her was a woman, and the image Aidane received was of someone just a few years older than herself, dressed in the tawdry clothing of a cheap strumpet. *You can't outrun him.*

Who?

Buka. The butcher. He'll hear you running. You can't hide. I know. I tried.

Aidane felt her heartbeat speed at the name of the killer. *I don't know where to go. I don't know where I am.*

In here. The ghost led her through a broken door and down a set of rickety wooden steps and into the basement of one of the abandoned buildings that lined the street. If it hadn't been for the faint luminescence of the ghost, Aidane would have been blinded in the darkness. *Down here. Hurry.*

Aidane followed the ghost warily, but she decided that whatever was in front of her could not possibly be as bad as what was behind her. The ghost led her through a narrow brick passageway that went from one cellar to the next, and then to another set of stairs. These steps were cut into the rock itself, and cool air rushed up to meet Aidane as she hesitated at the top.

He won't find you down here, but you have to hurry.

Where does this lead?

To the caves. You'll see. People are down there. Too many for him to follow.

Aidane saw no real choice. She heard footsteps in the distance, close enough to be in the first cellar. She took a deep breath and made her way carefully down the shallow stone steps. At the bottom, a mix of scents reached her. She could smell the damp and mildew of a root cellar or cavern, but she also caught the faint aroma of distant cooking, of sweat, and of smoky fires.

Don't dawdle! Hurry!

Following the glow of the ghost, Aidane stumbled along a corridor barely wide enough for her shoulders. They turned a corner, and dim light flooded a large cavern room. Aidane had to squint for a moment after the near darkness. A torch flickered in a rough sconce, enough to give light sufficient for Aidane to make her way across the room toward where the corridor continued. The room was empty of people, but it was obvious that many had come this way, and recently. Broken wine bottles, greasy bones, and tatters of soiled clothing littered the floor. It smelled as though more than one person had relieved himself along the room's walls. Swallowing hard, Aidane followed the orb of blue light that was her ghostly guide.

After a few steps, the corridor once again opened up to a large room. This was a tannery, and the smell of stale urine from the tanning pits almost made Aidane gag. A narrow walkway led among the pits. Under torchlight, two scabrous men and a few scrawny boys tamped the hides into the noxious brew. They looked up at Aidane's entrance.

"Come to cheer us up, dearie? Come over here, and I'll warm your bones."

Aidane did not look up, but kept her focus on navigating the narrow walkway.

"See, even the whores think they're better than the likes of us," replied the second man. "Roll me in flowers, darlin', and I'll show you I'm man enough for you."

Aidane let out a relieved breath as she left the tanner behind, following the path upward to a new room. Inside, a few women and half a dozen ragged children made their home in a squalid cave room barely a dozen paces wide. The room smelled of sweat and spoiled milk and rough liquor. Two hollow-eyed women barely spared Aidane a glance, though one of the young children raised a finger to point at the blue orb that led Aidane deeper into the caverns.

Where are we? Aidane asked the rescuing spirit.

In the bowels of Principality City. Where people go when there's nowhere left to hide.

Back in Nargi, Aidane knew of places like this beneath Colsharti, warrens of caverns, closed-off tunnels, and forgotten basements inhabited by the most desperate and destitute. She followed the blue orb through a series of places where the cave walls had been chipped and gouged into rooms. Some were home to cracked-tooth merchants who held out handfuls of dreamweed and stalks of bitwort, while in others, hunched-over hags called out to offer pessaries and worm fern to be rid of an inconvenient pregnancy. Only her fear of Buka enabled Aidane to overcome her terror and keep moving forward. Her ghostly guide, while quite visible to Aidane, did not seem to be noticed by anyone but the children. Perhaps, Aidane thought, it was because the adults gave her bleary-eyed looks that suggested they were too besotted by liquor or numbed by dreamweed to care. She lost count of how many squalid rooms and branching corridors the ghost led her through. Aidane despaired of ever finding her way to the open air again. Finally, the orb slowed as they approached yet another doorway. Even before Aidane reached the opening, she could hear the buzz of voices, the click of rolling dice, and peals of drunken laughter. Tendrils of pipe smoke curled from inside, and the air was heavy with the smell of river rum and the bitter ale that better innkeepers referred to derisively as "trough beer."

Aidane saw the orb change into the glowing outline of the ghost once more. *See the tavern keeper. Name's Kir. He was a friend of mine. He's down here because of bad luck, not on the run like most. Tell him you're a friend of Surrie. That's me.*

He'll find you a place to sleep and make sure no one bothers you. In the morning, he can help you get out.

Thank you. I don't know—

Watch out for Buka. He'll kill anyone, but he likes our kind best. Whores.

Is that . . . how you died?

Surrie's ghost nodded. *Caught me not far from where you were. Didn't want to take his pleasure, just wanted my blood. Cut me up like a pig and dumped what was left in the sewer.*

Why do you stay on? I'm not a summoner, but I can say a prayer to the Lady for your passage.

The ghost's expression grew bleak. *Even a summoner can't help me. Buka took my skull, breastbone, and right hand before he dumped the other pieces. Made an offering on an altar made of bones. Sang and danced and cut himself he did. I don't know who he worships and I don't want to know, but it's evil, that I'm sure.*

Shanthadura, Aidane thought with a sinking feeling. *Surrie, have you seen men in black robes in this part of town? Have you seen them with Buka?*

Surrie's ghost gave a harsh laugh. *No one's with Buka but the dead. Even the ghosts run from him. I've never seen black-robed men, with him or not.*

Thank you, Surrie. If you hadn't helped me—

You'd be dead, like I am. You're welcome. Now go see Kir. Mind you don't go wandering down here by yourself. I brought you in one way, but there are other entrances, and some places are filled with people sick with the plague who've come down here to die.

Surrie's blue orb faded. Aidane stepped through the doorway, into one of the largest rooms she had seen in the underground maze.

The underground tavern bore no sign, but it was full of patrons.

Four or five small tables made from barrels were surrounded by threadbare men and women. Some rolled dice, others played cards, and everyone drank. One of the men had a ragged trollop on his knee, while another man regaled all who would listen with obscene jokes as he stood with his arm around a scantily clad girl who was so thin that her bones jutted from her sallow skin.

At one end was a bar made of rough boards. Behind it were stacked a few barrels, as well as several pottery jugs. Aidane could smell the acrid scent of fermenting mash, suggesting that the tavern keeper distilled his own poitin. She mustered her courage and went to the bar.

"I'm looking for Kir."

A florid-faced man looked up from pouring a drink for a customer. "Who wants to know?"

"I'm a friend of Surrie's."

The barkeeper gave Aidane a hard stare. "Surrie went missing two nights ago. Do you know where she is?"

Figuring it best to keep her true source to herself for now, Aidane shook her head. "No. But she told me that if I ever needed somewhere safe, to come here and ask for Kir."

"Who ya runnin' from?"

"A man who hit me." Aidane pulled back her hood enough to expose the bruised cheek and blackened eye. It would be enough of a motivation, she thought, if Kir was the type of man to give shelter. And if not, invoking Buka's name was unlikely to help.

Kir paused as if making up his mind. "You'll need to earn your keep. How do you earn your coin?"

Aidane let out a long breath. "I'm a whore."

Kir chuckled. "Lots of those down here. Anything special?"

"I'm a bit of a hedge witch," she lied. "I read Jalbet cards and tea leaves for a message from spirits." Kir didn't need to know that neither the cards nor the tea leaves had anything to do with obtaining a message from the dead, but it might make her unusual enough without standing out too much.

"You can stay the night. There's room on the floor in the back, by the still. It's a mite warm, but better than too cold. It's angled off the main room, so you can take your customers there if you're quiet about it. I get half of whatever they pay, and you get two meals and two cups of poitin. Deal?"

"Deal." Food, shelter, a way to earn coin, and, possibly, a protector. It was the best she was likely to get.

She turned to find her way to the back room when a familiar face caught her attention. Ed the peddler sat against the wall. He was well into his cups, but he was sober enough to entertain a few of the tavern's customers with one of his tales. He looked up and a glimmer of recognition crossed his face.

"Aidane! Come on over here."

Aidane hurried to comply, fearful that Ed might say something that would give her away. One of the men got up and gave her his seat, but from his quick exit Aidane decided that a full bladder had more to do with it than any form of rough chivalry. She forced a chuckle as Ed finished his story and waited nervously as his listeners drifted up to the bar, leaving them to themselves.

"What are you doing in this nest of rats?"

Aidane could smell the river rum on Ed's breath, but she recalled from the journey from Margolan that the peddler held his liquor deceptively well. Ed knew for certain that Aidane was a *serroquette*, having used his own hedge witch magic to free her when hostile spirits had tried to possess her.

Aidane spread her hands, palms up, and shrugged. "What everyone else is doing here, I imagine. I ran out of places to go."

Ed looked at her skeptically and dropped his voice, further proof that he was quite sober. "I thought Jolie was looking after you. How did you end up in Principality City?"

Aidane sighed. Ed pushed his glass of river rum toward her and Aidane took a drink, letting the rough liquor burn down her throat, fortifying her. "It's a very long story."

She could see worry in Ed's eyes. "Principality City's not safe for the likes of you," he said in a voice just above a whisper. "Doubly so, with what you are, and what you can do. Buka—"

She cut him off and made a warning sign. "I know. The ghost of one of his victims led me here, told me the barkeeper would shelter me."

"Not Surrie—"

Aidane nodded, and Ed's face fell.

"She was a sweet girl, come to a bad place. I'm sorry to hear that."

Aidane took another drink of the river rum. "How is it you're here?" she asked, hoping to change the subject.

Ed shrugged. "You remember the musicians? Cal, Nezra, Bez, and Thanal? They crossed from Margolan with us." When Aidane nodded, he went on. "Cal had an old friend he thought would have a place for us in a tavern up this way. Thought there might be more business. Fie! We should have stayed in Dark Haven. The tavern was closed, boarded up tight. They ended up playing on the street for coins, and that's cold work with winter coming on. That's where they are tonight, playing for the festival crowds, hoping to make enough to keep them in food and ale for a few weeks, at least."

"And you?"

Another shrug, but this time, Ed looked away. "What's a peddler with naught to sell? I traded all that I had on the journey to Dark Haven. Meant to buy more with what I'd earned, but I was robbed and lost it all. I get by now by telling fortunes, mixing poultices, and doing a bit of healing when I can. On a good night, I can tell a few stories in here and someone will buy me a drink and share a bit of bread."

Aidane looked closely at Ed. He had a narrow, angular face that was more gaunt than she remembered. His clothes, hard worn a few months ago, were tattered. He seemed to be sizing her up as well.

"You look like things have been a little rough for you lately." His gaze went pointedly to the bruise on her cheek, and Aidane looked down.

"One of the hazards of my kind of work," she murmured.

"I thought that biter, the blond one, might have taken a liking to you," Ed said. "Thought he'd have looked after you. Course, I thought Jolie would have wanted someone with your skills in her house."

"I had business that brought me to Principality City, and with the war, I don't think I could make it back to Dark Haven on my own, so even if Jolie would take me, I can't get there, at least no time soon. As for Kolin . . ." Her voice fell, and she stared at her hands. "He has more important things to think about."

Ed took the meaning she intended him to take, and he clucked comfortingly. "Then he's blind as well as dead, if he left you on your own. Do you have a place to stay?"

"The barkeep said I could have the back room, by the still."

Ed's eyes narrowed. "Do you mean to use your gift when you work?"

Aidane shook her head. "I didn't tell him . . . what I was. I didn't think it was safe." She lowered her voice to a whisper. "Can you feel the spirits? They're all around us. I can barely think for having them crowd me."

She could see in Ed's eyes that he understood. "Aye. I feel them. Thick as thieves. Between Buka and the plague, there are plenty of souls so newly dead they can't find their way." He paused. "Probably as well to keep your gift under your hat, though you'd earn a bit more coin."

327

"Assuming my patron doesn't kill me."

Ed shrugged, and he reached for his river rum, knocking back the rest of his drink. "Just a matter of time before everyone down here is dead of the plague anyhow." He looked over Aidane's shoulder toward Kir at the bar. "No one's saying it, but they all know. Plague travels fastest in places like this. Bad air, foul water, people pressed on top of each other, and no real food to speak of. I'm afraid that we've come here to die, Aidane."

18

"Your Majesty, I must protest. This is far too dangerous." Tice crossed his arms and glared at Kiara, who turned back toward him exasperatedly.

"We accomplish nothing if I hide in the palace. I dare not fight in the front lines, like a proper queen, because I'm pregnant. But I have to do something, Tice, and this is important. If we succeed, we'll end the burnings in the city, cut off the chance that our troops might face an attack from the rear."

"And if we fail, the succession of two kingdoms is in danger."

Kiara sighed. "I know. I just don't see any way around it. I'm the only one who can do this."

"You're using yourself as bait."

"There isn't any other way."

"There's always another way," Tice said, glowering. "Use a double. Kings and queens have done that for centuries when situations were too dangerous."

Kiara shook her head. "If we want to draw out the Divisionists and the Durim, then we've got to take a risk. A public coronation—really public—will be too much for them to pass up. For once, our soldiers won't need to hunt for them; the Durim and the Divisionists will come to us."

"What makes you so sure that they'll come?" Tice fidgeted

329

as Kiara crossed to the window and looked down on the streets of the city.

"Oh, they'll come. The prize is too good to refuse. Allestyr is proclaiming the Sohan festival as a special celebration in honor of the unborn prince."

Tice turned to her, slack jawed. "I was not consulted. This is madness!"

"Blame Allestyr. He knew you'd worry. But it's perfect. There were going to be large public celebrations for Sohan night anyway. The ghost in the kings' crypt said that it takes one of the blood to rally the people. That's exactly what I mean to do, and the Festival of Changes is the time to do it."

"What makes you think that the sword of the clan lords will mean anything to a crowd of drunk revelers?"

Kiara gave a smirk. "Are you telling me you don't know from which of the eight clans you're descended?"

Tice stiffened. "Of course not."

"Uh-huh. Royster's done some digging in the last few days. Seems that all of the current nobility can trace a direct lineage back to the eight warlords and their clans. But we didn't know whether it was just the nobles, so Captain Remir and a few of his soldiers did a little experiment for us. They spread out to about a dozen pubs in the city, everything from the better inns to some of the taverns in the worst part of town. They had coin enough to buy drinks for the house and keep the ale flowing. Then they made a show of feigning an argument that the invaders could whip the asses of the eight old clan lords."

"And?"

Kiara's smile widened. "In every case, it nearly touched off a riot. Crofters may not feel especially cozy toward the crown at the moment, but the old warlords are still revered. Not only that," she said, grinning, "but everyone in the pubs, down to the drunk in the corner, claimed one of the clans for his own."

"I don't understand."

Kiara crossed to a writing desk and opened up a box. She withdrew a paper with a hand-drawn crest showing a sword cleaving apart the three-bone symbol of the Shrouded Ones. "The lords and the drunks aren't the only ones who have clan blood. Royster found this in the archives. Father's family isn't just the royal line. They're descended from the intermarriage between two of the eight old clans." Her hand fell to the sword that hung in a scabbard at her side. "I'm willing to bet that if the threat of invaders isn't enough to turn people against the Divisionists for the love of the crown, they'll do it for their family ties."

Tice looked at her skeptically. "Do I need to point out how many times war has pitted brothers against brothers? Blood ties aren't as thick as we'd like to think."

Kiara put the crest back carefully in the box and closed the lid. "Let's see what Balaren and Royster are able to find. If they bring me what Balaren promised, it could change everything."

The rest of the evening was consumed in consultations with Allestyr regarding the Sohan feast as well as a briefing from messengers from the front lines. A fitting for her festival clothing took two candlemarks, largely because the seamstress had little experience concealing chain mail and a hardened leather cuirass beneath a satin gown.

Throughout the meetings, Kiara had difficulty concentrating. Balaren and Royster were a day late, and the Sohan feast was the next night. She began to fear that the quest she had given them might have been impossible.

Her spirits rose when one of the guards hurried her way as she finished dinner. "Your Majesty," the guard said with a low bow. "You have visitors. *Vayash moru*," he added nervously.

Her broad smile was not the reaction the servant expected. "Bring them to the parlor. And make sure there are refreshments for both mortals and *vayash moru*."

331

The servant blanched and swallowed hard, and then nodded. "As you wish."

Kiara left the rest of her meal untouched and hurried to the parlor. She had just arrived and taken a seat near the fireplace when the guards knocked on the door to announce her visitors and one of the guardsmen swung the door open. Royster rushed into the room, his white hair forming a wild cloud around his excited features. The librarian looked fit to burst with news. Behind him, Balaren followed at a more leisurely pace, and his features did not reveal his thoughts.

Kiara's attention went to the third man, a *vayash moru*. He moved with the grace that she had come to associate with the oldest among the undead, and he was quite pale. The newcomer was built like a professional soldier, medium height but with muscular shoulders and arms earned from years of serious swordsmanship. Kiara found herself holding her breath in anticipation.

"Your Majesty," Balaren said, making a low bow. "May I present Olek, of the clan Kirylu, the last surviving warlord of the great clans." He turned to Olek. "Warlord Olek, I present Queen Kiara Sharsequin of Isencroft."

Olek regarded Kiara carefully. His ice-blue eyes seemed to miss nothing, and Kiara steeled herself to meet his gaze. Finally, just when she thought he would not yield to protocol, Olek gave a small nod and an equally shallow bow. "Your Majesty," he said, his tone neutral, but in his eyes Kiara thought she saw skepticism.

"Warlord Olek. Thank you for agreeing to come to the palace."

An ironic smile touched his lips. "How could I not obey the summons of the queen?" His eyes told Kiara what she already knew—that it was up to the Old Ones whether they recognized any mortal ruler.

"Please, sit down." Kiara led them to a grouping of chairs near the fireplace. A visibly nervous servant offered brandy to

Royster and goblets of fresh deer blood to Balaren and Olek.
A goblet of watered wine for Kiara went untouched as she
leaned forward, intent on Olek.

"It's true, then, that you are the last surviving warlord who
fought in the eight clans?"

Olek gave a cold chuckle. "How polite a phrase you turn,
m'lady. 'Surviving' covers a wide territory, does it not? And
yet, 'living' wouldn't be quite right, either." He paused and took
a sip of the blood. "Yes. I am the fifth warlord of Kirylu, the
fifth and last Olek. I was mortal over four hundred years ago."

"Do you recognize this?" Slowly, so as not to give any
indication of threat, Kiara unsheathed the sword that the spirit
ancestor had given to her. She held it out, blade flat across her
open palms, and extended her hands toward Olek.

It was satisfying to see an ancient *vayash moru* look startled.
"Where did you get that?"

"I went into the tomb of my ancestors for guidance. One of
the spirits gave me the sword with a stern reminder to look
to the old clans in order to unify my people."

Olek took the sword from Kiara and turned it in the light.
She could not read his expression when he finally handed it
back to her. "Balaren told me nothing of the sword. Yet I dreamed
of a sword just like it only a few nights ago. Did your spirit
give you any indication of what you are to do with it?"

"She said to raise the sword and remind my people who they
are."

Olek was quiet for a moment, still and silent. Finally, he looked
up at Kiara and seemed to be evaluating her anew. "You are the
one who saw a vision of Chenne on the battlefield years ago."

Kiara nodded. "Father had been wounded. It was my first
real battle. We were doing badly. I saw a vision of the Lady
and she told me to raise the flag and rally the troops. It gave
them heart again, and we won the day."

333

"I have paid scant attention to the whims of the crown for many, many years," Olek said. "Do you know why the spirit might have chosen to give you this sword, a sword I know was buried with its owner?"

"I'd like to hear your thoughts, and then I'll share my own."

Olek looked at the sword in silence for a moment. He did not meet Kiara's eyes, but he began to speak. "Five hundred years ago, the first eight warlords won their lands in battle from the savages and brigands. This land you call Isencroft was wild, nearly unsettled except for small groups of barbarians and men-at-arms who were nothing more than thieves. Those who became the warlords did not rise together. Each rose separately, out of the conviction that it would be better to unify sections of the land under one strong ruler than to have the constant bloody battles for territory that came from the warring tribes."

He paused and took another sip of the blood. "Generation after generation, the battles raged. My family conquered the lands in the northwest, against the coast and the lands of the Adair. Gradually, the seven other warlords brought their lands under control. War was constant in those days, and we feared it might always be so. Finally, the other warlords and I consolidated our control and war ceased."

"How did the warlords give way to a monarchy?" Kiara leaned forward, fascinated by Olek's account.

"Although eight warlords arose, we were not all equally powerful. Four of the warlords were already related by blood, descending from two pairs of brothers. When marriages and alliances took place between the strongest families of those four houses, it consolidated the power into those four families. One of those was my own clan, Kirylu. The four combined clans had more land and more men than the other four warlords, and when war broke out once more, the four allied lords won. To seal the alliance, a woman descended from two of the houses wed a man descended from the other two houses. Their son became the first king of Isencroft." Olek paused. "The sword that you were given in the crypt was forged for the coronation of King Jashan, the first king of Isencroft, who was the son of Lord Gavrill. It was buried with Jashan."

Kiara sipped the watered wine as she considered Olek's story. "But it wasn't until your lifetime that the followers of Shanthadura were driven out, and the worship of the Sacred Lady took its place."

A shadow crossed Olek's face, and he made a gesture of warding, something Kiara guessed was an unconscious mannerism left over from his mortal days. "As much as we sometimes hated the other warlords, all of us hated the Durim more. I have seen all the horrors war can provide, and yet I judged the Black Robes far worse. They were a greater scourge on our people than any famine or plague. Of all my victories, I was most proud of destroying the Durim."

"But they weren't really destroyed," Kiara said quietly.

Olek shook his head. "No. We thought we had rooted them out, but my guess is that a handful of them escaped into the mountains and wild places and waited. Balaren tells me that they have risen again."

"We have reason to believe that a dark summoner is behind the invasion fleet from Temnotta that lies in the harbor," Kiara said, straightening. She met Olek's gaze. "The Durim may not be working with him, exactly, but it appears that the dark summoner's power is related to the Durim's attempts to bring back the cult of Shanthadura." She paused and took a deep breath. "Are you familiar with the Sworn?"

Olek nodded. "I know of them, and the spirits they guard, the Dread."

"Then you know that the Dread guard even more fearsome

spirits, the Nachele. The Durim are trying to wake the Nachele from their slumber."

"Though the Nachele were bound long before my lifetime, the stories remained. I would not care to see them loosed once more." He paused. "Neither, I dare say, would my fellow warlords."

Kiara exchanged a glance with Balaren, who gave a slight shake of his head, indicating this was also news to him. "I thought you were the last surviving warlord?"

A cold smile touched Olek's lips. "The key word is 'surviving.' I am the only one of the last eight warlords who still walks among the living. But the spirits of the other seven never left the lands they fought so hard to claim. We are not infrequent visitors to each other." He shrugged. "I have long outlived my contemporaries, save for some among the *vayash moru*. As time passes, I find that I have few interests in common with the living, and the dead become very good companions."

"Are their spirits nearby? Can you find out if they would join us in stopping the Durim?"

Olek looked amused. "They are quite nearby, and they already know of the Durim's rise. In fact, they called to me from their crypts right before Balaren arrived with your royal summons. They are interred in the necropolis beneath Aberponte."

"To keep the Nachele from waking, we need to defeat Temnotta's dark summoner, and it would help a lot if the Durim weren't causing panic behind our lines." She met his eyes. "Would you like another chance at the Durim?"

Olek smiled so that the points of his eye teeth were plain. "I think I would enjoy that, and so might my fellow lords."

Kiara hid her smile. "I believe Isencroft would rally around the warlords, even though, in recent months, they will not rally for flag and crown." She met Olek's gaze. "Do you realize that every Crofter claims to trace lineage back to one of the eight old warlords? It's a point of personal pride and family heritage that runs deeper even than being of the kingdom itself."

Olek chuckled. "I will leave them their pride, but I truly doubt all the lineages claimed are, shall we say, legitimate?"

"No doubt you're right. But in this case, belief matters more than fact." Kiara let out a long breath and squared her shoulders. "I'll be frank. Isencroft is in a bad spot. Invaders on the coast, traitors among the people, and the Shanthadurists working their blood magic—most probably in support of the invaders. Alone, I don't think I can rally them. Together, I believe we can." She paused. "Will you help me? And do you think the other warlords would be willing to help as well?"

Olek looked at her in silence for a moment as if taking her measure. Finally, he nodded. "I will help you, Kiara of Isencroft. As for my fellow lords, I can't promise, but I will give you my word to plead your cause to them." A sad smile tugged at the corner of his mouth. "Old loyalties run deep. And if there was one thing every one of the warlords loved more than life, wealth, or family, it was this land. Even in death, that remains unchanged. I'll bring you their decision by tomorrow night."

The next evening, Kiara paced in her room. Cerise and Royster watched in silence while Kiara smoothed her dress down over her cuirass. The gown had a wide, full skirt that did a good job of camouflaging the armor. Cerise chuckled. "Don't worry. You'll be up on the balcony. From where the crowd is, the dress will look fine."

Kiara raised an eyebrow. "That's the least of my worries. What if the spirits won't come?"

Cerise chuckled again. "Having second thoughts?"

Kiara sighed. "Tice would certainly like it if I did. He and Allestyr had quite a row last night when they thought I couldn't hear them. But I don't see another way to stop the Durim, and maybe even the Divisionists."

Cerise held out a platter of cakes to Kiara, who stopped her pacing for a moment. "Then stop second-guessing yourself. Trust your instincts." She smiled. "Besides, you've always loved Sohan. It would be a shame not to enjoy your first feast night as queen."

Outside in the courtyard, Aberponte glowed in the light of bonfires celebrating Sohan night, the Feast of Changes. Even from a distance, Kiara could hear the music and revelers. While the war had diminished the number of jousts and skirmishes, not even the threat of an invading fleet could deny Isencroft its ale on this feast night.

Sohan was one of the more lighthearted celebrations. In celebration of the change from autumn to winter, changes of all kind were embraced, with a preference for the silly, the ribald, and the extreme. Musicians played popular tunes but sang different and often bawdy new lyrics. There was no shortage of noblemen disguised in the garb of soldiers, farmers, and tradesmen, while the ladies of the court played at being shepherdesses or milkmaids. Children powdered their hair and chalked their faces to look old, while elders relaxed their dignity and indulged in youthful pursuits. In years past, Kiara had seen farmers dress pigs as sheep and pretend horses were milk cows. It was a night for hidden identities, as rich young men were often known to go about in disguise as beggars, and nearly everyone pretended to be someone they were not.

Even the food was changed for the feast night. Flower dyes were added to ale and liquor to turn the drinks unusual colors, and breads, cakes, meats, and vegetables were cut or twisted into the appearance of animals, plants, and other objects. Games and wagers abounded, and Crofters of all walks of life were encouraged to wish on the Sohan moon for changes they desired to see in the next year.

A knock sounded at the door. One of the guards opened it. "Brother Felix to see you, Your Majesty."

"Let him in."

Brother Felix stood in the doorway, looking harried. "Allestyr sent me to let you know the ceremony is ready to begin. You've studied the ritual so you know what to expect?"

Kiara nodded. "I just hope I'm not so nervous that I forget the words."

Brother Felix smiled. "I'm told there's room for 'creative interpretation,' if such a thing occurs." He paused, and his smile faded. "There are a brace of palace guards here to escort you, and Balaren, Patov, and Jorven are already in place in the crowd below the balcony, where they'll be on watch. Tice said to tell you that every guardsman in the barracks is on duty tonight, some in uniform and some spread among the crowd. I wish the Veigonn were here, but they've gone to the front lines with Cam. Even so, we've done everything to assure your safety."

Kiara managed a smile. "Then let's go."

The aroma of roasting meat and freshly baked bread filled the castle as Kiara made her way down the stairs. Cerise and Royster stayed behind to watch the proceedings from another balcony. That was just as well; Kiara was happy to have them out of harm's way.

The guards escorted her to the large ballroom at the front of the palace, where a huge balcony opened out the second floor. It was designed to enable a monarch to speak to a crowd gathered in the courtyard below, and Donelan had often used the setting for feast day greetings and major announcements. Count Renate was waiting for her, as were Tice and Allestyr. Two guards took up their watch outside the room, while two others went to stand just to the side of the open balcony.

"Is Olek here?" Kiara asked, looking around the room.

339

"I am." Kiara startled as Olek appeared just behind them, without benefit of warning footsteps.

"And your 'friends'? Will they join us?"

Olek gave a cold smile. "Yes. There is no lure for a soldier so sweet as the opportunity for a final victory."

Kiara moved around the guards to where Allestyr stood behind a screen that kept the crowd in the courtyard from seeing beyond the balcony and into the room. "Is everything ready?"

"As ready as we can make it. Beyond the courtyard, there are large crowds in the streets tonight. I guess everyone's decided to forget the threat of war for a night," Allestyr said with a sigh.

"Well, then, let's get started. I'd hate to keep the crowd away from their feast night ale."

Trumpets blared as Count Renate stepped out onto the balcony. The autumn night was cold, but that did not seem to have tempered the crowd's appetite for revelry. A bonfire just in front of the balcony served to illuminate the regent's entrance and to cordon the crowd at a distance. A cheer went up from the assembly, though Kiara attributed its enthusiasm more to alcohol than to any true excitement over the crowning of a new monarch.

"Good feast night to you all," Renate said, with the aid of one of the court mages to project his voice over the noise of the crowd. "I would like to wish you all a happy Sohan night."

Again, the crowd roared its approval, tankards held high.

"I have served as regent in the trying weeks since the death of King Donelan. Now, it is time for me to step aside, time for Isencroft to crown a new monarch. I am honored to present Kiara, daughter of Donelan and Viata, to be crowned Queen of Isencroft."

Squaring her shoulders, Kiara stepped forward. A cheer rose from the crowd, but it was notably less enthusiastic than the response to Renate's feast day blessing.

Standing in the center of the balcony where Kiara knew most

of the crowd could see her clearly, she looked out over her skeptical new subjects. "I wish that I could join in the celebration, but tonight, Isencroft faces invaders from the north who would take this land and this crown by force," Kiara said, feeling her passion rise to the occasion. "Our armies have gone to fight, but there are traitors among us who would welcome both the invaders and their bloody ways."

The crowd had begun to stir restlessly. If they had expected a wave and a smile, they were now beginning to wonder just what was in store, Kiara thought.

"These traitors would not only challenge this crown, but they also invade the lands for which the warlord fathers of the eight clans fought and bled. The same enemy that the clan lords fought now seeks to return, the very same murderers who were driven out by the lords of old. Black Robes walk among us, Durim, the followers of Shanthadura, the Destroyer. You know what I say is true. You have heard the rumors, seen the tombs that were desecrated. It is time to end this, once and for all."

At her nod, Olek stepped onto the balcony beside her, and the crowd quieted nervously. "I am Olek, son of Olek, last of the eight warlords, ruler of the Clan Kirylu." Olek's voice carried across the cold night air, and the crowd fell silent. "And I am not alone."

At Olek's words, the temperature in the courtyard plummeted. As Kiara watched, a chill blast of air swept into the yard, and with it, a blue haze that glowed independent of the light of the bonfires. As the crowd murmured and drew back, the haze hovered over the yard for a moment and then slowly rose to the balcony, enveloping Kiara in the mist. Figures began to take shape in the haze, until the forms of seven men dressed in antique armor stood, ghostly swords in hand, a line of spectral defenders behind Kiara.

"Leksandr, of Clan Dunlurghan." Cheers rose from those

341

scattered throughout the crowd who claimed Clan Dunlurghan as their own. The ghost of a tall man with shoulder-length dark hair stepped forward to stand beside Kiara and Olek.

"Gavrill, of Clan Finlios." This ghost was shorter than Olek and Leksandr, but with powerful arms and broad shoulders.

"Illarion, of Clan Skaecogy." Another spirit stepped up beside Kiara. Medium height, solidly built. What caught Kiara's attention was the glint of intelligence in Illarion's ghostly eyes.

"Ceshilban, of Clan Dromlea." The fourth spirit carried the ghostly image of a huge war hammer. Long, light-colored hair hung shoulder length around a square face, and Ceshilban's eyes shone with implacable determination.

"Luka, of Clan Tratearmon. Minya, of Clan Veaslieve. Pyotir, of Clan Rathtuaim," Olek called, and each name was greeted by scattered shouts and cheers as the crowd showed its pride in their warrior ancestors. When all eight of the clan lords stood in a semicircle around Kiara, Renate turned to Allestyr, who handed him the crown. Renate lifted the crown for all to see.

Renate turned to the crowd. "In light of the fact that the clan lords honor us with their presence, I defer to Lord Olek," Renate said, ceremoniously passing the jeweled crown to Olek.

"People of Isencroft," Olek said. "Kiara of the House Sharsequin is your rightful ruler, as the daughter of King Donelan and the blood heir to the lands of the eight warlords." He placed the crown on Kiara's head. "Behold your new queen."

The crowd roared and clapped, but Kiara could see some among the revelers who did not look pleased and who remained still and watchful.

Olek bowed, and one by one, the ghosts of the eight warlords also bowed in tribute. Kiara swallowed hard, overcome for a moment. Olek's back was to the crowd, and he caught her eye and winked, letting her know that every movement was planned for its effect on the audience.

Kiara took a deep breath and stepped forward. Olek and the ghosts of the warlords formed a semicircle behind her. "Sons and daughters of Isencroft, your fathers have risen from their slumber to destroy the Durim and those who aid them." Kiara's voice carried over the exclamations of the crowd.

Behind the screen, in the ballroom, Kiara heard hushed voices. Tice peered around the screen, his eyes wide. "The guards just reported that thirty dead Black Robes have been dumped in the outer courtyard. The guards didn't see anyone, but suddenly, the bodies were there."

Olek's lips tightened in a chilling half smile. Kiara met his eyes, and she nodded approvingly.

Kiara had drawn the sword that the spirit queen had given her in the crypt. Now, she held it aloft. "Tonight, the ancient warlords have killed thirty of the Black Robes that trouble our land. The bodies of the traitors lie in the outer yard." The crowd gasped, and festivalgoers began to turn and strain for a look beyond the courtyard gate.

Kiara held the sword so that it gleamed in the torch light. "The dead have begun the work, but shall we leave it to the dead to do the work of the living?"

A roar went up from the crowd, even as some nervously eyed the queen and the ancient clan lords.

"Shall we leave it to the dead to protect us?" Kiara challenged. Another roar rose from the crowd, louder now.

"The Durim were not alone in their treason. They and the Divisionists murdered King Donelan, and they would hand Isencroft over to an enemy army and a traitor lord. We have seen the mettle of the dead. Do the living have the same courage to drive out the destroyers of Isencroft?"

The crowd found its voice, and the roar grew louder. "The

343

clan lords have brought me the Durim. But we will not be strong enough to fight the invaders until the Divisionists who burn our city and threaten your families are brought to justice." Kiara brought the sword of the clan lords down so that it pointed out to the crowd, and she held it in a two-handed grip.

"I ask no coronation tribute save this: Bring me the Divisionists. Bring me the traitors who would challenge the throne, the ones who murdered my father. Let their bodies be your tribute, and banish the flames from our city. For Isencroft, and for the eight clans, I bid you fight!"

"I-sen-croft! I-sen-croft!" The chant spread throughout the crowd until it rang from the walls of the palace and echoed in the streets beyond. The crowd cheered and shouted, and Olek gave Kiara a nod of approval. But the mood of the feast day crowd had shifted. The cries and cheers now sounded angry, and some among the crowd grabbed wood near the bonfires and lit torches, rallying into groups ready to storm the city in search of Divisionists.

There was a scuffle in the crowd, and several men emerged, holding two other men by the arms as they shoved the prisoners forward. "Here are two for you, right away, Your Majesty. These two be Divisionists. That I can state for sure."

Kiara looked down at the two prisoners. One of them had a growing bruise near his eye, while the other sported a split lip. "Is this true?"

"Death to the whore of Isencroft," the first prisoner spat. The second man said nothing, but nodded his assent.

Kiara moved to demand that the prisoners be taken to the guards, but before she could speak, the cold wind and its blue haze swept through the courtyard again. When the wind stilled, two of the ancient warlords stood in front of the terrified prisoners and their equally fear-struck captors. Before anyone could move, the ghosts surged forward, plunging their spectral swords deep into the chests of the prisoners. The Divisionists screamed and their captors shouted in alarm. Quickly as they came, the ghosts vanished. The Divisionists sagged in the grip of the men who held them.

"They're dead," one of the captors said, raising his head to look at Kiara with an expression of fear and awe. "But there's not a mark on them, no sword wound, nothing."

For a moment, it seemed as if the crowd held its collective breath. Then a voice shouted from its midst: "Death to all traitors to the clans!"

"Death to Divisionists! Death to the enemy!" The crowd took up the cry. Holding their makeshift torches aloft, the crowd surged toward the gate, spilling out of the palace courtyard and into the streets. The mob swarmed down toward the city, leaving behind them the litter of the feast and the two dead Divisionists.

Kiara paused for a moment, watching the torches of the mob head down the road toward the city, before she allowed Allestyr to guide her back into the ballroom. Kiara looked to Olek and the ghosts of the other clan lords.

"Thank you," she said, looking to each lord in turn. "I'm grateful for what you did tonight." She met Olek's gaze. "Have the clan lords really destroyed the Durim?"

Olek shrugged. "We were mistaken once before. We may again be mistaken now. But I would wager that, like long ago, any Durim who escaped the punishment will shed his black cloak and think twice about joining this battle." He smiled, revealing his eye teeth. "We discovered that the Durim's allegiance to their goddess came second to their desire to protect their own skin."

Kiara sighed and collapsed against the high back of the chair. "Goddess! What a night!" She closed her eyes and took a deep breath as the emotion of the night's events tempered into exhaustion. She opened her eyes and looked from Allestyr to Olek.

"We've set the mob on the Divisionists, as we intended to do. But I fear the justice of a vengeful mob. There will be innocents who die, as well as the guilty. We may pay a high price in blood for what we gain this night."

Olek nodded, and Kiara could see bitter wisdom in his eyes. "It was ever so, m'lady. Whether it be a mob or an army, innocents die when men take up swords for vengeance. There's no way to know until long after whether the price was just or steep."

Welcome to the burden of the crown, Kiara thought bitterly. *It's what Father knew too well, and what Tris has learned. Every decision I make changes the lives of everyone in the kingdom. Sweet Chenne! How can anyone be wise enough for this?*

"I will take my leave," Olek said, with a shallow bow. Kiara noted that he did not ask permission.

"Thank you," she said. "I am grateful. Isencroft is in your debt."

No one spoke until Olek departed and the spirits of the clan lords had vanished. Kiara let her head fall back against the smooth velvet of the chair. She felt Cerise's hand on hers, and she knew that, aside from the gesture of concern, Cerise was using her healing magic to check Kiara's health.

"I think it wise to let the queen rest."

Allestyr and the others murmured their assent, and though Kiara welcomed the chance to sleep, she knew that tomorrow, her reign would begin in earnest.

"Get some sleep, Kiara," Allestyr urged. "Tice and I will make sure one of us keeps in touch with the guards in case we have trouble in the city. There's nothing more you can do tonight."

Perhaps I've done enough already, Kiara thought darkly, but she nodded in assent and forced herself to open her eyes. "Tomorrow, we plan my trip to the battle lines. I may not be able to fight, but I want to be close enough to see what's happening for myself. All the regent magic in the world won't make a difference if I'm leagues away."

Allestyr nodded without protest, but Kiara could see the concern in his eyes. *I don't like it any better than he does, but I didn't return to Isencroft to hide in the palace. This war won't stay a standoff from much longer. We're running out of time.*

19

Kiara stood at the top of a rocky hilltop. Just days had passed since the coronation. The late-afternoon sun was brilliant, though the air was cold. She was far enough behind the battle lines to satisfy Allestyr's demand that she stay safe but close enough to satisfy her own requirement that she be able to see what was going on. Royster had insisted on accompanying her, as had Balaren, Patov, and Jorven, in addition to the two dozen guards who made the journey with her from the palace to the war front, and Cerise, who refused to make the battle healers responsible for the health of a pregnant queen.

Jae flew overhead, turning in broad circles over the battlefield. Kiara smiled, watching as the gyregon selected his targets on the ground below and swooped down at high speed, striking with razor-sharp talons before winging his way high into the sky.

"Do you think the old warlords might be persuaded to lend us a hand here on the battlefield, if they've still got their taste for blood?" Captain Remir asked, and managed a bleak smile.

Kiara sighed. "I think we're on our own now. Their fight was really with the Durim, and they delivered what I asked of them."

"And the Divisionists?"

Kiara turned away and sighed. "A victory . . . at a price. After seeing what the ghosts of the warlords did to the Durim, the mob turned on the Divisionists. I'd hoped they would bring the suspects to us, alive, to stand trial. Unfortunately, they were a little too inspired by what happened to the Durim. By morning we found seventy-five men—and a few women—hanged from trees in the common green or dangling from balconies. Some had Temnottan coins in their pockets, while with others, there's just no way we'll ever know for certain whether they really were Divisionists or whether it was just a convenient opportunity to be rid of a troublesome neighbor."

Remir nodded. His expression was grim, but he showed no surprise. "It's much the same in battle. Few of the men who get killed care much about the reasons for the war. They were conscripted, or they sign on because they want three meals and a tent to sleep in and what the army offers is better than what they left behind. If a truce were called midbattle, most of them would be game to sit down for a pint of ale with the men who were just trying to kill them." He shook his head. "I've been a soldier all my life, but I'm the first to admit war makes very little sense."

"And yet, here we are, with no other choices left to us," Kiara murmured, looking down over the rise toward where two armies faced each other across a burned and blasted no-man's zone.

"Here we are."

Kiara was dressed for war, though the battle lines were far down the valley. Allestyr had kept several armorers up all night long adjusting her armor to give better protection to her abdomen without adding to the armor's already substantial weight. The result was a hardened leather cuirass with an elongated and broadened front over a chain-mail garment that fell from shoulders to midthigh. She wore the cuirass at all times, but she left both the helmet and vambraces behind in her tent today. Though she had trained and fought in armor, Kiara realized that her recent duties as queen had left her out of practice.

Jae had perked up at the sounds and smells of the battlefield. Prized by the Eastmark aristocracy for their ferocity in war, gyregons were virtually unseen outside of Eastmark's boundaries. Jae had been a gift from Kiara's uncle, King Kalcen of Eastmark, though Kalcen may have never imagined Jae would actually see battle. Kiara watched the gyregon attack, and her soldiers cheered as clusters of Temnottan soldiers ducked and dove or flailed their arms unsuccessfully to ward off Jae's attacks.

Kiara's gaze followed the slope down to where the armies held their positions. The harbor was filled with Temnottan ships and the wreckage of both Temnottan and Croft ships. The beach was littered with the burned remnants of battlements and the unmistakable shapes of bodies, some of which still lay at the water's edge. Temnotta had managed to overcome the Isencroft fleet and land enough troops to force back Isencroft's army, so that the battle lines were now inland from the beach itself.

Captain Remir and his guards had followed Kiara to the battlefield, charged with assuring her protection. Come nightfall, Antoin, Patov, and Jorven would join them. "It could be worse." Captain Remir roused her from her thoughts. "We'll hear from the commanders tonight."

"There was a lot going on when we received Cam's report that the invaders had managed landfall. Go over it again for me, slowly. I want to know how they broke through."

Remir grimaced. "In a nutshell, Isencroft has too large a coastline for the army to hold every bit of it with troops. Alvior knows the coastline. The ships here laid siege to the main troop position, while a portion of the ships slipped farther down the coast, where they defeated the garrison and landed their men."

He drew a long breath. "Cam seemed to think that Alvior planned to launch the invasion from Brunnfen, but the fortifications that his brother, Renn, and Captain Lange put into place were enough to change Alvior's plans. Good thing, too, since the terrain below Brunnfen would have made it easier to march on the Palace City than the rocky hills here."

"So we've forced them to fight in the place of our choosing. That's something."

Captain Remir nodded. "It's something important. I'll take any advantage we can get."

Kiara managed a grim smile. "Me too." She looked down into the wide plain where several divisions of the Isencroft army faced off against a sizeable enemy force. "What I don't understand is how they managed to send so many troops so quickly."

Remir shook his head. "We've seen their ships going back and forth between the beach they took and the open water. My guess is that they had more ships beyond where we can see from shore, just waiting for an opportunity. They wanted us to think that the ships we saw were all they had. We were wrong."

The chill winter air whipped around them, whistling through the ruins of an old fortress where Kiara had made her headquarters. Little remained of the stone fortress except for a single crumbling tower and a network of broken walls and rubble.

"Any word from Antoin?"

Remir looked at the sky, and she knew he was mentally calculating the remaining candlemarks until sunset. "Not yet. It's still too early for him to be about. As you've mentioned yourself, m'lady, 'tis not an easy thing to rally *vayash moru* to fight for a mortal cause."

Kiara frowned. "The Durim who were doing the Temnottan's bidding were sacrificing *vayash moru* as well as mortals. To my mind, that makes it a common cause."

Remir chuckled. "I hope for our sakes that you've learned to think like a *vayash moru*. We could use the help." He paused and looked around them, as if to make sure that he would not be overheard.

"The old man who came with you from the palace, is he a mage?"

Kiara chuckled. "Don't let him hear you ask that or his head will swell! Royster is the Head Keeper at the Library of Westmarch. He's not a mage himself, but he keeps the largest library about magic in the Winter Kingdoms, and even the Sisterhood treats him with great respect. He was a great help when Tris fought to take back the crown in Margolan. He came with me from Margolan because he's also a chronicler, and he can't stand to let a good story get by him."

Remir's face fell. "Oh. I was hoping for a mage. A really powerful mage, someone who could send the Temnottans packing without more bloodshed."

"Don't we have battle mages?" Kiara asked, concerned.

"Oh yes, as many as we could find. But the battles have gone hard on them, and we didn't have that many to start with. The Temnottans tried to soften us up with magic before they brought the fighting in earnest. If we could find more mages, we'd welcome them."

Kiara grimaced. "Unfortunately, the Sisterhood doesn't want its mages involved in 'worldly' conflicts, so the mages who have come to us had to go rogue in order to do it. I think we'll see others join us. I'm hoping that when they have to choose between loyalty to Isencroft and loyalty to the Sisterhood, their homeland will win."

Remir gave her a half-smile, but the look in his eyes told her that he wouldn't bet money on their chances. "I hope you're right."

Later, Kiara listened in silence as Cam, Wilym, and Vinian recounted the main turning points of the battle. Morane, one of the senior mages, and Antoin listened to the report in silence. When the report was finished, Wilym met Kiara's gaze.

"I know we failed in keeping the enemy from landing, but

it's been a brutal fight to hold them where they are. I'd pit Isencroft's army against any in the Winter Kingdoms, but we've never fought a war of magic before, and it's taken a heavy toll on our soldiers."

Kiara looked to Morane. The mage was a man in his middle years. He had dark hair that was gray at the temples, and his clothing was unremarkable, with little to reveal him as a mage except for the vials and pouches on his belt. "What kind of defense can our mages make? Are they powerful enough for some offensive magic, or are we lucky to hold our wardings?"

Morane regarded Kiara for a moment before he spoke. "I'm reminded that my queen has been in the presence of some of the most powerful mages in the Winter Kingdoms," he said. "If you mean, do we have any mage equal in power to Martris Drayke, the answer is no. We have no one that powerful, nor any summoners among us. On the other hand," he added, meeting Kiara's eyes, "if Temnotta does have a dark summoner of its own, he—or she—is not in any of those ships or among the troops that landed. That kind of power is impossible to hide. I would expect such a valuable weapon would be deployed against its counterpart—in Margolan."

Kiara caught her breath. It made perfect sense that the Temnottans would wield their strongest mage against the greatest magical threat. Any sense of relief she might have felt knowing that the Temnottan summoner was not poised to strike in Isencroft was negated by her heightened fear for Tris's safety.

"We've used our magic to harry the Temnottans every way we can," Morane went on. "Our water mages have roiled the seas, but it's a delicate thing trying to sink their ships and not ours. The Temnottans have turned fire against us, and both our fire and land mages have worked hard to contain the blasts. The air mages have done their best to push the invading ships farther from shore. Remember, m'lady, that the enemy has their mages countering everything we do." Morane paused. "Our scryers and rune readers have done their best to advise the generals. It was because of them that we had advance warning about Alvior's flanking maneuver. We think Alvior's mages were using glamour to hide what they were doing, and it worked, for a while. When our mages broke through it, we were able to see what was happening and move the troops to meet them."

Kiara nodded. "Well done." She turned to Antoin. "I'm hoping you have news to report."

Antoin gave a predatory smile. "News I have—good news. I've found thirty *vayash moru* who will join our ranks, and nearly as many *vyrkin*. All of them asked that I pass along their deep thanks to Your Majesty for stopping the Durim. And in my travels, I also made some inquiries as to mages." His gaze darted to Morane, and then back to Kiara. "The *vayash moru* told me that there was a cluster of mages who were making their way toward the front lines. All I did was welcome them to the party and make sure they got to the right place."

Antoin dropped his gaze as he finished, giving Kiara to guess that there was more to the story. "What caused the mages to leave the Sisterhood?"

Antoin licked his lips, a mortal gesture that showed his uneasiness. "It wasn't completely voluntary, their leaving. Seems that all of them have been hearing a hum that they said nearly drove them mad. The other mages couldn't hear it, and decided that those who could must be unstable. These mages were driven out." He raised his gaze again. "I've seen my share of madmen, and none of these mages seemed mad to me."

Perhaps they hear the same hum that Cheira Talwyn heard, the hum that sent Cwynn into a frenzy. Not mad, just attuned to different magic. "I believe you," Kiara said to Antoin. "I've heard of this before, in Margolan."

Antoin looked relieved. "Then they're welcome?"

"Very welcome," Moranc affirmed. He looked to Antoin. "If you'll take me to them after this meeting, I'll assign them to battle stations."

Cam leaned forward. "I don't know whether to be glad you're here, or worried sick. I think the next battle will be the big one. Temnotta's been softening us up, testing our mages, trying to deplete our forces. But they're at a basic disadvantage: Their main point of supply is a long way from here. Even if there are more ships out to sea, they can't supply their army forever." Cam met Kiara's eyes. "They're going to have to break through our lines and make a big push, and do it soon."

"Any chance they'll try another flanking maneuver somewhere down the coast?"

Wilym shook his head. "We've got troops at all the accessible beaches, and catapults fortifying the cliffs. There's no other good strategic access except through Brunnfen, and that's bottled up. I think the battle will be here, and soon."

Cam lingered behind when the rest of the meeting's participants filed from the tent. He embraced Kiara in a bear hug. "Beggin' the queen's pardon, but it's damn good to see you, Kiara," he said.

Kiara managed a tired grin. "Good to see you, too, though you look a bit worse for the wear." Her gaze traveled from a slash on Cam's cheek to the cuts, scrapes, and welts on his knuckles and hands.

Cam shrugged. "I don't mind not looking too pretty as long as I come back alive."

"How's the leg?"

Another shrug. "It's still attached, and the limp hasn't kept me off the field, so that's something. Pains a little when it's damp, but so did my grandfather's gout. Guess that's how it is once something's been busted up. But I'll live." He grinned. "'Sides, anything that isn't fatal will make Rhosyn greet me with plenty of sympathy, if you know what I mean," he said with a broad wink.

Kiara could not help but chuckle. "So marriage agrees with you?"

Cam gave a sly smile. "That it does. I miss Rhosyn something fierce out here, though I'm glad she's safe, and I'll sleep better now that I know you've rid the city of those damned Divisionists. Rhosyn and Renn are conspiring to open a new ale house near Brunnfen as soon as the fighting is over. Rhosyn's got her daddy to agree to lend us one of his ale masters. And I met a brandy maker who's going to come brew up liquor for us instead of that gut-rot poitin the locals drink. Goddess knows, we need something to put coin in the coffers after Alvior spent it all, damn him to the Abyss!"

Kiara sobered. "No sign that Alvior's come ashore to fight with the troops?"

Cam spat and ground his heel into the spittle. "Alvior's a bully and a coward. He'll let other men fight and die as long as possible before he puts his own precious neck at risk. Don't worry: I have my men watching for him. When the time comes, I want to be the one who sends him to the Crone."

"He's all yours," Kiara promised. "But be careful. I don't want to explain any serious injuries to Carina after she just finished patching you up."

Cam chuckled. "Don't worry. I learned my lesson about blowing myself up. This time, I mean to do the real damage to Alvior."

Kiara watched Cam walk back toward the troops. His limp was more noticeable than Kiara had expected from Cam's casual dismissal, but it did not slow him as he crossed the camp. She turned back toward her tent, only to spot Royster waiting in the shadows. "I hope I'm not too late," Royster began, "but I think I've come up with something you might want to hear." Kiara took another look and realized that he had a large book and several scrolls tucked under his arm.

Wearily, Kiara waved him inside as the guards at the tent door stood away from the flap. Kiara crossed to where a small tea kettle simmered on the brazier and began to pour a cup for herself. She glanced over her shoulder at Royster. "Tea?"

He gave a tired smile. "Don't mind if I do. Here, let me pour." Quickly, he set down the book and scrolls and made himself a cup of tea, and then settled into a chair near where Kiara sat. "I've been spending a lot of time looking up the last two gifts your ghost ancestors gave you," he began, nearly spilling his tea as he tried to set out the scrolls on a small folding campaign table. "You've already figured out the necklace—that was to win the favor of the Western Raiders and get them to send us grain. The sword bought you the support of the eight warlords, and got rid of the Durim. That leaves us the lens and the runes.

"Let's start with the lens," Royster said breathlessly, tea forgotten in his enthusiasm. "I didn't want to talk about this in front of Morane, but everything I've found on lenses confirms that—if you have the right kind of magic—you can focus and amplify the magic of other mages." He looked up at Kiara excitedly. "Do you realize what this means?"

Kiara crossed her tent and removed the lens from her trunk. She took it out of its velvet wrap and placed it on the table, looking at the lens thoughtfully. "If it works, it might make up for our side not having as many mages."

Royster nodded enthusiastically. He nearly bounced in his seat with excitement. "That's not all. I spent some time with the old maps, and I located several shrines and temples in this area, as well as places that people seem to think have power. In my opinion, we need to think about where you use the lens during the next battle, so that you can focus any power from these nearby sites as well."

Kiara set her tea down and rubbed her temples. "I don't know, Royster. Just being a focus for several mages seems risky enough. I wish we had time to practice. I'm not sure about trying to focus anything bigger—"

"That's just it," Royster said, his eyes alight. "The Flow itself is rumored to run beneath these lands. You can bet that the Temnottan Volshe are drawing on it. If the Volshe weren't drawing on the Flow before the warlords destroyed the Durim, they'll need to now that you've stopped whatever power the Durim's sacrifices were generating." He paused. "Think about the potential, Kiara, if the lens would let you focus some of the Flow's energy as well as the mages' power."

Kiara shook her head. "We don't know whether the Durim's sacrifices actually did help the Temnottans, or whether they were using blood magic to raise the Nachele. What if I try to use the lens and it does something we don't expect, like make me burst into flames?"

Royster chewed his lip when he thought. "The reports of something like that happening are rare."

"Rare? How rare?"

Royster shrugged. "The records tend to be a little vague—"

Kiara fought a growing headache. "Great. That's great. I'd really like to have tried this once or twice on a small scale before we're in the thick of battle."

"Oh, that's easy." Royster brightened. "I can set that up. Just wanted to clear it with you first. We can try it with two or three of the mages, on something small."

"Let's start with that," Kiara said. She could hear the weariness in her voice, and she didn't doubt that Royster could also hear it, because he gave her a concerned look, which she dismissed with a shake of her head. "I'm fine, just tired." She paused. "Have you found anything interesting about the runes?"

Royster smiled. "They're very sympathetic to the working of magic. In other words, strong magic makes them move." He held up a hand at Kiara's worried expression. "Don't worry—I haven't cast them. But when I was working on the maps, I could hear some of the mages outside my tent reinforcing the camp wardings. The runes started to tumble around like mad inside their bag. So you might want to have them out when you use the lens, to see what they have to say."

Kiara sat up and stretched backward, yawning widely and arching her back. "Let's get some sleep, and in the morning, I want to do a test with that lens before we're under fire. Can you arrange that?"

"As you wish," Royster replied with a grin that told Kiara he was looking forward to testing his theory. "I'll meet with Morane and the mages and set up a meeting at ninth bells."

Royster left the tent, and Kiara heard a scuffing noise near the brazier. Jae waddled out from under her cot to linger next to the warm brazier and then gave a flap of his leathery wings and landed on her lap. Absently, Kiara stroked his scales, and Jae rumbled contentedly

The court might mistake Jae for a pet, but he had proven today just how well he could fight in battle. "I'll need you, more than ever, to watch my back if I'm supposed to concentrate on that stupid lens," she murmured. She drew a deep breath. *Look at me—I'm talking to my gyregon. Lady true! I need some sleep.*

Kiara put Jae down, and he waddled over to find a place close to the brazier for the night. Kiara was just unbuckling her cuirass to get ready for bed when Cerise stuck her head through the tent flap.

"Aren't there guards out there?" Kiara grumbled good-naturedly. "It seems as if everyone's paid a call on me tonight!"

Cerise chuckled and stepped inside, not waiting for an invitation. "Queen's Healer's privilege, my dear. Even your father knew better than to second-guess Trygve."

The words made Kiara duck her head and turn away. She'd done well today at holding back memories of her father, but every time she looked across the army camp, she expected to see him come striding up through the campfire smoke, healthy and alive and ready for action. "How is Trygve?"

Cerise shrugged and gave Kiara a look as if she could guess where Kiara's thoughts had strayed. "Busy. Still tending casualties from the last battle. Cam and Wilym have been his best customers."

"I didn't notice any visible new scars on Wilym, but Cam did look a little worse for the wear."

"Trygve was in the mood to vent a little, healer to healer. I guess Cam hasn't really changed his ways since he blew himself up to alert your father about the Divisionist stronghold. Still taking crazy chances, still at the front of the action."

"That's Cam," Kiara replied with a smile. She struggled with the last of the buckles on her cuirass, and Cerise stepped up to help her out of the armor, but when Kiara went to remove the chain mail, Cerise shook her head.

"No. You need to wear that all the time. No telling what damage a stray arrow could do. Keep the chain mail on."

Kiara scowled. "Easy for you to say. It's not comfortable to sleep in."

Cerise made a dismissive gesture. "You're in an army camp, not back at the palace. Think how good your bed will feel when we can go home and you can take it off."

Kiara grumbled, but she knew Cerise was right. "All your fault if I don't sleep," Kiara replied.

Cerise smile broadly. "I can help with that." She let Kiara dress for bed and brought her another cup of hot tea. Cerise mixed some powder into Kiara's tea. "There. You'll fall asleep quickly and sleep soundly, but if there's a real commotion or any danger, you'll wake with your wits about you." She winked at Kiara. "Part herbs, part magic. Always worked for your mother."

Kiara couldn't help smiling as Cerise handed her the cup. "Did you ever have to follow Mother to war?"

"Viata? No," Cerise said, shaking her head. "Don't forget, your mother was a long way from home, and being from Eastmark, she had no standing to lead Isencroft troops, no matter how well she had been trained as a warrior. I think your father was relieved, because there'd have been no denying her if she'd have been able to go. Sometimes, though, she would follow just close enough to be within a few candlemarks' ride, and we'd take a room at an inn or in the home of a nearby noble. Your mother would scry and cast runes and send messengers to your father with the results." Cerise chuckled. "They had quite a partnership, though only a few of us knew it."

Kiara managed a sad smile and met Cerise's gaze. "I'm sorry for dragging you out here."

Cerise made a dismissive gesture. "Tarra's a sweet girl, but she's never been outside the city, let alone this close to a war. In my younger days, I held a position much like Trygve's, a battle healer. I've seen the worst war has to offer." She chuckled. "It's hardly as if I'll be run ragged dressing you for court balls. In the field, you're lucky to get a single change of clothing, let alone an outfit for every occasion. As a 'lady in waiting,' I figured I got the best of the deal."

Kiara sipped at the hot tea and sat on the edge of her cot. Jae was curled up near the brazier, sleeping, and she watched the shallow rise and fall of his chest. She was silent for a while, until she realized Cerise was watching her, patiently waiting for her to speak.

"I'm nearly sick with worry about Tris. I'm not even sure he knows I've gone to Isencroft, and there's been no word about how the war is going for him. Tonight, Morane said that the mages think the Temnottans have sent their dark summoner to Margolan. I'm frightened for what that means for Tris." Without thinking, Kiara's hand fell to her abdomen.

Cerise looked at her and frowned. "Feeling poorly with the babe?"

Kiara shook her head. "Not too bad. Tired, mostly. A little nauseous, but that might be the camp cooking. I don't think tonight's gruel was fresh today."

"Army cooking's meant to be filling, not delicious. But I might have some herbs I can slip to the cook that would help, since it won't do to have a queen with the heaves."

Kiara was silent for a few moments while she drank her tea. Then she set the cup aside and looked at Cerise. "Tomorrow, at ninth bells, Royster wants me to test his theory about the burning glass lens. He wants to see how well I can use it to focus magic. I'm a little nervous about that. Will you come?"

Cerise stepped closer and took Kiara's hand. "Of course I'll come. Just promise me that your days of making magical glass objects explode are behind you."

Kiara chuckled. "I can't promise, but I'll do my best."

Cerise banked the fire in the brazier and turned down the oil lamp to a dull glow. She motioned for Kiara to get into bed. "Don't worry. I'll be there. Now let the tea do its work and get some sleep." Kiara tried to give herself over to the soothing warmth of the tea and Cerise's herbs, but her dreams, when they came, were of fire and runes.

True to his word, Royster was waiting in his tent at the ninth bells with maps set out on a broad campaign table and the burning glass lens sitting in the middle of the maps. With him were Morane and Brother Felix.

"I took the liberty of telling Morane and Brother Felix what we discussed last night," Royster said, clearing his throat. "We thought it best to try this with just a few participants, until we know how well it works."

The better to minimize casualties, Kiara thought dryly.

"Let's get to it," Kiara said. "The sooner we know, the more chance we've got to fit it into the battle plans. Cam and Wilym were pretty sure that the Temnottans are up to something, which means we'll need to strike sooner rather than later."

Royster led them from the tent to the rear edge of the camp. Captain Remir's guards trailed them at a respectful distance. Royster gestured toward a large boulder not far from where they gathered. "Brother Felix, I'd like you to try to move that boulder over to the road."

Kiara saw Felix size up the distance, which was about three wagons' length. "That's a big boulder," Felix said.

Royster smiled. "Just try."

Brother Felix closed his eyes in concentration and then brought his hands up to chest level, palms out, as if he meant to push the rock himself, though the rock was at least ten paces distant. Felix took a deep breath, and then exhaled. The rock, which was nearly the size of a large wagon, began to tremble. Trembling gave way to rocking back and forth to free itself from the ground around it, and then, slowly, the rock began to roll, gradually gaining speed until it was moving slowly toward the road. After a few minutes, the rock reached its destination, and Brother Felix opened his eyes. He wiped the sweat from his forehead. "That was one heavy rock."

Royster's smile widened. "Let's see how well you move it back again—with Kiara's help." Royster gestured for Kiara to bring the lens and stand next to him. "For the first test, I want you to try holding the lens and have Brother Felix touch the lens at the same time. You're already familiar with his magic." Royster motioned for Felix to move so that he could lay his hand on the top of the lens while Kiara held it on the sides.

"Kiara, I want you to think about Felix moving the rock back to where it was, and picture it happening in your mind, but imagine that you look through the lens like a window. If you have any sense of your regent magic, focus it on the lens and then on the image in your mind. Felix, use your magic again, but pay attention to anything that seems different this time. Begin."

Kiara closed her eyes. Before her coronation, the regent magic had always seemed elusive and very faint. Now, as Kiara held the smooth sides of the burning glass lens between her hands, she felt the regent magic flow through her, vibrant and strong. Kiara took two deep breaths, trying to concentrate. In her mind's eye, she saw the boulder move and then, slowly, begin to tumble. She concentrated on the image through the lens, feeling the regent magic flow through her. As she watched, the boulder began to move more quickly, until it was back in its original position.

Kiara took another deep breath and opened her eyes. The rock had rolled back to its original position.

"Very good," Royster said with a wide grin. "Very, very good."

"Did you see that?" Brother Felix said, turning to Morane. "That rock moved twice as fast with her help as it did when I moved it by myself."

"Now, let's try it another way," Royster said, but he moved off to the side a bit and drew a circle with a stick in the ground. He withdrew the pouch of runes from his belt, the runes that the ghost queen had given to Kiara. Carefully, he took each rune out one by one and laid them blank side up.

"What are you doing?" Kiara asked, straining to see.

Royster straightened. "When you helped Brother Felix move that rock, the runes in the pouch were positively dancing in response to the magic. It would seem that they're very sensitive to your power. If they moved when you focused one mage's power, let's see what they do when you focus both mages."

Kiara gave the circle with its runes a wary glance and then brought her attention back to the lens in her hands. She visualized the focused magic passing through the burning glass and the lens began to glow.

"Are you ready?" Royster's voice brought Kiara back to the task at hand. She nodded, and Morane stepped up to stand beside Brother Felix. He found room to add his hand to the lens as well.

"I'm not certain that the mages actually need to be in physical contact with the glass," Royster mused aloud. "Obviously, if they don't, it would mean you might be able to focus the magic of more mages than if they all have to stand close enough to touch. We'll try that next."

On Royster's count, Kiara closed her eyes again, focusing on the lens. Her magic seemed to leap up to meet the burning glass this time. Kiara saw the image of the lens glow even more brightly in her mind, and she felt Morane join his magic with Brother Felix.

Kiara concentrated on the boulder, and this time, it began to move almost immediately. She felt the magic flow through her, and then through the glass, as the boulder began to tumble faster and faster. It thudded to a stop in the middle of the road, moving too quickly to stop in its original resting place.

Kiara opened her eyes. Royster, Brother Felix, and Morane were staring at her wide-eyed.

"Damn! I've never seen a rock move like that when it wasn't falling down hill," Morane exclaimed. He grinned. "Oh, we can do some damage with this on the battlefield!"

Royster had crossed to look at the runes. He turned and shook his head. "Nothing. They moved in the pouch the last time, but nothing this time."

"Maybe they're too far away from the magic," Kiara suggested.

Royster nodded slowly as he considered her words. "Perhaps. If so, that may change on this next round." Royster brightened and looked from Kiara to Brother Felix and then to Morane. "This time, I want to see whether Kiara can focus the magic without you touching the lens. You'll try to do the same thing with the boulder, and we'll see what happens. Kiara, I want you to keep doing what you've done the last two times, only focus on the magic around you. Felix and Morane, I want you to imagine pouring your magic through the lens and then out to the boulder. Is everyone ready?"

Kiara could feel a pounding reaction headache and wondered how much effort it was costing her to channel the regent magic through the lens. Neither Felix nor Morane seemed to be feeling any effect. Kiara centered herself with several deep breaths with the lens clasped firmly between her hands.

"Ready?" Royster asked. Kiara gave a nod.

Kiara focused on the lens and visualized magic flowing from Felix and Morane like golden waves of light. She smiled to herself as magic touched the lens. She knew by its feel that it was Brother Felix. A second later, she felt Morane's magic touch the lens and begin to bend through it, toward the boulder.

She was unprepared as a flood of energy washed over her. The magic seemed to come from everywhere: from the land itself, from the camp below, from places of power that she saw only as glimpses in her mind, roadside shrines, family crypts, temples, and altars. The power hit her like a tide, rolling her beneath it like a powerful wave, taking her breath away. From somewhere nearby, she could hear a low thudding noise growing nearer.

366

"Break the contact, Kiara! Break it now!"

The crashing noise was closer, coming faster. But the power that washed over Kiara was as unrelenting as the sea, and nearly as limitless. It seemed hungry to find her, and to drain through the lens. The ground trembled, and as Kiara struggled to free herself, someone plowed into her, knocking her off her feet and landing hard on top of her. The lens fell out of her hands and she abruptly lost consciousness.

Slowly, light and memory returned. Kiara was still lying down, and her head was pounding. "Kiara, can you hear us?" It was Cerise's voice, worried and close. Kiara murmured, but even that effort was too much to bear.

Cerise pushed a wad of leaves between Kiara's teeth. In a few minutes, the pain of the headache receded and Kiara opened her eyes, squinting at the brightness of the sun. "What happened?"

Cerise had a dour expression. "Let's just say that there's no question about you being able to channel magic without the mages in physical contact."

Kiara moved her fingers and felt grass beneath them. "How did I end up here?"

"Thank Morane. He's the one who bowled you over and landed on top of you," Royster replied. "And it's a good thing, too, or else the boulder would have done it."

With Cerise's help, Kiara struggled to sit up. Her eyes widened. The boulder had moved far from its spot on the road, but instead of going back to its starting point, it had rolled twice the distance toward where she had stood with the lens and then past that point and down a small rise, to rest in a gully. "I did that?"

Brother Felix knelt next to her as Cerise finished checking Kiara for injuries. "Not exactly. To some extent, *we* did that. You channeled our energy without Morane and me needing to touch the lens. But it wasn't just our power. I felt part of what hit you, and I bet he did, too," Felix said with a glance toward Morane, who nodded, wide-eyed. "Somehow, I think you tapped into the power of the rest of the mages in the camp, maybe in the Temnottan camp as well, and I'm almost certain you touched the Flow."

"I saw images of shrines and temples, places I'd never seen before," Kiara murmured.

Royster frowned. "When you feel better, I'd like to show you the map I made of the nearby places of power. I have drawings of most of them. I'm betting we'll find more than a few matches."

"And the boulder?"

Morane chuckled nervously. "It moved, all right. Unfortunately, it headed straight for you as if it had been thrown by a giant. I'm afraid you'd have more than a headache if it had hit you."

Kiara looked toward where the boulder lay, and shuddered. Then she glanced over her shoulder to where Royster had spilled out the runes. "What about the runes? Do they say anything?"

"How about, beware of big, fast-moving rocks," Morane muttered.

Royster was frowning when he straightened and turned back toward her. "Very strange. Only four of the bones show their runes. The others remain blank. *Aneh*, the rune of chaos. *Sai*, the rune of death. *Est*, the rune of darkness, and *Tivah*, the rune for the Flow of magic." He shrugged. "I'm sorry, Kiara. The runes speak, but I can't interpret them for you."

Kiara squeezed her eyes shut against the headache. "It's probably just as well," she said. "The dead queen warned me about relying too heavily on runes and portents. Perhaps the runes just remind us that the outcome is in our own hands."

20

"Thank you for showing me the way out." Aidane gave Ed a smile as she drew a deep breath of fresh air for the first time in three days. It was late afternoon, and the winter sun cast long shadows.

Ed did not return the smile. "As dodgy as it is in the tunnels, it's more dangerous above, in my opinion. That Buka fellow doesn't come beyond the cellars, but he roams the streets. Watch yourself, Aidane. I'll make sure Kir keeps your spot for you."

Aidane gave Ed a peck on the cheek. "I'll be careful. I promise. I just need to earn some coin and I'd rather do it telling fortunes than . . . other ways . . . right now."

"Fair enough. You remember the way back to Kir's place?"

Aidane nodded. "Thank you, Ed. I'll buy you a drink when I get back."

Ed managed a grudging smile. "Since it'll mean you're in safely, I'll drink to that. Now best get going before the light fades."

Despite the assurances Aidane had given to Ed, she was jumpy once she reached the outside streets. She watched passersby warily, and cringed when anyone followed too closely. Though it was midafternoon, Aidane could not shake the feeling that she was being watched by someone other than the ghosts that clustered around her.

Has Buka been near here lately? If the ghosts were intent

on following her and pressing her for favors, the least she could expect in return was information.

At the name, even the ghosts recoiled. *We don't speak of him,* one of the spirits said. *But he's been quiet for a spell. No new killings; least, not that anyone's found.*

Makes it worse, chimed in another ghost. *The longer since he's killed, the more likely he is to kill again.*

What do you care? You're dead. Aidane felt the ghost shudder.

Dead isn't safe. Not now. Not when those Black Robes come around and hollow spirits so that there's naught left but anger and pain. Buka reaps and the cursed Black Robes glean the souls he harvests. It ain't right.

Have you seen Black Robes recently? Since the new queen came to the throne?

She thought that the ghosts might not answer. The subject seemed to frighten them, but finally, a response came.

Only a few. Just a few are left. Bad enough.

Aidane sighed. Although she and Thaine's ghost had done their best to warn the queen and help the soldiers arrest the Black Robes, it wasn't really a surprise to discover that a few had slipped the net. *At least it's better than it was,* Aidane consoled herself, drawing her cloak more tightly around her. *That's something I did to help.*

The winter air was cold, though the sun occasionally peeked through the sky between clouds. Aidane remembered passing several taverns on her way into the city, and it had occurred to her that telling fortunes might raise some coin without the need to resort to practicing her other services. Even though she had resolved not to use her *serroquette* abilities to broker reunions between the dead and living, Kir had been game enough to give her a place to sleep and enough food to get by on out of her wages as a common whore. But that wasn't something she could bring herself to face, not just yet.

Nothing says true love like a whore's chastity, she thought, chiding herself. She had not been with a client since the night she had enabled Elsbet's spirit to make a final reunion with Kolin. She was reluctant to have the memory sullied by the crudeness of a strumpet's tryst, not when the memory of Kolin was so fresh and her heart still ached.

He said he cared about me. Could it have been real? She sighed. *It was real for me. But even though Kolin knows I can't bring Elsbet back to him, it had to be her he wants, or the memory of her using me. He might be* vayash moru, *but he was a noble once. Nobles don't fall in love with whores, no matter how fancy. Better this way. I can imagine good things when I remember him, instead of finding out that he would have eventually grown tired of me. After all, he's immortal, and I'll be lucky to live twenty and five seasons.* She quickened her pace as if to leave the bleak thoughts behind her. "Enough of that. There's coin to earn," she muttered to herself.

Aidane stopped at an inn that was far enough from the palace to assure her that none of the guards who stopped in for ale would recognize her. It was early enough in the day that the inn was still mostly empty of customers. In the bar, a drunk dozed near the fire while two men drank and played dice in the corner. Aidane approached the man behind the counter. He was big and raw boned, with a broad face and unremarkable features topped by a shock of hair the color of dried cornstalks.

"What's your business here?"

Aidane managed a businesslike smile. "I'm a seer and a fortune-teller. I'd like to pass the evening in your common room telling fortunes, and I'd be willing to share my wages in return for a meal and a bed for the night if there's any to spare."

The innkeeper tilted his head to have a closer look at her and Aidane was grateful for her decision to leave her fancy clothes behind at the palace. Nothing about her very plain dress and cloak indicated her status as a *serroquette*. "Are you any good?"

Aidane took a deep breath and closed her eyes for a moment, reaching out to the spirits around her. She frowned, listening. Finally, she opened her eyes and looked at the innkeeper. "There's a little girl named Vivian who wants to know why you don't sing to her anymore. She liked to hear you sing, but you don't sing at all, not in a long time."

The blood drained from the innkeeper's face, and he made the sign of the Lady in warding. "You can see her?"

Aidane nodded. "Her head's just about as high as your hip, and she's got hair like you, but dark eyes and a nose that tips up."

The innkeeper steadied himself against the bar, looking as if he might faint. "That's my daughter, my little Vivian. Took fever last spring and died. I used to sing her to sleep, sang all the time she was sick, hoping it would bring her around. I haven't sung since I buried her."

Aidane swallowed hard and listened to the ghost before replying. "She'd like to hear you sing at the bar like you used to. She's sorry she had to go away, but she'll stay with you here if you'll sing to her now and again."

The innkeeper's pale blue eyes had gone as wide as saucers. He nodded, as if still overwhelmed by the message. "Yes, tell her I'll do it. It's good to know she's still with me. I miss her so much."

"She never left," Aidane said gently. "When you stopped singing, she thought you'd forgotten about her."

"Never," the innkeeper said, his voice breaking. "Never." He looked at Aidane for a long moment without speaking, and then nodded as if finishing an internal conversation. "All right. You've convinced me. And I owe you for that. Tell your fortunes for as long as you want. Pay me a third of what you make and I'll give you a meal and a room if there's one to spare; else, you can sleep in the hayloft out back." He managed a wan smile.

"Not as much traffic as there used to be, with the war and that Buka around, but maybe people will hear tell of you and that would be good for business, huh?"

Aidane thanked him and found herself a chair near the fire where she would be able to strike up conversations as the inn grew more crowded. As she turned away from the bar, she heard the innkeeper begin to sing in a faltering voice, quietly, as though to himself. She looked back and saw Vivian's ghost seated cross-legged at the end of the bar. The ghost smiled and waved at her, and Aidane waved back.

The evening was prosperous. With Sohan over, many travelers were on the road, returning to their homes after visiting the city, or resuming their travels after having paused a while for the festival. As the night wore on and word spread about Aidane's ability to communicate with the spirits and weave fortunes from their advice, she found her services in demand until late into the evening.

Aidane listened to the talk as the tavern's regulars gossiped. Tales of unfaithful spouses, hard luck, and unfair taxes circulated, much as in every tavern. One conversation made Aidane focus her attention.

"Said they found his body in the woods outside of town. Horse must've bolted," a soldier said with a shrug to the other guardsmen who listened to his tale. "Broke his neck when he fell. Snapped clean. Lord Norden's beside himself, so they say."

Lord Norden's son, Aidane thought, catching her breath. *It can't be an accident. Kolin must have found out. This is all my fault.*

"Lord Norden's got other troubles to keep his mind busy," said one of the other guards. "Heard the queen's guards took him for aiding the Durim. Wonder who'll get his lands, with his son dead and all." He tossed back the last of his ale. "Won't be me, that's for sure." The other soldiers chuckled and rose, leaving coins on the table for their ale.

The soldiers' conversation replayed itself in Aidane's mind throughout the evening. When the tavern was empty of all but the innkeeper and a patron who had passed out over his table, Aidane finally stood and stretched.

"Goddess, what a night! I hope you did as brisk a business in ale as I did in telling fortunes!"

The innkeeper stopped humming, glanced up, and then blushed self-consciously. "Aye, that we did. And I'll thank you for telling them good fortunes, for the most part, so that they were of a mind to drink a toast or buy a round for their friends." He winked at her. "Though come to think of it, the ones who found out they were to come to grief drank many a pint to ease their sorrows."

Aidane emptied out the apron where she had kept the night's earnings on the bar and counted the coins in front of the innkeeper, giving him his share. To her surprise, he pushed the coins back to her and shook his head. "Not tonight. I appreciate that you meant to hold up your end of the bargain, but you gave me back my Vivian, and I can't take your coin tonight." He managed a sad, crooked smile. "Now tomorrow night, if you're of a mind to stay a while, I'll take a cut. Sit down while I get you the food and ale I promised you. As for a bed, well, the rooms upstairs are full, but I can give you blankets to take to the hayloft. It's warm out there above the horses, and none of the guests should bother you."

Aidane was about to decline, but the thought of making her way back through the dark streets made the hayloft an attractive alternative. "Thank you," she said, gratefully accepting the heel of bread the innkeeper handed her and the bowl of steaming soup. Vivian's ghost scampered from her place at the end of the bar to sit across from Aidane and prattled on with tales and imaginings that kept Aidane entertained as she ate. When one of the girl's comments made Aidane chuckle aloud, the innkeeper gave her a sideways look.

Aidane pushed the empty bowl aside. "Your daughter is a charming girl. She's been telling me stories while I ate. Your singing has cheered her up tremendously, and she likes that I can hear her."

Sorrow darkened the innkeeper's eyes. "Aye, she was a spark of light, my Vivian. There's nothing good as having her live again, but since she can't, it's something to know she's still with me. Something important. Thank you."

To shake off his mood, the innkeeper began to bustle around, closing up the tavern and fetching two hard-used and threadbare blankets for Aidane. "It's all I've got," he said apologetically. "They should be right enough for you, with your cloak. Night's not too cold out."

Aidane thanked the innkeeper again and followed him to the back of the tavern. A small barn sat a few dozen paces from the inn's back door. "There's a ladder on your right to the loft. I don't fancy taking a candle or a lamp out there what with the hay and all, but the moon's bright enough you should be able to make your way. Sleep late as you want; not much happens at the bar until after midday."

With that, the innkeeper headed back inside, and Aidane made her way across the patchy grass in the small open area between the barn and the inn. Between the light that shone from the windows of the inn and the partial moon, Aidane could see well enough to avoid the well and the watering trough, as well as the hitching rail. Twice, she thought she caught a motion in the shadows, but no ghosts answered when she called, and when she turned her head, she saw nothing. With a sigh, she climbed the rickety wooden ladder to the loft.

Down below, horses snuffled and shifted. The loft was open in the center, all the way down to the horses and the packed-dirt floor below. Ropes and pulleys hung limply from the beams overhead. The barn smelled of animals, new hay, and sweet feed. Once more she thought she saw shadows move strangely toward the back of the barn, but when she stood still and stared, she saw nothing else, and she finally convinced herself it was just a trick of the waning moonlight. Stomach full and still happy about being able to do a good turn to Vivian and the innkeeper, Aidane wrapped herself in the blankets and settled down on the hay to sleep.

The moon had set when the voice woke her. *Wake up. Bad man coming. Wake up!*

It took Aidane a moment to realize that the warning had not been spoken but sounded in her mind. She shook herself awake to see Vivian crouched beside her. The child looked terrified. *Wake up. Bad man is downstairs. Hide!*

Just then, Aidane heard footsteps and the crunch of gravel. She reached out to sense if other ghosts might be able to tell her what was happening, but the spirits that had been plentiful earlier had fled, all except for Vivian.

Buka! Aidane thought. Only Buka or the Black Robes could inspire such terror among the dead. Just then, Vivian gave a choked sob of terror and winked out of sight. Aidane heard the ladder creak under someone's weight as the intruder began to climb.

Desperate, Aidane looked around the loft. She saw a pitchfork stuck tines down in a mound of hay and wriggled out of her blankets, stretching and shifting as noiselessly as possible until she could grasp it. She waited in the darkness, pitchfork poised, watching the space where the ladder opened into the loft.

A man's head and shoulders rose above the opening. In the dim light, Aidane could barely make out the form of a bald man's head and broad shoulders. The head turned until the man was staring straight at where she hid in the shadows. A dangerous smile crept across his features and his eyes glinted with malice.

"I know you're up here, ghost whore. I can feel your magic. I have a little of my own. Just enough to feel the souls when they slip from their bodies. All I need is your blood. Just blood. Blood to feed my amulets, to silence the voices for a little while. I have a charm to make them go away. You shouldn't have run from me. I'd have killed you quickly. Now," he said and clucked his tongue. "I don't have all my knives with me. It will take longer."

Aidane gave a loud *whoop* and ran toward Buka, pitchfork angled at his throat. His arms had not yet cleared the narrow opening in the floor, and Aidane sank the tines deep into his chest and shoulder and then ran for the edge of the loft as Buka howled in pain.

The long handle of the pitchfork thrashed as Buka struggled to free himself, and it caught Aidane on the knee, sending her sprawling. She had hoped to let herself over the loft's edge and drop to the floor below, but she fell, stumbling toward the edge. At the last minute, Aidane managed to grab one of the ropes dangling from overhead. It was enough to slow her fall to the stable below, though the rough hemp burned her hands. Aidane gathered her skirts and limped out of the barn, hearing Buka's footsteps pounding behind her.

Buka was gaining on her. She caught a glimpse of him, blood streaming down his shoulder and left arm. His face was twisted with hatred and the intensity of a hunter keen on his prey. She also saw the glint of metal in his hands—knives meant for her. She screamed, wondering whether the innkeeper and his guests would bother to rouse themselves. A sharp pain exploded through the back of her head, and Aidane stumbled as a rock bounced behind her. She could feel something warm and sticky begin to drip down her neck. She was almost to the back door of the inn, but there was no guarantee that the innkeeper hadn't thrown the bolt. Another rock caught her between the shoulders, and a third found its mark against the other side of her head.

Aidane fell but she kept on crawling, even though she could hear Buka just steps behind her. *Somewhere, there has to be a weapon*, she thought, but the ground near the hitching rail was bare. She dug her fingers into the dry dirt and flung a handful in Buka's face just as he reached down to grab for her, then rolled to the side as he clawed at his eyes. She kicked hard at his kneecap, scrambling to get back to her feet before Buka could see again.

Suddenly, the shadows began to move. Aidane caught her breath. Her magic sensed no spirits, and yet shadowed shapes were closing in on them from all around the yard. Featureless, yet with the bodies of men, the shapes moved silently and swiftly. Aidane braced herself to fight, curling her fists tight. The shadow shapes were nearly upon her.

A flash of silver streaked through the air. Crimson fountained from Buka's throat and a look of surprise crossed his face. His hands clutched at his open flesh as blood continued to gush down his chest. More silver streaks hissed through the cold night air, piercing Buka's body with deadly accuracy. The shadows grew closer. Their approach was silent and their movements had the fluidity of dancers. Buka gave a hoarse cry and collapsed in a pool of his own blood, his chest studded with silver knives.

The shadow shapes gathered around Buka, and one of them toed the body over and then bent to yank a charm from the strap around his butchered throat. He tossed the talisman on the dirt and ground it under his heel.

Aidane felt the ghosts clustering around her, abuzz about Buka's death. But more than that, Aidane could feel the ghosts swarming around the shadow men. Not just gathering around them, but entering them, bidden by the fighters whom Aidane could now see were dressed in head-to-toe costumes of black that hid all but a strip around their eyes, where the skin had been blackened with coal.

"What are you?" Aidane challenged. She had not relaxed

from her defensive stance. Buka was dead, but she had no idea what fresh horror the shadow men had planned. *Maybe they're just Black Robes, dressed in a different way.*

One of the figures stepped forward and slowly removed its black hood. To Aidane's surprise, it was a woman. She was tall and lean, with angular features that spoke of Trevath blood. "Don't worry, *serroquette*. We're not here for you. But we knew your ghost magic would draw Buka to you, as it drew us. That's why we followed you here."

"Assassins," Aidane breathed. Her eyes widened. "Then it's true? I'd heard tell that there were assassins that allowed the spirits of dead fighters to possess them. I thought they were just stories. The ghost blades are real?"

The woman's thin lips quirked upward, but not quite to form a smile. "Buka's dead. You're not. Might be safest for you to forget anything you saw out here and let rumors remain rumors."

Two of the ghost blades hefted Buka's body between them, and the woman replaced her hood. Aidane turned as she heard the sound of the bolt on the back door being drawn back, and when she looked again, the ghost blades were gone.

The innkeeper bustled out into the yard, armed with a cleaver from the kitchen. Two other men with swords followed unenthusiastically behind him, while Aidane could see faces pressed against the upstairs windows. "What in the name of the Crone is going on out here?"

Aidane took a shaky breath to steady herself and willed her hands to relax out of cramped fists. "There was a man in the barn. He came after me. I stabbed him with the pitchfork, but he chased me and threw rocks at me. He must have heard you coming," she said, licking her lips and stealing a glance toward the shadows where the assassins had disappeared. "He ran off."

The innkeeper looked from the pool of blood on the ground to Aidane, and his eyes widened. "Dark Lady take my soul!

You're bleeding. Come inside." The innkeeper shot a glance at his two unenthusiastic assistants. "Go fetch her cloak and blankets from the loft. Two sturdy men with swords shouldn't be afeared of a highwayman with holes in him."

Goaded to protect their honor, the two men glared at the innkeeper but set off at a trot for the barn.

"I'll clean her up. No reason for the rest of you to miss your sleep. Go on back to bed," the innkeeper said, waving off the onlookers, who gradually filed back into the building and left the windows now that there was nothing to see.

"Did you hear me scream?" Aidane asked as the innkeeper led her into the kitchen and bade her sit on a bench by the worktable.

The innkeeper soaked a rag in cold water from the pump and daubed carefully where the rocks had cut her. Now that the danger was past, Aidane could feel her head and knee throbbing, and she realized she felt light-headed.

"Drink this," the innkeeper said, pouring a measure of poitin into a cup and handing it to her. The raw, strong liquor burned her throat, but in moments, it also dulled her pain. "No, I didn't hear you scream. Sorry about that. I wouldn't have suggested you sleep out there if I'd any thought of robbers."

"Then what woke you?"

The innkeeper had gone behind her to finish cleaning the matted hair and blood from where the rocks had struck her head. "Vivian woke me. Funny, but in the year since she's been gone, she'd never made herself known by causing mischief. But she pulled the sheet off me and tugged at my feet, and then everything on a shelf in my room crashed to the floor and the window swung wide open. Well, you can imagine it woke me up. Thought there was a burglar in my room. When I didn't see anything except my sheet and the things from the shelf lying on the floor, I got up to close the window, thinking how it might have been the wind that done it. That's when I saw you down there." He paused. "And I saw the shadows."

Aidane's heart skipped a beat. *He might be safer if he never realizes what he really saw.* "Whoever it was must have been a blood mage. There were shadows all around, and they nearly got me. I'm so glad you came when you did. You scared them off."

The innkeeper nodded. "Thought it was something like that. I imagine magic like yours draws bad ghosts, too, like moths to a flame." He refilled her cup and pushed it back to her, shaking his head at her objections until she drank the clear, fiery liquid. Not only had the pain dulled, but Aidane found that it took a great deal of effort to focus her eyes.

"You'll spend the rest of the night inside, where it's safe," the innkeeper said. "You can sleep in my bed." At her raised eyebrow, he blushed. "No, not like that. I'll sleep down here. It's just that my room has the only available bed tonight, and you look like you need a good night's sleep."

Aidane went to stand, but her legs were wobbly from the shock and the poitin. The innkeeper got an arm under her shoulder and helped her make it up the stairs and into the bedroom. Vivian followed, keeping a watchful eye on Aidane. When they reached the room, Aidane saw the outline of an ample woman's form beneath the covers and a cloud of curly red hair on the pillow.

The innkeeper helped Aidane to get into bed and drew the sheet up over her. "Now get some rest."

Protesting her gratitude in slurred whispers, Aidane sank down onto the bed and was instantly asleep.

It took a day for Aidane to recover before she could even think of putting her gift to use for the amusement of the inn's patrons. The innkeeper refused her coin for lodging, and Vivian told her that it was out of guilt for not better safeguarding

Aidane. She noticed that the innkeeper's reticent humming had grown into a near-constant medley of tavern favorites and old songs sung in a passable baritone. Vivian, who had not left Aidane's side as she recuperated, was back at the end of the bar, happily swaying to the music.

The morning of the third day, Aidane came down to breakfast and found the innkeeper unusually pensive. She had gone to bed early with a throbbing headache and guessed he was unhappy that her earnings for the night would be less to share.

"A *vayash moru* came around looking for someone who sounds a lot like you," the innkeeper blurted before Aidane could say anything. "After you went to bed."

Aidane felt a chill. "What did he look like?"

The innkeeper leaned on the bar and gave Aidane a measured look. "Tall. Thin. Blond hair tied back. Had an odd accent, like he wasn't from around these parts."

Kolin. Aidane paused to make sure her voice was steady. "Did he say why he wanted to find me?"

The innkeeper went back to cleaning the bar. "Not really. Asked if I'd seen you, said he was looking for a fortune-teller who could see spirits. Then he asked if there'd been any disturbances round here. Had the feeling he knew just what he was looking for."

Aidane realized she was holding her breath. "What did you tell him?"

The innkeeper met her eyes. "Seein' as how I owe you for Vivian and all, I said I hadn't seen you and that we'd had a quiet couple of nights. But I don't think he believed me." He looked down. "If you want to avoid him, I don't think you can stay on here. Had the feeling he'd be back."

Aidane swallowed hard. "Thank you. I'll leave right away. I hadn't really intended to stay long but—"

The innkeeper shook his head. "I'm right sorry about everything. If that biter hadn't come around, I was thinking of letting you stay

382

on as long as you like. But for a nice girl, you seem to have some bad people looking for you. I don't think it's safe here."

"It isn't. You're right. And I'm sorry for bringing trouble on you. I'll be on my way."

The innkeeper insisted on packing a large cloth full of bread, sausage, and cheese for Aidane to take with her, and he gave her a full wineskin, though she protested that her journey was only back to the city. To her surprise, the innkeeper gave her an awkward hug before she left, thanking her profusely for letting him know that Vivian was still with him. Vivian regarded Aidane with sad eyes as she packed up her few possessions to leave.

Do you have to go so soon?

Aidane managed a sad smile. *I'm sorry I can't stay.*

Vivian considered this for a moment, and then nodded. *I hope I see you again. I like you. And my daddy sings to me because you told him I could hear it. I like that, too.*

Aidane knelt down to be on eye level with Vivian. *You're a brave little girl. You saved my life. Thank you.*

Vivian rushed forward, arms open, and Aidane dropped her shielding. For a moment, she felt Vivian's spirit cling to her, pass through her, and for a few seconds, the child's memories poured through her mind in a giddy profusion. Vivian drew back, separating them, and looked at Aidane wide-eyed.

Lady Bright! You can hug ghosts! I'll miss you, Aidane.

I'll miss you too, Vivian.

Aidane straightened and smoothed her skirts. The innkeeper and his wife were watching her, and Aidane smiled self-consciously. "Vivian just wanted to say good-bye. She'll stay close to you, so please keep singing to her."

The innkeeper swallowed hard and nodded. "Don't worry 'bout that. We will. Travel safely, so that you're safe by dark."

* * *

Aidane's sore knee slowed down her journey, and after a candle-mark her limp made progress difficult on the cobblestone streets. She reluctantly parted with two copper coins to pay a passing wagon master to take her into the heart of the city. The winter day was gray and rainy, matching her mood. Aidane felt exposed and vulnerable in the open streets. Here in the alleys and ginnels where the poor lived, no one had spread the word that Buka was no longer to be feared. People moved furtively, glancing over their shoulders.

Aidane drew a deep breath, trying to shake off her gloomy mood. *I've proven that I can earn good coin without whoring*, she thought to herself. *Maybe not the gold I earned as a* serroquette, *but enough to keep me warm and dry and fed. I won't have to live down in the tunnels for long. Maybe I can find a tavern or two topside to let me come round a few days a week.*

Kolin's visit to the innkeeper made her sigh as the wagon jostled through the busy streets. *If I show my face more than once in a tavern here in the city, Kolin's sure to find me. He doesn't understand the risk I am to the queen. Berwyn would feel honor-bound to take me back, but I'm only going to be fuel for her critics. She doesn't need that. No, maybe I need to keep to the tunnels until the war ends. After that, I can make my way back to Dark Haven, where Jolie said she'd have a place for me. And if Kolin still wants me, then who's to say it's not love?*

"I'll drop you here, but no farther," the wagon master called back to her. "Can't figure out why anyone in his right mind would be about in these parts, let alone a woman."

She paid the wagon driver, who seemed anxious to leave, and she made her way down the narrow, refuse-heaped alleyways. Aidane shivered as she ducked into the crumbling, abandoned building with its entrance to the cellars. Though she knew that

Buka was gone for good, other dangers lurked all too often in places like these. Cutpurses, drunks, and dreamweed addicts all stumbled their way here to die.

Aidane made her way amid the broken crockery, stray leaves, and scurrying rats toward the far side of the cellar, where the entrance to the tunnels was located. She slowed, noticing a movement in the shadows. But before she could scream or run, a voice called out to her.

"Aidane? Is that you?" The shadow moved, and Aidane recognized Ed. She let out the breath she was holding and felt as if she might collapse.

Ed opened up the shutters on his lantern, flooding the cellar with light. He gave her a hug and put an arm around her shoulder. "You're hurt. What happened?"

Aidane managed a shaky laugh. "I'll tell you once we reach Kir's place. But if you don't mind, I'd like to lean on your arm while we walk." She paused. "What are you doing here?"

Ed shrugged. "Been coming up to look for you each day round this time. Part of me hoped you'd done well enough for yourself that you didn't need to come back here, much as I'd miss your smiling face," he said with a playfully flirtatious grin. "But mostly, I was worried. I wanted to make sure you got in safely."

"What do you mean?"

Ed sighed. "The folks topside seem to have convinced themselves that the plague is all the fault of those down below. There's been a new bout of plague; lots of people have died. Another reason I was hoping you didn't come back was for your own safety. Anyhow, at some of the entrances to the tunnels, there've been men waiting with clubs to attack anyone who comes out. Couple of regulars got killed. Ugly stuff."

Aidane realized that Ed had a long, thick staff with him. "Thank you," she said, repressing a shiver.

She leaned harder on Ed's arm than she wanted to admit

as they made their way through the maze of tunnels back to Kir's place. The tavern was quieter than usual, though Kir greeted her with a shout and a mug of his watery home-brewed ale.

"Where is everyone?" Aidane asked, thankful to take a seat and rest her throbbing leg.

"That's what I was trying to tell you," Ed said, pulling up a chair next to her. Like most of the furnishings in the tunnel, the chair was a broken cast-off, with one leg splinted back together and still too short, so that the chair wobbled fiercely. "People are scared of the plague. Scared enough that they aren't even coming out to drink." He nodded toward Kir. "Yesterday, about the only coin Kir earned was going down the tunnels with a bucket of ale and a jug of poitin, clanging his ladle on the bucket. Those who wanted a drink put out a mug and a coin and he filled them up from outside the door."

"Damndest thing," Kir said, shaking his head. "I've seen people scared before, but not too scared to drink. I can't say I liked wandering around myself, but I need coin to pay for the supplies to brew with and the food to serve."

Ed gave Aidane a level glance. "Now, I'm guessing you've got a story to tell, Aidane. You've got a couple of good knots on the back of your head and a knee swollen twice its size. What happened?"

The two drunks in the corner of the tunnel bar were fast asleep and paid no mind as Aidane told her story to Kir and Ed. They listened raptly as she recounted her success with Vivian's ghost and the tavern's patrons, and were wide-eyed at her escape from Buka. Aidane omitted only the role of the ghost blades, but she ended the tale in a way that left no doubt that Buka was dead.

Kir and Ed both gave Aidane a round of cheers when she finished, and Kir slid another ale toward Aidane. "On the house, for the slayer of Buka! By the Lady, I'm honored to know you! Don't you worry none," he said, wagging a finger at Aidane. "You've got a warm bed here without having to take clients if you tell fortunes and speak to spirits in the tavern here instead of topside. That might be enough to coax people out of their holes once word spreads."

"Thank you," Aidane said wearily. "I wouldn't mind it being quiet for a day or two so I can recover, but then I'm happy to earn us both some money talking to the spirits." Kir went off to a side tunnel to tend the still, and Aidane leaned toward Ed.

"I'm sure the problems up above will blow over. Why don't you come topside with me a few days a week? We could work our way around the taverns, you doing your hedge witching and me with my fortune-telling. Come back here until we've saved enough to go back to Dark Haven. Maybe your musician friends would go back with us. What do you think?"

Ed considered for a few minutes and shrugged. "We could try. Not much coin to be earned down here, even with Kir's brew. I wouldn't mind going back to Dark Haven after what I've seen of Principality City."

A day later, when Aidane's knee was no longer swollen and her headache was gone, she and Ed made their way back up to the safe entrance she had used. But instead of a broken door on a cracked doorpost, they found freshly mortared bricks sealing the doorway.

Aidane and Ed exchanged glances. "What's this about?" Aidane murmured. Together, she and Ed retraced their steps and then headed for the next closest entrance. This time, they found a small group of people milling around a similarly sealed doorway.

Ed pushed forward. "What's going on?"

A thin, bearded man gestured toward the sealed entrance. "It's clear enough, innit? The topsiders have sealed us in here to die. It's the same all over the warrens. All the doorways out onto the street are sealed up with bricks or boulders, or boarded over. We've tried to break through, but it's no use. The walls are too thick. It's the city people who did it. They think if they seal us in, they seal the plague away."

"They've left us to starve," Aidane murmured. "We'll die."

21

A somber group trudged back into the depths of the tunnels. Aidane felt the press of spirits closer than ever. When they returned to the tavern, Kir met their news with a growl of outrage.

"Sealed us in! If the plague doesn't kill us all, we'll starve to death before too long." He turned away, cursing.

Several people had begun to drift into Kir's tavern, and Aidane guessed they wanted to drink their share of the ale before it ran out. She found a seat next to Ed and rested her head on his shoulder. "How long do you think we've got?"

Ed shrugged. "We've got water, that's not the problem. Plenty of cisterns down here, as fresh as you'll find up above. It's food and good air that are going to be in short supply. Without the doorways and openings to the above ground, the air will foul. Course, plague spreads faster like that, too. Food won't last long. Nothing grows down here except for some mushrooms, and there aren't enough of those for everyone, even if you were of a mind to eat them."

He shook his head. "Once people realize that there's no way out and they get hungry, some of them'll go mad, riot. It'll go from bad to worse pretty quickly then." He put an arm around Aidane like a protective big brother. "I'm sorry, Aidane. You shouldn't have come back. Unless something changes, none of us are likely to be alive for very long."

Spirits filled the air around them. The voices had a new urgency, and Aidane let them speak to her.

Please carry a message for me. My wife is dying. She's afraid. I'm waiting for her, just on the other side. We can cross the Gray Sea together. Please, please tell her.

My children are dying. They're alone. Please go to them and tell them that I'm here with them. Tell them I'll be with them soon. Please tell them.

Each ghost came with a fresh tale of woe, but the plea was always the same. These spirits had no desire for a carnal reunion with a living lover; they simply wanted to comfort the dying.

Aidane roused from where she leaned against Ed. "I need to go to where the plague victims are," Aidane said, meeting Ed's eyes.

Ed stared at her. "Are you crazy? Why would you want to do that?"

"Because it's better than sitting here waiting for the ale to run out and feeling sorry for ourselves," Aidane said, as purpose began to replace resignation with anger. "The spirits are all around us—can't you feel them?"

Ed sighed. "Not like you can, but I know they're here."

"They won't leave because they're trying to stay with their loved ones," Aidane said, taking Ed's hand as her resolve grew stronger. "They want me to carry messages for them, to comfort the dying. Ed, we don't have to wait around to starve to death or die pushed up against a stone wall in some Goddess-forsaken riot. Maybe we can do a little bit of good with the few days we have left. You're a hedge witch. You could ease some pain. I can carry messages. If you can find Bez and Thanal and the other musicians, maybe we can make it a little easier on the dying, since we'll soon be among them. Please, Ed."

"You're sure to die of plague."

Aidane gave him a level glance. "How long does it take to die of plague?"

Ed shrugged. "Cough in the morning, dead by nightfall."

"And it takes how long to starve?"

Ed sighed, and then nodded. "All right. We'll round up the musicians and then go to the lower levels."

They found the musicians crowded together in a dingy cellar. Their bedrolls and personal possessions were stacked against one wall. A torn, dirty sheet hung from a length of rope served as a makeshift divider in a room that was home to a dozen people. A bucket against the far wall served as the garderobe. A jug of poitin and several tin cups sat on a small, broken table next to a block of hard cheese and a half loaf of dry bread.

Cal, a portly older man, cradled his drone as he listened to Aidane's proposal. Cal's wife, Nezra, sat next to her dulcimer. Nezra had been plump on their journey from Margolan to Dark Haven. Now, she was much thinner and her face looked tired and old. Her dulcimer was scratched, with several broken strings. Bez, the young tattooed drum player, kept up a quiet rhythm all during their conversation, and his faraway expression made Aidane wonder whether he had mentally already left the caverns for somewhere untouched by death and sorrow. Thanal, the flute player, looked even shaggier than before, with his long, dirty hair tied back haphazardly.

"If we're all going to die; at least we can do some good," Aidane said, wrapping up her plea. She fell silent, waiting for what she was sure would be a quick rejection from the others.

Cal turned to Nezra. "Sounds like what we've talked about, doesn't it?" he said quietly. Nezra nodded.

"I'm in." Aidane looked up in surprise at Bez, who answered without altering the rhythm his fingers tapped on the drum.

"Me too," said Thanal, who withdrew his flute and his

pennywhistle from a pouch on his belt and turned them lovingly in his dirty hands. "Playing to an audience makes me feel alive, and I haven't felt like that since we came down here." He shrugged. "At least we won't be alone when the end comes."

"Follow me," Ed said.

Ed led them farther into the caves. Aidane had never been this far underground. They left the man-made tunnels behind and were soon following a maze of natural caverns.

After a long walk, the narrow passageway widened and Aidane and the others followed Ed out into a large open space. "Where are we?" Aidane wondered, squinting to see better. Bez and Cal moved up to the front with their lanterns, and Aidane gasped as the view unfolded.

The cavern opened out of what appeared to have once been a hillside, now just an outcropping of bare rock and dry dirt. A few paces away, a cobblestone road led off in either direction into darkness. Lanterns hung from posts at intervals along the street, casting everything in a smoky haze. On either side of the street, the first two stories of shops and buildings opened onto walkways, but at a second glance, Aidane could see that the buildings' windows were broken and their signs were missing or askew. What had once been a common area around a well was long barren of grass, now just hard-packed dirt. But when Aidane looked up, expecting to see sky, all she saw was total darkness.

"Welcome to Ford's Crossing," Ed said with forced joviality. "Fifty-odd years ago, this was a busy part of town: shops, taverns, plenty of merchants. Had a sky then, too, and the road actually went somewhere in either direction."

"What happened?" Aidane could see that Nezra and the others were also craning their necks for a good look around themselves.

"The street ran in a narrow place between two hills. A big

flood swept through the first two floors of the buildings, killed a lot of people. Instead of cleaning up and reopening the shops, the people just built arches from one side of the valley to the other and ran the road over this part. They abandoned the bottom floors of the buildings and built new over the top." Ed shrugged. "No one up there probably even remembers. But it didn't take long for the vagabonds to find it."

He swept his arm in an arc. "Now, this is where the sick gather, if they can make it this far." He pointed across the commons, toward a rocky outcropping in the far hillside. "The tunnels go on in that direction for quite a ways, too. But those tunnels filled up with the plague victims first, so there's naught down that way but corpses."

"Are ye dying?"

The strange voice startled them. Aidane and the others turned to see a pale, thin man in tattered brown robes making his way across the street toward them. "If you're not dying, best you go back the way you came, or you will be," the stranger warned.

Aidane stepped forward. "My friends and I aren't sick. We came to give comfort to the dying. They're minstrels," she said with a nod toward Cal, Bez, Nezra, and Thanal. "Ed's a hedge witch, and pretty good with herbs. I'm a seer."

The thin man looked at them sharply. "If you thought to loot the bodies, there's nothing to take. The people who come here have nothing and leave with nothing."

"No, of course not," Aidane protested. "We've come to help."

The thin man crossed his arms over his chest. "I've been down here for several months, I reckon, and no one else has come to help. I even marked the tunnels to keep people away and help the dying find their way here. Why would you come if you didn't mean to steal from the dead?"

Ed exchanged glances with Aidane. "The topsiders have sealed off all the entrances. I imagine there'll be more business for you in a few days than you'll be able to handle, once the hunger sets in."

The thin man's eyes widened. "Truly? We're sealed in?"

"I hope you weren't planning on leaving."

The man shook his head. "No. When I came down here, I knew I wouldn't leave." He paused, and then extended a hand to Aidane and to Ed in greeting. "I'm Brother Albert. Welcome to Ford's Crossing. To my way of thinking, it's a peaceful place on the shores of the Gray Sea."

"You're a healer?" Aidane asked as their unexpected guide greeted the musicians.

Brother Albert shrugged. "No, I'm not. But I do have a talent with potions and herbs, and a little bit of magic with plants. It was enough to win me a position at a noble house. Then fever took the lord's son, and he blamed me. He cast me out, and I wandered, since no other manor would have me."

"How did you end up down here?" Aidane asked.

He shrugged. "Truth be told, I blamed myself for the boy's death as much as his father did. I was tired of my existence, but not quite ready to end it."

Aidane watched Brother Albert carefully, trying to reconcile what her magic was telling her. She met his gaze. "You're *vayash moru*."

Albert nodded. "I lived here in Ford's Crossing long ago. Before the flood. Before I was turned. After I left the noble's employ, I was going house to house with my powders and elixirs, treating whatever ills people would pay coin to cure." He grimaced. "It's a myth, you know, the idea that all *vayash moru* are well-off. I wasn't wealthy before I was turned, and my luck didn't change after I was dead. I still had to earn a living.

"Anyhow, Buka had started terrorizing the people in the lower parts of the city, and some of the ruffians blamed the *vayash moru*." His gaze was haunted. "There were burnings, innocent people staked through the heart, heads cut off. I thought if Ford's Crossing still stood, I could come here and be safe. I have seen too much killing."

Brother Albert gave a bitter laugh. "I wasn't the only one who remembered the stories of Ford's Crossing. Others came, fearing Buka, the mobs, the war. But they didn't bother me, and I didn't mind the company. Down here, we were safe from Buka, but they couldn't hide from the plague. I realized that I had a chance to atone. I hadn't known how many people were living down in the tunnels, but it didn't take them long to find me. Now, they come as soon as they start to sicken, or they bring their dying to me and stay on to die themselves. There's naught to be done for them except to give them some water, wipe their brows with a cold rag, and say a litany over them when they die, but it didn't seem right for them to die alone."

"Why do you stay?" Ed was looking at Brother Albert skeptically.

Brother Albert laughed. "Why, indeed? I ask myself that question each day, and I have no answer. Perhaps the Lady has her share of fools and isn't in a hurry to add a new one to her collection. But for now, I have nowhere else to go, no one who will miss me when I'm gone, so at least here, I'm needed."

He looked at the musicians and their instruments. "Well, if I haven't frightened you off, then follow me. I've done a little bit of singing to keep my own sanity and comfort the dying, but my voice is no treat to listen to, I assure you. I'd welcome some music, and I know it would give comfort." He looked at Ed. "You're a hedge witch?"

"I can do a little magic, very little."

Brother Albert harrumphed. " 'Very little' is quite a bit when I've been accustomed to doing everything myself. I've got work for you." He grew quiet as he studied Aidane.

"I sense magic in you, but not a mage's power. You're not a healer. What are you?"

"I'm a seer. I can carry messages from the dead," Aidane said, meeting Brother Albert's gaze. "They're the ones who asked me to come. They want me to comfort their loved ones."

Brother Albert regarded her in silence for a moment, and she felt a tingle as his magic touched her. "Your magic has a strange feel to it. You're more powerful than just a fortune-teller. You're a *serroquette*, aren't you?"

Aidane sighed and looked down. "I used to be. Not any more. I had to run away from a powerful employer. It was dangerous for me to stay. I meant to earn a living topside talking with the ghosts instead of letting them use me, but things didn't work out."

Her sincerity seemed to win over Brother Albert's skepticism. His expression relaxed. "No one expects to end up down here, but it's where our paths lead us. If you can make their passing easier with messages from beyond, you're welcome."

"How is it the people haven't starved down here?" The question came from Thanal, the young flute player, and it was so unexpected that they all turned to stare at him. "Just wondering," he said, turning his hands palms up as if to indicate that he meant no offense.

Brother Albert chuckled. "Two of the buildings had storage cellars that partially collapsed during the old flood. No one bothered to make the effort to see what was in them when the top was covered over. Turns out, there were several rather large wine cellars, a hundred or so casks of brandy, and a nice deep cistern, plus some storage rooms full of pickled vegetables and dried fruits, all kept high and dry with powerful preservation spells." His smile widened. "I move the spell back a little at a time to take just what I need to feed everyone. Most of the people who come down here aren't well enough to eat more than broth, and I don't eat much. Once or twice, I've ventured up above for some dried meats and sausages, waxed cheeses, things I can preserve with a keeping spell of my own. It's held us well enough."

Ed looked at Brother Albert warily. "How about you? What do you eat?"

Albert turned to look at him. "I assure you, I don't drink from the sick. There are more than enough rats to keep me fed. As I told you, I've seen too much killing."

As Brother Albert walked with them toward the largest of the buildings, Aidane looked around at the eerily silent former street. "Are there other tunnels that lead here, besides the way we came?"

Brother Albert nodded. "Most of the main tunnels have a way to connect to Ford's Crossing. Back in its day, it was quite a popular place, and after the flood, it was still a main cut-through between the caves. So the people who need me find me." He opened a warped door to usher them into what had once been the fine entranceway of a grand building. Its walls were stained from the water of the long-ago flood, and the soot from torches marred the marble walls. Rooms opened off the huge entranceway, and in the dim light, Aidane could see bodies lying shoulder to shoulder on ragged blankets. Low moans greeted them, and a few of the sick called out incoherently.

"This is my hospital," Brother Albert said. "There are three rooms here, and sometimes they're all full. I live upstairs. There's room for you up there, if you really plan to stay."

"What happens to the dead?" Aidane asked in a low voice.

Brother Albert met her eyes. "Every morning, I gather them up, wrap them in their blankets, and carry them to the empty buildings across the street. Nothing I can do except to stack them like cordwood and put a stabilizing spell on them so they don't stink. In the time I've been here, I've filled two of the buildings' first-floor rooms with bodies stacked high as my waist."

"And you do all this yourself?"

Brother Albert gave another sharp, bitter laugh. "Who else would be crazy enough? When I'm gone, that will be the end of it, I imagine." He looked to an hourglass on a shelf. "Nearly time for my evening rounds. You can come with me," he said with a nod toward Aidane and Ed. He looked toward Cal and the other musicians.

"Why don't you set your instruments up here in the entrance? That way all the rooms can hear you. Play whatever you want for however long you like. I can bring up some water for you, and later on, I'll make some soup." He paused. "I'm sorry for not being more welcoming when you arrived, but I've been alone down here for a while now." He paused. "You do know, you're taking a terrible risk, coming here. You'll get plague sooner or later."

Ed nodded. "It's no different than staying in the tunnels. They sealed our fates when they sealed up the doorways."

In the lightless underground, day and night became meaningless. Brother Albert cheered considerably when Cal and the musicians began to play, and he took Ed and Aidane at their word and put them to work.

"Here are some herbs and a few elixirs I've mixed up," Brother Albert said to Ed, handing him pouches and vials that Ed stuffed in his pockets. "Why don't you take the room on the far side of the entranceway, while I take the room on the right? If you need me, just shout." He then handed Ed a pitcher of water, a rag, and a goblet. "Some of them can take a little water, and if they seem to be in great pain, add some herbs. It will help them sleep. For the worst cases, I put enough herbs in the water so they'll just drift away peacefully without waking up. There's nothing you can do for the fever except the water." He shook his head. "Some nights, it's like a madhouse in here. Especially up against the north wall. Don't know what it is, but lately, they howl like wild things." He drew a ragged sleeve across his forehead. "It's been a bit better this week. Things reached a frenzy and then got quiet again."

Aidane shot a glance at Ed. "When did that happen?"

Brother Albert thought for a moment. "About two nights ago. Why?"

The night Buka died. Maybe all his killing really did tie into the dark magic that's been about. Aidane shrugged and looked away. "No reason. Just wondered." She straightened her skirts and dusted off her hands. "Now, where would you have me start?"

Brother Albert shrugged. "Wherever the ghosts pull you, I imagine. When you're tired, go upstairs. You'll find several open rooms; take the one you like. Rest when you need to. There will be patients aplenty when you come back."

Cal, Nezra, and the other musicians had set up on the landing of the stairway, and soon the lively strains of a popular tavern song filled the air. Despite everything, Aidane smiled, swaying with the music for a moment. But soon enough, the spirits clustered around her, as if they, too, were drawn to the tune.

Take my message first!

No, mine!

My mother is dying. I need to reach her before she's gone.

The spirits crowded around Aidane shouting so loudly in her thoughts that she covered her ears and closed her eyes. *Quiet, all of you! I'll work with all of you, but you've got to take turns.*

After a few moments, the spirits calmed, and Aidane chose one of the nearest ghosts. He was a short man with thick, dark hair that stuck out in every direction and a scraggly beard. *That's my wife over there. She doesn't have much longer to live. Please, tell her that I'm waiting right beside her, and that I'll go with her to the Gray Sea.*

Aidane nodded and made her way carefully in the dim light among the moaning forms. The man's ghost guided her to the side of an emaciated woman who lay under a ragged blanket. The woman's skin was mottled and covered with blisters filled with dark blood.

Tell me your name, Aidane said to the ghost.

Noris.

And what is her name?

Ella. Her name is Ella.

Aidane nodded. "Ella," she said quietly. The woman stirred slightly. "I have a message for you from Noris. Can you hear me?"

At that, the woman slowly opened her eyes. Her eyes were unfocused and watery. "Ella, Noris's ghost is here with me. He wants you to know that he's next to you. You can't see him, but I can."

The ghost nudged Aidane. "Noris doesn't want you to be afraid of dying," Aidane went on, speaking in a calm, low voice. "He says he'll wait right here for you, and walk with you to the Gray Sea. You won't be alone." Aidane listened for a moment as Noris added to his instructions.

"Noris said he believes the Lady will honor all the offerings you made to her, and she'll let you and Noris cross the Gray Sea together to your rest. Do you understand?"

The woman made an almost imperceptible nod. "Thank you," she said in a voice that was a low croak, the syllables stretched out along her whole, weak breath. She twitched a bony hand toward Aidane, and it when it brushed against Aidane's skirt, Aidane could feel the heat of the woman's fever.

"Sleep now," Aidane said gently. "When you wake, you'll be with Noris."

The woman visibly relaxed, and her lined face smoothed as if her pain had eased. Aidane looked up at Noris's ghost, who knelt beside her.

Ella was a strong one, but no one's stronger than plague, Norris remarked. He met Aidane's eyes. *Thank you, seer. I've been trying to talk to her for days now. You've done us both a great kindness.*

Aidane swallowed back tears as she got to her feet, leaving Noris sitting beside Ella. Before she could turn, the ghosts crowded in on her again.

Candlemarks passed, and Aidane moved through one room and on to the next, following the direction of the spirits. Finally, when she was overwhelmed with exhaustion and light-headed from hunger, Aidane sank down on the bottom step of the staircase to listen as the musicians played.

Cal wound his drone in a steady hum and played a clever fingering that was a perfect counterpoint to the melody Nezra coaxed from her dulcimer. Bez sat behind them, drumming with a look of relaxed bliss, eyes closed, body swaying to the music. Thanal played a counterpoint on his flute. The music gave Aidane a mental image of trees swaying in the sunlight of a summer day and birds in flight, and she realized that she was unlikely to see either of those things again.

Just then, Brother Albert appeared with a tray of wooden bowls filled with soup. "The broth's a bit thin, but it's warm. I baked some bread, and there's more than enough to go around." Brother Albert gave a self-conscious smile. "Looks like it was a good thing that I ventured up above to get some supplies before they sealed us in. I bought enough to last for a while."

Perhaps longer than we will, Aidane thought. She accepted the soup gratefully. A few minutes later, Ed joined her, and Brother Albert reappeared with a bowl of soup for Ed and hot, flat flour cakes wrapped in a stained cloth.

"I really never expected to have dinner guests," Albert said with a chuckle.

When the minstrels finally stopped playing, Aidane realized she felt as tired as if she had put in a full day's labor. Even Brother Albert looked exhausted, but he waved his new guests upstairs, saying he would be along in a bit.

The upstairs was musty, filled with cobwebs and dust from disuse. Aidane could glimpse the old high-water mark on the plaster walls. It was clear that no one had bothered to make the empty rooms habitable, except for the small room Brother Albert had claimed as his own. Aidane ventured back downstairs to fetch a broom, and before long, she and Nezra had swept out two of the rooms. Any furnishings had long ago been looted, so they made do with their cloaks. Brother Albert supplied them with two small oil lamps and a flint. Aidane was tired enough that sleeping on the floor did not bother her in the least.

She woke at the sound of Nezra's uneven breathing. The older woman was restless, quietly moaning in her sleep. The next time Aidane woke, the others were rousing and stretching. Aidane cast a worried glance at Nezra, but the old woman said nothing. They made their way downstairs to find Brother Albert awake and singing cheerfully to himself in an off-key tenor. He motioned them to follow him down the hallway, where he led them to a small, smoky kitchen. A dented cauldron simmered over a small fire in a sooty fireplace.

Ed cocked his head and looked at where the fireplace and chimney met the ceiling. "Think there'd be enough room to get out that way? Above ground?"

Brother Albert chuckled. "Nice idea, but no, the passageway is partially collapsed. What I can see on this end is an opening no wider than my fist." He motioned them to take seats on the floor, and proceeded to ladle out a thin gruel into a few dented bowls. Then he set a pitcher of water out for them to drink.

"Not much variety down here, but you won't starve," Albert said cheerfully. He worked at the stove as they ate and accepted their gratitude for the meal with a self-conscious smile. Already, Aidane could feel the spirits clustering around her with more requests. When the group finished their breakfast, Cal, Nezra, and the others took their places on the steps with their instruments right after breakfast, launching into a vast repertoire of tavern songs. Ed followed Brother Albert from room to room, falling easily into the role of assistant. Aidane found a routine, moving from one huddled patient to the next, holding out a ladle of water or offering words of comfort if the patient had a ghostly visitor with a message to convey.

Aidane heard a series of soft thuds from the front hallway and heard Cal cry out in alarm. She set her water bucket aside and ran to the front. Nezra lay in a heap at the foot of the stairs. Cal cradled her in his arms calling for her to wake, but Aidane could see Nezra's spirit, disembodied and confused, hovering near her still body.

"She's gone," Aidane murmured. Bez and Thanal had rushed to Nezra's side, but Aidane shook her head.

"She can't be dead," Cal argued. "She's not even feverish."

Aidane remembered Nezra's restless night, and she listened as the ghost murmured to her. "It's not the plague; it's her heart. She's been having pains for a while now, but she didn't want to worry you, seeing how there was nothing you could do."

"I would have taken her topside to a healer. I would have done something," Cal cried.

Again, Aidane listened to Nezra's spirit, and then looked back to Cal. "She was afraid to go above ground, afraid of Buka, and of the mobs. She wants you to know that the pain is over now. She'll stay with us, until it's our time to go," Aidane said.

Cal bowed his head, and Bez put an arm around the older man, comforting him as he wept. Thanal rose, walked a few steps to retrieve his flute, and then began to play a lively tune that had been one of Nezra's favorites. It was a spirited piece often played at parades during feast days, especially on Haunts, the Festival of the Departed. After a moment, Bez joined Thanal, adding the rhythm of his drum. Brother Albert and Ed had quietly slipped up alongside the group. Aidane knelt next to Cal, slipping an arm around his shoulders, while Albert and Ed wrapped Nezra in her cloak and Brother Albert said the passing-over litany. Then Brother Albert and Ed gently lifted Nezra's body and headed for the door. Cal came next, leaning heavily on Aidane, while Thanal and Bez took up the rear, still playing their jaunty song, keeping up the tune until Nezra's body was laid to rest in the building across the street.

Aidane thought that Cal might leave them for the solitude of the rooms upstairs, but when they returned to the hospital building, Cal squared his shoulders, sniffed back tears, and took his place on the steps beside Nezra's abandoned dulcimer, playing his drone.

Another "night" passed, and when Aidane awoke and came downstairs, she was alarmed to see that Ed was not with the others at breakfast.

"He said he was beginning to feel poorly last night," Brother Albert said, ladling out porridge. "He slept down here, in the hallway. When I came down this morning, he was flushed with fever and soaked with sweat. He's in the second room, with the others. By the sound of his cough, he may not make it until evening." As Aidane scanned the room for Ed, a ghost slipped up beside her.

Can you take a message to Ed for me? I've been waiting a long time. Startled, Aidane regarded the new ghost. She was a young woman with long, dark hair and a pretty, sad smile. Just then, Aidane spotted Ed, and she motioned for the ghost to join her.

Picking their way across the crowded room, Aidane made her way to where Ed lay. Flushed with fever, Ed lay still, breathing shallowly.

Tell him Cora's come back for him. I promised him that I'd come back for him.

Aidane wiped Ed's forehead with a cloth dampened with cool water, and he opened his eyes, managing a weak smile of recognition. "Sorry to leave you like this," Ed said in a raspy voice. "I thought I'd last longer."

"Cora is here. She said to tell you she's come back for you."

Ed's eyes widened, and then he focused his gaze on where the woman's ghost sat next to him. "Good," he murmured, closing his eyes. "It won't be long now."

Cora reached out a ghostly hand to pat Ed's chest. *We were married when we were young, many years ago. I took sick from bad water and died two winters after we were wed. I told him on my deathbed that I'd come back to him when it was his time to cross over. He kept the ashes of my bones in a pouch with him, so that I could travel beside him.*

"That's how he knew so much about spirits," Aidane murmured.

Cora's ghost nodded. *Over the years, he learned how to draw me close and keep bad things away.* She met Aidane's gaze. *Go on. You have others to care for. I'll stay with Ed. He'll be all right.*

Weary with sadness, Aidane nodded and began her rounds. Her throat, which had been scratchy when she awoke, was rapidly growing sorer. It hurt to talk, and she found herself whispering. Aidane busied herself with the influx of new refugees, meeting them at the doorway and directing them to where there was room.

There were enough newcomers that Aidane had stopped looking at faces, just noting the numbers on a tally and pointing to direct them. A man stopped in front of her.

"There's room to my left," Aidane rasped without looking up.

"Aidane."

With a gasp, Aidane looked up to see Kolin standing in front of her. "What are you doing here?"

Kolin steered her out of the crowded front entrance and into the quiet of the hallway. "I came to look for you. I came to bring you back to the palace."

"But the tunnels were sealed up. How did you get in?"

Anger glinted in Kolin's eyes. "I brought a contingent of the queen's guards and smashed through the wall. You have to believe me; the queen never ordered those entrances to be bricked up."

Aidane nodded. "I know. It was the topsiders. They're afraid."

"We've been helping all those who want to leave find other lodging," Kolin said. "I came looking for you." He paused. "Why did you run away?"

Aidane sank down on the floor and Kolin sat next to her. "I heard the talk in the palace. My presence was hurting the queen. Berry has so much to worry about now, with the war and the invasion. I didn't want to give anyone a way to hurt her."

"I tracked you to a tavern near the edge of town. I knew you were there, even though the innkeeper lied," Kolin said, and he reached out to gently smooth the hair back from Aidane's face. "It was too crowded for me to come in and take you back. I feared there would be an outcry about *vayash moru* kidnappings. The Truce is too fragile; I couldn't risk it. When I rose the next night, you had disappeared, and by the time I realized that you must have gone into the tunnels, they'd been sealed." He paused. "Scian and the ghost blades confirmed that they had seen you. Because of you, Buka is dead. The queen is grateful, but she's also beside herself with worry about you."

"I'm not that important."

"You've saved the queen's life, averted a bloodbath at the coronation, and provided the key to destroying Buka. You're a hero."

Aidane swallowed with effort, trying not to grimace at the pain. "I'm sorry, Kolin. I didn't think anyone would bother to come after me. But I can't go back. I don't feel well. I can't take the fever back to the palace."

Kolin looked at her in silence for a moment. "All right then. I'll stay here with you. Plague can't hurt me." He reached out to take her hand. "I love you, Aidane."

Aidane stifled a cough. "This is why you shouldn't fall in love with a mortal. We break too easily." She lifted his hand to her cheek and kissed his fingers. "Goddess help me, I love you, too."

Aidane insisted on carrying messages from the ghosts throughout the afternoon. By evening, Cal's drone had fallen silent, and the musician lay slumped on the stairs with Nezra's ghost attending him. Thanal looked pale and sweaty, and Aidane noticed that he was missing more notes on his flute. Bez kept up a steady beat on his drum, his eyes distant, as though he were far away in thought.

Aidane stumbled, and Kolin caught her. "You're hot with fever," he murmured. He sat against the wall and cradled her in his arms.

"I never thought I'd see you again," Aidane murmured. "Will you stay with me?"

Kolin held her close against his chest. Aidane knew that with the heightened senses of the *vayash moru*, Kolin was well aware of her slowing heartbeat and of the shift in her temperature between fever and chills. "Did you mean it, when you said you loved me?" he murmured from behind her ear.

"I love you. Forever." The words came out as a raspy whisper.

"Then I will stay with you. Forever."

Aidane gave a slight gasp as Kolin's teeth closed on her shoulder. She sank back against him, feeling the fever and plague slip away from her with her life blood, growing drowsy in his arms. Her heart slowed, skipped a beat. Kolin turned her so that she lay across his lap, and her head lolled. He lifted his left forearm and tore back his shirt sleeve, and then he dug a fingernail into his wrist, opening a slit from his wrist up his forearm. Dark ichor welled from the gash.

Kolin looked into her eyes. "If you love me and you want us to be together, then drink."

Aidane pressed the wound against her lips and let the cold ichor slip down her swollen throat, managing to take in several mouthfuls before she felt her heart stagger to a stop and her breath leave in a ragged gasp. The last thing she saw was an expression of pain and hope on Kolin's face.

Aidane stirred. Panic filled her as she searched her memories.

"You're safe." Kolin's voice was quiet, nearby in the darkness.

"Am I dead?"

"Undead."

"Where are we?" Aidane realized that she could not feel her lungs expanding with breath and that her heart did not beat, but her senses told her that the air in this place was cold and fresh.

"In a safe place, a house in the city owned by another *vayash moru.*"

"The tunnels . . . Brother Albert . . ."

"Brother Albert sent us on our way with his blessing. The two musicians chose to stay behind. They were already sick. Brother Albert said he'd continue to manage on his own."

A sudden memory came to her. "Lord Norden's son—"

Kolin's expression hardened. "The stable hands weren't happy to be questioned, but in the end, I found out who attacked you.

The problem has been eliminated." He held up a hand. "And before you feel guilty about it, I've kept an ear out for the gossip below stairs. Seems Lord Norden's son made a habit of forcing himself on the servants and roughing up any man who tried to stop him. He doesn't deserve your sympathy."

"Was his father really helping the Durim?"

Kolin nodded. "Yes. And we have you to thank for making us look in his direction. The queen thought Norden was obnoxious, but she hadn't realized he was disloyal."

"What happened to him?"

"He's in the palace dungeon, awaiting execution. Once again, the queen says she is in your debt."

Aidane's hands rose to her chest and carefully slid down her body. "My clothes. They're different."

Kolin chuckled. "Making the transition is . . . messy. I brought you here, cleaned you up, and let you sleep while I went out to find a gown for you."

Aidane's hands fluttered to her throat and then down to the bodice of the gown. She sat up and realized that even without the light of a candle, she could see as if the room was cast in moonlight. Although she could not make out the color of the dress she wore, she knew it had a high bodice and a proper neckline, a gown fit for court. The trim waist was tied with satin cords, and the full skirt fell in yards of rich brocade. Aidane felt something slip against her arm and she looked down. The onyx bracelet Kolin had given her in the palace was fastened around her wrist.

"Kolin, I can't wear this dress."

"Why not?"

"It's a proper lady's gown. This . . . it's a gown for a married woman, not a . . . whore."

Kolin clasped her right hand in his and reached over to her belt, wrapping their wrists in its silken cords. "Aidane, I take

409

you as wife and lover. I will teach you the ways of Those Who Walk the Night, and I will hunt beside you forever."

Aidane stared at him, dumbfounded, until he nudged her with his other hand.

"You're supposed to say something."

She swallowed hard, still caught off guard. "I accept . . . I take you, Kolin, as husband and lover. Forever."

Kolin smiled broadly, and she saw his long eye teeth. Gingerly, she lifted a hand to her own lips, drawing away startled as her fingers found that her teeth had changed.

"When you're fed and rested, we can go back to the palace. I burned your old clothing and took the liberty of giving you a full bath while you slept off the change, so there's no fear that you can carry any plague back to the queen." He smiled. "By the way, I sent a messenger to tell her that I'd found you. She's expecting you to return to the palace, and that, my dear, is an order from the queen."

22

Tris Drayke looked up as the guard at the entrance to his tent announced a visitor. Coalan went to greet Sister Fallon as she entered. Fallon stopped and eyed Tris with a mixture of concern and resigned frustration.

"Aren't you supposed to be getting some rest?"

Tris shrugged and pushed the book away that he had been reading by the light of a small lamp. "I could ask the same of you."

Fallon made her way to sit down across the table from Tris as Coalan busied himself making a cup of tea for their guest. "What's so important that you're reading instead of sleeping?"

Tris hesitated, and then slid the slim, leather-bound book toward Fallon. Her eyes widened as she picked it up and began to flip through the yellowed pages filled with cramped handwriting. "Please tell me this isn't—"

"The third journal of the Obsidian King," Tris finished for her.

Fallon handled the book gingerly, as if it might bite. "Everyone thought this was destroyed long ago."

"Grandmother gave it to Riqua to safeguard. Riqua gave it to me, two years ago. Like Nexus, I put it away, hoping I'd never need it." Tris patted the sword that hung by his side, and Fallon shook her head.

"We still don't know the full power of that blasted sword—or exactly what the repercussions will be if it steals a breath of your soul."

Tris shrugged. "Better my soul than all those souls out there," he said with a jerk of his head toward the crowded campground of the Margolan army.

"Every man—and woman—on that field lives to serve the king, and if need be, to die for you and for Margolan."

Tris gave a tired sigh. "And too many of them have been dying. That's why I turned to the diary—to see if there was something I could find that might turn the tide, something I could use against Scaith." He looked at the careful handwriting on the journal's yellowed pages. "The Dread mentioned my grandfather. They hinted that there was a way his power might serve me."

Fallon looked wary. "Your grandfather was tricked by the spirit of the Obsidian King. Lemuel was nearly destroyed because of it, and he brought the Winter Kingdoms to their knees. We don't need that kind of help."

Tris gave a harsh, mirthless chuckle. "If the book was full of incantations to destroy enemies, you might have something to worry about. Unfortunately, it seems to be a collection of notes on Margolan history." He sighed. "I was hoping for something more helpful. This daily skirmishing is like slow death."

"It's better since you're back from the barrows. While you were with the Sworn, it was as if Scaith knew you weren't here to fight, and the attack was brutal."

"Soterius told me. Trust me, it was pretty brutal in the barrows, too."

"But when you sent Cwynn's essence back to his body,

Scaith's troops backed off. That tells me Scaith is powerful, but not more powerful than you are."

Tris shrugged. "Maybe. But two equally matched summoners fighting a battle to the death are likely to take a whole lot of people with them."

Fallon was quiet for a moment. "Still, there's something else going on. Twice now, when it seemed the Temnottans were winning, they've suddenly fallen back for no apparent reason. I felt something in the magic, as if power was wind and the sails had just gone flat."

Tris nodded. "But it wasn't the Flow. It was blood magic—I'd stake my crown on it. Something disrupted the blood magic Scaith's been drawing on to enhance his power. It's weakened him. That's why this next push has got to work, before he can rally."

"Have you figured out how to do what the Dread told you, to meld your magic with the Flow?"

"Not and live to tell about it." Tris took a sip from a goblet of brandy as Coalan handed a cup of tea to Fallon.

"And there's nothing in the journal?" Fallon asked, nodding toward the leather book on the table.

Tris grimaced and stretched. "I expected a sorcerer's working notebook, full of notes on potions, instructions for rituals, maybe even incantations. I thought it might have even been a logbook of his 'experiments.' But it's not. It's a collection of old stories and legends, about two kings—Hadenrul and Gustaven."

Fallon frowned. "Hadenrul I know about. You met his spirit in the tomb. But Gustaven I don't recognize."

"Both of the kings died in battle. I know that's true about Hadenrul from his tomb paintings, and from what he told me. In the tomb, there was a painting of the Nameless holding out her hand for Hadenrul's bloody heart." Tris shook his head.

"Hadenrul died defending Margolan, and his death spurred his army to victory. But as far as I can tell, Gustaven was just a coward. In the thick of battle, when his army was overwhelmed and losing badly, he rode away from the fighting with his trusted steward and fell on his own sword. He didn't even have the courage to fight to the end. His army rallied and won the day despite him." Tris frowned. "His name is damnably familiar, but I can't remember why. I know I've heard of him before."

Tris savored another sip of the brandy, swirling it in his cup. "And here's the other strange thing: Neither Hadenrul nor Gustaven were mages, let alone summoners. Marlan was a summoner, and that's how he brokered the arrangement with the Dread. But grandfather had very little interest in him. There is only one story about him, the story of how he sent the Dread away to guard the Nachele." He took a velvet pouch from his belt and carefully shook out the talisman Marlan's ghost had bid him take from the tomb.

"I'd hoped there would be something in the journal to explain why Marlan wanted me to take his talisman, why he said to wear it into battle. But there's nothing." He turned the talisman in his hands, and the gold shimmered in the lamplight. "There's one place I've seen something like this before."

"Where was that?"

Tris looked up to meet Fallon's gaze. "When I went into the barrows to save Cwynn, the Dread gave me passage tokens so that I could pass through the gates of the Abyss to confront Konost. One of the passage tokens was a necklace with a hammered gold disk that looked a lot like this."

"What, exactly, did Marlan tell you when he said to take the talisman?"

Tris closed his eyes and leaned back in his chair. "He said

for me to wear it into battle, and if my offering was sufficient, it would open the magic of my fathers to me."

"So it's a passage token of another kind."

Tris nodded tiredly, opening his eyes and leaning forward to lay the talisman gently on the battered campaign table. "I believe so. The question is—passage to where?"

"Can you speak to the spirits of Hadenrul and Marlan? Or Gustaven?"

Tris shook his head. "I wish it worked that way. The spirits are bound to the crypt. We're on our own."

Fallon reached out to take the old leather journal and opened the cover. "*The third testament of he who is called by many names. Darkness. Slaughterer. Blood-Sower. The Obsidian King,*" she read, almost to herself. "An intimidating heritage for a grandson."

Tris's head snapped up. "What did you say?"

Fallon looked nonplussed. "I just read the names he inscribed here in the front of the book, and said that it was an intimidating heritage."

Tris reached for the book and stared at the page. "Darkness. Grandfather was called by many names, and one of them was Darkness."

"I don't understand why that's so important."

Tris met her gaze. "Because the night Donelan died, Beyral came to me with a rune scrying. She knew that a king had been killed. The runes spoke of war in the places of the dead, and of chaos, and succession. But they also spoke about something neither of us understood. According to Beyral's runes, the fate of the war depended on the 'son of darkness.' At the time, I thought it had to mean Scaith, because he's a dark summoner. But what if—"

"Lemuel, the Obsidian King, was your grandfather. You're his mage heir, his son of power. That makes you—"

"The son of Darkness."

Fallon sat in silence for a moment, thinking. "What about Cwynn?"

"What do you mean?"

"The Dread told you that the poison that nearly killed Cwynn blew open his magic to the Flow. Talwyn and Alyzza both called him a bridge, and the Dread told you he could channel the Flow itself without harm."

"I felt some of that power when I freed his spirit in the Underrealm."

"Alyzza also called him a 'key' and a 'voyager.' Well, now we understand that, at least," Fallon said. "She was talking about his power in the Flow."

"Talwyn was right—Cwynn is one of the spoils of war Scaith wants from this conflict." Tris's expression hardened. "He'll have to take that over my dead body."

Fallon shivered. "I'd really rather you not use that turn of phrase."

"And if Cwynn can channel the Flow, that explains 'voyager.' I've touched the Flow directly, channeled it for a few moments. It's like falling into a huge, swift river that carries you through the most amazing places—"

"As it burns your life thread to a crisp."

Tris shrugged. "For any normal mage, yes."

"No. No normal mage gets close enough to touch the Flow before turning into ash. For an extraordinary mage, the most powerful summoner in the Winter Kingdoms, you get a glimpse of wonders before you fry."

"Thanks to Carina, I didn't fry."

"I was there, remember? It was too damn close."

Tris shook his head. "But it's not about what the Flow can do to a normal mage—or even to an unusually powerful mage. I get the feeling that when Cwynn comes into his magic, he's going to be in a class by himself. But the question is—can his magic affect this war?"

"You mean, other than Scaith laying siege to the Winter Kingdoms and brokering a deal with a forgotten goddess to steal part of his soul? I'd say Cwynn's magic has already affected this war."

Tris shook his head. "Indirectly, yes."

"It would have been quite direct if you had died in the Underrealm trying to free him."

"That didn't happen, now did it?" he replied with a grimace. "The Dread said that they would assure his safe return to Shekerishet. But they also said that when Cwynn felt Scaith searching for him, Cwynn instinctively knew to hide, and that part of him, his consciousness, followed Kiara to Isencroft. We don't know what that means for his power—or his life." He spread his hands, palms up, questioning.

"Scaith thought he could draw on Cwynn's power. Cwynn fought him, even if it was just instinctive. If some part of Cwynn's soul or consciousness followed Kiara to Isencroft, how did he do it? Where did he hide that part of him? And if his power is guided solely on a child's instincts, what is he capable of doing if it ever senses that Kiara's in danger?"

A few candlemarks later, Tris Drayke looked out over the battle-field from astride his warhorse. His generals had been unanimous that he must stay back from the front lines, and it rankled with Tris even as he grudgingly acknowledged their wisdom. He felt the same irrational irritation for the *Telorhan* who followed him everywhere he went. But the ever-present bodyguards were a small concession for managing to be closer to the battlefront.

"You really think Scaith will make his move today?" Sister Fallon had refused to leave Tris's side. Her large roan horse shuffled impatiently.

"I'm sure of it. I don't know how or when, but I've never felt his presence as clearly as I do today. That's why I wanted to be the first to strike."

A deafening war cry went up from the front lines as infantry and horsemen charged forward at General Senne's command. Another cry on the left told Tris that Soterius had led his division against attackers who had landed a sizeable number of troops on the eastern flank of the battle. With luck, Tris thought, Senne and Soterius would catch the invading army in a pincer movement to drive them back toward the beaches.

The armies met with the crash of steel and the cries of soldiers. Hoofbeats thundered on the clear, cold winter day, and the ground beneath Tris's feet shuddered with the tide of men and horses.

The battleground had not shifted far from the opening salvos of the war. Margolan's army were dug into positions to hold the invaders as close to the shoreline as possible, while the Temnottans brought wave after wave of ships bearing fresh troops. Neither side had been able to gather their dead, and the press of battle pushed back and forth across a field of war strewn with the corpses of both armies. Out beyond the bay, Pashka's fishermen and Tolya's privateers did what they could to harry the Temnottans, picking off straggling ships and launching night-time attacks that nipped at the invaders' heels. But while the armies appeared to be evenly matched once on land, it was clear that Margolan's ragtag maritime presence was no match for the power of the Temnottan navy.

"I'll keep the wardings. Go find Scaith!" Fallon raised her arms and began to chant, and Tris did his best to block out the banging of battle drums, the din of the pipers, and the howling maelstrom of war.

Tris felt the shift in magic even before he heard the cries of alarm from the battlefield. As he stretched out his mage sense, he could feel a massive tide of dark magic pouring across the killing grounds, touching the bloated corpses of the Temnottan dead and forcing their souls back into their rotting bodies.

"If they mobilize all their dead, they've got us seriously outnumbered," Fallon shouted.

It is forbidden for a Light mage to compel a soul to return to a dead body, on peril of his soul, Tris thought in horror.

But not if we go willingly. In a breath, Tris was surrounded by the Margolan battle dead, rank upon rank, fully fifteen hundred soldiers strong. A young man stepped forward, and by his insignia, Tris knew him for one of Soterius's captains. *We swore our lives to you. We will rally in death. Send us, and spare the living.*

Tris gathered his power. Once, by accident, he had sent a soul back to reanimate its corpse, and Alyzza had warned him of the consequences of such gray magic. *What does my soul matter when Margolan hangs in the balance?* Tris marshaled his magic and sent it forth in one powerful, rippling blast. The magic swept past the living like an unexpected wind, but it touched each of the fallen Margolan soldiers. Tris felt the magic stir in their cold, stiffened forms, felt the dead flesh tremble as magic coursed through their sinews and, as the tide of his power receded, it left in its wake not shambling puppets but corpses possessing the mind and will of their original soul, bent on taking their vengeance.

"What have you done?" Fallon breathed.

Tris drew back, staggered from the massive drain of power. In the distance, he could hear the shouts of terror as soldiers saw their fallen comrades rally to their feet, and above the din, he heard Senne and Soterius shouting for order, heard the bugles signal an advance.

Tris drew a deep breath, fighting a massive reaction headache, and gathered his power around him once more. Before Scaith could regroup, Tris sent out another blast of power, this time directing his magic at the advancing lines of the reanimated Temnottan dead. He saw the image of the walking corpses clearly in his mind. Unlike his own ghostly soldiers, the Temnottans had not returned willingly. They had been violently forced back into the rotting shells of their bodies, and Tris could feel their pain, terror, and utter confusion.

In his mind, he reached out for the sickly green glow of the reanimated Temnottans' life threads and snapped the cords, releasing the dead souls from bondage. A row of undead soldiers collapsed, and Tris sent his magic out across the ragged lines of the Temnottan walking dead, breaking the faltering threads and freeing the enslaved souls as the decomposing bodies fell to the ground midmotion.

"Brace for it," Tris shouted only an instant before a shockwave of magic swept toward the Margolan line with the force of a storm tide. It was Scaith, and mingled with the powerful magic, Tris felt rage. Tris sent an answering salvo, drawing on his waning power. Magic met magic midfield as soldiers on both sides scrambled away in terror. As Tris's stamina wavered, he reached out to the life forces of the dead Margolan soldiers, shielding them from Scaith's retaliation and borrowing from the spark of their energy to hold a defensive wall of power against Scaith's attack.

The energy burned across Tris's skin, as if every nerve were on fire. Tris could feel Scaith trying to pull energy from his life force, but the Flow welled up to replenish him, even as the fallen Margolan soldiers offered what they could of the dim glow of their souls. Just when Tris thought his magic could hold out no longer, Scaith pulled back, departing with such suddenness that Tris reeled, nearly falling from his horse. He clung to the pommel of his saddle, his vision blurred and his breath ragged, fighting a headache that throbbed like a blade embedded

420

in his skull. With his remaining power, Tris released the Margolan dead, too exhausted to sustain them. The live Margolan soldiers surged forward, intent on retribution.

Tris felt the tendrils of the Flow slip away and with a deep exhalation, he murmured the passing-over ritual to send the souls of the Margolan dead on their way to the Lady. Exhausted and aching from the effort of his fight, Tris felt a surge of alarm as new, unfamiliar magic tingled along his senses.

Without warning, dozens of the scavenger birds that had been circling high above the battlefield plummeted at full speed, their sharp beaks and talons trained on the Temnottans. The invaders screamed at the onslaught as the birds beat at the soldiers with their wide, powerful wings and ripped at their flesh with beaks and claws.

A new flicker of powerful, wild magic surged over the battle ground, and the Temnottans found themselves pelted with a hail of dark objects that rose from the trampled ground and then rained down from the sky.

"Is that *horse manure*?" Fallon breathed, caught between a startled intake of breath and a strained laugh.

The unmistakable odor of a barnyard accompanied shouts and curses from the Temnottans. Undaunted, Soterius and Senne urged their men forward. Tris heard a cackle of laughter behind him and turned.

On the ridge behind the soldiers, an old, hunched woman danced with mad glee, her hands rising and falling in precise correlation to the offal that flew through the air at the Temnottan army. Farther down the ridge, a gaunt man made wide, swooping motions with his hands, orchestrating the attack of the carrion birds.

Rocks flew up from the ground, pelting the Temnottans from all sides as a third figure joined the first two. The third mage was a heavy man who held a large rock in either hand, striking them together so hard that sparks flew, and with each shower of sparks, more rocks sailed through the air.

A giddy shriek of insane glee accompanied a blast of fire. With amazing precision, the flames ignited the pants of one of the Temnottan commanders, causing him to leap from his horse and beat at his legs and then drop to the ground and roll. Another blast and then another caught soldiers and officers alike, setting their uniforms ablaze.

Tris strained to make out the figures on the ridge, when a familiar singsong voice reached him. *Alyzza!*

The Temnottan bugler bleated a jumbled retreat. Rocks, offal, birds, and fire pursued the Temnottans until they were running from the field to the jeers and catcalls of the Margolan army.

As the certainty of their unlikely victory became clear, Tris felt fatigue utterly overwhelm him. He would have tumbled from his horse, but he felt Fallon's hands steadying him as he slid to the ground.

"It worked," Fallon murmured, and Tris could feel her magic reaching out to him, doing what she could to temper the headache and fatigue. "Senne and Soterius have them on the run." She paused. "But what you did—"

"Is forbidden," Tris whispered, his throat dry. Fallon lifted a wineskin and splashed warm wine into his mouth. "If it matters, our dead gave their consent. The Temnottans had no say with Scaith."

"I did my best to shield you and the troops from that last blast of power, but if Scaith strikes again while you're down, I don't think even all of us together can hold him off."

Holding onto the reins in one hand and with Fallon under his shoulder on the other side, Tris began to make his way toward the rear, surrounded by a contingent of guards. He could see the looks on the soldiers' faces as the ranks parted to let him through. Fear and horror mingled with duty and discipline as they began to grasp, possibly for the first time, the true implication of a Summoner-King.

As they reached the open ground behind the troops, Tris saw a short, robed figure running toward them. As the figure neared, she threw back her hood. Panting and breathless, Sister Rosta managed a hurried bow as Tris's guards parted ranks to permit her access.

"Apologies, Your Majesty, that we did not give you advance notice of our arrival."

Despite his headache, Tris managed a tired grin. "You can surprise me like that any time, Rosta." He shot a teasing glance toward Fallon. "Why didn't your battle mages ever think of throwing horse shit at the enemy?"

Fallon gave a good natured shrug. "We will now." She grinned at Rosta. "And while the rocks were a nice touch, setting their pants on fire was truly inspired."

Rosta rolled her eyes. "That was Brother Gernon. He's a fire mage who's gone a bit senile. He was sent to Vistimar because he kept lighting the hems of the other mages' robes just to watch them dance."

"But the horse shit was all mine." Tris looked around to see Alyzza stride up behind Rosta. Alyzza's eyes were bright with madness and excitement, but her face was animated and her expression knowing and shrewd. For a moment, she was every bit the canny old sorceress who had trained him.

"It's good to see you, Alyzza."

Alyzza barked a harsh laugh. "All the iron and salt in the world wasn't enough to hold back the darkness, was it? But we drove him back, aye, that we did."

One by one, clad in threadbare robes, the mad mages of Vistimar assembled behind Sister Rosta. "The 'hum' they hear in their minds reached a crescendo a fortnight ago," Rosta said apologetically. "They reacted so violently and with such a burst of magic that Vistimar is in ruins." She sighed and spread her hands, palms up. "Alyzza was insistent that they come to fight the invaders, and the other Sisters and I thought it better to set them loose on the enemy than have them wandering around the countryside, so here we are."

"You're a welcome sight," Tris replied. "We've lost several of our battle mages. The other side seems to have plenty to spare, so I'll accept all the help we can get."

"Volshe," Alyzza spat, and for a moment, her eyes lost their mad glint. "I'd know the touch of Volshe magic even in my grave. It was from a Volshe that Lemuel learned of the Obsidian King. I've got an old score to settle with them."

"We'll find you tents," Tris promised, filing away Alyzza's comment for future thought and turning his attention back to Sister Rosta. "And we'll scrounge provisions. Another bad harvest has made for rather slim rations, but no one's gone hungry yet."

Rosta nodded wearily. "Thank you, m'lord. Even warm gruel and watered wine would be welcome. There's less to be had inland, because of the plague. We'll be grateful for whatever you can spare."

Coalan came bounding up, sword ready in one hand, and took in Tris's condition with a worried expression. "I was headed to find you to tell you that the mages were here, but I see they've beat me to it."

Tris pretended not to notice the glance that traveled between Coalan and Fallon, and he assumed that they wordlessly confirmed that Tris needed nothing so much as his cot and a goblet of brandy. "Coalan," Tris said, getting the young man's attention, "while Fallon sees me back to my tent, I need you to get Sister Rosta and her mages set up with tents and provisions."

"As you wish, Your Majesty," Coalan said, grinning at the show of formality he reserved strictly for company. He gave a bow and sheathed his sword. "If you'll follow me back to camp, we'll see about getting you settled in."

When the new mages had left them, Fallon returned her attention to Tris with a critical eye. "At least we've got reinforcements if Scaith strikes before you're back on your feet."

"I did my best to make sure Scaith's in as bad shape as I am," Tris replied. His voice was a dry rasp, and his head pounded with every beat of his heart.

"So with both of you flat on your backs, the rest of the battle should be up to the army?"

"Goddess, I hope so."

They reached Tris's tent without incident, and Tris handed his horse's reins off to a groomsman. Fallon followed Tris into his tent, giving instructions to his guards that he not be disturbed. She looked askance at Tris when he collapsed into a chair. "Here, drink this," Fallon said after she had rummaged in Tris's trunk for a bottle of brandy. She added powders from the pouches on her belt to help with his reaction headache and handed the mixture to Tris, who knocked it back, then gasped at the raw burn.

"What exactly did you do out there?" Fallon's voice was a mixture of curiosity and suspended judgment. She drew up a chair and reached out to take Tris's pulse and then touched his temples lightly with her fingertips, letting the warmth of her healing magic wash over him.

Tris was quiet for a moment, letting the brandy and the powders begin to ease the pain. Speaking quietly so as not to make his pounding headache worse, Tris told Fallon what he had done. When he was finished, Fallon sat back. From her expression, Tris knew she was thinking hard to process what he told her.

"So you reached out to the souls of the dead, and the Flow? Damn. That took a lot of energy."

"Don't forget the souls of the Temnottan dead. I set them free."

"No wonder you're so drained. I'm impressed. A year ago, lesser workings knocked you out for days at a time."

"I guess it's true—you gain strength from the things that don't kill you."

"Let's not push that idea too far," Fallon replied wryly. She was silent for a moment. "Do you think Scaith will try that trick again?"

Tris closed his eyes and slouched in his chair, letting his head fall back. "Goddess, I hope not. I'll do my best in the next battle to help the dead cross over as quickly as possible so their souls can't be violated. Scaith's troops weren't fighting out of their love for Temnotta or their loyalty to him. All I felt was fear."

"How long do you think it will take him to regroup? Can you be on your feet first?"

Tris tried to sit up and groaned. "It was a strain for him—I could feel it. I had the distinct feeling that Scaith hasn't come ashore yet, so he was casting his power over a greater distance. That cost him, and I think he'll make sure he's closer the next time." Wincing as movement made his head throb, Tris staggered from his chair and dropped heavily onto his cot. "As for how quickly I can be on my feet—the sooner I sleep this off, the sooner I can get back out there."

"We've got the new mages," Fallon said, moving to stand beside Tris. She bent down and touched his temples again, blurring the pain and hastening sleep. "The sheer unpredictability of what they'll throw at Temnotta should keep the enemy at bay until you're ready for action again." She shook her head. "It's easy to forget the mage and focus only on the madness, but of the mages who I saw with Rosta today, they were all considered quite powerful in their day. Mad or not, they're a force to be reckoned with."

"Then let's leave it in the hands of the madmen, at least, for a little while," Tris murmured, as Fallon's magic took effect and he fell into a deep, healing slumber.

23

"You're certain Buka is dead?"

Scian inclined her head and leveled a measured glance at Jonmarc Vahanian. "Quite certain. I put the blade through his heart myself."

"There's no mistake that it was Buka you killed?"

Scian shifted her whipcord-thin frame in the campaign chair, meeting Jonmarc's eyes. "Absolutely no mistake. He'd set his eye on a specific target, a *serroquette*. She barely escaped from him once, and we were just steps behind them, but Buka got away from us. We watched for her, and tailed her. Our ghost blades found it easy to focus on her magic. When she left the tunnels, we followed her to an inn outside of town and waited. Buka followed her, too. When he struck, so did we. Buka is dead."

Jonmarc frowned. "A *serroquette*? Aidane?"

Scian shrugged. "The same ghost whore who was with the queen at the ceremony on Haunts."

"Why was Aidane outside of the palace—not to mention the tunnels?"

Scian looked bored. "How should I know? Lucky for us that she was; Buka knew the area he was using as a killing ground as well as the ghosts themselves did. His blood magic charms made it difficult for my ghost blades to get a fix on him. Aidane drew him out into the open for us, out of his usual hunting area. We severed the head and burned the skull, hand, and breastbone separately, then set the rest of the body on fire. The ashes were scattered over a very wide area. I used a *damashqi* dagger when I killed him; it was spelled to destroy the soul. He's gone. Permanently."

There was a rustle at the tent door, and Jonmarc looked up to see Ansu, the *vayash moru* mage, framed in the doorway. "Glad you could make it," Jonmarc said, motioning for Ansu to join them. Scian regarded Ansu warily.

"I thought your ghost blades were an extinct breed," Ansu said, regarding Scian with a look that seemed to take her measure.

"As the *vayash moru* know, large numbers aren't always necessary."

"Very true." Ansu looked from Scian back to Jonmarc. "In my mortal days, nearly every warlord employed a handful of ghost blades among his personal retinue. They were regarded as prized weapons."

"As were *vayash moru* assassins," Scian replied in a tone that implied far more than it stated.

"Indeed. I have no desire to see those days return."

Scian shrugged. "Peace may suit the farmer, but it's hell on the fighter. Turn us loose on the enemy."

Jonmarc had been quiet, letting the two dodge and parry. He looked up and glanced at Ansu. "The timing is right. It has to be connected."

"Hmm?"

"Scian's told me about how her ghost blades finally caught and killed Buka. That was four days ago. It matches, to the candlemark, when Imri pulled his troops back."

"That *is* interesting," Ansu agreed. "It would make sense, if Buka's butchering was somehow feeding the invaders' power. But what about the other time?"

Scian leaned forward. "Other time?"

Jonmarc nodded. "Not long after Sohan. We were in a pitched battle—just as we were on the night you killed Buka—and if I had to place bets, I would have said Imri's side had the advantage. All of a sudden, it felt like the energy completely changed on the battlefield. Imri's troops lost their will to fight. They called back their troops when they were winning, for Crone's sake, and the ones that didn't hear the call milled around lost until we cut them down."

"I hadn't come to the battle lines yet, but I think I know the night you speak of," said Ansu. "I, too, felt a shift in the magic, but it was blood magic, not the Flow, that waned. I'd wager that on one of the battlefronts, someone struck a deathblow to the one of the dark summoner's sources of power, and without their blood offerings, the Volshe lost some of their power."

"Just like with Buka," Jonmarc murmured. "I'm grateful for anything that hands us a victory." He looked to Scian. "If Imri is using blood magic, how does that affect your ghost blades?"

Scian grimaced. "It depends on how the power is being used. If the blood magic targets ghosts, then my assassins can't let the spirits possess them. They lose the edge that the spirit warriors provide. On the other hand, if the blood magic is set against mortals, our ghost blades may have an advantage."

"If you're right, Imri and his Volshe have lost the extra power they were getting from Buka's murders and from somewhere else, maybe the Black Robes. They've come too far to retreat, so that means they'll throw everything they've got into the next battle." Jonmarc leaned back in his chair, thinking. "I wish we knew how the war was going in the other kingdoms. Temnotta took a big risk when it decided to attack the entire coastline. If Margolan and Isencroft are holding their own, then it has to have taken a toll on Temnotta's manpower and mages." He let out a long breath. "And if Margolan and Isencroft haven't been able to hold them off, Goddess help us."

By the time the sun was high in the sky on the next day, Jonmarc was looking out over the lines of battle from astride his warhorse. Gethin and the *Hojun* priests were to his left, while Taru was to his right.

"With Gregor gone, Exeter had to cover the flank. We'll miss his mercs on the advance," Jonmarc commented to Taru.

"We've still got a sizeable force, between your men and Valjan's," Gethin added.

"How sizeable depends on what Imri still has to throw at us. I don't think he's out of tricks."

"No, but he won't throw the same trick twice," Taru said dryly. "My mages have made sure of that."

"Something feels wrong," Jonmarc muttered. Valjan's division had made the first assault of the day, while Jonmarc's soldiers hung back to enable an onslaught of fresh troops later in the fight. Exeter's mercs were intent on forcing back the flanking invaders who had gained ground at Gregor's expense. "I don't think Imri is throwing his full weight against us. It's not like him to fight defensively."

"Maybe getting rid of Buka hurt him more than we realized." Taru followed his gaze out over the battlefield, and Jonmarc guessed from her look of concentration that she was seeing with her magic as well as with her vision.

"Much as I'd love to believe that, it's too convenient. He's waiting, trying to wear us down, or hoping our guard slips," Jonmarc replied. It wasn't magic that informed his skepticism, but rather hard-won intuition, born of more life-and-death battles than he cared to remember. And every fiber in his body told him that the fight had not yet really started.

As the light began to wane, neither side had gained ground. Despite pitched skirmishes up and down the battlefront, the line of fighting retreated and advanced like the tide, gaining precious yardage only to surrender the same ground moments later.

At the front of his division, Jonmarc watched the position of the sun. As dusk fell, he raised his arm to signal his unit to advance. On the ride behind them, he saw Ansu join Taru and the mages. Vygulf stepped up beside the *Hojun* priests. The *vyrkin* in their wolf form slipped among the ranks of the waiting soldiers, awaiting the order to charge. And although he couldn't see them, Jonmarc knew that Scian and the ghost blades were somewhere in the fight, as were the *vayash moru*.

"Move out!" Jonmarc shouted, and he heard the order echoed down the line. He gripped his reins and raised his sword high, leading the advance. The moon was waning, and the night was dark as clouds blotted out the stars. Here and there, torches lit the darkness. Barrages of mage fire from both sides split the night like lightning strikes. Imri's forces showed no sign of falling back; instead, Jonmarc noted that the rogue shapeshifters' army seemed invigorated as darkness fell. *That's exactly what I was afraid of.*

He heard shouts and the screams of men coming from his right, and he saw that Exeter's troops were fully engaged, yet their enemy did not appear to be the Temnottan soldiers. Jonmarc rode into the thick of the fighting. Cries of horror rose from the soldiers at the front.

"What is *that*?" Gethin's voice carried above the fray.

"The missing dead."

Hundreds of walking corpses staggered over a rise to their right. Jonmarc felt his blood chill. Dressed in ragged clothing and tattered shrouds, these weren't the fresh dead of the battlefield. They weren't battle dead at all. Jonmarc remembered the panicked farmers and bewildered townspeople who sought a reason for why someone had snatched the bodies from their crypts. Staring at the shambling corpses, Jonmarc now knew the answer.

"Hold your ground! They're already dead. Cut them down!" With a cry, Jonmarc spurred his horse onward, toward the ranks of the dead. Only when he reached the front did realization hit him.

These were not mindless puppets, crudely moved by distant mages. Nor were they *ashtenerath*, men driven to madness by magic and potions. These corpses moved with sentience and malice. Armed with famers' scythes or the scavenged swords of the battle dead, the corpse fighters moved with purpose. Two of them fixed their eyeless stares on Jonmarc and advanced.

The night suddenly grew colder. Across the battlefield, a horrific wail split the night, the keening of the damned. Opaque shadows flitted across the sky or wound between the soldiers, stretching into shapes with dangerously long arms and gaping maws. Jonmarc brought his sword down hard on the nearest corpse fighter, swinging his blade to send the head rolling from the body. His blade glowed and tingled in his hand as it made contact, and as the corpse fighter fell, another of the black shadow shapes rose from its headless body.

Sweet Chenne. Imri might not be a summoner, but he's enticed the hollowed spirits to possess the dead he stole from the tombs. How in the name of the Lady do we fight that?

Four of the corpse fighters advanced on Jonmarc, trying to encircle him. He cut down two with his sword. He heard a growl and the snap of teeth, and one of the *vyrkin* leaped past him, taking the third corpse fighter to the ground and ripping into the dead flesh of its throat, breaking its spine. Jonmarc reared his horse, and a powerful kick from the sharpened shoes on his stallion's front hooves shattered the fourth corpse's skull.

Men screamed as the hollowed spirits attacked with fury. In

the gray fog, Jonmarc spotted Tevin, the fire mage, lobbing bursts of flame to drive back the ravening shadows. Vygulf's ghost *vyrkin* joined the attack, and when they leaped at the dark shapes of the hollowed ghosts, the shadow ghosts shrieked and drew back.

To his left, Jonmarc glimpsed the *Hojuns*' spirit stawars prowling across the battlefield, hunting the hollowed spirits that had suddenly gone from predator to prey. Two of the corpse fighters launched themselves at Jonmarc. As Jonmarc used his sword to cut one of the corpses from shoulder to hip, the other attacker leaped from the other side, colliding with Jonmarc with such force that he was thrown from his saddle as his panicked horse reared.

Mottled teeth snapped a breath away from his throat as Jonmarc bucked to free himself from his attacker. This close, he could smell the stench of the grave. The corpse fighter tore at him, and the exposed bone and leathery darkened flesh of its hands ripped at Jonmarc's armor. Momentarily winded by his fall, Jonmarc twisted to throw the attacker clear, but it fought with a *dimonn*'s fury.

Mage lightning flared across the sky, and Jonmarc saw it glint on steel. A blade swung down as Jonmarc heaved with all his strength to tear his attacker loose and throw it into the path of the blade as he rolled clear.

Gethin's sword pinned the corpse fighter to the ground through the ribs, and the dead form began to shudder and writhe until the opaque shadow within wrested itself free. Gethin fell back a pace, one hand going to an amulet at his throat, while Jonmarc rolled to his feet, sword raised. The hollowed spirit stretched into a tall, menacing shape with long arms that ended in sharp talons. The shadow surged forward, slashing its talons toward Gethin. The prince raised his sword, deflecting the worst of the blow, but Jonmarc heard the clatter of talons across armor and

Gethin cried out, staggering backward as four gashes appeared on his right shoulder. The shadow reared back for another strike as Jonmarc rushed forward to pull Gethin from its claws. A spirit wolf raced past him, leaping into the air, plunging into the center of the dark form. The hollowed spirit gave a shrill scream. Jonmarc grabbed Gethin by his uninjured arm and pulled him to his feet, dodging away from where the shadow and the spirit wolf battled.

Gethin was ashen, and his arm was soaked in blood. "We've got to get you back to the *Hojuns*," Jonmarc said, getting his shoulder under Gethin's good arm.

"Leaving so soon?"

Astasia stood blocking Jonmarc's path. Jonmarc looked up and saw a row of figures silhouetted in the dim moonlight on the high ground to the right, and in the blink of an eye, they moved with immortal speed into the battle, attacking Exeter's troops first.

"Get out of my way."

"Or what?"

Gethin allowed himself to slip from Jonmarc's grip as Jonmarc drew his sword. "I don't give a damn whether you're Blood Council or not. If you're not here to fight on my side, you're the enemy."

"Then fight."

Astasia's movement was swift enough to blur. Jonmarc's parry was equally swift. More than a year of training with Laisren and Gabriel had honed his already-legendary sword skills to be fast enough to fight *vayash moru*. The war against Malesh and his rogue *vayash moru* had pushed Jonmarc's skills even further. And while Astasia's hatred for Jonmarc was clear in her eyes, he also saw that she was shrewd enough to recognize his skill.

Astasia came at him with a sword in one hand and a dagger in the other. He parried her sword easily and caught her dagger with his vambrace, letting the blade slide harmlessly against the leather.

Astasia drew back, scything her blades as she twirled, then let the dagger fly. It nicked his ear, sending a rivulet of blood down his neck. Astasia met his eyes and licked her lips.

Jonmarc pressed the advantage of her momentary distraction and delivered a pounding series of sword strikes that drove Astasia back a pace. He moved forward to score a hit and felt a rush of air behind him as Gethin cried out. Too late, he saw a *vayash moru* grab the injured prince in a vise-like hold and lift him off the ground, rising into the dark sky.

Astasia's laugh spurred Jonmarc to fury, refocusing him on the battle at hand. She gripped her sword two-handed, parrying blows that would have shattered the bone of many mortal fighters. "Where are your *vayash moru* protectors, Lord Vahanian? Will your girl-queen be able to save you from Eastmark's wrath when we deliver their prince's corpse to the palace steps?"

Jonmarc closed his mind to her taunts, to the noise of battle around him, to Gethin's cry of alarm. He circled Astasia warily, intent only on vengeance.

"I'd like nothing better than to drain your body to a husk and leave it as a warning."

"Someone already tried that, and failed."

Astasia's gaze flickered to Jonmarc's throat, where two healed puncture wounds remained from Malesh's failed attempt. "Malesh only tried to kill you. I'd prefer to bring you across, force you to my bidding."

"Good luck with that."

Behind Astasia, a fast-moving shadow collided with the rising *vayash moru* that held Gethin, who was struggling to free himself. At first, Jonmarc took it for one of the hollowed spirits, until he realized it had shape and mass. He dared to spare only a glance, enough to see the newcomer's sword glint in the faint moonlight as it swept toward Gethin's attacker, neatly slicing head from body.

Gethin plunged toward the ground along with the body of the headless *vayash moru*. The severed head bounced on the hard ground, rolling under the feet of soldiers as they battled the sudden wave of enemy *vayash moru*. The body of the headless *vayash moru* crumbled as it fell, and the cold wind carried its gritty ash across the killing ground. A dark form snatched Gethin by the waist before he could strike the ground, landing softly with the shaken prince. Jonmarc recognized Laisren in the instant before Astasia charged toward him, fangs bared and snarling in rage.

"I will finish what Malesh started!" Astasia gripped her sword with both hands, driving it straight for Jonmarc's heart. Jonmarc's sword swung as he dodged her blow, and his sharp blade struck across the side of her face, laying bare her white skull and tearing through her throat. Undeterred, Astasia swung again with blind fury, a powerful blow that Jonmarc barely blocked, feeling the force ache through his bones as he let it carry him in its arc so that it did not shatter his arms.

The attack had put Astasia slightly off balance. Jonmarc wheeled with the force of her strike, and a dagger from a sheath on his left wrist fell into his hand. He let it fly, and it buried itself hilt-deep in Astasia's chest.

Astasia's sword fell from her hand as her ruined face stared in disbelief at the ichor that stained her tunic. She collapsed to her knees, and Jonmarc swung once more. His sword snapped through Astasia's exposed spine before her eyes could register the end of her immortality. Jonmarc watched as the cold wind blew past Astasia and her body began to crumble and then collapsed into ruin.

"Get him behind the lines," Jonmarc shouted to Laisren, who lifted Gethin despite the prince's protests and disappeared into the night sky.

No sooner had Laisren vanished than Jonmarc looked up to see a new *vayash moru*, one he did not recognize, heading toward him with a deadly expression on his face. Still feeling Astasia's final strike as an ache in his bones, Jonmarc resolutely gripped his sword with both hands, ready to fight. In his peripheral vision, he saw two more *vayash moru*, one from his left and one from the right. *This isn't good.*

The three *vayash moru* charged at once. Jonmarc pivoted in a high Eastmark kick, catching one of the attackers in the chest and throwing him clear. He let the momentum of his first strike carry him as he met the second *vayash moru*'s sword with enough power to tear the grip from the hand of a mortal opponent. Jonmarc saw the glint of steel and knew that he could not dodge the third blade streaking toward him.

With a clang, a new blade interposed itself, knocking aside the third opponent. Jonmarc had only a glimpse of his rescuer, but it was enough to make him question his own sanity as he pounded back a defense against the first two *vayash moru*. Clad all in black, swords gleaming in both hands, Uri fought back the third *vayash moru*.

The advance of his two attackers left Jonmarc no time for greeting. Out of the corner of his eye, he saw that a fourth attacker now circled Uri. Jonmarc and Uri were back to back, holding off the press of four of Astasia's brood.

Jonmarc feinted to the left, then dropped and rolled to the right, coming up close enough to his attacker to thrust his sword up and into the *vayash moru*'s unprotected belly, slitting him open to the ribs. Ichor and entrails spilled down on the ground as Jonmarc reached his feet and evaded the worst of it, though the foul mixture spattered his armor. Seizing the advantage,

Jonmarc drove his sword into the *vayash moru*'s chest and through his heart. The body crumbled into ash.

He could not spare a glance to see how Uri fared. Jonmarc's remaining opponent eyed him with a feral gleam in his eyes. "I'll take your head back to Imri to have it put on a post and raised for all to see."

"You wouldn't be the first to try."

Fire and mage lightning arced across the sky, illuminating the battlefield in hues of flame. Jonmarc's attacker rushed forward and Jonmarc braced himself for the strike, realizing an instant too late as the sword locked with his own blade that attack was merely distraction for the fangs that snapped just shy of his throat. Jonmarc managed to miss the worst of the attack, but pain flared through his body as the *vayash moru* grabbed him by the back of the neck in a grip strong enough that a twitch of his attacker's fingers could break bone.

"I will be a hero for killing you."

Jonmarc's left hand closed around a knife slung low on his leg. As the *vayash moru* leaned in for the kill, Jonmarc jerked the knife blade up and jammed it into his attacker's chest.

Cold dark ichor covered Jonmarc as the *vayash moru* began to tremble. The attacker eased his grip on Jonmarc's neck, and with a few inches more room, Jonmarc twisted the blade and drove it deeper. The *vayash moru*'s body bucked and quivered, and then crumbled into dust, leaving Jonmarc holding a dark-stained blade coated with ash.

Jonmarc looked up in time to see Uri finish off his last opponent. What Uri's sword work lacked in proper salle style it made up for in the blunt, efficient strokes of a street fighter. Uri disarmed his attacker, wrestled him to the ground, and then straddled him and brought his blade down through the heart and into the dirt below. In the blink of an eye, the body crumbled into nothing, and Uri straightened.

Covered with ash and ichor, his black tunic and pants ripped and bloodied, Uri looked more like a brawler than a lord of the Blood Council. Jonmarc met Uri's gaze and saw grudging acknowledgment.

"When you were a fight slave in Nargi, I never lost a bet on you," Uri said, as a gash on his lip rapidly healed itself. "Nice to see that you haven't gone soft."

"Thanks for the assist."

Uri's lip twitched into a bitter half-smile. "This doesn't make us friends. Let's just say that I dislike you less than I hated Astasia."

Jonmarc looked out over the battlefield. The battle showed no sign of waning. Magic crackled in the air as the mages on both sides launched and parried deadly salvos overhead. Exeter's troops were still embroiled in combat, but to Jonmarc's eye, their opponents appeared to be alive and not the corpse fighters of a candlemark earlier. Those shambling forms had disappeared, and Jonmarc guessed that they, at least, had been defeated. Gone, too, were the deadly shadows. *Vyrkin* still prowled among the combatants, and he spotted a stawar spirit in a clearing surrounded by the bodies of Temnottan soldiers.

"Rafe's brood is fighting on the queen's side, as are my people," Uri said quietly. "I have a feeling that Imri intends to make his final stand tonight." Uri's gaze was fixed far down the field of combat, where the core of the Temnottan troops were fighting fiercely.

"For once, you and I agree on something. I think it's going to be a very long night."

24

"Surely you can feel the power rising," Talwyn said, turning toward Jair.

Jair shook his head. "I don't have your magic. I can't feel power; I've just got a gut feeling that something is going to happen very soon."

Armed for battle, the Sworn's warriors held vigil along a line of barrows that ran south of the battlefront, only half a candlemark removed from where the army of Margolan made its stand against the Temnottan invaders. In the distance, Jair could see flashes of mage lightning flare against the night sky, and the answering streaks of blue and green that lit the clouds. He could hear the pounding of the catapults and trebuchets and an unholy cacophony of death screams and war cries from the men who fought and died.

The *trinnen* were even more heavily armed than the other Sworn warriors, with a second, shorter *stelian* blade and an array of small blades on a baldric across their chests. Many of the *trinnen* were on horseback, but this night, Jair awaited the enemy on foot, along with Talwyn, Pevre, Emil, and Mihei.

The rest of the Sworn, the elders, pregnant women, and young children, had been sent inland and far from the battle, guarded by a small group of warriors. The rest waited here along the barrow line, called to action by Talwyn's vision.

A burst of red light lit the sky bright as day, casting the entire landscape in a bloody glow. A blast of power accompanied the light. It shook the ground under Jair's feet and whipped the wind as the temperature plummeted enough so that his breath misted in the air.

A deafening boom shook the ground. Jair saw a crevice open along the barrows. He turned just in time to catch Talwyn as she staggered.

"They're coming," she breathed. Her face was ashen, her voice slightly slurred as the blast of magic caught her with its backlash. Pevre stepped between Talwyn and the widening chasm. His hands were weaving through the air in a complex series of wardings. Talwyn caught her breath and stood, returning to Pevre's side as Jair, Emil, and Mihei drew their swords.

As bright as the night sky had been, it turned to inky black. Neither stars nor torches lit the night. Jair knew he stood only an arm's length away from Talwyn, but he could not see her. The ground trembled once again, and dozens of high-pitched shrieks sent a shiver down Jair's back. He gripped his *stelian* tightly. Blinded by the darkness, he had no idea how to defend himself or the others if an attacker rose out of the night.

Total darkness faded to a dull gray and then to a night sky lit once more by stars and torches. Yet the screeching wails continued, and as Jair watched, red and blue balls of light floated from the chasm. Wraiths followed the lights, streaming from the jagged crevice in the ground. Smoke and mist when they rose, the beings became solid as they stepped onto the ground in the realm of the living. Jair caught his breath.

The creatures that formed out of the cleft belonged in nightmares. Some of the beings had green-gray skin clinging to their protruding bones, bones that were too long to have once been those of men. Other beings were the mottled blue-gray of a bloated corpse, with distended bellies and gaping jaws. Yet others were muscular creatures with the sinewy lines of a large cat but the general form of a man, covered in a skin that was a yellowish purple like an old bruise. The beings walked upright, though with a forward lean that reminded Jair more of a bear on its hind legs than a man. Several of the beings had four or six arms, and each ended in sharp-clawed fingers or in hands that wielded great scythelike blades. Some of them wore bones, blackened, shriveled fingers, hands, and ears as ornaments, while one of them had wrapped rotting entrails around his brow like a headpiece. As one of the risen creatures turned toward him, Jair saw a face that did not look to have ever been human. Folds of blue-gray skin hung from its high, broad forehead down to its jowls. Wide-set, large eyes held a glint of both cunning and madness. A broad, sharp-toothed maw opened wide on a snakelike hinge. A three-forked tongue flicked from between the double row of daggerlike teeth. The stench of putrefaction rose with them from the depths.

"What are those things?"

"Nachele," Mihei replied.

A blast of yellow light flared from the wardings Talwyn and Pevre had set, streaming toward the emerging creatures, punching through the mist of forming shapes. For an instant, the mist slowed and swirled.

Down the line of barrows, Jair heard the horn blast to attack. Jair had assumed that the Nachele might move with the lumbering power of a large bear. Instead, they struck with the speed and power of *vayash moru*. Jair let himself slip into the fighting trance of the Sworn's warriors, following the energy of his attacker with his instinct as well as his senses. Though his opponent had only two arms, each ended in long, jointed whip-like fingers that lashed at Jair and curled around his *stelian*, threatening to wrest it from his grip. Red eyes with vertical black slit pupils gazed hungrily at Jair out of their deep-set sockets, a contrast to the gray-green of its leathery skin.

Jair jerked his *stelian* back, freeing it from the creature's hold, and charged forward, thrusting his blade toward its chest. With a sibilant cry, the Nachele flailed its whip-fingers again, opening up bleeding welts where they grazed the skin on Jair's hands and one cheek. The Nachele made a clicking sound as Jair circled it, and Jair let his left hand slip to the tunic of his shirt, grasping Talwyn's amulet.

The amulet flared with light, nearly burning his palm, and the light arced from the amulet to Jair's *stelian* blade. He charged forward recklessly, dropping his hold of the amulet to grip his blade two-handed, striking at the Nachele with all his strength. Just as he gained an advantage and began to press the creature backward, it dissolved into mist and vanished, leaving Jair to stumble forward with his own momentum.

It took only a glance to see that Emil was engaged with an equally fierce foe. Around him, Jair could hear the cries of the Sworn warriors and nightmarish clicks, hisses, and screeches from beings that had not walked above ground in over a thousand years.

Talwyn, Pevre, and Mihei had stopped their chanting and taken up their swords as more of the Nachele advanced. Mist began to swirl around them. The Nachele did not have to rely on their speed to surround an enemy; the mist also did their bidding, swirling and solidifying into shapes.

Before the mist could fully form, Talwyn and Pevre lurched forward, swords held in a two-handed, shoulder-height thrust. Chanting as they ran, they plunged their *stelians* into the churning mist as their swords flared a brilliant orange. From the mist where they struck, an earsplitting shriek echoed from the rocks around them. The mist rolled back. Jair and Mihei held their ground. With a thunderous crack, the mist around Talwyn's and Pevre's swords vanished, but just as Jair hoped that the shamans' spells had turned the attack, shapes solidified out of the haze, rushing toward them.

Mihei and Jair took the brunt of the attack, using their talismans to borrow from Talwyn's magic. The Nachele reared back and then came at them as swiftly as the wind, so that Jair was almost knocked from his feet with the momentum of the attack. He swung his heavy *stelian* with all his might, in blows that would have easily cleaved through the body of a mortal. His attacker, a six-armed warrior with blue-gray shriveled skin, cackled as it parried his blows, though some of the strikes cut through its skin enough that rivulets of a puslike liquid began to stream down from its many wounds.

Across the open plain, along the line of barrows, Jair could hear the cries of soldiers and the clash of steel. Behind his attacker, Jair glimpsed one of the Nachele plunging its long, sharp talons through the chest of a Sworn warrior. It lifted the dying man in its many arms and bent him backward, snapping his spine. The Nachele plunged its sawlike teeth into the soldier's exposed belly, gorging on the flesh as fresh blood stained its matted hair and covered its chest in gore.

Jair and Mihei were fighting back to back against two of the Nachele, while Talwyn and Pevre worked in tandem, striking with both sword and magic to interrupt the Nachele's attack. Yet even as Talwyn forced one of the Nachele back with a blast of magic, Jair knew that they could not hold them off indefinitely.

A sound like the loudest rolling thunder Jair had ever heard drowned out the clang of swords and the battle shouts of soldiers. In the pale moonlight, Jair could see openings appear in the sides of the barrows, yawning black caverns. The rolling thunder moved across the open ground like a physical force, echoing from the barrows and the rocky hills. Behind the thunder swept silence like a suffocating blanket. Everything was shrouded by the silence, and though the battle raged and Jair could see soldiers' faces grimace with screams of pain or twist in rage as they roared battle cries, no sound escaped the weight of the silence. Jair could not hear his breath or the pounding of his heart that had been deafeningly loud just seconds before.

The Nachele did not ease their attack, despite the unnatural silence. But as Jair struggled to hold off the press of his Nachele opponent, he saw motion coming from the barrows and braced for another attack.

Twice the height of a man, garbed in what appeared to be flowing black shrouds, the newcomers to the field of battle swarmed from the barrows with the fleetness of an insect horde. As they moved, Jair saw that what he had taken to be swirling capes of fabric were long tendrils that fell from the creatures' shoulders down to the ground. Beneath the swaying tendrils Jair glimpsed long, thin arms with powerful, clawed hands.

The Nachele began to turn their attention from the Sworn to the ominous black shapes that rose from the barrows. The two Nachele that battled Jair and Mihei dissolved into mist, fleeing from the fearsome newcomers. Jair turned, *stelian* raised, to add his strength against the other two Nachele, who remained locked in battle with Pevre and Talwyn.

These must be the Dread, Jair thought. If the Dread were to be their salvation, then their rescuers were every bit as terrifying as their adversaries.

Pevre's lips were moving in a chant and it seemed to Jair that the older man fought with twice his usual speed, beating back the Nachele's attack. Talwyn also mouthed silent protections, and her *stelian*'s aim was true, scything between her attacker's two blades to rake the razor-sharp tip of her sword across the Nachele's chest.

Jair raised his *stelian* and swung with his full might, aiming his blade for the back of Talwyn's attacker. As his blade fell, the two Nachele moved with blinding speed. The Nachele Talwyn had been fighting pivoted out of position to attack Pevre with its barbed-bladed swords. Pevre's opponent, a blue-gray creature with long, whiplike fingers of claw and bone, whirled to confront Talwyn. Pevre's swords blocked his attacker's onslaught, though his parry nearly drove him to his knees.

Jair's blade fell just short of the Nachele that had turned on Talwyn. In the stifling silence, Jair saw the whip cords of the Nachele lash out at Talwyn, watched as they snaked past her sword, which had not yet corrected its angle for the new attack. Jair screamed a warning that Talwyn never heard as one of the long, bony whips struck her in the chest, penetrating her leather cuirass. Mihei and Jair reached the Nachele at the same time, beating on its ridged back with their *stelians*, and while the razor-sharp blades cut through cloth, armor, and skin, the Nachele did not turn its attention from Talwyn.

The whip cord jerked back from Talwyn's chest and a look of astonished disappointment crossed her features as blood pulsed from the wound and she sank to her knees. She was still mouthing an incantation, but her tawny skin had grown ashen.

Jair marshaled all his strength to bring his *stelian* down point first into the back of the Nachele, while Mihei angled his blade to strike under its arm. The Nachele stumbled and then its whole form shuddered, blurring around the edges as if it were attempting to vanish into mist. Talwyn's lips moved again, and she thrust out her palm, sending a flare of power toward the staggered Nachele, which writhed for an instant in the glare and then crumbled to the ground in a heap of bone.

Before Jair could take a step toward Talwyn, two of the Dread swept up behind them, intent on the remaining Nachele that battled Pevre. Too late, the Nachele realized its peril, but the Dread's presence kept it from fleeing into the mist. The curtain of black tendrils swept out in the blink of an eye, wrapping around the Nachele and pulling it into long, bony arms hidden beneath the tendrils. The Nachele disappeared into the Dread's deadly embrace, and suddenly, the silence was shattered.

Jair's throat was already raw from screaming when the silence ended. Heedless of the Dread or the Nachele, he rushed forward, reaching Talwyn at the same time as Pevre. Wordlessly, Mihei stood guard as Jair and Pevre eased Talwyn back to lie on the dry, brown grass.

Pevre's chanting took on a fevered intensity, and Jair dared not speak for fear he might break the shaman's concentration. Jair took Talwyn's hand, and her fingers wound around his, though her grip was weak.

"Hang on," Jair murmured. He shot a glance at Pevre. "Can't you do for her what she did for Tris? Can't you call on the life energy of the Sworn?"

"That energy is shattered," Pevre said, as his hands moved over the wound in Talwyn's chest, tracing burning lines of power in the air. "Too many dead and dying. There is no energy to spare."

"You can't just let her die!"

Talwyn's eyes struggled open, and Jair could see that she labored to make her gaze focus. "Promise me," she whispered. "Promise me that Kenver will know both our worlds."

Jair swallowed hard. "I swear to you."

There was a rustle like wind through dead leaves, and one of the Dread stood at Talwyn's feet.

The damage is too great. Too much of the Nachele's poison has reached her heart. Even we cannot heal a mortal of it. But Cheira Talwyn's spirit may dwell with us, safe among her people and the souls of her ancestors. The voice did not speak aloud;

Jair heard the words echo in his mind, slow and deliberate, as if the speaker were trying to remember how to make himself understood to mortals.

Talwyn's gaze rose to the amulets Jair wore at his throat, to one of silver and leather, wound with strands of her own dark hair, the amulet that had enabled her spirit to visit him in his dreams in the palace at Dhasson. "If I go with the Dread, I can watch over Kenver, and the amulet will bring me to you in your dreams."

Jair held her hand in both of his, clutching it as if by holding on he could bind her soul to life. He did not care that Pevre and Mihei saw the tears that streaked down his face or heard the sobs that robbed him of his breath. "I love you, always," he managed.

Talwyn gave a weak smile. "And I will be with you, always, my love." Her voice was faint, and Jair could feel her breath slowing, see the light of her spirit leaving her eyes. As Talwyn's body stilled, the Dread reached forward with two of its long, black tendrils, sweeping them across Talwyn's face as if by catching her final breath it retrieved her spirit.

She will rest among the guardians who do not sleep, and keep watch with those who cannot die. Do not mourn her, son of Harrol. She is with you still.

25

"That's him, all right. I'd know the son of a bitch anywhere," Cam said, lowering the spyglass with a curse. "I wondered when my traitor brother would bother to put himself at the slightest risk by joining the war he started."

"By the crest and regalia, the Temnottans look to be indulging Alvior's fantasy of becoming the next king of Isencroft." Wilym turned to the side and spat, as if the very mention of Alvior's name poisoned his tongue.

"Of course they are. They need a puppet king, and Alvior wouldn't fuss about the terms of the agreement so long as he got a crown out of it."

"How much do you think it'll damage the invader's cause if Alvior dies?"

Cam grimaced. "I doubt they've grown that fond of him, except for his usefulness. He's not the type to inspire loyalty. He probably doesn't know that most of his former Divisionist followers are hanging from gibbets outside the palace. But it will certainly raise my spirits to part his head from his shoulders."

Cam looked across the battlefield. What had once been thousands of acres of farmland and pasture leading down to the shore of the sea was now a pockmarked and burned killing ground. Huge boulders lay where they had landed from the near-constant two-way barrage of catapults and trebuchets, war machines that thundered day and night.

Benhem and his mages had discovered the secret of the invaders' Destroying Fire, casting waves of flame back on the advancing troops. Between the two entrenched camps, a charred and blackened no-man's-land attested to the range over which both sets of mages could hurl their curtains of flame. Ingenious use of the Destroying Fire coupled with the reach of the catapults lobbed fiery missiles deep behind both lines.

"We've given them a pounding," Wilym observed, "and they've given it back. I had hoped that if we showed fierce resistance, they'd pack up their ships and go home to Temnotta. Maybe they're more afraid of what's behind them than what's in front of them, but now I'm convinced that we'll have to destroy every last one of them before this over."

Cam nodded soberly. "I had come to the same conclusion."

Wilym glanced at Cam. "Is the queen ready for her part in the assault tonight?"

Cam let out a breath and nodded. He was sure that Wilym could read his uneasiness in his face. "I don't like it, but she's ready. Damn it, Wilym, if it were Donelan, I wouldn't think twice about seeing him place himself at risk. Many's the skirmish that you and I had to chase him to keep up if his blood was high in a battle. But it's not Donelan. It's Kiara and she's pregnant. Two kingdoms hang in the balance. If I had my way—"

"She'd be under house arrest back in Aberponte with an entire division of mages and soldiers to protect her," Wilym finished for him with a laugh. "I guarantee she wouldn't be happy about it!"

Cam grimaced ill-humoredly. "If you'll recall, Donelan didn't much like it either when we had to put him under guard for his own protection."

Wilym's expression grew sober. "And we both know how well that turned out." He met Cam's gaze. "Donelan was murdered in his own bed, in a locked room with guards at the door and the two of us in the other chamber. We can do our best, Cam, but we can't guarantee Kiara's safety, just like we couldn't guarantee Donelan's. It's the price of the crown, and she accepts it."

"It doesn't mean I have to like it."

Later, Cam and Wilym joined Edgeton, Vinian, and the other generals for a briefing before the night's attack. Rhistiart, Cam's valet-turned-squire, was wide-eyed and silent as he kept the group's cups full of watered wine and refreshed a trencher with cheese and hard sausage. Kiara sat at the head of the assembly, with Cam and Wilym on her right and left. Brother Felix was there, along with Morane and Benhem from the mages. Jae rested near the brazier, exhausted from harrying the enemy. Royster sat on the floor just inside the tent doorway with a leather folder filled with parchment, ink, and a pen, poised to chronicle the moment for history.

It took just under a candlemark to finalize the last details for the battle and to assure that every resource was in place. Throughout the conversation, Cam thought Kiara was quieter than usual, although she leaned forward to listen intently. He guessed that her thoughts strayed to her own, untested role.

"We'll make an all-out assault once you and the mages are ready, Your Majesty," Vinian said. "We'll have the catapults and trebuchets firing in waves, and if we can't use the Destroying Fire, we'll settle for good ol' regular fire. If you're able to put their mages completely out of action, we'll drive the bastards back into the sea and drown them."

Kiara nodded. To Cam's eye, she already looked older than when she had returned to Isencroft, and in her eyes, he saw the burden he had so often glimpsed in Donelan's expression.

"Well done," Kiara said. "Drive the invaders toward the sea. As soon as we're confident that the attack on their mages has succeeded, the water mages will bring down a large wave to drown the Temnottans and a wicked current to drag them under and out to sea. Mind that our men are well back from it. An ocean is not a precise weapon."

Vinian chuckled dourly. "Warning taken, m'lady."

Kiara stood. Even with her armor, it was evident that her pregnancy was advancing. Cam took a deep breath, forcing back protective instincts, reminding himself that Kiara undertook both her risk and her role knowing the danger involved.

"I ask the favor of the Lady on our venture. May Chenne bless you with her sword and protect you with her shield. Tonight, we determine the future of Isencroft. Go with the blessing of the crown."

Cam lingered to be the last to leave the tent. He looked to Rhistiart and then Royster. "I want both of you to accompany Kiara behind the line of battle tomorrow," he said. Rhistiart opened his mouth to protest, but Cam shook his head.

"Tomorrow is going to be bad. We're evacuating all noncombat personnel, so don't take it personally. I'll feel better knowing that you two are well behind the lines. Help her any way you can."

He turned to Kiara. "I need to ask you, have you determined how you want to deal with Alvior? Is he to stand trial?"

Kiara's eyes took on a hardness Cam had not seen before. "Alvior of Brunnfen abetted the Divisionist plot to murder my father and put the crown of Isencroft under the heel of invaders. He arrives on our shores with a foreign army, to fight against his own countrymen and seize the throne. He is guilty of treason. The sentence is death." She met Cam's gaze. "You are the

Champion of the Queen of Isencroft. Execute Alvior, in the name of the crown."

Cam nodded grimly. "That's all I needed to hear."

Another candlemark passed before Kiara was in position. The late afternoon was cold, and clouds gathered on the horizon, threatening rain. Despite her armor and her woolen cloak, she shivered, and wondered whether it was the cold or nervousness about the workings of the evening to come that sent the blood from her fingers and chilled her to her core.

Kiara stood in the center of a large circle whose boundary was set out with the rune stones from the ghost in the crypt, each carefully turned facedown to present blank bone. At the four points of the compass, Brother Felix carefully laid thin disks of iron that he had blessed and charged with protective wardings. A thin stream of salt ran from disk to disk. As Felix laid the iron and salt, Morane followed behind him, smudging the circle with a burning bundle of pine and sage, and then returning to the center to raise and lower the smoking bundle bathing Kiara in its sacred smoke. High in the air, Jae flew in wide circles, serving both as protection and as an early warning should anyone approach.

Kiara stood atop a parchment map Felix had made showing their position relative to places of power throughout the kingdom. Aberponte was on the map, said to be located above one of the rivers of the Flow. Temples and sacred burying grounds, shrines, and sanctified groves were included. Felix and Royster had done a remarkably thorough job of marking them all and drawing lines to run from each place of power back to Kiara, the better for her to call upon their energy.

"You look like you're about to be sick, my dear," Brother Felix murmured to her. "Is it the baby?"

Kiara gave him a wan smile. "Not this time. I'm just a little nervous about what we're going to do."

Felix chuckled. "You're wise to be nervous. But after the demonstration you gave us a few days ago, this may be our first real chance to push Temnotta back where they came from."

Kiara nodded. "I know, but that doesn't make my stomach any happier about it."

Benhem, Felix, and Morane took their places on the quarter marks of the warded circle. Joining them was Sister Eunice, one of the rogue mages who had left the Sisterhood to aid the army. Royster sat off to one side, parchment, pen, and ink at the ready to record everything as it transpired. Rhistiart had been put to work as a healer's helper, should the magic go wrong. He stood next to Cerise, who had refused to remain in the camp despite the danger.

At Felix's nod, Kiara lifted the lens. She took a deep breath and tried to still the nervousness she felt. Morane began a low chant, and Kiara closed her eyes, feeling the power build around her. She focused her thoughts on the lens in her hands and on sensing the magic that radiated from the four mages in the circle. In her mind's eye, she saw their power begin to stream to her in bright yellow tendrils, and the lens began to glow.

Once Kiara felt confident that the magic of the four anchor mages was channeled through the lens, she took another deep breath and cast her regent magic farther, down beyond the slight hillock that shielded them from the view of the enemy, to the dozen battle mages among the soldiers who were ready to take an active part in combat. As her magic touched them, she saw golden tendrils of power unwind from around them, undulating through the air, seeking the lens.

The burning glass was growing warm in her hands. Kiara cast her thoughts toward the map at her feet. She had memorized the position of the sacred places, and she began to work her way around the map clockwise, fixing her thoughts on each place of power in turn, using her regent magic to call to it to aid them. For a few moments, there was nothing except the slow inhale and exhale of her own breath. Then Kiara felt a nudge from the magic as new tendrils of golden light slipped through the wardings that opened for them and found their way to the glass in her hands. As she slowly turned her attention from one shrine to the next, she could see each of the places of power clearly. Not only were their images clear to her, but for each, she had associations of sound and scent so that their waterfalls and fountains, their fragrant groves and burning incense were as real to her as if she stood in each of the sacred spaces.

As Felix and Morane had taught her, Kiara lifted the burning glass into the air, holding it firmly with one hand on either side, turning its broad lens toward the battlefield. In the distance, her regent magic identified the location of the enemy mages. Kiara could feel their power. She fixed their places in her mind, making them glowing red dots on her mental image of the battlefield. But unlike during their practice, Kiara did not focus her magic on drawing in the power of the Temnottan mages. Instead, with a forceful exhale of breath, Kiara willed the combined magic in the lens to release its power toward the enemy mages, an invisible, lethal blast that crackled along the currents of magic, traveling at the speed of thought.

Kiara felt the magic burn its way toward its intended targets. As the power struck the first Temnottan mage, Kiara was unprepared for the momentary link opened up by the magic, a link through which she felt the enemy mage's surprise, his terror, and then the awful, consuming fire.

Kiara staggered but held fast to the burning glass. Eight, then nine, then ten of the Temnottan mages fell, and Kiara reeled from the momentary, intimate link as the magic burned its way toward its victims. She doubted that she would ever silence their death cries in her memory, or the blinding instant of pain as the power burned them from within. A pounding reaction headache was severe enough to make her nauseous. She fought every instinct to drop the lens and fall to her knees retching.

I have killed before in battle with a sword, she told herself, struggling for control. *A blade brings no less of an agonizing death. If I were able, I would be with Cam and Wilym in the thick of the fighting, killing soldiers myself. The magic changes nothing.* Yet in her heart, Kiara knew that the momentary connection to her quarry changed everything, because for one awful instant, she felt their pain and knew their fear. *Now I know something of what Tris feels on a battlefield, when he can see the spirits rise from their bodies as they die. If all men could feel this, surely no one would ever choose to wage war.*

Before the magic reached the eleventh Temnottan mage, Kiara felt a warning tingle and an undulating crimson wall of power slammed up to deflect her magic. Even at a distance, the crimson wall stank of blood magic and death. Kiara took a deep breath and mustered the magic once more, and this time, she shattered the wall of power. She heard the screams of the dying mage in her mind as she turned the power in search of the next Temnottan sorcerer.

Again, a blood-red curtain of magic rose to block her. "They know they can't stop you, but they're hoping to wear you out before you can strike all of them," Brother Felix warned. "Draw on the power of the lens. Don't draw on your own power."

The crimson wall became a lightning bolt, streaking back across the tendrils of power. Instinctively, Kiara moved the lens to intercept the bolt, bracing herself as the bolt slammed into the concave surface of the burning glass with a force that shuddered down her arms like a sword strike. She gasped for breath, staggered by the sheer force of the blow. A pounding headache throbbed in her temples, but she grasped the lens more firmly, using it to absorb the full power of a strike that was meant to kill. Kiara sank to one knee, still holding tightly to the lens.

"Kiara, are you all right?" She could hear Felix's voice, but it sounded far away. For a moment, Kiara swayed, drained almost to the point of losing consciousness. She heeded Brother Felix's warning and gathered the strands of magic around her, from the mages in the circle, the Isencroft mages on the field, and the distant places of power. Magic rushed toward her with her incoming breath, easing the pain of her headache and giving her the strength to stand. Grimly, Kiara turned just as another bolt of crimson lightning burned toward her, ready this time for the onslaught. *There are still at least ten of them, and only one of me. This is going to be a contest to the death.*

Cam and the generals led their soldiers into battle with a fearsome shout and the din of drums and pipers. The Isencroft army swept toward the invaders in a thunder of hoofbeats and the pounding footsteps of armored men. Though Cam possessed no magic, he was certain that anyone with a beating heart could feel the power that crackled in the air just above them.

"Look there!" Cam's head snapped up at the cry that rose from his men. The horizon had taken on a greenish glow, setting the battlefield in an eerie foxfire light.

"Best we be about our business, and leave the mages to theirs," Cam muttered.

The din of battle rang out over the field as torches rose and the thunder of catapults rivaled the steady beat of the drummers. A large, fiery lump of something heavy landed only yards away from Cam, crushing two foot soldiers beneath it and lighting four others afire. Cam's horse shied, but he reined in the frightened beast, intent on cutting a swath through the invading line to clear a path for the foot soldiers behind him.

Cam blocked and parried, using his size and strength to batter through the defenses of the enemy host that swarmed toward them. As he fought his way through the tide of soldiers, he watched for a glimpse of Alvior's standard or the green crest of Brunnfen.

"By the Whore! What in the name of the Crone is that?" One of the foot soldiers pointed in horror toward an open spot amid the fighting. Cam caught his breath. The ground was littered with the bodies of the dead and dying, both men and horses. But where the soldier pointed, the bodies were sliding together. Broken bodies of Isencroft and Temnottan soldiers and the carcasses of downed horses, drawn together by an invisible bond, gradually took the shape of a giant man.

The Temnottans surged forward, heedless of the horror, and Cam wondered if a trick of their mages had robbed the men of normal fear. The Isencroft soldiers met the charge, but Cam could see across part of the battlefield, where more of the monstrous creatures rose out of the assembled corpses of the dead.

"How in the name of the Crone do we fight that?" One of Cam's captains reined in his horse within shouting distance.

"I don't have the slightest idea," Cam admitted. "Hard to kill something that's already dead."

"You'd better think of something fast."

Cam looked up to see the corpse-giant begin to move. It had no actual hands; instead, two long chains of bodies hung from what might be regarded as its shoulders, and as the monster lumbered forward, it swung its shoulders from side to side, knocking men out of its way with the force of its powerful sweeps, or stepping on those who fell in their mad scramble to get out of its way.

"Close ranks!" Cam shouted above the fray, grateful that this new horror had at least silenced the pipers. *Nothing drives a man into a killing frenzy as quickly as a dozen damn pipers*, he thought.

"Strike in a tide, like the sea," he shouted. "Topple it."

Cam could see the terror in the eyes of the men who surged forward, and he wondered if they saw the same fear in his face. While he hoped that the sheer momentum and weight of the running troops and galloping horsemen would take the corpse-beast off its feet, he had no idea how to vanquish it once they had it on the ground.

Rage drove him forward as he watched the corpse-beast use the bodies of their fallen comrades against them, wielding the dead as bludgeons. Its long "arms" hit with the force of a catapult strike, crushing soldiers beneath its weight or sweeping a line of men and horses out of its way. The survivors of the first wave reached the "feet" of the beast and began to push against it to knock it over, but it swept them away as casually as a child might flick a gnat, sending men flying through the air.

Goddess help me, I have no idea how to fight a thing like this, Cam thought. The green glow in the sky grew brighter, replacing the dying light of the sunset with its own sickly glare. *It will take a river of blood to fight our way out of this.*

Kiara tipped the burning glass, barely averting the crimson fire that blasted toward her. Morane and Benhem were chanting new wardings, while Felix and Sister Eunice sent more of their own magic toward her. If the Temnottan mages had merely sent lightning, the wardings would have been sufficient to keep it beyond the circle. Instead, they sent their defensive blast along the same tendrils of power Kiara had used, following the trail of her own magic back to her.

Kiara could feel herself growing weak from the onslaught. Her head was pounding too hard for her to think clearly. Taking a deep breath, Kiara grounded her energy and held up the burning glass once more, marshalling her power to go on the offensive.

She reached out for energy from Brother Felix and the mages

in the circle and from the Isencroft mages, taking all she dared without weakening them. Kiara returned her focus to the parchment map at her feet, working her way across it, concentrating on each place in its turn. As she turned her concentration to the palace at Aberponte, a bright blast of crimson fire surged through the channel of power she had opened toward the Temnottan mages. Before she could move to block it, the fire hit her, immobilizing her and sending a wave of excruciating pain through her body.

Sudden power welled up in Kiara, rising from the ground beneath her feet. It rose so quickly that she gasped as it drove out the pain of the crimson fire, and she felt the new energy like a fever, burning inside her. The power rose from nowhere and everywhere; it flowed upward from the ground, through the map, up her body, and into the lens. In her mind, Kiara could see a blinding light of coruscating colors, and for an instant, the radiance of the new power threatened to consume her with its intensity. Kiara felt the channels of magic burn raw with the sheer power that coursed through her.

White light blasted from the lens, visible, Kiara was sure, even for those without magic. It streaked across the sky in a dozen directions at once. But what amazed Kiara most was that, for an instant, as it coursed through her body, the light seemed to have a primal sentience of its own. It was angry over the strike that injured her. And in a blind, primitive rage, the power struck back at her attackers with wild force.

As quickly as it came, the light went dark, and Kiara collapsed to the ground, completely spent. She was barely conscious as Brother Felix hurriedly dismissed the wardings. Cerise and Rhistiart ran to her side. Felix and Morane joined them a moment later. Morane and Felix hung back as Cerise attended Kiara, and Rhistiart scrambled to do the healer's bidding. Finally, Cerise sat back on her heels and motioned for the others to come closer.

"What in the name of Chenne was that?" Kiara managed, her whole body still tingling uncomfortably.

Brother Felix exchanged a nervous glance with Morane. "I believe you managed to channel the Flow," Morane said uncomfortably. "What were you thinking right before the power surged?"

Cerise pressed a wineskin of warm wine to Kiara's mouth, and she took a sip. "I was working my way across the map, drawing power from the sacred places. I had gotten as far as Aberponte when the Temnottans attacked," Kiara said.

Brother Felix nodded. "The Flow runs beneath Aberponte. It might be possible that you accidentally tapped into that power to protect yourself. The Temnottan blast could have easily killed you."

Kiara swallowed hard, grateful for another sip of the wine. "There was something else. The power . . . was aware. Not completely sentient, but aware in a primitive way, as if it was striking out on instinct. I had the strangest feeling that the Temnottan attack made it angry, and that it was protecting me."

Brother Felix met her eyes. "There is something else besides the Flow in Aberponte, something in a box in the necropolis," he said quietly.

Kiara gasped, remembering the *nenkah* and the part of Cwynn's consciousness that had taken refuge there. "How is that possible?"

"I don't know. But if it's true, if he has an innate ability to wield the Flow, and if he was aware enough for his consciousness to flee to you when he was in danger, then it might be possible that your power grasped at everything within reach when you were focused on Aberponte and the attack came. Your power might have woken him as you pulled the Flow to you, and that consciousness would have reacted in very simple terms. Before, he chose to flee. This time, he chose to fight."

* * *

The Dread

The long chain of dead bodies swung across the field, sweeping Cam and his soldiers out of its way. Cam flew backward, landing hard on his back. Tossing him through the air was no easy feat, yet the corpse-giant had managed it effortlessly. Cam groaned and decided there were no broken bones. As he struggled to his feet, he saw that others had not been so lucky. Several of his men lay with a leg or an arm badly twisted beneath them, broken by the force of their fall.

"Ready for another charge!" Cam shouted to the soldiers to regain their feet.

Without warning, the sky above them turned a dazzling white, as if the sun itself had drawn near. Yet this light bore no heat, though it nearly blinded Cam. Reflexively, he threw his arms over his face and dared another glance through slitted eyes. The brilliant light struck the corpse-giant square in the center, so that the monster began to tremble from top to bottom. Mouthless, it could make no cry, but the whole infernal conglomeration shuddered as if with a sudden, violent fit. Cam's eyes burned from the glare, but he could not look away. As he stared in amazement, the bonds that held the corpses together broke, and the monster collapsed into a heap of motionless bodies.

A cheer went up from Cam's men and Cam breathed a sigh of relief. Yet as he turned to help one of the injured soldiers to his feet, he spotted a green banner fluttering in the wind not far to the right.

"Any man who can fight, follow me!" Twenty men rallied, battle-bloodied but still combat ready.

"What was that light? Where did it come from?" The soldier looked around, frightened and bewildered.

"If it's what I think it is, it's on our side," Cam replied, with a quick glance toward where he knew Kiara and the mages were hidden on the hillside. "Let's make it expensive for those invading bastards."

Anger burned fresh through Cam's veins as he charged forward, intent on reaching Alvior's banner. Isencroft forces had seized the offensive, taking advantage of the shock from the brilliant white light. Across the field, Cam could see Isencroft's soldiers fighting with renewed energy, heartened by the unexpected show of power. Cam forced down his concern for Kiara's safety, focusing on one goal: Alvior.

They fought their way through a line of Temnottan soldiers who found themselves badly outnumbered and cut off from their regiment. The Temnottans fell to their knees, arms raised in surrender. Cam glanced down the line, looking for anyone of rank. He found an injured and terrified young lieutenant and grabbed him by the arm.

"Where is Alvior of Brunnfen?"

"I don't know."

Cam brought the tip of his sword up beneath the young soldier's chin. "That bastard doesn't deserve your loyalty. There's no need for you to die on his account. After all, I don't see him fighting to save you. So I'll ask only one more time: Where is Alvior?"

"He's heading back to the coast," the lieutenant managed, taking a deep breath. "We were supposed to cover his escape."

Cam removed his sword from his captive's throat and cursed. "Damn his soul to the Crone!" Cam looked around and saw that, along with abandoning his banner, Alvior had also left behind the shield that bore his crest and had torn the colors from his armor. "Bloody coward! He didn't have the stomach to finish the war he started."

Still cursing, Cam rallied his men. "You there," he said, gesturing with his sword to five of the soldiers who had come with him. "Disarm the prisoners, tie them up, and walk them back to our lines. The rest of you, come with me. Archers, make ready. We've got a traitor to hunt."

Clouds of smoke hung over the battlefield from the burning missiles. The clouds overhead had grown more threatening, and in the distance, thunder rumbled. A cold rain began to fall, darkening Cam's mood further. He grumbled an increasingly creative litany of curses as he made his way over the battle-scarred ground.

Without his colors, it would be more difficult to spot Alvior. "Keep your eyes open," Cam shouted to his men. "He's a hands-breadth taller than I am, but not as broad. I'd expect him to have armor befitting his fancied role as king, and you might see a bit of green cloth where he's torn off his tunic. Spread out the line. We win a victory for the queen when we destroy the pretender."

They doubled their pace. The fiercest battle had moved off to their left, as had the bulk of the troops from both sides. Cam had no illusions that Alvior would put himself into harm's way. No, he thought, it would be like Alvior to skirt the thick of battle, intent on saving his own skin. One of his soldiers came running toward him, breathless.

"There's a group of Temnottan soldiers ahead, maybe fifteen of them at most. They're moving around one man in the center, and they seem more intent on reaching the coast than rejoining a regiment."

Cam smiled tightly. "That's Alvior. Lead the way."

Within a few minutes at forced march pace, they closed the gap. Cam gave the signal for his archers to circle around, flanking Alvior's small group on both sides. When Cam could see that the archers were in position, he ran forward.

"Alvior of Brunnfen. Stand and fight!"

At that signal, the archers let fly a volley of arrows. Six of Alvior's guards dropped in their tracks, arrows protruding from their chests. As the archers readied for a second strike, Cam broke into a dead run, sword raised, along with the rest of his soldiers.

Alvior's guard rallied around him, forming a ring with Alvior in the center. The archers sent another flight of arrows, but these soldiers were better armored than the others and only three fell to the archers' assault. The surviving guards launched themselves at Cam's soldiers with desperate ferocity.

With a battle roar, Cam and his soldiers attacked. One of Alvior's soldiers stepped in front of Cam, sword raised in challenge. With a curse, Cam swung hard, a blow the soldier struggled to parry. Within three strikes, Cam's strength beat through the soldier's defense, and his powerful two-handed blow cleaved the man from shoulder to hip.

Alvior did not run. Instead, he raised his own sword and charged at Cam, rage reddening his features. Cam stepped into the charge, throwing aside Alvior's blade in a parry that pushed Alvior off balance. Cursing, Alvior regained his footing and came at Cam slashing with his full might, broad, fierce strokes meant to eviscerate an opponent or cut a man in two.

"You murdered Father," Cam shouted, as Alvior came at him again.

"I should have murdered you."

Steel screeched as their swords met, throwing off sparks at the force of the blow. Alvior's height gave him an advantage in his reach, while Cam's bulk and surprising speed were a formidable asset. "You betrayed the king. You funded the Divisionists. And you nearly killed Renn."

Cam saw a deadly smile touch Alvior's mouth. "Should have killed that scrawny pup, too. And yes, I betrayed Donelan. Brunnfen never received the honor it deserved, despite the way Father fawned over the king. It was time to change the order of things in Isencroft. Time to take control."

"So you sold out for the promise of a puppet's throne?" Cam put his weight into a downward stroke that nearly broke through Alvior's guard. Alvior managed to parry, barely, and Cam smiled

466

in satisfaction as a series of brutal, pounding strokes beat Alvior back several paces. The battleground around them was littered with broken spears and shattered swords and the bloated, discolored bodies of the men who had no more need of their discarded weapons. It made for tricky footing, and more than once, Cam had to maneuver at the last minute to avoid putting a foot down on a rotting corpse or tripping over a downed body.

"Better than a starving kingdom and a Margolan alliance." Alvior took the offensive, striking with surprising force and speed. He pressed forward, and his reach nearly got inside of Cam's guard. Alvior's blade missed its target, but he swung into a side kick that took Cam in his bad knee, the leg the Divisionists had shattered. The knee buckled under him, and Cam went down as Alvior swung again, a blow Cam barely blocked, shattering Cam's sword.

Cam's leg throbbed, but the pain rekindled his rage. Alvior was standing over him, both arms drawn back over his head to plunge his sword point down in a killing thrust.

Cam lurched forward, heaving his heavy body toward Alvior's legs. He brought the shattered hilt of his sword up with all his might, digging it deep into Alvior's right knee just above the joint and leaning his weight into it, to separate the knee cap from the joint itself.

Alvior screamed in agony and went over backward, landing hard on his back as Cam threw his bulk onto the bloody sword hilt, driving it deeper into the joint. Alvior's blade sliced wildly, barely missing the top of Cam's head. Cam took the brunt of the swing on his metal vambrace, trapping the blade with the vambrace's curved spikes and wresting it out of Alvior's hand.

Alvior gave a shriek of rage and pain, twisting underneath Cam, his right hand scrabbling for a weapon. Alvior's hand closed around a broken spear on the ground, and he rammed it toward Cam's neck with his full strength. Cam caught Alvior by the wrist, twisting until Alvior released the weapon with a curse.

With a sudden burst of strength, Alvior bucked, throwing Cam off him. Alvior seized the broken spear and lunged. Cam reached back to break his fall, and his hand closed around the pommel of Alvior's discarded sword. Cam fell onto his back and angled the sword toward Alvior. Alvior's momentum left him no way to evade the gleaming blade angled at his heart and the blade tore through his cuirass, sinking deep into his chest.

Alvior's body began to tremble as blood poured from the heart wound and trickled from the corner of his mouth. With the sickening screech of ring mail against the steel blade, his body sank against the blade until the hilt was flush with his armor. Alvior struggled to lift his head, and Cam thought that his brother might finally have an admission to make. Instead, Alvior spat in Cam's face.

"Alvior of Brunnfen, you have been accused and found guilty of patricide and high treason," Cam said coldly, using his sleeve to wipe away the spittle. "By the order of Kiara, Queen of Isencroft, the sentence is death." Cam's eyes narrowed. He met Alvior's gaze. "And may the Formless One feast on your faithless heart for all eternity."

26

"We've got to hold the ridge. Tell them to dig in and hold fast. I have a feeling Imri's going to come at us with everything he's got."

Jonmarc watched the runners disperse in both directions with his order. He let out a long breath and wiped his forehead with a grimy sleeve. The battle had raged all night, back and forth over the same ground, each side gaining only a temporary advantage. He looked out over the hastily dug earthworks, staying low to avoid tempting the Temnottan archers. While the night's battle had been grueling, it had not cost as many lives as he feared. He looked out over his soldiers, an unlikely group of last-minute volunteers and seasoned mercenaries. In their faces, filthy with the mud, blood, and ash of the battlefield, he saw a weariness that rivaled his own.

By the Dark Lady! How long can we keep this up? Imri's thrown magicked beasts, hollowed spirits, the walking dead, and forced shapeshifters at us and we've managed to push him back. That's worse than most men see in a lifetime of battle. Why do I feel so certain we haven't seen the end of it?

He looked up to see one of the *Hojun* priests striding toward him, hunched to keep his head below the trench. Jonmarc frowned in concern. "How's Gethin?"

"He had a rough night of it. The wound festered quickly and the sickness went to his blood. It took both my fellow priest and me to cleanse it."

"Will he live?"

The *Hojun* nodded. "Yes. And we saved the arm. But it was close. He's too weak to return to battle."

"Is he conscious?"

The *Hojun* managed a slight smile. "Barely. And already, he argues to return to the fight."

"He's made his point. The last thing I need is to end up at war with Eastmark because Gethin's gone and gotten himself killed."

The *Hojun* priest sobered. "I assure you, while King Kalcen loves his son, he knew what was at risk when he sent Gethin to Principality in such dangerous times. His death in battle would be mourned, but it would not provoke a war."

Jonmarc gave him a sideways glance. "I'd rather not take your word on that. Knock Gethin out if you have to, but keep him behind the lines. I have a feeling it's going to get nastier than ever tonight."

"I, too, would not want to see the prince put needlessly at risk. He won't be healed enough to fight for several days. Perhaps by then this war will be over."

The *Hojun* gave a stiff half-bow and left just as Valjan sprinted up from the other direction. "By the Whore, Jonmarc! You look as bad as I feel."

Jonmarc shrugged. "I'm getting too old for this shit."

Valjan laughed. "You're a good ten years younger than I am. If an old War Dog like me can take the punishment, I don't doubt that you'll make it." He grew serious. "Were your *vayash moru* able to scout the field before daybreak?"

Jonmarc nodded. "Casualties on both sides, to be sure, but they estimated no more than two thousand new dead." He looked out over the battlefield. "Of course, we don't know how many of the bodies they counted were the old dead that Imri sent at us with those damned hollowed spirits."

Valjan let out a potent curse. "I thought I'd seen everything war had to throw at me, but this battle has been a thing of horrors." He followed Jonmarc's gaze toward the devastated land between the two army's entrenchments. Hastily dug trenches carved shallow scars across the burned and pockmarked battle zone.

"The catapults and trebuchets have been moved," Jonmarc said, fighting an overwhelming exhaustion no amount of *kerif* could revive. "I've put a mage with each grouping. They'll see to the lighting of the missiles and offer some defensive cover. We can't spare men to protect the war machines."

Valjan nodded. "Exeter's in position. He's either crazy or brilliant, but his men were willing to see if they could slip around behind the enemy, and at this point, I don't see how we have much to lose."

Jonmarc grimaced. "I try not to say that, because there's always more to lose than you think. But I agree: It's worth a try. He's still got a contingent to strike from the flank?"

"They'll be in place by nightfall. They intended to draw off the Temnottans and open a gap for the others to slip in behind." He shrugged. "We'll see." Valjan was quiet for a moment, and Jonmarc found the other's gaze uncomfortable.

"There's more on your mind than the war, Jonmarc."

Jonmarc let out a long breath and looked away, annoyed that his old commander knew him quite so well. "If I've got the date figured right, and there's no guarantee of that out here, Carina's due with the twins. At one point, I hoped to be home by then. Now . . . now I just want to live long enough to see them."

Valjan clapped him on the shoulder. "I always said that the Dark Lady had her hand on you. I can't guarantee that you won't take a few more scars with you, but I've no doubt that you'll make it home." He managed a tired grin. "You might find battle more restful than two squalling babes and a woman who's gotten no sleep. I'd fight the Crone herself in battle rather than relive those days in my own house!"

Jonmarc forced a chuckle he did not feel. "Point taken. But after this, I have a mind to retire from war altogether. I've had my fill."

Valjan gave him a sideways glance. "I've tried twice to retire from service, and twice circumstances made it impossible to say no when the call came to return. So I wish you well with that, Jonmarc."

"Let's just hope we both have the luxury to plan a long, comfortable retirement when this is over."

The sun had no sooner dipped behind the horizon when screams rose from the Temnottan camp. Jonmarc smiled. Laisren and the *vayash moru* had orders to fly into the midst of the Temnottans and pluck men from the fortifications, sowing terror and confusion. The strike lasted just minutes, followed by a barrage from the catapults. Men had worked through the night to move the catapults into new, fortified positions. Mages positioned with each catapult or trebuchet lowered their defense of the war machine long enough to lob several burning volleys at the enemy, only to slam the magical defenses back into place while another catapult picked up the offense.

"Go!" Jonmarc signaled the attack. Men and *vayash moru* swarmed over the embankments, their advances timed to correspond with the cover provided by the catapults. Each attacking division had at least one battle mage with it near the front lines, with instructions to lay down a barrage of fire to force the enemy from its fortifications. A second wave of men and *vyrkin* was poised to fill in gaps in the assault and reinforce where needed.

Jonmarc let the battle coldness take him, reacting on instinct as the hand-to-hand fighting grew increasingly intense. Whether or not Imri's forces feared death less than defeat Jonmarc did not know, but the invaders fought with tenacity.

Two of the Temnottan fighters came at him. Jonmarc crouched, and then swung into a high Eastmark kick that sent one of his opponents reeling. He rose from the swing with a blade in each hand and let the momentum deliver a shattering blow to the first attacker. With a cry, the second soldier regained his feet and ran headlong at Jonmarc, fury blazing in his eyes. Jonmarc dove and rolled, neatly slicing through the second attacker's heel to drop the man in agony midstep, unable to regain his footing. Jonmarc rose from the roll closer than the first soldier expected, enabling him to come up inside the man's guard, sinking his blade deep into the man's chest before the soldier ever realized what was happening.

The dying man swung hard with the last of his strength, a blow Jonmarc did not expect. He parried, but the attacker scored a gash on Jonmarc's arm between his vambrace and his chain-mail shirt. As the dying Temnottan sank to his knees, his eyes showed unreasoning fury, making a final grasp for Jonmarc's boots to pull him from his feet. Jonmarc stepped back to evade the man's reach. Behind him, the hamstrung soldier threw a dagger, lodging it high on Jonmarc's thigh. Despite his wound, the man was trying to drag himself closer to Jonmarc, cursing in Temnottan as he clawed his way across the ground.

With a swing, Jonmarc severed the man's head from his shoulders, and then let out a curse of his own at the wound in his thigh. Blood was running down his leg. He tore off a strip from his shirt to bind up the wound. His leg throbbed, but he judged that the gash wasn't deep enough to take him out of the fight.

Jonmarc felt a wave of sheer rage flow over him as he bound

up the wound. It lasted only seconds, leaving him reeling as it receded. *Where the hell did that come from?* Years of battle had taught him that while anger was a part of war, fighting fueled by rage was a sure path to an early grave. He thought about the unreasoning fury he had seen in both of his attackers' eyes, and he glanced out over the battlefield. It took only a glance to confirm his suspicions. All around him, men fought with the frenzy of *ashtenerath*, berserk with rage.

To his right, one of the Principality mercs cut down his opponent with a fierce two-handed swing, not satisfied to step away until he had hacked his adversary to pieces. To his left, Jonmarc saw one of the Temnottans run through a Principality fighter and then stab the downed body a dozen times before turning to find a new foe.

"Imri has chosen his weapon." Ansu's voice came from behind him, and the *vayash moru*'s silent approach startled Jonmarc. An instant later, Laisren joined him, looking as dour as Jonmarc had ever seen him. Laisren took hold of him and lifted off, whisking him out of the heart of the battle to the shelter of a nearby trench.

"How is it that Imri can bewitch the men on both sides?" Jonmarc asked, appalled. He had seen every atrocity war had to offer, yet the carnage unfolding around him was a new level of barbarism that far transcended the norm of battle.

"Imri's strength is to force the shift between man and beast," replied Ansu. "He has called their beast."

Jonmarc turned to him. "Those men aren't shifters. They have no beast to call."

"No animal form, that is true. But there is a beast within every man: the rage of madness."

"I felt the rage touch me, and recede," Jonmarc said slowly, thinking through Ansu's statement.

Ansu nodded. "As Gabriel has no doubt told you, you have

474

unusually high resistance against magic for a mortal. Ordinary compulsion does not work on you, nor are your thoughts easily read without your permission. Most men do not have that natural resilience."

Jonmarc ventured a glance above the entrenchments. The fighting was so heavy it was difficult to be certain, but in some of the clashes, it looked as if Temnottans had turned upon their own soldiers, and Principality troops skirmished with each other. "Are you telling me that bastard Imri is willing to see his own troops slaughtered just to send a killing rage through the ranks?"

"Willing—and able," Laisren answered. "For all we know, once we've weakened ourselves, he may have another assault planned to sweep in and finish the job."

"Could the three of us take Imri?"

Ansu smiled, showing his long eye teeth. "That's exactly why we came for you. It's time to end this."

Jonmarc looked from Ansu to Laisren. "What about you? Can he call your beast?"

"Imri is powerful, but he's not a summoner. While he can animate dead bodies by calling hollowed spirits to fill them and provide a beast, we are not mere corpses. A dark summoner I would fear. Laisren and I should be immune from this."

"*Should*," Jonmarc repeated skeptically. "Should as in, if you're wrong, I become lunch?"

Ansu gave a cold chuckle. "I hope not. I believe the odds are in your favor."

"That's better odds than I have now. Let's go."

No matter how often Jonmarc found himself lifted into the sky by a *vayash moru*, the experience was distinctly unsettling. Laisren's hold across his chest was like iron bands, and while Jonmarc had no fear of being dropped, the sensation of being whisked into the air and just as suddenly plummeting back to ground left his stomach uneasy.

"Imri's just behind those embankments," Laisren murmured as they touched back down in a grove, momentarily sheltered from the battle.

"I saw. I don't care for flying, but I envy you the reconnaissance advantage."

Laisren smiled broadly with a predator's grin. "Undeath has its perquisites."

"So did you have a plan or do we just fight our way over there and hope he doesn't blast us before we get to him?"

"I'll strike from above, while Laisren gets the two of you into position," Ansu replied. "I'll draw off his magic while you and Laisren attack. It will likely take all three of us to bring him down."

Once more, Jonmarc swallowed hard at the sickening lurch of the rapid ascent and equally fast descent. Ansu struck at Imri from the front, sending a powerful wave of magical force that nearly pushed the rogue shapeshifter to his knees. As Imri struggled to shield against Ansu's attack, Laisren and Jonmarc touched down behind Imri, charging with swords ready as a dozen of Imri's guards attacked.

Open yourself to your beast, Jonmarc. Ansu's voice sounded in Jonmarc's mind, forcing its way through Jonmarc's formidable resistance. *Just this once, let your beast rule your sword.*

Jonmarc met Laisren's eyes, and without words, Jonmarc knew they were of one mind. Jonmarc took a deep breath and opened himself to the magic that surged around them, letting Imri's call to fury feed on his own anger, deadening the pain of his wounds and filling him with new vigor. A feral rage unlike anything he had ever felt flowed through every vein in his body, druglike in its intensity, driving out any thought except an overwhelming lust for blood. The pain of his wounds was overpowered by the desire to kill. His own survival meant nothing to him. All that mattered was Imri's death.

476

Too late, Imri sensed his mistake, but the magic already flowed through Jonmarc's blood. Jonmarc attacked.

Jonmarc let the rage consume him. Honed by more than a decade of war and fueled by rage, Jonmarc moved with exceptional speed and accuracy. Laisren had the advantage of *vayash moru* reflexes, but as they fought their way through the dozen guards, Jonmarc was nearly his equal. He moved with deadly efficiency, fighting with swords in both hands, scything through his attackers with no wasted movement, no hesitation, the perfect killing machine. He and Laisren finished off the last of the guards. Jonmarc stood for a moment, heaving for breath, bloodied to the elbows, as the beast inside called for more.

Imri sent a blast of mage fire at Ansu, forcing the *vayash moru* to dodge and shield. He swung back toward Jonmarc and Laisren. It was the first time Jonmarc had gotten more than a glimpse of the Temnottan leader. Imri's battle armor had a golden sheen, and the torn and bloodied tunic over his cuirass bore the crest of a half-shifted man-wolf, lethal claws at the ready. Imri struck with the strength of a *vayash moru*. Laisren and Jonmarc, long accustomed to each other's fighting styles, came at him as a team. Laisren swung his long sword with enough power to cleave a mortal opponent. Imri met him with equal force, giving Jonmarc an opening to strike from the side.

Imri howled with rage as Jonmarc's blade connected with his hip. The blow struck just below Imri's cuirass, and while it did not quite penetrate his long chain-mail tunic, the force was sufficient to bruise bone. Imri turned his attention to Jonmarc, landing a series of fast, brutal strikes that drove Jonmarc back several paces. A sudden gust of wind surged between Jonmarc and Imri, raising the dust in a maelstrom around the shapeshifter. Jonmarc had just enough time to catch a breath and regain solid footing before Ansu let the dust storm drop and both Jonmarc and Laisren attacked in unison.

Imri gave a cry of feral fury. He sent a streak of orange mage lightning crackling toward Ansu. Laisren angled his sword to pierce under Imri's arm, just above the opening in his cuirass. His blade sank deep enough to severely wound a mortal, but it did not reach Imri's heart. Imri cursed at the pain, though it did not slow his defense, and both Jonmarc and Laisren knew the shifter would begin to heal the second the blade was withdrawn.

Ansu kept up a magical barrage that kept Imri's magic occupied, breaking his concentration on the two men who circled him. Imri struck back at Ansu, his aim growing wilder as Laisren and Jonmarc harried him. An errant blast of magic sizzled past Jonmarc, blistering the skin on his cheek as he dodged aside at the last instant.

Jonmarc was the lone mortal in the fight, and while the others could draw on their immortal strength, he knew he would be the first to weaken, despite the mage-sent fury. Imri threw a blast of fire at Ansu and a wall of flame at Laisren, clearing the way for him to pound Jonmarc with a savage series of nonstop blows that tested Jonmarc's reflexes and jarred his bones with their brutal power. Jonmarc was between Ansu and Imri, making it difficult for the mage to strike at Imri. Imri wheeled, bringing his sword down hard enough to snap Jonmarc's blade and, with it, his right forearm. Jonmarc parried with the sword in his left hand, and Imri's eyes gleamed with the light of expected triumph.

Jonmarc stepped back, opening a space between himself and Imri, sword raised in his left hand, blocking with the vambrace on his injured right arm. Imri dove forward, his sword angled for Jonmarc's heart. There was a blur of motion between them, and the sword sank deep into flesh. Imri's sword impaled Laisren through the belly. Laisren's face was ashen, his body trembling with the agony of a wound that could slow but not destroy him.

Imri's sword was still plunged deep into Laisren's body.

Jonmarc launched himself at Imri as Laisren jerked his right arm up, sending his blade into Imri's body, immobilizing the shifter. Jonmarc's sword sliced through Imri's neck, severing his head.

Imri's headless body fell backward as Jonmarc grabbed Laisren by the shoulders, freeing him from Imri's bloody sword. As Imri's body hit the ground, Ansu struck the corpse with a wall of fire hot enough to burn the body to ash within seconds. Jonmarc felt the killing rage drain from him, and the pain of his wounds made him stagger.

Jonmarc knelt next to Laisren. Dark ichor flowed between Laisren's hands where they were pressed against the gash that had nearly eviscerated him.

"Ansu can get you behind the lines," Jonmarc said, aware that the mage stood behind them, giving them cover.

"No need," Laisren managed between gritted teeth. "Already healing."

"Imri meant that strike for me," Jonmarc said soberly. "Thank you."

"You fight like one of us, but you don't heal as fast." Already, the wound was closing, and within a few minutes, the flesh had closed. Laisren accepted Jonmarc's hand to get to his feet.

"Look," Ansu said, giving a nod toward the battlefield.

With Imri's death, a sudden pause came over the fighting. It was as if the fighters had suddenly lost the wind from their sails and found themselves becalmed. The silence lasted for only a few heartbeats before the Principality mercs seized the advantage, setting on the befuddled Temnottan fighters with a vengeance that was born of honest anger instead of magicked fury.

From across the battlefield, Jonmarc heard a wild battle cry and saw the standard of Exeter's mercenary guild rise high into the air as the merc fighters attacked from behind the Temnottan army. Beset from three sides, the Temnottans fell like rabbits to the hunt. Imri's magic was gone. Principality's mercenaries gave no quarter and took no prisoners. Within a candlemark, the battlefield was silent, a bloody slaughter.

"We need to get you both back to camp," Ansu said with a glance toward Jonmarc, who cradled his broken arm close to his chest. Laisren was already recovered from his wound, showing no more than a tear through his chain mail and tunic. "I think it's fair to say that we've won."

Jonmarc stared out over the killing ground. Though Imri's magic was gone, the memory of unreasoning bloodlust haunted him. He had killed many times before in the heat of battle, for vengeance, for survival, and, as a Nargi fight slave, for the entertainment of his tormentors. But never before had he fought and killed in unreasoning, mindless fury. In those few moments, he had glimpsed something in himself that he had never faced before, a beast he prayed to the Dark Lady might never surface again. A chilling thought struck him, and he looked at Ansu and Laisren.

"What if Imri didn't care about winning? The Durim killed to strengthen their magic. All the blood they shed was just a way to gather power. What if we were just a distraction?" he said, new horror dawning with every word as he realized the implications. "How much power could a dark summoner draw from the slaughter of thousands of men?"

27

Two days and nights of battle left the Margolan battlefield awash with blood and entrails. Tris moved by sheer will, bone weary. Esme, his battle healer, refused to leave his side. Tris knew that Esme feared he would collapse from fatigue or be felled by a backlash from the powerful magic that crackled through the air around them.

"Tris, you've got to rest," Sister Fallon urged.

Unshaven and filthy, covered in the spattered blood and muck of battle, eyes red from lack of sleep, Tris was sure he looked more like one of the mad Vistimar mages than the king of Margolan. "I don't dare. Every time I try, Scaith attacks."

"He's trying to break you."

"He's doing a damn good job of it."

"What I want to know," Esme said, "is why he's not as exhausted as you are."

Tris drew a long, ragged breath. "He's drawing energy from somewhere. It's not the Flow; I'd feel that. Right now, the Flow is all that's keeping me on my feet. But more than once, I've felt a surge in his power. I don't know where it's coming from. It's felt different each time. But there's a shift in the magic, and it's favoring Scaith."

In the distance, Tris could see a tall man dressed in mage's robes. His long arms swooped and arced. In a wide circle around the man, birds of prey hurtled toward the ground, striking at the Temnottan soldiers and bloodying their faces and arms before rising high into the sky, nimbly evading the enemy's swords. Falcons, kestrels, and eagles yielded to the mad mage's power, harrying the Temnottans so that the soldiers within one hundred yards of the mage's position broke ranks and fell back.

Tris looked around, but he did not see Alyzza, though he spotted Brother Gernon, the crazy fire mage. In the last battle, Gernon's magic had been almost playful, driving off the Temnottans by setting fire to the hems of their tunics or trews. Today, Gernon was not in a playful mood. Mad or not, Gernon grasped that the Temnottans were the enemy, or perhaps Scaith's blood magic amplified the maddening hum Gernon and the other addled mages heard in their minds. Gernon strode fearlessly across the battle-field, snapping whiplike tendrils of flames around him. Margolan troops scurried out of his way, but Gernon paid them no heed. He scythed the blue-white flames right and left, lashing the Temnottan soldiers with lightning or immolating them on the spot.

"He's going to get himself killed," Tris muttered under his breath.

"I doubt Rosta or anyone else can stop him," Fallon replied. "He's mad enough to be without fear, and sane enough to recognize the enemy."

"Do we know where the rest of the Vistimar mages are?"

Fallon smiled. "Verant, the rock thrower, is with one of the catapults. I suggested it to Rosta, and she was quick to pair up as many of her mages as she could with the catapults or the trebuchets. It should make for some surprising attacks. Verant was able to split large rocks into smaller ones in flight and accelerate their force. Rosta told me that some of her mages can make iron burn or blood freeze. The air mages can make the catapult missiles and the archers' arrows travel twice as far. As long as they remember whose side they're on, I welcome the help."

"Scaith's magic has been an annoying hum that's bothered them for months," Tris replied. "All interest in throne or kingdom aside, I think they're fighting to silence that damn noise."

Amid the smoke and confusion, Tris thought he glimpsed a pack of *vyrkin*. Kolja had assured him that he and the other *vyrkin* would harry the edges of the Temnottan forces. Tris looked skyward, hoping to catch sight of Trefor or one of his *vayash moru*. This war had gone hard on their numbers, but many of the undead fighters owed the allegiance of several lifetimes to Margolan and its kings and had no intention of seeing the kingdom fall to outsiders.

"This might be a good time for reinforcements," Tris said. His right hand closed around the talisman of Marlan the Gold that hung from a chain around his neck and brushed against Talwyn's amulet.

"Reinforcements?" Esme questioned, and then her gaze fell to the talisman. "You've expended a lot of energy. Don't push yourself too far."

"If I'm right, this might save some lives. It's worth what the magic costs." Tris reached out his power and felt a strong tug at his magic. Tired as he was, he sent a flicker of magic toward the spirits that sought him. Through the smoke, Tris saw three ghosts. One man was dressed in leather and animal skins. He wore a necklace of shell and bone and carried a crudely forged two-handed sword. The second man wore armor of a style common in Tris's grandfather's reign. The third ghost carried a shield with the crest of King Hadenrul from four hundred years earlier. These were the ghostly commanders of long-dead armies who had once fought on this same battlefield: Vitya, sworn to fealty to Marlan the Gold a thousand years before; Estan, loyal to King Hadenrul even after four centuries; and Dagen, liegeman to King Larrimore, Tris's grandfather.

The three ghosts stood before Tris and bowed. "We have offered you our fealty," Dagen said. "Legions of our spirits lie beneath these fields. Your men grow weary. We can fight against the living if you call to us with your power."

"I accept your offer. If your dead will rise in spirit, we would be grateful for their help." With his right hand, Tris touched the talisman he had taken from the tomb of Marlan the Gold. He held out his left hand to the three ghosts, who each in turn clasped his hand and bent to kiss the signet ring of the House of Margolan. As each of the ghosts touched his ring, Tris let his power flood through the connection, down into the hard ground of the battlefield, to the mass graves of long-forgotten soldiers.

Vitya was the first to kiss the ring. His soldiers lay buried beneath a millennium of soil, their bones now mostly dust. Tris's magic touched the jumbled bones that lay together in trenches, buried long ago.

"Rise and fight. The lands of Marlan the Gold are under attack." Tris knew that the language of these long-dead men was not the same Margolense that he spoke, but saying the words aloud enabled him to focus his power. As he had done in the crypt with Marlan, Tris sent images to accompany the words, letting the ancient dead see the battle that now unfolded above their battlefield tomb. Vitya called to them in a language Tris did not understand, but by Vitya's tone and gestures, Tris could guess well enough at the meaning. After a millennium, Vitya was calling his fallen soldiers to arms.

The spirits responded sluggishly to Tris's touch, but they knew the magic of Marlan's talisman, and they rose to meet the call. Row upon row of the long-dead soldiers rose as spirits, empowered by Tris's magic. Vitya shouted to them, raising his spectral sword over his head. Vitya's soldiers replied in a war cry that was unmistakable in intent, and the ancient spirits swept into the fray. Tris spared a flicker of magic to make the advancing horde visible to living soldiers. They did not need his magic to fight. Fueled by vengeance long denied, the ghosts rose with a fury, sweeping across the battlefield toward the Temnottans. While their swords and daggers would pass harmlessly through their enemies, the ghosts themselves could also step through living flesh, chilling the unlucky soldiers to the bone and stopping a beating heart. A weak-willed soldier might find himself possessed, forced to turn on his own comrades. Vitya and his men would be avenged.

It took a moment for Tris to gather himself after the first working. He swayed and nearly fell. Fallon reached out a hand to steady him.

"Once is enough," Esme said sternly. "If you raise the dead of all three, will you have the power to sustain it?"

Before Tris could answer, he heard a high-pitched, chilling wail. It came from the deepest shadows at the edges of the battlefield, but Tris felt it in his magic like a sudden winter blast. As he and Fallon looked out over the field, shadows like a thick black fog began to swirl toward the Margolan army. Tris knew that the dark fog was hollowed spirits. Darker shapes streaked through the fog, and even at this distance, Tris could feel the power of *dimonns*, called at Scaith's command. Margolan's fire mages sent volleys of flames at the hollowed spirits and the *dimonns*, which twisted and swirled out of the way.

"What choice do I have? Something is feeding Scaith blood magic power. Let the dead battle the dead and the *dimonns*. We don't have enough soldiers or mages to fight both the living and the dead. I'd rather spend myself to a husk and go down fighting." Tris saw the concern in Fallon's eyes and knew that she was right to worry, but it did not change what he had to do. Reaching out to the Flow to steady his magic, Tris held out his hand to Estan.

Estan's soldiers lay deep within the ground, but not so far beneath the surface as the ancient dead. These men had fallen in battle four hundred years ago, and their bones and rusting armor were still intact. "Armies of Margolan, rise and fight."

Tris heard his voice echo through the Plains of Spirit, touching the dry bones of the dead. These spirits understood his words, even though Estan seconded the command, adding a familiar voice to the edict of a new king born generations after these soldiers' death. By tens and then by hundreds, the spirits struggled clear of the land that had entombed them. Estan gave a curt salute and faded from his position beside Tris, to reappear at the head of his army of revenants. Estan's soldiers swept down the battlefield to place themselves as a gray line of defenders between the hollowed spirits and the overwhelmed Margolan troops.

This time, it took longer for Tris to rally. He waved off help from Fallon and Esme, and he drew once more on the power of the Flow. *If I keep this up, I'll be as dead as the kings that Vitya and the others served.* Yet the howls and screams that rose from the battlefield gave Tris no choice. He took a deep breath and extended his hand to Dagen.

Dagen's soldiers lay only a few feet beneath the battleground. The death and turmoil of the weeks of war had already roused the recently dead from their slumber. Only sixty years dead, these spirits were intact enough to have sensed the threat to their homeland, and they rose with a surge of energy and anticipation at Tris's first call.

"Army of King Larrimore, my father's father, rise and defend your homeland." Dagen did not have to translate Tris's call. The signet ring grew warm on Tris's left hand. These spirits were not as weakened by their slumber as the ancient dead, and much to Tris's relief, they required only his call to rise from their graves, barely needing any of his magic to make themselves visible.

Dagen wore a predator's grin as he turned away from Tris. It didn't matter to the ghostly general who the invaders were. To him and to his army of the dead, this battle was an opportunity for redemption, a chance to rewrite the ignominy of their long-ago defeat for the glory of king and crown. If he survived this battle, and that was looking far from certain, Tris promised himself that he would make sure Royster chronicled the heroics of the dead as well as the living. *If I live through this, I'll make sure Carroway writes a ballad or two about the old battles, to give the dead their due. Let's just hope that what he writes for me is a victory song and not a requiem.*

Amid the smoke of the torches and the haze left by the burning catapult missiles, Tris saw a figure dancing toward them. The figured neared, and Tris recognized Alyzza. Alyzza's mage robes were ripped and bloodied, filthy with the muck of the battlefield. She swayed to music only she could hear, seemingly deaf to the screams and death cries of those around her. But even at a distance, Tris could feel the wild magic that streamed in waves from Alyzza, once one of Margolan's most powerful sorcerers.

Alyzza lifted up her hands as she sang and chanted, like a child dancing in the rain. But it was lightning, not raindrops, that fell at her command. With uncanny accuracy, streaks of lightning cracked down from the sky, striking only amid Temnottan soldiers. Men screamed and fled to the cheers and catcalls of the beleaguered Margolan army. The air around her was heavy with power, as streak after streak blazed to the ground, leaving shallow, burned holes in their wake. Alyzza threw off the power with apparent effortlessness, and the lightning struck with mad unpredictability. More than once, Tris saw Alyzza's mage lightning send the *dimonns* and hollowed ghosts fleeing.

"'What shall be done with all the dead, m'lord, when the crypts are full to bursting and the ground will hold no more?'" Alyzza's singsong voice carried across the noise of battle, and Tris recognized the words from a play that was popular on Haunts.

"'Consign them to the sea, and let the fish feed on their marrow,'" Tris replied, making an effort to remember the words to the play. A reaction headache throbbed with blinding intensity, and it was difficult to think. When Alyzza was lost in the madness, normal conversation was impossible, and only the words to a play or song she currently remembered reached her. Tris wished with his whole heart he had paid more attention to all of Carroway's storytelling.

"'What now, when blood and iron no longer serve and darkness mutes the day?'" Fallon asked. Tris glanced up sharply to see Fallon step forward, and he was grateful that she remembered another line from the play.

Alyzza brought down a streak of red-tinged lightning just behind the nearest Temnottan line, and the ground shuddered beneath their feet. "'If iron and salt can hold the tide no longer, 'tis only the red blood of kings twill stem the flood.'"

Alyzza's words brought the edge of a memory to Tris's mind, but before he could grasp the full memory or its significance, a cry went up from the soldiers behind them. Tris, Fallon, and Esme turned to see what was enough to turn the men from battle. Tris caught his breath. Through the haze of smoke that hung over the battlefield, Tris made out the fast-approaching forms of beings that appeared neither human nor undead. Grotesque, misshapen forms moved with frightening speed toward the Margolan army, which now found itself caught between Scaith's army and a new horror. Balls of blue and red light floated in the smoke and then took shape into creatures that were the stuff of legends and nightmares.

Voices shouted up and down the battle line as the commanders rushed to redeploy their men. Tris and the mages fell back, but caught between the approaching force and Scaith's army, there was nowhere to go.

Alyzza gave a shrill laugh and raised her hands as if she were welcoming the first rains of spring. Fire, not water, came at the call of her magic, striking amid the advancing figures. They avoided the lightning, but it did not deter them, nor did the white-hot bolts seem to instill any fear. Some of the beings stalked upright on two feet, while others slithered or crawled, an infernal bestiary of beings Tris might have said belonged to the fevered visions of a mystic or the terrors of a child. Their strange and frightening silhouettes were oddly familiar, and Tris realized with a start that he had glimpsed many of the same twisted visages and taloned profiles in an illuminated manuscript of *dimonns* and beings of the Underrealm.

"What are those things?" Fallon's voice was an awestruck murmur.

Tris felt the ancient magic, and it chilled him to the bone. "Nachele," he said. "We'd better hope the Dread are planning to show up, or this battle won't be ending in our favor."

Until now, Senne, Soterius, and the other generals had managed to keep their harried soldiers in position despite the onslaught of *dimonns* and hollowed spirits. The Margolan soldiers stayed at their posts, even when reinforcements came in the form of revenants. But at this new horror, men dropped their weapons and fled, although the advancing Nachele cut off any hope of retreat, pushing the terrified soldiers closer to the line of Temnottan attack.

Estan, Dagen, Vitya, we need your men here! The ghost armies materialized amid the chaos of mortal troops that scrambled to

489

fend off the new attack. The dead commanders saw the Nachele and gave Tris a curt nod of acknowledgment, understanding their new orders. Three legions of the dead massed in front of the living troops as the Nachele closed the distance with long, predatory strides.

The Nachele stalked forward as if the mass of spirits and men meant nothing to them. Their long, clawed arms and lashing barbed tails swept through the spirit soldiers as if they were nothing but smoke. Yet everywhere the Nachele touched, their power burned, so that even the dead writhed. Linked by magic, Tris sensed the rending power that drew the essence from the revenant soldiers, until they winked out into nothing, their souls extinguished.

Senne's soldiers were the front line of mortal fighters, and Tris guessed that Senne had left Soterius with the task of holding back Scaith's soldiers. Archers launched flight upon flight of blazing arrows toward the approaching Nachele. Where the arrows hit, they stuck, still burning in the Nachele's flesh, as if they represented nothing more than gnat bites. Tris had no illusions about Senne's soldiers being able to hold off this new assault.

Around him, Alyzza rained down bolts of lightning and Fallon's magic called to the winds, trying to hold the Nachele at bay. Tris mustered his magic and let a shadow of himself slip into the Plains of Spirit. He sensed the approach of the Dread.

When you called to me, I came and I met your challenge. Help us, as you aided Marlan the Gold. We can't fight these things alone. Long ago, you also made a pact with Marlan, whose blood flows in my veins. Honor your blood bond.

Power stirred the air. The hair on Tris's arms stood up, and the back of his neck prickled in warning. A sound like a hundred thunderclaps rolled across the battlefield as the ground at their feet tore open. Soldiers staggered back from a crevice that quickly widened to a chasm. From the maw of the chasm rose the massive, dark silhouettes of the Dread. Tris had seen the Dread in the spirit realm. Here among the living, their appearance was quite different. Swirling black shrouds covered the huge beings, but as Tris watched, he realized that the dark fringe was moving, a covering of tendrils that bent and reached.

Some of the Nachele had broken away from the others. Tris saw dark shapes moving to intercept, and he knew that Trefor and Kolja had interposed the *vayash moru* and *vyrkin* to slow the Nachele's advance. Men screamed and scattered at the approach of a new horror. Even the *dimonns* and hollowed ghosts fled before the Nachele, or wilted beneath the Nachele's deadly touch. The valor of the *vayash moru* and *vyrkin*, Tris feared, would not be enough. It did not seem to worry the Dread that some of their quarry had wandered free. *Time means nothing to the Dread. They may be confident that they can defeat the Nachele, but we may all be dead by the time their victory happens.*

"King Martris!" Tris turned at the unexpected voice. Coalan had hailed him, and the young man was breathing hard as he climbed the ridge. Coalan was covered in dirt and blood, as if he had fought his way to the hilltop.

"You've got to do something," Coalan panted. "Uncle Ban's troops can't hold out much longer. It's bad down there. Two of the catapult crews have been wiped out, mages and all. The camp is a shambles. If there's anything you can do, now would be a good time to do it."

Alyzza danced closer to Tris, her face alight with madness. "The blood of kings, a sacrifice. King Gustaven knew what you must learn."

Tris met her mad gaze, and a memory clicked into place. The Obsidian King had written about Hadenrul and Gustaven, kings who died in battle. Tris had seen the mural in Hadenrul's tomb that showed the Formless One requiring the king's heart in exchange for victory. But now Tris realized where he had heard

Gustaven's name. A play at the Haunts feast day about a long-ago battle had told the tale of King Gustaven. And while it had been years since Tris had thought about that play, he remembered its ending clearly. Gustaven hadn't fallen on his sword out of cowardice. He had invoked an ancient, powerful magic that required the most potent and precious ingredient for success: the life blood of a king.

Not all magic that involves blood is to be feared, my son. Blood can damn, and blood can redeem. It is the first magic, and the strongest. Tris could hear the voice of Hadenrul's ghost clearly in his mind, and with a growing sense of certainty, the words began to make sense.

"Go fetch Soterius," Tris said to Coalan. "There's no time to lose. Bring him here. There's one more thing I can do, but I'll need his help."

The moments slipped by as Tris waited for Soterius to return. He refused to answer Fallon's worried questions, even as he mustered his own courage for a desperate bid for victory. Alyzza hummed and sang to herself, paying no attention to them. Tris had learned in his first battles how to shield himself from the part of his magic that saw the souls of the battle dead rise from their corpses, but exhausted as he was, that shielding did not hold. He looked out across the battlefield and saw a cloud of newly riven souls floating above their sundered bodies. With a flicker of his magic, he sent those that were willing back as revenant fighters, while the others he freed to pass over to the Lady, eliminating the possibility that Scaith might force their spirits back into their corpses to be used against their comrades.

A candlemark later, Coalan and Soterius returned to the knoll. "By the Whore, Tris. We're in the thick of it. This is a bad time for a meeting."

Tris met Soterius's gaze. "We're losing, aren't we?"

Soterius took a deep breath. "It's slaughter. Senne is dead.

The troops are barely on their feet. There's no strategy except individual units trying to stay alive. It's a rout." He shook his head. "We'll fight to the last man, but we can't hold off what Scaith's thrown at us."

"I believe Scaith has been drawing his power from the other battle fronts," Tris said. Fallon and Esme listened in worried silence. Alyzza danced closer to hear. "I think that's why he's had the huge surge of magic to call the *dimonns* and the hollowed spirits. It's what's giving him the ability to draw the Nachele. We can't win this unless I find the same kind of power."

"What do you need from me?" Soterius replied. "Whatever it is, take it. Just find the power to keep Scaith from conquering Margolan."

Tris paused and glanced at the *Telorhan* guards who surrounded them. "Captain," he said. "Leave us."

"But, Your Majesty—"

"Leave us."

When the guards were gone, Tris looked back to Soterius and Fallon. Alyzza danced closer. "I know why the Obsidian King was obsessed with Hadenrul and Gustaven," he said quietly. "They both worked very old, very powerful magic to win their wars. Magic that has only one source. A king's life blood."

Soterius's expression was a mixture of horror and disbelief. "You can't possibly—"

Tris withdrew his sword from its scabbard. At his touch, the runes along Nexus's blade flared into life, realigning themselves. *Heir of blood and power*, the runes read in a fiery, swirling script, just a flicker of the magic that thrummed within the sword. He offered the blade, hilt first, to Soterius.

"I don't know if the magic will let me return. Neither Hadenrul nor Gustaven were summoners. I'm also sure that it has to be a mortal wound, willingly sustained. A blood sacrifice. That's why the blood of combat doesn't work, or blood shed from assassination, like Donelan. If the power requires blood but it doesn't take my soul, I may be able to use my magic to come back. There isn't anything in the legends about a summoner working this magic."

"You're asking us to murder the king," Fallon said incredulously.

"Aye, that he is." It was Alyzza who spoke, but in this moment, her eyes had lost their madness. "It's old magic he speaks of, very powerful. He's right that the Obsidian King lusted after it, but not enough to risk himself. Only a king's blood can work the magic."

"Drive the blade straight into my heart," Tris said levelly, meeting Soterius's eyes. "Leave Nexus in the wound. It holds a shadow of my soul; I saw that when I walked among the Dread. That may help me find my way home. Fallon and Esme can put a preservation spell on my body, at least for a little while. With any luck, my magic and theirs will bring me back."

"This is madness," Soterius protested.

Tris saw fear and confusion in Soterius's eyes. "Ban, we've been together since we were boys. I'm asking this as a friend. Please don't make me order it as a king." Reluctantly, Soterius accepted the sword.

Tris removed his helmet. Coalan stepped up to help Tris remove his cuirass. Tris could see that Coalan's hands were shaking. Tris stripped off the chain-mail tunic and the linen shirt beneath it. Finally, he was naked to the waist, and he closed his eyes and then took a deep breath, centering his magic and forcing away his fear. He opened his eyes and met Soterius's gaze.

"I'm ready."

"Goddess, forgive me," Soterius murmured, as he grasped the hilt and drove the sword between the ribs, deep into Tris's heart.

Tris gasped at the pain and caught a ragged breath. Fallon and Esme were both chanting under their breath as each grabbed

494

a shoulder and helped Tris fall gently onto his back with Nexus still impaled between his ribs. He caught a glimpse of Soterius's ashen face and knew what loyalty had cost.

Blood poured from the wound, first with a gush as his heart tried to beat, and then more slowly as his heart quivered and went still. Breath ceased. Dimly, he heard Fallon and Esme finish their preservation spell, but by then, his spirit was seeping with his blood deep into the ground.

Unlike the many times he had left behind his body to travel in the Plains of Spirit, this time, Tris felt the blue-white strand of his life thread unravel, felt his body recede from his reach. Yet the blood that seeped through the ground around him gave him warmth and held his power and his essence. But more than that, Tris could feel the power that emanated from the blood sacrifice, felt it swell like a wave out over the battlefield and knew that the mages and the Dread could turn that power to their advantage as Scaith had drawn on the carnage for his own purposes.

Sacred Lady of the Eight Faces, hear me. I have made the sacrifice of king's blood. Grant me deliverance for my people.

In the Nether, Tris could feel the energy of the men, monsters, and spirits that moved above, in the realm of the living. Nexus, able through its magic to be present in the world of the living and the places of the dead, felt solid and real in his hand. To his surprise, Marlan the Gold's talisman had also followed him into the Nether, as did Talwyn's amulet.

In the Nether, Tris's summoner-magic seemed heightened as never before. The life energy of the soldiers, locked in mortal combat, pulsed around him, surging and vibrant in its desperate intensity. All around him, souls fled the mangled bodies of the dead, and Tris could sense the magic that fed on the energy of their death and the carnage of the battlefield.

The Nether flickered and glistened. Tris recognized the signature of power before the form could take its full shape. Scaith.

He didn't wait for the figure to solidify. Tris sent a blast of magic, disrupting the shimmering cloud. Tris felt Scaith's power crackle around him, as the cold magic of the dark summoner slammed against Tris's own shields. Scaith's power had lost its iridescent shimmer. Now, it roiled like storm clouds in the Nether. Tris readied for another strike, but before he could act, a tendril of power lashed toward him. It cut across him, an agonizing touch that staggered him. Though he possessed no physical form in the Nether, Tris had learned through bitter experience that injuries were no less real on the Plains of Spirit than in the world of the living. Where the tendril struck, it left a trail of pain and a momentary depletion of his magic.

Another tendril lashed toward him. Tris blocked it with Nexus, and the ghost sword flared as the blood-red tendril sought to wrap itself around the blade. Nexus grew brighter and brighter, until the tendril blackened and withered.

"Show yourself!" Tris shouted to the storm cloud. "You've fought this war through proxies. If you would take this kingdom, be man enough to show your face!"

The storm clouds roiled again, growing darker and more ominous.

"I'm not impressed with parlor tricks," Tris shouted, barely dodging another crimson tendril. "Are you too much a coward to show your form?"

A man's image began to take shape amid the dark clouds. Scaith stepped from the shadows. Dark hair was shaved to stubble on his head, and runes were both carved into the skin and shaved into the hair, encircling his brow like a crown. He wore a white robe, the Temnottan color of death, and both his hem and sleeves were stained crimson with blood. Tris could not guess his age. One eye was green and the other nearly black, but there was no mistaking the madness and rage in Scaith's mismatched eyes.

"You've cheated me out of my prize." Scaith's voice was the dry rasp of old bones grinding together. "I had your execution planned. It would have been slow and painful, to savor every gobbet of power that drained with your life."

Two more of the power tendrils cracked like whip strikes toward Tris. He dodged the strike that sought his sword arm, but the tip of the other tendril lashed across his chest and left arm with immobilizing pain. Tris gritted his teeth and lurched forward with Nexus, aiming for Scaith's heart. He saw Scaith gasp in pain as Nexus's glowing blade severed the crimson tendril like a hot iron through tender flesh.

"You took your own life rather than face my sword." Scaith's eyes were alight with fury and anticipation. "Your son eluded me once, but not again. When I bend his power to my will, nothing will be able to stand against me, not even the Dread."

"Not in my lifetime," Tris said as he swung once more. This time, Nexus's tip slipped between the fiery tendrils to score against Scaith's shoulder.

"Your lifetime is over. I will rule Margolan. Your crown, your sons, your queen are forfeit to me."

Tris felt Scaith drawing on the life energy of the Temnottan troops. Behind him, the clouds grew even blacker, crackling with stolen energy as Scaith drained his troops for a final strike. Tris felt Scaith pull suddenly at the energy, felt a rush of power, and knew that hundreds of soldiers had fallen dead to bolster Scaith's power. Strange magic crackled along the bond, and Tris knew that the death magic had also called the power of the Nachele to Scaith's command.

Tris stretched out his power, reaching to the Flow and to the blood that had worked its magic, strengthened by the sacrifice of a king and from the life blood of thousands of soldiers who had gone willingly to their deaths for crown and kingdom. This time, as the power arced around them, dozens of fiery crimson tendrils snapped out toward Tris. It was impossible to avoid them all as they snaked and moved, and while Nexus's blade blocked and cut through tendril after tendril, more of the crimson whips sliced into Tris's spirit form. They struck with blinding agony, each one a drain on his energy. He staggered as the pain lanced through him, and he knew he could not withstand much more.

"You are defeated. I am the new king of Margolan," Scaith exulted. "I am the true lord of the dead."

Each of those soldiers pledged you his life. They would willingly die for you. Soterius's words rang in Tris's mind as he fought the onslaught. And in that moment, he understood.

I am a dead man on the Plains of Spirit. I belong here. Scaith splits his power between the place of the dead and the lands of the living. The advantage is mine. With all of his remaining strength, Tris sent his magic down into the Flow and out among the living, where the life energy of the souls of the Margolan army thrummed with the frantic pulse of blood and breath. It was that energy he tapped, channeling it, not to snuff it out as Scaith had done but to feel the living tide of those souls couple with the raw power of the Flow. Tris's left hand reached up to clasp the talisman of Marlan the Gold, remembering what the king's ghost had told him. *If your offering is sufficient,* Marlan's ghost had said, *it will open the power of your fathers.*

Focusing on Marlan's talisman, Tris called to the spirits of the ancient dead, to the bones and souls of all the fighting men who lay buried beneath Margolan's soil. The Nether trembled, and Tris felt that power yield to him, sustaining him. Another power added itself to the rush of energy, power that trod the gray line between the living and the dead, the magic of the Dread.

Knowing he would not have another chance, Tris focused his magic in Nexus as his athame and charged at Scaith. Tendrils lashed and cut him, making each step forward agonizing. But as the whip welts of the crimson tendrils stripped away his essence and lashed at his soul, Tris's consciousness remained focused on the white-hot tip of Nexus's blade.

Tendrils wrapped themselves around Tris's sword arm, snaked around his legs, and lashed around chest and waist, sending ripples of blinding pain through him, drawing him into Scaith's deadly hold. Nexus thrummed with power as he gripped its hilt two-handed. The runes on its blade became a river of fire, sending arcs of flame streaking from the steel to burn away the tendrils that tried to hold Tris back as he pressed its tip closer and closer to Scaith. Tris wrested one more surge of power and sent his magic toward Scaith, binding him to the Plains of Spirit even as Tris lunched forward, spending the last of his magic to drive Nexus's glowing blade into Scaith's chest.

"I am lord of the *living* and the dead," Tris said, as Nexus sank hilt deep into Scaith's form. The power that tied them together began to hum, and the pitch rose until it was a shrill scream. Tris could feel Scaith's magic still bound to the spirits of the Temnottan soldiers. Steeling himself for what he must do, Tris stretched out his power. *I am the Son of Darkness, heir to the one they called Blood-Sower, Slaughterer. Let me reap these souls, and if damnation comes, let it be on my head alone.*

Tris flung his power wide. He slashed through Scaith's bond to the Temnottan soldiers, severing his hold over them. At the same time, his magic called to the souls of all the hollowed and stolen spirits Scaith had enslaved. Tris let his power sweep across them like a wind through a bank of candles, setting them free. Impaled on Nexus's blade, Scaith began to tremble, his mismatched eyes wide with fear and pain.

"Go to the Abyss," Tris whispered, as he wrenched the blade to the side. The tendrils withered and blackened, dropping away from where they had wound themselves around Tris's form, smoking and smoldering as they fell. Heat surged through Nexus's blade, and Scaith screamed in agony as the white light burned through him from the center out, until his body charred and his screams ended, and the great Temnottan dark summoner fell in a rain of ash. Tris fell to his knees. He steadied himself on Nexus, quivering with the pain of Scaith's attack. Though the tendrils were gone, he felt their burn. Nexus's glow faded to gray steel, and its fiery runes became mere script. Tris was utterly spent, as if the massive blast of power that channeled through him had left an empty shell.

Even if Nexus still holds a whisper of my soul, I don't have the power to return to my body. I'm going to die here. Grief washed over him, for Kiara, for Cwynn, for the son he would never know.

The Nether shifted around him, and he found himself kneeling in the cold, wet sand of the ocean's shore, on the rim of the vast Gray Sea. A figure was coming toward him through the mist, and even at this distance, Tris's magic recognized the power of the goddess. The figure blurred in the mist, but as she grew closer, and Tris saw which of the Aspects came for his soul, he trembled. The shape that emerged from the mist was not the Mother, to whom he had paid homage all his life, nor Istra, the Dark Lady, patron of the outcast, nor Chenne, the warrior. Hunched and gimping, it was the gnarled figure of the withered Crone that emerged from the mist, the Aspect in whose cauldron souls were rendered in payment for misdeeds.

Stand before me, Martris Drayke, Summoner-King. I require an accounting of your soul.

Tris staggered as he struggled to his feet. His battle wounds still burned over most of his skin, and the wild magic had blasted through him with such force he felt charred within. Death, an end to pain, would be a mercy. Tris managed to stand and square his shoulders, raising his chin and meeting the unforgiving gaze of the Crone.

"I have done the unforgivable. I have forced living souls into dead flesh, no matter that the souls begged for me to do so. I accept the consequences. Punish me as you will, but spare my people."

You are indeed the Son of Darkness, Lemuel's true heir. He, too, used his summoning to draw power from blood and death. Yet you did not grasp this power for yourself. You made the sacrifice that Hadenrul and Gustaven paid to me, the price of blood. You have fought the Shrouded Ones and won.

"How so? I fought only Konost, and I won back my son's soul not by my magic alone, but with the help of the Dread."

The Crone gave a harsh laugh. *Peyhta is the Soul-Eater, the harvester of the spirits of those who fall in battle. Shanthadura is the Destroyer, She Who Bathes in Blood. You stole Peyhta's harvest and Shanthadura's tide and turned blood and spirit to your own ends, for your kingdom's sake.*

You have done well, Martris of Margolan. Yet for your deeds, you must still be judged. Hear my words. I judge the soul that stands before me. Regardless of intent, you have used magic that is forbidden. You must pay the penalty.

Tris had steeled himself for the verdict, yet its reality sent a surge of mortal fear through him that, for a moment, overwhelmed the pain. "I accept your verdict. My soul and my life are forfeit."

Perhaps not. The Crone's gaze was wily, and her thin, pressed lips quirked in something of a bitter smile. *I have not judged the whisper of your soul that remains with your body. You did not gain by your forbidden magic. You were prepared to sacrifice all that you held dear for the sake of your kingdom and your vows. You set the souls of the Temnottan soldiers free, as you freed the hollowed and stolen spirits. You paid the blood price, and you have returned to me the passage token that was given long ago.* The Crone gazed at the talisman of Marlan the Gold, whose spectral shadow hung on a chain around Tris's neck.

Marlan's spirit was given a choice: to bring me this passage token and stand for judgment when he, too, made forbidden use of magic, or to walk the tombs for eternity. A thousand years I have waited, and he did not return. But his blood runs in your veins, and it was the coin of your offering.

Hear my judgment. I will honor the whisper that remains. I will grant passage for you to return to your body. But you must pay a price for the magic that was forbidden. Decide, Martris of Margolan. Ten years of life is the penalty. You need not pay with your own life. Will you give me those years from the life of the next summoner, your son, Cwynn?

At the Crone's words, it seemed as if his spirit self took on flesh and blood. Tris could feel his heart beating and breath filling his lungs, feel the warmth of the sun on his skin and hear Kiara's distant laughter. He felt the life that thrummed through every sinew, every vein. It was a cruel reminder, here on the shores of the Gray Sea, of how much he loved life itself.

Tris met the Crone's eyes. "No. Not Cwynn. Send me to the Abyss. Refuse to let me cross the Gray Sea to my rest. Just leave my son alone."

The Crone's black eyes glittered. *It is not yet your time to cross the Sea. Your work is not complete. But payment must be made. Hear my judgment. Ten years of your life is forfeit. I will claim your soul before your body would have yielded to time. And know this: The power of the king's blood can be paid only once. You cannot walk these paths a second time.*

Exhaustion swept over Tris in an overwhelming tide. *Even if I had the energy to try, I don't know how to find my way back from here.* Then he felt heat against his chest, and raised his hand to find Talwyn's amulet, warm and glowing.

It will guide you in dark places, Talwyn said when she had given him the amulet. Tris closed his fingers around its stone and metal, hoping for a sign.

A new presence joined them on the shore. Here in the place between life and death, the being that appeared by the Crone's side was not immediately familiar. Hidden partly by the mist, it had the silhouette of a broad-shouldered warrior, head held high, wrapped in a billowing cloak. The mist parted, and one of the Dread emerged.

My servant will lead you back along the paths of spirit to rejoin the whisper of your soul. Farewell, Martris of Margolan. Know that we will meet again.

The Crone vanished into the mist, and the cold, damp clouds closed in around Tris. In an instant, the Gray Sea was hidden from view. The dark silhouette of the Dread stepped out from the mist, and its black tendrils wrapped around Tris. It took all his will not to flinch away, remembering the torment of Scaith's crimson fire, but the Dread's touch was as cold as dead flesh. Everywhere the Dread touched him, the pain of his wounds faded.

The mist parted, and Tris stood with the Dread back on the battlefield, beside his pale body which lay on its back where he had fallen, in a pool of his own blood, Nexus still protruding from his chest. Thin red welts, like the lashes of a whip, covered his arms and chest, mirror images of the wounds Scaith had inflicted. Fallon and Esme knelt beside him, chanting through their tears. Coalan knelt a distance away, weeping, and would not be comforted. A man's voice joined the chant, and Tris saw that Pevre, the Sworn shaman, stood a short distance away. The candle with the tribe's mingled blood burned at his feet. In one hand he held a flask of *vass*, and in the other, a bowl of *tepik*.

Beside Pevre stood another of the Dread, an imposing figure, silent and still.

Touch your sword to your sword, the Dread who had guided Tris from the Gray Sea advised. Tris still held Nexus in his spirit form, as real as the blade that jutted from his motionless body. Tris touched Nexus's tip to the hilt of its solid double and felt a surge of power ripple through him, coursing from the Dread's tendrils through his body, down the length of Nexus's ghostly blade. The runes on both the ghost sword and its real counterpart burst into flames simultaneously. *Light sustains.*

The icy tendrils of the Dread were gone. With a shudder, Tris was back in his body, struggling for breath, consumed by the pain of the blade in his chest. In the blink of an eye, the Dread who stood with Pevre was beside Tris, and its dark tendrils wrapped around Nexus's hilt, pulling the blade free and laying the sword against Tris's side so that it still touched the bare skin of his chest. Magic cocooned Tris, and he recognized its signatures. Esme, trying frantically to knit the muscle and sinew of his body. Fallon, sending magic and life energy to strengthen Esme's healing power. Pevre, whose ancient chant held the power tightly confined within the circle of salt and iron. The primal power of the Flow, coursing through them all, the source of magic. There was another power as well, and Tris knew it came from the Dread, channeled through Nexus, replenishing blood and sustaining Tris's spirit in his damaged body as the healers worked.

Tris gasped for breath, and a final jolt of magic convulsed his heart. He was cold, so cold, and his arms and legs tingled painfully, burning as blood forced its way through his body. The Dread glided away, loosing its hold on Nexus, and Pevre pushed forward, holding the container of *vass* up for Tris to drink, and then forcing him to take a mouthful of the *tepik* to bind his soul back to the world of the living. Tris lay still, overwhelmed by the sensations as life returned. The feel of the *vass* burning down his throat and the cool *tepik* that followed. Of his beating heart and the rise and fall of his chest. It took another heartbeat before he remembered how to move, now that he was a being of sinew and not merely spirit. He opened his eyes, and a deafening cheer rose.

"Thank the Lady!" Esme murmured, throwing her arms around him from one side as Fallon embraced him from the other. They helped him sit up, and Tris shivered, still shirtless in the cold winter night. He looked down at his bare chest and realized that the whip welts were merely thin, raised scars, their pain only a memory. Coalan handed him a blanket, too overcome to speak, but his red-rimmed eyes told all.

"What of the battle?" Tris's voice was a rough croak.

"It's over." The voice was Trefor's and Tris looked up as the *vayash moru* commander strode toward them and then knelt beside him.

"Tell me."

"We knew nothing of the magic here, or your sacrifice," Trefor recounted, the look in his eyes silently critical of the risk. "The Nachele broke through the mages' line to the battlefield, worse than any magicked monster or spellbound beast we had ever fought. We meant to make it costly, though I saw no way for us to win. Scaith's army seemed unstoppable, and we were retreating." Trefor shook his head.

"By this time, Soterius and I were the only senior commanders left on the field. In the fiercest part of the battle, it felt as if something invisible . . . shifted. My mortal soldiers told me it was as if something stole their breath; I felt weakness and insatiable hunger, a drain on the power of the Dark Gift. All at once, Scaith's soldiers threw down their weapons and surrendered," Trefor said, spreading his hands wide in utter amazement. "For a moment, the whole battlefield was silent. No one had expected to survive. Then our soldiers began to cheer, until Soterius found me and told us what price we'd paid for victory." He shook his head. "My liege, it was too dear a bargain."

"Where is Soterius?"

"Resting," Trefor replied. "He returned from the hilltop and fought with such fury that the men thought you had bespelled him like an *ashtenerath*. He cared nothing for his own safety; he went after the Temnottans like the Soul-Eater. His men followed his example, and the Temnottans scattered and fled, sure they were all bewitched." He paused. "When the killing stopped, we realized that Soterius was badly wounded. He had worked himself past feeling the pain, until he collapsed. He'll need time to heal, but he'll live."

Trefor managed a wan smile. "When he told us what had happened, what you'd ordered him to do, I understood. If you had died, he did not want to live with it on his conscience, king's command or not."

"Tell him thank you," Tris said, his voice still a dry rasp. "It really did turn the tide."

Beyond the circle of people who were crowded around Tris, there was a stir of motion and the distant, terse questioning of guards. A moment later, a man struggled to the center of the group. It was Nisim, the mage-Sentinel.

"The Temnottan navy, what's left of it, has pulled back. We've had reports from the Sentinels in Isencroft and Principality to the same end. They're going back to Temnotta. It's over."

Tris pulled the rough wool blanket across his shoulders. He picked up Nexus in one hand, taking comfort in the sword's familiar grip. Trefor helped Tris to his feet, bearing most of his weight while looking as if he merely gave support. Trefor headed toward a wagon that waited to take Tris back to camp.

"Stop for a moment," Tris said as they neared the edge of the hilltop. "I want to see the battlefield." Leaning heavily on

Trefor, Tris looked out across the ravaged land that swept down to the ocean. He knew that his magic permitted him to see what the others did not. Above the war-scarred ground and the scattered ash, the spirits of the dead still lingered. Silently, Tris sent his power over the field and whispered the passing-over ritual, granting the spirits passage to their rest.

Tris drew a deep breath. "Burn the bodies. Gather the living. Let's go home."

28

Jair Rothlandorn felt the winter wind against his skin. It made his eyes sting and it gusted with enough force to take his breath away, bringing the blood to his cheeks. The pain of it reminded him that he was alive. That, and the small hand nestled in his own. He glanced down to see that Kenver was watching him. In the days since Talwyn's death, Jair often caught Kenver sitting silently, watching him. Whether it was a small child's way of dealing with overwhelming grief or a glimmer of the magic that would someday claim Kenver as the Sworn's next chief and shaman, Jair did not know. It was enough that they were together, and that they had an understanding that did not require words.

Kenver's gaze met his. "Don't worry, Daddy. She's here."

Jair swallowed hard as his throat closed to any reply he might have made. True to her word, Talwyn's spirit had come to him often in his dreams, and in that meeting place between dream and wakefulness, she was as warm and solid as life. Those outside of the Sworn might dismiss such a thing as the fantasy of a grief-stricken husband, but Pevre had made a point to take Jair aside and assure him that Talwyn's presence and their conversations were as real as anything in the tangible world. He looked down again at Kenver. More than once, he had heard the boy humming to himself as he fell asleep, humming the harmony to the tune Talwyn used to sing for him. Kenver did not speak of it, but Jair was sure that Talwyn sang for him still.

"I don't want you to go back to Dhasson."

"I don't want to go back, either." Two weeks had passed since the battle that cost Talwyn her life. Pevre had carried back the tale of what had happened when the Dread and the Nachele made their way to the battlefields to the north, of Tris's heroic sacrifice, and the victory over Temnotta. Once Scaith's blood magic was eliminated, the Nachele found themselves cut off from the power that called to them and the Dread forced them into exile once more. Jair suppressed a shudder. It would be a very good thing if no one glimpsed either the Dread or the Nachele for another millennium, or longer.

"But you're going, aren't you?"

Jair sighed. Every fiber of his being yearned to stay here with the Sworn, to remain with Kenver and Pevre, close to the barrow where Talwyn was buried. It was already a few weeks past the normal end to the Ride, but that was more a factor of the war than of his desire to linger. And while King Harrol would not begrudge Jair time to grieve, Jair knew that his father expected him to treat his responsibilities to Dhasson with equal respect as his duty to the Sworn.

"I don't have a choice, Kenver. I'm sorry. I want to stay, but I can't. I hope you'll understand when you get older." Jair had said "understand," but what he really meant—what he dared not say—was "forgive."

Raised voices in the distance made both Jair and Kenver turn. Someone was arguing with the warrior who guarded the perimeter. Voices carried across the meadow, and Jair noted that Pevre, too, had joined the conversation. It took another instant for him to recognize that the voice arguing the loudest was speaking Dhassonian.

"Come on," Jair said, giving Kenver's hand a squeeze of

reassurance Jair did not feel. Before they could walk the full way back to the camp, a man Jair did not recognize came running toward them. He had neither the coloring nor dress of the Sworn. The newcomer was unshaven, and while a glance at his cloak and clothing told Jair that the man came from Dhasson, he was splattered with mud and covered with the dust of the road. One glance at his haggard face gave Jair to wonder if the man had ridden without sleep for days at a time.

Abruptly, the newcomer fell to one knee and bowed his head. "Forgive me for intruding, Your Majesty."

Jair froze. A chill of premonition slipped down his spine. He realized that he was scarcely breathing, and it felt as if his heart had stopped. "What did you say?"

The messenger remained kneeling and did not look up. "Please forgive me for bearing this news. King Harrol was stricken by the plague. His healers could not save him. The king is dead."

Jair thought he could grieve no more after Talwyn died, but fresh pain washed over him, settling in a lump in his stomach. "When?"

"A month ago, m'lord. Your travels take you far from Valiquet. I set out the day after the king died, but it has taken this long for me to find you."

Jair hoisted Kenver into his arms. Kenver had never met his grandfather, but the boy had the intuition of his mother's people, and Jair was sure that Kenver sensed the gravity of the situation even if he did not fully understand its import. Jair held on to him tightly, unwilling to admit just how much he needed to hold his son close as the world crumbled around him.

"My orders were to find you and to deliver this," the messenger said, reaching into the satchel he carried on a wide strap across his chest and shoulders. He withdrew a piece of folded parchment, closed with the wax seal that Jair recognized as the mark of Valiquet's seneschal. With the parchment was a wide velvet pouch, and Jair knew its contents from the feel of the thin, rigid ring inside. The circlet of the king of Dhasson.

Pevre strode across the field to join them and laid a steadying hand on Jair's shoulder. Jair felt Pevre's magic, as well as his support, flow through the contact, making the unthinkable bearable. Still holding Kenver on his hip, Jair cracked open the seal and read down through the seneschal's careful script. Paragraph upon paragraph detailed Harrol's last days, his struggle against the plague, and the futile attempts by the healers to save him. Jair's hand tightened to a fist, crumpling the parchment, and Kenver reached up to wipe a tear as it streaked silently down Jair's cheek.

"My prince. Your Majesty. Dhasson grieves with you. I beg of you, come back with me now. Your people need their king."

Pevre gently took Kenver from Jair and let the boy stand beside him. Then Pevre took the velvet pouch from Jair and carefully unwrapped the gold circlet inside. It was beautiful in its simplicity, a battle crown, intended not for the pomp of court but for the leadership of troops. As chief and shaman of the Sworn, Pevre had the power to convey the crown. Jair could see sadness and pride in Pevre's eyes as the older man bade him kneel.

The messenger scurried out of the way as Jair sank to one knee. Pevre began to chant in the language of the Sworn, and while Jair knew the words would be meaningless to the messenger, he recognized them as the ritual said over a new shaman, a call to power. Jair felt a tingle of magic as Pevre placed the circlet on his head.

"Hail, King Jair of Dhasson."

Jair rose and struggled to find his voice. Kenver stood between him and Pevre and reached up to take Jair's hand, his eyes fixed on the glittering circlet. Jair turned to Pevre. "This leaves me no choice about leaving for Dhasson immediately," he said, his voice thick with grief.

Pevre nodded. "Kenver has his people to guide him. He's heir to my title and his mother's power, as well as to your crown. I'll make sure he learns to wield a sword as well as a *stelian*. We'll take good care of him."

"I'll pack my things," Jair said tersely to the messenger. "Mihei and Emil will ride with us to the border. We can exchange horses at the garrison there." He gave a curt nod of dismissal to the messenger. "Wait for me in the camp. We'll leave at dawn."

With a bow, the messenger left, and Jair knelt in front of Kenver. "I'm sorry," he said, looking into his face and thinking for the millionth time how much he reminded him of Talwyn.

"You're the king. You have to go. They need you."

I'm your father. I have to stay. You need me. He did not say the words aloud, but they tore at his heart, even though he knew that Pevre was right and that the tribe would see to Kenver's healing and his safety.

Instead, Jair took Kenver in his arms and hugged him tightly, memorizing the smell of his skin, the silk of his dark curls, and the fierceness with which Kenver hugged him back. "When it's safe, when things are quiet again, I'll send for you. You'll learn the ways of both worlds, your mother's and mine. The court will know you are my son."

He stood, lifting Kenver in his arms, and gave a last look at the stars that glowed in the night sky above the barrow. Wordlessly, he felt Talwyn's presence slip around him, embracing him and Kenver, and his hand touched the amulet at his throat, the charm that linked them over the distance of space and death. "I'll be back," Jair whispered, as much to Talwyn as to the boy who burrowed his head into Jair's shoulder.

And I'll be with you, came the silent reply.

29

"Jolie's going to be disappointed when she hears you won't be returning permanently to Dark Haven." Jonmarc Vahanian grinned and took another swallow of brandy. He walked a few steps to a chair near the fireplace, satisfied that the remaining pain of the battle wound to his leg did not demand too prominent a limp. His right arm was held close to his chest by a sling, still needing a few weeks for the bones to knit despite the healer's work. For now, he wore his scabbard on the right.

"If I know Jolie, she's probably got all the talent she needs to set up the most profitable brothel in Dark Haven," Aidane rejoined. "But Kolin and I will be keeping an eye out for other *serroquettes* who need to leave Nargi, so I'm sure to find her a replacement." She laughed and met Kolin's gaze with a lingering look.

Jonmarc rolled his eyes. "Newlyweds." He finished the last of his brandy and shifted with a wince to accommodate his leg. Though the battle healers had assured him everything had been set as right as their magic would allow, the injuries twinged painfully. He knew that Carina's magic could fix the rest, but that was the least of his reasons for wanting to return to Dark Haven as quickly as possible.

"Speaking of which," Kolin murmured as the doors to the small parlor flung wide and Berry burst into the room, with Gethin trailing several steps behind. If Berry was worried that her entrance was not sufficiently queenly, she gave no indication, though Gethin was shaking his head in good-natured amusement.

"Jonmarc! Thank the Goddess you're free of the healers." She gave a critical look. "How's the leg?"

Jonmarc shrugged. "Nothing Carina can't put right. By the Dark Lady, she's patched up worse."

"True enough." Berry paused just long enough for breath. "I figured that as soon as you could sit a horse you'd be riding off for Dark Haven, so I wanted to make sure you knew that we've set a wedding date."

Jonmarc looked from Berry to Gethin, unsure of what reaction was expected. Aidane looked astonished, while Kolin's expression gave nothing away. "You've set a date? So this means you've decided to accept Gethin's . . . alliance?"

Berry grinned. "As if you hadn't expected that, after all the notes you sent me from the front about him."

Gethin looked warily from Berry to Jonmarc. "You were reporting on me? To her?"

Jonmarc gave another shrug. "Only the truth. Someone had to make sure you were . . ."

"Not going to be a ruthless maniac," Kolin supplied.

Gethin grimaced. "Thank you . . . I think."

"Just part of the job of the Queen's Champion," Jonmarc replied. "Have to admit I was relieved; your father only just lifted the old death warrant on me, and if she'd have turned you down and there was a fuss, I didn't fancy having the warrant reinstated if I had to kill you."

Gethin gave him a sideways glance, as if he considered asking whether or not Jonmarc was kidding, and thought better of it. "Then I guess we all have reason to celebrate," he said dryly.

"We've set the date in the spring," Berry continued, dropping unceremoniously into a chair next to Jonmarc. Although her gown attested to her rank, Berry's auburn hair fell loose around her shoulders, and it was clear that Principality's new queen had no interest in stuffy protocol when no one official was watching. Jonmarc chuckled to himself. *Gethin has no idea what he's gotten himself into.*

"That'll give you time to go home to Carina and spend some time with the twins before you have to come back to the palace."

Jonmarc's attention snapped back to Berry. "Return?"

Berry turned her most calculatedly innocent grin on Jonmarc. "You're Queen's Champion. The Queen's Champion stands at her side throughout the handfasting to make sure the bride and groom live through the wedding. It's tradition. "

Gethin chuckled out loud, and Jonmarc glared at him, but he gave a resigned sigh. After everything they had been through, Jonmarc often felt as if Berry was his oldest daughter rather than his monarch. "Just as long as the chaperoning ends before the wedding night."

"Yes," Gethin said.

"Now there's a thought," Berry said simultaneously with an impudent grin.

"I happen to know a healer who could give me a convenient outbreak of hives," Jonmarc replied with a pointed look at Berry.

"And if I don't send you on your way soon, Carina may be tempted to give hives to me, instead," Berry said and chuckled. "Much as I hate to see you go, your horse is ready at the stable, and everything's provisioned. Am I correct that Kolin and Aidane will go with you?"

"Yes. Lord Uri's made connections in Nargi for us to smuggle *vayash moru* to safety," Kolin replied. "We'll go back to Dark Haven to gather what we need, and then head to Nargi." He made a shallow bow. "We're grateful for your hospitality, but there's work to be done," he said and took Aidane's hand.

Berry sobered as she looked from Kolin to Aidane and then to Jonmarc. "I'll miss you," she said quietly. "Besides, with everyone else, I have to wear those awful, stiff gowns and pretend to act like—"

"A queen?" Gethin finished with a grin.

"Exactly."

Jonmarc chuckled. "Here's a thought. Once the wedding is over, you're welcome to slip away to Dark Haven for a visit. I'm certain we'll be up to the rafters with *vayash moru* and *vyrkin* refugees when Kolin and Aidane get back from Nargi, and Carina would be glad to have her best assistant back to lend a hand."

Berry looked wistful. "You don't know how good that sounds." She sat up taller, changing from hoyden to young monarch in a breath. "We've got a kingdom to put back together now that the war's over, and while I know it seems silly to put so much effort into a wedding, it's an historic first alliance between Eastmark and Principality, so it's a huge diplomatic issue." She sighed. "On the other hand, now that Gethin's actually here in the palace instead of off at war, it won't hurt to have a few months to get to know each other." A grin spread across her face. "Although it's too late for Gethin to back out now."

To Gethin's credit, the glance he gave Berry assured Jonmarc that he had reasons beyond affairs of state for staying in Principality. Though Berry had confided to Jonmarc that she was "pleasantly impressed" with the Eastmark prince, she knew that it was in Principality's best interests to go forward with the marriage, regardless of sentiment. Jonmarc hoped that time would forge a bond of affection, if not love. On the other hand, it was clear that Gethin was quite taken with Principality's feisty queen, and that he had gone from sullen pawn to willing consort.

"Maybe I can convince Carina to bring the twins to the wedding," Jonmarc said with a wink. "Just to liven it up."

"I'm counting on it," Berry replied. "Bring the Blood Council and the *vyrkin*, too. If we're going to make a fresh start of things, let's do it right." She could not resist casting a mischievous glance toward Jonmarc. "Of course, when the time comes for an heir, I'll be expecting the queen's favorite healer to make the trip up to take care of everything."

A look of momentary panic crossed Gethin's face and Berry burst out laughing. "Don't worry—I think we can wait on that for a while. A long while. I just thought Jonmarc should let Carina know . . . for later."

"Later," Gethin replied, swallowing hard as he regained his composure. "Much later."

"Good to see you back in one piece, Jonmarc," Neirin, the Dark Haven grounds manager, greeted Jonmarc, though he looked askance at the sling that bound Jonmarc's right arm. A stable hand ran up to take the reins of Jonmarc's horse, and he looked up at the moonlit façade of the Dark Haven manor house and let out a long, relieved breath.

"Not as good as it is to be back," Jonmarc replied, running a hand through his hair as he looked for a light in the window of the upstairs room that was the nursery. He matched Neirin's pace as they headed for the broad front steps. "Thank you for the updates you sent to Principality. It's nice to have some idea of what's going on when I get home." He stopped halfway up the steps and looked out over the courtyard. "What's the refugee count?"

Neirin shrugged. "A couple of hundred, give or take a few. Lord Rafe has started taking some of the new *vayash moru* to his villa, and the Blood Council voted to turn the properties they seized from Astasia into lodging for the refugees, which has taken some of the burden off Dark Haven."

"Astasia's manor housing refugees? I like it. She won't be needing the place anymore." Jonmarc paused. "Where's Carina?"

Neirin smiled. "Awaiting your arrival. Kolin and Aidane arrived just before dawn with news that you weren't far behind. No guarantee on whether she's had any sleep—I'm told that the twins have a very healthy appetite."

Jonmarc gave his cloak to Neirin and sprinted up the steps two at a time, ignoring the pain in his leg. He paused for a moment at the door to the nursery, listening, and then turned the knob and eased the door open.

Carina sat in a chair near the fire, holding a sleeping infant. Lisette was walking slowly back and forth near the windows, singing quietly to the bundle in her arms and glancing at the night sky. Both Carina and Lisette turned as Jonmarc entered, and for a moment, the scene in front of him was so much as he imagined it would be that he felt unable to move.

"Welcome home," Carina whispered, with a nod toward the child in her arms. Jonmarc felt his heartbeat speed as he grew closer, straining to get a first look at his daughter. He bent to kiss Carina's cheek. She looked at him with concern. "You're limping. And your arm—"

He shrugged. "Nothing you can't fix. I didn't want to stick around Principality City until it was properly healed."

"In other words, you left against healer's orders."

"Maybe."

Carina smiled warmly. "I'm glad some things never change." She edged back the soft cloth that wrapped the infant she held. "Corinn, this is your daddy," she whispered to the sleeping child. At her words, the baby stretched, opened her blue eyes just a sliver, and then settled back into the curve of Carina's arm.

Jonmarc found himself entirely at a loss for words. He realized that he was holding his breath, and that his heart was pounding in his throat. Strong emotion was nothing new to him; he was well accustomed to fury and vengeance, hatred and fear. Before this moment, he thought he had some experience of love: with the strong bond he shared with Carina, the intense and tragic feelings he had for his late wife, Shanna, and for the parents and brothers he had loved and lost as a young man. He was unprepared for the ferocity of the emotion that swept over him, an unsettling mixture of tenderness and a viscerally primal need to protect, whatever the cost. Jonmarc looked down on the perfect features of Corinn as she slept, and he knew without question that the price of his soul had been named.

Lisette moved silently to stand beside him. "There's someone else you need to meet," she said, and gently held out the sleeping baby. Jonmarc took the bundle awkwardly in his left arm. He was aware of how large his calloused and scarred hands seemed, broadened by years of wielding a sword and before that a blacksmith's hammer, compared to the tiny child nestled within the blankets. Once again, he caught himself holding his breath, afraid that any movement would wake the baby. He forced himself to breathe, and he let himself relax as Lisette nudged the blanket aside to reveal a tiny face.

"And that's Kai," Carina said, her voice just above a whisper.

"You're holding her well," Lisette said with a chuckle. "Carina and I weren't sure whether you'd ever held a baby before."

"I was the oldest of four," Jonmarc replied absently, trying to memorize the tiny, perfect features of Kai's profile. "My mother had no problem handing the youngest to whoever was available. It was a simple choice. If I wanted to eat, someone had to hold the baby. And I always wanted to eat."

Kai shifted at the sound of his voice, and her small lips pursed. Her eyes opened, blue like her sister's, and she stared at him with a wide-eyed, unfocused gaze. Jonmarc found himself awkwardly at a loss for words.

"Hello, little one," he murmured. Kai gave a little hiccup and her eyes slowly drifted closed. Gingerly, Jonmarc made his way to a chair facing Carina and sat down, holding Kai close to him, marveling at the steady rhythm of her breath.

"They're beautiful," he said, and his voice caught. "I just can't believe—"

"That you're a father?" Carina chuckled.

Jonmarc shook his head, his eyes fixed on Corinn's face as she slept in Carina's arms. "That I could have had anything to do with something so good."

"Oh, they're not always this sweet," Carina replied with a quiet laugh. "You should see them in a mood. They have your temper, all right." She was quiet for a moment. "Do you think the prophecy was true?"

The same question had been on his mind for the entire ride home from Principality City. At their wedding, an ancient *vayash moru* had made a prediction: *Twin daughters will each bear a son. One will wear a crown, and the other will wield a sword, and together they will challenge the abyss.* While Jonmarc and Carina had rarely spoken of the prophecy throughout her pregnancy, he was sure it had never been far from either of their minds.

"I don't know," he said, letting Kai snuggle into his shoulder. "Personally, I've had my fill of making history. But I suspect that they'll make their own choices and their own destiny, the same way everyone else does." He gave Carina a sideways glance. "But just in case, whether or not they turn out to be healers like you, I'm still teaching them to fight."

30

Kiara Sharsequin Drayke, Queen of Isencroft and Margolan, looked with a mixture of anticipation and sadness at the satchels and trunks waiting next to the door of her room.

"*Skrivven* for your thoughts," Allestyr said quietly.

Kiara gave a self-conscious smile. "Just thinking about the trip back to Margolan. It's so funny that when I'm there, and I talk about Isencroft, I call Aberponte home. But now that I'm here, and I think about going to be with Tris and Cwynn, it's home there, too."

Allestyr chuckled. "I understand completely, my dear. Though with the official residence of the joint monarchy moving to Margolan, it will be some time before your travels bring you back here again."

Kiara sighed. "I don't see any way around it, but I'm afraid you're right. Once the boys are older," she said, and her hand slid to her abdomen, which was now undeniably rounded, "we'll have to work out a way for them to feel as much at home here as in Margolan." Jac rubbed against her leg and she leaned down to stroke his scaly back.

"Do you have any idea of when you'll know whether Cwynn will be able to be king? It would certainly simplify things if he is able to take the throne. Two boys, two crowns."

Kiara nodded and began to pace. "Somehow, I doubt things are ever that simple. At least we know that some of the unusual ways Cwynn's acted have to do with his power. But what it will mean for him, growing up with that kind of magic, and whether or not it lends itself to kingship . . . we just won't know for a while." She patted her belly. "And as for Ghent, we know he'll wear a crown, the question is, will it be one throne or two?" She shook her head. "It seems crazy, imagining them being kings when Cwynn's so little and Ghent hasn't even been born."

"Ghent?"

Kiara smiled. "Tris and I chose the name before he left for war."

"I'll expect you to include drawings of them along with the official papers we send back and forth to you," Allestyr said with mock sternness. "I want to watch them grow up, not just meet them when they're old enough to be sent for fostering."

"Oh, you can count on seeing some drawings," Kiara said with a chuckle. "Expect them to speak Croft and Markian, too. I'll send for tutors when they're older. If they're to rule Isencroft, then they must be *of* Isencroft."

"And how will you work out the choice between the worship of the Mother and Childe versus Chenne?"

Kiara gave him a knowing smile. "The same way Mother did. They'll learn to make all the appropriate official offerings to the Mother and Childe in public, as good princes of Margolan. And they'll learn to worship Chenne at the altar in my room, so that they make the Crofters happy."

"I happen to know Viata raised you to worship the Lover, as she did in Eastmark."

"Fortunately, the Lover Aspect isn't as jealous as some of the other faces of the Lady. I'll teach them to make their private devotions to the Lover, just as Mother taught me."

"You've discussed this with Tris?"

"Tris is a summoner. He's seen the Lady in all her aspects, in person. It's made him rather . . . broad-minded . . . on the topic."

Conversation stopped as servants came to load Kiara's bags into the carriages that would take her to Margolan. Jae stirred from his place on the hearth and rubbed against Kiara's legs, as if to ensure that he would not be left behind. At nightfall, Captain Remir and his guards would escort her on the first part of her journey, along with her *vayash moru* and *vyrkin* protectors. Cerise and Royster would travel with her, and both of them were as eager to return to Margolan as she was, Kiara knew. At the border, Margolan soldiers would replace the Isencroft guards, a concession to politics. *Something we'll need to work out, eventually*, she thought.

A knock at the door made both Kiara and Allestyr turn. The guards had a very short list of permissible guests. Cam stuck his head and shoulders into the room. "Are we too late to say good-bye?" The door swung open, and Cam entered with Rhosyn, arm in arm. Kiara noticed that Cam's limp was more prominent than before the war, and that Rhosyn seemed to be providing support as much as a gesture of affection.

"Not at all. I'm glad you could stop in before I had to leave."

Cam greeted Kiara with a bear hug. "I guess I should quit doing that now that you're queen and all, but old habits die hard."

"There are exceptions in the rules for old friends," Kiara said with a grin. "Are the two of you heading for Brunnfen?"

Cam and Rhosyn exchanged glances. "In a while. Brunnfen's not the warmest place to spend the winter, trust me. And while we work out the details of this whole 'shifting the monarchy to Margolan' thing, Tice and Allestyr thought it would be better for Count Renate and me to stick around to help keep familiar faces involved."

"Does Renn know you won't be moving back right away?"

Cam laughed. "Renn and Captain Lange made a great team. After all Alvior's plotting, he couldn't land ships at Brunnfen at all. In fact, the ships didn't even get close enough to do any serious damage, so instead of cleaning up a mess, like the rest of the coast, Renn can put his time into building the ale house and distillery that Rhosyn's father's invested in." He grinned. "I've persuaded Rhistiart to move into Brunnfen to lend a hand. He's got a decent head for business. When the tavern and distillery are up and running, who knows? Rhistiart might stay on with us, or he may head back to Dark Haven. There was a *vayash moru* silversmith who offered him an apprenticeship there."

"And Renn doesn't mind standing in as lord of the manor for a while longer?"

"He says he doesn't. Truth be told, I've been gone from Brunnfen for so long, it's probably best to have Renn in charge. Bum leg or not, I'm not sure I'm ready to sit still long enough to run a manor house just yet, at least, not the way it should be run. Renn will do just fine, and we'll visit when we can." He grinned again. "After all, we'll need to inspect the quality of the ale and spirits, now won't we?"

After Cam and Rhosyn said their good-byes, Brother Felix came to the door. "If you're ready, m'lady, something requires your attention," he said.

Allestyr accompanied Kiara and Brother Felix as they made their way into the necropolis, down the long corridor to the warded room where Kiara had one last piece of unfinished business. Kiara and Allestyr stood back and let Felix release the wardings on the ornately carved door. It swung open, and with a flicker of magic, Felix lit the torches. On the table in the center lay the closed box that held the *nenkah*.

"Is it . . . the way we left it?" Kiara asked, daring to move to the edge of the table, but hesitant to touch the box.

Brother Felix smiled. "See for yourself." He opened the box. Inside lay a crude cloth doll. Kiara watched for several minutes, but the doll showed no movement. "I don't know for certain when the magic ended, but my guess is the night you turned the battle with the burning glass, when you told me that you felt Cwynn's magic protecting you."

"So much was going on," Kiara said quietly. "There was a moment when I was truly afraid, and that's when I felt a rush of power. My intuition said it felt like Cwynn, but I don't know how to be sure."

"If I had to guess, I'd say that the same instinct that led the boy's soul here for protection also felt your fear and, by instinct, went to his mother."

"And afterward? How was the *nenkah* when we returned from the battlefield?"

Felix spread his hands, palms up, and shrugged. "When I came down to check, the magic was gone. The *nenkah* was as you see it, nothing but cloth and the bits and pieces we used to create it. I'm guessing here, but it could be that whatever magic frightened Cwynn in the first place may have gone away, and he simply went home." Felix gave a wan grin. "It's not the kind of magic you see every day."

"No, it's not," Kiara replied, deep in thought. "I wish we knew for certain about the timing. We've heard from the mage-Sentinels that the last of the fighting ended when Tris defeated Scaith. I'd love to know if that's when Cwynn 'went home,' as you put it." She gave Felix a worried look. "And I wish I knew whether he made it home safely."

Felix chuckled. "Any 'child' capable of projecting his soul across that kind of distance and giving you the boost of power he sent at the battle is likely to be able to find his way back without our help." He sobered. "He's not going to be the typical child to raise, even with the magic you and Tris possess. You know that, don't you?"

The same concern had kept Kiara awake for several nights since she had returned from battle. "It's crossed my mind. The trick is going to be keeping him safe—from himself and from others—until he's old enough to control his gift."

Felix clapped a hand on her shoulder. "You'll figure it out. I have no doubt of that."

"What will you do with the *nenkah*?"

Felix looked uncomfortable. "It's dangerous to leave it as it is. We created it from items that held a personal resonance for you. If someone were to get a hold of it, it could be used to harm you. Now that we know that Cwynn's soul is gone and you've fully assumed the regent magic, there's a small ritual of unbinding to turn the *nenkah* back into bits of linen and hair and such. Once that's done, I'll take the *nenkah* apart and burn the pieces separately. But before I did, I wanted to show you, just so you'd be certain that Cwynn won't be harmed."

"What do we need to do for the ritual?"

"Much less than was required to create the *nenkah*." Kiara watched in silence as Brother Felix warded the room. He lit a candle from the torch and placed it next to the box that held the *nenkah*. Then Felix took a small knife from his belt. "The closing ritual requires a little blood," he said.

Kiara held out her hand, and Felix made a shallow cut on her palm, just enough to coat the blade. "Sacred Lady, guardian spirits, kings and queens of Isencroft, withdraw the magic from this proxy now so that the circle may be closed. May you lend your wisdom and protection to Kiara, Queen of Isencroft and Margolan, throughout her days." Felix shook three drops of the blood onto the candle so that the blood fell onto the wick, extinguishing the flame.

"That's all there is to the unbinding ritual," he said quietly. "See for yourself."

Kiara reached out and stroked the doll with one finger. It was as Brother Felix had said, mere cloth and stuffing. "Thank you," she whispered, but whether she spoke to Brother Felix or to the *nenkah* and the soul that had departed it, even Kiara was not sure.

31

Tris Drayke stood on the front balcony of Shekerishet, looking out over the palace city. Two restless wolfhounds brushed against his legs, as did the ghost of a large mastiff. Absently, Tris reached down to pet them.

He closed his eyes for a moment. In some ways, it seemed as if nothing at Shekerishet ever changed. If he tried, he could almost believe that his mother and sister and father were elsewhere in the palace, that he would see them at dinner, that none of the last two years of treachery, war, and bloodshed had ever happened. Tris opened his eyes and the comforting illusion disappeared. The days he remembered were gone forever, leaving him—and his kingdom—forever changed.

A knock at his door made him turn, and from habit, his hand fell to the sword at his belt, although he knew a contingent of guards outside his door made it highly unlikely that anyone unexpected would approach. Ban Soterius opened the door and stepped inside, letting the guard pull it shut behind him.

"I figured I'd find you at a window." He chuckled. "You know, watching for Kiara's carriage won't make it come any sooner."

Tris sighed and turned away from the window. The wolfhounds padded over to the hearth, and the mastiff stretched his long, ghostly legs out behind a chair. "I know. But one of the *vayash moru* guards came ahead to say she would arrive tonight. Goddess, it seems like she's been gone forever!"

Soterius walked over near the fire. He moved stiffly, and Tris knew that although Soterius downplayed the wounds he had received in the last battle, he had nearly died from his injuries. Tris poured two glasses of brandy and walked over to where Soterius stood. He handed one glass to Soterius and sat down, swirling the brandy in his goblet in silence.

"Alle told you what happened with Cwynn while we were gone?"

Soterius let himself carefully down into a chair and took a sip of his brandy. "It wasn't the first thing we talked about," he said, flashing a wicked grin, "but it did come up. So it really was Cwynn that Scaith was after?"

Tris shrugged. "Cwynn was certainly one of the prizes. Mikhail says the soldiers intercepted several suspicious strangers who might have been sent to kidnap Cwynn, but we had Cwynn too well protected, physically at least. When Scaith couldn't snatch him, he tried to take his soul. That's the part that gets tricky. Fallon and I don't pretend to understand exactly what happened. I'm sure that Royster will have a wonderful time looking for clues in the Library at Westmarch's archives."

"You rescued a piece of his consciousness when you went into the barrows."

Tris nodded. "And from the letter Kiara sent, I gather a part of him fled to where she was for safety. Alle and Eadoin were beside themselves to tell me the story as they lived it. From their perspective, Cwynn had a bout of night terrors, and then became completely unresponsive. They called in healers, and it was clear that Cwynn was still alive, but they couldn't rouse him."

Soterius nodded. "I suspect the version Alle gave me was

even more complete than what she told you. She and Eadoin were terrified. They were sure Cwynn was bewitched, but neither the healers nor the mages could figure out how to break the spell."

"Until I went after the part of his soul Konost stole."

Soterius repressed a shiver. "Let's not talk about that, huh? That whole thing is unsettling."

Tris chuckled. "It was worse in person, believe me." He sighed. "And I'm sure Kiara will have her own story to tell, since she was rather guarded in her letters. If Cwynn really can touch the Flow—and I believe he can—it's going to be a challenge raising him. His magic may take him down another path, away from the throne."

"That's why you've got another son on the way, isn't it?" Soterius took another sip of brandy. "And just so you know, all the time Alle spent with Cwynn has made her rather set on having a child of her own, so don't be surprised when we make an announcement one of these days."

"The only thing that surprised me was that you didn't have that project underway before we left for war."

"Not for lack of trying." Soterius grinned, and then grew serious. "What about Sister Rosta and the mad mages? Vistimar was destroyed when the mages broke through the wardings. Where will Alyzza and the others go?"

"Mikhail suggested a perfect solution. Lord Guarov's manor has stood empty since he was hanged for treason last winter. Since he died a traitor, his lands revert to the crown." Tris paused. "In gratitude for the role the Vistimar mages played in the battle, I've granted Lord Guarov's land and manor as a sanctuary, on the condition that it remain outside of the Sisterhood's control and that the rogue mages are welcome there as well."

Soterius chuckled. "I'll bet Sister Landis loved that."

Tris shrugged. "It was her choice to keep the Sisterhood out of the war. The mages who joined us did so at their own risk. They earned their reward."

Tris grew quiet. He finished the last of his brandy and set the goblet aside. The logs in the fireplace danced with flames that did not quite heat the large old castle room.

"So now what?" Soterius broke the silence. "The war's over. For the first time since you've taken the throne, no one's trying to kill you. By all the reports I've heard, even the plague seems to have run its course. What next?"

Tris drew a deep breath and managed a tired smile. "With luck, we get down to the business of actually running a kingdom, instead of defending it. Father reigned for over thirty years, and most of those years were utterly boring. Nothing could make me happier than to see the next several decades be normal, prosperous, and completely uneventful." *Except that I'll see ten less of those years. But so be it.*

Soterius raised his glass. "I'll toast to that." He finished the rest of the brandy in one swallow, and sighed. "There was a letter from Danne, Coalan's father—my sister's husband. While we've been off saving the kingdom, he's kept working on repairing Huntwood." He shook his head. "I still can't believe the mess Jared's soldiers made of it. But the good news is that Danne thinks he'll have at least part of the main house habitable by spring. The *vayash moru* refugees who stayed there before the war helped quite a bit." He paused. "After all this time, Coalan and I can finally go home." He grinned. "At least, when the king grants us leave from his service and we're not needed here, of course."

Tris gestured toward a pile of papers on a desk. "You're not the only one who had letters waiting. There was one for me from Carroway. He and Macaria are planning to head back from Dark Haven now that Carroway's hand is healed and Carina's had the twins. She'd asked them to stay with her and play music during the birth, since Jonmarc wasn't back from the war in time."

"Jonmarc, a father," Soterius mused with a grin. "Now that is going to take some getting used to." He glanced toward the pile of papers and sobered. "Anything from Jair?"

Tris shook his head. "Just the note he sent before he left for Dhasson. From what he said in the note, the plague hit Dhasson's nobility pretty hard. It wasn't just Uncle Harrol who died; several of the key lords in his council were also killed. Jair's going to have his hands full for a while."

Soterius stared into the fire. "Amazing how everything can change in such a short time, isn't it? Two years ago, the thrones of the Winter Kingdom looked as constant as the sunrise. Your father, Staden, Donelan, Harrol—they all could have easily ruled another twenty or thirty years. Now, those kings have all fallen. It really was a War of Unmaking. Everything's been turned upside down, and a whole new generation is in power."

"Let's hope that we can keep any surprises to a minimum for a long, long time."

Soterius frowned. "There's still the matter of Jared's bastard, hidden in Trevath."

Tris shrugged. "The child's no more than a year old. It'll be years before anyone can make much of that. By the time that's something to worry about, I'm hoping that we'll know for certain what Cwynn's capable of, and have the Isencroft issue settled." He stretched. "Right now, I just want to keep the people fed through the winter and get the crops planted. No war. No magic. No excitement of any kind, if I can help it."

"Do you think that will actually happen?"

"No, but I can dream, can't I?"

A candlemark before dawn, Tris stood on the landing of Shekerishet's broad front steps, watching as a shadow drew closer to the palace. In the still, cold air, the sound of hoofbeats carried over the distance, and before long, he could hear the crunch of carriage wheels in the snow. Three *vyrkin* arrived first, effortlessly loping ahead of the entourage, their thick fur glistening with snow in the torch light. Behind the *vyrkin* rode a dozen guards, and Tris recognized some as *vayash moru*. Kiara's carriage followed, drawn by six large geldings. Behind the carriage rode another dozen guards.

Tris realized hc was holding his breath as the carriage door opened and servants hurried to help Kiara down from the coach. He smiled. She wore a sensible, if somewhat unconventional, traveling outfit of trews rather than a gown, and Tris had no doubt that she also wore a sword and cuirass under her heavy cloak. He hurried down the steps toward her and took both Kiara's hands in his, sending a flicker of magic through the touch to assure himself that both Kiara and the child she carried were well. Then he caught her up in a tight embrace and kissed her, heedless of the small group of guards and servants around them.

"Welcome home," Tris murmured, his throat tight, as he took Kiara's arm and escorted her into Shekerishet. Royster and Cerise alighted after Kiara and followed at a distance. Jae stirred sluggishly from his spot on the carriage floor, flexed his leathery wings, and flew to the top of the stairs.

"It's good to be back," Kiara replied. Behind them, Mikhail took charge of assigning servants to see to the queen's belongings. A servant took Kiara's cloak and Tris gave instructions for food to be brought to his rooms. Tris and Kiara made the way up the stairs to the privacy of the king's parlor. Tris opened the door, and Kiara gasped. Alle and Eadoin waited inside with Cwynn. Kiara rushed toward the baby, and then slowed, not wanting to wake him. Tris watched as emotions played across Kiara's face: joy, longing, and hesitation, as if Cwynn might not know her when he woke.

"Since the war ended, he sleeps through the night," Alle confided, gently transferring the bundle in her arms to Kiara. "Whatever he heard, it's gone now. And what an appetite!"

Lady Eadoin patted Kiara on the shoulder. "Alle and I will stay as long as you need us, my dear. We thought you might welcome some time to rest and get reacquainted with the king," she added with a sly smile as Kiara blushed.

"Thank you," Kiara replied, looking down at Cwynn with an expression that combined both wonder and sadness. "And I want to hear all about how he's been, but maybe not tonight."

Eadoin smiled. "Those tales will keep. I warrant you've got some stories for us as well." She stroked the back of Cwynn's small hand, and his fingers curled reflexively. "So small to be the crux of such large intrigue, isn't he?"

Alle and Eadoin took their leave as a servant appeared with a tray of food and a pitcher of warmed wassail. Kiara brought Cwynn and sat next to Tris by the fire, nestling Cwynn into the crook of her left arm as she sipped from a mug of the warm drink. Kiara rested her head on Tris's shoulder and relaxed against him as he wrapped an arm around her. "I missed you," she murmured.

"Not as much as I missed you."

"Don't be too sure." As Cwynn slept, Kiara and Tris took turns recounting what had happened in their time apart. Kiara picked at the food as Tris told his part of the story, and finally she set the empty mug aside.

"Royster's taken custody of the burning glass while he's here at Shekerishet. He wants to study it and make notes for posterity. After that, we'll need to find a suitably safe place to store it—if there is such a place." She grinned. "Royster's written quite a bit in his chronicles about the war and the way it played out in Isencroft, so don't be surprised if he hunts you down to hear your side of things, for the archives."

"So the gifts of your ancestors' spirits actually turned the tide?"

Kiara nodded. "Thanks to the necklace, Tice was able to broker a truce with the Western Raiders. They've agreed to sell us grain, which should stave off famine and help get Isencroft through the worst of the winter. The burning glass made all the difference in the battle. As for the runes, they've been mostly silent, but I wonder, now that I'm here with you and Cwynn, what they might say."

Carefully, so as not to wake the sleeping child in her lap, Kiara found the velvet pouch of rune stones that hung from her belt and took the bits of polished bone in her hands. "They're warmer than usual," she murmured. "That's odd."

Tris cleared the table surface and Kiara held the runes tightly in her fist next to her heart for a moment and then gently let them fall across the wood. This time, only one of the bones refused to speak. Tris rose and went to the door, speaking a few words to the guard outside, who returned in minutes with Sister Beyral, who did not look fully awake.

"We thought you might be able to help Kiara interpret," Tris said, as Beyral bent closer to look at the runes.

"This is very interesting," Beyral mused. "*Katen*, the rune of succession, lies akimbo. Something about the succession of the throne is not clear, but of which kingdom the rune speaks, I don't know. *Telhon*, the rune of family, lies at cross quarters to *Est*, the rune of days. In that position, it refers to an eldest son. So this reading is specific to Cwynn. *Aneh*, the Chaos rune, lies beneath *Tivah*, the rune for the Flow of magic. There will be tension between the power of chaos and the power of the Flow, and Cwynn will be at the center of that conflict."

Beyral indicated the next three runes. "*Sai*, the death rune, is inverted and lies next to *Vasht*, the burial rune. That's the 'summoner's couplet'— it confirms that Cwynn will inherit his father's abilities, but differently, as the rune for the Flow indicates. *Vayash moru* will play a significant role, but how that will happen isn't clear. *Fia*, the power or crown rune, is face down. It would appear to mean that Cwynn will not ascend the throne." She held up a hand to forestall their comments. "But look. *Lyr* lies face up and at the top of *Fia*. *Lyr* is the rune of swords and athames. In this position, it speaks to distinction as a warrior or mage, perhaps both."

Beyral spread her hands, palms up. "That's all the runes tell me. I'm sorry it's not clearer, but the runes rarely are."

"Thank you," Kiara replied, still staring at the runes as Tris and Beyral walked to the door and conferred in low tones before the seer left them.

"Did Beyral have anything to add?"

Tris smiled and sat down next to her. He swept the runes into his palm and placed them carefully into the velvet bag, which he returned to Kiara. "Only that we shouldn't read too much into the runes or expect them to chart a course. Cwynn will have to do that for himself."

Kiara twined her fingers through his. "How about your magic? Does it tell you anything?"

Tris took a deep breath and sent a tendril of magic along the paths of spirit. But for the first time in many months, nothing stirred in response. "Nothing," he reported. "No strange hum of power, no looming dark presence, no message from the spirits, no rift in the Flow. I suspect this means we'll have to figure this out ourselves, one day at a time." He squeezed her hand. "That's good enough for me."

Names and Places in *The Dread*

Aberponte—The Isencroft royal palace

Adares—The name the Western Raiders call themselves

Aidane—A ghost whore who finds herself at the center of political unrest because she bears messages from the dead

Alcion—A traitor to the Eastmark crown, uncle of Prince Gethin; wrongfully court-martialed Jonmarc Vahanian years ago

Aldo the Wise—Long-ago king of Isencroft

Alle—Niece of Lady Eadoin, wife of Ban Soterius, former spy during the rebellion against Jared the Usurper

Allestyr—Seneschal to the monarch of Isencroft

Alvior of Brunnfen—Traitor to Isencroft, brother of Cam, Carina, and Renn

Alyzza—Powerful elderly sorceress now presumed mad; a friend of Tris's grandmother, Bava K'aa

Ansu—*Vayash moru* mage

Antoin—*Vayash moru* assigned to protect Kiara

Ashtenerath—Men who have been turned into mindless weapons by a combination of blood magic, potions, and torture

Astasia—One of the *vayash moru* Blood Council, now gone rogue and presumed to have joined enemy forces

Athira/The Whore—One of the eight aspects of the Sacred Goddess

Avencen—Eastmark diplomat and adviser to Prince Gethin

Balaren—*Vayash moru* soldier assigned to protect Kiara

Ban Soterius—Margolan general, close friend of Tris Drayke, a leader of the rebellion against Jared the Usurper; married to Alle

Bava K'aa—Tris's maternal grandmother, a famed and powerful sorceress who fought the Obsidian King and who mentored Tris in magic

Benhem—A clever Isencroft mage

Berwyn (Berry)—Queen of Principality, daughter of King Staden, friend of Jonmarc and Carina Vahanian

Bez—Tattooed drum player in a roving band of musicians

Black Robes—Also known as Shanthadurists; blood mages and devotees to the banished goddess Shanthadura the Destroyer

Brightmoor—Lady Eadoin's manor

Brother Albert—Monk who tends the dying in Ford's Crossing

Brother Felix—Monastic mage who is an adviser to Kiara

Brother Gernon—A crazy fire mage formerly held in Vistimar

Brunnfen—The manor held by Cam and Carina's family

Buka—A mass murderer in Principality City

Cal—Drone player in a group of traveling musicians; partner to Nezra

Cam—Queen's Champion of Isencroft, Lord of Brunnfen, twin brother to Lady Carina Vahanian, close friend of Kiara's; brother to Renn and Alvior the traitor

Captain Remir—Loyal soldier to Kiara

Captain Vyn Lange—Captain of a garrison protecting Brunnfen

Carina—Twin sister of Cam, wife of Lord Jonmarc Vahanian, former court healer to King Donelan, cousin to Kiara, one of the most gifted healers in the Winter Kingdoms

Carroway—Master Bard of Margolan, close friend to Tris Drayke, married to Macaria

Cerise—Personal healer to Kiara

Ceshilban, of Clan Dromlea—One of the ghostly Clan Lords of Isencroft

Cheira—A shaman leader among the Sworn

Chenne the Warrior—An Aspect of the Sacred Goddess, especially revered in Isencroft

Childe—An Aspect of the Sacred Goddess, especially revered in Margolan

Clan Dromlea—One of the ancient clans of Isencroft

Clan Dunlurghan—One of the ancient clans of Isencroft

Clan Finlios—One of the ancient clans of Isencroft

Clan Kirylu—One of the ancient clans of Isencroft; led by Olek, son of Olek, the last of the great warlords

Clan Rathtuaim—One of the ancient clans of Isencroft

Clan Skaecogy—One of the ancient clans of Isencroft

Clan Tratearmon—One of the ancient clans of Isencroft

Clan Veaslieve—One of the ancient clans of Isencroft

Coalan—Valet to Tris Drayke, nephew of Ban Soterius

Cora—Ghost of Ed the peddler's wife

Corinn—Daughter of Jonmarc and Carina Vahanian

Count Renate—Loyal noble of Isencroft, regent until Kiara takes the throne

Crofters—Residents of Isencroft

Curane—Traitor lord in Margolan, loyal to Jared the Usurper

Cwynn—Infant son of Tris Drayke and Kiara Sharsequin

Daciana—Advisory spirit to the *Hojun*

Dagen—Ghostly liegeman to King Larrimore, Tris's grandfather

Dark Haven—Manor home and land holding of Lord Jonmarc Vahanian, given to him by King Staden

Darry—Court arms master of Isencroft and loyal friend to Kiara

Davin—Messenger from King Harrol

Detri—Ghost of a wronged woman

Dhasson—Neighboring kingdom to Margolan, Principality,

Eastmark, and Nargi; ruled by King Harrol, father to Jair Rothlandorn and uncle to Tris Drayke

Durim—Black Robes, also called Shanthadurists, blood mages loyal to the Destroyer Goddess Shanthadura

Eastmark—One of the Winter Kingdoms, ruled by King Kalcen, uncle of Kiara and father of Prince Gethin

Ed—A peddler and friend of Aidane

Edgeton—An Isencroft general

Elsbet—Kolin's dead lover

Elya—Redheaded air mage

Emil—Sworn warrior

Esiteran—"Life drinkers," demonic shadows that drain energy instead of blood

Essel—Rogue mage from the Sisterhood who comes to help guard Cwynn

Estan—Ghostly warrior who served King Hadenrul

Exeter—Head of the Principality Mercenary Guild

Formless One—One of the eight Aspects of the Sacred Lady; her worship is banned throughout the Winter Kingdoms

Gar—Round, portable Sworn dwelling

Gavrill, of Clan Finlios—One of the ancient clan lords

General Gregor—Isencroft general, older brother to Ric, a mercenary who was a long-ago lover to Carina

General Senne—Margolan general

General Valjan—Former leader of the War Dogs mercenaries, Principality general

Ghent—Second son born to Tris Drayke and Kiara Sharsequin

Hant—Principality palace spymaster

Harrol—King of Dhasson, father of Jair Rothlandorn, uncle of Tris Drayke

Hojun—Mystical priests from Eastmark

Illarion, of Clan Skaecogy—Ghostly clan lord of Isencroft

Imri—Temnottan mage and shapeshifter

Isencroft—Neighboring kingdom to Margolan, formerly ruled by King Donelan; now to be jointly ruled by Kiara, daughter of Donelan, and her husband, Martris Drayke of Margolan

Istra/Dark Lady—One of the eight Aspects of the Sacred Lady, especially revered in Dark Haven and among the *vayash moru*; protector of the outcast

Jae—Gyregon belonging to Kiara

Jair Rothlandorn—Son of King Harrol and heir to the throne of Dhasson; cousin of Tris Drayke, warrior of the Sworn, married to Talwyn, father of Kenver

Jared—Eldest son of King Bricen of Margolan, half-brother to Tris Drayke, became Jared the Usurper when he took the throne by treachery

Jencin—Seneschal of the Principality palace

Jodd—Faithless husband of Detri

Jolie—Madam and owner of Jolie's Place, friend to Jonmarc Vahanian and Tris Drayke

Jonmarc Vahanian—Former mercenary and smuggler, now brigand lord of Dark Haven; Champion of Berwyn of Principality, husband of Carina, one of Tris Drayke's best friends

Jorven—*Vyrkin* guard to Kiara

Kai—Infant daughter of Jonmarc and Carina Vahanian

Kalcen—King of Eastmark, son of King Radomar, youngest brother of Kiara's mother, Viata; father of Prince Gethin

Kellen—Loyal Isencroft bodyguard

Kenver—Son of Jair Rothlandorn and Talwyn, grandson of Pevre

Kiara Sharsequin—Daughter of King Donelan of Isencroft, heir to the Isencroft throne, wife of Martris Drayke of Margolan, cousin of Carina Vahanian, mother of Cwynn and Ghent

King Donelan—King of Isencroft, father of Kiara Sharsequin

King Gustaven—Long-dead king of Margolan

King Hadenrul—Long-dead king of Margolan

King Jashan—First king of Isencroft, son of Lord Gavrill

King Larrimore—Long-dead king of Margolan, father of Bricen and grandfather of Tris Drayke

King Martris (Tris) Drayke—King of Margolan, husband of Kiara, father to Cwynn and Ghent; the most powerful Summoner in the Winter Kingdoms

King Radomar—Former king of Eastmark, father to King Kalcen and to Kiara's mother, Viata

King Staden—King of Principality, father to Berwyn

King Vestven—Long-dead king of Isencroft

King Zoccoros the Third—Long-dead king of Isencroft

Kir—Barkeep in the tunnels beneath Principality City

Kolin—*Vayash moru*, leader of the Ghost Carriage, liege to Lady Riqua of the Blood Council

Konost, the Guide of Dead Souls—Forgotten goddess, one of the Shrouded Ones

Lady Eadoin—Elderly patron of Master Bard Carroway, aunt of Alle

Lady Riqua—Member of the Blood Council

Laisren—*Vayash moru*, Dark Haven's weapon master, friend to Jonmarc Vahanian

Lienholt Palace—Royal palace of Principality

Leksandr, of Clan Dunlurghan—Long-dead Isencroft warlord

Lemuel—Mage who was possessed by the spirit of the Obsidian King, lover of Bava K'aa, grandfather to Tris Drayke

Lisette—*Vayash moru* lady's maid to Carina Vahanian

Lord Alarek—Member of the Principality Council of Nobles

Lord Antony Norden—Member of the Principality nobility

Lord Gabriel—*Vayash moru*, member of the Blood Council, seneschal of Dark Haven, friend to Jonmarc Vahanian

Lord Gavrill (Clan Finlios)—Father to the first king of Isencroft

Luka, of Clan Tratearmon—Long-dead clan lord of Isencroft

Macaria—Musician, wife of Carroway, friend to Kiara

Margolan—One of the Winter Kingdoms; ruled by King Martris Drayke

Markian—Language spoken in Eastmark

Marlan the Gold—First king of Margolan

Martris Drayke—Summoner-King of Margolan, mage heir and grandson of Bava K'aa, husband of Kiara Sharsequin, father of Cwynn and Ghent

Mihei—Warrior of the Sworn

Mikhail—*Vayash moru*, liege of Lord Gabriel, friend to Tris Drayke

Minya, of Clan Veaslieve—Long-dead clan lord of Isencroft

Morane—Isencroft senior mage

Mother—One of the eight Aspects of the Sacred Lady, especially revered in Margolan

Nachele—Dark spirits entombed in the barrows and guarded by the Dread

Nardore—Rogue mage of the Sisterhood sent to protect Cwynn

Nargi—One of the Winter Kingdoms known for its devotion to the Crone Aspect

Necropolis—Crypt beneath Isencroft palace

Neirin—Dark Haven grounds manager

Nenkah—Rag doll used for magical rituals

Nexus—Magic sword forged by Bava K'aa and given to Tris Drayke

Nezra—Dulcimer player in a group of traveling musicians, partner to Cal

Obsidian King—Ancient evil being that possessed the mage Lemuel and was imprisoned in the Soul Catcher by Bava K'aa and later destroyed by Martris Drayke

Pashka—Margolan fisherman who leads the flotilla

Patov—*Vayash moru* guard to Kiara

Pevre—Sworn chieftain, shaman, father of Talwyn, grandfather of Kenver

Prince Gethin of Eastmark—Son of King Kalcen, arranged suitor to Berwyn

Peyhta the Soul Eater—One of the Shrouded Ones

Pyotir, of Clan Rathtuaim—Long-dead clan lord of Isencroft

Queen Tanisia—Long-dead queen of Isencroft

Queen Viata—Former queen of Isencroft, wife of Donelan, mother of Kiara, sister to Kalcen of Eastmark, daughter of King Radomar

Rafe—*Vayash moru*, member of the Blood Council

Renn—Younger brother to Cam and Carina

Rhistiart—Squire to Cam

Rhosyn—Wife of Cam

Royster—Scholar, Keeper of the Library at Westmarch, friend to Tris and Kiara

Sathirinim—An Eastmark vulgarity, literally "corpse flesh," an ethnic slur against lighter-skinned people

Scaith—Dark summoner and leader of the Temnottan invasion against Margolan

Scian—Assassin, one of the ghost blades

Serg—*Vyrkin* emissary to Principality

Serroquette—Ghost whore

Shanna—Jonmarc Vahanian's late wife

Shanthadura, the Destroyer—One of the Shrouded Ones

Shanthadurists—Blood mages loyal to Shanthadura; also called black robes and Durim

Shekerishet—Margolan palace

Shrouded Ones—Trio of dark goddesses whose worship fell out of favor with the cult of the Sacred Lady

Sinha/The Crone—One of the eight Aspects of the Sacred Lady, especially revered in Nargi

Sister Beyral—Mage, rune reader, adviser to Tris Drayke

Sister Fallon—Mage, adviser to Tris Drayke

Sister Glenice—Mage, healer, helper to Carina Vahanian

Sister Rosta—Mage, administrator of the madhouse at Vistimar

Spirit Guides—Ghostly advisers to the Sworn

Stelian—Sworn sword

Surrie—Ghost who leads Aidane into the warrens

Talwyn—Sworn shaman, daughter of Pevre, wife of Jair Rothlandorn, mother to Kenver

Tarra—Allestyr's niece, personal assistant to Kiara

Telorhan—Elite bodyguards to the Margolan king

Temnotta—Warring kingdom from across the Northern Sea

Temnottan—People or things from the kingdom of Temnotta

Tevin—Principality fire mage

Thaine—Ghost of a whore who was a long-ago lover to Jonmarc

Thanal—Flute player, part of a group of traveling musicians

The Dread—Ancient spirits that guard the Nachele within the barrows

The Sworn—Nomadic warriors who guard the barrows of the Dread

Tice—Trusted adviser of King Donelan

Tolya—Head of the privateers aligned with Margolan

Trevath—One of the Winter Kingdoms, located to the south of Margolan, long an adversary of Margolan and an ally of Nargi

Trinnen—Elite Sworn warriors

Trygve—Personal healer to King Donelan

Uri—*Vayash moru*, one of the Blood Council

Valiquet—Dhassonian palace

Vayash moru—Vampire residents of the Winter Kingdoms

Ved—Innkeeper at the Goat and Ram tavern

Veigonn—Elite Isencroft warriors, personal bodyguards to the Isencroft monarch

Verley—Lady's maid to Lady Eadoin and wet nurse to Cwynn

Vistimar—Madhouse for insane mages, managed by Sister Rosta

Vittor—Healer in the palace of Queen Berwyn
Vitya—Ancient Margolan warrior
Vivian—Ghost of a little girl
Volshe—Temnottan mages
Vygulf—*Vyrkin* shaman
Vyrkin—Shapeshifters
Warlord Ifran—Long-dead Isencroft warrior, one of the eight clan lords
Warlord Olek—Long-dead Isencroft warrior, *vayash moru*, one of the eight clan lords
Wilym—Head of the Veigonn warriors
Wivvers—Margolan weapons inventor

Acknowledgments

Writing is a lot of time spent stuck in your own head, so it's a wonderful thing to pop up for air and rediscover wonderful people around me. Thanks certainly to my agent, Ethan Ellenberg, and to Evan Thomas at the agency, for all their hard work. Thanks also to my editor, DongWon Song, and all the wonderful people at Orbit who help my books go from manuscript to finished product and do such a great job of it. Thanks to all my con and bookstore and Renaissance festival friends, both writers and readers, who show up for panels and readings and make the crazy travel stuff much more fun. Most of all, thanks to my family, who helped with the creation of this book in a million little ways and a lot of big ways. I couldn't do it without you.

extras

www.orbitbooks.net

about the author

Gail Z. Martin discovered her passion for science fiction, fantasy, and ghost stories in elementary school. The first story she wrote—at age five—was about a vampire. Her favorite TV show as a preschooler was *Dark Shadows*. At age fourteen she decided to become a writer. She enjoys attending science fiction/fantasy conventions. Renaissance fairs, and living-history sites. She is married and has three children, a Himalayan cat, and a golden retriever. Find out more about the author at www.chroniclesofthenecromancer.com

Find out more about Gail Z. Martin and other Orbit authors by registering for the free monthly newsletter at www.orbitbooks.net

if you enjoyed
THE DREAD

look out for

THE HEIR OF NIGHT

Book One of the Wall of Night series

by

Helen Lowe

1

The Keep of Winds

The wind blew out of the northwest in dry, fierce gusts, sweeping across the face of the Gray Lands. It clawed at the close-hauled shutters and billowed every tapestry and hanging banner in the keep. Loose tiles rattled and slid, bouncing off tall towers into the black depths below; as the wind whistled through the Old Keep, finding every crack and chink in its shutters and blowing the dust of years along the floors. It whispered in the tattered hangings that had once graced the High Hall, back in those far-off days when the hall had blazed with light and laughter, gleaming with jewel and sword. Now the cool, dry fingers of wind teased their frayed edges and banged a whole succession of doors that long neglect had loosened on their hinges. Stone and mortar were still strong, even here, and the shutters held against the elements, but everything else was given over to the slow corrosion of time.

Another tile banged and rattled its way down the roof as a slight figure swarmed up one of the massive stone pillars that marched along either side of the hall. There was an alarming creak as the climber swung up and over the balustrade of a wooden gallery, high above the hall floor—but the timbers held. The climber paused, looking around with satisfaction, and wiped dusty hands on the seat of her plain, black pants. A narrow, wooden staircase twisted up toward another, even higher gallery of sculpted stone, but the treads stopped just short of the top. She studied the gap, her eyes narrowed as they traced the leap she would need to make: from the top of the stair to the gargoyles beneath the stone balcony, and then up, by a series of precarious finger- and toe-holds, onto the balcony itself.

The girl frowned, knowing that to miss that jump would mean plummeting to certain death, then shrugged and began to climb, testing each wooden tread before trusting her weight to it. She paused again on the topmost step, then sprang, her first hand slapping onto a corbel while the other grasped at a gargoyle's half-spread wing. She hung for a moment, swinging, then knifed her feet up onto the gargoyle's claws before scrambling over the high shoulder and into the gallery itself. Her eyes shone with triumph and excitement as she stared through the rear of the gallery into another hall.

Although smaller than the High Hall below, she could see that it had once been richer and more elegant. Beneath the dust, the floors were a mosaic of beasts, birds, and trailing vines; panels of metal and jeweled glass decorated the walls. There was a dais at the far end of the long room, with the fragile remains of a tapestry draped on the wall behind it. The hanging would have been bright with color once, the girl thought; the whole hall must have glowed with it, but it was a dim and lifeless place now.

She stepped forward, then jumped and swung around as her reflection leapt to life in the morrored walls. A short, slightly built girl stared back at her out of eyes like smoke in a delicately chiseled face. She continued to stare for a moment, then poked her tongue out at the reflection, laughing at her own fright. "This must be the Hall of Mirrors," she said, pitching her voice against the silence. She knew that Yorindesarinen herself would have walked here once, if all the tales were true, and Telemanthar, the Swordsman of Stars. But now there was only emptiness and decay.

She walked the length of the hall and stepped onto the shallow dais. Most of the tapestry on the rear wall had decayed into shreds or been eaten by moths, but part of the central panel was still intact. The background was darkness, rimmed with fire, but the foreground was occupied by a figure in hacked and riven armor, confronting a creature that was as vast as the tapestry itself. Its flat, serpentine head loomed out of the surrounding darkness, exuding menace, and its bulk was doom. The figure of the hero, dwarfed beneath its shadow, looked overmatched and very much alone.

The girl touched the battered figure with her fingertips, then pulled back as the fabric crumbled further. "The hero Yorindesarinen," she whispered, "and the Worm of Chaos. This should never have been left here, to fall into ruin." She hummed a thread of tune that was first martial, then turned to haunting sadness as she slid forward, raising an imaginary sword against an unseen opponent. Her eyes were half closed as she became the fated hero in her mind, watching the legendary frost-fire gleam along her blade.

Another door banged in the distance and a voice called, echoing along silent corridors and through the dusty hall. "Malian! Mal—lee-ee—aan, my poppet!" The Old Keep caught the voice and tossed it into shadowy corners, bouncing echoes off stone and shutter while the wind whispered all around. "Where are you-oo-oo? Is this fit behavior for a Lady of Night? You are naught but an imp of wickedness, child!"

The door banged again, cutting off the voice, but the damage was done. The bright figure of Yorindesarinen faded back into memory and Malian was no longer a hero of song and story, but a half-grown girl in grubby clothes. Frowning, she smoothed her hands over her dark braid. The hero Yorindesarinen, she thought, would not have been plagued with nurses when she was a girl; she would have been too busy learning hero craft and worm slaying.

Malian hummed the snatch of tune again and sighed, walking back to the stone balcony—then froze at a suggestion of movement from the High Hall, two storeys below. Crouching down, she peered between the stone balusters, then smiled and stood up again as a shimmer of lilting sound followed the initial footfall. A slender, golden figure gazed up at her through the twilit gloom, his hands on his hips and his sleeves flared wide, casting a fantastic shadow to either side. One by one the tiny golden bells on his clothes fell silent.

"And how," asked Haimyr, the golden minstrel, the one bright, exotic note in her father's austere keep, "do you propose getting down from there? Just looking at you makes my blood run cold!"

Malian laughed. "It's easy," she said, "especially if you've been trained by Asantir." She slid over the balustrade and made her way back down the finger- and toe-holds to hang again from the gargoyle. She grinned down at the minstrel's upturned face while she swung backward and forward, gaining momentum, before arching out and dropping neatly to the stairs below. The staircase swayed a little, but held, and she ran lightly down, vaulting up and over the second balcony, then scrambled through its wooden trusses to descend the final pillar. The minstrel held open his golden sleeves, scalloped and edged and trailing almost to the floor, and she jumped the last few feet, straight into his arms. He reeled slightly, but kept his balance, catching her in a brocaded, musical embrace. A little trail of mortar slid down the pillar after her.

"I had no idea you were due back!" Malian exclaimed, her voice muffled by the brocade. "You have been away for-*ever*! You have no idea how tedious it has been without you."

Haimyr stepped back and held her at arm's length. His hair was a smooth curve along his shoulders and no less golden than his clothes, or the bright gleam of his eyes. "My dear child," he said, "you are entirely mistaken. I have every idea how tedious it has been, not to mention dull and entirely unleavened by culture, wit, or any other redeeming quality. But you—I go away for half a year and you shoot up like a weed in my absence."

She shook her head. "I'm still short, just not *quite* as short as I was."

"But," he said, "every bit as grubby and disheveled, which will not do, not if you expect to embrace me in this wild fashion." He looked around with the lazy, lambent gaze of a cat. "This is a strange place for your play, my Malian—and what of the danger to your father's only child and heir, climbing about in that reckless manner. What would any of us say to him if you were to fall and break your neck?"

"Oh, he is away at present, riding the bounds and inspecting the outposts," said Malian. "You would all have time to run away before he got back."

Haimyr regarded her with a satirical eye. "My dear child," he said, "why do you think your good nurse and the maids are all out hunting for you, high and low? Your father is back." Mockery glinted in his smile. "On the whole, my Malian, I think that it would be better for you and your household if you were on time for his returning feast."

Malian pulled a face. "We all thought the patrols would be away another week at least," she said, with feeling. "But thank you for coming in here after me. You're right, I don't think anyone in my household would brave it, even to prevent my father's anger." She grinned again. "That's why I like it, because no one else ever comes here and I can do what I want. They think it's haunted," she added.

"I know," said Haimyr. "They have been telling me so since

before you were born." He shrugged, his tall, fantastic shadow shrugging with him on the wall. "Well, folk have always liked to frighten themselves, by daylight or by dark, but they may be partly right about this place. The shadows of memory lie very thick here."

"It is a strange place," Malian agreed, "but I don't think it's dangerous. It seems sad to me, because of the decay and the silence, rather than frightening. And the memories, of course, are very bitter."

The minstrel nodded. "All the histories of your people are tragic and shot through with darkness. But the memories here must rank among the darkest."

"You are not afraid to come here, though," she said.

Haimyr laughed, and the sound echoed in the high stone vault overhead. "Afraid? Of the past's shadows? No. But then, they are not my shadows. They are your blood heritage, my Malian, not mine."

Malian frowned. "I am not afraid either," she declared, and Haimyr laughed again.

"Of course not, since you choose to come here," he said. "And rather often, too, I suspect."

Malian smiled in response, a small secret smile. "*Quite* a lot," she agreed, "especially when you and Asantir are away." She drew a pattern in the dust with her foot. "It has been very dull without you, Haimyr. Six months was far too long a time."

He smiled down at her. "I apologize for condemning you to a life of tedium. Will you forgive me if I say that I have brought back something you value, to make up for my neglect?"

Malian considered this. "New songs and stories?" she asked. "Then I may forgive you, but only if you promise to teach me every one."

Haimyr swept a low, extravagant bow, his sleeves tinkling

and his golden eyes glinting into hers, one long slender hand placed over his heart. Malian smiled back at him.

"Every one, remember," she said again, and he laughed, promising nothing, as was his way.

It was only a few hundred paces from the old High Hall to the gate into the New Keep, which was barred and soldered closed, although there was a locked postern a few yards away. Malian's customary means of coming and going was a narrow gap between the apex of the gate and the corridor's arched roof, but she was resigned, rather than surprised, when Haimyr took the postern key from his pocket. "Oh dear," she murmured, "now I am in trouble."

Haimyr slanted her a mocking smile. "Didn't you hear poor Doria calling to you? She summoned the courage to put her head around the postern for love of you, but even a lifetime's devotion wouldn't take her any further. Nhairin, of course, is made of sterner stuff, but we agreed that I was better suited to hunting you out."

"Because you could hope to catch me if I ran?" she inquired, with a smile as sly as his. "But I cannot see you scaling the walls, Haimyr, even to save me from my father's wrath."

He closed the postern behind them, locking it with a small, definite click. "You are quite right. Even the thought is an abhorrence. The ghosts of the past are one thing, but to scramble through the rafters like an Ishnapuri monkey, quite another. I would have absolutely no choice but to abandon you to your fate."

Malian laughed aloud, but sobered as they turned into the golden blaze of the New Keep. Darkness never fell in these corridors and halls where jewel-bright tapestries graced the walls and the floors were patterned with colored tiles. Pages sped by on their innumerable errands while soldiers marched with measured tread and the vaulted ceilings echoed with all the commotion of a busy keep. Malian's eyes lit up as the bustle surged around them. "It's always like this when my father comes home," she said. "He sets the entire keep in a flurry."

Haimyr's laugh was rueful. "Do I not know it? And now I must hurry, too, if I am to prepare my songs for the feast."

"Everyone will be eager for something new," Malian agreed. "But only after you have sung of the deeds and glory of the House of Night—for are we not first and oldest?"

"Oldest, first, and greatest of all the Derai Houses on the Wall, in deeds and duty if not in numbers," a new voice put in, as though reciting indisputable fact. A spare figure rose from an alcove seat and limped forward. She was as dark and reserved as the minstrel was golden and flamboyant, and her face was disfigured by the scar that slashed across it from temple to chin.

"'For it is the House of Night that holds the Keep of Winds,'" Malian chanted in reply, "'foremost of all the strongholds on the Shield Wall of Night.' It was you who first taught me that, Nhairin."

The newcomer's dark brows lifted. "I have not forgotten," she said, taking the postern key from Haimyr. She had soldiered once for the Earl of Night, until the fight in which she gained both limp and scar, and she liked to say that she soldiered still in the Earl's service, but as High Steward of the Keep of Winds, rather than with a sword. "I do not forget any of the few lessons that did not have to be beaten into you," she added meditatively.

"Nhair-rin!" said Malian, then a quick, guilty look crossed her face. "Have I caused you a great deal of trouble, having to look for me?"

The steward smiled, a slight twist of her mouth. "Trouble? Nay, I am not troubled. But I know who will be if you are not clean and in your place when the feast bell strikes." The smile widened at Malian's alarmed look. "That bell is not so very far off, so if I were you I should be running like the wind itself to my chamber, and the bath that is waiting there."

Haimyr clapped Malian on the shoulder. "The good steward is right, as always. So run now, my bold heart!"

Malian ran. Her father held strict views on the conduct appropriate to an Heir of Night, and exacted the same obedience from his daughter as he did from the warriors under his command. "We keep the long watch," he often said to Malian, "and that means we are a fighting House. The Wall itself is named for us, and of all the fortresses along its length, this one stands closest to our enemy. We cannot let our vigilance or discipline waver for an instant, and you and I must be the most vigilant of all, knowing all others look to us and will follow our example, whether good or bad."

Malian knew that upholding discipline included being on time for a formal Feast of Returning. Her nurse and the other maids knew it, too, for they did not stop to scold but descended on her as one when she ran through the door, hustling her out of her grimy clothes and into the tepid bath-water. Nesta, the most senior of the maids, caught Malian's eye as she opened her mouth to complain, and Malian immediately shut it again. Nesta came from a family that had served the Earls of Night for long generations, and she held views on the value of discipline, tradition, and truancy that were remarkably similar to those of Malian's father.

Doria, Malian's nurse, was more voluble. "An imp of wickedness, that's what you are," she said. "Running here, and running there, and never in sight when wanted. You'll be the death of me yet, I swear—not to mention the wrath of the Earl, your father, if he ever finds out about your expeditions."

"We'll all die of fright on that day, sure enough," said Nesta, in her dry way, "if nothing worse happens first. But will our fine young lady care, that's what I ask? And none of your wheedling answers either, my girl!" She struck a stern attitude, with arms akimbo, and the younger maids giggled.

"Well," said Malian meekly, "it hasn't happened yet, has it? And you know I don't mean to be a trouble to you, Doria darling." She hugged and kissed her nurse, but poked her tongue out at Nesta over Doria's shoulder.

The maid made a snipping motion with her fingers, imitating scissors. "Ay, Doria knows you don't mean to cause her trouble, but it won't stop trouble coming—especially if we don't get you down to dinner on time." She held up an elaborate black velvet dress. "It had better be black, I suppose, since you welcome the Earl of Night."

"Black is good, thank you," agreed Malian, scrambling into it. She waited, as patiently as she could, while Doria bound her hair into a net of smoky pearls.

"You look just like the ladies in the old tapestries," the nurse sighed, as her fingers twisted and pinned. "You are growing up, my poppet. Nearly thirteen already! And in just a few more years you will be a grand lady of the Derai, in truth."

Malian made a face at the polished reflection in the mirror. "I do look like a scion of the oldest line, I suppose." She kicked the train out behind her. "But can you imagine Yorindesarinen wearing anything so restrictive?"

"That skirt would make worm slaying very difficult," Nesta observed, and Malian grinned.

Doria, however, frowned. "Yorindesarinen is nothing but a fable put about by the House of Stars to make themselves feel important." She sniffed. "Just like the length of their names. Ridiculous!"

"They're not all long," Malian pointed out. "What about Tasian and Xeria?"

The nurse made a sign against bad luck, while Nesta shook her head. "Shortened," the maid said. "Why should we honor that pair of ill omen with their full names?" She pulled a face. "Especially she who brought ruin upon us all."

Doria nodded, her mouth pursed as if she had filled it with pins. "Cursed be her name—and completely beneath the attention of the Heir of Night, so we will not sully our lips with it now!" She gave a last tweak to the gauze collar, so that it stood up like black butterfly wings on either side of Malian's face. "You look just as you should," she said, not without pride. "And if you hurry, you'll be on time as well."

Malian kissed her cheek. "Thank you," she said, with real gratitude. "I am sorry that I gave you all so much trouble."

Nesta rolled her eyes and Doria looked resigned. "You always are," she said, sighing. "But I don't like your gallivanting off into the Old Keep, nasty cold place that it is. Trouble will come of it—and then what the Earl will do to us all, I shudder to think."

Malian laughed. "You worry too much," she said. "But if I don't hurry I really will be late and my father will make us all shudder, sooner rather than later."

She blew a butterfly kiss back around the door and walked off as quickly as the black dress would allow, leaving Doria and Nesta to look at each other with a mixture of exasperation, resignation, and affection.

"Don't say it," the nurse said to the younger woman, sitting down with a sigh. "The fact is that she is just like her mother was at the same age—too much on her own and with a head filled with dreams of glory. Not to mention running wild, all over the New Keep and half the Old."

Nesta shook her head. "They've been at her since she was a babe with all their lessons, turning her into an earl in miniature, not to mention the swordplay and other skills required by a warrior House. I like it when she acts like a normal girl and plays truant, for all the anxiety it causes us."

Doria folded her arms across her chest. "But not into the Old Keep," she said, troubled. "That was her mother's way, always mad for adventure and leading the others after her. We all know how that ended." She shook her head. "Malian is already too much her mother's daughter for my comfort."

Nesta frowned. "The trouble is," she said, pitching her voice so that no one else could hear her, "does the Earl realize that? And what will he do when he finds out?"

Doria sighed again, looking anxious. "I don't know," she replied. "I know that Nhairin sees it, plain as I do—and that outsider minstrel, too, I've no doubt. It's as though the Earl is the only person who does not see it."

"Or will not," Nesta said softly.

"Does not, will not," replied Doria, "the outcome is the same. Well, there's nothing we can do except our best for her, as we always have."

"Perhaps," agreed Nesta. Her dark eyes gazed into the fire. "Although what happens," she asked, "if your best is not enough?"

But neither the nurse nor the fire had any answer for her.